U1011428

比较文学与世界文学阅读系列教材

丛书主编　邹建军

比较文学文献精读：经典与案例

主　编　曾小月　李卫华

副主编　常　芳　李伟荣　黄　惠

WUHAN UNIVERSITY PRESS
武汉大学出版社

图书在版编目(CIP)数据

比较文学文献精读:经典与案例/曾小月,李卫华主编.—武汉:武汉大学出版社,2018.4

比较文学与世界文学阅读系列教材/邹建军主编

ISBN 978-7-307-19846-3

Ⅰ.比… Ⅱ.①曾… ②李… Ⅲ.中国文学—文学研究 Ⅳ.I206

中国版本图书馆CIP数据核字(2017)第276574号

责任编辑:胡 艳 责任校对:李孟潇 版式设计:汪冰滢

出版发行:**武汉大学出版社** (430072 武昌 珞珈山)

(电子邮件:cbs22@whu.edu.cn 网址:www.wdp.com.cn)

印刷:湖北民政印刷厂

开本:787×1092 1/16 印张:25.5 字数:603千字 插页:1

版次:2018年4月第1版 2018年4月第1次印刷

ISBN 978-7-307-19846-3 定价:48.00元

版权所有,不得翻印;凡购我社的图书,如有质量问题,请与当地图书销售部门联系调换。

总　序

比较文学在中国是一门年轻的学科，同时也是一门显要的学问，在文学与语言及相关学科群中，往往发挥着引领潮流的作用。世界文学在我国并非一门学科，而是一个重要的研究领域，有时候几乎等同于外国文学。外国文学是一个研究对象甚广、从业人员众多的专业，然而，在20世纪90年代中期，教育主管部门将其与比较文学合并一起，成为比较文学与世界文学学科，成为中国语言文学学科之下的二级学科之一。

比较文学与外国文学一样，研究对象范围甚广、队伍庞大，对于两者的合并与融合，学界部分学者虽有不同意见，却也认可两者在研究内容与批评方法上的关联性和同一性。因此，比较文学与世界文学一起作为一门重要的学科进行建设，不仅成为了教学与科研的实践，并且积累了丰富的经验，取得了很高的成就，在理论上也富于创见，而有所建树。正是基于这一背景，我们主编了比较文学与世界文学阅读系列教材（六册），由武汉大学出版社陆续出版。

教材的编写，一个方面是由于学术研究的推进和学科的发展，另一个方面是出于教学实践的需要。因此，本系列教材的编写遵循以下四个基本原则，并将此贯彻于编写的每一个环节之中：

一是阅读原则。编写本系列教材的目的在于为学生提供阅读的方便，从而有一个基本的阅读选本，与相关文学史类教材配套使用。因此，虽然分文体而编选，合起来却是一部全面的、具体的和多作品形态的文学史。

二是文献原则。收入本系列教材中的文学作品与相关文献，英文的文献尽量保持原貌，其他语种的文献尽量选择权威版本，除长篇之外一般不节选，节选之作品也尽量保存作品的完整性。所有入选作品都在文末注明原始出处，让本系列教材成为可信可靠的文学文献。

三是导读原则。由于有的文学作品年代久远，有的文学作品晦涩难懂，同时由于中外文化的异质性存在，对每篇收录作品进行导读是有必要的。但导读不可长篇大论，也不重复前人说过的东西，当抓住所选作品的重点、难点和关键之点，进行必要的说明与阐释。

四是创新原则。本系列阅读教材虽以文学文献为主体，却并非一般的文学作品选读。选文尽量不与前人所编重复，并且要拉开相当的档次，以体现新的审美眼光教材编写思想。导读更要体现创造性，自我的阅读体验与独特的价值判断尽量融合其间。

比较文学与世界文学阅读系列教材的编写，是为了适应新时代的需要，培养高水平的专业人才，也是为了推进比较文学与世界文学的学科建设，从而加强本学科以及相关学科的理论建设。

由于水平有限，加之时间仓促，缺失和不当在所难免，请各位同道与教材使用者提出宝贵的意见和建议，以便在适当时候进行修订。

邹建军

2017 年 12 月

目　录

比较文学名称与实质

（节选）

[法]费尔南·巴登斯贝格

【导读】

费尔南·巴登斯贝格（1871—1958）生于法国洛林地区孚日省的圣迪埃市。对日耳曼文化很有研究，1899年发表博士论文《戈特弗里德·凯勒》和《欧伦施莱格》。1901年，巴登斯贝格接替戴克斯特主持里昂大学的比较文学讲座；1902年，巴登斯贝格接手贝茨的《比较文学书目》的编订工作，至1904年，《比较文学书目》正式出版时已增至6000余条。1910年，巴登斯贝格离开里昂大学执教于法国索尔本的巴黎大学。1921年，巴登斯贝格和巴黎大学的同事阿扎尔共同创办《比较文学杂志》。与阿扎尔一起推动了比较文学法国学派的发展，是公认的"法国比较文学的教父"。

《比较文学名称与实质》是巴登斯贝格在《比较文学杂志》创刊号上发表的一篇文章。本书节选其中第一部分至第四部分的内容。《比较文学名称与实质》在比较文学界影响巨大，是法国比较文学史上的第一篇纲领性文献，对法国比较文学名称与实质进行了具有指导性意义的探讨。这篇文章几乎揽括了比较文学名称与实质的方方面面，通过阅读它，可以了解法国比较文学的历史，同时，对法国比较文学的研究特色会有更加清晰的把握。本文第一部分通过对"比较文学"与"文学比较"的界说，指出"比较"的意义在于两个不同对象的真实性。第二部分列举一些例子说明"比较"应该富有探索性质。第三部分提出问题，一百多年来人们怎样比较，以及比较了什么，认为"比较文学"从18世纪末开始在文学实践与文学理论的历史范围内发生了某种奇异而有教益的演变。第四部分认为文学史效法了生物学方面的"比较"科学。

巴登斯贝格对学界的观点进行了批判性的总结，在研究外国文学和法国文学的相互影响时，采用了严密考证的方法，对法国比较文学的发展脉络进行了历史性的探寻，从而总结出法国比较文学实证主义的研究特色。

（白阳明）

一

有人说："'比较文学！'文学比较！这是毫无意义又毫无价值的吵闹！我们懂得，它只不过是在那些隐约相似的作品或人物之间进行对比的故弄玄虚的游戏罢了，而且凭了某些类似的表面现象，便将高乃依和阿尔菲耶里，将德博尔德—瓦尔莫夫人和伊丽莎白·布朗宁，将儒贝尔和柯勒律治，罗宾汉和歇洛克·福尔摩斯进行比较！人们是不是将提醒我们注意，拉辛与莎士比亚的美学原则是截然不同的，弥尔顿的史诗并不是塔索的史诗，莱辛和拉丰登的寓言差不多只是名字相同罢了？……"

不消说，一种被人们这样理解的比较文学，看来是不值得有一套独立的方法的，或者说，至少它可能把精神的本能进程的重要性强调到了荒谬的程度。人们一旦熟悉一些诗人，阅读了一些作品，就开始进行比较。知识渊博的马蒙泰尔在他的《文学要素》一书中，就曾经期望每一个当之无愧的批评家来进行比较活动，因为只有那些"拙劣的批评家"，缺乏比较范例和比较对象的人才自行其是。这就是一切真正批评活动的预备阶段，但是，它还仅仅是由于阅读面比较广，了解的情况比较多，认识类似现象比较随便所产生的结果，所以带有偶然性。这种比较可能得益于这样的情况：通过记忆，将维尼的《军人的屈辱和伟大》同克莱斯特的《洪堡王子》进行比较；就认识对象本身来说，他们在中心思想上仍然采取他们各自的立场。如果有所发现的话，也正如普鲁斯特的《追忆逝水年华》那类作品，在许多方面都令人记起让·保尔那种迂回曲折、追溯往事、捉摸不定、华而不实、冗长啰嗦，加上大量插入句、引号和十分含蓄的隐喻的手法一样，如此而已。因为事实上，任何实际上的巧合都不能造成一种从属关系，从而也不能用来解释从这一作家到那一作家的起点，而我愿意建立起的对比，不会更令人满意(如果它不再向前发展的话)，正如同18世纪的一位大胆的生物学家把一朵花和一个昆虫之间的形状和色彩进行精巧的比较那样。十分清楚，真实性不在那里。仅仅对两个不同的对象同时看上一眼就作比较，仅仅靠记忆和印象的拼凑，靠一些主观臆想把可能游移不定的东西扯在一起来找点类似点，这样的比较绝不可能产生论证的明晰性。

二

显然，法语的"比较文学"一词不过只是局部地取代了各种不同的表达方式而已。让我们试举一些例子，这些例子可以说富有探索性质，而不是令人厌烦的流水账。

一般的"比较"在1760年的《外国杂志》和1754年的《文学年鉴》中，用得已经比较自如；而在1749年9月的《学者报》中几乎认为它是一种方法："运用这种比较总可以获得巨大的好处……"在1780年2月的《法兰西信使报》上，伽拉(Garat)笔下的"比较研究"已有完整的纲领："对那些拥有文学的民族引以自豪的作家进行比较研究，也许是最适宜于孕育和培养大量人才的研究……"

让我们继续探求，如果不是在相同的领域，那也是在相邻的领域。1802年，特雷桑神父尝试性地写了《神话学与历史的比较》；维莱尔的《比较色情》显得既放肆又笨拙；而德热朗多在1804年《哲学体系比较史》中，运用了培根所欣赏的“联系原则”，并自命为是这种总体的完整文学史中的一部分。此外，还有1810年索布里的《文学与绘画比较教程》，1814年斯科帕神父的“比较考察”等。

在这些探索之后，紧接着，人们突然发现了那个初具形迹的术语，以及开始确定的观点。诺埃尔和拉普拉斯于1816年起发表他们的《比较文学教程》。维尔曼在他的《十八世纪概况》(1827年和1828年的课程)的序言中谈到一种“比较文学研究”。安贝尔在马赛公学的第一堂课(1830)上，预见到“各国人民的文学艺术比较史”将产生出文学艺术的哲学。1832年，他在巴黎大学的讲课中说道：“先生们，我们将进行这一项工作，没有这种比较研究，文学史将是不完备的……”总之，安贝尔在他的论文集《文学和旅游》的前言中指出，他的这些论文都与比较文学的历史有关联(1833)。也就在这个时候，《历史科学学报》为《比较语文学》开辟了专栏。

两年以后，即1836年1月17日，夏斯勒在公学的第一堂课中，就自己选择的“比较外国文学”这一用语表示歉意：“这一题目，我曾感到唯一合适的题目，从许多方面来看，都缺乏准确性。”为了对夏斯勒在这一领域中的活动作一番分析，1841年肖德-埃格在他的《法国现代作家》中坚持了“比较文学史”这一工作；维尔曼和皮比斯克则在1842年和1843年坚持了“文学比较史”的说法，同样，邦洛埃维于1849年在第戎提供了一篇“文学比较史导言”；上一年，安贝尔在法兰西学院入院演说中，再次谈到“比较文学研究”。A. 杜凯内尔在1846年，把“比较文学教程”作为他的《文学史》的副标题。

所有这些更加全面、更加确切的各种表达方式，几乎都没有给适当的简称让位。

甚至在圣伯夫的这种语言“政变”之后，老的用语也并没有销声匿迹。洛德把他于1886年在日内瓦开设的课程命名为“论比较文学”；埃纳坎在他的《科学批评》的序言中提到波斯奈特的《比较文学》一书，并用英文原文引用了这一书名。J. 戴克斯特将他的《欧洲文学研究》中的第一篇，题名为“论文学比较史”，他通常使用“比较批评”和“比较方法”这些词。同样，布吕纳介在各种较为明确的表达方式和一个虽不确切但比起所有其他表达方式来有其最大好处——简短——的术语之间犹豫不决。F. 罗力耶的《比较文学史》出版于1903年，而由我再版的贝兹的《比较文学》是在1904年出版的。最后，关于文学比较教学的官方批定是，《比较现代文学》和《比较文学》同时并存。

三

人们不厌其烦地进行“比较”，难免出现那种没有价值的对比；在这150年里，人们比较了什么，怎样比较？在那些习惯的方法——美学批评、教条主义的批评、心理分析批评、历史批评和编年史的方法——之侧，比较文学以怎样的形象出现？有时她被认为有野心、不知趣，有时她被迫沉默寡言，但是她的姐姐们从来没有能够把她变成“灰姑娘”。从18世纪末开始，无论在文学实践还是在文学理论的历史范围内，这方面都已发生某种奇异而有教益的演变。

起初大多数的情况是这样：爱国主义的敏感性把原来学说上、习惯上和趣味上的对立情况加深了。国别文学一被唤醒，意大利人、法兰西人、德国人和英国人各自玩弄了一种归根结底为了鼓励本国文学创作的手段，今天，当这些作品开出丰硕果实的时候，他们又尖刻地将它们的价值进行比较，而这些价值又往往是无法估量的，他们这样做是为了证明什么？证明莎士比亚的成就高于或低于高乃依；证明现代的古典主义是否真正的古典主义；证明法兰西人绝不可能了解但丁。拉哈尔普或莱辛，约翰逊或巴雷蒂，他们以不同的优点在“比较”中寻找进攻的或自卫的武器。弗雷隆·兰盖则在一部名著中，孜孜以求一些外来的东西，致力于那种渊源探索的雕虫小技，他们不是从中找出一些独创性，而是贬低创造性和揭露“剽窃行为”……赫尔德和维柯，他们将文艺复兴以来从未被人遗忘的思想明确起来，把各国人民的语言、文学和精神状态当作一个整体来看待，因而有机地利用一切决定因素来制约精神生活，通过这样的方法，把比较工作从由于人们的偏爱而把它作为理由和论据的贫乏的教条主义之中拯救出来。从那以后，人们就可以用历史的批评方法对文学现象进行比较和对照；它们的失调就可以用怪现象和不规则等现点来加以解释了；人们可以通过在不同趣味中发现一些社会的，也可能是种族的迹象来避免那种白费口舌的强词夺理；同样，人们也会感到那种肤浅简单的比较的华而不实：1808 年，西斯蒙第在给阿巴尼夫人的信中写道：“机灵的人将不同语言的戏剧进行比较，无疑是对艺术大有裨益的；但是接着就从这种比较中得出一通结论，却不可能。每个民族的戏剧都有一种本质上不同于其他民族的诗学，它为自己确定的目标不同于其他民族，并受制于不同的法则……”因此，艺术的相对性(随着它的广泛运用，创作的活力能从中得到鼓励)能在 1880 年取得胜利，就是由于人们对比较作出了新的努力。在斯达尔夫人，贡斯当，司汤达，《地球》杂志，歌德和曼佐尼那里都显示了这种努力；同时被日益激起的“环境”决定论，也迫使艺术史接受那些不严谨的系统化理论。

另一方面，18 世纪人们对原始的和自然的作品所发生的好感，由于各种争执而变得更如强烈，于是在 1800 年出现了民间诗歌的理论，这些理论探讨民间诗歌在一切名副其实的文学中的崇高地位和内在性。通过 F·史雷梅尔、格林兄弟和他们的浪漫主义门徒，通过普里埃尔及其可尊敬的后辈，一系列新的探索激起了学者们的努力。渊源的共同性，雅利安各民族之间存在的最初潜在的亲属关系，由于民间意识的作用而显得真正重要的全部材料所必然引起对于神话的喜爱，所有这些浪漫主义的准备阶段都导致产生了一种有意义的研究工作：“民俗学”或“题材史”，形形色色的比较文学，都向这个中心靠拢。这种研究似乎对材料比对艺术更感好奇，对隐秘的遗迹比对艺术家的创造性更感兴趣；在这里，人们对杂乱东西的关心胜过事物的特征。因此，当谈到真正的文学作品时，流浪的犹太人①，伊诺克·阿登②，浮士德原型或唐璜等，都可能被作为这种研究的对象，但其目的则几乎和艺术活动的目的相反……

① 欧仁·苏《流浪的犹太人》中的人物。

② 丁尼生自由体叙事长诗《伊诺克·阿登》中的人物。他是一名水手，流落海外十年，回家后发现妻子已与旁人结婚，为避免破坏她的幸福，自愿隐蔽，孤寂而死。

四

生物学方面的“比较”科学，在19世纪前三分之一时期内形成了专门的学科，文学史自然会效法它的方法。居维叶在比较解剖学方面(1800—1805)，布朗维尔在比较生理学方面（1833)，科斯特在比较胚胎学方面(1837)，都已经凭借不同的对象发表了他们从比较研究这一角度写成的著作。他们不是简单地比较“同一群体”的类似事物——这对任何一个观察者来说，显然太容易办到了——以求达到分门别类的目的，而是比较“群体间在某种关系下被人忽视的种种现象，这些现象最正常地属于群体，但必须通过比较，他们之间的共同特征才能显示出来，这时人们得到启示：从前被认为毫不相干的群体，相互间是有着亲缘关系和发展过程中的联系的”。

重要的是不要忘记了这个出发点，而“比较”这一术语有时却使人忘记这一点(生物学方面的比较学科，甚至在欧文和热让博尔的著作发表之后，也不得不常常提醒人们注意，它应该成为一门学科，这点是很能说明问题的)。对于文学史来说，向生物科学借用一种方法和一些手法的确是不可能的，但是它从中发现了一种倾向，这种倾向有助于活跃文学史的各种研究。利特雷是一这样的以为学者，他在我国各派学说众说纷纭、莫衷一是的情况下，坚定地支持了比较观点的合法性。利特雷，他在中学毕业后，就爱上了比较语言学，并在1830年介入了由于比较解剖学所引起的纠纷，在“统一单位”的支持者和反对者之间表明了态度，在1874年最后一部著作《文学和历史》的序言中，他还提醒人们注意，各种文学都是“姐妹”，不管有什么东西将它们分开。

此外，在物质学科和精神学科的“比较主义”之间，不只在一个方面已经出现了中间状态；在A. W. 史雷格尔的著作之后，语言学中的比较方法产生了包布和迪茨的著作，其他的学科，如比较神话学、比较地理学、比较立法学等也依次出现，且不谈本质就是比较性质的在浪漫主义的荫庇下不孚重望的民俗学。

如果安贝尔能够走完他在充满希望时期所开辟的道路，无疑能更自由地建立起比较文学。凭着他对生活和个人的兴趣，凭着一位旅行者与心理学家的好奇心，以及一位研究者本身所具有的遗传意识，他是能够摆脱那个欧洲内部沟通已成为明显事实的时代的；但是，他的性格和好奇心的多变，却使他备尝苦难，这也就是天才所受的磨折。

他的同代人不安地看到，在我国逐渐和丹纳的名字联系在一起的思想在文学艺术史中取得了位置。无疑，这种超群的才智没有抛弃已经越出了过分狭窄范畴的大量概述性的东西。丹纳在他的著作中，处处暗示人们注意整体的联系，机敏地启发读者。多少次，他马不停蹄，对那些通过比较能得到更明确阐述的关系进行对照，如莎士比亚和拉辛，缪塞和丁尼生，古代人和现代人，浮士德和曼弗雷德，弗朗德和意大利等的关系；或者进行有利于说明思想互相影响的类比，如法兰西的专制主义和英国的复辟，意大利的文艺复兴和德国的宗教改本等……可是，他所偏爱的原则是“汇集”，是力量和效果的协调，他认为，“艺术作品由整体所决定，而整体则是精神和周围环境的总的状况”，他在一首诗歌和一个种族中同时发现“内部结构”，他的这些日益增多的论点和各种比较方法最大量的实践却是背道而驰的……

如果和丹纳的名字有着关联的这些理论的严格性没有被不同的概念削弱的话，比较文学能否向前迈进一步呢？这种可能性是不大的。不管怎么说，在将近19世纪末的时候，我们几乎到处都看到一种努力，它正力图用一种更直接的比较方法，并列于在降低了要求的丹纳的整个学说旁边，而且常常还是叠架于这些思想之上。一些小国的历史学家和批评家们，他们国家的民族性较弱，因而他们具有某种世界主义的本能，尤其是G. 勃兰兑斯，Ed. 洛德，马尔克·莫尼埃和V. 罗塞勒等人的名字，和这种"欧洲主义"有着关联，无论怎么说，"欧洲主义"对囿于小国范围的情感来说是一种飞跃。1886年，波斯奈特把他的比较文学理论建立在人类文明不断发展的各阶段的基础上，这说明他对人类社会学的主要分类看得特别重要。对于他对于美国、英国任何一个由他发起的小团体来说，社会的进化——从氏族过渡到城邦，从封建集团到国家集团等——有力地支配着种族的从属关系或者物质环境的决定作用；比较文学随着艺术和社会的变化之间多少有意识的关系的变化而变化，……

（徐鸿　译）

（节选自费尔南·巴登斯贝格：《比较文学名称与实质》，干永昌、廖鸿钧、倪蕊琴选编，《比较文学研究译文集》，上海译文出版社1985年版，第32-40页。）

The Crisis of Comparative Literature

［美］René Wellek

【导读】

韦勒克的《比较文学的危机》从内容上可分三部分，首先主要指出了比较文学研究“岌岌可危”的处境，接着分析了这种情况出现的原因及其危害，最后提出解决方法。“岌岌可危”的处境主要表现是：第一，未能确定研究内容和专门的研究方法论；第二，从狭义上理解比较文学，机械地把比较文学局限于研究渊源和影响，导致比较文学成为研究国外渊源和作家声誉的附属科学；第三，比较文学研究中的文化民族主义动机，使得文学被当成争夺文化声誉的舌战，导致研究本身失去了其客观性。基于以上种种弊端，韦勒克提出要彻底废除“比较”文学和“总体”文学之间的人为界限，重新调整理论、评论和评论史，这样才能解决比较文学的危机处境。一些比较文学家，如梵·第根、伽列和基亚巴斯登贝格等，尝试建立比较文学研究的内容和方法，但都宣告失败。梵·第根试图将比较文学和总体文学划清界限，把比较文学局限于研究两国文学间的相互关系，而总体文学则着眼于席卷几国文学的运动和风尚。韦勒克指出这种区分不切实际，在比较文学和总体文学之间构筑了一道人为的障碍。这是一种仅研究外部情况的狭义做法，把比较文学局限于研究两国文学间的“贸易交往”，致使比较文学成为了仅研究国外渊源和作家声誉的附属科学。伽列、基亚则把研究范围扩大到包括对民族幻想的研究，以及对国家之间相互渗透的固定看法的研究。韦勒克认为，这种研究范围的扩大，已经超越了文学研究的研究范围，意味着承认研究内容贫乏，而且还把文学研究融入了社会心理学研究、文化研究和文化史研究的领域。巴斯登贝格提出文学研究的范围应当扩大到包括一些次要作家，同时注意同时代人的评价。韦勒克不同意这种看法，认为这种划分暗示了历史相对主义。关于在“比较文学”的心理动机和社会动机方面，存在着一种矛盾现象：一方面，充当两国之间的中间人和调停人反对19世纪学术界的狭隘民族主义，对法、德、意、英等国的文学史家的孤立主义表示异议；另一方面，这些人的真诚愿望总是为当地狂热的民族主义所淹没和歪曲，从而导致了把比较文学当作文化扩张和实现民族虚荣心的手段这种现象的产生。

韦勒克不仅看清了比较文学研究中存在的危机及其原因，还提出了相应的解决方法。在研究内容和范围上，他主张把“比较”文学和“总体”文学之间的人为界限彻底废除，要把文学研究视为不受语言限制的统一学科，让人人都有权讨论任何问题，甚至研究历史、哲学和任何其他课题。同时指出，文学研究界很有必要确定研究内容和中心，回归到对文学艺术作品本身的研究上来，应当把文学研究同思想史研究、宗教及政治观念和情绪的研究区分开来，正确理解文学研究的概念。关于方法论，他强调必须正视“美学性”的问题，因为它是美学的中心问题，是文学艺术的本质；他提出要克服内容和形式的分离、打破文学史和文学评论之间的界限、反对在历史研究和形式研究之间树立起一道藩篱，要把艺术作品看成是一个有机体，要用理论、批评和历史通力合作来描述、阐释和评价一部或一组艺术作品，而不要死死抱住“事实联系”、渊源、影响、媒介和名望；比较文学应当回到文学研究和文艺批评的洪流中去，评论不能也不应该被逐出文学研究领域。虽然该文发表时至今日已半个多世纪，但韦勒克所披露的不少问题如今仍富有挑战性。

（李伟荣）

The world (or rather our world) has been in a state of permanent crisis since, at least, the year 1914. Literary scholarship, in its less violent, muted ways, has been torn by conflicts of methods since about the same time. The old certainties of nineteenth-century scholarship, its ingenuous belief in the accumulations of facts, any facts, in the hope that these bricks will be used in the building of the great pyramid of learning, its trust in causal explanation on the model of the natural sciences, had been challenged sharply even before: by Croce in Italy, by Dithery and others in Germany. Thus no claim can be made that recent years have been exceptional or even that the crisis of literary scholarship has reached anywhere a point of solution or even temporary accommodation. Still, a re-examination of our aims, and methods is needed. There is something symbolic to the passing, in the last decade, of several of the masters: Van Tieghem, Farinelli, Vossler, Curtius, Auerbach, Carré, Baldensperger, and Spitzer.

The most serious sign of the precarious state of our study is the fact that it has not been able to establish a distinct subject matter and a specific methodology. I believe that the programmatic pronouncements of Baldensperger, Van Tieghem, Carré, and Guyard have failed in this essential task. They have saddled comparative literature with an obsolete methodology and have laid on it the dead hand of nineteenth-century factualism, scientism, and historical relativism.

Comparative literature has the immense merit of combating the false isolation of national literary histories: it is obviously right (and has brought a mass of evidence to support this) in its conception of a coherent Western tradition of literature woven together in a network of innumerable Interrelations. But I doubt that the attempt to distinguish between "comparative" and "general" literature, made by Van Tieghem, can succeed. According to Van Tieghem "comparative" literature is confined to the study of interrelations between two literatures while "general" literature is concerned with the movements and fashions which sweep through several literatures. Surely this distinction is quite untenable and impracticable. Why should, say, the influence of Walter Scott in France be considered "comparative" literature while a study of the historical novel during the Romantic age be "general" literature? Why should we distinguish between a study of the influence of Byron on Heine and the study of Byronism in Germany? The attempt to narrow "comparative literature" to a study of the "foreign trade" of literatures is surely unfortunate. Comparative literature would be, in subject matter, an incoherent group of unrelated fragments: a network of relations which are constantly interrupted and broken off from meaningful wholes. The *comparatiste* qua *comparatiste* in this narrow sense could study only sources and influences, causes and effects, and would be even prevented from investigating a single work of art in its totality as no work can be reduced entirely to forcing influences or considered as a radiating point of influence only toward foreign countries. Imagine that similar restrictions would be imposed on the study of the history of music, the fine arts, or philosophy! Could there be a compress or even a periodical exclusively devoted to such a mosaic of questions as, say, the influence of Beethoven in France, of Raphael in Germany, or even Kant in England? These related disciplines have been much wiser: there are musicologists, art historians, historians of philosophy, and they do not pretend that there are special disciplines such as comparative painting, music, or philosophy. The attempt to set up artificial fences between comparative and general literature must fail because literary history and literary scholarship have one subject: literature. The desire to confine "comparative literature" to the study of the foreign trade of two literatures limits it to a concern with externals, with second-rate writers, with translations, travel books, "intermediaries"; in short, it makes "comparative literature" a mere sub discipline investigating data about the foreign sources and reputations of writers.

The attempt to set apart not only the subject matter but also the methods of comparative literature has failed even more signally. Van Tieghem sets up two criteria which supposedly distinguish comparative literature from the study of national literatures. Comparative literature is concerned, he tells us, with the myths and legends which surround the poets and it is preoccupied with minor and minimal authors. But it is impossible to see why a student of a single national literature should not do the same: the image of Byron or Rimbaud in England or France has been successfully described without much regard to other countries and, say. Daniel Monet in France or Josef Nadler in Germany have shown us that one can write national literary history with full attention to ephemeral and forgotten writers.

Nor can one be convinced by recent attempts by Carré and Guyard to widen suddenly the scope of comparative literature in order to include a study of national illusions, of fixed ideas which nations have of each other. It may be all very well to hear what conceptions Frenchmen had about Germany or about England-but is such a study still literary scholarship? Is it not rather a study of public opinion useful, for instance, to a program director in the Voice of America and its analogues in other countries? It is national psychology, sociology, and, as literary study, nothing else but a revival of the old *Stoffgeschichte*. "England and the English in the French novel" is hardly better than "the Irishman on the English stage" or "the Italian in Elizabethan drama". This extension of comparative literature implies a recognition of the sterility of the usual subject matter at the price, however, of dissolving literary scholarship into social psychology and cultural history.

All these floundering are only possible because Van Tieghem, his precursors and followers conceive of literary study in terms of nineteenth-century positivistic factualism, as a study of sources and influences. They believe in causal explanation, in the illumination which is brought about by tracing motifs, themes, characters, situations, plots, etc., to some other chronologically preceding work. They have accumulated an enormous mass of parallels, similarities, and sometimes identities, but they have rarely asked what these relationships are supposed to show except possibly the fact of one writer's knowledge and reading of another writer. Works of art, however, are not simply sums of sources and influences: they are wholes in which raw materials derived from elsewhere cease to be inert matter and are assimilated into a new structure. Causal explanation leads only to regresses ad infinitum and besides, in literature, seems hardly ever unequivocally successful in establishing what one would consider the first requirement of any causal relationship: "when X occurs, Y must occur." I am not aware that any literary historian has given us proof of such a necessary relationship or that he even could do so, as the isolation of such a cause has been impossible with works of art which are wholes, conceived in the free imagination, whose integrity and meaning are violated if we break them up into sources and influences.

The concept of source and influence has of course worried the more sophisticated practitioners of comparative literature. For instance, Louis Cazamian, commenting on Carré's book *Goethe en Angleterre*, sees that there is "no assurance that this particular action made this particular difference." He argues that M. Carré is wrong in speaking of Goethe's "having, indirectly, provoked the English romantic movement" merely because Scott translated *Goetz von Berlichingen*.① But Cazamian can only make a gesture toward the idea, familiar since Bergson, of flux and becoming. He recommends the study of individual or collective psychology which, with Cazamian, means an elaborate, totally unverifiable theory of the oscillations of the rhythm of the English national soul.

Similarly also, Baldensperger, in his programmatic introduction to the first number of Revue de literature compare (1921) saw the dead end of literary scholarship preoccupied with tracing the history of literary themes. They can never establish, he admits, clear and complete sequences. He rejects also the rigid evolutionism propounded by Brunetiere. But he can substitute for it only the suggestion that literary study should be widened to include minor writers and should pay attention to contemporaneous evaluations. Brunetiere is too much

① "*Goethe en Angleterre*, quelques réflexions sur les problemes d'influence," *Revue Germanique*, 1921 (12), 374-375.

concerned with masterpieces. "How can we know that Gesner played a role in general literature, that Retouches charmed the Germans more than Moliere, that Deville was considered as a perfect and supreme poet in his time as Victor Hugo was later and that Heliodor us counted perhaps as much as Aeschylus in the heritage of antiquity?" (p. 24). Baldensperger's remedy is thus again attention to minor authors and to the bygone fashions of literary taste. A historical relativism is implied: we should study the standards of the past in order to write "objective" literary history. Comparative literature should plant itself "behind the scenes and not in front of the stage" as if in literature the play were not the thing. Like Cazamian. Baldensperger makes a gesture toward Bergson's becoming, the incessant movement, the "realm of universal variation" for which he quotes a biologist as a parallel. In the conclusion of his manifesto Baldensperger abruptly proclaims comparative literature a preparation for a New Humanism. He asks us to ascertain the spread of Voltaire's skepticism, of Nietzsche's faith in the superman, of the mysticism of Tolstoy: to know why a book considered a classic in one nation is rejected as academic in another, why a work despised in one country is admired elsewhere. He hopes that such researches will furnish our dislocated humanity with a "less uncertain core of common values" (p. 29). But why should such erudite researches into the geographical spread of certain ideas lead to anything like a definition of the patrimony of humanity? And even if such a definition of the common core were successful and would be generally accepted, would it mean an effective New Humanism?

There is a paradox in the psychological and social motivation of "comparative literature" as practiced in the last fifty years. Comparative literature arose as a reaction against the narrow nationalism of much nineteenth-century scholarship, as a protest against the isolationism of many historians of French, German, Italian, English, etc., literature. It was cultivated often by men who stood themselves at the cross- roads of nations or, at least, on the borders of one nation. Louis Betz was born in New York of German parents and went to Zürich to learn and teach. Baldensperger was of Lothringian origin and spent a decisive year in Zurich. Ernst Robert Curtius was an Alsatian convinced of the need of better German-French understanding. Arturo Farinelli was an Italian from Trento, then still "irredenta", who taught at Innsbruck. But this genuine desire to serve as a mediator and conciliator between nations was often overlaid and distorted by the fervent nationalism of the time and situation. Reading Baldensperger's autobiography, *Une Vie parmi d' autres* (1940, actually written in 1935), we feel the basic patriotic impulse behind his every activity: his pride in foiling German propaganda at Harvard in 1914, in refusing to meet Brandes in 1915 in Copenhagen, in going to liberated Strasbourg in 1920. Carré's book on Goethe in England contains an introduction arguing that Goethe belongs to all the world and to France in particular as a son of the Rhineland. After the second World War Carré wrote *Les Écrivains Français et le Mirage Allemande* (1947) where he tried to show how the French nourished illusions about the two Germanies and were always taken in at the end. Ernst Robert Curtius thought of his first book, *Die literarischen Wegbereiter des neuen*

Frankreichs (1918), as a political action, as instruction for Germany. In a postscript to a new edition written in 1952, Curtius declared his early concept of France an illusion. Romain Rolland was not the voice of the new France as he had thought. Like Carré, Curtius discovered a "mirage" but this time it was a French mirage. Even in that early book Curtius had defined his conception of a good European: "Ich weiss nur eine Art ein guter Europäer zu sein: mit Macht die Seele seiner Nation haben, und sie mit Machete nähren von alum, was as Einzigartiges gibt in dear Steele dear andiron National, dear befreundeten odor der feindlichen."① A cultural power politics is recommended: everything serves only the strength of one's nation.

I am not suggesting that the patriotism of these scholars was not good or right or even high-minded. I recognize civic duties, the necessity of making decisions, of taking sides in the struggles of our time. I am acquainted with Mannheim's sociology of knowledge, his *Ideology and Utopia*, and understand that proof of motivation does not invalidate the work of a man. I clearly want to distinguish these men from the base corruptors of scholarship in Nazi Germany or from the political doctrinaires in Russia who, for a time, declared "comparative literature" taboo and called anybody who would say in print that Pushkin drew the story of "The Golden Cockerel" from Washington Irving a "rootless cosmopolitan kowtowing to the West".

Still, this basically patriotic motivation of many comparative literature studies in France, Germany, Italy, and so on, has led to a strange system of cultural bookkeeping, a desire to accumulate credits for one's nation by proving as many influences as possible on other nations or, more subtly, by proving that one's own nation has assimilated and "understood" a foreign master more fully than any other. This is almost naively displayed in the table of M. Guyard's little handbook for students: it has neat empty boxes for the unwritten theses on Ronsard in Spain, Corneille in Italy, Pascal in Holland, etc.② This type of cultural expansionism can be found even in the United States which, on the whole, has been immune to it partly because it had less to boast of and partly because it was less concerned with cultural politics. Still, for instance, the excellent cooperative Literary History of the United States (ed. R. Spiller, W. Thorp, et al., 1948) blithely claims Dostoevsky as a follower of Poe and even of Hawthorne. Arturo Fraxinella, a comparators of the purest water, described this situation in an article contributed to the *Mélanges Baldensperger* (1930) entitled "GI'influssi leterari e l' insuperbire delle nazioni." Farinelli very appropriately comments on the absurdity of such computations of cultural riches, of the whole creditor and debtor calculus in matters of poetry. We forget that "the destinies of poetry and art are fulfilled only in the intimate life and the secret accords of the soul". In an interesting article Professor Chinard has most opportunely pronounced the principle of "no debts" in the comparison of literatures and quoted a fine passage from Rabelais on an

① Franzosischer Geist im zwanzigsten Jahrhundert (Bern, 1952), p. 237.

② M. F. Guyard. La Litterature Comparee. Paris, 1951, pp. 124-125.

ideal world without debtors and creditors."①

An artificial demarcation of subject matter and methodology, a mechanistic concept of sources and influences, a motivation by cultural nationalism, however generous—these seem to me the symptoms of the long-drawn-out crisis of comparative literature.

A thorough reorientation is needed in all these three directions. The artificial demarcation between "comparative" and "general" literature should be abandoned. "Comparative-literature has become an established term for any study of literature transcending the limits of one national literature. There is little use in deploring the grammar of the term and to insist that it should be called "the comparative study of literature", since everybody understands the elliptic usage. "General" literature has not caught on, at least in English, possibly because it has still its old connotation of referring to poetics and theory. Personally I wish we could simply speak of the study of literature or of literary scholarship and that there were, as Albert Thibaudet proposed, professors of literature just as there are professors of philosophy and of history and not professors of the history of English philosophy even though the individual may very well specialize in this or that particular period or country or even in a particular author. Fortunately, we still have no professors of English eighteenth-century literature or of Goethe philology. But the naming of our subject is an institutional matter of academic interest in the most literal sense. What matters is the concept of literary scholarship as a unified discipline unhampered by linguistic restrictions. I cannot thus agree with Friederich's view that corporatists "cannot and dare not encroach upon other territories", i. e. those of the students of English, French, German, and other national literatures. Nor can I see how it is even possible to follow his advice not to "poach in each other's territory".② There are no proprietary rights and no recognized "vested interests" in literary scholarship. Everybody has the right to study any question even if it is confined to a single work in a single language and everybody has the right to study even history or philosophy or any other topic. He runs of course the risk of criticism by the specialists, but it is a risk he has to take. We corporatists surely would not want to prevent English professors from studying the French sources of Chaucer, or French professors from studying the Spanish sources of Corneille, etc., since we corporatists would not want to be forbidden to publish on topics confined to specific national literatures. Far too much has been made of the "authority" of the specialist who often may have only the bibliographical knowledge or the external information without necessarily having the taste, the sensibility, and the range of the non-specialist whose wider perspective and keener insight may well make up for years of intense application. There is nothing presumptuous or arrogant in advocating a greater

---

① "La Littérature comparée et l'histoire des idees dans l'étude des relations franco-américaines". in: *Proceedings of the Second Congress of the International Comparative Literature Association*, ed. Werner P. Friederich. Chapel Hill, 1959. pp. 349-369.

② *Yearbook of Comparative and General Literature*. 1955, p. 57.

mobility and ideal universality in our studies. The whole conception of fenced-off reservations with signs of "no trespassing" must be distasteful to a free mind. It can arise only within the limits of the obsolete methodology preached and practiced by the standard theorists of comparative literature who assume that "facts" are to be discovered like nuggets of gold for which we can stake out prospectors' claims.

（选自 René Wellek. *Concepts of Criticism*. Edited and with an introduction by Stephen G. Nichols, Jr. New Haven and London：Yale University Press, pp. 282-293.）

Comparative Literature, Its Definition and Function

[美]Henry H. H. Remak①

【导读】

自诞生之日起，有关比较文学的定义就一直存在争论。1961 年，亨利·雷马克(Henry H. H. Remak, 1916—2009)在《比较文学：其定义和功用》(Comparative Literature, Its Definition and Function)一文中对比较文学下了一个明确的定义，这一定义在比较文学界一直被奉为经典。他认为，“比较文学是一国文学与另一国或多国文学的比较，是文学与人类其他表现领域的比较。”

首先，雷马克把比较文学从两国之间文学的事实性联系和法国实证主义方法论的束缚中解放了出来，将比较文学延伸到超出国别文学界限和跨越学科界限的研究中去。他驳斥了法国学派把文学批评排斥在比较文学领域之外的观点，认为“法国人对文学研究‘可靠性’的要求现在已经显得陈腐了……这个时代要求更多的想象力”。随后，他指出了影响研究的一些问题，并提出“影响研究主要限于找出和证明某种影响的存在，却忽略更重要的艺术理解和评价的问题”。在雷马克看来，比较文学的研究必须综合，否则文学研究就是支离破碎的；而且，他指出，只有把文学以外的领域作为独立连贯的学科来研究，才算是“比较文学”。其次，雷马克论述了比较文学的“功用”，即：使学者、教师、学生以及广大读者能更好、更全面地把文学作为一个整体来理解，而不是看成某部分或彼此孤立的几部分文学。再次，雷马克试图厘清“民族文学”、“世界文学”和“总体文学”三个概念的含混之处。他首先陈述了民族文学与比较文学的区别，认为二者的研究方法相似，而具体研究内容上有重合，但又不尽相同。此外，民族文学分类复杂，作家的民族、国籍和写作语言都是影响其分类的原因。值得一提的是，雷马克似乎认同这些问题“没有严重到足以混淆民族文学研究和超出民族文学研究的界限”这一观点，但“国别文学”与“民族文学”的界限却实在成为一个研究难题。例如，属于不同民族，使用不同或相同语言，但同属于中国的那些文学作品应该怎么划分呢？这似乎超出了民族文学的范围，但似乎也不应属于“国别文

① Henry H. H. REMAK, Professor of German at Indiana university, has published extensively in the fields of Franco-German literary relations (Goethe and French literature, French Realism in Germany) and principles of comparative literature. He is a corresponding member of the Academie des Sciences, Lettres et Beaux-Arts of Marseille.

学”。遗憾的是，雷马克并未就此给出答案。此外，雷马克拓宽了比较文学的研究领域，将其分为空间、时间、质量和感染力四方面，并就此论述了世界文学和比较文学在程度上的区别。而二者更基本的差别在于：美国学派认为比较文学包括研究文学与其他领域的关系，而世界文学不包括这类研究；甚至法国学派也有一套针对比较文学的特殊研究方法，而世界文学却没有。至于总体文学，雷马克的定义是，“不能方便地归入某一类的东西和似乎使研究某一民族文学以外作品的人感兴趣的东西”；它可以指“总”的文学潮流、问题和理论，或是美学；和世界文学一样，也没有规定一种比较的研究方法。

雷马克在本文中对比较文学下了明确的定义，对其功用的总结也很符合研究需求，因此受到广泛推崇。他对比较文学功用的划分也较为合理，将其归为一个非常必要的辅助学科，这一切都为比较文学的跨学科发展打下了坚实的基础。然而，在涉及比较文学与民族文学、世界文学、总体文学的概念辨析时，雷马克的论述仍有尚待完善之处。首先，虽然他批判了梵·第根的概念分类方式，但雷马克本人并未提出确定的“民族文学”的定义，这一概念仍然模糊不清。其次，雷马克只进行了民族文学与比较文学、比较文学与世界文学的两两对比，后简要介绍了总体文学，至于剩余概念间的比较则没有表述，因此比较也不够完整。

（李伟荣）

Several areas and terms are contiguous to or seem to overlap with comparative literature: national literature, world literature and general literature. A clarification of their meanings is indispensable for the delimitation of comparative-literature terms.

There is no fundamental difference between methods of research in national literature and comparative literature, between, for example, a comparison of Racine with Corneille and of Racine with Goethe. There are, however, subjects encountered in comparative-literature research which go beyond national-literature scholarship: the contact or collision between different cultures, in general, and the problems connected with translation, in particular. Other topics inherent in the study of national literature occur in somewhat different patterns and tend to occupy a place of greater importance in comparative-literature research: vogue, success, reception, and influence of literature; travel and intermediaries.

Even geographically speaking, an air-tight distinction between national literature and comparative literature is sometimes difficult. What are we to do with authors writing in the same language but belonging to different nations? We should probably not hesitate at all to assign a comparison between George Bernard Shaw and H. L. Mencken, or between Sean O'Casey and Tennessee Williams, to comparative literature, but when we go back to English and American literature of the colonial period the case, as Wellek has suggested, becomes much less clear-cut. Maeterlinck and Verhaeren were Belgians writing in French; would a study of their intimate connections with French Symbolism be classed as comparative literature? What about Irish authors writing in English or Finnish nationals composing in Swedish? Similar difficulties arise in investigations of the Nicaraguan Ruben Dariô place in Spanish literature, or of the eminent positions of the Swiss Gottfried Keller and Conrad Ferdinand Meyer, the Austrians Adalbert Stifter and Hugo von Hofmannsthal in German literature (not to speak of the still more complicated cases of Rilke and Kafka). To what extent should legal naturalization be taken into account? There is surely a difference, in the consequences for their literary work, between the British citizenship of T. S. Eliot and the American citizenship of Thomas Mann.

Inversely, there are authors belonging to the same nation but writing in different languages or dialects. Welsh literature in relation to English, Low German literature in relation to German, Flemish literature in relation to French (in Belgium), Sicilian literature in relation to Italian, Ukrainian literature in relation to Great Russian, Basque and Catalan literature in relation to Spanish or French, raise questions that must be answered from case to case. In general, we may state the rule that a scholar asserting that a transitional topic of this nature is comparative must assume the burden of positive proof that he is dealing with significant differences in language, nationality or tradition.

Most comparatists, while admitting complications and overlapping, will agree that these difficulties are neither frequent nor serious enough to invalidate the distinction between literature studied within and across national boundaries.

Between comparative literature and world literature, there exist differences of degree as well as more fundamental differences. The former comprise elements of space, time, quality and intensity. Comparative literature (geographically speaking) involves, like world literature, an element of space, but frequently, though not necessarily, a more restricted one. Comparative literature often deals with the relationship of only two countries, or two authors of different nationality, or one author and another country (e. g., Franco- German literary relations, Poe-Baudelaire, Italy in the works of Goethe). The more pretentious term "world literature" implies recognition throughout the world, ordinarily the western world.

"World literature" also suggests an element of time. As a rule, the acquisition of world renown takes time, and "world literature" usually deals with literature consecrated as great by the test of time. Contemporary literature is, therefore, somewhat less frequently covered by the term "world literature," whereas comparative literature, at least in theory, may compare anything that is comparable no matter how old or how recent the work(s) may be. It must be readily admitted, however, that in practice many, perhaps most, comparative literature studies do deal with literary figures of the past who have achieved world-wide fame. Much of what we have been and shall be doing is, in effect, comparative world- literature.

World literature deals therefore predominantly with time and world-honored literary productions of enduring quality (e. g., the *Divine Comedy*; *Don Quijote*; *Paradise Lost*; *Candide*; *Werther*), or, less markedly, with authors of our own day who have enjoyed very intense applause abroad (e. g. Faulkner, Camus, Thomas Mann), which, in many cases, may prove transitory (Galsworthy, Margaret Mitchell, Moravia, Remarque). Comparative literature is not bound to the same extent by criteria of quality and/or intensity. Illuminating comparative studies have been, and many more could be done on second-rate authors, often more representative of the time-bound features of their age than the great writers. Such investigations would include authors once thought great or known to have been very successful (e. g. , Lillo, Gessner, Kotzebue, Dumas father and son, Scribe, Sudermann, Pinero), or even minor authors who never made headway abroad, but whose production might illustrate pan-European trends of literary taste (in Germany alone, such writers as Friedrich de la Motte-Fouque, Zacharias Werner, Friedrich Spielhagen, Max Kretzer).

In addition, certain first-rate writers not yet acclaimed by world literature are eminently fitted for comparative-literature studies. The latter may actually contribute to their acceptance as figures of world literature. Among the men of letters of the past, just recently "discovered" or resurrected (or in the process of being so) by the western world are Donne, Blake, Holderlin, Buchner, Gerard de Nerval, Lautreamont, and Melville. Others, equally worthy of international attention, are still waiting for commensurate recognition outside their own countries: Espronceda, Larra, Galdos, Azorin, Baroja (Spain); Herder, Hebbel, Keller, Trakl, Hofmannsthal, Hesse (Germany, Austria and Switzerland); Petofi (Hungary); Creanga, Eminescu, Sadoveanu (Rumania); Jens Peteivjacobsen and Isak Dinesen (Denmark); Froding (Sweden), Obstfelder (Norway); Willa Cather...the list is endless. Baltic, Slavic (except Russian) and literatures outside the occidental tradition have hardly been touched; they are bound to contain many surprising literary nuggets.

Elements of space, time, quality and intensity provide differences of degree between world literature and comparative literature. But there are more fundamental distinctions. In the first place, the American concept of comparative literature embraces inquiries into the relationship between literature and other orbits; world literature does not. In the second place, even the more restricted, "French" definition of comparative literature (where the material to be studied is entirely literary, as it is in world literature) specifies a method; world literature does not. Comparative literature requires that a work, author, trend or theme be actually compared with a work, author, trend or theme of another country or sphere; but a collection of essays on, let us say, Turgenev, Hawthorne, Thackeray and Maupassant, under one cover, might very well be called *Figures of World Literature* without containing any or perhaps only incidental comparisons. Webster defines "comparative" as "studied systematically by comparison of phenomena...as, *comparative* literature."

Many courses devoted to the analysis of literary masterpieces from various countries, mostly read in translation, are now being offered in American colleges, and many anthologies designed for such courses have been published. These courses and textbooks should be, and usually are designated by the term "world literature" rather than "comparative literature", since the works read are by and large studied as individual masterpieces, not (at least fairly) systematically compared. It would be up to the instructor or editor to make such a course or book truly comparative, provided the choice of texts lends itself to comparative treatment.

A comparative literature study does not have to be comparative on every page nor even in every chapter, but the overall intent, emphasis and execution must be comparative. The assaying of intent, emphasis and execution requires both objective and subjective judgment. No rigid rules can and should, therefore, be set down beyond these criteria.

The term "general literature" has been used for courses and publications concerned with foreign literature in English translation, or, more loosely yet, for offerings that do not fit into departmental pigeonholes and appear to be of interest to students outside one national literature. Sometimes it refers to literary trends, problems and theories of "general" interest, or to aesthetics. Collections of texts and of critical studies or comments dealing with several literatures have been assigned to this category (e. g., many anthologies and such historical and critical works as Laird [ed.], *The World through Literature*, Shipley [ed.], *Dictionary of World Literature* and *Encyclopedia of Literature*. See Bibliography). It must be remembered that, like the term "world literature," general literature fails to prescribe a comparative method of approach. While "general literature" courses and publications may afford an excellent basis for comparative studies, they are not necessarily comparative in themselves.

The very haziness of the term "general literature" seems to have worked to its advantage in this country. A much more precise definition of "general literature" by the French scholar Paul Van Tieghem (Sorbonne), though not widely accepted beyond France, deserves nevertheless our attention. To him, national literature, comparative literature and general literature represent three consecutive levels. National literature treats questions confined to one national literature; comparative literature normally deals with problems involving two different literatures; general literature is devoted to developments in a larger number of countries making up organic units, such as Western Europe, Eastern Europe, Europe, North America, Europe and North America, Spain and South America, the Orient, etc. Expressed visually, national literature would be the study of literature within walls, comparative literature across walls, and general literature above walls. In a comparative-literature study, national literatures would remain primary factors, serving as anchors of investigation; in a general-literature study, national literatures would simply provide examples for international trends. According to van Tieghem, a study of the place of Rousseau's *Nouvelle Heloise* in literature would be part of national literature; a paper on the influence of Richardson on Rousseau's *Nouvelle Heloise* would belong to comparative literature; a survey of the European sentimental novel would be general literature. Van Tiegliem himself has written a number of works illustrating his ideas of general literature: *Latin Literature of the Renaissance*, *Literary History of Europe and America since the Renaissance*, *Pre-romanticism*, *European Romanticism*, and the *Discovery of Shakespeare on the Continent.* Other syntheses of this kind include Curtius' *European Literature and the Latin Middle Ages*, Farinelli's *Romanticism in the Latin World*, Friederich's *Outline of Comparative Literature*, and

Hazard's masterful twin works, *The European Mind*, 1680—1715 and *European Thought in the XVIIIth Century*.

Van Tieghem's definitions raise at least one question. Is it not arbitrary and mechanical to relegate the term comparative literature, as he has done, to comparative investigations limited to two countries, while studies involving more than two countries are reserved for general literature? Why should a comparison between Richardson and Rousseau be classified as comparative literature, whereas a comparison between Richardson, Rousseau and Goethe (as undertaken years ago by Erich Schmidt) would be assigned to general literature? Is not the term "comparative literature" sufficient to cover syntheses encompassing any number of countries (as it does in Friederich's *Outline of Comparative Literature*)?

In setting up his distinctive categories, Van Tieghem was probably thinking less of logically coherent units than of a necessary division of labor. The number of creative, historical and critical works to be absorbed by a scholar before he can hope to portray adequately even a limited period or aspect of *one* literature has become so enormous that we cannot expect the same scholar to take on one or more additional literatures. In turn, for reasons of inclination, aptitude and longevity, scholars specializing in comparative literature will, Van Tieghem fears, probably be unable to assemble and integrate the researches of more than two national literatures. A third group of scholars is therefore needed to pull together the findings of national literature and comparative literature and merge them into general literature.

The dangers of such an arrangement, aside from its very hypothetical workability, given the cherished individualism of the scholarly profession, are readily apparent. Comparative-literature and general-literature scholars would have to be content with organizing the findings of others (in itself a Herculean task), an assignment bound to expose them to loss of contact with the literary text, and carrying the seeds of mechanization, superficialization and dehumanization of literature. Van Tieghem's own books certainly have not escaped this peril altogether. On the other hand, Hazard, in his two syntheses, has njagnificently succeeded in presenting the spirit of an age (preenlightenment and rationalism) without depriving the bones of the flesh.

We are inclined to think that a rigid division of labors between national-literature, comparative-literature and general literature scholars is neither feasible nor desirable.[16] National-literature scholars should realize and act on their obligation to widen their perspectives, and should be encouraged to undertake, now and then, excursions into other literatures or spheres related to literature. Comparative-literature scholars should return, from time to time, to the more circumscribed areas of a national literature to make sure that at least one foot is firmly planted on the ground. This is precisely what the best scholars in the comparative field, both here and abroad, have consistently done.

None of the terms discussed are completely clear-cut. Overlapping exists among all. The definitions of and distinctions between national literature and comparative literature are, however, sufficiently clear to be useful. While we subscribe to the more inclusive American concept of comparative literature, we urge that topics claimed to belong to this field be subjected to closer scrutiny, on the basis of stricter criteria, than heretofore. World literature, in the sense of literature of such outstanding merit or success as to have gained international attention, is a serviceable term, but must not be laxly used as a sort of alternative for comparative literature or general literature. It is to be hoped that the term general literature will be avoided, whenever possible. It means, at least at present, too many different things to too many people. In its place, we should use synonyms for the intended connotation: comparative literature, or world literature, or literature in translation, or western literature, or literary theory, or the structure of literature, or just literature, whichever the case may be.

Notes

…

10. The quarterly bibliographies of the *Revue de littérature comparée* contribute to the same confusion. What are such titles as *Erzählformen in den Werken Gerhart Hauptmanns* or *Zur erlebten Rede im englischen Roman des* 20. *Jahrhunderts* doing in a comparative bibliography (xxxm, 148-49, January-March, 1959)?
11. The terms "international literature" and "universal literature" are more or less synonymous with world literature, but have not been able to establish themselves. The Dutch scholar J. C. Brandt Corstius gives, in his De Muze in het Morgenlicht, Zeist, 1957) pp. 149-70, an excellent account, both descriptive and critical, of the evolution of the term "world literature" from the threshold of history via Herder and Goethe to the twentieth century.
12. August Wilhelm von Schlegel's pioneering *Lectures on Dramatic Art and Literature* (1808) may serve as an illustration. They belong to comparative literature not because he covers the literatures of Greece and Rome in the first, and the literatures of Italy, France, England, Spain and Germany in the second volume, although, were they restricted to independent discussions of these literatures, his essays would still provide a rich nutrient for comparative literature. They *are* comparative literature because, e. g. , in his first lecture, he compares not only Greek with Latin drama but the classical with the romantic drama, and brings in the Spanish, Portuguese and German drama; because he constantly refers back to the classical literatures when he treats, e. g. , Italian and French literature; because he avails himself of every opportunity to draw general comparisons (between the dramatic literatures of England and Spain, of Spain and Portugal, of France and Germany, etc.); because he consistently keeps the general polarities of the drama in mind (tragic-comic, poetical-theatrical, "Ernst und Scherz", etc.); because, wherever possible, he directs attention to the fine arts. It is the combination of these factors which makes this work clearly comparative. But not every one of his chapters would (or need) qualify for the overall label "comparative": e. g. , his eleventh lecture is completely limited to France, his thirteenth to England.

13. Julius Petersen makes the interesting point that *any* treatment of a foreign literature is, in a way, comparative, inasmuch as it utilizes, consciously or unconsciously, criteria derived from the writer's own national environment. (*Die Wissenschaft von der Dichtung*, Berlin, 1939, I, 7). This is a valid observation, but it is clear that the comparative angle of a literary study must be explicit rather than implicit if we are going to have standards at all.
14. Sometimes Van Tieghem uses the alternate term "Synthetic Literature."
15. This definition was suggested by Professor Craig La Driere in addressing the Comparative Literature section of the Modern Language Association of America, New York, December, 1950, and elaborated on by him in the Proceedings of the Second Congress of the International Comparative Literature Association, I, 160-175.
16. Equally unacceptable, because artificial, is Werner P. Friederich's compromise suggestion that comparative-literature scholars might well restrict themselves to the "French system" in teaching but could indulge in the "American point of view" in their researches ("Zur Vergleichenden Literaturgeschichte in den Vereinigten Staaten" in *Forschungsprobleme der Vergleichenden Literaturgeschichte*, II, eds. Fritz Ernst and Kurt Wais, Tübingen, 1958, 186.)

（选自 Henry M. M. Remak. Comparative Literature, Its Definition and Function. in: Newton P. Stallknecht and Horst Frenz eds., *Comparative Literature*: *Method and Perspectives*. Carbondale: Southern Illinois University Press, 1961, pp. 7-19.）

比较文学的目的、方法、规划

(节选)

[法]雷内·艾金伯勒

【导读】

该文源自于法国比较文学家雷内·艾金伯勒(René Etiemble)教授的论著《比较文学中的危机》第三部分。该部分的主要内容是，批评法国学派只重视文学作品外在关系，忽略文学作品内在美学价值的急症，同时勾勒出比较文学未来的研究规划。首先，重新确定比较文学研究的目的。艾金伯勒教授继承性地对法国学派“事实联系”研究展开批评，认为比较文学应该强调文学作品的美学价值与内在规律。其次，提出了比较诗学的主张。艾金伯勒教授推崇具有共同诗心的，而没有事实联系的两国(或多国)文学的比较分析。例如，他在解释欧洲前浪漫主义文学作品时，曾用古代中国的诗歌加以评述，认为二者虽无“事实联系”，却存在着美学上的共通性。面对此种文学现象，比较文学研究者势必要超越法国学派的传统方法，而上升到比较诗学。由此，各个国家尤其是跨越东西方异质文化的文学进行比较时，必然要走向文学理论的比较研究。再次，倡导跨学科研究。论者勾勒出比较文学的未来趋势，即从历史分析、案卷研究和社会学角度切入到文学批评，重申了比较文学跨学科研究的可能性。这同时也是对雷马克《比较文学的定义与功能》一文(1962年)中提倡跨学科综合研究的全力支持。最后，给予比较文学研究以世界关怀的眼光。在展望比较文学研究与教学工作中，艾金伯勒教授非常强调第三世界国家与民族的作用和和地位，他认为，一名真正的比较文学研究者应当放弃自我中心论，以平等心态审视其他民族的文学作品。

艾金伯勒教授在文中充分尊重每一个民族的独特性，也客观认识到各民族之间文学的交流性。作为一位法国比较文学家，艾金伯勒教授对中国文学投以热切的关注。他曾以个人授课经历为例，指出从屈原到宋代的中国古代诗歌，完全能胜任评述欧洲前浪漫主义的诞生问题，由此而否定没有“事实联系”的二者同样可以进行比较研究。这不但这体现了论者平等的文学情怀，更昭示出后继者应具有的世界眼光。

(曾小月)

假定这一显然无法解决的难题①获得了解决，那么，比较文学的目的，以及随之而来的方法，规划应当是什么？在一个世纪的四分之三时间里，有关这一课题的书籍已经多得足够摆满一个普通的受过教育的人的藏书室了；让我们在当中再添上几页，希望能够认清1958年在教堂山和1962年在布达佩斯召开的大会所提供的经验教训。

……

历史主义者

某一阵营里聚集着这么一些人，他们以为，或者说自称他们是在把朗松②的历史方法运用于比较文学。但是他们老是忘掉它的实质，那就是，对这位最正统的文学史经典的创立者来说，历史方法远不能构成文学教学的本质特性，而只能够、事实上也只应当构成探讨文学的一种方法。这一点在朗松著名的《法国文学史》这部支配了我们的教学长达半个世纪的书中讲得很清楚。然而，这部书的用意却一直没有得到正确理解。人们是否读过书的序言？不管怎样，下面这段文字很值得推敲：

> 所以，我想不出一个人学习文学除了想提益自我修养外，还能出于什么其他理由；除了他喜欢它外，还能出于什么其他原因。无疑，那些打算当教师的人必须使他们的知识系统化，使他们的学习遵循一些方法，和那些仅仅作为文学的"业余爱好者"的人们相比，需要在他们的学习中运用更加精确的（如果他们愿意的话，我想说更加科学的）概念。但是，决不能忽视这两点：其一，如果他不能首先努力去培养学生对文学的鉴赏力的话，他将是个蹩脚的文学教师……；其二，如果在成为学者前，他本身并不是个"业余爱好者"，那么，对于如何使他的教学富有这方面的成效，他就会不得要领。

你"成为学者之前"就一直在正确地阅读。普雷沃（Jean Prévost）就把自己说成是"诗歌的业余爱好者"。普雷沃这位人文学者不仅翻译西班牙、英国、德国、现代希腊的诗歌，而且还在一位中国文学家帮助下，借助一些拙劣的法文译作，翻译中国诗歌。普雷沃的杰作之一《诗歌爱好者》使他跻身于比较文学的忠实的解释者，也就是说比较文学的忠实的信徒的行列；之所以能这样，是因为这位作家能够遵奉朗松提出的那些要求，他在第二次大战期间，在里昂曾为一部著名的、出色的论述"司汤达的创作"的论文进行答辩，而同是这位作家，对一些中国诗人喜爱得如痴如醉（象他自己说的那样）。

在被盗用了的"朗松主义"的名义下，那些最低能的、因而也是最顽固的效颦者们，追随那位老一代的大师已有半个世纪，却仿佛他提出的先决条件是失效了的：对他们来说，那些最没有价值的文献汇编、遗闻轶事、附属文件构成了比较学者的工作的核心部分；无论怎么说，这些也是他们的范围以内的唯一的工作。某些法国学派的代表人物机械

① 指比较文学学科在世界范围内使用统一的工作语言的问题。

② 朗松（Custave Lanson，1857—1934），法国文学史家。

地将这种走了样的“朗松方法”运用到比较文学中来，而在朗松看来，历史的、信实的、确凿的研究是文学研究的前奏，作家欣赏的前奏[并且同时保证“业余爱好者”免受妄自尊大的批评，有关这类批评，勒梅特尔(Jules Lemaitre)以及其他许多文学方面的报刊撰稿人在当时提供了出色的然而是令人沮丧的例子]。这些热心分子自作主张，把文学研究、甚至比较文学划入历史研究的范围。不过，甚至象让马里·伽列这样眼光敏锐的大师，故世前不久在同意为基亚的《比较文学》撰写前言时，也犯了同样的错误。虽然急于想继巴登斯贝格和梵·第根之后划定我们学科的范围，他在下面这些话中还是没有给出这样一个定义，使我们确实应当称之为“法国式的”正统：

> 比较文学是文学史的分支，它研究国际性的精神联系，研究拜伦与普希金、歌德与卡莱尔、司各特与维尼之间的事实联系，研究不同文学的作家之间在作品、灵感，甚至生活方面的事实联系。
>
> 它不是主要探讨作品原有的价值，而是着重关心一些国家和作家如何改造他们借用来的东西……说到底，比较文学不是美国学校里教的那种“总体文学”。它最终可能导致总体文学的产生；对某些人来说，它必须这么做。但是，象人文主义、古典主义、浪漫主义、现实主义、象征主义这样的大略的平行关系(还有共时性关系，synchronisme)，因为系统性过强、时空延展太开而有化成为抽象空泛、主观臆断的东西、只剩下些标签的危险。尽管比较文学能够领出条通向这些综合的路来，它本身并不能完成这些综合。

并不是说所有这些话在我看来都应当受到批评。为了把这些观念引向荒谬(但毕竟，这些观念往往是文学史家杜撰出来或加以系统化的)，我从我们的历史学者的教科书里收罗了所有适合归类的欧洲前浪漫主义的题材：“自然”、“情与景”、“爱情与激情”、“宿命”、“敏感性”、“过去的时光”、“古代遗迹”，等等；随后我在蒙特贝里埃(Montepelier)大学开设了18世纪末叶欧洲前浪漫主义的课程。我讲授了一门再正统不过的课，最后，我用这些话作结语：“我想指出，所有我用来评述欧洲前浪漫主义的诞生的引语均出自中国诗歌，从生活在纪元前的屈原到宋代。”我是以这种方式在为伽列的审慎辩护，并且为那些人辩护(同时也偷偷捅了他们一拳)，他们认为，作家之间、流派之间或文学类型之间的“事实联系”的历史并没有穷尽我们这门学科的内容。原因在于，如果说我能够引用公元前和公元后十二个世纪的中国诗歌来解释十八世纪的前浪漫主义的所有题材的话，显而易见，这是因为那些形式存在着，类型存在着，不变因素存在着，一句话，有人存在，文学也就存在。

……

理想的比较学者

让我把意思讲清楚！我并不打算将历史的方法从我们的训练中排斥出去。正象人们说的，我们都置身于历史之中：历史无所不在地压着我们，重重地压着我们，常常把我们压碎了。我感到，从历史的观点去研究至少是某一个"事实联系"起着明显作用的时期，对所有的比较学者来说，是合适的，甚至是必要的。我希望我们的比较学者在考察案卷和收集小型杂志方面得到很好训练。除了受到一个历史学学者应受的训练外，我也希望他受到一个社会学学者应受的训练，我甚至不去阻止他接触总体文化。此外，他应该具备他所选择的那个时期有关造型艺术和音乐的较完备的知识，而不满足于一知半解，以便能在这方面产生他自己的见解！今天我们有时称之为"交叉学科"(sciences diagonales)的东西，在我年轻的时候仍叫总体文化，或说的更朴素些，叫文化；它成了供奉我们这个世纪的恶魔的牺牲品，在这个过分专门化的时代，任何一门学科——至少我们这门学科——都应该认识到它的重要性，这样才妥当。是的，我希望我们的比较学者尽可能博学多闻；我甚至希望他具有百科全书编纂者那样的雄心，狄德罗那样的雄心。18世纪，孟德斯鸠和伏尔泰这两位参与当时哲学运动的人物能意识到、甚至能阐述我们学科的某些原理和准则，这不是偶然的。伏尔泰在他的《论史诗》中，试图把史诗的根本性要素——那就是，一个统一的动作：单纯，重大，有趣——从另外一些要素中分离出来：诸如小插曲的选择，事件的不可思议的性质，某某天神力量的降临，这些要素可以随各民族的不同特点、历史的偶然事件、作家的幻想的不同而改变。以同样有见地的眼光，孟德斯鸠从这种或那种语言的声调重音入手，以便推导出为这种或那种语言的诗歌所独有的特性：这种语言用抑抑扬格或抑扬—抑抑扬格更可取，那种语言用扬抑格或扬抑抑格更好。说到那些百科全书式的学者(二十世纪在各种各样学科中我认识一些这样的学者)，我希望这样的人在我们的领域里更加众多。没有谁是受法令强迫而成为比较学者的，除非他具有博学强记的能力专长。

我同样希望我们的比较学者是有情趣和会享乐的人。我希望他的所有初步性研究对他来说仅仅是手段，通过这种研究，他比起那些对作品背景情况了解得很少或一无所知的人来，在阅读作品本文时更能发挥自己的才智，因而也就更能从中得到乐趣，更加兴致勃勃。

我希望他是一个诗歌、或戏剧、或小说的"业余爱好者"，就像朗松要求于他的文学史家的一样。所以我们应当认为1958年教堂山大会是有收获的。在那儿，"美国学派"的一些学者再三强调了那些在《比较文学》杂志上阐述过多次的观点，从而有力地恢复了在"法国学派"那儿往往被忽视的文学批评的地位。和我一样，雷内·韦勒克没有忘记，在"比较文学"中有"比较"一词，但和我一样，他也相信，另一个词"文学"是不应被忘记的。

这并不意味着我对某些美国学者也举手赞同，他们在纯批评、或所谓的纯批评的名义下，拒绝接受我们学科中一切看上去类似他们不屑一顾地称为"实证主义"经验的东西。有些人以文学是人类想象力的产物为理由，断言(如果我们打算相信他们的话)它不能成为分析的对象。举例来讲，如果马隆(Malone)局限于对那些借口研究来源和影响、胡乱堆砌了一些丝毫不说明问题的历史的或社会学方面的资料的人进行嘲讽，我就完全赞同他了！来源的研究从来就解释不了为什么一只绵羊根据不同情况被改变成一头狮子、一只老虎、或一头豹，甚至一条五颜六色的岩间巨蟒。但是，对"实证主义"的谴责如果导致了纯唯美主义观点，我对此表示怀疑，我坚持认为，美学的一切都要从确凿的研究那儿获得，正象我们从1937年于巴黎召开的第二届"美学与艺术科学大会"中看到的。在不久的将来，处于最理想状态的比较学者会是这种人：具有极为广泛的爱好，通晓几种将在二〇〇〇年前后用来写作的最重要的语言，并且具有对文学的美的深切体会。巴登斯贝格、伽列、哈扎都曾经尝试写非学术性著作，并获得了不同程度的成功：巴登斯贝格尝试写诗，伽列写游记；哈扎很早以前曾经私下向我透露，他一直想写小说（后来甚至出版了）；至于维维埃，他作为诗人是丝毫不会辱没他作为教师的名声的。如果说巴达庸能在当今法国的比较研究中高人一筹的话，他这一地位的确立不应仅仅归功于他的学问；他对《塞莱斯蒂娜》和《土耳其的旅行》的阐释完全出自艺术家的手笔。

……

从比较文学到比较诗学

历史的探寻和批判的或美学的沉思，这两种方法以为它们自己是势不两立的对头，而事实上，它们必须互相补充；如果能将两者结合起来，比较文学便会不可违拗地被导向比较诗学。这种美学不再是从形而上的原理中演绎出来，而将从具体文学的细致研究中归纳出来，要么是研究文学类型的历史演进，要么是研究不同的文化中创造出来的与文学类型相当的每一种形式的性质和结构；因此，与一切教条主义水火不容，它能成为真正具有实用价值的美学。我们知道，伟大的作品总是以它新颖的风貌超出我们的意料。不管我们对美学如何痴情，我们当中有谁梦想把自己的那套雄辩奉为准则，纵使它是由类型的历史推断出来的？但是，我们为什么不去尝试概括出一个由诸不变因素构成的系统呢？这种系统如果是用极为严格的标准制定出来的，它可能会有助于使当代文学从那种错乱、混杂、丑态中摆脱出来；当代文学如果不说是完全醉心于其中的话，也在其中荒废掉不少时间。现在，诗歌可以摒弃诗韵，接着是节奏，言语、词义、停顿，最后是词本身，以便用一些孤立的字母，或是用几组无法读音而且任意地分散在书页上的辅音字母构成诗的形式；小说则以一扎文稿的形式出售，读者可以把它当作一副扑克牌那样来洗。在这种情况下，诗的结构的比较分析（不管所研究的文化之间是否有历史联系）可能会帮助我们发现诗歌或小说本身必须具备的特性。今天，那么多人不是用嘲讽就是用挑衅拒不接受一切美学标准，或者拿与他们声称属于他们的艺术毫不相容的一些原则硬是自相标榜；在这样的时期，文学的比较研究，甚至对那些相互之间没有影响关系的文学的比较研究会对当代艺术的复原作出贡献。是啊，比较学者干嘛老是被动呢？说到那些对布莱希特和“间离化”推崇之致的人们，他们为什么就不能证明“间离化”这个东西很早就存在了，只不过那位伟大人物推广了它的名称呢？他们为什么就不能设法用演出“能乐”的方式来提倡“能乐”理论，从而使欧洲或美洲的戏剧恢复其活力呢？伍德贝里（G. Woodbery）在第一期《比较文学杂志》中写道：“比较的方法是一切古典主义之母。”他说的是否就那么一无是处呢？

我们还需要重建我们的规划

无论如何，我们必须重建我们的规划。我们现在培养的学生在某一天就是别人的老师了，他们将承担为这个世界培养他们自己的学生的责任，而这一世界可能会由这样的成分组成：将要宣布列入世界强国的最前列的十亿或二十亿中国人；几亿伊斯兰人，在表明了他们的独立意愿后，再次表明了（他们也确实已经这么做了）他们对宗教帝国的信仰；还有印度半岛，在那儿，几亿人，包括泰米尔人，北部印度人，还有孟加拉人，马拉斯特拉人，等等，将不再沉默；拉丁美洲的几千万印第安人，他们一直在呼唤着重新成为人的权力，成为拥有充分权力的人；除了当今世界的两大强国，俄国和美国外，还有至少一亿二千万的日本人，它们也许有一天会结成联盟以与新的野心抗衡；幅员辽阔的巴西、拉丁美洲也许最终将摆脱美帝国主义的控制；整个黑非洲，赞扬或贬斥"黑人特性"（négritude）的人们等等。至于我们法国人，我们非常愿意创建一种"现代文人学衔考试制"（Agrégation），但要假定不包括中国和阿拉伯世界才行。卡尔（Adrien Cart），这位公共教育监察主任、学衔考试审查委员会主任以"要预见遥远的未来人们在智力上可能会关注的东西以及那时的志趣所向"就得靠肆意妄为才行作为借口，把他的培养目标局限于训练那些将来能基本胜任1970年左右的教学工作的青年人。我们将继续讨论亚里士多德、《堂吉诃德》、《一千零一夜》。但那些"和法语教授或比较文学教授惯常所关注的东西相去甚远的课题"被他从我们的规划中一笔勾销。在我看来，恰恰相反，我们选择了这一职业并不是为了盲目遵从一些缺少素养、随波逐流的头脑里的"惯常占所关注的东西"。同样，我们学科的性质鼓励我们对某种足以影响形成之中的文学的辩术梦寐以求，我们的学科也要求我们引导我们的学生不仅去思考今天正在提出的问题，而且更着重去思考将来会出现的问题。

……

组织起来进行我们的研究

一个由世界范围内的比较学者精心拟定、并首先意在弥合我们学科中出现的隔阂的研究规划，应当能引导我们把那些被培养来研究新鲜课题的研究者们组织起来，从事研究。我感到奇怪的是，在当今这个世纪，既然我们终于明白了，再也不能听凭或者是人们的生活状况，或者是国家的经济状况变化无常，采取放任自流的态度；那么，我们怎么还听凭至少是人们的精神生活的这一部分处于一种危险的混乱状态之中，这种精神生活能够，实际上也必须把自己安排得井然有序。如果根据我和我的同行共同达成的协议，我被指定更着重地讲授我们学科中那部分我感到自己对此具有某种能力和某些感想的内容，和其他任何人同样程度地关心自由的我，并不会感到我是在受到别人强迫。如果一个真正的国际性组织赏识一位来自另一国度的同行的才华和学问，建议他致力于比较韵律学的研究，我看不出他如何还会感到受了压制。这样的话，隔阂将弥合，同时用不着担心由于重复劳动而浪费精力，鉴于我们学科的所有有意义的工作都在等待我们去做，这些精力可以使用得更加富有成效；这样，对我们的后继者就更好了。

（戴耘　译）

（节选自雷内·艾金伯勒：《比较文学的目的，方法，规划》，干永昌、廖鸿钧、倪蕊琴选编，《比较文学研究译文集》，上海译文出版社1985年版，第93-120页。）

比较文学的新动向

（节选）

[美]勃洛克

【导读】

此文为美国纽约市立大学比较文学教授勃洛克（Haskell M. Block）于1969年写就。这篇论文不仅被视作法国学派与美国学派十年论战的经验总结，而且更体现出一位比较文学家对国际比较文学发展动向的敏锐把握。

文章前半部分以回顾的口吻完成了对法国学派的功绩肯定与不足批评。勃洛克指出，法国学派"机械地研究来源和影响、事实关系、际遇、名望，或者一个作家、或一部作品受到的待遇，以及文学作品之间所谓的有决定性的因果关系"，比较文学研究失去生命力和创造性，从而导致了危机产生。鉴于此，勃洛克提出了个人的主张。

在重新调整比较文学的目标与方法问题上，勃洛克开出了如下良方：其一，强调文学内在价值与国际关系的并置研究。以往人们多进行双项研究（X作者对Y作者的影响），而忽视了作品内质的挖掘，由此论者以为，比较文学研究者在研究一部著作时，可以既分析其内在价值，又探寻其国际联系。这种研究方法由于破除了假定一个唯一来源问题的局限，因此能让评论更加自由，也更多地符合文学本性。其二，修改比较文学的定义。比较文学不应是强调它的研究内容或者学科之间的界限，而是一种前景、一种观点、一种坚定的从国际角度从事文学研究的设想。因此，其研究旨归是总体文学。其三，重新梳理比较文学与文学研究的关系。勃洛克指出，对诗学和文学理论的深入分析，能强化比较文学对国别文学的研究价值。当人们打算彻底了解一种艺术形式的成分时，必定要涉及他国文学，这就使得未来的文学研究更侧重于比较文学方向。其四，比较文学研究应更注重评论精神。今后的比较文学家应着重考察文学作品的价值关系，而非事实关系。强调每一件艺术品的特性和个性，推崇文本细读。其五，在文学作品的历史价值与批评价值的问题上，提倡从文学研究本身的特殊性与直接性角度出发。

综上所述，勃洛克认为，比较文学新的最重要的动向是，人们已逐渐意识到比较文学研究中各别艺术品的内在价值，以及从文体论和结构角度展开分析的重要性。这些，对未来的文学研究提供了很有意义的可能性。

（曾小月）

现在来为比较文学作一总结，为时尚早。很可能战后没有别的与人文科学有关的学科曾得到同样的发展。每一年似乎都为比较文学活动的日益开展和人们对它的兴趣的增长提供新的佐证。比较文学研究本身并非新鲜事情。过去好几位大作家——但丁、拉伯雷、密尔顿、拉辛、伏尔泰、歌德——无论在态度上还是方法上都是出色的比较文学研究者，他们是当代博学之士和文学评论家们真正的先驱者。比较文学就其最广泛的意义而言跟文学本身同样古老。它迅速成为一种建制，并且作为人文科学的一个分支被正式列入大学课程，足以表明它在我们时代具有特别重要性。虽说比较文学当前的目标和任务主要归入大学里的文学研究范围，但我们却不能因此把它局限为纯学院课题。

尽管比较文学不久前才进入大学圈子，它却可以被看作人文科学中最具活力、最能引起人们兴趣的科目之一。近十年来，多亏国际比较文学学会的历届大会及其他活动，新的努力层出不穷，蔚为大观，这表现为制订新的大学教育计划，召开全国性的和国际性的大会和讨论会，出版新的杂志和论文集，以及长论、短评、文章、书籍数目的持续增长。人文科学界愈益认识到，比较文学可以为理解并培育我们的文化遗产作出贡献。

怎样解释这一新的重要性呢？部分原因是二次世界大战结束以来，世界各部分的居民之间的文化交往迅速扩展。我们所处的国际化和世界主义的时代赋予学者以世界公民的身份，这不能不激起他们对比较文学研究的兴趣。这一新的重要性也可以用学者们的性格来解释，是他们把我们的学科引向一个方向并且给它一个尊严的地位。如果没有这一批相对来说数量不多但才华出众、精力充沛的学者作出的努力，比较文学不会有今天的发展。其次，这一发展曾享有有利的条件。国别文学研究日趋专门化，分工过细，以及关于各别作者的若干专题研究的支离破碎性，使得相互沟通成为一个严重的问题。比较文学研究为在明显不同领域工作的人文学者之间进行重要的交流和对话提供了方便。攻读文学的学生为摆脱民族和语言的束缚，以便使文学研究接近文学的本质，也越来越转向比较文学。

……

通过比较文学在它达到战后的发展以前的历史，我们可以部分理解为什么关于比较文学研究的性质与功能的解释如此繁多，而且往往相互矛盾。本世纪头几个十年里，一群杰出的法国学者在比较文学研究中占领导地位，特别是巴登斯贝格、梵·第根和伽列。梵·第根的教科书《比较文学论》(1931)长时期内曾是唯一的入门书。《比较文学评论》以及规模可观的《比较文学评论丛书》为传播巴登斯贝格及其同行们确立的原则与目标出了不少力。然而不能认为所有这些学者以及他们的学生对于原则和方法都持相同见解。他们肯定没有以比较文学研究的"法国学派"的代表自居，但是他们的集体努力为重新估价作为一项研究任务的比较文学提供了基础。

应当感谢1958年在教堂山举行的国际比较文学学会第二届大会鼓励了这一重新估价的努力。韦勒克的报告《比较文学的危机》是这一努力的最有力、最富论战性的表现。该文在大会记录中发表，后来收入作者重要的论文集《批评概念》(1963)。这以后，艾金伯勒的《比较不是理由》1966年在美国出版时用了一个类似的标题：《比较文学中的危机》。

我们不应该纯粹从否定方面去看我们的学科中的危机观念。很可能形成危机的条件今天不仅在人文科学中，而且在日常生活中一直具备着。但是也可能意识到这一危机——甚至自愿接受这一危机，会导致产生一种创造性的努力。精神生活是一种永久紧张的对话和运动的生活。有危机未必就是混乱和不协调。不同态度和价值的充满活力的交锋是人类为实现其企图而需要的能量和力量的必不可少的源泉，而危机能使这一交锋带上戏剧性。我以为确认比较文学当前的危机本身不是一件坏事，恰恰相反。

我已指出比较文学的发展特别迅速。回过头来看，过去的十年可以代表一个几乎难以置信的发达时期。至少以后再也不可能回到教堂山那种气氛里来了。如果我们援引韦勒克1958年的意见，我们还应该承认这些意见——特别是针对在场的外国学者——主要是法国学者们而发的。我还得补充，由于韦勒克的报告采用论证性的语调，他详尽地重复了他在别处，特别是在他与华伦合作的《文学理论》(1949)一书中曾经阐发的论据。如果他是在对美国学者作报告，口气可能会不一样，不过我不以为他的立场会有什么实质上的改变。

现在让我们来进一步看看这份报告。韦勒克要求的正是全盘调整比较文学研究的方向。报告一开头，他宣称："我们学科的处境岌岌可危，其严重标志是，未能确定明确的研究内容和专门的方法论。"比较文学的主要理论家巴登斯贝格，梵·第根和他们的合作者们的纲领性述作"把陈旧过时的方法论包袱强加于比较文学研究，并压上十九世纪事实主义、唯科学主义和历史相对主义的重荷"。这些看法相当有见地。比较文学往往局限于机械地研究来源和影响、事实关系、际遇、名望，或者一个作家、或一部作品受到的待遇，以及文学作品之间所谓的有决定性的因果关系。韦勒克还指出，许多比较文学研究虽然有潜在的世界主义倾向，其起因却是出于爱国主义的和民族主义的考虑。

这些研究通常只能成为一种国别文学的附庸；菲利普·梵·第根的《外国文学对法国文学的影响(1550—1880)》便是明证。大部分影响研究——菲利普·梵·第根说，仅仅关于外国文学与法国文学之间的关系的研究著作已有1200多种——确实如韦勒克说的那样毫无可取之处，即便其中最成功之作提供的文学研究手段，在方法上也与在一种国别文学的范围内研究相互影响的做法没有什么差别。按照韦勒克的说法，死抱住事实不放，使得比较文学不能从当代充满生命活力和富有创造性的冲动得到好处："直截了当地说，在方法和方法论见解方面比较文学已成为一潭死水。"

依照韦勒克的看法，比较文学已落到这步田地。在抨击这种状态的同时，如果说他没有提供调整方向的手段，至少他提出了这样做的原则。他摒弃死气沉沉的事实，要求人们能领悟价值和品质；他对文学史不持伪科学的见解，强调要承认文学评论在任何文学研究中的根本作用；他不从外部关系来考察一个艺术品，而是坚持作品是一个"符号和意义的分层结构"这样一种见解，认为正是这一结构能确定作品的性质。所以调整方向表现在美学和文学评论领域，在这一领域里文学史将自觉地、毅然决然地变成评论史，变成"象艺术本身一样的一种想象的行为"。

虽说韦勒克对于比较文学研究应朝什么方向努力发表了坦率的、清醒的声明，他的发言主要还是攻击错误的观念和方法，指责过去的谬误，指明比较文学不应该是什么样子。未必每个读者都全盘接受他对最近的过去的分析。但是我以为他有许多观点是绝对正确的。这一如此有力、如此清晰的批评性分析，对我们大有好处。不过我认为应该补充说明，照我的看法他的论证稍嫌过火。他举出近五十年应用的方法和取得的成果中最薄弱的部分，否认这一时期的比较文学家作出的积极建树。比较文学在最好的情况下并非是他的分析试图一笔抹煞的那个僵化的、愚蠢的分支学科。方法论远远赶不上实践，我们与其听取那些对于比较文学应遵循什么标准的议论，不如去审查研究成果本身，这样我们才能对过去的成就有一个比较准确的看法。

……

对于教堂山上发端的那一场有关比较文学原则和方法的争论，肤浅的观察家们很容易认为有一个“美国学派”在与“法国学派”相对抗。我以为谈论典型的法国方法或者典型的美国方法都是完全错误的。在大西洋两岸都能找到关于比较文学的富有想象力的或者有密切联系的见解。在美国与在欧洲一样，人们越来越意识到比较文学研究中各别艺术品的内在价值以及从文体论和结构角度去进行解释的重要作用。我认为这一觉醒标志着比较文学新的最重要的动向。作品的内在价值不仅在韦勒克与艾金伯勒的述论文中，而且也在最近在欧洲和美国举行的有关比较文学的讨论中得到广泛承认。任何适当的比较文学研究都要求同时应用分析方法和关系方法。

如同科修斯在他出色的《比较文学研究导论》中指出的那样：“一般说来，学文学的学生应该既能体会各国文学的个性，又能对文学作为一个共同体有所认识。”对于文本(text)，应该既能把握它的特殊性，又把它放在最广阔的文学背景下来考察。冉纳不久前说过：“比较文学家经常需要从事一种最地道的文学评论：文本阐释。他从事这项工作的时候要运用他的全部鉴赏力，可能的话还要读懂几种原文。”冉纳在那篇重要的、内容丰富的论文中认为，作比较解释至少需要重叠两个文本；但是我看不出来，为什么用心阅读并解释单独一个文本必须取决于字面上的比较。

如同里奈尔(Sven Linner)为我们指出的那样，比较作为一种语文学(philolgy)和文学评论方法，并非比较文学家的专用手段。任何攻读文学的学生都可以使用它。此外，比较只是比较文学研究应用的许多方法中的一种而已。需要指出，在有关比较文学的新著作的作者中，许多比较文学家——但并非全体——都强调拿文本作为研究的出发点。将来再有某些比较文学研究者只研究一部著作，既考察它的内在价值，又探索它的国际联系，可能就不会是什么异乎寻常之举了。我认为这样的研究要比双项研究(X作者对于Y作者的影响)更有价值。不幸的是，大部分比较文学研究仍是双项研究。最优秀的双项研究——我想到诸如弗莱德曼(Alice Green Fredman)的《狄德罗与斯托恩》，加埃德(Edouard Gaede)的《尼采与瓦莱利》，或者威斯盖白(Jean Weisgerber)的近作《福克纳与陀思妥耶夫斯基：汇合与影响》——既考虑亲和性与汇流，也考虑影响；同时探索这些作品特有的价值，以及它们包含并加以发扬的文学传统。大部分双项研究都从假定有一个唯一的来源出发。这样一来，它们甚至在最好的情况下也局限了评论解释的范围。为数太多的语文学家仍旧如此理解比较文学，他们认为除了这一形式之外，几乎不能有别的形式；只消阅读任何一期《比较文学》、《比较文学评论》、《比较文学研究》或者《阿卡提亚》，就能发觉这一点。但愿我们的方法以及我们的学生们的方法将更多地符合文学的本性。在作品的分析与解释方面最近取得的进展，使得这一研究方式逐渐在比较文学界占据主要地位，并逐步引向重新调整比较文学的目标与方法。

……

如果有理由认为我们美国人不喜欢这个术语，我们的法国同行对之也不见得满意。巴达庸(Marcel Bataillon)写道:“比较不过是我们称之为比较文学的那门学科应用的手段之一。而这个名称是相当词不达意的。”在给比较文学下定义的时候，与其强调它的研究内容或者学科之间的界限，不如强调比较文学家的精神倾向。比较文学主要是一种前景，一种观点，一种坚定的从国际角度从事文学研究的设想。据弗莱德里克·罗(Frederick C. Roe)说，赫福德(C. H. Herford)教授早在1886年，即波斯奈特出版《比较文学》一书的那一年，就称他的研究项目为“国际文学”。阿贝克隆比(Lascelles Abercrombie)在纪念赫福德的一篇论文中恰如其分地指出，赫福德的研究的特色在于他经常关注语文学与评论的相互作用，与传统的忽视价值问题的比较文学研究适成对比，甚至在他着手对文学关系与文学传统进行大规模研究的时候，“他也知道他始终应该回溯到各别艺术品”。

……

比较文学研究与国别文学之间这一持续的相互关系可以表现为对诗学与文学理论的重新增长的兴趣。当人们对一种艺术形式的成分，对于术语及一般概念，对于文学体裁与风格的内在活力所作的研究，涉及好几国文学，当人们既研究它们的相互关系又研究它们的个性时，人们实际上做的就是比较文学研究。我指的是，举例来说，关于小说的基本研究，如凯赛尔(Wolfgang Kayser)的《谁来叙述小说》和缪勒(Gunther Muller)的《讲述的时间和讲述出来的时间》；或者，在戏剧文学方面，如古叶埃(Henri Gouhier)的《戏剧的本质》，宗第(Peter Szondi)的《现代戏剧理论》。韦勒克很有理由强调要取消比较文学与总体文学之间业已过时的区别。对于梵·第根来说，总体文学是某种与它今天的样子全然不同的东西。对他来说，总体文学是国际文学史的大型综合。基亚在他的教科书《比较文学》中宣称，如果说“总体文学”这个名词有一个特殊含义，那正是因为人们把 它应用于广泛的比较文学研究。《比较文学与总体文学年鉴》前编辑弗里德里希(Werner P. Friederich)承认说:“我不知道什么是‘总体文学’，几年来，我一直寻求某个有学问的人写的一篇有学问的文章，希望这篇文章能廓清各种各样的定义……使我们最终能弄个明白，我们这个年鉴本应该做些什么工作。”与此同时，过去和现在的编辑们还是体面地完成了他们的任务。但是从比较文学观点出发，我们应该多加注意为任何文学表达形式所共有的因素。

……

我们感谢大西洋两岸的比较文学家如此聪慧地确定了问题的性质，同时我们还应该考虑如何确定历史价值与批评价值的相互作用。这个问题并非只限于比较文学；今天人文科学各个部门都面临这个问题。一种能把事件的活力与个性，以及它们彼此的活跃关系都考虑在内的历史观，可能会为这个问题提供一种解决方法。但是一种历史哲学只能指出一个方向；如何在文学研究中运用这一历史哲学，必然是个人的事情。没有什么秘诀，也没有普遍适用的解决办法；但是任何关于历史与批评之间的相互关系的思考都应该从文学研究本身的特殊性与直接性这个角度出发。

……

其实，评论才能只不过是一个见解高低的问题。评论才能与其取决于一种预先设定的方法，不如取决于在解释一个艺术品的时候需要动用的全部经验。不管应用什么方法或者什么方法组合，文学研究的目的应是使我们对于由重大的文学表现出来的巨大想象力及人情味能有新的、更扩大的领悟。由于比较文学对文学一般性的理论问题以及个性丰富、各不相同的艺术品同时怀有兴趣，它能为文学研究提供一种有益的、甚至是唯一的可能性。

危机不等于灾难。佩尔在他关于比较文学现状的论文《瞻前顾后》的结尾写道："比较文学家们如果这么认为也不算狂妄：他们在最近二三十年间形成这个国家以及其他几个国家最开放、最有进取心的文学史家团体。"把比较文学研究局限于事实领域的倾向正在消失，而把事实关系降到次要地位的倾向却是不可避免的，但是我们对于比较文学家将怎样承担他们的新的责任，却不是那么有把握。个别情况下，对于方法论问题和文学理论问题的思考会引出好的结果；在最好的场合，方法论可以成为激励研究者作出新的努力的泉源。

但是我认为，当前比较文学需要更多的是伟大的榜样，而不是抽象的方法论公式。为了取得有效的结果，我以为灵活性、努力的多样性，甚而彻底的主观性都是必不可缺的条件。佩尔有理由要求研究者具备胆识和想象力。一个学者具备这两种品格未必就会在语文学上不负责任。当前没有任何一个文学研究领域能比比较文学更引起人们的兴趣或有更如远大的前途；任何领域都不会比比较文学提出更严的要求或更加令人眷恋。

巴登斯贝格曾设想通过比较文学的发展来"为新的人文主义做准备"。二十世纪的混乱历史为他这个设想作出辛辣的评注，但是想法本身仍旧延续下来了。由于比较文学要求研究者具备聪明、机智的态度，它将把我们引向人类的相互同情和团结。我们彼此需要。我们正投入一项集体合作的事业，很可能，通过发现、解释和妙悟，我们将对这个人文主义有新的体察，而我们的文明的存亡有赖于这个人文主义。

（施康强　译）

（节选自勃洛克：《比较文学的新动向》，干永昌、廖鸿钧、倪蕊琴选编，《比较文学研究译文集》，上海译文出版社 1985 年版，第 185-206 页。）

我们：从何来，是什么，去何方
——比较文学的永久危机
（节选）

[美]乌尔利希·维斯坦因

【导读】

乌尔利希·维斯坦因（Ulrich Weisstein），生于德国，后加入美国籍，著名比较文学家，文学史家，艺术评论家，翻译家。比较文学著作主要有：《比较文学导论》（德语版1968年），修订后改名为《比较文学与文学理论》（1973年），还有《比较文学——第一个报告：1968—1977》（1981年）等。

《我们：从何来，是什么，去何方——比较文学的永久危机》发表于1984年，是在比较文学遭遇又一次危机的情况下，通过对其发展轨迹的梳理，来澄清问题，探索出路。本文首先对比较文学的危机进行讨论，作者表达了对这门学科的信念。接着通过对史前史的追述，探讨了早期比较文学与民间文学的关系，明确了比较文学跨语言与跨国界等基本问题。结尾部分则从具体方法的层面提出自己的设想。文章主体部分主要从时间、空间、论题、理论和方法等几个轴心描述分析比较文学发展轨迹。

在时间轴上，作者主要讨论了以梵·第根为代表的早期比较文学研究对于中世纪的忽略，最终这一时间方面的限制被打破。在空间轴上，作者批评了西方比较文学界长期流行的欧洲中心主义思想，同时指出，企图打破各国文学之间的传统区别，创造一种所谓的“平均主义”，同样是过激的。他肯定了“言语文学”对比较文学的意义，意识到对在语言上统一，政治、经济和文化上却属于不同体系的文学进行比较研究，关注“文学区域”，已经成为一种研究趋势。他认为，正是尼日利亚、澳大利亚、中国等国家成立了全国性协会，才将比较文学的全球性推进到一个高潮，但是仍未实现真正的全球性。他表达了对比较文学中存在的新的所谓“中心主义”的担忧，希望比较文学能够真正形成一种不带偏见的、跨国别的观点。上述讨论都体现了维斯坦因的开放性与包容性，这在西方学者中是难能可贵的，而这种精神正是比较文学精神的内核。研究论题方面，他认为“比较文学”这一名称应该会保留下去，应该始终立足于文学，但又会突破“纯文学”，主要表现在对文学与其他艺术、文学和自然科学之间的关系、文学与社会科学的关系的研究上，从而肯定了跨学科研究的价值。但是他又对总体文学（即“一般文学”）研究颇有微词，认为总体文学与比较文学只是数量上的差异，而无实质区别，这有点过于轻视总体文学的价值。维斯坦因认为，接受美学并没有为比较文学带来新的突破。这一观点在异质文化背景下就会受到挑战，跨异质文化的文学接受因为存在着文化过滤与误读的问题，将会远远超出他所说的“老方法”，而具有实质上的突破。维斯坦因对翻译理论和翻译实践的称赞，预示着翻译研究与比较文学之间的关系愈益密切。他认为“意象学”（现一般称为“形象学”）及“心理状况史”研究的出现及发展说明比较文学“文学性”的削弱。

在理论与方法论方面，维斯坦因对比较文学过分依赖文学理论的倾向提出质疑。他指出比较文学的理论问题与文学理论、文学史及文学批评三者的联系与平衡有关。比较文学最初是作为文学史的一个分支，在遭遇多年冷落之后，比较文学史的编撰又得到重视。与文学批评相比，比较批评是后来者，对比较批评的重视与对价值判断的兴趣的恢复密切相关。在三者之中，理论是最热门的一个，以致作者担心比较文学会被文学理论所吞噬，或者变成文学理论的附庸。作者希望比较文学能够更多地致力于方法论的探讨，并能真正立足于实践，论文最后对编撰目录、术语辞典、比较文学史的呼吁及对加强教学问题的强调即体现了这一思想。

维斯坦因捍卫比较文学的学科独立性，致力于比较文学理论与方法论的建构，对比较文学的来龙去脉有着清晰的把握，对于富有争议性的问题有着自己明确的立场，对容易走向极端的现象又能给予冷静的提醒，他既是比较文学的守护者，也是其培育者。

（常芳）

……

我所要探讨的五个论题中的第三个论题，是与第四（理论）和第五（方法论）紧密联系在一起的，因为科学中每一种新发现或重新发现的研究领域，必定需要新的技术和理论根据。尽管近来有人试图为它重新命名，① 但我们的学科很可能会保留“比较文学”这一名称。既然如此，任何对其目的所做出的定义，必定会把自己限制在那一文艺的氛围之内。这就是索尔本的创立者们的目的。他们要求比较文学（“对不同文学中的作品彼此之间的关系的研究”）②和一般文学（研究“国际文学史”同时属于几种文学的范畴现象）③，虽然后来还包括了思想史这一类的研究④，都严格地立足于文学（尽管它不断地引起一些法国人和德国人做出努力来复兴“一般文学”，但它还是应该被放在一边，因为它所要求的差异是数量上的，而不是质量上的）。

除了早期试图将比较文学的范围扩展出“纯文学”的断断续续的努力之外，⑤ 不顾名

① 梵·第根《比较文学》，第57页。

② 梵·第根《比较文学》，第174页。

③ 在Simon Jeune的《一般文学和比较文学：论方向》中最为明显。

④ 最明显的是Dyserinck的《比较文学：导论》第二卷的第二部分，标题为“一般文学作为比较文学的分支”。

⑤ 早在1901年，英国批评家G. G. 史密斯便在“比较文学的衬托”一文中提出扩展的建议。见《黑林爱丁堡杂志》第189期，第38-49页。

称而与传统决裂的努力，直到第二次世界大战以后才产生效果。布朗(C. S. Brown)设想，既然文学是一种艺术，它是可以与其他艺术的关系进行有意义的研究的。布朗成为第一个进行这项“冒险尝试”的比较学者。他在《乔治亚评论》第一期中，在他为我们这个领域所下的定义中，首先呼吁将比较艺术里涉及文学的那一方面包括进文学中去，并作为其术语之一。① 从那时起，他的观点尽管在当时还很有争议，但在学科内却变得如此流行，如此广泛，即使不算普遍，但也被看作是常规了。②

构成比较文学内核的第二个更大一些的圆周环，是对文学和科学之间关系的研究。它超出了美学范畴，因此更有争议——这并非由于其本身(因为有谁会否认，从当代人对传统遗产的看法的角度研究左拉的《萌芽》，或由所谓的“南特学派”所做的精神心理试验来分析斯特林堡的《父亲》呢？我们可以从中得到很多结果)，而是由于它的地位，这种明了、极易辨认的附属地位，正如亨利·H. 雷马克在其著名的文章中为其所命名的那样，雷马克是唯一的在试图为其下定义时严肃提出该问题的学者。③

韦勒克在《比较文学的性质与名称》中对雷马克的观点表示反对，说它是“为了一个实用的目的而定的，即在一所美国研究生院中，在那些没有同情心并又怨恨你闯入他们所擅长的领域的同事们面前，你不得不为你那属于比较文学的论题去作出论证”。④ 但这个误解的根子，它所引起的逻辑上的错误既多又深。就是说，各种现象必须真正地对等才具可比性，例如文学不可与科学比，只有文艺学和科学才能相比。作为学术研究对象，文学是与社会学、植物学、动物学和心理学相互联系而起作用的。这些就像文艺学一样，是在理论和方法论上产生作用的，因此，也就像纽保尔(John Neubauer)在一篇文章中⑤所表示的，是可以从某个角度进行比较的。从主题上来说，科学材料、观察和技术都可以是很好的文学形象的研究对象(因此也可用在比较文学中)。它们可以作为一种尺度来衡量不同语言文学作品中对这方面的问题的处理。这是无可非议的，但还不足以说明应对比较文学重新作出定义。

从历史上来说，社会科学与文艺学的关系要比自然科学密切。在比较文学史上，它们对接受研究起着主要的作用(机会、成功、传播等)。对接受的研究与对“影响”的研究是相对的[“影响”是鲁狄格(Horst Rudiger)的术语，指美的影响的最好名称]。⑥ 事实上，法国波尔多会议(1970年)的组织者们是文学社会学的倡导者，他们将“文学和社会、结构

① 布朗很明智地提出了恰当的界限，他说：“并不是所有这些关系都属比较文学的范畴，如巴洛克建筑和马洛克音乐之间的平等关系就与比较文学者无关。”(《乔治亚评论》1959年第13期，第175页。)

② 极少数量的比较文学手册包括《文学和其他艺术》。

③ 《比较文学：其定义和功用》，见：N. P. Stalkencht 和 H. Frenz：《比较文学：方法与角度》，第8页。

④ 这篇论文首次出现在《工作中的比较学者：比较文学研究》中。后来收入韦勒克的《区别：批评概论新编》。

⑤ 这篇题为《文学与科学：它们的比喻和变形》的论文是匈牙利—美国文化委员会举办的座谈会的一部分。这次座谈会资料发表在《比较文学和一般文学》第32期(1983年)。

⑥ 见 Rudiger 的《国别文学和欧洲文学：比较文学的方法和目的》。

的问题和交际的问题”作为那次国际会议的两个主要论题之一。① 近来，把接受美学的原理运用到我们这门学科已形成一股风，虽然它并非完全没有学术上的长处，然而，它只不过是在一个较高的水平上(介于形式主义和文学社会学之间)，修改和复兴了在新术语掩饰下的老方法而已。在这种情况下，奥地利因斯布鲁克会议的资料汇编，即《文学交流与接受》一卷，几乎没有什么令人吃惊的东西。其中既没有新的方法上的突破，也没有为比较文学打开新的途径。实际上，尧斯在“引论”中写的纲领性的第一句话(“在此，我的开头部分的任务是：把比较文学中的接受美学进行如此的介绍，即根据前者理论建立的目前形势和后者的实际问题来予以讨论”)，② 给人的印象就具有一种无意的讽刺性。根据最近对这一复杂问题的处理情况来看，在这一领域里没有取得多大的进展。③

就第三个，即研究论题而言，最近出现或恢复了几种比较文学的情况，最令人兴奋的发展是对翻译理论和翻译实践方面兴趣的增长。对于翻译，我们这门学科的前驱者们是有所注意的，当然他们对译者(作为媒介者)的兴趣要大于对翻译本身。④ 在过去几十年中，整个翻译的质量大大提高，系统地研究这种语言交流工作的基础已经奠定。对翻译理论的强调，在安东·波普维奇(Anton Papovic)创立的斯洛伐克奈特拉学校所做的工作中得到反映，虽然对系统化的强求有些过分，⑤ 但还是应该受到欢迎。在国际比较文学协会内部，这种新的发展导致形成了一个格外活跃的“翻译委员会”。它有好几个项目，其中包括由 F. 麦吕格利(Meregalli)在一篇没有发表的文章中建议和初步规划的一部文学翻译史。

M. F. 基亚在其关于文学手册方面的文章中赞扬了卡瑞所做的研究，即法国接受德国文学中的意象与幻象的性质与功用方面的工作，并且试图建立一个新的接受研究领域。他称之为“所见的外国”。⑥ 后来，因为韦勒克站在新批评的立场上对其进行攻击，说研究“意象的社会史”导致文学研究“被瓦解成为心理和社会学”，⑦ 这朵小花似乎被扼杀在萌芽状态之中了。然而，《意象和幻象及其在比较文学范围内的研究》⑧论文中，代瑟林克(H. Dyserinck)又提出了这个问题。他争辩说，意象学——这门新的辅助学科的名称——将着重点放在意象的三种表示方式上，可以得到文学上的一定地位：(1)它在某些文学作品中的存在；(2)它在通过翻译或原著传播到当时即将出现的国别文学种类之外；3)在文艺学和批评中所占的主要地位。

主要由于代瑟林克的强烈干预，作为一种文学研究课题的意象学，当时已经受到人们的尊重。正如菲歌尔(M. S. Fischer)(他的文章《比较意象学：民族意象种类系统的跨学科

① 那次会议的主持者是 R. Escarpit，当时他是 Bordeux 大学文学和艺术技术学院院长。

② 康斯坦丁·诺维克等编：《第九届 ICLA 资料汇编》第二卷，第 35 页。

③ 这可以运用到 F. Rinner 和 K. Zerinschek 的《比较文学作为接受美学的引发者》，也可运用到 M. Gesteiger 的《比较文学和接受美学》中。

④ 在《比较文学》中，梵·第根声称：“翻译……在文学影响中起着重要作用。”

⑤ 《文学翻译分析辞典》可作为此趋势的例证。该书由 Alberta 大学比较文学系和 Popovic 出版。

⑥ 这是基亚的手册第三版第三章的标题。

⑦ 《比较文学概论》，见《比较文学和一般文学年鉴》第 2 期(1953 年)，第 4 页。

⑧ 《阿卡狄亚》第 1 期(1966 年)，第 107-120 页。

研究》①是介绍这门课题的最佳论文）所说，“比较意象学正象语言学介绍结构元素那样，主要是研究其他国家的现象”。但这个定义有个漏洞。正如“主要”一词所示，意象学者们继续与人类学和民族心理学“调情”②——这是在我们这门学科的一个日趋热门的分支中，社会角度正在逐渐占优势的又一迹象。③

我们这个不断扩大的家庭中的一个最新成员被命名为“心理状况史”。布加勒斯特的东南欧研究院的亚历山大·杜图(A. Dutu)最热心于这一学术事业。根据杜图在几本书和发表在《综合》以及最近的《比较文学杂志》④中的文章的阐述，“心理状况史”并没有什么特别新的出发点，它可被忽视为“精神史”的一个分支，它并不很强调对艺术和发达的文化进行研究，而是要追溯非理智或理智的现象。因而它也削弱了比较文学中的“文学”成分。

当论题转到理论和方法论问题上时，我们应该注意克本(Erwin Koppen)在一篇题为《比较文学有自己的理论吗?》⑤的论文开头所谈的看法。克本认为，与德国人所称的“一般文艺学”(它与法语“比较文学”一词不一样，这一术语跟文学理论几乎是同义词)不同的是，比较文学“从定义上来说不是一门以建立理论为任务的科学，而是一种用比较方式，凭经验从事的科学，它或多或少地是要去探讨历史事件和文学作品”。对于那些把这项指令放在心上的人来说，此处作出的划分极为重要，因为它指明了这样的事实，由于我们这个跨学科的研究不允许创建自己的理论，最好的办法还是借用现存的理论。这主要是一个技巧和权宜手段，因此，没有理由像一些人那样，去相信“比较文学的前途”⑥取决于其对形式主义、结构主义，符号学⑦等的采纳和吸收。佛克玛的“比较文学和新范例”⑧是为文学理论所做的雄辩呐喊。像他这样的学者也错误地认为这才是比较文学的出路所在。

我认为，对于一个比较文学学者有意义的理论问题之一，是同文学学者所从事的三个方面(即文学理论、文学史、文学批评——译者)之间的联系和变化着的平衡有关的。正如韦勒克和渥伦在《文学理论》第四章里说到的：

---

① 《社会心理学杂志》第10期(1979年)，第30-40页。

② 他们经常引用《人种心理学：各民族心理学评论》这一期刊作为例证。

③ 这一发展可从D. 克拉克的“文学与社会：比较的角度”得到证明。

④ 《新时期、新文化和比较文学》，《比较文学杂志》第56期(1982年)，第5-20页。N. Simms在《亚历山大·杜图和心理史》一文中评论了杜图的工作，见《比较文学研究》第16期(1979年)，第250-261页。

⑤ 见H. Rudiger编：《比较文学理论》，第41-64页。这篇文章正如其副标题“文学影响一例”所示，是关于影响问题的。

⑥ 这是亨利·雷马克为国际比较文学协会布达佩斯会议写的文章的标题(汇编第二卷，第429-437页)。文章中对各种理论体系在比较文学中的运用问题进行了乐观的讨论。

⑦ 符号学没有能帮助艺术之间是的相互解释。S. P. Scher有理由说，“在符号学研究各种艺术的早期阶段”，他对“最后结果是抱怀疑态度的”。参见他的《文学与音乐的比较：批评理论和方法学的趋势和前景》，见《第九届ICLA会议资料汇编》，Innsbruck 1981年，第三卷第215-221页。引文出自第200页。

⑧ 《加拿大比较文学评论》第9期(1982年)第1-18页。福克玛认为，“比较文学和理论研究的目的在原则上是一致的”(第3页)，并试图表明可将后者运用到前者的可能性，但仅仅部分成功。

在我们所谓“适当的研究”中，文学理论、批评和历史（叫历史编撰更好）之间的区别显然是最重要的。首先，把文学视为一种同时存在的体系，和把文学看作是一系列按时间顺序排列的作品及其在历史进程中的必要部分，这些不同看法之间有着区别。然而，还有对文学原理和标准的研究与对具体的文学作品研究——无论我们单独研究它们，还是按时间顺序去系统地研究它们——之间的区别。要强调注意这些区别，我们最好是把对文学原理、类别、标准等这一类的研究称之为“文学理论”，而把对具体文学作品的研究称之为“文学批评”（方法上主要是静态的）或“文学史”。①

至于这些与比较文学有关的区别及其在历史中的“换位”，我已经强调过，我们这门学科最初仅仅是作为文学史的一个分支的。经过了多年的不景气后，现在比较文学史的编撰才又复苏，这在很大程度上应归功于历史学家们，特别是法国人所得到的新见识；② 同时也要归功于马克思主义对比较文学的看法及其在西方的传播。③

虽然这三位一体中的历史编纂，素来是国际比较文学协会及其成员所关注的主要问题（参看自1967年便已开始编写的《比较文学史》……），但它远没有占取舞台中心，还需与它的两个伙伴竞争。先看文学批评：前驱者们对它予以抵制，因为他们那实证主义的热情使得他们讨厌做分析判断的事情，其效果当然是极为不利的；甚至在“新批评”占统治地位的几十年里，这一情况亦未能形成一个比较有利的气候。比较批评是个后来者，它是在60年代末70年代初才得到承认的。当时斯特瑞卡（Joseph Strelka）在美国，佛利查在英国同时兴起这一专业。斯特瑞卡在1968年创办了《比较批评年鉴》，并在其《比较文学批评：三篇文艺学方法论文》（1970年）一书的引言中，解释了他的嗜好。文章中，他的术语是混乱的，把理论和批评等同起来了：“在区别首先致力于文学作品本身的比较文学史中，比较批评是将其重点建立在从文学理论和文学批评那里得到的各种比较方式上的。”④

佛利查具有启发性的，但颇为古怪的论文《比较批评：比较文学和精神史的趋于一致》⑤要合乎规矩得多。他对文学史（历时方法）和理论的公然舍弃是同他对同行们的恳求连在一起的：“应该在教条的形式主义和刻板的历史循环论之间选择一条中间的道路。”在英国，比较文学协会的正式刊物叫《比较文学批评年鉴》，这一术语似乎已经确立了下来，其部分原因是对人为的体系和死板的教条的厌恶而产生的务实传统。

从定义上来说，价值是相对的，因此也是可比的。最近，比较批评要在比较文学领域

---

① 《文学理论》，第30页。

② 这一发展在C. Guille（奎勒）《文学是一体系：文学史文学理论文集》中有关部分得到很好的反映，特别是在《文学阶段再议》一文中。

③ 特别是通过德文版D. Durisiz的《比较文学的问题》（1976年），L. Richter将标题译为《比较文学研究：方法和概论尝试》（东柏林1972年），以及G. Kaiser的集子《社会主义国家中的比较文学研究》（斯图加特，1980年）。

④ Strelka的著作由弗朗克在波恩发表。Dyserinck的《比较文学引论》较好地区分了“比较历史分支”和“比较体系”。他认为后者包括“比较文学理论和方法论”。

⑤ 这篇文章收进了M. 布雷伯利和D. 帕英的《当代批评》，第107-129页。

里争得显著地位的要求，是与对评价和判断的兴趣再度恢复密切相关的。在布达佩斯的“方法论会议”上，我们这门学科的创始人竭力回避“文学史，美学价值”这一论题，但在8位来自东西方的学者之间却进行了讨论。① 这一论题在恩姆利齐(Wilhelm Emrich)，哈斯(Hans Egon Hass)、凯塞(Wolfgang Kayser)和塞德尔(Walter Muller-Seidol)等德国学者开创先例后，便成了蒙特利尔—渥太华会议和好几家刊物以及近期的纪念文集中的争论焦点——多而又多，以致事实上，与“意象学”和“心理史”一道，“价值判断”形成了比较文学近代史上的三足鼎立的主流。②

然而，目前人们对这三种主流的崇敬同对理论的醉心相比，真可谓不值一提。随着文艺学所引起的一种潮流以及被一些民族语言学(英、美、法，甚至西班牙和德国)推动所兴起的理论，在比较文学学科中也获得了热门论题的地位。目前，这一形势的发展是如此之快，以致完全有理由担心我们这门学科，有朝一日会被这一巨人生吞活剥地吃掉。在这方面，将理论包括在现行的国际比较文学协会规章中，那略为有些多余的比较文学目标里——从国际比较角度进行文学史、文学理论、原文理解等研究③——意味着将在国际比较文学协会内成立一个理论研究组。比较文学将会成为文学理论的女佣这一危险，无论是真的还是想象的，都由于以下事实变得更为明显：两年前在蒙特利尔举行了一次座谈会，之后决定编写《文学理论手册》，并一直在积极地准备。虽然这项工作有出色的和忠实的比较学者参加，但在此书后记中，对比较文学方面却一带而过。

……

（韩冀宁　译）

（节选自乌·维斯坦因：《我们：从何来，是什么，去何方——比较文学的永久危机》，孙景尧选编，《新概念　新方法　新探索——当代西方比较文学论文选》，漓江出版社1987年版，第33-47页。）

① 《新赫利孔》第1/2期(1973年)，第27-111页。

② 此处指的是S. 维斯格伯有鉴别力的论文《比较文学中的价值判断：比较为艺术价值判断服务》，见《文学研究》第7期(1974年)，第229-243页。我同时推荐亨·雷马克的《比较文学在价值判断中的作用》。

③ 正式的法文原文规定，国际比较文学协会以发展比较文学的研究为目的，以文学史，文学理论，原文的解释从国际的比较观点着手。B. Scholz的《比较文学理论？论国际比较文学协会的新的任务规定》中对此定义做出了极为尖锐的评论。见《比较文学和一般文学年鉴》第28期(1986年)，第26-30页。

对文学进行历史比较研究的问题

（节选）

［苏联］维克多·马克西维其·日尔蒙斯基

【导读】

维克多·马克西维其·日尔蒙斯基（В. М. Жирмунский，1891—1971），前苏联著名文艺理论家、语言学家，彼得堡学派的集大成者。日尔蒙斯基在历史诗学思想基础上，对史诗进行比较历史研究，从而建立了历史类型学理论。他的历史类型学理论集中体现在《突厥英雄史诗》（1974 年）与《比较文学东方与西方》（1979 年）这两部著作中。作为苏联比较文艺学理论体系的创立者，日尔蒙斯基突破了对某种文学现象的研究，走出了一条由分析到综合的发展之路。得益于广阔的学术视野，日尔蒙斯基超越了西方中心主义立场，提出了东西方文化跨文化比较研究的构想。本文是作者在苏联“各民族文学的相互联系和相互影响”研讨会上的发言，他在文中提出的原则和方法论基本上代表了苏联学派的观点，在一定程度上影响了我国比较文学学科的发展方向。

日尔蒙斯基首先把“比较”定义为：判明历史现象之间的异同并作出历史的解释。他反对把“马克思主义方法”与“比较方法”相对立。他认为，人类历史发展的共同过程具有一致性和规律性的思想，是历史比较的研究各民族文学的基本前提。关于不同民族文学发展的类似道路的问题，是和关于国际性的文学相互影响的问题交叉在一起。在今天社会主义革命的时代，苏联文学成为社会主义现实主义思想艺术影响的主要策源地，它在全世界都具有的巨大影响。因此，东方国家不必再重复欧洲文学所经历过的从古典到浪漫到现实主义的各个发展阶段，可以直接学习苏联先进的社会主义现实主义文学。当然，各民族在向苏联学习的同时，也应重视利用伟大经典作家的遗产。但是对经典作家文学遗产的创造性认识，不能太随心所欲，不能把重新认识变成主观曲解。

在研究国家之间文学相互影响的问题时，必须考虑到以下两点：第一，影响不是偶然的。维谢洛夫斯基曾经提出过文学的“汇流”现象。历史类型的类似和文学的相互影响是辩证的、相互联系的，在文学发展的过程中应该被看成是一个历史现象的两个方面；第二，任何文学影响都同被借用形象的社会变化相联系。作者最后强调文学的联系和相互影响是历史的范畴，在各种具体的历史条件下，活跃的程度和采用的形式都是不同的。比如许多民间故事的情节具有国际性，原因是童话故事没有对民族、历史和地理的直接依存关系，散文的形式也便于翻译和流传。最后，在浪漫主义时期，各民族文学逐渐成型并独立出来。与此同时，消除民族差异的资本主义倾向也发展起来，这使得歌德提出“世界文学”的口号。作者呼吁克服传统的外国文学研究中的欧洲中心论，使总体文学真正成为全世界的文学。

（霍晓珊）

比较，也就是判明历史现象之间的异同以及对它们作出历史的解释，我认为，这是任何历史研究的必要因素。比较并不取消所研究现象（个人的、民族的、历史的）的特性；相反，只有借助于比较，也就是判明异同，才能正确判明其特性之所在。……而科学研究的道路则是从指出异同的简单对比向着对这些异同作出历史解释的方向发展。

……

人类的社会历史发展的共同过程具有一致性和规律性的思想，是历史比较地研究各民族文学的基本前提，而这一共同过程决定着作为意识形态的上层建筑的文学或者艺术的合乎规律的发展。正像由生产力和生产关系的类似状况决定的封建时代的社会政治关系，在欧洲最西部（尽管它有某些地域性的区别）与比如在中亚细亚（封建土地所有制，手工业作坊等方面的发展）就显露出类型学的类似特征，同样，在意识形态领域——艺术，其中包括作为对现实的形象认识的文学，在不同民族的社会发展同一阶段上，会出现大量的类似。这种类似的特点，不管是普遍的或是特殊的，在没有直接的相互影响和接触的情况下，也可以称之谓历史的类型学的类似或者吻合。它们在文学中出现的情况比一般想象的更为多；而且它们还是在文学之间产生相互影响的前提。同时，正像在社会生活的其他方面一样，它们不可避免地会带来重要的、更具个别性的差异，这些差异由历史过程的地域性特点和由这些特点造成的民族的、历史的独特性所引起。对这些特点的比较研究之所以重要，是因为可以确定在社会制约中文学发展的共同规律，同时确定作为比较对象的各种文学的民族特性。

……

一

如果研究资产阶级社会形成以来的文学史，我们就可以确定各种欧洲民族的文学社会思潮的相同的、有规律性的序列，可以确定与各种思潮相联系的主要文学艺术流派的更替和斗争，这些流派的类似应以这些民族社会发展的类似条件来解释：文艺复兴，巴罗克风格，古典主义，浪漫主义，批判现实主义，自然主义，现代主义。而在我们今天，随着社会发展新的历史时代的开始，出现了社会主义现实主义，一种本质上全新的、现实主义艺术发展的更高阶段。社会发展的矛盾和不平衡导致这些现象在不同的文学中出现的时间不一。由于具体的社会历史条件，由于民族文学的传统不一，这些思潮和流派在不同的国家具有不同的民族特点。虽然在某些文学思潮和流派之间，还可能存在过渡性质的现象。我们正是在这种意义上评论前文艺复兴时代或前浪漫主义的；19 世纪批判现实主义的早期代表巴尔扎克、狄更斯、果戈理，不同于福楼拜、萨克雷、托尔斯泰，他们与浪漫主义紧密相联，而且浪漫主义是他们艺术手法的非常重要的、在创作上起作用的因素。对这些过渡现象的深刻的比较研究，会显示出他们的类似的、合乎历史规律性的特点。共同的文学过程的某些阶段，在不同民族中可能较鲜明地表现在(对某一文学思潮来讲)所谓典型的形式中，或者表现在不太典型的形式中(19世纪法国和英国的传统的现实主义与德国的相比较)。

东方伟大的文明民族的文学，在中世纪不仅和欧洲的文学平行发展，而且还走在它们的前面，因为东方国家本身，长期保持着封建性质，从资本主义的原始积累时代开始，逐步成为资本主义国家殖民主义剥削的对象，结果就被排除在资产阶级发展的过程之外。在帝国主义和民族革命的时代他们的民族觉醒，是与在社会和文学发展中的跃进相联系的，在这种情况下，利用先进的文学经验，当然不必再简单重复欧洲文学所经历过的所有阶段了。如启蒙运动，浪漫主义，批判现实主义，自然主义，现代主义，而在我们的时代——首先在苏联各民族中——还有社会主义现实主义正在这些国家取代封建时代的文学传统，同时，以各种不同方式来利用民族的文学遗产。

……

二

关于不同民族文学发展的类似道路的问题，关于文学过程的历史类型学的吻合的问题，总是和关于国际性的文学相互影响和作用的问题错综交叉在一起，完全排除后一种情况显然是不可能的。人类社会的历史事实上，不存在其个别部分之间缺乏相互影响而绝对孤立的社会和文化(因而也有文学的)发展的例子。越是文明的人民，与别国人民之间的联系和相互影响就越活跃。让我们回忆一下马克思在《资本论》序言中的话："一个国家应该而且可以向其他国家学习。"

这些话也适用于文学的专门领域。任何一种伟大的民族文学都不能在排除与其他民族文学之间的积极而富于创造性的相互关系的情况下得到发展，而那些想要提高自己本民族文学的人，同时肯定，仿佛它只能在地区性的民族的土壤上成长，那么他们因此却使它遭受甚至不是"光荣的孤立"，而是地方的狭隘性和"自我服务"。

这种相互影响的最简单的情况乃是某一个在社会发展上超过其他民族的较为先进民族的文学，影响那些在社会关系方面较为落后的民族的文学。说明阶级社会发展的不平衡性、矛盾和落后现象是这种相互影响的基本前提。在同一社会历史过程的不平衡条件下，当存在共同发展倾向时，一个在工业方面比较发达的国家，照马克思的说法，"向工业较不发达的国家所显示的，只是后者未来的景象"。由此可见，较落后国家并不总是独立走完先进国家已经走过的道路的这一个阶段。

在欧洲，国与国之间的文学相互作用的过程中，随着资本主义关系的萌芽，民族国家和民族文化就开始形成，可以勾画出明显的文学(一般说意识形态的)影响的连续性，这一影响的策源地由在某一阶段中是社会发展的先进地区的国家轮番充当。15、16世纪意大利的文艺复兴，17世纪法国的古典主义，18世纪英国和法国的资产阶级启蒙运动，19

世纪法国和英国的批判现实主义，就曾有过这种国际性的影响。

在我们今天，在社会主义革命的时代，苏联文学，先进的社会主义国家的文学，就成了社会主义现实主义的思想、艺术影响的主要策源地，它影响着人民民主国家的文学和资本主义国家的进步文学及革命文学，不仅在欧洲，而且在全世界的范围。

……

同样也不应该简单地、片面地把国与国之间的文学影响，仅仅理解为先进的文学、社会思想和流派的影响。在有些历史形势下，相反的反动作用也是可能的。作为帝国主义时代颓废文学的产物的法国现化派的全欧影响，在目前可以说是全世界的影响就是一例(或者西班牙和意大利在封建复辟和天主教反动时代对欧洲文学的影响，与此相联系的是17世纪欧洲的巴罗克文艺风格问题)。如果忽视存在于文学过程每一阶段中的社会矛盾和斗争，那么在这一问题中，将会不正确地把文学思潮和风格的连续性想象为一股“统一的潮流”。

……

如果过去时代经典作家的影响只限于和他有着同样社会基础的文学范围内，那么莎士比亚对浪漫主义作家的影响将是完全不可能的。更谈不上莎士比亚的永恒的生命力了，也就更不能谈他对不同流派、时期和民族的文学之影响，包括对我们苏联戏剧的影响在内，不能谈在俄国文学历史发展的各个阶段中歌德的命运了。伟大经典作家是丰富而复杂的，有时在历史上矛盾的遗产中，那些属于不同文学流派和不同社会集团的作家，可以在不同历史时代找到某些合乎他们的时代要求，为他们解决某些迫切的创作任务所必需的观点和基础。

当然，对过去遗产的创造性的认识和重新认识的程度也不是无止境的，其极限在于作家或作品本身客观的、历史制约的特点中。超越了可能有的思想上或艺术上相近的一定界限，就会产生冷淡或者甚至论争性的排斥(如莎士比亚和法国古典主义)，或者重新认识变成主观的曲解，转变为赝制品。……虽然如此，作家仍有相当大的余地，能不同程度地流传后世，引起对自己文艺遗产某些方面的理论兴趣和创作上的共鸣，对处于发展过程中每个新阶段的外来文学来说，这种选择本身是具有代表性的。

三

为了历史地正确提出国与国之间文学相互影响的问题，必须考虑到以下这些方法论方面的意见：

(一)影响不是偶然的，来自外部的机械推动力，不是一个作家或一批作家个人生平所经验过的事实，不是偶尔熟悉一本新书或迷恋一种文学时尚的结果，也不是偶尔存在两种语言的“媒介者”，旅行者或政治流亡者的结果，搜罗这类人，是持经验主义立场的梵·第根和法国比较主义者十分关心的。任何思想的(其中包括文学的)影响都是有规律性和受社会制约的。这种制约性取决于前一时期的民族、社会和文学发展的内在规律。为使影响成为可能，就必须存在这种思想输入的要求，必须有在一定社会、一定文学中多少已经定型的发展的类似倾向。为此，维谢洛夫斯基讲到过外来文学中的“汇流”现象。许多情况下，都存在类似“汇流”现象，这使得解决是否有来自一方的“影响”问题就困难了。

……

因此，历史类型的类似和文学的相互影响是辩证地相互联系的。并且在文学发展的过程中，应该被看成是一个历史现象的两个方面。

(二)任何文学影响都是和被借用形象的社会变化相联系的。所谓社会变化，我们指的是形象的创造性的改造和对那些成为相互影响的前提的社会条件的适应，民族生活和在社会发展一定阶段的民族性格特征的适应，对民族文学传统，同样也对所借鉴作家创作个性的思想和艺术上的独特性的适应。

马克思说，17 世纪的法国戏剧“正是依照他们自己艺术的需要来理解希腊人的，而在达西埃和其他人向他们正确解释了亚里士多德以后，他们还是长时期地坚持这种所谓的‘古典’戏剧”。

……

四

文学的联系和相互影响是历史的范畴，在各种具体的历史条件下，其活跃的程度是不同的，并且采取不同的形式。在民间创作的各种体裁中，比如人民的英雄史诗，总的说来最少受国际性影响的渗透，因为史诗是人民的英雄主义理想化了的过去的历史，在富于诗意的形式中，体现人民对自己的过去的理解和评价；相反，许多民间故事的情节——妖魔的、动物的、故事的、奇闻笑谈的——却具有国际性，促进这一现象的是童话作品的美妙的、引人入胜的特性，没有地区性民间口头传说特有的对民族、历史和地理的直接依存关系，以及散文的形式，因为它使一种语言转述成另一种语言和创造性的更换地方情调，使之适应另一种民族环境，比较容易进行。

……

随着资产阶级民族的发展，新时代的各国文学开始具有鲜明地表现出来的民族性格。它们比起中世纪文学来，在更大程度上互相区分和迥然不同；随着个性的发展，个人的世界观(在社会、历史和阶级的范围内)和文学技巧的个人特色(在民族传统和艺术流派的范围内)都开始具有空前的意义。与此相联系，在国与国之间的文学相互影响的领域里，表达新的社会意识，创立艺术的新流派的艺术个性的个人主动精神也起作用了；与此相适应，我们就谈到拜伦对浪漫主义时代欧洲文学的影响(“拜伦风格”)，说到乔治桑的较为有限的影响(“乔治桑风格”)，说到歌德或者狄更斯、陀思妥耶夫斯基、托尔斯泰或者契诃夫的影响。

但是，在各民族文学的形成和更明显独立出来的同时，另一种“全世界的、历史性的消除民族隔阂，抹煞民族差异的资本主义倾向”又发展起来了。

……

在 1848 年革命前夕，马克思和恩格斯在《共产党宣言》里从理论上确定了“世界文学”的概念是新的资产阶级社会发展的历史标志之一。“过去那种地方的和民族的闭关自守和自给自足状态已经消逝，现在代之而起的已经是各个民族各方而互相往来和各方面互相依赖了。物质的生产如此，精神的生产也是如此。各个民族的精神活动的成果已经成为共同享受的东西。民族的片面性和狭隘性已日益不可能存在，于是由许多民族的和地方的文学形成了一个世界的文学。”

正像批评界多次指出的，歌德在自己的创作中提供了最为鲜明的“包罗万象”的新时代诗人的范例，他创造性地汲取和改造了世界文学的传统的多样性。歌德对西方的诗(古典的和当代的)表现出了真正的兴趣。对莎士比亚和拜伦，对拉辛、伏尔泰和法国的浪漫主义者，对波斯和中国的抒情诗，对德国的民歌和塞尔维亚的叙事诗都极感兴趣。对德国民族的过去遗产，对古代希腊、罗马以及被他发现的近东的诗歌的掌握，构成他自己创作发展的阶段，永远成为民族的，同时又具有最深刻个性的形象。

……

五

对历史的发展，整个历史过程的(因而也是文学的)规律性和共同性的法则的马克思主义的理解，使得不仅是世界通史，而且还有世界文学史的真正历史的体系成为可能。这种体系应该依靠文学的比较研究，它既估计到文学发展的平行现象和由此引起的文学之间的合乎规律性的历史类比的相似，也考虑到由其制约的国际性的文学相互影响。这些现象，如上所述，辩证地相互联系着，应该从这些联系的各个方面加以考察。

自然，这种与苏联历史科学的精神相适应的真正的“总体”文学必须克服传统的外国文学研究中的“欧洲中心论”，使它成为真正全世界的，而不单是全欧洲的文学史。为此，必须首先使那些由于在地理上远离欧洲世界或者在自己的文化发展中较落后和成了资本主义欧洲的殖民地、半殖民地而很少为我们所知的民族的文学对我们来讲，不再是“异国情调”，就像对18世纪欧洲艺术中的“中国热”一样，或者像在西欧现代派中对黑人的雕塑的迷恋一样；换句话说，我们一定要在这些民族中揭示出那种共同的历史的以及文学史的规律性，这些在地理上离我们遥远，并在世世代代形成了民族独特性的文学，也服从于这种规律性。对文学进行历史比较的研究，为我们打开实现这个重要的历史和文化任务的道路。

(倪蕊琴　译)

（节选自维克多·马克西维其·日尔蒙斯基:《对文学进行历史比较研究的问题》，干永昌、廖鸿钧、倪蕊琴选编，《比较文学研究译文集》上海译文出版社1985年版，第284-300页。）

现代比较文艺学问题

（节选）

[苏联]康拉德

【导读】

在《现代比较文艺学问题》一文中，康拉德首先指出自20世纪以来文学相互渗透的情况不仅存在于地理位置相邻近且文化同质的欧洲国家内，而是“真正包括了整个文明的人类”。事实上，文学的相互渗透现象不仅在规模上有所扩大，在其程度及社会意义上均呈现出朝前发展之势，因此，康拉德认为现代文艺学最迫切的任务之一就是要研究这种国际性的文学联系。接着，他引入了“国别文学”和“文学共同性”这两个概念，进一步详细论证比较文学研究的必要性。

有关比较文学的定义历来众说纷纭，康拉德在文中主要列举了三种定义，比较文学可以是“对过去历史上彼此具有共同性的两种或某几种文学的研究”，也可以指“对各国别文学中所产生的现象进行比较类型学的研究”，还可以理解为“研究不同国家文学之间的联系”，第三种定义基本与法国学派的观点相吻合。接着，康拉德集中梳理了法国学派的核心概念，其基本思想是为了很好地了解本国的文学现象必须注意这一文学和其他国家文学的联系。基于此，法国学派崇尚文献考据，重事实联系，以揭示不同文学间的影响，这种影响可以是单向的，也可以是双向的。除此之外，法国学派还发展出一套文学影响内部构造的理论，认为这种内部构造共包括“放送者”、“接收者”、“传递者”（或“媒介”）这三大要素，媒介既可以是个人，也可以是集体，如文学组织。法国学派的局限性在于以实证为基础的影响研究，因为它将揭示文学间的影响作为研究的最终目的，这势必会极大地限制比较文学作为一门独立学科的生命力。此外，法国学派的欧洲中心主义也是其致命缺陷之一。

法国学派界定的研究对象是17世纪至19世纪欧洲各国文学领域所产生的现象，康拉德认为这种研究在空间和时间上都有明显的局限性。尽管这一时期东西方文学的联系是双向的，然而，东方文学对西方文学的发展所做出的贡献却往往被囿于欧洲中心主义的西方比较文学研究者所忽视，甚至连东欧各国以及俄国的文学也被排除在研究范围以外，因此他认为比较文学研究的第一个任务便是“要断然扩大空间的界限，要把整个文明人类的文学间的联系纳入研究的轨道”，而不能将文学相互关系的过程简化为“影响—接受”的静态二元对立机制。随后，康拉德提出比较文学研究的第二个任务即扩展研究的时间幅度，将中世纪也纳入研究的轨道。虽然文学联系一直到

17 世纪才初具各国文学相互联系的性质，但这并不意味着在此之前不存在文学间的彼此交流。最后，康拉德重申了扩大比较文学研究的空间界限和时间幅度的重要性，并区分了中世纪的部族文学与盛行于 17 至 19 世纪的民族文学。

遗憾的是，康拉德未能摆脱时代的局限性，在第三部分谈及研究整个文明人类的文学关系时，他写道："必须经常考虑每国的阶级关系，政治和思想上的斗争。离开这些是不能了解各种文学相互关系的真正性质的。"诚然，了解阶级关系、思想和政治上的斗争对于研究文学的相互关系有一定帮助，但是是否真如他所言，不了解这些就无从研究文学的相互关系呢？

（李伟荣）

一

对"比较文艺学"这一名称可以有许许多多的看法。它可以指的是对过去历史上彼此具有共同性的两种或者某几种文学的研究。在这里，问题归结为研究某些文学从以前的共同性中区分出来的过程，它们作为独立现象而形成的过程。例如波斯和塔吉克两个伊朗民族的国别文学的形成过程就可以这样来研究。

其次，可以把比较文艺学理解为对各国别文学中所产生的现象进行比较类型学的研究。这种研究可以涉及由某种历史共同性的因素而产生的一些现象，对于 19 世纪的古典现实主义文学的研究就可以是这样。这样的研究是以比较类型学的观点来对比法国、英国、俄国、欧洲其他国家，甚至亚洲某些国家的文学。在这种场合，研究的结果可能是：第一，很好地理解现实主义这一创作方法的本质，了解这种创作方法的全部复杂本性；第二，揭示具有这种文学共同性的各国文学所产生的现实主义各个变种。

以比较类型学的观点也可以研究各国文学在没有任何历史共同性、彼此缺乏任何联系的条件下所产生的现象，甚至也可以研究在不同历史时代产生的现象。例如，对于在基督教影响所及的欧洲各国和在佛教影响所及的亚洲各国所产生的传记文学，就可以这样进行比较研究。在这种场合，研究的任务可以是分析这里的每一种现象，这种分析在它们相互对比下，比之孤立研究要充分得多。

比较类型学的研究的任务，也可以是从事发现彼此独立地兴起的各现象所具有的类型共同性。例如，依我看来，可以证明西欧文学中的骑士小说和日本文学中的"军事记"、欧洲启蒙时代的讽刺小说和中国 19 世纪的暴露小说之间的类型学的相似。

最后，也可以把比较文艺学理解为研究不同国家文学之间的联系。这里的任务，第一是显示联系本身，弄清楚它们的历史原因，联系的性质，联系的途径与方式；第二是揭示这些联系对有关的某些文学或是所有文学所产生的后果。上述全世界的文学方面的实际状况所引起的首先是进行最后这个意义上的历史比较的研究。因此，我们必须来探讨在现代文艺科学的这个领域中已经具有的东西。

二

比较文学先驱者在许多方面是不同的。布兰代斯及其《十九世纪文学主潮》是一种现象，玛克斯·科赫及其《比较文学史杂志》又是另一种现象；波斯奈特所代表的又是独特的现象。对于布兰代斯的观点说来，最重要的是这样一种想法：一个民族的天才，“为了不致使他凋谢”(像他所说的)，常常需要同其他民族的天才相接触，这常常给他本身和自己的发展以新的力量。如果观察上世纪末在玛克斯·科赫主持下发行的一卷杂志，那么，除开德国人称之为 Stoffgeschichte 的某些非常明显的特点外，可以看到有一种意向，要以双方面的影响和假借，把不同民族的文学联系起来。对波斯奈特所代表的流派说来，其特征是以十九世纪的社会学为方向，他之所以运用社会学，是为了发掘不同民族的文学的共同特点。无疑的是，戴克斯特所提到的文艺学家们是各不相同的，但他正是采取他们的方针，而不是任何别人的方针，这是很有意义的。然而，起源于上世纪末的法国比较文艺学的代表，显然想走上与他们的先驱者所走的不同的道路。

这种新道路的实质，在 1924 年，第根在其论著《前浪漫主义》中曾经表述过：“每一民族在其存在的任何一个时代的政治史，离开了这一时代、这国家所属的世界的那一地区的共同历史，是不能充分理解的……对于每一国家的文学史每一发展时期说来也是如此，如果不把它作为某种巨大的整体的部分来考察，也是不能充分和正确地认识的。……”“当然”，第根补充说，“每一民族文学有其自己的传统，而且是非常巩固的传统。这些传统允许它永远保持自己独特的面貌；但是每一种这样的文学常常接触到艺术中新的思想和感情，这些思想和感情使它加强，使它完全变样。研究这些国际思潮与研究民族传统是同样必要的”。

1931 年，第根在自己的《比较文学论》里写道(如所周知，这是他的探讨新学派的历史、表述它的原则、规定它的任务、确立它的方法的头一部著作)：“比较文学只是补充那些本国的文学史并把它们联合在一起。同时，它在它们之间以及它们之上，纺织一个更普遍的文学史的网。”

在第根这些话里很重要的是，强调指出主要的事情是研究国别文学，亦即各个国家的文学。这个流派在日本的代表之一——中岛，在强调指出所涉及的是研究本国的文学时也坚持这样一种想法，即研究者本身也正是属于、而且应该属于本国文学的研究者之列。

这也就是现代比较文艺学的代表人物的言论，这些言论尤其是遵照这个文艺学学派的精神而写成的著作本身，都指明了比较文艺学的现阶段实际上与先前的比较文艺学大不相同。

……

如果观察比较文学的代表们所写出的大量学术文献，就会知道，事情主要在于揭示影响——单方面的和双方面的。

在许多研究甲文学对乙文学影响的著作间，在我看来，其研究法上很典型的是梅格龙的论著《浪漫主义时代的历史小说》(1912)与艾格黎的论著《席勒与法国浪漫主义》(1927)。前一书的作者追溯历史小说在法国的兴起，从而指出，在这个过程中司各特的创作起着怎样的作用。这部论著可以作为法国研究者揭示在某种体裁范围中甲文学对乙文学发生影响的一个例子。艾格黎的论席勒在《法国》一书指出，人们怎样提出了甲国的文学现象对于乙国戏剧的流派的形成发生影响，以及通过戏剧对乙国整个文学发生影响的问题。哈扎的《法国大革命和意大利文学》指出法国文艺学家如何研究一国的文学影响别国的整个文学。

可以作为研究两种文学相互影响的论著的例子的是艾斯忒夫的著作《拜伦与法国浪漫主义》(1907)。作者在开头阐明拜伦的创作在法国作家影响下得到发展的那些方面。例如，艾斯忒夫认为，在《海盗》中的个人主义与崇尚情感，在许多方面来自卢梭的《新哀洛绮思》；在《堂璜》中的怀疑态度，在很大程度上是在伏尔泰的《老实人》的影响下产生的；在《曼弗雷德》与《查尔德·哈洛德》里“世界性的悲哀”的基调中的某些东西溯源于夏多布里安的《勒内》。然而，拜伦创作里这些由内因而发生、因法国作家影响而加强的因素，是在这英国诗人的极有个性的创作里经过熔化与陶铸，而且在其复杂的交织中获得新的艺术品质的。

从法国得到这许多东西，拜伦以后也偿还给它。他的《查尔德·哈洛德》、《海盗》与《曼弗雷德》在艾斯忒夫看来，也帮助法国作家离开夏多布里安的《基督教真髓》，——这二十年代天主教反动派与政治上的保守主义的旗帜，并且重新使浪漫主义文学成为进步思想与时代情绪的表现者。拜伦有助于所谓左派的、民主的浪漫主义的确立。

这里不多的几个例子说明了“比较文学”的代表人物的基本思想——为了很好地了解本国的文学现象，必须注意这一文学和其他国家文学的联系。但是艾斯忒夫这本书也阐明了怎样从事发现包括几国文学的共同性的工作。

……

除了研究文学间联系的具体表现的实际工作外，法国的比较文艺学代表们也探讨这种研究的理论。在他们的理论体系中最有意思的，依我看来，是他们所提出的文学影响的内部构造的观念。

他们认为这种内部构造是三种因素的作用“放送者”、“接受者”与“传递者”。与术语“传递者”并列的还有术语“媒介”。被特别详尽地探讨的正是后一问题——传递者与媒介的问题。媒介可以是个人的——一个人；可以是集体的——文学的联合组织、杂志。……

构成法国比较文艺学理论的一个特别部分是关于 success、fortune、influence(成就、命运、影响)的学说，“成就”指的是一国文学的任何一种现象在别国文学中所具有的意义的大小；“命运”指的是该文学现象在别国的生活史；而“影响”则指这种生活的后果。

由于这样的研讨比较文学研究的理论和研究方法，主要的由于大量精心撰写的具体论著，法国比较文艺学保证了自己在现代西方整个比较文艺学中的主导地位。

三

怎样看待这一工作呢？我认为，它自己证明了自己。比较文艺学在其历史发展的现阶段上，是二十世纪的孩子。但是文学理论常常是为一种“跋”，是对以前存在过的东西而言的。上面提到过的第根的著作指出了这个“以前”的最远界限是文艺复兴时代；而绝大多数的研究著作则是以十七至十九世纪所产生的现象为其对象。

这立刻阐明了问题的实质。

文艺复兴时代，是可以开始追溯现代欧洲各国的国别文学形成过程的时间上的最远点。十七世纪，是国别文学已清楚地显示轮廓的时期。十九世纪，几乎是所有欧洲国家的国别文学大规模发展的时代，是竭尽其典型形式发展的时代。同时，从文艺复兴时代起，国际文学联系就开始广泛发展；在十七世纪，它们初具各国文学的相互联系的性质。在十九世纪，文学间的联系获得了巨大的规模。

法国文艺学家注意到这个双重的过程，并努力在实践和理论上理解它。它们在这个领域做了许许多多工作。研究十七至十九世纪欧洲文学史，是不能撇开他们的著作的。

然而，研究这个过程时，必须弄清它的历史实质，同时也要弄清它的真正范围。过程的实质，是各国文学、亦即一定的社会历史性质与一定的结构的文学的形成；范围是构成世界资本主义体系的所有的国家。

……

在十七至十九世纪间形成的世界资本主义体系不仅引起了经济上与商业上的联系，也引起了文化上、随之是文学上的联系，而且这些联系遍及全世界。大家知道得很清楚，在这个时期内西方各国的文学开始传播到印度、土耳其，稍后则传播到日本与中国。东方各国现代的文艺学者当研究该时期的本国文学史时是很能理解这个事实的意义的。

然而，联系是双方面的，而西方文艺学者的论著在分析上述各个世纪文学发展过程时都没有从应有的程度上估计这个事实。……

因此，在比较文艺学领域里应该作的头一件事——甚至在西方研究者所划出的时间范围上(即十七至十九世纪)——要断然扩大空间的界限，要把整个文明人类的文学间的联系纳入研究的轨道。

在研究这样一些联系，而在更广泛的观点上—研究各种文学的相互关系时，应该注意到各国的政治关系，它们的文化水平，以及在思维方式和世界观、信仰、生活方式上、甚至在各个民族的趣味上的相似或差异。必须经常考虑每国的阶级关系，政治和思想上的斗争。离开这些是不能了解各种文学相互关系的真正性质的。

当然，不能把这些相互关系中的一切归结为影响。……

一国文学的活动家对别国文学的事实和现象这种不同的关系，是由于许多原因：作者的不同阶级立场，世界观的差别，创作个性和生活经验的特点。文学联系按其内容和性质来说不仅可以是相去悬殊，而且在每一种文学里可以产生极其不同的后果。引力与拒力的复杂结合也正构成了各种文学相互关系的实质。

四

现代比较文艺学所面临的第二个任务是扩展研究的时间幅度。必须把中世纪也包罗在研究的范围内。

各个国家的文学在范围和意义上的这样或那样的彼此交流，是向来存在的。它在中世纪也存在过。我们已经知道许许多多，但是在最近又发现了新的事实，对以前早已知道的情况带来了重要的补充。

这样的事实之一是敦煌石窟的全部藏书的发现。……

“变文”的发现是意义非常巨大的事件。当然，它首先涉及的是中国文学史：今后中国文学史的某些篇章将要重新改写，而主要的是，在许多方面将要改变中国中世纪文学的总的观念。其次，“变文”的发现使我们能够提出更宽阔的问题：关于在世界的两端——西欧与中国——产生类型学上相近的、即使不是完全同类的现象，即西方文学中称之为‘传说”、“传记”的文学体裁。……

第二个事实，也属于近年的发现，是关于中世纪早期西欧文学同阿拉伯文学的联系问题。允许我们重新解释这种联系的尼克尔的论著《西班牙的阿拉伯诗歌及其同古老的普洛旺斯的吟游诗人的联系》(1946)中所包含的材料。尼克尔该书的大部分是叙述西班牙的阿拉伯人诗歌创作史的。在这一部分里作者继续久已进行的研究工作。而这一论著中新的东西是由确凿的证据所证明的西班牙的阿拉伯诗歌对十一至十三世纪普洛旺斯人的诗歌的影响……

因此完全可能，文化上的交流是双方面的。如果说在中国唐代已发现有“西方的”，其中包括阿拉伯文化的因素，那么中亚细亚与伊朗已有相当明显的中国文化的遗迹。文化联系的存在是毫无疑问的，应该也有文学上的联系。几乎可以确信无疑地说，这样的联系将会逐步发现。……

五

这样，如果把研究十七至十九世纪世界文学的界限扩展到当时整个文明世界的极限，我们就会克服西欧比较文艺学的空间上的局限性，这种局限性不仅反映在我们所展示的文学联系的真正规模和历史实质的认识上，而且也反映在对各个国家文学过程的全面评述上。而如果把中世纪也纳入研究的轨道，我们就可以克服现代比较文艺学的时间上的局限性，这种局限性不仅表现在国际文学联系全部历史的结构上，而且也表现在历史比较研究的理论本身的完整性上。

把中世纪文学包括于研究范围，就可以指出区别民族文学和部族的文学是如何重要。……十七至十九世纪，亦即民族时代，欧洲各国文学史的特征是相反的两种倾向：一方面是经历着国别文学的形成和发展的过程，亦即从语言和民族的特征上明确表现出的各种文学的特殊化过程，另一方面是国际文学联系强烈发展的过程，亦即单独的、独立的文学包括于某些共同性的过程。对于中世纪，亦即部族时代，富有特征性的是另一幅画面：一方面，没有如此轮廓分明的各种独立的文学；另一方面，给它们相互联系以巨大影响的常常是族与族之间以及语言的界限的模糊不明，这些界限的动摇不定，在很大程度上是语言的相互渗透。

也必须注意到部族的时代国际文学语言的存在。这样的语言——对不同区域而言——有：梵文，希腊文，拉丁文，古斯拉夫书面语言，中国古文，波斯文，阿拉伯文。这里的一种、甚至是几种语言的知识是当时教育必要的组成部分，因为这样的语言成为各族文学许多作品的语言。这样的作品的存在，区分出单独的部族的文学，因为除了用国际语言写成的作品外，每个族还有用自己的部族的口语写成的作品。但同时，国际语言的作品使各部族彼此联络，成为巨大的文学共同性形成的基础。这样共同性的存在，是部族时代世界文学史最有代表性的现象之一。但是这些共同性按其本质与构造说来与民族时代的文学世界的共同性完全不同。

最后，必须充分估计在不同历史时期里文学存在的形式本身的差异事实。对民族时代，文学存在的通常形式是书写的；在部族时代的文学，则很多以口头形式而存在。而这绝不仅在民间创作——民间口头诗歌创作的专门领域内。正如上文以“变文”为例指出的那样，这种文学体裁的形成正是通过口头创作的，甚至当记录下来以后，这些“变文”在讲故事人的转述中，还继续以口头形式而存在。同样的现象我们在中国以及其他文学领域内都可以看到。这种现象的基础是这样一种情况——记录形式的作品对当时大多数中国人民是无从接受的；因此，甚至“书写的”作品对当时的中国人民也以口头故事形式而存在。与此同时，文学作品的这种存在形式，给讲故事人打开了发挥文学主动性、参与该作品的流传并使其进一步发展的广大余地。正因如比，在许多场合，很难说出作品的“作者”。

如果注意到对于该作品的讲述，起直接影响的是听众，亦即人民群众的兴趣与爱好，那就可以毫不夸张地说，中国许多中世纪文学的叙述作品甚至从著作权来说也是人民的。

这就是我认为要加入现代文艺学的一般理论的一些论点，这是为了使现代文艺学能够作出对文艺科学说来是新的成果来。

（周南　译）

（节选自康拉德：《现代比较文艺学问题》，干永昌、廖鸿钧、倪蕊琴选编，《比较文学研究译文集》，上海译文出版社 1985 年版，第 262-283 页。）

比较文学

(节选)

[法]基亚

【导读】

马里奥斯·法朗索瓦·基亚(Marius-Francois Guyard),法国比较文学学者,影响研究的代表人物。《比较文学》(1951)是在梵·第根、卡雷等人的基础上,对法国学派比较文学思想的进一步完善,是针对法国学派所受质疑而确认其合法性的努力。“比较文学的范围”选自该书第二章第二节,主要讨论比较文学的研究领域,包括文学交流的媒介、流传、渊源、异国形象等问题,是全书内容的总括。

基亚指出文学交流的媒介包括两个方面:“书籍”和“人”。“书籍”主要指承担了国与国之间文学交流功能的文字资料及其相关媒介,尤其是接受者国家的外语掌握情况、评论文章、旅行轶事等,现在仍有巨大研究空间。在“人”的方面,他认为对于那些在国与国之间充当“文化联络员”的人,不仅要研究其作品,了解其在异国的生活及对异国的看法,而且比较文学工作者也应对异国语言、文学、文化有相当的了解。如今对文化身份的重视可谓是对这一思想的发展。文学类型、题材与作家的命运都属于流传的问题。基亚认为,文学类型的流变既是历史问题,也是现实问题,应与作家身份气质、社会历史与民族性格等联系起来,这大大拓展了影响研究的领域。基亚指出题材的沿袭构成文学的传统,但只有那些“文艺性的、可以显示出一个人或一个民族的心理特点”的题材才是值得研究的,这避免了比较文学研究肤浅化的弊病,但也会限制问题在更大范围内的展开。在作家方面,基亚特别强调要研究个人名望与作品的声誉同样高的作家,体现出精英主义思想倾向,实际上,有些非经典作家也会在特定情况下对他国文学产生影响,不应被排除在比较文学研究之外。基亚指出要仔细区别“传播”、“模仿”、“成功”与“影响”,及影响的多种模式。在渊源研究方面,基亚肯定了影响过程中作家的个性与创造性。渊源研究要重视作家对异国的印象以及相关资料,还要注意辨别是巧合还是真正意义上的思想或技巧的交流。文学思想和潮流问题涉及多个国家,又与其他学科的发展紧密相联,对研究者提出了更高的要求。他并不认同梵·第根将比较文学与“总体文学”进行区分的做法,而是将文学思想与潮流问题仍然作为比较文学研究的一部分。他提出,这类研究容易把巧合当作影响,但是又肯定巧合同样有研究价值,属于巧合的部分其实包含了后来美国学派平行研究的内容。

“阐明一个国家”属于形象学范畴，讨论了对某个国家的阐述是如何产生及发展的，即一个国家的形象是如何在异国被塑造并得以确立的。既要了解作家如何看待他国形象，以及为什么这样看待，以此观照两国的民族心理并进而认识自我，加强两国之间的沟通与理解；还要了解作家通过何种途径熟悉异国，思想上受到哪些影响，以及他如何传达自己所受的影响。这一思想受到韦勒克的批评，他认为会导致文学研究被瓦解成为心理学和社会学，但是形象学研究现在已经走向成熟，并受到学者们的重视。基亚的这本书也成为最早在理论上确认形象学研究的专著。

基亚进一步规范了比较文学法国学派的思想，与其前辈一样，强调基于事实联系的国际文学间的关系，研究范围同样局限于欧洲文学，忽略了文学的审美性及欧洲之外文学的情况，但是他又兼顾到比较文学的新动向，比如平行研究与形象学研究，因此是对之前比较文学研究的丰富，也为之后比较文学研究模式的转变做了一定的准备。

（常芳）

第二章　对象与方法

Ⅱ　比较文学的范围

现在我们沿着已选定的轨道前进，那么对象和方法也就相应地会明确起来。

1. 世界主义文学的传播者

每一个时代都有一些书、一些人在帮助人们了解别的国家和它的文学。这就是比较文学所要研究的主要对象。

A. 书籍

比较文学首先可以使人们精确地知道一个作家、一个集团或一个时代对某种外语的掌握情况。这种比较的研究在文学上肯定只有好处——人们常常为一部译作感到兴奋，不过要能真正地欣赏它却只有阅读原作。怎样才能确定某个人或社会对那种语言的了解程度呢？如果是一个人的话，有时他会承认自己对某种语言是一无所知的，一旦收集到了这种坦白的承认，调查工作自然也就结束了。不过多数情况却是这个人初步掌握了一点英语或意大利语，并期望把它变成更深的知识，在这种情况下，比较文学工作者就要探寻一下这位作家曾否用这两种语言中的一种来进行过写作。伏尔泰的英文书信可以帮助研究者了解他的进步情况，指出他未能超越的水平。译文是另一种检验，而且是更能说明问题的检验。按照所需的审慎态度和方法来运用这种检验，是可以解决一些与自尊心有联系的疑难问题的。

如果是与一个社会集团有关的话，那么唯一的办法就是：研究该社会集团经常使用的字典、语法书、教育学书等。比如我国到1763年还重版的安托南(Antonini)神甫(1735年编纂出版)的《拉—意—法字典》，就很能说明十八世纪时意大利文在我国的传播情况。更明显的是这位作者还出版了一本女用意大利语语法。

除了这类使人厌烦的，但又是必要的研究之外，还可以看些译作。这是任何时代都被广泛采用的了解外国作品的手段。如果要想知道大革命时期①和帝国时期②对歌德情况的了解，比较文学工作者就得给他的作品的法文译本编制一份清单。当然这纯粹是一种广采博收的办法。继之而来的就是分析和评论工作了：这些译文忠实于原作吗？完整吗？对一些被改动的地方有什么想法？对时代的敏感性有什么启发？等等。

评论文章也是了解外国情况的一个来源。读者可以把它和作品(原文或译文)合起来看。一般来说，读者是会感到满足的。把一定时期里在法国出现的有关雪莱(Shelley)或济慈(Keats)的书籍和文章挑出来分析分析，体会它的价值，估计一下它的影响，这也是一种比较工作。在这方面，尤其重要的是要研究那些对传播外国作品曾作出贡献的杂志和报纸——一些专业的杂志如十八世纪的《外国日报》(Journal étranger)；尤其是那些广大读者较易接受的、又有普遍意义的出版物，如十九和二十世纪的《两个世界评论》(Revue des deux mondes)或《新法兰西评论》(Nouvelle Revue Française)。这些工作都需要秩序和耐性。只有它们才能对作品的影响提供严肃的调查。马尔洛③(Malraux)发现了福克纳④(Faulkner)、那是个人的偶然事件，有关福克纳的评论文章不断在杂志上出现，却是一件具有社会意义的事件，是时代的一个标志。

总之，人们往往满足于阅读别人所写的有关外国的东西。1840年《两个世界评论》的订阅者多数是从来没读过歌德和海涅(Heine)的作品的人，但他们却从头至尾地阅读了署名安培或基内的描绘他旅德的故事。这说明知道一些“旅行轶事”对了解一个国家或有关作者的传说是至为重要的。从天主教神甫们所写的“可资借鉴的书信”到哲学家们的寓言，都把中国人描绘成有道德的形象，甚至把它提高到了一个象征性的地位。这里也如此，搞一份清单是首要的任务。继之，就要搞清楚一本书的流传情况和它的影响——图书馆的图书目录、发行者的账簿、有关通信的考证等等，都要反复查对、比较和评价。

B. 人

为了叙述的方便，到现在为止，我们一直把那些字典、译作和游记跟它的作者分开来观察，原因是这些作者往往不能提供什么使人感兴趣的东西，有些作品也只具有提供统计资料的价值或只反映了一种普遍存在的舆论而已。假如作者是伏尔泰的话，光研究他的《英国通讯集》，而不去了解他在英国是怎样生活的，他对英文、英国、英国人了解得怎么样，那就是不可思议的事了。

在不著名的作者群和在文学生活里起着重大影响的人物中，比较文学往往只着眼于那些天赋的使命是向外国介绍自己祖国文化，更多的是向本国介绍外国文化的人物，如：狂

---

① 指1789年法国大革命时期。

② 指拿破仑统治时期。

③ 马尔洛(1901—1976)法国现代小说家、考古学家、艺术理论家。二次大战时的反法西斯战士，戴高乐政府部长。

④ 福克纳(1897—?)美国小说家，著有《圣殿》、《忿怒之声》、《八月之光》。

热崇拜英国文学的法国人絮阿德①(Suard)、想要本国同胞接受自己所热恋着的法国文化的乔冶·摩尔(George Moore)、德德扬(Dédéyan)以毕生之力予以研究的"文学方面的世界主义"的作者迪博(Du·Bos)等。在这种情况下，一个比较文学工作者运用的不外是所有传记者所运用的方法。至于要想评价一个译者的译文是否忠实、一种批评的精深度、一个旅行者的可靠性等等，比较文学工作者本人就必须对这种语言、这种文学和这个国家具有最可靠的知识才行。

2. 文学类型的命运

上面介绍的研究对象是必要的，但主要只是针对文学上国际交往的工具(译作·游记)或传播者(译者·旅行者)，而不是针对这些国际交往的本身——因为它只具有提供方法的价值。

当这种交往被估计得相当高的时候，最引人注目的则莫过于那些在不断产生着、成长着和消失着的文学类型的命运了。而这些过程的出现却又往往是毫无明显理由的，比如：为什么现在人们不再用诗来写五幕的悲剧？为什么十九世纪初期所有的欧洲国家都写历史小说？为什么文艺复兴时期整个西欧的诗人都用十四行诗这一诗体来抒写自己的爱情？也许有人会问，为什么尽谈这些死了的问题，我们二十世纪的文学不是也曾涌现出许多可敬的作家吗？不过，历史总是由无数死者构成的。再说，又有谁敢肯定说，相似的事情——如果不是完全相同的，不会重新再现呢？1950 年的法国小说固然不曾像古典悲剧那样囿于死板的形式，可是我们的小说家们难道没有采用过某些方法、某些流行的形式吗？同时叙述法、内心独白法、梦幻的象征，这许许多多技巧和结构形式，都可以从外国找到它的渊源。类型的概念在"技巧"面前消失了。作家不再考虑必须忠实于某种既成形式的戒律，而是要对所发生的事件表达自己的观点了。不管这些观点是属于时间的还是属于精神分析的，它都要受到某些规矩的约束。于是人们就会发观，类型原来是被改换了，并不是被摧毁了。

研究文学类型的命运是一个历史问题，同时也是一个现实问题。这种研究需要具备两个条件：固定的类型和接受这种文学类型的环境(时间和空间都明确限定的)。如果比较文学工作者只研究一个国家的文学形式的命运，他的任务就此较容易完成——比如研究十七世纪西班牙喜剧在法国的情况，或英国移植我们古典悲剧的情况等。当然，比较文学工作者也可以把目标定得更高一些，如写十九世纪欧洲历史小说的历史或十六世纪十四行诗诗体的历史等。

方法就是：

A. 给文学类型下定义

如果涉及的是一种比较模糊的形式或甚至是一种文风的话，研究工作就很可能变成徒劳。如象研究的对象是一些外国的、往往要通过译文才能了解的文章，怎么能精确地探索这种文风的影响呢？提出十八或十九世纪某诗人的表达形式是奥西昂(Ossian)的风格②，

---

① 法国新闻工作者和评论家(1733—1817)。写了很多有意义的回忆录。

② 奥西昂：苏格兰传说中的诗人。1760 年麦克费森(Macpherson)以他的名字出版了一本诗集，诗的风格忧郁悱恻。以后形成一种艺术风格。

也只不过是给勒图尔纳(Letourneur)①记上一些明确的借鉴记录罢了。相反，如果是一种具有严格规则的文学类型(彼特拉克(Pétrarque)②的十四行诗、拉辛(Racine)③的悲剧、历史小说)，那么在外国译者的译作里是可以看得出来的。有模仿或改造的地方也是能比较准确地提出来的。

B. 要验证借鉴——可能是直接的，也可能是间接的

伏尔泰、雨果、克洛代尔(ClaudeI)④、布莱希特(Brecht)⑤都曾怀着不同的意图去从莎士比亚戏剧理论那里获得启发，这是直接借鉴。对这种借鉴也需要估计它的影响范围。伏尔泰、雨果、克洛代尔或布莱希特也去启发自己的竞争者。某些竞争者在某些时候只能从其启发者那里接受莎士比亚的戏剧理论，这就是间接借鉴。离开第一个借鉴者越远，问题就越不易得到证实。

C. 评价文学类型和作者之间的相互作用

如果是属于自由选择的话，那么为什么作者要做这样的选择？在这样的选择中他受到了什么限制或丰富了什么？如果是出于一种时尚或接受了权威的影响，那么作者在自己所处的地位上又是如何觉得有这种必要的呢？他是否被一种专横的形式压制了呢？人们都知道，在国内，高乃依(Corneille)曾长时间地与所谓的亚里士多德(Aristote)戒律进行过斗争。比较文学将指出，比如，英国古典主义者跟拉辛悲剧形式的搏斗。这样一种研究将可以使人们对这些作家的气质，甚至对一个民族的性格获得一些很有意义的了解。

3. 题材的命运

每一种伟大的西方文学都有它自己的浮士德⑥和唐璜⑦。季洛杜(J Giraudoux)⑧成了第38个东道主。这些随处都可以再见到的典型、这些在每一个时代都曾被不同的作家采用的传说都是从哪儿来的呢？这里，研究的方向该是由主题提供而不是由形式提供。德国人称这类工作为“主题的历史”，他们很自然地把比较文学往这个方向推进。克罗齐(Benedetto Croce)所支持的法国学派则认为这种研究太枯燥，而且往往会不由自主地陷入繁琐之中。其实，要把这种工作做好，也只不过要“一些完整的事例”，再用一篇文词轻松的评论充实一下就行了。主要还在于作者的才华和所选的题材。而题材又往往只能给文章提供一种人为的统一，如在法国和德国的文学作品中，连一只跳蚤也可能成为“创造性论述”的题目，这能算是比较吗？然而，有关浮士德在法国和德国作家笔下的情况的研究，却一直是沿袭着歌德、瓦莱里(Valéry)直到托马斯·曼(Thomas Mann)等人，它是以

---

① 勒图尔纳(1736—1788)法国文学家，曾翻译过莎士比亚的作品。

② 彼特拉克(1304—1374)意大利名诗人，文艺复兴最早的代表人物。

③ 拉辛(1639—1699)法国古典主义第二期诗人，最有代表性的古典主义悲剧作家。

④ 克洛代尔(1868—1955)法国作家和外交家。著有《人质》等。

⑤ 布莱希特(1898—1956)现代德国著名戏剧家和诗人，创立了“史诗剧”的理论和表演体系。

⑥ 浮士德：法国传奇人物。1587年在大众读物里出现。1590年被英剧作家马娄当做自己剧本的主人公。后歌德又用做自己剧作的名称。

⑦ 唐璜：西班牙传奇人物。后成为西方诗歌和戏剧中风流荡子的典型。

⑧ 季洛杜(1882—1944)法国作家。曾任外交官。作品中宣扬个人主义，充满宿命论思想。写有剧本《特洛伊战争不会再发生了》等。

文艺性的、可以显示出一个人或一个民族的心理特点这样的题材来进行的。从事这种研究工作的人不妨参考一下特鲁逊(Raymond Trousson)1965年留下的“方法论笔记”。

4. 作家们的命运

A. 这里，起点是非常明确的：一个作家创作的全部或一部、一位个人名望与作品的声誉同样高的作家，这二者是不可分割的整体。如下面这三种情况：莎士比亚的戏剧、哈姆雷特(Hamlet)、歌德。

B. 接受者同样也可能是广泛的或少量的：一个国家、一个集团或一个作者。研究的原则是相同的但范围将是多样的。比如：《莎士比亚在法国》、《哈姆雷特在法国》、《歌德在法国》、席勒对浪漫主义戏剧理论的影响、歌德对卡莱尔①(Carlyle)的影响，等等。

C. 在我们这里，很久以来人们把这类研究工作看成是比较文学，因为这是法国学者们经常采用的方法。从原则上看似乎比较简单，但仔细观察，问题就复杂了，因为我们需要把“传播”、“模仿”、“成功”与“影响”都仔细地区别开来。一本“畅销”书是一本成功的书，但它的文学影响却可能等于零。马拉美(Mallarmé)②的诗传播的范围并不广，但它启发了相当多的外国作家。研究一部作品的传播、模仿和成功情况是一件需要耐性和方法的工作，识别一种影响，更是一件细致的工作。首先，因为存在许多种影响：

个人方面的：对卢梭生前和死后的崇拜。

技术方面的：莎士比亚剧作在法国浪漫主义时期的威望。

精神方面的：伏尔泰思想的传播。

题材或背景方面的：我们十七世纪的戏剧理论家借用了西班牙戏剧的一些题材、浪漫主义时期奥西昂式风景画的兴时等。

其次，就像教皇比十一世(Pei XI)曾经对保罗·阿扎尔(Paul Hazard)说过的那样：要注意，不要把“原是干扰的地方看成为有因果关系的联系”。除了明显的蹈袭，再也没有比都德(Daudet)受到了狄更斯(Dickens)的影响更为荒诞的了。因为都德从来就没有接触过狄更斯的作品。应该承认事实，比如说某时代、某国家对歌德或陀斯妥耶夫斯基(Dostoievski)情况的了解仅此而已，要避免不切实际地去证实影响。

D. 采用的方法要与不同的研究内容相适应。不过，任何方法都需要事先满足一些共同的条件：研究某人的著作时，首先要对这个人和他的创作进行深入的了解，对环境也是如此。要一丝不苟地核查书籍、报纸、杂志；经常注意一些年表，对提出结论的报告要审慎地分辨什么是成功，什么是影响——还要分辨出各种不同的影响。

5. 来源

用逆向的推理方法会使人误把传播影响的作者看成是接受影响的人，这就需要把无关紧要的来源剔除出去。若有人冒然地去搞这类研究，就会碰到困难，甚至会宣布这种研究是徒劳的。其实这里面存在一种创作秘诀的问题。如何才能在重视一些印象(如歌德游历意大利印象记)、一些口头资料(如拉马丁(Lamartine)和艾克司丁(Eckstein)有关印度的交谈)、一些造型资料和照片(左拉(Zola)的说明)等的同时，又能不陷入尴尬的境地——否

① 卡莱尔(1795—1881)苏格兰作家。著有《英雄对英雄的崇拜》等。

② 马拉美(1842—1898)法国诗人。象征主义理论家，认为诗歌应当表现“理想世界”。

定天才的个性，让它湮没在一堆证明书的下面，甚或只是编制了一份永远也找不出差别的对照表——呢？如果一个比较文学工作者富有批判精神，列一份对照表还是好的：在负数项目里可以记下，比如夏多布里昂(Chateaubriand)流亡英国时阅读的英文书目，在正数项目里则写上《基督教精神》(Génie du Christianisme)。有时，当某种作品的形式或内容与所仿效的对象发生违谬时，就需要辨别它是由于作者某种模糊的记忆形成的呢，还是由于一种创作上的巧合。在找不出令人易于错乱的抄袭迹象或缺乏作者本人的申明时，对作品来源的研究就只能限于对作者的读物进行一番统计了。

6. 各种思潮

一旦问题已经不属于文学样式、题材或某些个别的作者，而是关系到具有敏感性的思想和潮流时，要识别某种影响所发挥的作用就更难了。比较文学工作者必须要通过对许多国家和文学作品的了解来观察他所要研究的那种思潮的发展情况。保罗·阿扎尔的一些巨著表明，类似的工作是完全可以做得好的。我们不像梵·第根过去在阐明自己的"总体文学"研究方法时那样富有野心，那类综合性的工作只有在一位学者已经广泛阅读作品之后才能进行。即便如此，要认为肯定会有收获也还未免有点自负呢。在这里，更具有危险性的是误把巧合当做了影响。不过，巧合还是具有教益的。它能给每一种文学的历史增添一点它单独存在时缺少的相对感。保罗·阿扎尔的《欧洲意识的危机》就这样给1680年至1715年的法国文学提供了一个远观的回旋余地。这些往往是在有关法国文学的专著中缺少的东西。今天，像《艺术、思想、历史》(*Arts*，*idées*，*histoire*)(斯基拉 Skira)这类丛书已说明一种接近于多学科的著作在如何帮助人们认识一种潮流、一个时代了。

7. 阐明一个国家

每个民族都能以自己的性格为别的民族提供一种比较持久的模式，而且传说往往比实事更起作用。一位拙劣的作曲家倒可能获得声望，正如每个法国人都知道"葡萄牙人是快活的人"这首歌一样。还有一些更深刻的原因，如法国人不像德国人那么能够欣赏和理解英国人民族性格中的同一个特点。而在塑造这些民族典型的过程中，文学、旅游故事、小说、戏剧都起着决定性的作用。试问，能有多少人愿意费神去找机会来验证莫洛亚(Maurois)①有关英国的一些说法，或史达尔夫人有关德国的说法呢？比较文学的任务就是要研究对某个国家的种种阐述的产生及发展情况。

A. 通过外国的文学。比如，英国在我们十九世纪文学中的情况：有哪些法国人曾向自己的同胞提供过英国的情况？英国人有哪些偏见、哪些知识？他们来过法国吗？他们看到了些什么？一些小说、戏剧中提到过英国人物吗？如果有，又赋予他们些什么特点？为什么会这样？这不属于影响问题而是有关阐明的问题。对这些问题的研究会使我们懂得我们是怎样看待英国人的，以及为什么是这样看待的。这种工作要求人们在仔细阅读法文作品的同时，对英国还要有亲身的体验。在这方面，比较文学可以帮助两国进行某种民族的心理分析——在了解存在于彼此之间的那些偏见的来源之后，双方也会各自加深对自己的了解，而对某些相同的先入之见也就更能谅解了。

B. 通过外国的作家。哪怕研究范围只限于一个作家，也要设法了解这个作家对某个

---

① 莫洛亚(1885—1967)法国现代作家，写过许多有关英国的作品。

外国是如何阐明的，而不能只在他的作品中去寻找他所受到的影响。对《伏尔泰与英国》(*Voltaire et l' Angleterre*)这样的书，当然要研究我们这位哲学家从洛克(Locke)①那儿吸收了些什么，主要的还得说明这位流亡者是怎样熟悉这个国家的，是怎样学习这个国家的语言的，又是怎样交朋友的。他回法国以后，又让人们了解了英国哪些方面的情况，为什么让人了解这些情况而不是另外一些。

这些工作的优点是可以避开“影响”这个暗礁。从事这种工作的人，首先应该尽可能广泛地分析整理一下所有有关那个国家的看法——当时流行的或那个作家本人所表现出来的。如果是关系到英国的话，那就要考察一下到英国旅行过的人的旅游笔记、英国名人的言论以及一些有关英国和英国人的评价，等等。同时还要知道作出这些评价或创造出这些人物形象的人是谁。然后把那些来源已经清楚的考察成果收集起来——收集时要注意时间的次序、作家的成就以及那些能使人一目了然的在一定时期里对英国普通形象的重点阐明。

这些似乎有点抽象的意见在帮助比较文学工作者弄清楚自己应走的道路这点上是必要的。现在我们将相继沿着这些道路走去。对每条道路上的情况——哪些领域已经开发了、哪些还有待于人们去开拓，我们也将尽量详尽地指出来。

(节选自马·法·基亚：《比较文学》，颜保译，北京大学出版社1983年版，第7-17页。)

① 洛克(1632—1704)英国哲学家。他发展了经验主义，推动了这一时期的唯物主义和自由思想的传播。他排除思想天赋论，认为人的知识是从实践中得来的。作品有《论人类智力》。

比较文学论

（节选）

［法］梵·第根

【导读】

保罗·梵·第根（Paul Van Tieghem，1871—1948），比较文学“法国学派”的奠基人之一。他的《比较文学论》（1931 年）是比较文学的代表性著作，集中阐述了法国影响研究的主要观点，使影响研究系统化、规范化。该书探讨了比较文学影响研究的意义、学科发展的过程、法国学派的基本研究方法以及总体文学等问题，不但确立了影响研究的基本原则与研究路径，而且对于平行研究与总体文学的相关问题都有涉及，可谓意义深远。

此书第二部第一章“一般的原则与方法”是影响研究的核心理论，从总体上对影响研究的一般原则与方法、比较文学的具体研究领域做出了界定。

一、文学的疆界与影响研究的三要素

梵·第根指出：比较文学是本质地研究各国文学作品的相互关系，这可谓是影响研究的基本界定了。其范围包括希腊拉丁文学、中古世纪以来近代文学与古代文学、近代各国文学之间的关系，后者是比较文学最重要的研究对象。对中世纪的忽略，对欧洲以外文学的无视，是梵·第根不可避免的局限性。经过东西方学者长期的争论与努力，这样的局限性才得以纠正。作者区分出语言与国家疆界的三种关系，对于当语言疆界与国家疆界不一致时如何确定影响关系，他并没有给出明确的结论。这关系到比较文学跨越性该如何界定的问题，梵·第根的困境揭示了以语言作为衡量标准的不合理之处。作者还明确了影响研究的三个基本要素：放送者、接受者与传递者。

二、基本研究方法

梵·第根认为，比较文学与国别文学是相互平行的关系，研究方法既有重合交叉之处，也有其独特性。首先应该将总体的影响分解为无数小的影响，一一加以考察检验，要避免似是而非的判断，还强调了做札记的重要性。对于如何确定影响或者假借的来源，梵·第根肯定了基于作家的阅读书目和作家所处环境的假设的必要性，以及社会事件、文学团体、人们的交谈、作家生活、年谱等在文学影响中的重要意义。这就把研究对象置于一个总体的历史语境之中，有效地避免了研究的片面性。对研究方法的阐述，集中体现了影响研究注重实证性的特点。

三、学者的素养

比较文学学者要懂得多种语言，能够流利地阅读原作，并能自如地处理以第三国语言写成的相关材料；不仅应该熟知超越国家范围的文学史，还应该对文学潮流、相关作家作品及其风格与思想了然于心。梵·第根强调应将作家作品置于其所处的时代氛围之中以更好地突显其价值；要重视文学与其他学科的关系及媒介者的重要性；研究者应该到异国居住。这里包含着跨学科研究及文化研究的因素。梵·第根区别了比较文学学者与一般的文学史研究者的差异，以及作家在本国文学史中的定位和价值与其作为"放送者"和"传递者"在异国的定位和价值之间的差异。

四、研究领域

"文学假借性"，包括文学的文体和作风(即作家风格及特定的艺术手法)，题材、主题、典型或传说，思想或情感等。经过路线，从放送者出发，则为后来所说的"流传学"研究；从接受者出发，则为"源流"亦即"渊源学"研究；以"媒介者"为考察对象，则为"媒介学"研究。在具体的研究实践中，这些方法往往交错使用。此类研究是对国别文学研究的扩大，同时其成果又成为本国文学史的一部分。

虽然该书有些思想并不成熟，概念表述稍欠明晰，欧洲中心主义思想随处可见，但是作为比较文学的奠基之作，它提出的观念与方法一直影响至今，其中有些思想仍然值得进一步挖掘与发展。

(常芳)

第二部 第一章 一般的原则与方法

【语学与文学的疆界。放送者，接受者，传递者】——我们上文已经说明过了，比较文学的对象是本质地研究各国文学作品的相互关系。在这那么广泛的定义之下，如果只就欧洲而论，它便包含希腊拉丁文学之间的关系，以及从中古世纪以来近代文学对于古代文学所负的债，最后是近代各国文学之间的关系。这最广阔复杂的最后一类的问题，是普通所说比较文学所从事研究的；这完全是为了那我们已在"导言"的后面所说明的，那些特别是实际上的理由。

现在我们应该阐明第一点。在指定的一个时代，一国的文学的界限是什么呢？那我们可以从而说"外国"，说外国影响或谈外国的界限是什么呢？在那些语言学的幅员和政治的领土准确地或甚至近似地符合的各点上，回答是很容易的：法兰西和英吉利或西班牙便如此。可是两者不相符合是常有的事，而且对于许多例子，我们是难以找到并不容易运用一个一般的解决的。一个国家的支配的语言往往是在疆域以外被人所说、被人所写；我们应该把那些这样产生的文学作品归附到本国文学中去吗？那些德国人遇到和他们有关的时候以为这样做是对的：他们把瑞士人哈勒(Haller)、鲍尔美尔(Bodmer)、凯勒尔(G. Keller)、奥国人罗赛格尔(Rosegger)和盎森格鲁伯尔(Anzengruber)，都堂皇地归在德国文学史中。在法国，国家的统一是那么的早，而人们对于这统一的情绪又是那么的深、那么的热烈，所以人们对于这个问题，只是带着一种时常探索着并有时是不合理的胆小的态度去解决。根据一些正大的理由，我们把日内瓦人卢骚、沙伏阿人美斯特尔(Maistre)算作法国作家；我们普通总承认瑞士人维奈(Vinet)、薛雷(Schérer)、洛德(Rod)、式尔布力(Cherbuliez)以及比利时人洛登巴克(Rodenbach)和魏尔哈仑(Verhaeren)是法国作家，因为他们多少总把巴黎作为他们的文学重心；可是我们却让瑞士拥有它的多泊费(Toepffer)，比利时拥有它的加米尔·勒莫涅(Camille Lemonnier)，因为他们很愿意留在他们的本国。很合理地，我们应该把左拉(Zola)对于勒莫涅的影响作为比较文学的一个主题。同样，浪漫主义在日内曼或在伏县(Vaud)应作如是观，法国对于加拿大、哈伊达等的法语文学的影响亦应作如是观。由于一种类似的差分，那些英国人并不把美国作家们归在他们的文学中；因此，我们应该从喀莱尔(Carlyle)对于爱麦生(Emerson)或爱伦浦(Edgar Poe)对于英国短篇小说家的影响中，去找比较文学的命题。

前面所说的那些国家或其他国家，可以被好几种语言划分(而且我们还只说那些有文学作品的语言)。左里克(Zurich)的作家凯勒尔和美易尔(C. F. Meyer)对于某一伏县或日内瓦小说家的影响，无疑是属于比较文学的(译者按，两者均在瑞士境中)；一位弗兰特(Flaudre)的诗人所能对于一位华龙(Wallons)的诗人发生的影响，也应当归在比较文学的研究中的(译者按，两者均在比利时境中)。更使人为难的例子还很多。英国文学把苏格兰大诗人洛勃特·彭斯(Robert Burns)引为自己的骄傲，可是他却是用苏格兰方言写诗的，他的国籍是“半外国的”[加萨勉(Cazamian)语]；人们谈着他所受到的“英国影响”，好像他是属于另一国的文学一样。还有我们的米斯特拉尔(Mistral，十九世纪法国南方大诗人——译者注)是用泊洛房斯语写作的；我们的文学史一点地位也不让给他；我们应该认为他和法国诗人们的关系是属于比较文学的。我们还很可以举出许多别的例子，提出许多别的场合来。这往往是一些争讼的问题；总之，人们往往是按照所研究时代而不同地提出这些问题的。

在两国文学的疆界既已确定之后，我们便要着手研究那在文学的领域中从这一边移到那一边而发生一种作用的一切了。这种发生的作用的性质往往是很不相同的；由于知识之获得而来的心智之发达；由于艺术手段之模仿而来的技巧之改善。那因为和外国的感觉协洽而颤动着的感觉的同情；以及还有那往往也是很丰富的反感、反动。我们不久就可以看到，我们如何可以把这一大群的现象加以整理，而终于划分出比较文学的领域来。

在一切场合之中，我们可以首先去考察那穿过文学疆界的经过路线底起点：作家、著作、思想。这便是人们所谓“放送者”。其次是到达点：某一作家、某一作品或某一页、某一思想或某情感。这便是人们所谓“接受者”。可是那经过路线往往是由一个媒介者沟通的：个人或集团，原文的翻译或模仿。这便是人们所谓“传递者”。一个国家的“接受者”在另一个说起来往往担当着“传递者”的任务。在1769年，勒·都尔纳(Le Tourneur)天知道怎样翻译了杨(Young)的《夜思》；他的译本在意大利和西班牙代替了原本。但是，那译文已把原文改得不成样子，实际上，这些国家所看到的简直是另外的一部《夜思》了。所以，我们对于“传递者”应该像对于“放送者”和“接受者”一样地注重。

【原本的探讨和研究】——我们前面已经说过，从今以后，比较文学已经被视为一种独立的学问，但和各国的本国文学平行着。它的方法，一部分就是本国文学史的方法，一部分却更专门一点，是专为它的特殊任务而用的。

比较文学家第一应该避免那些早熟的似是而非的批判；那些批评诱惑着心智，但它们的立脚点却是一些近似或一些错误，而它们又只会把人引导到空泛或不确的概论去。在这些不生效力的批评的起源上，我们差不多总可以发现一些混淆。人们往往把有一些字的种种意义混错：自由、性、理、真、情……因为他们没有仔细读原文，而在原文的某一段中，它们的意义是说明白的。他们常常把同一部书中所表现或带来的各种思想、各种倾向和各种很不同艺术成绩混淆，而不小心地加以分析，以便区别出它们的因子来。反之，我们应该把"放送者"、"接受者"或甚至"传递者"的这些因子隔绝，以便个别地去探讨它们，并确切而有范围地证明那些影响或假借。在那些原文的复杂的织物中，我们需得带着一种一切真正的文学史家所必要的心理学上的细腻——即心灵——去寻出思想的、感情的或艺术的种种不同的丝缕来，以便再去探寻那一些丝缕是在别处可以发现，是织在别的织物中的。如果没有这种小心，那么我们一定会有一种太空泛、太混沌的批判——特别是对于影响这方面——而在那些并不充实而徒有其表的结论中，把真、伪以及可疑的都混在一起。一切整个的影响都可以分为无数特殊的小影响，而我们是应该把它们一一地加以考验的。

这样说来，我们就应得做许多详细的札记，或如人们所说的做札记片，许多的札记片。人们往往嘲笑某一些学识不全的学者们的"札记片癖"。如果这种嘲笑会使那些初步的研究者避免了以为把一切感情一切局面都录在纸片上就认识了一首诗、一出戏曲、一部小说的这种可笑的事情和拙劣的行为，那么这种嘲笑倒是有益于人的了。可是，我们应该把内容或形式的每个变化不同之处，好好地分别札录下来，以备不忘，以后便把这些变化不同之处，用我们上文已证明了其必要性的微妙的心理学的分析隔绝开来。这样，我们可以把那在表达出来的时候常常混错的东西分别清楚；而这样地组成的每一组，将来便可以做那影响或假借的探讨的基础。

我们还应该知道什么地方可以找到那些影响和假借，我们不能任意乱翻乱找。正如在许多别的学问中一样，对于比较文学家的工作，假设往往是必要的。不论关于一个思想的起源也好，关于一件作品的可能的影响也好，一位有见识的史家往往会向某一个方向去探讨，这或者是因为一些类似的移转已经证明了这个方向，或者是因为他觉得他很像能从这一个方向找到那提出的问题。他的探讨往往会毫无结果，可是这种反证却已经是一个有意思的成绩了；或者，在这方面探寻着的时候他会找到什么别的结果出来。可是，一般地说，那些由他对于一位作家，这作家所读的书以及这作家的环境等的深切的认识所提示的假设，总有丰富的结果的。夏都勃里昂的基督教义之精髓中的护教辩证是哪里采取来的？当他草订这本书的计划的时候，他是在英国；他会不会用当时英国新起来的那些护教论者的论证的？但泊赛女士(Dempsey)便是从这个假定出发的；她用着许多断然的符合，去证明那把现成的论证供给了新入教的青年法国人的有点无经验的热忱的，的确是那些英国牧师们的著作。马都尔加女士(Matulka)探讨季兰·德·加斯特罗从什么地方找到他戏曲中的那已经成为熙德所特有的局面和感情(高乃依便是从加斯特罗那里借来了这位可爱的英雄)，而这些熙德所特有的局面和感情等因子又是在加斯特罗以前熙德的传说中所没有的。她提出了这个问题：加斯特罗会不会从什么特别是西班牙的艳侠小说中受到影响？的确，在当时《阿马第斯》(*Amadis*)那一系小说非常风行。马都尔加女士把这些现在已被人遗忘了的小说一部部地加以探讨，而在《弗洛里赛尔·德·尼葛阿》(*Florisel de Niquea*)中，找到了加斯特罗从洛特里格(Rodrigue)的传说中借来，而造成了我们现在所熟稔的熙德这位传说的英雄的种种细节。

探讨的工作不应该只限于把文章加以比较。思想感情的显示和散布，是可能从一件历史的或社会的事实，从一个文学的团体，或只从一次会话出发的；我们将在讨论“媒介”的那一章中举出一些例子来。在作品的起源中，我们应该让一个大地位给作者的生活。当然，年谱在这方面会有一种至高的权威：它足够排除某一假设，使某一很可能发生的关系不生效力。要做这任务，年谱应当尽可能的详细：单是知道某一个诗集在哪一年出版还是不够的，我们应该知道这诗集中的每一首诗是在什么时候第一次发表的——这往往是在什么没有出了几期就停刊的销路不广的刊物上发表的。有时候，一部著作的某一部分的原稿，在未印行之先很久就流传于世了。这些情形就使我们能够提出那些最初似乎被传统的出版年代观念所打破的假设。

为要尽可能多地容纳事实和文献，我们第一应该小心地去检查所研究的时代中的各种定期刊物。批读许多二流或三流作家的作品和各种文学杂志也有用处，因为这样一来那探讨者可以知道所研究的时代的智识温度之高低，并以那与我们现在不同的当时人的观点去看。如果没有这种对于一个时代的一般的初步知识，人们对于那已证实的事实，是有误解的危险的。有一些比较文学的研究成绩——专对于某一点的很精密的探讨的结果——便显得对于接受国的当代文学总体，并没有充分的稔读。

……

【比较文学之各种不同的领域】——比较文学的研究可以用种种很不相同的主题来做对象。一种分类法是不可少的；那我们所采用的分类法将允许我们在后面的各章中合方法地遍历比较文学的广大的领域，这或许还会增加一些新的陌生的领域。在那些我们将去巡历的各区域之间，有些是还没有十分开拓的，而另一些却四面八方都耕耘过了。

我们已经说过，整个比较文学研究的目的，是在于刻画出“经过路线”，刻画出有什么文学的东西被移到语言学的疆界之外去这件事实。可是就是最小的一条经过路线，也是一件复杂的事，因为有种种物质的和心理学的因子跑了进去。为要研究它们，我们可以取两种不同的观点。

有时我们把考察加在经过路线这对象本身之上，加在那被移过去的东西之上。我们把尽可能多的事实聚集在一起——而在这事实之中的共同因子，与其说是环境和状态，还不如说是“文学假借性”；于是我们便把这一种假借或这一群假借记录起来。那人们假借得最多的，或是文学的“文体”或艺术形式、“作风”式表现法；或则是“题材”、主题、典型或传说；或则是“思想”或“情感”；在这第一类中也有同样多的部门，我们均将一一加以考验。

有时候却相反，人们处身在这一方面或另一方面，去观察那经过路线是如何发生的。于是人们便在这两者之间取其一：如果他是置身在放送者的观点上的，他可以研究一件作品，一位作家、一种文体、一种全国文学，在外国的“成功”，它们在那儿所生的“影响”，以及在那儿以它们为模范的各种模仿(在这些种种不同的表现之间，本位是在发送者那里的)；如果他是置身在接受者的观点上的，那么他便要去探讨一位作家或一件作品的可以任意变化的“源流”，而这时本位便在接受者那面了。最后，他会碰到那些促进影响之转移的“媒介者”；那时每个主题的本位便在传递者那里了。

我们将说明，许多这类的研究只不过把一个本国文学史在国内所研究的问题，迁到国外去而加以扩大，并很有用地补充了本国文学史所给与的部分的研究而已。当奈里先生(F. Neri)在他的《岂亚勃雷拉》和《法国七星诗社》中，或莫干先生(Maugain)在他的《龙沙》和《意大利》中研究龙沙在意大利的际遇和影响的时候，他们的探讨所获得的成绩便延长了岛赛尔·雷蒙研究16世纪龙沙的诸模仿者的时候所获得的成绩。同样，当研究“主题”、“源流”等的时候，比较文学家便有总括那一国文学诸史家的探讨，并因此在他们的结论之上加了新的成绩的任务，这种新的成绩我们前面已经说过了，在获得了之后便应该作为本国文学史全体中的一部分。

在同一个研究之中，却也有这些方法的交错。例如说明龙沙或杜·伯莱是怎样地模仿贝特拉尔格或班波(Bembo)，便是写一章“商籁体”(sonnet)或情诗之在法国的历史(“文体”)；便是贴近地研究那形成贝特拉尔格主义的“作风”、“情感”和“思想”等的移植；便是写了贝特拉尔格在法国的“成功”及其“影响”的历史的一部分；又便是(如果我们是从龙沙或杜·伯莱的诗作出发的话)辨认出他们的诸主要“源流”之一。

（节选自梵·第根：《比较文学论》，戴望舒译，吉林出版集团有限责任公司2010年版，第37-43页，第46-47页。）

比较文学的挑战

（节选）

[美]乔纳森·卡勒

【导读】

乔纳森·卡勒(Jonathan D. Culler，1944—　)，康奈尔大学教授、美国艺术与科学院院士，在文学批评、文学理论和比较文学研究中都取得巨大成就。代表性著作有《结构主义诗学》(1975)、《论解构》(1982)、《理论中的文学》(2007)等。《比较文学的挑战》是他在清华大学的演讲，主要讨论了比较文学在当今时代的发展动向及其所面临的挑战，提出了许多独特而富有启发性的见解。卡勒简单回顾了比较文学的学科史，接着指出，中国、印度、日本等国家的加入，他们对民族国家文化身份的强调为比较文学带来新的动向；欧美比较文学则表现出对理论问题的强烈兴趣，对各种理论体系的敏锐与热情使比较文学成为一门先锋学科。但是比较文学现在却面临着身份问题的困扰，与国别文学相比已经不具有区别性，而其欧洲中心主义的模式也开始显得不合时宜。卡勒指出当前比较文学的挑战主要在于走向全球化的困难与文化研究的兴起。对于发端和兴盛于欧美的比较文学来说，过去确立的可比性一旦遭遇跨文化问题，则必然丧失其先天的合理性，在欧美文化范围内确立的一系列比较文学的规范准则也要经受重新拷问。文化研究视角的引入使比较文学的范围迅速扩展，其边界被抹消。卡勒为此提出的解决之道是：比较文学将成为某种最广维度上的跨国现象的一般文学研究，成为比较诗学的发展场域。这一路径的提出，一方面是试图在保持传统与应对全球性问题之间寻求一个两全之策，另一方面也是卡勒本人向来致力于理论研究的必有之思。卡勒认为比较文学虽然经历了各种各样的危机，但是仍然应以文学为其立足点。开放性是比较文学的重要特征，但无论开放到什么程度，文学性始终应该成为比较文学最基本的坚守。

比较文学的身份危机在某种意义上说就是可比性的危机，寻找新的可比性已经成为关乎比较文学合法性的重要议题。西方中心的比较文学话语体系是以同一性的文化空间为前提的，在异文化空间背景之下，其适用性也必然要经受考验。卡勒检讨了西方旧有的标准或规范在开辟新的文化价值方面的限制作用，这也成为比较文学走向全球化的最大障碍。对这一问题的反思体现了一个有担当的理论家的学术理性，也是比较文学学科发展对研究者提出的新的历史任务，斯皮瓦克的“星球性”主张即体现了视角转换的企图。所谓“相互陌生化”，就是在对他者的观照之中重新反观自身，寻找自身的局限性，这是比较文学跨文化研究的必经途径。奥尔巴赫的“出发点”概念对比较文学可比性问题极具启迪意义，对可比性的界定也可以采取一种更为开放的姿态，只需确立基本的关联性原则或曰“出发点”，而其离心性辐射的特点将会为比较文学带来更加多样化的可能性。

卡勒结合具体的研究实例，说明不同文化的相互参照可以帮助纠正西方理论具有普泛性价值的偏见，使人们认识到西方理论不再具有不证自明的先天优越性。他指出：“正是这种朝向其他文化的比较性的、横向的运动，与对我们自己的范畴加以反思的元运动(meta move)的结合，才成为这一学科最突出的特征。”这也使人们确信，所谓比较文学的危机，其实也是其机遇，正像过去多次发生过的那样，比较文学会因此而变得更为丰富，更具包容性，也因此而更具挑战性。

（常芳）

……

那么，比较文学的第一个挑战就是一种全球性视角的必要性。在这里，我或许应该加上一句，佳娅特里·斯皮瓦克曾经催促我们要言说或者思考一种“星球的”(planetary)视角，而不仅仅是一种“全球性的”视角，以抵制被国际资本所操纵的有关全球化的思想。要想让比较文学走向“全球化”或者“星球化”是比较困难的，这是因为比较需要某些规范标准或者相似点，而总存在这样的危险：西方的比较文学将只会关注那些看上去与西方形式相似的文学。而这一困难又由于这样一个事实而变得更加复杂：在西方，从18世纪末开始，原来那种基于文类标准或模式的关于文学的概念已经被这样一种概念所取代：文类范畴倒被看做是一种压抑的标准，而想象力则应该从这种压抑中摆脱出来；许多人现在认为，最伟大的文学作品应该被看做是唯一的、独一无二的，而这恰恰又使我们更难确立比较之或然性的基础。我很快将回过头来讨论如何在全球化或“星球化”的比较文学中进行文学比较这一问题。

比较文学的第二个挑战是由文化研究的兴起而造成的，后者与文学研究领域内的一些变化相关，这些变化是由我们在西方所谓的“理论”所引起的。在今天，被囊括在“理论”范围以内的很多理论都不是文学理论，因为它们并不是阐释文学作品的性质和研究文学的方法，而是关注一般的语言和文化、表意的种种机制、心理的运作、个人与社会之间的关系，等等。对于“理论”而言，文学是文化生产的一种形式，文学系所的教授们所做的研究不仅仅聚焦于文学，而且也将研究的范围扩大到文化方面的话题和表意实践(signifying practices)。我或许需要强调指出，这并不是一种彻底的变化，因为先前所做的很多对表面上是文学话题的研究，在本质上其实是历史性的；这些研究重新建构起该文学作品和作家的创作时代。但是在过去，这种研究表面上看来最终都是指向对文学的某种理解。而在文化研究中，对文学文本的研究则经常意在理解社会话题、政治话题或文化话题，作为其他什么东西的某种症候。当比较文学将如此多不同的文化纳入自己的研究范围时，就已经变成了一个范围广大、无法操控(unmanageable)的事业；当文学与其他社会产品和文化产品之间的边界被消抹，当比较文学学者也开始研究电影、电视、流行文化、广告和各种各样的文化表现形式时，该学科所要面对的材料绝对多得令人窒息(completely overwhelming)。

上述的每一个挑战都十分重要，但它们的结果都走到了一起，走向“全球化”，走向“文化”研究；其所涉及的范围是如此广大，以至于它似乎已经不再是一个学术领域了，潜在地是对全世界的话语和各种各样的文化产品的研究。比较文学的研究范围迅速扩展，以至于根本无法把握，这一问题在比较文学的会议上显得尤为突出，大会上所提交的论文所涉及的范围常常如此宽泛，以至于你很难觉得你与很多其他的参会人员是属于同一个研究领域的，因为你与他们几乎没有多少共同的知识背景或相互之间的参照。

我在上文中已经指出，研究国别文学的系所越来越重视理论，或者更加准确地说，它们允许文学研究和文化研究围绕那些来自理论辩论的问题，而非那些传统的文学—历史阶段，去重新组织自己，随着这些系所越来越多地将更大范围的文化产品带入它们的视野——不仅仅是电影和流行文化，还包括性别话语(discourses of sexuality)、身体的建构、民族身份和文化身份的形成等——它们实际上已经变成民族文化研究的系所了：英国研究和美国研究、法国研究、德国研究、西班牙研究等。这种文化转向对于国别文学而言是有意义的：通过国家界限或语言界限所做的划分总是十分可疑的，但是，这种国别的划分对于组织对文化的研究和考察是十分合理的。随着德国文学系转向德国文化研究，法国文学系转向法国研究，国家的名称最终将代表那些在知识上更为相干的学科领域。而且，随着国别文学系所转向文化研究，我认为，它们给比较文学系所留下了一个十分独特的角色。① 由于比较文学在很大程度上已经使文学研究扩展为文化研究，它或许可以具有讽刺意味地通过逆向移动，去做那些其他系所现在所忽略的研究，从而使自己获得某种新的身份。它也许可以获得一种新的身份：作为最广维度上的文学研究场域——作为某种跨国现象的文学研究。其他领域的权力移交最终将会给比较文学留下一种独具特色而又弥足珍贵的身份。比较文学作为一般的文学研究的场域，将为诗学——一种比较诗学(a comparative poetics)——提供一个家园。

但是，这并不意味着我们不鼓励比较文学系所的研究者去研究相关于其他文化实践的文学研究，或者甚至不鼓励他们去从事那些与文学关系较远的研究项目。我绝对不是这个意思。正如我们一直认为的那样，比较文学学者将参与人文学科中那些最有意义的方法论研究和理论研究，不管这些研究会将他们带到哪些领域。既然文学并不是自然的，而是一种历史的建构，那么，相关于其他话语的文学研究就不但是不可避免的，而且相对于人文学科中的其他系所，比较文学将把文学研究作为自己最核心的责任和任务，这一任务将以各种各样的方法来完成。

我认为比较文学应该接受由于文学研究和文化研究的演化所创造出来的这种差异的可能性(the differential possibility)，也就是作为跨国现象的文学研究，但我的这一观点并没有得到多少人的支持(尽管我还将一如既往地拥护它)，而比较文学应该是什么这一问题

① See Culler. Comparative Literature, at Last. in: Charles Bernheimer, ed. *Comparative Literature in the Age of Multiculturalism*. Baltimore: Johns Hopkins University Press, 1995, pp. 117-21, and, revised, in: Culler. *The Literary in Theory*. Stanford: Stanford University Press, 2007, pp. 254-68.

依旧充满了争议，不过我们都同意：比较文学的性质决定了它是人文学科各种不同的选择在其中角逐争战的一块场域。但十分引人注目的是，20 世纪 90 年代比较文学中文学的角色似乎受到咄咄逼人的文化研究的威胁，而时至今日，情况似乎发生了变化。这种发展确实让人欣慰。我们可以说，虽然不牵涉文学的比较文学研究的合法性已经确立，但文学的核心作用(centrality)却不像以前那样受人质疑了——即便这只是由于来回摇摆的钟摆又摆回来了。苏源熙在谈到比较文学就是"用文学进行比较"(comparisons with literature)时，假定文学具有核心作用，他的意思是说比较文学牵涉到阅读各种各样的文本，但这种阅读是"文学的阅读"(reading literarily)。实际上，当我看到后殖民研究领域内的某些比较研究(它们是聚焦于社会问题和政治问题的，其实根本不必去涉及文学)似乎也包括好几章对英语作家的研究时，我也为此而感到吃惊。这一类的研究向人们展示，一种新的超经典的英语作家产生了：拉什迪、阿切贝、沃尔科特、库切等。在今天，比较文学内文学的角色似乎仍然生气勃勃，即使文学作品经常被症候式地阅读，即使同事们并非急于支持我的观点：比较文学的身份仍应该重新建基于文学之上。

但是，文学又将我们带回到可比性(comparability)这一问题上，而比较文学的命运似乎不可阻挡地被绑缚在可比性上，这真是见证了一个名称的巨大力量。我在前文指出，以前的比较文学是建基于经过验证的接触关系，进而建基于渊源和影响，后来逐渐拓展到范围更广的文本间的研究，因而，原则上任何文学作品之间都可以进行比较；但随着比较文学自身从上述可比性上解脱出来，我们便开始听到关于"比较文学的危机"的说法，这无疑是因为人们难以解释这种新的可比性的性质，而这种新的可比性的作用就是要建构比较文学的结构，而且在原则上是要建立起比较文学的合法性。

随着我所描述的比较文学从一种欧洲中心的研究转向一个全球性的学科，上文所述的可比性这个问题便变得更加突出，虽然在某些方面这个问题对我们来说是隐而未显的。我们可以说，有这么一个阶段，可比性这一问题或许在表面上可以被暂时放到一边，因为大量的新作品都聚焦于后殖民社会中的和殖民霸权的文学作品中的跨文化接触和混杂性。事实上，大量令人激动的作品都是对渊源和影响研究的复杂版本和现代化版本：在对德里克·沃尔科特的《奥梅罗》(*Omeros*)或者塞尔曼·拉什迪的《魔鬼诗篇》(*The Satanic Verses*)中的各种文学影响和文化影响所做的比较研究中，其比较都是基于直接的文化接触和有迹可循的影响的。但是，原则上可比性这一问题仍旧未能得到解决，而是比以前更加突出了。在我们这个新近全球化的空间里，什么东西能够使得把某些文本放在一起合法化呢？

意义的互文性特征——意义位于某一文本或者某个话语和另一文本或者话语之间的差异处这一事实——使得文学研究从本质上看、从根本上看是可比较的，但意义的互文性特征也产生了这样一种情形：可比性有赖于某种文化体系，一个支持比较的一般的领域。文本的意义有赖于它与某个文化空间中的其他文本之间的关系，譬如说西部欧洲文化空间，这也是为什么比较文学的重心是如此倾向于保持在西方和欧洲范围内的原因之一。一个人对于话语的理解越是深刻复杂，他就越是难以对西方和非西方的文本进行比较，因为这二者中的每一种的意义和身份都依赖于它们各自在其话语体系中的位置，而这些性质相异的体系似乎使得文本之间那种公认的可比性要么虚无缥缈，要么至少也是误导性的。最近的一些比较文学作品中的比较研究之所以成为可能，主要是由于它们采用了后殖民理论中的认同观，该理论探讨的是一种普遍的后殖民语境，而在这种语境中就产生了一种可比性。

那么，什么样的可比性能够引导比较文学从一种以欧洲中心主义的学科向一种更加全球化的学科转化呢？这里有一个难题。正如娜塔莉·麦拉斯(Natalie Melas)所指出的，那种赋予某个学科以合法性的比较，巩固了某种标准或者规范，这种标准或者规范又赋予了那些符合或达到这种标准的作品以价值，并且排除掉那些不符合其标准的作品——对于西方人而言，西方的实践变成了标准或者框架，因此比较——比较性原则——不仅不为文化价值去开辟新的可能性，反而常常对其加以限制并将其整合为一了。①

今天的比较文学学者都迫切地要避免用外在于某种文化的标准去评价来自这种文化的文本所产生的隐含的结果(this implicit result)，但是，这当然是很难做到的。在主张一种“星球性”比较文学而非“全球性”比较文学时，斯皮瓦克督促我们，不仅要抵制那种麦当劳遍布每个城市(这是我想到的例子，不是她的)的全球化，而且要避免把我们自己变成比较的标准，而将他人看做知识的场域(sites of knowledge)。她写道：“地球在我们的电脑上，没有人住在那里。它让我们认为我们能够控制它。这个星球属于变异的物种(species of alterity)，它属于另一个体系；而我们居住在其上，是临时租借的……如果我们将自己想象成星球的主体而非全球性的代理、星球上的生物而非地球上的实体(global entity)的话，那么变异性(alterity)就仍旧无法从我们身上得出(underived)；它不是我们的辩证否定。”

对于西方人而言，从地理上来定位他们的比较视角(而非只是去想象自己具有某种普遍性)将非常具有启发意义。譬如说，比较欧洲文学与非洲文学，考察欧洲文学与非洲某个特定时期的文化产品之间的关系。这种总体的想法(general idea)的另一个版本就是，比较文学和文学理论也应该包括所谓的“相互陌生化”(reciprocal defamiliarization)，意思就是他人的规范或者标准会对你自己的规范或标准提出质疑。

采纳这样的策略确实是一种挑战，无疑需要各方进行合作，因为极有可能的情况是：你很难不透过那些你已经知道的文化框架，而轻易地识别出另一种文化的标准。不过，将其他文化看做知识的场域而非知识对象这种思想就容易对付多了。然而，我自己却不太热衷于去获得某种星球性的视角，而是更偏爱从某种承认自身也具有局部性(partialness)的视角去进行研究：试图去详尽地写出支撑自己的比较的那些假设和规范，以便它们不会变成隐含的条件或者暗地里做出判断。这里有一个例子，就是艾瑞克·奥尔巴赫(Erich Auerbach)关于“出发点”(*Ansatzpunkt*)的概念，它指一个具体的出发点，它不是被设想为一个外在的掌控位置，而是作为一个“把”(handle)，或者是一个带有偏好的有利位置(partial vantage point)，它使批评家能够将多种文化客体带到一起来。奥尔巴赫这样写道：

---

① Natalie Melas “Versions of lncommensurability”, World Literature Today 69: 2(Spring 1995). See also her book, *All the Difference in the World*: *Postcoloniality and the Ends of Comparison*, Stanford: Stanford University Press, 2007.

“一个有利的出发点的特征就是，一方面它具有具体性和准确性，另一方面是它具有离心性辐射的潜能”。该出发点也许是一个主题、一个比喻、一个细节、一个结构性问题，或者一项经过充分定义的文化功能。我们可以做这样的设想：将跨文化比较建基于这些关联性的原则之上，这些关联性原则的偶然性将阻止它们产生某种标准或者是什么理想的类型。

……

（节选自乔纳森·卡勒：《比较文学的挑战》，生安锋译，载《中国比较文学》2012年第1期，第5-10页。）

《罗摩衍那》在中国

（节选）

季羡林

【导读】

季羡林（1911—2009），山东临清县人，教授，北京大学比较文学研究会会长，著名梵文专家和外国文学研究家。有关比较文学的主要论著有：《〈罗摩衍那〉初探》（1979）、《中印文化关系史论丛》、《漫谈比较文学史》、《泰戈尔与中国》、《印度文学在中国》等。季羡林先生于1986年发表的此篇论文，主要分析印度两大史诗之一——《罗摩衍那》在中国的流传情况，及其影响问题。季羡林先生研阅了当时所有的《罗摩衍那》文献，涉及梵文、巴利文、汉文、傣文、藏文、蒙文、古和阗文和吐火罗文A（焉耆文）八种语言，展开了详细、确凿的考证与分析，此文属于流传学研究的范例。

论文分两个部分，其一为文献材料的罗列与整理，其二为相关结论的归纳与总结。首先是文献梳理。论者按汉、傣、藏、蒙、新疆的顺序，简述《罗摩衍那》在中国的传播情貌。第一，《罗摩衍那》在汉译佛经中的流传。论者分别从《罗摩衍那》的若干故事与《罗摩衍那》中的小故事（如寓言、童话等）两方面进行爬梳。在谈论骨干故事时，论者选择汉译佛典《十奢王缘》、《六度集经》第五卷第四十六个故事同印度蚁蛭《罗摩衍那》进行比较。发现，《十奢王缘》与《六度集经》第五卷第四十六个故事两相结合，便是一个完整的梵文《罗摩衍那》。因此得出结论："汉译佛经中这两个故事同蚁侄的《罗摩衍那》几乎完全一样，它们属于同一个发展体系，这一点非常值得注意。"在分析书中插入的小故事时，论者选取了两个典型进行讨论。第一个是鹿角仙人的故事。通过经文比照，印度《罗摩衍那》鹿角仙人故事在汉译佛典中有了变异："一、不是鹿角，而是鹿斑。二、讲明了身上长鹿斑的原因；三、破坏鹿斑的道行不是为了求雨，而是天老爷害了怕。"第二个是睒子的故事。论者研阅发现，睒子故事在《六度集经》与《罗摩衍那》中的书写基本一致，唯独故事结尾有稍许差异，即原本在印度《罗摩衍那》中的悲剧结局，到了中国《六度集经》这儿便成了个喜剧收场。论者推测，或许是顺应为了中国读者的心理。第二，《罗摩衍那》在傣族地区的流变。论者以为，傣文本与梵文《罗摩衍那》在主题思想与情节方面基本相同。不同之处在于，主题上，梵文《罗摩衍那》宣传的是婆罗门教，宣扬种姓制度和封建伦理道德。而傣文《罗摩衍那》（即《兰嘎西贺》）宣传的是佛教，美化封建领主制。情节上，由于傣族化使然，促成了一系列小故事的变异，譬如，印度地名被替换成了云南地名等。第三，《罗摩衍那》在西藏的传播情况。论者将藏本与梵本相比较，发现二者的骨干故事、细节基本相同。不同之处在于，藏本《罗摩衍那》加入一些新情节，且藏本在结构、结尾上均有本土化改写。第四，《罗摩衍那》在蒙古的流传情形。由于结合本民族历史与习俗，蒙古文罗摩故事表现出非常浓厚的地方化色彩。第五，《罗摩衍那》在新疆的传播。在新疆境内，没有《罗摩衍那》的维吾尔文全文介绍，但却有《罗摩衍那》的故事记载。论者以为，维吾尔文与梵文《罗摩衍那》的故事基本相同。最后是论文的结论。在罗列了《罗摩衍那》梵文与其他本子的异同之后，季羡林先生总结出以下几点：一、罗摩故事宣传的是印度教——婆罗门教思想，并以讲述人民道德观念的传奇故事为主要形式。二、罗摩故事传入中国地区之后，汉、傣、藏、蒙、维等民族加以利用，为自己的政治服务。三、《罗摩衍那》汉译本十分强调伦理道德。四、再次印证了中国读者不大喜欢或欣赏悲剧的接受心理。五、《罗摩衍那》在傣族与蒙族地区流传时，表现出的地方色彩和民族色彩最为明显。

值得关注的是，季羡林先生在分析《罗摩衍那》之中国流传与演变时，还论及《西游记》中孙悟空形象的来源问题。通过材料得出，《罗摩衍那》神猴哈奴曼影响了中国孙悟空形象的形成。诚然哈奴曼与孙悟空形象的关系分析非本文重点，但季羡林先生通过《罗摩衍那》的中国之旅，推衍出了中印文化交流的新观点与新途径。此做法不仅彰显出其学术研究的敏锐感与开拓精神，更为中国比较文学流传学研究提供了一个典范。

（曾小月）

印度两大史诗之一《罗摩衍那》写成或纂成以来，至今至少已有将近两千年的历史了。它在印度、亚洲，以及世界其他地区的影响之巨大、之深入，是众所周知的。至于对中国的影响，过去学者们多半强调《罗摩衍那》没有译成汉文，言外之意就是说，它对中国影响不大，至少对汉族影响不大。实际上并不是这样子。最近有一些学者，特别是研究云南少数民族文学的同志，对于这个问题作了一些深入的探讨，得到了可喜的成果。我自己也对《罗摩衍那》在中国传播的情况以及它的影响，搜集了一些资料，形成了一些看法，现在介绍给大家。

为了有利于把中国境内的各异本同梵文原文的《罗摩衍那》进行对比，我在这里先把罗摩的故事介绍几句。《罗摩衍那》的精校本虽然长达将近两万颂，但骨干故事是比较简单的。十头罗刹王罗波那肆虐，欺凌神人。大神毗湿奴化身为四，下凡生为十车王的四个儿子。长后憍萨厘雅生子罗摩，小后吉迦伊生子婆罗多，另一后须弥多罗生子罗什曼那和设睹卢祇那。罗摩娶遮那竭王从垄沟里捡起来的女儿悉多为妻。十车王想立罗摩为太子。小后要挟他，放逐罗摩十四年，立自己的儿子婆罗多为太子。罗摩、悉多和罗什曼那遵父命流放野林中。十车王死，婆罗多到林中来恳求罗摩回城即国王位。罗摩不肯。十头魔王劫走了悉多，把她劫到楞伽城。罗摩同猴王须羯哩婆联盟，率猴子和熊罴大军，围攻楞伽城。神猴哈奴曼立下了奇功。后来魔王被杀。罗摩同悉多团圆，流放期满，回国为王。

梵文《罗摩衍那》整个故事的梗概就是这样。巴利文本《Jātaka461》内容大同小异。最显著的差异是：悉多是十车王女，与罗摩是兄妹，两人后来结婚。

现在我就把目前能够找到的资料和我的一些分析的结果和看法，按汉、傣、藏、蒙、新疆的顺序，简要叙述如下。

一、《罗摩衍那》留在古代汉译佛经中的痕迹

中国古代译佛经为汉文的佛教僧侣，包括汉族、少数民族以及印度僧侣在内，确实对《罗摩衍那》这一部史诗是熟悉的，不过可能因为它与宣传佛教无关，所以他们只在译经中翻译过它的故事，提到过它的名字，而没有对全书进行翻译。陈真谛译《婆薮槃豆法师传》说："法师托迹为狂痴人，往罽宾国。恒在大集中听法，而威仪乖失，言笑舛异。有时于集中论毗婆沙义，乃问《罗摩延传》，众人轻之。"马鸣菩萨造、后秦鸠摩罗什译的《大庄严经论》卷第五说："时聚落中多诸婆罗门，有亲近者为聚落主说《罗摩延书》，又《婆罗他书》，说阵战死者，命终生天。"《罗摩延书》就是《罗摩衍那》。

这里讲的只是书名，书里面的故事怎么样呢？

关于这个问题应该分两部分来谈，第一部分是《罗摩衍那》全书的骨干故事；第二部分是书中插入的许多零碎的小故事，其中包括寓言和童话。

首先谈本书的骨干故事。骨干故事比较简单，已如上述。唐玄奘译的《阿毗达磨大毗婆沙论》第四十六卷里说："如《逻摩衍拏书》有一万二千颂，唯明二事：一明逻伐拏(罗波那)将私多(悉多)去，二明逻摩将私多还。"同这个骨干故事相当的故事在汉译佛典中可以找到。我在这里抄上两个。《杂宝藏经》第一卷第一个故事，《十奢王缘》：

……

《六度集经》第五卷第四十六个故事：

……

我现在对照印度蚁垤的《罗摩衍那》对上面的两个故事稍加分析。

首先从整个结构上来看。这两个故事，一个只讲十奢(车)王同三位夫人四个儿子，只讲由于宫廷阴谋罗摩和弟弟罗漫被流放十二年。罗漫就是罗什曼那，婆罗陀就是婆罗多，灭怨恶是意译，就是设睹卢祇那。故事内容，同梵文《罗摩衍那》完全一样。连细节都并无二致。比如梵文中罗什曼那那种李逵式的性格，这里也表现了出来。婆罗多率军至森林中，罗什曼那对他怀疑，都说得清清楚楚。这些细节相同到令人惊异的程度。至于孝悌忠信那一套封建思想，这里也表露无遗。虽然着墨不多，但却完整无缺。可能受到中国旧时代士大夫的赞赏。

第二个故事只讲一个大国王，避敌让位，带着元妃住在山林中，元妃被海中恶龙劫走。国王与同病相怜、命运相同的猕猴联盟，终于渡海登洲，消灭了恶龙，夺回元妃，皆大欢喜。从出场的人物来看，它与梵文相差颇远。但从骨干故事的情节来看，则几乎完全一样，连细节都一样。恶龙就是梵文的罗刹，鸟就是梵文的大鹫。倘若把国王名字改为罗摩，把王妃名字改为悉多，把舅舅改为小后吉迦伊，则是活脱脱一个罗摩、悉多故事了。

这两个故事合起来，就形成一个完整的梵文《罗摩衍那》。这暗示，在古代印度大史

诗《罗摩衍那》形成时确实是把两个故事合并起来的。我们不要忘记，这个骨干故事在印度本土也是多种多样的。各个邦、各个民族几乎都有自己的罗摩、悉多故事，内容有时甚至有相当大的差异。虽然蚁垤的《罗摩衍那》可能由于思想性对头、艺术性高超的缘故，因而占据了相当重要的地位，可是也没有能定于一尊。汉译佛经中这两个故事竟然同蚁垤的《罗摩衍那》几乎完全一样，它们属于同一个发展体系，这一点非常值得注意。

以上讲的是第一部分，是全书的骨干故事。现在再来谈第二部分，是书中插入的许多零碎的小故事。

这样的故事数量大得惊人。我眼前没有可能搞得太多。我只能选出几个有典型意义的来加以探讨。按在《罗摩衍那》中出现的先后排列顺序，第一个是鹿角仙人的故事。这个故事在印度文学中不知出现过多少次。德国梵文学者 Lüders 有一篇文章，专门谈这个问题：Die Sage von Rsya'srnga，Schlingl-off① 也有一篇文章：Unicorn② 讲同一个问题。在《罗摩衍那》中，这个故事出现在第一篇第八、九两章。十车王想行祭乞子，大臣苏曼多罗给他讲了鹿角仙人的故事。故事的内容大体如下：一个婆罗门的儿子住在森林中，对外界的事物什么都不懂，不懂有女人的幸福，不懂感官享乐。这时候，一个国王犯了错误，上天罚他，久旱不雨。他很苦恼。婆罗门给他出主意说，只要把林中婆罗门童子引诱到城里来，天就会下雨。国王就派妓女入林。这个童子不懂什么叫男人和女人，碰到这些妓女，觉得她们很可爱，最后终于被引诱走出山林，进入城市。这个故事没有讲他为什么是鹿角。这个故事在汉译佛典中也多次出现。……我也只能简略叙述一下内容，以资对比。故事首先讲仙人小解，不净流出，母鹿吞下，怀孕生子，身有鹿斑。仙人告诫他："可畏之甚，无过女人。"命终后，鹿斑苦修，天老爷害了怕，怕有人夺他的宝座。于是派天女下凡破坏鹿斑的道行。对比两个故事，其中有几点是不同的：一不是鹿角，而是鹿斑；二、讲明了身上长鹿斑的原因；三、破坏鹿斑的道行不是为了求雨，而是天老爷害了怕。

第二个我想选睒子的故事。这个故事出现在《罗摩衍那》第二篇(参阅《罗摩衍那》2. 56. 2；③ 2. 57. 8-39；2. 58. 1-46)。内容大体如下：十车王把儿子罗摩流放后，心中悔愧万分。他告诉长后，他年轻的时候，能闻声放箭，射中目的物。有一次他到萨罗逾河边玩耍，忽然听到黑暗中有瓶子灌水的声音，他误以为是大象，射了一箭，结果射中的是一个苦行者——他正到河边给盲父母汲水。苦行者死后，国王见到盲父母，盲父母让他带路来到儿子尸体那里，他们呼天抢地，大放悲声，盲父最后诅咒国王，也让他尝一尝失子之痛。

汉译佛典中，这个故事多次出现。我只举一例：《六度集经》：

……

对比一下《罗摩衍那》与《六度集经》这两个故事，可以发现，两个故事内容是一致的，连一些细节都一样或者相似。国王的名字当然不会一样，但这无关大局。最主要一个差别是，《罗摩衍那》的故事是一个悲剧，童子死掉，其父发出诅咒。而在《六度集经》中则转

① Philologica Indica Göttingen 1940 年，第 1-43 页。

② German Scholars on India vol. I. Varanasi 1973 年，第 294-307 页。

③ 指第二篇，第 56 章，第二首诗。

悲剧为喜剧。童子得群神福祐，死而复生，皆大欢喜。这是否为了适应中国读者的心情而改变的，不得而知。

……

我在这里想顺便谈一谈《西游记》中的主角孙悟空。这个猴子至少有一部分有《罗摩衍那》中神猴哈奴曼的影子，无论如何标新立异，这一点也是否认不掉的。如果正视事实的话，我们只能承认《罗摩衍那》在这方面也影响了中国文学的创作。这个问题我在这里不细谈。

我只谈一下孙悟空与福建泉州的关系。这一点过去知道的人是非常少的。最近日本学者中野美代子教授送给我一篇《福建省与〈西游记〉》。我觉得这是一篇有独到见解的文章。我在这里简略地加以介绍。

在泉州开元寺，南宋嘉熙元年(公元1237年)修建的西塔第四层壁面上有一个猴子浮雕，戴着金箍，脖子上挂着念珠，腰上挂着一卷佛经，右肩上有一个小小的和尚像。这和尚是否就是玄奘？这不敢说。在西塔第四层其他壁上有玄奘的像。另外在泉州的一座婆罗门教寺院里，大柱子上有一个猴子浮雕，尾巴拖得很长很长，手里拿着像草似的东西。这让人自然而然地想到《罗摩衍那》中的哈奴曼。他曾用尾巴带火烧毁楞伽城，并手托大山，带来仙草，救了罗摩和罗什曼那的性命。

这明确地说明了，南宋时期《西游记》的故事还不像以后这样完备，只能算是一个滥觞。中野美代子研究猴行者的来源，说是在宋代《罗摩衍那》经过南海传到泉州。泉州当时是中国最大的港口，与阿拉伯和印度等地海上来往极其频繁。说猴行者不是直接从印度传过来而是通过南海的媒介，是顺理成章的。我推测，在这之前关于神猴的故事，一方面中国有巫支祁这个基础，再加上印度哈奴曼的成分，早已在一些地方流行。泉州的猴行者并不是最早传入的。在八、九世纪以后，《罗摩衍那》已逐渐传入斯里兰卡、缅甸、泰国、老挝、柬埔寨、马来西亚等地。从这一带再传入中国，是比较方便的。

福建泉州发现了孙悟空，这一件事实虽简单，我觉得却给我们提出了非常值得考虑的问题：研究中印文化交流的学者，不管是中国的，还是外国的，大都认为中印文化交流渠道只有西域一条，时间都比较早，也就是说在唐宋以前；现在看来，这种想法必须加以纠正：中印文化交流从时间上来说，宋以后仍然有比较重要的交流。从空间上来说，海路宋代才大为畅通。此外，还有一个川滇缅印道，也往往为学者所忽略。

二、傣　　族

我国云南的傣族，由于与缅甸接壤，而缅甸受印度文化影响较早；又因为傣语与泰语同系，泰国也早已受到印度影响，近水楼台先得月，因而比较早地接受了印度的文学、宗教等。印度《罗摩衍那》虽然没有全部传至中国内地，却传到了傣族地区，在这地区的民间流行极广①。根据现在的调查，至少有这样一些不同的本子，首先有大小《兰嘎》，即

① 以下叙述主要根据高登志、尚仲豪：《〈兰嘎西贺〉与〈罗摩衍那〉之异同》《思想战线》1983年第5期，页74-79；王松：《傣族诗歌发展初探》，中国民间文艺出版社(云南版)，1983年，第三编，第二十节。

《兰嘎竜》和《兰嘎囡》之分，在大《兰嘎》中又分为《兰嘎西贺》与《兰嘎双贺》。在中国傣族地区，罗摩故事译本极多，这里无法详细列举。大概每一个罗摩故事的民间演唱者，都根据当时当地的情况而随时有所增删，以适应听者。这充分显示了傣族艺人的才能，但也产生了另一结果：异本蜂起，头绪纷繁。

对比一下梵文《罗摩衍那》与《兰嘎西贺》，从主题思想、故事内容、人物形象来看，印、傣的本子基本上相同，连名字都差不多。比如：

罗摩	召朗玛
悉多	婻西拉
罗什曼那	腊嘎纳(这显然是从巴利文传过来的)
婆罗多	帕腊达
哈奴曼	阿努曼
维毗沙那	被亚沙
楞伽	兰嘎
阿逾陀	阿育塔

《兰嘎西贺》诗共分为二十二篇，内容可分为五个部分。第一至第四部分，主要情节与《罗摩衍那》大体相同。罗摩被流放十四年，而召朗玛只有十二年。第五部分叙述召朗玛为儿子选妃，同勐哥孙发生了战争，最后两国联姻，召朗玛传位于儿子洛玛，死后升天。这些大半是傣族人自己创造的。

在情节方面和人名方面，有不少不同的地方。在《罗摩衍那》中，是大神毗湿奴化身为四，而在《兰嘎西贺》中则是众神上天告捧玛加的状，说他欺凌群神，大神英达为了惩罚十头王，指令天神波提亚弟兄四人下凡投生。三个王后是吃了香蕉，而不是喝了仙酒，才怀孕生子的。《罗摩衍那》中的悉多是从垄沟里捡起来的，在《兰嘎西贺》里婻西拉被说成是十头王的女儿，被他抛入江中。召朗玛是私自出走，不是由于宫廷阴谋被父亲流放。帕腊达回宫后也进入森林修行，由最小的弟弟达鲁嘎为王。《兰嘎西贺》诗西双版纳本说十头王的姑妈变成金鹿引诱召朗玛走开，乘机劫夺婻西拉。此时腊嘎纳在嫂子西拉周围画了一个圆圈，请土地神保护她。这个情节在《罗摩衍那》中已经删掉。大战前夕，是十头王派女妖化身为西拉，以骗召朗玛，而不是由于因陀罗耆的妖术。阿努曼到兰嘎城侦察，带给婻西拉的不是只戒指，而是手镯等信物。召朗玛与妻儿相会，是在放马追踪过程中遇到婻西拉的，从而父子相认，消除误会，而不是在举行马祠时，听两个青年歌手演唱《罗摩衍那》才认子团圆的。这样的不同之处还有一些。

在细节方面也有一些值得注意的地方，比如误杀盲道人之子，《兰嘎西贺》诗刀秀廷翻译本有这个情节，而岩温扁、刀兴平翻译本则没有。这个情节在罗摩故事中不是重要情节，而《兰嘎西贺》有的本子竟然能有，反而证明二者关系之密切了。

西双版纳纳岩罕翻译的小《兰嘎》，同梵文《罗摩衍那》差异更大。比如说婻西拉原是天神叭英的妻子苏坦玛，夫妻七天相会一次。十头王窜到天宫，摇身变成了叭英，奸污了她。她为了复仇，下凡投胎为十头王的女儿婻西拉。十头王将她绑在筏子上，丢进大海，为仙人帕拉西救起，抚养成人。

在傣族、崩龙族和布朗族中流传着的《兰嘎西贺》的故事，有一些情节与《罗摩衍那》

不同。比如在森林比武招亲时，高僧帕拉西既要求婚者拉神弓，又要他们抬石桌子，十头王旁观不动。等到召朗玛娶了婻西拉以后，他变为金鹿劫走了她。又如说十头王的母亲是一个寡妇；十头王陷害婴儿婻西拉，把她和妻子一齐放到竹筏上，任其漂流，竹筏被浪打翻冲到岸边，妻子上岸天天骂十头王，后与猴子婚配，生了两个儿子，其中之一就是阿努曼，长大后报了母仇。再如十头王抢走婻西拉，是在召朗玛到深涧中去找水的时候，十头王学着召朗玛的声音，喊腊嘎纳去取水，乘兄弟俩不在，劫走了婻西拉。所有这一些不同之处，都说明这故事在传播中的演变。

现在归纳起来，再进行一下对比。从主题思想上来看，傣文本与梵文《罗摩衍那》基本相同。都是宣传正义战胜邪恶，这充分表现出，中印两国人民人同此心，心同此理。从情节方面来看，两者基本上相同。连一些细节都一样。当然也有不同之处。从主题思想方面来看，《罗摩衍那》宣传的是婆罗门教，主角是刹帝利，有婆罗门仙人相助；它宣扬种姓制度和封建伦理道德。而《兰嘎西贺》宣传的则是佛教，辅佐召朗玛的是佛教高僧。它美化封建领主制，表现出了外来的佛教与本地原始宗教的矛盾。从情节方面来看，不同之处有：婻西拉(悉多)是十车王女，下凡为了报仇；毗湿奴换成了英达(因陀罗?)；王后们吃香蕉怀孕；金鹿诱走了召朗玛，留守的腊嘎纳在嫂子周围画一个圈，让妖魔不敢进去。这些情节在别的地方也可以看到。

总起来看，这故事大大地傣族化了，也就是中国化了。好多印度地名都换成了中国地名，也就是云南本地的地名。比如阿努曼丢下来的仙草山，就落在云南傣族地区。此外，还有不少的本地民间故事串入整个故事之中。这些都是难以避免的，也是合乎规律的。第五部分，召朗玛与勐哥孙之间爆发战争，故事就发生在傣族地区，这已不仅是中国化，而是中国的创造了。

除了傣族以外，《罗摩衍那》在云南别的少数民族文学或民间故事中，似乎也留下了痕迹。比如在景颇族的文学中，有一首长篇叙事诗①：《凯诺和凯刚》，主题思想是反映人民和自然界的斗争，善与恶的斗争，歌颂英雄气概和除恶务尽的精神。十一章的内容有以下几段：歌头、诞生、成长、打刀、激战、恋歌、寻找、风洞、重逢、拉弓、歌尾等。在故事的两个主人公中，哥哥凯刚代表恶，娶猴子为妻，弟弟凯诺代表善，娶扎英为妻。凯刚嫉妒凯诺，并想夺取扎英，他把凯诺骗到一个风洞口，把弟弟推进风洞，然后去诱骗扎英。这与《罗摩衍那》猴国两兄弟之争几乎完全一样，不能不承认这里有《罗摩衍那》的影响。

……

结 束 语

我在上面介绍了《罗摩衍那》传入中国的情况，以及它在中国的影响。材料大概还不止这样多，我目前能够搜罗到的，就是这样一些了。

我介绍的范围包括八种语言：梵文、巴利文、汉文、傣文、藏文、蒙文、古和阗文和

① 《云南少数民族文学资料》第Ⅰ辑：景颇族文学概况，第117-147页。

吐火罗文 A（焉耆文）。给人总的印象是：内容从大的方面来看，基本上相同；但是从细节来看，又有差别，有的甚至是极大的差别。关于梵本与其他本子之间的异同，我在上面已经作了一些分析，现在再归纳起来，谈几个问题。

一、罗摩故事宣传什么思想？

从印度本国罗摩故事的两个本子来看：一个是梵文的《罗摩衍那》，一个是巴利文的《十车王本生》，这两个本子代表两大教派。故事本源肯定是来自民间，根据天鹰《中国民间故事初探》的分类，《罗摩衍那》是属于"反映人民道德观念的传奇故事"这一个范畴。印度教的《罗摩衍那》除了宣扬三纲五常等道德教条之外，着重宣传一夫一妻制，保证统治者财产继承确有把握。而佛教的《十车王本生》则似乎把重点放在宣扬忠孝上。总之，两大教派（其他教派亦然）都争相利用。《罗摩衍那》宣传的是婆罗门教，以后的印度教。《十车王本生》宣传的则是佛教思想。佛教在印度后来消失了，只剩下印度教的一统天下。《罗摩衍那》的影响完全是在印度教方面。然而罗摩故事传到国外以后，大概是由于都是通过佛教传出来的，所以国外的那许多本子毫无例外地宣传的都是佛教思想。

《罗摩衍那》在印度与佛教的关系，我在《〈罗摩衍那〉初探》中已有所涉及。但是问题并没有全部解决：梵本《罗摩衍那》和佛教都产生于东印度，时间也相差不多，为什么竟好象是互不相知，其中原因还有待于进一步探讨。我在《〈罗摩衍那〉初探》中曾表示了一个意见："佛教在当时还并不十分流行，并不象一些佛教研究者所想象的那样。"（第 35 页）近读 Ananda Guruge 的《〈罗摩衍那〉的社会》，其中说到，《罗摩衍那》的故事晚于梵书，而早于释迦牟尼。它不提佛教，也就可以理解了。

二、罗摩故事传入中国以后，各族都加以利用，为自己的政治服务。汉族在下面来谈。傣族利用它来美化封建领主制，美化佛教。藏族通过对罗摩盛世的宣传，美化当地的统治者。和阗文本最后十头王被打败，打倒，请求饶命，称臣纳贡。这种宣传也有利于统治集团。所有的本子都是通过对佛教的宣传来为各自的政治服务。

三、汉译本特别强调伦理道德的一面。汉族好象对伦理道德（封建的）特别重视。我常常发现汉译佛典中强调忠和孝的地方很不少。我有点怀疑，我不相信印度原文如此，而是汉译者加上的。罗摩的故事也不例外。梵文《罗摩衍那》也有这种情况，我在《〈罗摩衍那〉初探》中已有所论述（第 57-59 页）。但是汉译本对这方面，特别是对孝，更是特别着力加以宣扬。在《杂宝藏经》中明确讲到罗摩的话："违父之愿，不名孝子。"下面又说："年限未满，至孝尽忠，不敢违命。"其他兄弟之道，夫妻之道，朋友之道，无不如此。在《六度集经》中也强调睒子是"孝子"。译者或编译者的用意是很清楚的：宣传这一套伦理道德，讨好中国的统治者，巩固统治，从而巩固了佛教的地位。

四、很多学者认为，同古希腊比起来，中国人不大喜欢或欣赏悲剧。这意见有一定的道理。古代希腊文艺理论中的 Katarsis（净化作用）对我们来说，了解起来比较困难。中国古代文学中真正的悲剧很少。罗摩故事在印度是一个悲剧，但到了中国却多被改成喜剧结尾，以适应中国人的心情和爱好，最突出的是插曲睒子故事。这本来是一个悲剧。但《六度集经》却让天老爷出马干预，使被射死的睒子复活。

五、涂上了地方色彩和民族色彩最突出的例子，一个是傣族，一个是蒙族。我在上面已经谈到，这里不再重复。

最后我还想讲一个问题。明洪楩编《清平山堂话本》卷三有一个话本叫《陈巡检梅岭失妻记》。有人认为这一篇话本受了印度影响，其中包括《罗摩衍那》。故事讲的是陈巡检带着妻子如春到广东去上任，来到了梅岭这个地方。梅岭之北，有一个申阳洞，洞中有妖怪，名叫白申公，是猢狲精。他弟兄三人：一个是通天大圣，一个是弥天大圣，一个是齐天大圣，另有一小妹名叫泗洲圣母。白申公施展妖术把如春劫至洞中。如春在洞中保持贞操，后来被紫阳真君救出。从故事的梗概来看，一方面与《罗摩衍那》故事有某些类似之处；另一方面又与《西游记》有某些类似之处。这三者可能有渊源关系。这对于解决印度神猴哈奴曼与中国孙悟空之间的关系，解决孙悟空与巫支祁之间的关系，也提供了重要线索，是一个很有趣的问题。我在这里暂且不谈，以后当专文论述。

（节选自季羡林：《〈罗摩衍那〉在中国》，《中国比较文学》1986年第1期，第1-35页。）

歌德与中国抒情诗

陈　诠

【导读】

德国人对中国抒情诗的移植始于歌德。由于歌德的翻译改写，中国抒情诗第一次引起了德国人的关注。歌德是站在世界文学这一角度来欣赏中国抒情诗的，不同于其他译者的逐字翻译，他更倾向于关注主人公的精神状态，创造性地将中国诗翻译成一种艺术品。此后，雷克特和司乔士的翻译达到较高水准。德国人在不同的历史阶段对中国文学的兴趣也会发生相应的起伏变化。在20世纪初，德国人经启蒙运动“中国热”、狂飙突进和浪漫主义运动时期的“中国冷”之后，欧洲思想界的又一次“反动”：“老子哲学，刚好切合欧洲现代人类的向心运动，所以东方和西方，现在又有第二次会面携手了。”伴随着对于老子哲学的兴趣，中国古典诗歌的德译迎来一个高潮。

《抒情诗》里，作者首先系统梳理了中国抒情诗对德国文学的影响史。由歌德的改作开启了德国人民对于中国诗歌的兴趣，随后是雷克特和司乔士的继承与发扬，以及第三阶段，德国的学者、诗人较好地翻译了《诗经》以及李白、白居易、陶渊明等人的诗，得出中国抒情诗对德国文学产生了较大影响的结论。在谈到歌德改作中国诗歌的时候，作者反复强调了歌德的世界文学观。歌德所追寻的目标是不分国界的人性，他对中国的抒情诗产生浓厚兴趣的原因恐怕还在于中华文化的魅力。中国古代有很多世界一流的伟大作品，如《诗经》、《道德经》等。这些中国文学蕴藏着与外界相同的宝贵的财富，可贡献于世界文学，而且还可以影响世界文化的发展。同时，作者还详细评述了德国作家学者们研究中国文学的作品的特点、成就与不足。比如，作者把歌德的译作与卫礼贤和汤姆斯的翻译进行了对比分析。以唐明皇曾宠幸梅妃的一首诗为例，因为他们三人都翻译过这首诗。卫礼贤是学者，尊重原作，保留了中国诗里特有的意味，这样在德文里就会生硬而不自然。歌德本身就是诗人，在忠实于原作的基础上，他还适当进行了创新，删掉对本国人来说不亲切的词，用德文里最纯熟的词，结合自身经验，翻译成属于德国人的诗。而汤姆斯既不是学者也不是诗人，他的翻译简直没有可取之处。此外，作者还提供了丰富的历史文献资料。不论是讲歌德的开创时期，还是雷克特和司乔士的发展与完成时期，作者都用实例来凸显这几位作品的价值。如司乔士翻译的《式微》，“没有一点儿不自然，没有一点是勉强杂凑。他的翻译不单是忠实的翻译，同时也是艺术的作品”。“虽然中国抒情诗对于德国文学的影响根本上还没有超过翻译时期，但是比起戏剧小说，已经要算有满意的成绩了”，不管是古代的《诗经》、唐朝的绝句，还是陶渊明等的诗句，都是饱含真情的，也就是因为这种真挚亲切的感情，德国学者才能较好理解、传播中国文化。与这种平民化、简单的诗句相比，以屈原为代表的富贵化、复杂的诗句更难理解，而且屈原的作品中有很多神话的背景、晦涩的比喻，这些对中国学者都有一定的困难，更别提对外国人了。

德国学者对抒情诗的翻译及研究，很大程度上促进了中国文学对德国文化的影响。与此同时，我们也感受到了作者对于传播中国文化的良苦用心、历史担当和美好愿景。

（李伟荣）

我们一直到现在，曾经将德国翻译改编的中国小说戏剧分析研究，我们发现翻译工作异常困难，因为中国语言、中国人的人生观同德国不太一样。这一种困难，到了抒情诗，可以算到最高点了。有许多人都认为中国抒情诗根本上就不能翻成德文。除了直接读中国文字，绝对不能赏识中国抒情诗的美丽。但在德国方面，尤其是在近代，总不断有人去努力移植中国抒情诗到德国。这一种工作起首于歌德，继续于雷克特（Friedrich Ruckert），完成于司乔士（Viktor von Strauss），大规模努力于近代许多德国的文人。

赫尔德分翻译的人为两种："一种把原文按字翻译，并且能够办得到的时候，把每字的声音都仿效过来。这一种我们叫做翻译的人，我们叫的时候，把'翻'字特别念得重。另外一种，只去表现原作者的意思，就好像他自己用他自己的话向我们表示意思一样。这一种是男性的翻译：因为无论如何正确，无论为旁的目的，有多少用处，你总不能达到目的，因为你不能把一种语言变成另外一种。"这一种主张，当然有讨论的余地，但是如果我们把它认为说明歌德翻译仿效中国的抒情诗，那么我们一定要说歌德属于第二种翻译。

歌德究竟为什么对中国抒情诗发生了兴趣，这很不容易找着满意解释。我们也不知道，歌德在1981年读了杜哈尔德《中国详志》里边的中国诗没有。不过无论如何，这本书里面翻译的中国诗，非常的坏，对歌德没有发生任何的印象。我们只能猜想，因为自从1827年1月30日以后，歌德在日记里也没有下任何价值的批评，只写出他诵读工作的事实：

> 星期三，一月三十一日。艾克芒博士。后来同他讨论过许多事情。关于中国诗的性质。
>
> 星期五，二月二日。研究中国诗。
>
> 二月三日。《花笺记》。晚上自修，续读《花笺记》。
>
> 二月四日。晚上《中国的诗》。
>
> 二月五日。同约翰。《中国女诗人》。
>
> 二月六日。抄写《中国女诗人》。
>
> 二月十一日。晚上艾克芒博士。——向他读中国诗。

从歌德日记的记载，我们可以知道他用的本子，是英国汤姆斯1824年英译小说《花笺记》，此书附录，载有英文译诗几十首。我们还知道歌德就汤姆斯译诗，重译了五首诗成德文。起初他题为《中国的诗》，后来改题为《中国女诗人》。

至于歌德的翻译同汤姆斯原本有多少出入，歌德根据了多少，自己凭空想象了多少，我们可以把两人译文同注解参考比较：

汤姆斯 下面女人传记简单的笔记，系由《百美新咏》钞出，前面几种笔记，也出于此书。原书在乾隆三十二年出版。

歌德 下面从一本传记的书《百美新咏》摘录出来的笔记和诗，使我们相信，虽然在这一个奇怪特别的国家有种种的限制，一般人仍然不断地生活，爱恋吟咏。

从歌德增加的几句话，我们可以略窥见歌德对中国了解的程度，同时我们知道，歌德对中国抒情诗发生兴趣，居然去重译它，是因为"虽然在这一个奇怪特别的国家有种种的限制，一般人仍然不断地生活，爱恋，吟咏"。

歌德同莱布尼兹、里格尔一样地相信一种共同的人性，世界的人类靠它可以互相连结起来。人性表现的一种就是诗，照歌德的意思，就是人类共同的产业。从这一个信仰，歌德在他1827年1月31日与艾克芒的谈话里，预言一个世界文学的新时代。他说："我看诗是人类共同的产业，无论什么地方，什么时候，都有千千万万的人出来。这一个人比那一个稍好一点，这进行得稍远一点，也就不过如此。"马蒂生先生不应当自命为他是唯一的诗人，我也不能自命为唯一的诗人，我可以讲，他有诗才，并不是特异的事情，没有人因作了一首好诗就敢因此目空一切。但是当然，如果我们德国人不愿意自己把眼光放远一点，我们一定会有这样孤陋的思想。所以我很喜欢研究旁的民族，我要忠告别人也这样作。民族文学从现在起没有多少可说了，世界文学的时代已经到了，每人都应该努力来促进这一个新时代。"

对于人类共同公有，不分国界的人性，是歌德寻求的目标，这也是歌德最浓厚的兴趣。因为使自己是诗人，所以他在世界民族文学方面，已经熔铸成功他们世界观、人生观的成绩里去寻求。顶有趣味的，就是当歌德去体贴、了解、介绍旁的民族的精神思想的时候，他自己的创造力也借此机会发展出来。从旧有的材料，他又给它以新的内容形式。我们可以把歌德同汤姆斯的翻译两相比较。

> 汤姆斯　薛瑶英夫人为容泽爱妾。貌美，工舞，能诗。有人听见她唱歌，看见她跳舞，作了下列一首诗送她。
>
> When dancing you appear unable to sustain your garments studded with gems,
> Your countenance resembles the flower of new-blown peach.
> We are certain, that theEmperor Woo of Han dynasty,
> erected a screen lest the wind should waft the fair Fe-lin.
>
> 歌德　薛瑶英女士，貌美能诗，人称慕她为最轻灵的舞女。有一个羡慕他的人，作诗称赞她如下：
>
> Du tanzt leicht bei Pfirsichflor,
> Am lustigen Fruhlingsort:

Der Wind, stellt man den Schirm nicht vor,
Blas't euch zusammen fort.
Auf Wasserlilien hupftest du,
Wohl in den bunten Teich,
Dein winziger Fuas, dein zarter Schuh,
Sind selbst der Lilie gleich.
Die anderen binden Fup fur Fuss,
Und wenn sie ruhig stehe,
Gelingt wohl sie noch ein holder Gruss,
Doch konnen sie nicht gehen.

歌德的诗，虽然不及汤姆斯对原文那样接近，文学的价值比他高尚十倍，自然不成问题。歌德的翻译，正是赫尔德所说的“男性的翻译”。歌德本来就是诗人，不是学者。他并不想求科学翻译的正确，他要求艺术价值的增高。他要作一种新的创造，汤姆斯的翻译，不过引起他创造的活动。他的想象力，不能仅仅靠忠实地翻译来满足，他还要借此机会，创造新的东西。其实这样也未尝不好。因为如果歌德仅仅把汤姆斯的译文一字不差地重译，对我们倒是一点意义没有，因为汤姆斯的翻译本来就没有多少价值。歌德增加的两首诗和一段注解，讲薛瑶英的金莲，特别令我们奇异。歌德在注解里说：“关于她穿金色袜子的小脚，相传诗人称美是为金莲，并且说因为她这种长处，使宫里其他的女人，都把脚用布缠小，如果不能同她一样，至少可以同她相像。他们说，这一个习惯，后来风行全国。”歌德从那儿知道这一段故事呢？汤姆斯译的《花笺记》里边有两处讲金莲：

Her golden Lilies (her small feet) do not measure three inches. (S. 29.)
When, as they walk along, the golden lilies lighty trod on the green moss. (S. 84)

关于头一句，汤姆斯有详细的注解，讲中国小脚的起源。但是这并不是薛瑶英乃是潘妃的事情。想来歌德曾经读过这一段注解，到作诗的时候，已经记不十分清楚，所以把名姓弄错了。

歌德翻译的第二首诗，是关于梅妃的事情。梅妃是唐明皇最宠幸的妃子，诗才敏捷、容貌美丽。但是后来杨太真进宫以后，明皇就把梅妃居于别宫置之不理。有一天，外国进宝珠，明皇忽然想起梅妃，命人把宝珠赠她，她却把宝珠退还，作一首诗寄明皇。

这一首诗，除了歌德、汤姆斯而外，卫礼贤也有德文翻译。① 我们把原文列出来比较他们三人翻译的特点。

梅妃：
柳叶蛾眉久不描，残妆和泪湿红绡。长门尽日无梳洗，何必珍珠慰寂寥。

① Münchner Neuste Nachrichten vom 3, Febr. 1926 Die Einkehr no 10.

卫礼贤：

Die Kassiabaltter-Augenbrauen babe ich lange nicht gemalt.
Schminkreste und Tranen feuchten die rote Seide.
Den ganzen Tag wasche und kamme ich mich nicht.
Warum sollen nun Perlen und Edelseine meine Einsamkeit trosten?

汤姆斯：

The eye of the Kwei flower, have been long unadorned：
Beijing forsaken my girdle has been wet with tears of regret.
Since residing in other apartments, I have refused to dress,
How think by a present of pearls, to restore peace to my mind?

歌德：

Du sendest Schatze, mich zu schmuckenl
Den Spiegel hab'ich langst uicht angeblickt：
Seif ich entfernt von deinen Blickon,
Weip ich nicht mehr, was ziert und schmuck.

卫礼贤的翻译，一点没有走失原文的意思，不愧学者的工作。他极力去保持中国诗原来的色彩。中国女人妆饰用的东西，他都——写出。但是就是因为这个原故，他这一首诗，在德国话里，生硬不自然。歌德把凡是德国人不亲切的字眼，淘汰罄尽，完全用德文里最纯熟的词句。他不描写任何的装饰，只形容梅妃精神上的状态。他只顾内心的经验，不管外形的渲染。自然这样一来，这一首诗，也就由中国的变成德国的了。汤姆斯既不是学者，又不是诗人，所以他的翻译，没有什么可取的地方。

还有开元宫人的诗，歌德也译的很好，颇带滑稽的趣味。有一次，皇帝的军队到边庭出征，皇帝叫人运大批冬衣，赠给军士。大部分的冬衣，都是宫女亲手作的。有一个军士，在衣袋里发现了一首诗，立刻报告长官，长宫报告皇上，皇上传旨叫作诗的宫女，自行出首。有一个宫女讲诗是她作的，她应该万死。皇上很可怜她，命她嫁给得诗的军士，他说我现在给你们结今生缘。

汤姆斯：

While in the field of battle contending with the enemy,
And unable to sleep from intense cold.
I make you this garment,
Through I know not who will wear it.
Being anxious for your preservation, I added a few extra stitches.
And quilt it with a double portion of wadding.
Though in this life we are unable to dwell together,
I desire we may be wedded in a future state

歌德：
Aufruhr an der Cranzezu bestrafer
Fechtest wacker, aber nachts zu schlafen
Hinder dich die strenge Kalte beissig,
Dieses Kriegerkleid, ich nahtes fleissig,
Wenn ich schon nicht weib's tragen sollte;
Doppelt hab'ich es wattiert, und sorglich wollte
Meine Nadel auch die Stiche mehren
Zur Erhaltung eines Mannes der Ehren
Warden hier uns nicht zusammen finden.
Mog'ein Zustand droben uns verbindenl.

关于冯小怜一首诗，歌德的译诗，同汤姆斯的英文完全不一样，我们简直可以说是歌德自己创作的一首诗。冯小怜本来事奉一位君主，后来君主国破身亡，冯小怜被俘虏去奉侍新主，但是她仍然不能忘记旧主的恩情。

汤姆斯：
Though I thank you for the kindness which you daily manifest,
Yet, when I remember the love of a former day;
If desirous of knowing whether my heart be broken,
It is only for you to look at the strings of my Pe-pa.
歌德：
Bei geselligem Adendbroth,
Das uns Lied und Frende bot,
Wie betrubte mich Selinel!
Wie sie, sich begleitend, sang,
Und ihr eine Saite sprang
Fuhr sie fort mit elder Miene:
Haltet mich nicht froh und frei;
Ob men Herz gesprungen sei—
Schaut nur auf die Mandoline.

中国诗对于歌德作品最有成绩的影响，要算他的《中德季日即景》。这里我们仍然发现汤姆斯英译《花笺记》的来源。但是从一首诗到一首诗《花笺记》的色彩，慢慢变淡，老年成熟的歌德，渐渐出来，他的观感、他的思想，都得了艺术形式的表现。在这种地方，我们很用不着逐字逐句地去作一篇索隐，像彼德芒那样，说歌德某字某句是从《花笺记》某处来的，结果不但穿凿附会，而且把原诗的美丽，摧毁无余①。歌德从他自己的世界

① Woldemar Freiherr von Bledermann：*Goethe-Forschungen*，neue Folqe，Leipzig 1886 S，420 ff.

观，把中国的材料，重新改变创造，把它弄成功一种艺术品。他绝不会一字一句地，像直译家一样地翻译。如果我们像彼德芒那样，一定要去证明，歌德第一首诗里边两位官员，一定是《花笺记》里边的梁大人、刘大人，或者歌德第六首诗富于象征意义的一句话"永远停留我的东方"，解释作"那儿可以看见他的爱人：梁生第一次在他姑母花园里，正向东方走的时候，看见耀仙"，那未免太笑话了，歌德的诗，要真是如此还有什么意义呢？

所以我们研究这一首诗，不应该太注意外形相互的影响，而应当考察精神一贯的关系。我们要看怎么样中国的精神，同这一位世界诗人的精神，根本相同。歌德从《花笺记》中所得来实际上中国的印象，本来就是模糊不定的，他把这些浅淡的印象，用他的想象和他创造的本事，独立形成。不过顶有趣味，顶奇怪的，就是歌德越是从自身出发来写诗，他同中国人性接触越近，因为他能够从他个人，到世界的全体。如像他第十一首诗，讲宇宙上的万事万物，时时刻刻都在变易，但是在一切变易中又有不变易者在。我们看见世界上所有的东西都风驰云卷地飞去，我们忍不住害怕，但是我们一想变易是宇宙的基本原理，事物可变，宇宙的基本原理不变，那么我们又未尝不可以自慰。歌德对于宇宙人生这一种深刻的认识同中国孔子、老子，有许多共鸣的地方。孔子平生最用工夫的书就是《易经》，《易经》中间所讲的道理，同歌德这一首诗中所讲的道理主要的地方完全一样。因为易与不易，相生相成，不易的地方，正要在易中表现。有一次孔子站在川上，说："逝者如斯夫，不舍昼夜！"在老子的道德经里边，也有无数的地方讲到同一的道理。

第十三首诗，令我们想到李太白咏酒的诗，因为诗里大意说："你要烦扰我清静的快乐吗？让我对着我的酒杯。同别人在一块儿，别人可以教益我，但是真正快乐的时候还是只有独自一个人。"最末一首诗，教人努力当时此地，同孔子实践道德的教训，也很相同。歌德这一集诗里最美的一首，要算第八首：不但写情写景到了登峰造极的地步，而且全诗充满中国的精神。卫礼贤对于这一首诗，曾经有最中肯的称誉，他说："德国诗同中国诗连结的地方，就是静的情状，完全解除，变成动的情状。一点没有描写，一切都是预备，动作经过。这一种精神上最细致的动作我们在中国画和中国空间里可以看见。这里我们在他的影响里听见世界上看不见的，无为的，然而永远影响的意义。"①

德文里面，翻译的中国抒情诗，大体可以分成三种：(一)学者式的翻译，(二)就其他欧洲语言的改译，(三)自由的改作。头一种翻译，根据原文，译者了解中国语言文学，努力把原文的意思，尽量地表现出来。这一类的译者，最重要的要算：查赫、瓦奇、卫礼贤、佛尔克、伯哈蒂、康亚蒂。查赫深通中国文学，对于汉文的了解尤令人惊异。他翻译的《李白》《杜甫》《韩愈》，把原文的意义彻底表现出来。但是音乐同形式，完全丧失不成其为诗。瓦奇翻译的《白居易》，伯哈蒂翻译的《李太白》《陶渊明》，也犯了同样的毛病。康亚蒂翻译屈原的《天问》(1931)，只能算是一种科学贡献，不能算是艺术的作品。比较有系统的选译，要算佛尔克的《汉六朝诗选》(1899)同《唐宋诗选》(1929)。一部很有趣的诗集是卫礼贤的《中德季日即景》(1922)，在里边中国诗人对四季的感情变化，分类介绍。卫礼贤在这一本集子里边，也收集了一些散文，翻成德文诗的体裁，如像陶渊明的《桃花源记》，周子《爱莲说》，苏东坡的《前后赤壁赋》。佛尔克同卫礼贤的翻译，已经比查赫、

① Münchner Neuste Nachrichten vom 3, Febr. 1926. Die Einkehr no 10.

伯哈蒂的，自由得多。此外还有无数在报章杂志书籍上的翻译，我们也不能详细讨论了。

第二种翻译，就是从其他欧洲语言改译出来的，大半是那一些既不懂中文，又没有诗才的作者闹出来的。这一类的翻译，异常地多，它们的价值也很小，虽然他们常常自称根据原文，其实他们往往还不懂一打的中国字。有时他们讲他们是自由改译，但是实际上只是他们对原文可笑的误解，或者把其他一种翻译，改得更糟。这一类著作，当然不值得我们仔细研究。他们的意义，只在大量的数目，可以证明德国人对中国文学有很高的兴趣。

顶有趣味的翻译，还是第三种自由的改译，他们多半是近代德国诗人的作品。他们也不懂中文，他们根据的本子，多半是英法拉丁文，或者其他德文的译本。他们同第二种翻译家不同的地方，就是他们都有诗人的天才，他们不过借别种译本得一点感兴，放笔来做自己的创造。他们的诗，因此往往不合中国的精神，但是他们的工作，并不算白费。他们创造了新的格调，新的内容有时成为很美丽的艺术品。

（选自陈诠：《中德文学研究》，商务印书馆 1936 年版，第 130-172 页。）

《万叶集》对《诗经》的借鉴

王晓平

【导读】

《〈万叶集〉对〈诗经〉的借鉴》一文采用了比较文学影响研究的方法，即从文化交流角度讨论《诗经》对《万叶集》的客观影响，以及《诗经》和《万叶集》作为文学作品在主题和表达技巧上的相似之处。

在正文的第一部分，作者从主题的角度分析两部作品的共同点，包括丰富性和现实主义精神。首先是丰富性。《万叶集》涉及不同阶层人的生活，有皇室争斗的影子、下层人民的反压迫反剥削，以及歌颂自然、美好爱情和浓厚的思乡之情等。其次是现实主义精神。作者指出《诗经》是“言志”之作，具有政治教化功能——针砭时弊、讽喻假恶丑、赞扬真善美。同时，作者指出“真实性”同样是《万叶集》的显著特色。歌人取材现实生活，创作真实自然、不忸怩作态。接着，作者指出这两部古典文学作品对民歌都极为重视。“饥者歌其食，劳者歌其事”，这是《诗经》中民歌的共有特色。而《万叶集》中，卷十四的东歌，卷二十的防人歌，卷十三的歌谣都产自于山乡水滨的民谣，以方言和乡音直接描写了底层人民生活的喜怒哀乐。再次，这两部歌集均产生于各自民族文学发展的开端，极具研究价值。《诗经》是中国古代诗歌的开端，是最早的一部诗歌总集；而《万叶集》则昭示了日本文学意识的开端。在正文的第二部分，作者从词汇和表现手法出发，以文本精读的方式具体地分析《万叶集》对《诗经》的借鉴。作者以《万叶集》卷七的“羁旅作歌”、卷十二的“悲别歌”为例，分别指出诗中“临照”、“言经绪兮”均改编自《诗经》中的“照临”、和“吾经绪兮”；“鸡鸣”、“展转”直接取自《诗经》。另一方面，《万叶集》受《诗经》影响，大量地运用比兴的手法以增强诗歌的艺术效果。中国古代诗歌的优良传统——赋比兴手法是从《诗经》开始。名篇《关雎》中，成双成对的雎鸠象征着美好爱情的结合，这个意象在《万叶集》亦频频出现，譬如《寄物沉思》；卷十二《悲别歌》中，行舟远去、水边送行的离别愁绪亦和《诗经》中的《二子乘舟》有异曲同工之妙。在《诗经》中，棠棣色彩艳丽、芳香扑鼻，是美好的代名词，诗人不仅联想到美艳的王姬，还有深厚的手足之情。在《万叶集》中，棠棣也总是和美好事物联系在一起，如卷十二：“棠棣艳，如阿妹，身着红装，梦中曾会面。”《万叶集》的现实主义精神更多地体现在诗歌内容贴近人们的现实生活，但不具备强烈的批判精神。与中国诗歌“文以载道”的使命不同，《万叶集》里的歌人更注重歌咏自然和恋爱，抒发个人的生命体悟，因而忧民忧天下的山上忆良更像是《万叶集》里的一枝独秀。

最后，作者对全文进行总结，并表达了观点。他认为江朝以后，全盘唐化、复制移植的官方文学是没有生命力的。只有像《万叶集》这种深扎于民族土壤，表达本民族声音的和歌才能经久不衰，流传至今。虽然《诗经》对《万叶集》有较大影响，但两者仍有多方面的差异，比如《诗经》的针砭时弊精神在《万叶集》里并未得到广泛的体现。

（李伟荣）

我国最早的诗歌总集《诗经》，编成于约2500年前的春秋时代，收集了周初到春秋中叶约500年间的合乐歌词，其产生地域相当于今天陕西、山西、河南、河北、山东、湖北数省的广大地区。作者既有人民群众，也有贵族士大夫。这部作品，对我国后代文学产生了多方面的影响。

在《诗经》产生以后约1000年的唐代，在与我国一衣带水的日本，伴随着两国长期的文化交流，诞生了一部宏伟的和歌总集——《万叶集》。

《万叶集》共收和歌约4500首，最古老的作品产生于仁德天皇在世时代，最晚的和歌产生于淳仁帝时。这期间约440年。其作者上至天皇，下至广大普通民众。作者包括以大和(今奈良县、日本古国)诸地方为中心，直到陆奥、东国、北陆、九州各地的和歌作者和来这些地方旅行的人。《万叶集》的诞生标志着日本文学发展跨进了一个崭新的阶段。它是日本文学发展的第一个里程碑。

《万叶集》和《诗经》在思想、艺术和艺术价值方面，都有一些共同点。《万叶集》编撰本身和其中一些作品，还曾受到《诗经》的影响。同时，这两部古典文学作品，又都表现出各自文学的民族特色。对它们进行对比研究，可以帮助我们窥见古代中日两国文学交流之一斑。在这篇短文中，仅就《万叶集》对《诗经》的借鉴问题，谈一点不成熟的看法。

（一）

《万叶集》和《诗经》具有一些共同的特点。首先是它们的丰富性。两部歌集所收诗歌，作者十分广泛，诗歌多方面地描写了现实生活，表现了不同阶级和阶层的人们的切实感受。《诗经》的作者，既有天子诸侯的贴身近臣、史官、武将，也有猎手、农夫、弃妇、乞丐。那些出于下层的反剥剥、反压迫的诗歌，反映了当时社会中本质的现象，那些来自民间的情歌，歌颂了劳动人民纯洁、真挚、纯朴的爱情，那些产生于统治阶级内部的怨刺之作，揭示了社会动乱及统治阶级内部的矛盾，那些下层官吏抒发内心忧愤不平的诗歌，勾勒出一幅社会上苦乐不均、劳逸悬殊的画图。这些诗篇从不同的侧面，为我们展示出广阔的人生画卷。同样，《万叶集》的作者，从身份和阶级来看，上至天皇，下至东国地方的农民、军人、流浪女子。这样广搜博采，使《万叶集》的和歌具有丰富多采的内容。和《万叶集》相比，《敕撰集》选歌就显得狭隘和死板得多。从《万叶集》中，我们可以看到“班田制”下农民饥寒交迫的惨状，也可以读到被征调而远离家乡的防人对恋人的思念。

我们为富士山下迷人的风光所陶醉，也为东国女子缠绵的情意所感动。皇族的作品使我们看到当时激烈派阀斗争的影子，宫廷诗人们的作品字里行间吐露着苦闷和哀痛。可以说，一部《万叶集》是当时社会的一个缩影。在艺术上，这两部歌集都具有多种风格的美。《诗经》中，特别是《小雅》和《国风》中那些优秀篇章，如《板》、《荡》的怨深恨切，《大东》、《鸿雁》的不平之鸣，《采薇》、《黄鸟》的声情凄婉，《硕鼠》、《伐檀》的炽烈反抗，以及《野有死麇》、《静女》的脉脉深情，都会使我们受到巨大的感染。《万叶集》中，除收了大量的短歌外，还收集了施头歌、佛足石歌等。歌集有着《人代集》以下的诗集中看不到的千姿百态。柿本人麻品的作品使人感受到壮阔宏大的美，如名山大川在人目前，东歌、防人歌使人看到素朴敦厚的美，如山野清风轻拂人面，这些都是后代和歌史上缺乏的独特的东西。《万叶集》反映社会生活面的广阔、选材的丰富、语言的多样、情趣的复杂，使后世一些歌人和评论家如正岗子规和左千夫等倍加赞赏和推崇。

其次，在于它们的现实主义精神。除了那些谀媚权贵的作品外，《诗经》中的优秀篇章，都恰如刘鳃所说："风雅之兴，志思蓄愤，而吟诛情性，以讽其上，以为情而造文也。①"这些诗篇，不是达官贵人、骚人墨客的无病呻吟，而是人们把诗歌创作和政治紧密联系超来，，针砭社会，讽谕假恶丑、赞颂真善美的"言志"之作。这种现实主义情神，影响着历代进步诗人，促进了大量具有讽刺意义的作品产生。和这十分相近的是：真实性，也就是子规赞为"真诚"的一点，也是《万叶集》的显著特色⑤。不少歌人的创作毫无虚情假意，反映社会不加粉饰，吐露真情实感而不扭捏作态。读者能从歌中听到歌人的心声和脉搏的跳动，从而受到强烈的感染。除去奈良中期以后的宴饮、相闻、季节歌以外，《万叶集》中大部分和歌充满了现实主义精神，在表现方法上也采用"写实"的手法，往往是选取现实生活中的素材，真实地抒情写意，而不是着眼于再现梦幻、陈述空想、臆构虚境。

对于民歌的重视，为这两部作品在文学史上增添了灿烂的光采。《诗经》中的《国风》及《小稚》中和风诗相近的作品，或痛斥剥剥者、寄生虫，或咏歌狩猎、耕作和采集，或赞美始终不渝的爱情。同是恋歌，有大胆率直的表白，也有微妙细腻的心理活动；有活泼纯真的对话，也有弃妇、赘婿的悔怨。这些民歌，玲珑剔透，闪耀着迷人的艺术之光。它们风格各异，而具有共同的特色：健康、直率、纯朴。《万叶集》中，卷十四的东歌、卷二十的防人歌、卷十三的歌谣，都是产生于山乡水滨的民谣。这些民谣，直接描写了生活在底层的人民的喜怒哀乐，带着浓郁的生活气息。他们直接使用方言和乡音，抒写他们健康的生活情趣。从这些歌谣中，我们可以直接感受到日本劳动人民敦朴、真挚、善良的情怀。它们和《诗经》中的优秀篇章一样，是"饥者歌其食，劳者歌其事"之作，其健康、纯真的情感，是那些高踞于庙堂之上的贵族文学，侍从文学无法相比的。在《万叶集》以后的日本古典歌集中，很难找到这样多优秀的民谣了。

再次，这两部歌集都产生于各自民族文学发展的幼年期，今天都具有极重要的研究价值。《诗经》为我们研究我国古代社会的历史、经济、音韵、文字，甚至地理、生物等提供了丰富的材料。同样，《万叶集》除了艺术价值之外，还有着重要的学术价值。它和《日本书纪》，《古事记》一起，理所当然地被作为了解古代历史、风俗习惯、思想等的重要材

① 刘勰著《文心雕龙 · 情采》。

料。特别是在探索中古代日本语言学及日本文学史的研究方面，它可以称得上最集中的资料了。即探寻日本长歌的衰亡、短歌的诞生、日本民族文学意识的发生、古代文学的性质，等等，都必须回顾《万叶集》①。

看来，中国的《诗经》和日本的《万叶集》在某些方面确是“何其相似如兄弟”。这当然不纯属历史的巧合。仅从文学的角度讲，从日本内部看，和歌到万叶时代已有很大发展，有可能编撰这样一部规模宏大的和歌集；从外部的影响来看，唐朝是我国诗歌空前繁荣的时代。日本为了吸收汉文化，进行了巨大的努力。汉文学的影响推动，和促进了日本民族文学的发展，读完《万叶集》，我们可以想见，当时的人们是怀着怎样浓厚的兴趣和强烈的求知渴望，学习着中国古代和当时的文艺作品。他们写的诗，像唐诗一徉深入浅出、明白如话；他们作的文，骈四骊六辞才华艳，颇具齐梁遗风，也正反映了初唐时的文风。当时的人们从唐文学中吸收了多方面的有益的东西，也从中国古典文学作品，其中包括《诗经》中吸取了多方面有益的东西：真实地反映社会现实的“写实”精神，比兴的表现手去，对民歌的喜爱，大量汉语俗语的运用。这种借鉴和学习，成为《万叶集》能够编撰完成的重要条件之一。

（二）

我们今天阅读《万叶集》，仍然可以找到许多足以说明它对《诗经》有所借鉴的论据。这首先表现在语汇上。正岗子规认为，大量地运用汉语俗语是《万叶集》的特点之一。在《万叶集》中，就有一些语汇，直接来源于《诗经》。如卷七的“羁旅作歌”：

夏日忙刈麻，烟波浩淼海上郡，在那大海滨，绿竹如箫百鸟鸣，喊妹妹不应。

这里的“绿竹如箦”，出自《卫风·淇奥》：“瞻彼淇奥，绿竹如箦”。又如十一卷的“寄物陈思”：

隔窗望，皎皎明月光。山风劲吹夜，思君意深长。

这里，描写明月照耀，用的是日语“临照”一词，脱胎于汉语“照临”一词，这恰恰出自《诗经》中《邶国·日月》：“日居月诸，照临下上。”

再如：卷于二的“悲别歌”，原文是：

京师边　君者去之乎　孰解乎　言经绪兮　结乎懈毛

意译如下：

---

① 《日本文学大辞典》第七卷。

阿哥你不在，你去京城人在外，谁来解衣带？让我来解懒得解，没精又打采。

这首短歌描写心爱的人远去之后心烦意乱的清景，和《卫风、伯兮》宛如姊妹篇。“自伯之东，首如飞蓬；岂无膏沐，谁适为容。”心上的人出门了，连打扮的心思都没有了，生活也好象变得索然无味了。一种深深的怀念之情在凝炼的诗句中吐露出来。在这里，作者把“吾经绪兮”写成“言经绪兮”，让“言”来代替“吾”，可能是受了郑笺的影响。郑玄把《诗经》中不少本来用作语首助词、语中助词的“言”字，都解作“我”。

《周南·葛覃》：“言告师氏，言告言归。”
郑笺：“言，我也，重言我者，尊重师教也。”
《周南·芣首》：“采采朵曹，薄言采之。”
郑笺：“薄言，我薄。”
《卫风、氓》：“言既遂矣，至于暴矣。”
郑笺：“言，我也。遂，犹久也。”

像这样直接从《诗经》中吸取的语汇，铂“鸡鸣”、“展转”等，还可以举出一些。

从表现手法上看，重视比喻，是《万叶集》受《诗经》影响的又一个重要方面。《诗经》里大量运用比兴的手法，获得显著的艺术效果，对后代文学产生了不小的影响。在我国，汉代已较普遍地注意到赋、比、兴是诗歌的艺术手法。齐梁时期刘勰在《文心雕龙》中对比兴作了专篇论述，并以《诗经》为例，对比兴的作用、要求作了比较全面的论述。赋比兴作为我国古代诗歌创作的一个优良传统，引起日本歌人的注意。《万叶集》中，有一种被称为“譬喻歌”的相闻歌，是完全借用他物以言志的一种体裁。作者并不直抒胸臆，而是把借用来的他物作为主体。在被称为“寄物陈思”的相闻歌中，也使用着比喻的手法。在这些和歌中，有的比喻和《诗经》中使用的比兴，具有相同或相近的含意。

“关关雎鸠，在河之洲，窈窕淑女，君子好逑。”《关雎》是《诗经》的首篇。诗中以河洲之中雎鸠成双成对和谐地鸣叫起兴，赞美有情人幸福的结合。在这里，雎鸠这种常在江边水中捕鱼的水鸟是爱情美好的象征。在《万叶集》中，雎鸠或写成水沙儿，或写成三佐吴、三沙吴、美沙，它被作为美丽的形象出现在爱情的画图中。如卷十一的《寄物陈思》：

雎鸠在海滨，大海茫茫波涛涌，拍岸浪纷纷，不知你亦往何方，我的心上人。

又如卷十二的《寄物陈思》：

飞落雎鸠鸟，深深海底长海藻，海藻名“莫名”，阿哥芳名决不讲，母父虽知晓。

卷十二的《悲别歌》：

雎鸠在洲畔，洲畔有条离岸船，浆起船去远。心上人儿可在船，日后难相见。

这首歌作为送别诗，还使我们想起《邶风、二子乘舟》：

二子乘舟，他们俩坐着一条船，
汎讯其景；水上的船影摇颠颠：
愿言思子，对他们心头多挂牵，
中心痒痒。为他们揪心心不安。

二子乘舟，他们俩坐着一条船，
汎讯其逝；山船儿飘飘欲行远；
愿言思子，对他们心头多挂牵，
不瑕有害。他们该不会遭祸患。

《邶风、二子乘舟》和《悲别歌》在表现手法上是相同的，都是抓住水边送别、行舟远去的一瞬间心中的感受，抒写离情别绪和对重新相会的祝愿的。

在《诗经》中，棠棣以它那色彩艳丽、芳香朴鼻的繁花，给人留下美好的印象。《召南、何彼襛矣》，诗人是这样深情地盛赞它穠丽的花姿：

何彼襛矣，它多么艳丽惹人爱，
唐棣之华；那正是唐棣花儿开；
易不肃雍，那车铃响得多和美，
王姬之车。正是那王姬车儿来。

毛传：“兴也，襛犹戎，戎也。唐棣，移也。”郑笺：“何乎彼戎，戎者乃移之华，兴者喻王姬颜色之美盛。”作者由唐棣的美艳联想到王姬的美貌，为诗涂上一层欢快的色彩。又如《小雅・棠棣》：

棠棣之华，棠棣花儿朵朵明丽，
鄂不韡韡；花粤也就光彩照人.
凡今之人，当今世上所有人们，
莫如兄弟。有谁能比兄弟更亲。

诗人从棠棣芳香明丽的花朵起笔，写到兄弟之间美好的情谊，棠棣使人产生美的联想。在《万叶集》中，棠棣也同样使我们感到赏心悦目，总是和美好的事物联系在一起。如卷十二：

棠棣艳，如阿妹，身着红装，梦中曾会面。

不仅如此，它还被用来作为鲜艳的粉红颜色的代称，被作为某些词的枕词(和歌中冠在某词上用以修饰或调整语调并无任何意义的词。

类似的例子不胜枚举。如遍地蔓延、连绵不断的葛藤，被用来比喻缠绵不绝的情意，或被用来比喻游子远离故土和亲人四方飘泊的遭遇；往下弯曲的樛木覆盖着葛藤，被用来比喻福禄代代相继，等等。这些比喻，恰恰是在《诗经》中首先出现，并在后代被人多次引用的。

在《诗经》中，那些怨刺之作曾使许多后世的有进步倾向的作家产生强热的共鸣。这些诗篇是作者满怀忧国忧民之情奋笔直书的，对最高统治者的荒淫无耻、糊涂昏庸、反复无常、听信谗言、任用小人提出的控诉，对劳动人民的苦痛表示了同情。这些诗篇使人惊醒，让人们把视野从统治阶级的上层转向劳动群众。在《万叶集》中，我们从山上忆良的作品中，可以感受到这种强烈的忧愤。山上忆良曾被任命为遣唐少禄（遣唐随员）来过中国。他学识渊博，从他后期的诗作中，可以看到儒家思想的巨大影响。他写的《贫穷问答歌》，直接继承了《诗经》的现实主义精神[①]。

《贫穷问答歌》是一首由两个贫苦农民的对话组成的长歌，写"班田制"下穷困潦倒的农民，在寒冷的风雪之夜，御寒无术，冻馁难熬，手持笞杖的里长还来追逼骚扰。作者描写一家妻儿老小在破败的矮屋里挨冻受饿的情景："灶里无火灶烟断，锅里有蛛网丝缠。"这和《豳风·七月》里"无衣无褐，何以卒岁"的控诉，情感是相通的。《豳风·东山》曾用"伊威在室，蛸蛸在户，町畽鹿场，熠耀宵行"描写征人离家之后故园的荒芜。作者抓住屋内的潮虫、门上的蜘蛛、院内的鹿迹、飘动的嶙火，写尽了庭院的冷落和荒凉。而在《贫穷问题歌》中，作者用寒夜中灶无烟火、锅有蛛网，人忘炊爨，写出了久已绝粮的惨状。两诗的作者都是用典型化的细节来表达了凄楚，哀怨的愁苦之情。《贫穷问答歌》激愤地质问：

虽云天地广，
何以于我却狭偏？
虽云日月明，
何以照我无火焰？

读到这里，我们自然会想起"谓天盖高，不敢不局；谓地盖厚，不敢不蹐"（《小雅、正月》）的有力揭露。这种从现实生活痛苦遭遇中体察到的对天地、日月信仰的动摇，是可贵的，都是作者对不平的现实强烈不满的反映。

在《贫穷问答歌》的结尾，作者愤怒地喊出："难飞高，身非鸟。"这和《邶风·柏舟》中的"静言思之，不能奋飞"同样蕴藏着反抗的火焰：他们都想离开这丑恶的现实，飞往自己心目中的理想王国，然而却找不到实现这个愿望的道路。

我们从《万叶集》中运用的汉语俗语，比兴方法和某些作品的思想和艺术技巧看，《万叶集》的编撰和其中某些和歌，对于《诗经》是有所借鉴的。这里需要说明的是，《万叶集》受汉文学的影响是多方面的，不仅是《诗经》这一部书在那里孤立地起作用。同时，万叶歌人采用的是日本人民喜闻乐见的和歌形式，描绘的是日本民族的社会生活，抒发的是自己的民族情感。他们的借鉴是大胆的、多方面的，同时又基本上是"中为日用"的，和当时某些为卖弄学识，自命风雅而纯粹模仿写出的汉文，汉诗不同。近江朝以后，贵族们从国家的一切制度乃至服饰，都尽量从唐朝移植。柿本人麻吕以后，在贵族社会中汉诗成了官方文学①。这种文学的“全盘唐化”，终被证明是没有生命力的东西。虽然它在传播知识方面起了不小的作用，但和深深扎根于民族土壤的和歌相比，它不过是纸扎的鲜花，终究缺乏新鲜动人的魅力。然而，《万叶集》却因其真实地反映日本古代社会风貌而作为具有无限生命力的古典作品，散发着诱人的清香，一直流传至今。

回顾唐代日中两国的文学交流，对照研究《诗经》和《万叶集》，对我们很有启发。我们为自己的祖先编撰的一部伟大的《诗经》自豪，在世界文学宝库中，它的确堪称一颗光彩夺目的明珠，值得我们珍视。同时，我们对日本民族吸收外国文化所作的惊人努力，深感钦佩。《万叶集》的一些作者喜爱本民族的文学传统，而又勇于对外国的先进文化实行“拿来主义”，繁荣了民族文学的百花园。他们的经验对于我们今天创造社会主义新文艺的伟大事业来说，不也是很有意义的吗？

（选自王晓平：《万叶集》对《诗经》的借鉴，《外国文学研究》1981年第4期，第52-56页。）

① 西乡信纲等著《日本文学史》。

美国诗中的禅与道

（节选）

赵毅衡

【导读】

1985年四川人民出版社出版了赵毅衡先生的《远游的诗神：中国古典诗歌对美国新诗运动的影响》一书，这本力作主要考察了中国诗学、宗教、哲学等对美国现代诗歌转型时期的影响，在新时期比较文学研究领域引起了强烈反响。作者在美国潜心研究的求学经历练就了其扎实的中西文化素养，并且在长期的教学科研中不断增补完善，近20年后上海译文出版社在2003年出版修订版，书名更名为《诗神远游：中国如何改变了美国现代诗》，把美国现代诗的考察范围从美国新诗运动阶段（1912—1922）扩展到上溯1910年前，下至当代，以翔实的材料梳理了现代美国的“中国诗群”，影响的中介，及影响的诗学和诗学的影响，其研究的广度和深度都得到了相当程度的拓展。十年之后，在世界多元文化的背景下，研究“中国如何改变了美国现代诗”这一重要课题，依然洋溢着时代的魅力。为此，四川文艺出版社在2013年第三次再度出版了该书，内容未作大的变动，为后来的比较文学研究学者提供研究方法、研究路径、研究内容等方面的启迪。旧版第二章“影响的中介”中道家思想及禅宗思想之西传，在新版中被放在第三章“影响的诗学与诗学的影响”中单独成节“美国诗中的禅与道”，以着重论述。庞德对博大精深的中国文化推崇备至，认为美国现代诗能够从中吸取营养而获得新的生命力。他本人就深受儒家思想的影响，并在其毕生力作《诗章》中集中体现，对其后的许多诗人产生了深远的影响。然而，赵毅衡先生认为禅宗和道家才被众多美国诗人看做是“中国诗学的真髓”，并被纷纷吸纳。

据作者的统计发现，由于诸多西方汉学家陆续英译道家有代表性的老子、庄子著述，如《道德经》在欧美颇受欢迎，其出版发行量仅次于《圣经》，所以道家思想因为译介的繁荣得以在西方广泛传播，并对西方文化的影响可见一斑。在美国的新诗运动中，中国的道家思想还未被深入理解，仅停留在粗浅层次的“阴阳说”，而真正体现道家思想的则是三位美国现代诗人：罗宾森·杰弗斯，卡尔·桑德堡和威廉·卡洛斯·威廉斯。其中，卡尔·桑德堡的名诗《冰冷的墓》和《草》就体现了道家的齐生死观。道家不像儒家追求人的责任感和使命感，它追求一种更本真、更率性的生活方式，即使面对死亡，也怀持一种自然达观的人生态度。

除了儒家、道家思想对美国现代诗歌影响甚大外，禅宗佛教的影响也相当显著。

对禅学西传做出过重大贡献的有日本人铃木大拙、中国学者胡适、英国汉学家韦利，而对美国现代诗产生重大影响的则是美国禅学家艾伦·瓦茨，他的《禅的精神》及《禅》在美国诗人中引起了广泛而持久的兴趣。禅，是梵文的音译，意思是静思冥想。面对苦难的人生，禅宗主张通过顿悟，破除执著，超越尘世的烦忧，摆脱外在的束缚，以出世之心获得内心的安宁和智慧通透的人生。至于禅意在美国现代诗歌中的存在，赵毅衡先生选取了有代表性的美国现代诗人进行论述，麦克娄用诗解禅，晦涩难懂，但其开拓精神具有不可低估的价值，而鲁伊特和斯特利克则都在诗歌中营造了一种朴素的禅境，令人神往。

“美国诗中的禅与道”仅仅是《诗神远游》这部学术专著中体现“东学西渐”的一个方面，纵观美国现代诗的发展历程，赵毅衡先生做了全方位多角度的考察，得出了令人信服的结论：中国文化、宗教、哲学对美国现代诗歌塑形起了至关重要的作用，使其成功地摆脱了欧洲传统诗艺的约束，从而催生了具有美国民族特色的现代诗。同时，这也展现了一位长期从事比较文学研究的学者广阔的学术视野和脚踏实地的科研态度。

（马礼霞）

一、道学西传

庞德对儒家的迷恋与过分政治化，被认为是庞德的个人怪癖，幸好他的理解与推演相当特殊，没有变成一个统治体制崇拜者。在大部分美国诗人心目中，禅宗与道家很快被认为是中国诗学的真髓，成为美国诗人所理解的真正中国精神。与其说是中国诗学的确舍儒而趋禅道，不如说这是现代美国诗人的选择性误读（或者说，是现代社会的选择性误读，因为中国诗人自己也越来越倾向于把儒家排除在中国诗学之外）。

西方汉学对道家思想的研究一直是受重视的。1842 年出现了《道德经》第一个法文译本；1868 年出现了第一个英译本；1870 年出现第一个德文译本。据统计，自 1886 年到 1924 年，光《道德经》的英译本就有 16 种之多，而从 20 年代到 60 年代，有 40 多种英译本。据说《道德经》是欧美印数之多仅次于《圣经》的书，几乎是每年一种新译本。

至今，有些美国文人诗人依然喜欢在译《道德经》的玄妙语句上一试身手。他们甚至不必懂中文，译本译文之多已足够作为依据母本。翟理斯 1889 年的全译本《庄子》，至今为学界珍视。

对老子思想的阐释，则很早就有人做。著名社会学家韦伯（Max Weber）的《儒家与道家》有多种英译本。20 世纪初，荷兰人亨利·波雷尔所作《无为》［英译名改为《生活的节奏》（*The Rhythm of Life*）1921］。在二三十年代被译成各种西方文学。瑞典汉学家高本汉（Bernard Karlgren）的《老子诗学思想》（*The Poetical Parts in Lao-tsi*, 1932）则直接讨论了道家思想与中国诗学的关系。

对道家思想西传作出重要贡献的有冯友兰，他英译的《郭象注庄子》1993 年由上海商务出版；林同济的《另一个中国》(*The Other China*)1944年出版于重庆。韦利1931年译出《长春真人西游记》，让人注意到道家与中国政治史的关系。

近年来道家研究方面较突出的学者有勃罗菲尔德(John Blofeld)，1973年他出版了《道家之神秘与魔法》(*Taoist Mysteries and Magic*)，1985年出版了《道教：长生之路》(*Taoism：The Road to Immortality*)，而集道家大成并提高到中国文化真髓地位的，则是李博翠(Joseph Needham)的多卷本《中国科学技术史》。

二、新诗运动中的道，杰弗斯

在新诗运动阶段，道与中国艺术的关系在西方鲜为人知，翟理斯的《中国文学史》有20页讲道家，依次讲解并摘译了《老子》、《庄子》、《列子》、《淮南子》，是作为古典散文讨论的，没有论及它们与中国文学思想的关系。

新诗运动诗人作品中经常提到"道"，但没有超出对"阴阳"的最粗浅了解①，重讲庄周梦蝶之类的故事，实在太多了一些②，只有宾纳1922年在《诗刊》上发表论王维的文章，才比较仔细地讲了王维与道家的关系。

在作品中真正应和道家思想的，是三个美国现代最重要的诗人：罗宾森·杰弗斯、卡尔·桑德堡和威廉·卡洛斯·威廉。

卡尔·桑德堡是以惠特曼的继承人自居的，但是他也明白，在这个成熟期工业社会中，不可能像惠特曼那样保持对人生，对历史的昂扬的、乐观的精神。1920年的诗集《烟与钢》中，大部分诗都是"工业大都会诗"，也有深沉的"低调"的思虑：

更早一些，1918年的诗集《剥玉米者》(*The Cornhuskers*)中两首诗，《冰冷的墓》(*Cool Tombs*)和《草》(*Grass*)，当时的美国评者指出其中有道家的齐生死观③。桑德堡这些诗，正是他最受美国现代读者欢迎的诗，《冰冷的墓》和《草》实际上是任何美国现代诗选必选的作品。他那些格调昂扬的力作，如长诗《人民，是的人民》，今日几乎无人再读。

> 完美地理解无声
> 总有音乐安慰孤独的心
> 如果音乐停歇，只剩无声。
> 它却像乐章一样进展。
> 完美地理解无声就是理解音乐。

几乎是老子"大音希声"的译解，桑德堡想必如大部分诗人一样仔细读过《道德经》。

罗宾森·杰弗斯(Robinson Jeffers，1887—1962)在新诗运动阶段已开始写诗，但缺乏新意，没有受注意。当时他在伯克利加州大学攻读医学、林学与文学。毕业后，他出于对

① Eunice Tietjens：Chinoiserie，Dial，April，1922，p. 358.

② Joseph Washington Hall. op. cit，p. 168，p. 169.

③ Joseph Washington Hall，op. cit. p. 170.

欧战的厌恶，避居到当时很荒凉的太平洋卡梅尔海岸。这里的大自然万象森列、奇景嵯峨。隐居的生活，使他诗风大变，在二三十年代，成为美国诗坛上独标一格的诗人。

杰弗斯的思想，即来自尼采的悲观主义，也来自老子的厌世倾向。他笔下的大自然，景色壮丽，是为了证明现代文明堕落而且命运短暂。这首《夏天的假日》，是他的文明观的典型表现：

太阳狂呼，人头拥簇，
叫人想起曾经有石器时代、青铜时代，也有铁器时代；铁，不稳的金属，铁制的钢，不稳定一如其母；巍然高耸的城市
将成为石灰堆上几点锈斑。
草根一时插不进，慈悲的雨能解决问题，
此后铁器时代无物存留，所有这些人，只剩一根大腿骨，几块碎片
一首诗
插在世界的思想上，像碎玻璃
混在垃圾堆里，混凝土坝远在深山中。

文明是一种疾病，短暂，非常态，与大自然相比，文明可怜，社会更可怜。杰弗斯的立场与老子相当契合："故飘风不终朝，骤雨不终日。……天地尚不能久，而况于人乎?"

杰弗斯与道家思想的另一个契合点是对文字之不信任。这首《改凿石工》把对文明的厌恶与对文字的悲观结合起来：

用大理石与时间斗争的石工，你们，命定失败的向忘却挑战的人，
你们勉强糊口，你们知道石头会碎裂，文字记载会消失，
那方臂方腿的罗马字母
在解冻时剥落，在风雨中消蚀。诗人也同样嘲弄似地建起他的纪念碑
因为人类将被一笔勾销，欢乐的大地将死亡，壮丽的太阳将瞎了眼死去，透心发黑：
然而石碑已屹立千年，痛苦的思想
在古老的诗歌中找到安宁的蜜

哪怕勒石刻碑也不足以保证文字的传达能力。煌煌巨文至多剩下悠远的回忆。正如老子所说："至誉无誉，不欲琭琭如玉，珞珞如石。""如石"并不解决问题，不如"万物并作，我观其复"。这样，痛苦的思想才能在"古老的诗歌"中找到"守静笃"的力量。

……

五、禅学西传

佛教各派籍典西传，一直局限于学术界，而西藏喇嘛教，因为在美国的庙宇甚多，作

为一种活的宗教，有学术界之外的人感兴趣（例如金斯堡在醉心于印度教之后，长期崇奉喇嘛教）。但禅宗佛教，则由于它对中国诗学和知识分子的人生哲学起过重大影响，由于它在日本多少世纪至今依然是活的宗教，本世纪来，对西方思想界起过影响，对美国现代诗的影响尤为显著。

本书只谈诗歌与诗学，因此禅宗在其他领域的传播（例如美国众多的禅宗佛教中心的传教活动）则远远超出本书所能注视的视野之外。

对禅学西传作出最大贡献的是日本人铃木大拙（Suzuki Daisetz Teitaro，1870—1966），1927 年铃木用英文发表《禅宗佛教论文集》（*Essays in Zen Buddhism*），此书被一再重版，并译成西方其他文字；1934 年他又出版《禅宗和尚之修炼》（*The Training of the Zen Buddhist Monk*）和《禅宗导论》（*An Introduction to Zen*）二书；1950 年他出版的《依照禅生活》（*Living by Zen*）则更注意到作为一种生活精神的禅。他多年禅宗研究的英文结集出版于 1956 年。铃木的教义看来是临济宗在现代之发展，但他用现代西方人能理解的语汇解释禅宗，并且与现代哲学相结合，形成自己的一家之言，所谓“铃木禅学”。

另一个在学识上，在对禅的热情上，或许足以与铃木匹敌的学者，是胡适。胡适曾有介绍禅学的论文多篇。1953 年他在《东西哲学》杂志上发表的论文，作单本印出，题为《中国禅学：其历史，其方法》（*Ch'an Buddhism in China, Its History and Method*），胡适有意把禅在西方通用的日文拼写法 Zen 改为中国写法 Ch'an，而且此书实际上是对铃木禅学的批判。铃木立即起而回答，驳难文集于 1955 年日英文书《禅学研究》（*Studies in Zen*）。

此处我们无意深入到二位学者争论的公案中。二人的分歧，既是二人身份不同（胡适是学者，尤重哲学史的理性分析；铃木是禅师，认为禅超越理智理解之障），也因为二人的民族性（禅在现代中国的影响，主要作为一种哲学，而不是活的宗教）。但他们的争论因为都用英文发表，从而引起普遍注意。

西方学者中，对禅学贡献较大的有韦利，他的《禅宗佛教与艺术的关系》（*Zen Buddhism and Its Relation to Art*）早在 1922 年就指出：对西方来说，禅的主要意义是诗学的、美学的。这也是西方理解禅的主要方向。

但是，禅与美国五六十年代以来的反文化与反学院诗相结合，则主要需归功于美国禅学家艾伦·瓦茨（Alan Wilson Watts，1915—　）。他从年轻时就研究禅学，20 岁时出版《禅的精神》（*The Spirit of Zen*，1936）。二次大战后他的几本书，如《禅学新纲要》（*Zen Buddhism, a New Outline and Introduction*）、《禅》（*Zen* 1948），与铃木相呼应，在美国掀起了对禅学的持久兴趣。1957 年，正在垮掉派运动兴起之时，他的《禅之道》（*The Way of Zen*）一书引起轰动的欢迎。相当多垮掉派诗人（以及他们的嬉皮士读者）幡然成为禅宗的信徒，成为佛教居士，甚至出家做和尚。对禅之“普及化”，瓦茨的“美国式讲禅”起了很大的作用。

六、禅与随机诗学

禅在美国诗人中引起广泛的影响，本书第一章第三节，介绍的韦尔契、惠伦、斯特利克、吉福得等人，都大书不讳地标榜禅。美国“第一位”后现代主义小说家布罗提根

(Richard Brautigan)也是加利福尼利的嬉皮士，他的成名作长篇小说《在美国钓鳟鱼》(*Trout-Fishing in America*)写得像禅宗公案集。《在美国钓鳟鱼》有时是人名，有时是地名，有时是游戏，文字之虚幻，比诗更像诗。

把禅看作是中国诗魔力的最终解释，从诗中找到解决人与自然，感觉并超越对立，这个任务太迷人了。相比之下，威廉斯为美国诗立下的信条"不要思想只要事物"，都显得过分拘泥。

禅立足凡人的生活，假定人人都有顿悟的可能，超越出凡俗生活。而诗就可能有能力把这种顿悟传送给其他人。悟之传送，自然不能靠语言文字，但诗又不可能不用语言。这个悖论，非但不是诗的障碍，反而成为诗开展的动力。

试图在这悖论中一试身手的众多诗人中有麦克娄。前面已经介绍过。他属于被成为"语言诗"的实验诗派，他们的作品不容易懂，但他们的开拓精神令人钦佩。

麦克娄有数首诗解禅，也就是说用诗讨论禅的诗学。这不是一件容易的事。试看他的一首诗"心理分析与禅宗佛理"。全诗较长，只能抽几段。是开始即说：

> 多产状态尚称作最高，只是左边有否定状态
> 我依然故我
> 没有歪曲

禅体验否只是未歪曲的程度不同，麦克娄在否认状态中感受。然而，他反对否定即生活——注意诗的写法很特殊，引号有上半无下半，问句无问号，句子常不合语法，而逻辑常跳跃至不成逻辑。这或许是以诗论禅的唯一方法。诗人回答自己的问题：

> 禅什么也不体验
> 而是理解
> ……是的，你的故事即睡眠。
> "又是?""不。""禅
> 是否即启示。"不
> 存在。无疑对付依赖他是创造者中的大师。

这一段应当说极为精彩，对禅的独立思考价值，是相当出色的阐述。禅不能依赖来得容易的理解，那不是真正的禅悟。

> 禅体验：新
> 但是无意识发现驱使有尽管做着
> 追求扇面。依然变化发生打开需要一个听见的更加强烈，我说
> 一个否定决断。

这是全诗收结的段落。遇到潜意识问题，语言便混乱了，此段第二行"但是无意

识……”下面是一大串乱糟糟不相联续的动词副词联接词，几行下来，“我说一个否定决断”。无意识无法形成禅，因为它还是在渴望联接。在一阵迷惘混乱之后，全诗的结论却是很诗意而且很明朗：

禅检查现刻
变成宇宙消失。晨光存在，如果脚步大都说可能

麦克娄的诗走了一个悖论大圈，他只是否定了复杂的逻辑语言传达禅悟之可能，而最后为他提供可能的诗句写晨光中的脚步，活生生的诗歌意象。

与麦克娄的艰涩正成对比，鲁伊特笔下的禅境是朴素的，向道家的齐物观靠拢。比如这首《晚》：

草的暖意
脚下的岩石
这幅古老的中国风景
我一直待到此地
对自己，我得老实说：
我一无所知
我一无所失
还有什么能告诉你，兄弟？
我能告诉你金花鼠如何敲钟
告诉你在我脚下鼬鼠优雅的动作
那么多花，粉白，淡红
紫的、红的、橘黄的，每一点
细节，关于白昼，关于
流动的湖水，关于花岗岩的峰顶

在当代美国，还能找到许多这样“朴素的禅宗”诗人，对他们来说，把禅理复杂化，是一种做作，甚至是一种亵渎，是违背禅悟的本意。斯特利克(Luaien Stryk)是这种朴素禅诗的阐说者，本书在第一章第三节已介绍过他。这里引一首他的典型作品《朗诵会前，作于黑鹧鸪林》：

不久就全是文词，文词，文词，现在
林中一片寂静
在这蓝领城市。
正午。大卡车震震晃晃
拉着木材
驶向芝加哥。突然，四周

工厂汽笛齐鸣。那位
给这林子命名的
诗人在哪里？我脚上有泥
伊利诺伊州勒蒙特的孩子们
我和他们在一起
一小时之久，谈鹧鸪，谈诗。

诗人被请去演讲，很可能是去讲他的专长课题：诗与禅。但那种给俗人讲的禅太实用，只剩下文词。真正的禅，只有童心未泯的孩子才能理解，在这个蓝领工人之城(勒蒙特是芝加哥的石油加工和钢铁工业中心)，禅渗透在日常生活之中。

……

（节选自赵毅衡：《诗神远游：中国如何改变了美国现代诗》，上海译文出版社2003年版，第314-318、325-330页。）

《赵氏孤儿》杂剧在启蒙时期的英国

（节选）

范存忠

【导读】

范存忠（1903—1987），英语语言文学家、比较文学杰出学者。著有《英国语言文学论集》、《英国文学论集》、《约翰逊博士与中国文化》等。逝世后出版《中国文化在启蒙时期的英国》。本文原载《英国语言文学论集》，是比较文学影响研究的典范之作，充分体现了范存忠的治学特点与实证性影响研究的一般理路。论文共分九个部分。

第一至三部分首先考证了《赵氏孤儿》在英法的传播情况。法国《水星杂志》和杜赫德《中国通志》先后登载了马若瑟的法文译稿。马若瑟译本以宾白为主，歌唱部分几乎一概不译。20世纪40年代初，英国有瓦茨和凯夫两个版本的《赵氏孤儿》，50年代又有帕西的译本。批评方面，法国的杜赫德和阿尔央斯侯爵以当时流行的新古典主义原则为标准，认为中国戏剧既不遵守三一律，也不遵守当时欧洲戏剧的其他惯例，因此不能与欧洲戏剧相提并论。启蒙时期的英国批评家并不像法国同行那样严格遵循新古典主义规律，理查德·赫德指出《赵氏孤儿》在故事情节、主题、情感表达、布局结构等方面都与古希腊悲剧相近。他运用亚里士多德的模仿说对此现象进行解释，认为好的作品都是模仿自然的结果。第四至八部分讨论《赵氏孤儿》改编情况。哈切特改编本《中国孤儿》将人名改得面目全非；保存了原剧的轮廓及主要段落；没有严格遵守三一律；增加歌曲以表达情绪。作为坚定的新古典主义者，伏尔泰认为《赵氏孤儿》不能跟法国当时的戏剧相提并论，他看中的是剧作体现出来的理性、智慧与道德的力量。伏尔泰遵照古典主义原则缩短了戏剧时间，简化了情节，还加入恋爱故事与风土习俗的描写，突出道德主题。英国剧作家谋飞的《中国孤儿》角色姓名和身份、场面与台词及道德说教意味都是对伏尔泰的承袭，而其故事轮廓、人物形象、结局安排等方面又体现出《赵氏孤儿》的直接影响。谋飞《中国孤儿》的舞台具有浓厚的东方色彩，演员的表演充分传达了角色的性格与精神气质。范存忠强调了哈切特和谋飞改编本的政治意义。最后，作者指出《赵氏孤儿》传入英国在中英文学关系上是一件富有意义的事，对于在英国引起的评论，应该结合当时的历史条件和思想倾向去认识，既要看到批评家机械照搬古典主义原则的局限性，又不能忽视某些批评家的客观评价。作者认为该剧在英国的影响主要不在它的艺术形式，而在它的题材。

该论文主要有以下特点：1. 翔实可靠的资料。范存忠早年留学国外，接受了严格的学术训练，且精通多门外语，这篇文章就是建立在准确、可靠、丰富的第一手资料的基础上，因此具有不容置辩的说服力，也成为后学相关研究的资料库。2. 严密有序的论证。《赵氏孤儿》在英国的流传情况涉及传播、翻译、批评、改编、表演等复杂的过程，又与在法国等其他国家的流传紧密相关，还要考虑到当时的文学思潮与社会状况，头绪繁多，作者却安排得井井有条、环环相扣，堪为典范。3. 富有创见的观点。以翔实可靠的资料、严密有序的论证为前提，文中随处可见富有启发性的原创观点也就不足为怪了。如作者认为谋飞的改编有不少地方直接取材于《赵氏孤儿》；《赵氏孤儿》在英国的影响，不在艺术形式，而在它的题材，这对同类研究都具有启发意义。但是，也要认识到作者对于改编作品政治意义的强调带有一定的时代特点。

（常芳）

三

阿尔央斯侯爵对于《赵氏孤儿》的看法是不是启蒙时期欧洲文艺界一致的看法呢？那也不尽然——至少在英国不是(或则不完全是)那种情况。从十七世纪中期到十八世纪后期，英国戏剧家和戏剧批评家，在法国影响之下，也讲究新古典主义的规律与惯例，不但根据这些规律与惯例来进行创作，也根据这些规律与惯例来改编(当时称为“改善”)莎士比亚的伟大的戏剧。可是，创作家和批评家不断地发出反抗的呼声。就三一律来说吧，十七世纪后期的戏剧家、批评家屈莱顿就已指出这根本不是古代希腊戏剧的规律；十八世纪初年的戏剧家法夸尔(Farquhar)进一步说明这些规律的不切实际、不合情理;① 到了十八世纪中叶，以维护传统出名的批评家约翰逊，也通过名演员加立克，当众宣称这些规律窒息了悲剧的创作。② 启蒙时期英国的戏剧家、批评家，谁都受到新古典主义戏剧规律的束缚，但谁都没有严格遵守那些规律，而不少人还有意无意地破坏了那些规律。③ 在这种情况之下，如果英国批评家对于《赵氏孤儿》的看法跟法国新古典主义者不一样，那不是一件偶然的事件。

在当时英国批评家之中，对《赵氏孤儿》进行比较详细讨论的是理查德·赫德。④ 我们说过，法国批评家阿尔央斯谈《赵氏孤儿》，主要是列举这本戏在哪些地方不合于新古典主义的规律，从而指出它的缺点。赫德则不然。他主要列举这本戏在哪些地方跟古代希腊悲剧相似或相近，从而肯定它的优点。赫德说，《赵氏孤儿》的故事跟古代希腊悲剧家

① 尼科尔：《戏剧理论》，第 42-44 页。

② 约翰逊：《德罗如瑞剧院开幕词》(1747)，第 29-34 行。

③ 尼科尔：《十八世纪前半期英国戏剧史》(1929)，第 51-66 页。

④ 赫德(Richard Hurd)于 1751 年出版他编著的《何瑞思致奥古斯特的诗篇》(Horace，Epistles to Augustus)，后附《论诗的模仿》一文，其中论及《赵氏孤儿》。这本集子从第 3 版起不收《论诗的模仿》一文，原因不详。但帕西认为该文极有价值，收入其所编的《中国诗文杂著》。

索福克勒斯的《厄勒克特拉》(Electra)很有相似之处。在《厄勒克特拉》里，阿加门侬被他的妻子和她的情人刺死以后，他的孤儿俄瑞斯忒斯不是由于一位老师父的拯救而脱险吗？瑞斯忒斯不是出由这老师父带往另外一个地方藏起来，培养长大起来吗？这一故事的轮廓跟《赵氏孤儿》是相似的。《赵氏孤儿》的主题是"怨报怨"，《厄勒克特拉》的主题也是"怨报怨"。再谈到复仇的动机，在《厄勒克特拉》里来自神座的谕旨，在《赵氏孤儿》里则来自父亲临死时的遗命。赵朔自尽前不是嘱咐过公主吗？("公主，你听我遗言，你如今腹怀有孕。若是你添个女儿，更无话说；若是个小厮儿呵，我就腹中与他个小名，唤做赵氏孤儿，待他长立成人，与俺父母雪冤报仇也。")赫德指出，《赵氏孤儿》里有多少表达愁苦的词句、格言式的话语、道德性的情绪，很像《厄勒克特拉》。此外，《赵氏孤儿》里，在情感激扬部分，"渗杂着歌曲，提炼而为壮丽的诗句，有些像古代希腊悲剧里的和歌"。①

赫德说，《赵氏孤儿》就它的布局或结构来谈，跟希腊悲剧是很相近的。他指出，这本戏的"特殊的单纯性，通体没有做作"，特别表现在人物介绍方面："演员上场，开口就把姓名、角色、任务，一一交代清楚。"②这样，阿尔央斯认为违反或然律的演员自我介绍，在赫德看来，不但不是缺陷，反而说明了结构的简朴、单纯。赫德说，戏剧结构有两条规律，一是动作需要完整、统一；二是事件需要联贯、紧密。他仔细考察了马若瑟的译本，认为《赵氏孤儿》是相当准确地符合这两条规律的；他觉得，就这本戏的前面三折来谈，动作是完整、统一的，就是诛灭赵氏，而且这动作"进展得差不多达到亚理斯多德所要求的那种速度"。同时，赫德也指出，依照古典戏剧的标准，这本戏还不够完善，在技术上还存在着一些缺陷。他说，为了连贯、紧凑起见，戏的动作最好能更接近结局或煞尾。《厄勒克特拉》的动作不是从俄瑞斯忒斯跟老师父回来复仇那里开始吗？因此，他说，这本戏的动作的开始应当跟复仇事件接得更近一些，应当从孤儿定计复仇那一段开始。赫德没有具体指出哪一段，不过他的意思大概是说，应该从第四折的末尾开始。在这一点上，赫德的意见跟阿尔央斯有些相似，可是在那篇论文里，他没有搬用三一律、或然律、措置得体惯例等来机械地衡量《赵氏孤儿》，而且他断言："中国诗人(《赵氏孤儿》的作者)对于戏剧作法的最本质的东西并不是不熟悉的。"③

那么，中国戏剧怎么会跟希腊古典悲剧有那些相近或相似之处呢？赫德根据他的文艺理论作了解答。他相信亚理斯多德的模仿学说，认为想象的创造(诗的创造)，就是模仿自然，而好的作品，就是模仿自然的、成功的作品。希腊的《厄勒克特拉》是这样，中国的《赵氏孤儿》也是这样。他认为，中国作家正同希腊作家一样，是自然的学生。正因为如此，尽管条件不同、情况不同，中国戏剧跟西方戏剧在做法上有相似的地方，也有一致的地方。他说：

> 这一个国家，在地理上跟我们隔得很远。由于各种条件的关系，也由于他们人民的自尊心理和自足习惯，它跟别的国家没有什么来往。因此，他们的戏剧写作的观念

① 帕西：《中国诗文杂著》，第2卷，第230-231页。

② 帕西：《中国诗文杂著》，第2卷，第231页。

③ 帕西：《中国诗文杂著》，第2卷，第229页。

> 不可能是从外面借过来的。我们可以肯定地说，在这些地方，他们只是依靠了他们自己的智慧。因此，如果他们的戏剧跟我们的戏剧还有互相一致之处，那就是一个再好也没有的事实，说明了一般通行的原理原则可以产生写作方法的相似。①

这里所谓“一般通行的原理原则”就是他的“诗的模仿”学说。他认为凡是模仿自然的、成功的作品，在写作方法上必然有些相似或一致之处。他就拿《赵氏孤儿》与《厄勒克特拉》来证明这理论，同时也拿这理论来将两者比较。赫德在当时作家中有“巧妙”之名，对任何东西都能说得头头是道。② 他的模仿学说曾引起诗人格雷(Gray)、诗人梅逊(Mason)、批评家华尔顿(Joseph Warton)与历史家吉朋(Gibbon)的注意。③ 他对《赵氏孤儿》的批评也曾引起民歌采集家帕西、谐剧家谋飞，以及当时文艺报刊《每月评论》的注意。④ 对我们来说，赫德的那篇论文的重要性，倒不在他的理论是否准确，而在于他能够摆脱新古典主义者的机械规律来考虑一个传统不同的外国文学作品。他对《赵氏孤儿》的估价是不低的。他的基本论点是：《赵氏孤儿》是模仿自然的、成功的作品，是中国人民的智慧的产物，是可以跟古代希腊的悲剧相比。这一种别开生面的说法，对中国文物在当时英国的传布，无疑起了一定的作用。

……

九

谋飞的《中国孤儿》，就十八世纪欧洲来说，还不是《赵氏孤儿》的最后一个改编本。德国文学史家们指出，在八十年代，诗人歌德对那本中国戏剧也曾发生兴趣，着手写他的《额尔彭诺》(*Elpenor*)，准备献给他的朋友斯旦因夫人。可是，就英国来说，谋飞的《中国孤儿》是《赵氏孤儿》的最后一个改编本，因此我们的讨论就在这里结束。关于《赵氏孤儿》怎样从法国传入英国，传入英国后得到怎样的注意，引起了怎样的批评，经过怎样的改编，改编本怎样上演，以及上演后取得怎样效果，——这些，我们都谈了，还加上了一些疏证和解释，余下来的只有一些结束语了。

我们谈这一个文学关系，很容易低估它的价值。翻译也好，介绍也好，批评也好，改编也好，搬上舞台也好，不但都有缺陷，而且有很多、很大的缺陷。翻译不完整；介绍不全面；批评不深入；改编本跟原剧差别很大，仅仅保存了一些轮廓；至于舞台表演，从中国人的眼光来看，在许多地方好象是一个讽刺。这些是很明显的，我们也提供了一些材料。可是，从历史主义的眼光来看，从比较文学的观点来谈，这许多工作——翻译、介绍、批评、改编、上演——都有其意义，因此也都有一定价值。

---

① 帕西：《中国诗文杂著》，第2卷，第222-223页。

② 鲍士韦尔：《约翰逊传》，第4卷，第189-190页。

③ 参阅舍伯恩(G. Sherburn)：《复辟时期与十八世纪英国文学》，见鲍(A. C. Baugh)主编的《英国文学史》(1948)，第977-978页。

④ 《每月评论》(Monthly Review)曾介绍赫德的主要论点，见第9卷(1573)，第122页。

我们知道，英国和中国的文学关系，不是从启蒙时期开始的。我们可以把它追溯到乔叟：马可波罗的游记曾经给《坎特伯雷故事》贡献了一些浪漫情趣。后来呢，莎士比亚的戏剧里提到过中国与中国人，弥尔顿的《失乐园》里也提到过中国与中国人。可是，英国跟中国文学艺术作品的接触，只能从十七世纪后期谈起。散文家、批评家坦帕尔爵士（Sir Willism Temple）介绍过中国的儒家哲学，也介绍过中国的园林布置；戏剧家赛特尔（Elkanah Settle）曾经把崇祯帝吊死煤山的故事搬上舞台；报章家艾狄生与斯梯尔曾经在他们有名的小型刊物《旁观报》里模仿过中国的高文典册"东方文体"；自然神论者高林斯（Anthony Collins）、丁特尔（Matthew Tindal）、鲍林勃洛克（Lord Bolingbroke）等人在批判启示宗教的著作中都曾谈到中国的哲学与道德；散文家、政论家切斯特菲尔德（Chesterfield）还运用过《晏子》、《新序》里的一些故事来讥刺当时的在朝党。……可是，谈到那中国人喜闻乐见的文学作品的传入欧洲、传入英国，《赵氏孤儿》杂剧是最早的一个。我们引过哈切特的话："多少年来，中国把它的农产品供给我们，把它的工艺品供给我们；这一次，中国诗歌也进口了。"这里所谓"诗歌"，是指诗剧。《赵氏孤儿》的传入英国，的确是中国诗剧的进口，在中英文学关系上不是一件小事。这是第一点，值得我们注意。

其次一点值得注意的是：《赵氏孤儿》在英国"进口"以后得到比较广泛的流传，也引起一些同情的批评。我们说，这与当时的历史条件和思想倾向是分不开的。启蒙时期前期的英国是这样的一种情况：一方面，资产阶级革命的胜利产生了自信、自足、自满的心理，人们惯用现成的尺度来衡量一切；另一方面，前几个世纪的地理大发现，扩大了人们的视野，激发了他们对于域外事物的兴趣。举当时比较保守的约翰逊为例。他是一个传统主义者，可是他也说了：

> 要用远大的眼光来瞻顾
> 人类，从中国一直到秘鲁。

正因为对域外事物有兴趣，人们并不束缚于原有的传统——希腊的、罗马的、希伯莱的传统——而以"远大的眼光来瞻顾人类"。就当时介绍和批评《赵氏孤儿》来说，凯夫和瓦茨的抢译《中国通志》并不单纯是两个书贾的企业竞争，赫德和帕西的介绍《赵氏孤儿》并不纯粹是几个作家的偶然好奇。这是一方面。在另一方面，正因为惯用现成的尺度来衡量一切，人们对域外事物的看法总摆脱不了古典主义的规律。赫德对于《赵氏孤儿》的批评就是这样。他企图说明哪些是合于亚理斯多德的理论的，哪些不是的。可是，我们也应该注意，他并不像法国阿尔央斯与伏尔泰那样机械地搬用新古典主义的规律。他也比较恰当地认识中国戏剧的一些优点。他从亚理斯多德的模仿学说出发来考察《赵氏孤儿》，指出中国的戏剧艺术与欧洲的古典传统在原则上颇有共通之处，但同时也指出中国戏剧不是从外面借过来的，而是中国人民智慧的产物。他的批评对中国文物在英国的传布上发生了作用。这一点，也值得我们注意。

再次一点是关于《赵氏孤儿》在英国的影响。一般说，它的影响，不在它的艺术形式，而在它的题材。元剧的说唱传统，它的结构体制，它的表演方式——这些，就当时情况来谈，都属不易理解，更是难于移植。哈切特在他的《中国孤儿》里插着歌曲，说是仿照中国格式，但与中国的说唱相去甚远。至于题材则不然。弄权、作难、搜孤、救孤、除奸、报恩——这题材有丰富的内容。这里有外部冲突，也有内部冲突；有残酷惊人的场面，也有凄婉动人的场面；有无可奈何的悲剧世界，也有人民大众喜闻乐见的“诗的正义”。这个题材，到了欧洲剧作家手里，不是一个历史故事，而是一个传说、一个寓言，可以采摘，也可以增删。哈切特采用了绝大部分情节，加以简化，写了他的“历史悲剧”；伏尔泰取用前半部分情节，加了许多穿插，写了他的“孔子之道”；最后，谋飞采用后半部分情节，也加了许多穿插，写了他的“悲剧”。这些改编本子，除了哈切特的以外，都在舞台上演，而谋飞《中国孤儿》得到很大的成功。

为了具体说明《赵氏孤儿》在英国的影响，我们对哈切特和谋飞的两个改编本作了较详细的讨论，并结合当时社会现实，阐明它们的意义、它们的作用。哈切特的《中国孤儿》是四十年代英国资产阶级政治斗争中的产物，在反抗瓦尔帕尔的运动中发生作用。它是采取戏剧形式的讽刺作品之一，表面上是一个东方故事，实际上揭露了瓦尔帕尔专政时代的政治现实，——贪污、腐化、搜括、剥削、政客的险恶与民间的疾苦——在历史上有一定价值。至于谋飞的《中国孤儿》，一向认为是伏尔泰的《中国孤儿》的改编本，我们考察了作者的创作过程，分析了这一剧本的情节发展，说明它与马若瑟的《赵氏孤儿》的关系，——说明谋飞也是根据《赵氏孤儿》来进行改编工作的。谋飞介绍了不少中国思想，也运用了一些“东方色彩”，结合了当时英国的内外局势，宣扬了爱祖国、爱自由的思想。谈文学关系，必谈影响；可是谈影响，往往易于笼统，难以明确，难以具体。我们在这方面作了一些企图。

《赵氏孤儿》在启蒙时期英国的这一个问题，不仅是文献考订，也是中英文学关系上一个值得注意的章节。我们贡献一些材料，也设法明确一些论点，用备全面研究中国文物在启蒙时期英国的影响的参考。

一九五七年五月

（原载《英国语言文学论集》）

（节选自范存忠：《〈赵氏孤儿〉杂剧在启蒙时期的英国》，张隆溪、温儒敏选编，《比较文学论文集》，北京大学出版社 1984 年版，第 91-95、117-120 页。）

歌德与中国

（节选）

杨武能

【导读】

杨武能是著名的德语翻译家、四川大学教授，毕生致力于中德文化交流，特别是对德国著名思想家、作家和科学家歌德作品的译介工作贡献卓著。其译著有《浮士德》、《魔山》等经典著作30余种，论著《歌德与中国》、《走近歌德》等5部，编著《歌德文集》等十余种，散文随笔集《圆梦初记》、《感受德意志》等，另有《杨武能译文集》(11卷)。

《歌德与中国》是中德比较文学研究领域较为重要的成果，为比较文学学者研究中德文学与文化交流以进一步了解中德两个民族的社会历史文化及其相互间关系提供了重要的参考。该书主要分为“歌德与中国”和“中国与歌德”两个部分，第一个部分“歌德与中国”是对西方研究歌德与中国关系成果的一个概述和分析。百年前就已经有西方学者开始研究歌德如何受到中国文化影响以及这种影响在其作品中的体现。所以这个部分是对西方学者研究成果的一个总结，作者也进行了一定分析。当时中国文化自东向西对欧洲持续两个世纪产生巨大影响——不仅中国丰饶的土地和物产在传教士们绘声绘色的描述下让人们神往，中国生产的精美商品通过贸易来到欧洲在当时社会引发热潮，人们争相效仿中国的艺术风格和生活习俗，而且人们对中国的社会、政治、伦理、道德乃至文学等渴望了解，于是出现大量关于中国的书籍，包括各种著述，有游记、报告，对中国经典的译介，研究中国的书籍，以及一些以中国为题材创作的文学作品。也要看到民众这种把中国看作是“王道乐土”的愿望与当时欧洲到处战乱、德国四分五裂人们渴望一个和平的理想社会的状况有很大关系。在这样的背景下，歌德开始关注中国，并从图书馆借阅有关中国的书籍进行研读，主要包括游记、哲学、小说和诗歌方面的材料，有的书籍一借再借，虽然这些书籍多是英法译本，与原著有一定出入，但是也不妨碍他对中国文学的热爱，甚至创作了十四首《中德四季晨昏杂咏》组诗以表达他对这个东方古国的憧憬。在他读完《好逑传》之后，与他的助手艾克曼的谈话中对中国文学的特点进行了分析，并提出了著名的预言，“世界文学的时代已快来临了”(艾克曼辑录《歌德谈话录》，朱光潜译，人民文学出版社，1982年，第112页。)第二个部分“中国与歌德”是本书主体部分，约占三分之二篇幅。作者在这个部分充分运用其所掌握的第一手资料对歌德及其作品在中国的传播及其影响进行了全面而较为详细的梳理，并进行了分析和评论，在谈到从事歌德及其作品在工作的译介和研究的学者时，用专门用一节重点提到了郭沫若的贡献，认为郭沫若对《少年维特的烦恼》和《浮士德》的成功翻译在文学界迄今仍然有巨大的影响。

（黄惠）

一、德国和欧洲启蒙运动前后的“中国热”歌德认识中国并受其影响的历史文化背景

源远流长的中西文化交流，在十六、十七世纪之交开始出现前所未有的高潮。这是由于葡萄牙商人打开了从印度前来中国的海上航路，中西交通较前方便多了①。接着，大批基督教传教士涌来中国，据统计，到1780年为止，仅耶稣会一个教派派遣的神父和一般传教士就达456名之多②。他们大都学识渊博。为了取得明清朝廷和士大夫阶级的信赖，他们在宣传耶稣基督的教义的同时，还有意识地向人们介绍西方的近代科学文化，像意大利人利玛窦、闵明我，法国人金尼阁、杜哈德和德国人汤若望等，都是他们的杰出代表。在他们影响下，我国明清之际出现了徐光启、李之藻、王徵等一批学习和引进西学的著名学者。

然而，中西文化交流这第一次高潮的主要流向，却应该讲是自东而西的。通过传教士们的大量报道、著述和通信，中央之国地大物博、人口众多、历史悠久、文化发达、道德高尚以及康熙时代政治清明的情形，详细地介绍到了西方，使三十年战争(1618—1648)前后历经劫难的人们惊羡不已，由此造成了持续近两个世纪的“中国热”。在德国，这“中国热”于歌德出生前后的启蒙运动和罗珂珂时期，达到了它的顶点。

“中国热”最明显和充分地表现在，人们普遍地爱好来自中国的物品，热衷于模仿中国的艺术风格和生活习俗，以致形成一种时髦，即所谓Chinoiserie(汉风)。当时源源传入欧洲的除去早已闻名的丝绸和茶以外，还有瓷器、漆、漆器、糊壁纸、皮影戏乃至轿子，等等。人们不但从中国大量进口这些东西，还竭力自行仿制，例如1709年在德国迈森，波特格尔(Bottger)终于烧制成了第一窑中国式的瓷器；自那以后，迈森这个地方一直以出产精美瓷器闻名全欧。人们不但引进这些东西本身，还引进使用它们的排场和方式，例如1727年，维也纳王宫中就下了一道懿旨，规定只有皇上的御轿才允许是黄色的，其他官员、贵族的轿子一律为黑色，等等，以通过颜色和造型来区分坐轿人的品级。在德国，也曾时兴过坐轿子，据记载，科伦大主教克勒门斯·奥古斯特(Clemens August)就喜欢像个中国大老爷似的让人抬着去巡视自己的教区；而迟至1861年，纽伦堡的市政府还郑重

① 在此之前，从中东经河西走廊或蒙古来中国的陆路充满了艰险，使想来中国的西方人大多要么望而生畏，要么半途而废。

② 参见L. Koch：Jusuiten—Lexikon. Paderborn 1934，S. 326.

其事地颁布了一套乘坐轿子的新规定。① 与此同时，中国园林建筑艺术也在十七世纪传入欧洲，先得到法王路易十四的赞赏，1670 年在凡尔赛建起了中国情调的特里亚依宫（Trianon）；随后又传到英国，与重视自然天成、反对雕琢修饰的英式庭园艺术融为一体，形成了中英合璧的新风格。这种风格很快也在德国流行开来。于是，在波茨坦的无忧宫（Sanssouci），在慕尼黑的水仙宫（Nymphenburg），在卡尔斯鲁的雉园，以及其它许许多多皇家宫苑和庭园中，都出现了亭、榭、塔、桥等中国式的建筑以及曲径假山。

然而，人们并不仅仅满足于这些物的方面，还渴望对中国的社会、政治、伦理，道德以及文学，等等，也有所了解。因此，“中国热”的第二个表现，就是大量出版关于中国的书籍，包括传教士的著述、商人的报告和旅行家的游记。除去 1298 年问世的马可·波罗的《东方旅行记》再次得到印行并引起极大重视以外，新出版的重要著述又有：1. 奉西班牙国王腓力二世派遣于 1580 年来到中国的奥古斯丁派传教士门多萨（F. L. G-de Mendoza），于 1585 年在罗马出版《支那王国述新》，这部书四年后就出版了德文版 *Neue Beschreibung des Konigreiechs China*；2. 法国耶稣会士金尼阁（N. Trigault）于 1615 年出版《耶稣会在华开教史》，此书两年后出版了德文版 *Historia von Einfuehrung der christlichen Religion in dass grope Konigreich China durch die Societet Jesu*；3. 意大利耶稣会士卫匡国（M. Martini）于 1654 年出版《鞑靼战争史》，次年又出版了《中国新地图》（*Novus Atlas Sinensis*）；4. 1665 年，出版了荷兰人诺依霍夫（Neuhof）的《使华游记》，这部书附有许多他自己绘制的铜版画插图，使西方人对中国第一次有了直观的认识；5. 1677 年，德国耶稣会士基尔歇尔（A. Kircher）用拉丁文出版了《中国图志》（*China Monumentis illustrata*），此书内容更深刻，插图更丰富，被誉为“十七世纪的中国百科全书”；6. 1696 年，法国耶稣会士李明（L. D. Le Comte）出版《关于中国目前状况的新观察报告》（*Nouveaux memoires sur l'etat present de la China*），此书译成德文出版题名为《今日中国》（*Das heutige Sina*）。②

在大量印行这些西方人自己的著述的同时，人们也开始翻译介绍中国的经典。最先出版的是耶稣会士英托塞塔（P. Intorcetta）用拉丁文翻译的《大学》（1662）和《中庸》（1673）。接着，比利时耶稣会士柏应理（P. Couple t）又重译了这两部典籍和新译了《论语》，收在他著的《孔子哲学》一书中（此书出版于 1680 年后不久，所用语言也是拉丁文）。1711 年，在布拉格印行了拉丁语的《中国六经》（Sinensis imperil libri classicl sex），除收柏应理上述三种译著外，还收了比利时耶稣会士卫方济（F. Noel）新译《孟子》、《孝经》和《三字经》。总的来看，十七、十八世纪被介绍到西方的，还只限于在中国占统治地位的儒家的经籍。

这里特别值得一提的是法国耶稣会士杜哈德（J. B. Du Halde）的《中国详志》（*Discription Geographque, historique, chronologique, politique et physique de l'Empire de la china et de la Tartarie chinoise*）。这部 1735 年在巴黎出版的四卷对开本巨著，不仅如原文题名所标示的那样包含着有关中国地理、历史、政治、民俗、科技等方面的丰富内容，而

---

① 详见：A. Reichwein：China end Europa. Berlin L923，S. 41.

② 关于这些著作的详细情况，可参阅：U. Aurich：China im Spiegel der deutschen Literatu r des 18. Jahrhunderts. Berlin，1935；E. H. V. Tscharner：China in der deutschen Dichtung. Munchen，1939.

且还收进了译成法文的元曲《赵氏孤儿》和《今古奇观》的四个短篇小说以及十几首《诗经》的诗。也就是说，在《中国详志》里，欧洲人第一次直接读到了中国的文学作品，虽然它们的翻译都不怎么好，特别是《诗经》里的那些诗，拿陈铨的话来说更叫"闹得一塌糊涂"。① 继《中国详志》之后，1761 年又出版了英国商人韦金生(J. Wilkinson)翻译、白尔塞(T. percy)润色的《好逑传》；白尔塞是以在美国刊行英国的《古诗笺存》著名的杰出作家，经他润饰的译文相当不错。此后，到了十九世纪初，还出了英国人托姆斯(P. P. Thoms)翻译的《花笺记》(1824)和法国人锐慕萨(A. Reemusat)翻译的《玉娇梨》(1926)。所有这些在中国文学中充其量只能算二流乃至三流的作品，在欧洲曾经十分流行，歌德也全都读过。

这些大量介绍中国的书籍，中国经典以及文学作品的译本的出版和流传，产生了广泛而深远的影响，不只增进了人们对中国的了解和认识，还唤起了不满现状的学者文人对于远在东方的文明礼义之邦的无限钦敬和渴慕。由此便导致了"中国热"的第三个表现，那就是在十七、十八世纪的启蒙运动和罗珂珂时期，第一出现了许多积极研究中国的思想文化，主张与中国进行文化交流和虚心向中国学习的重要思想家和学者；第二产生了一大批或以中国为题材，或假借中国人之名所写的讽喻时世的各种体裁的文学作品。

先说第一个方面。

德国启蒙运动早期的代表人物托马修斯(Ch. Thomasius，1655—1728)，他在 1689 年以前就读了柏应理出版的《孔子哲学》以及收在里边的《大学》、《中庸》和《论语》，并且对儒家的哲学思想作过详细的评论。但他还说不上对中国哲学有深刻的认识，因此对之评价也不很高。

真正对中国的思想文化有深入研究、对中国称赞备至的是莱布尼茨(G. W. F. V. Leibniz，1646—1716)。早在 1666 年至 1667 年在纽伦堡学习的时期，他已接触到了诸如基尔歇尔的《中国图志》之类的出版物。他还通过朋友，向一位叫缪勒(A. Muller)的也可能是欧洲最早的汉学家提出了一系列关于中国语言文字的问题。1669 年，他已发表第一篇谈论中国的文章。1687 年，他读到了《孔子哲学》这部书，对孔子十分钦佩。但作为莱布尼茨一生中的重要转折点，则是他 1689 年在罗马遇见从中国回来的耶稣会传教士闵明我(C. Ph. Grimaldi)。从闵明我的口中，莱布尼茨自称"得到了许多关于中国皇帝本人以及他那非常进步的人民的十分可贵的消息"。通过与闵明我的交往，莱布尼茨心中燃起了对于有关中国的新知识的越来越强烈的渴望。他阅读了一切能得到的有关中国的书籍，潜心钻研中国的经典。1692 年，闵明我接受康熙的邀请，再次动身前往中国，以便接替已故南怀仁(F. Verbiest)原任的钦天监监正的职务。他刚离开罗马，莱布尼茨已寄出一封长信，向他提出了三十个有关中国的问题，涉及的内容可谓无所不包。从此，莱布尼茨与闵明我以及其他许多传教士书信往来不断，直至 1705 年他们之间的关系才渐渐疏远。

1697 年，莱布尼茨用拉丁文出版了著名的《来自中国的最新消息》(*Novissima Sinica*)。这部在当时极受欢迎、很快便获得再版的书，收集了关于中国的报道、通信和文献(如

---

① Chen Cbuan(陈铨)：Die chinesische schone Literatur im deutschen Schrifttu. Inaugur Dissertation, Kiel, 1932. 此书中文题名为《中德文化研究》，商务印书馆 1936 年版。

1689 年的中俄尼布楚条约），以及一些当时在欧洲难得一见的图片资料，如西安府的大秦景教流行碑、北京的观象台和穿着满清官服的汤若望（Adam Schall）的画像等。特别值得注意的是，在序言中，莱布尼茨将中西文化进行对比分析，指出西方长于思辨哲学、理论科学以及军事技术，中国长于伦理哲学、政治哲学、礼仪道德，认为中国（Tschina）和欧洲乃是人类文明发展的两个高峰，只要两者结合起来，便可达到最完美的和谐，实现世界的大同；强调西方要向中国学习，在学习许多具体的东西之前，首先要学习中国的实践哲学和养身之道。他说："鉴于欧洲的道德沦丧的情况日趋严重，简直没个尽头，我就觉得几乎有必要将中国人的传教士请到我们这儿来，向我们传授自然宗教的教义和实践，正如我们派人去向他们传播启示的教义一样。因此我想，设若选一位贤明的人来作裁判，要他判定的不是三位女神中哪位最美，而是判定哪一国的人民最优秀的话，那他一定会把金苹果扔给中国人的，因为我们仅仅只在一个非人力的方面，即在我们神赐的对于基督的信仰这一点上，才优越于他们。"①

经过莱布尼茨这位大学者的积极宣传和推崇，中国成了人们向往的理想乐土，康熙皇帝——《来自中国的最新消息》第二版加进了白晋（J. Bouvet）绘的他四十一岁时的肖像——就成了人们景仰的贤明圣君，儒家哲学就得到进一步的介绍和传播。

作为莱布尼茨的后继者，克里斯蒂安·沃尔夫（Ch. Wolff，1679—1754）这位德国启蒙运动的大思想家以创立理性主义的理论体系而著称于世。他在研读了儒家的经籍以后，对其重理性、重实践的教育思想和教育制度极为赞赏，对其"以德化民"、"爱民如子"的政治主张和国家哲学十分推崇。他相信，只要实践这些思想和主张，便可挽救颓败的世风，祛除时弊，而不是如当时流行的观点所认为的那样只有等待上帝的恩典和拯救。1721 年，他在接受哈雷大学副校长职务的典礼上作题为《中国的实践哲学》（De Sinarum Philosophia Practica）的报告，大胆地阐明了自己的上述观点。为此，他被当局指为"无神论者"，失去了大学副校长的职务，被驱逐出哈雷市。但是，沃尔夫的《中国的实践哲学》却流传开来，引起了极大的注意，1740 年又由其他人从拉丁文译成德文出版，在整个欧洲产生了巨大影响。因为，在这篇报告中，古老的儒家哲学在西方第一次得到了系统、全面和详细、深入的阐述。②

在全欧范围内，还有伏尔泰和狄德罗这样伟大的启蒙思想家，也是中国文化思想的热情景仰者和传播者。伏尔泰视孔子为自己的思想的先驱，认为他是"自然的原始启示"的化身，说他认识了"最高的存在"的意义，因而也完成了一个人在世上所能完成的最伟大的业绩，自称："我非常专心地读了他的书，在这些书中谈的都是最纯净的道德。"③狄德罗称孔子为"中国的苏格拉底"，甚至将孔子置于这位古希腊哲学家和柏拉图之上。一次，他在海牙和人谈到中国的古代贤哲时说："荷马是个糊涂蛋，普利琉斯（古罗马学者）是个

① 关于莱布尼茨大力推崇中国文化和积极促进中西文化交流的情况，详见 B. F. Merkel：Leibniz und China，Berlin 1952.

② 详见 Tscharner：China in der deutschen Dichtung.

③ 转引自 Aurich：China im Spiegel der deutschen Literatur des 18. Jahrhunderts.

大傻瓜，中国人才是最可敬的君子。"①至于伏尔泰还将我国的元曲《赵氏孤儿》改编成《中国孤儿》搬上欧洲舞台，则也早已是众所周知的中西文化交流史上的一段佳话了。

再说第二方面，即欧洲十七、十八世纪出现的一大批以中国为题材或假托中国人之名写的各类文学作品。

远在十七世纪的巴洛克时代，就有不少文学作品写到中国，例如被誉为"德语诗歌之父"的奥皮茨(M. Opitz)的长诗《歌颂上帝的战争》(1628)，开德国流浪汉小说先河的格里美尔斯豪森(H. J. Ch. V. Grimmelshausen)的《痴儿西木传》(1669)，以及葡萄牙人平托(F. M. Pinto)的《平托奇遇记》(1671)和英国人希德(Th. Head)的《扬·彼鲁斯流浪记》(1672)等模仿《痴儿西木传》的作品，都是其中较有名的。在这些作品中，对中国的描写大多出自作者的想象，目的仅是满足读者对中国的好奇而已。

真正以中国为题材并且有事实为基础的作品，是洛恩施坦(D. C. V. Lohenstein)的《阿尔米琉斯》(1689)和哈格道恩(W. Hagdorn)的《艾全》(1670)。这两部卷帙浩繁的小说，都主要取材于卫匡国(Martini)的《鞑靼战争史》(1654)，写的是明末清军入关前后的事。如在《艾全》中，就具体写到了李自成起义、吴三桂勾结清兵从北京赶走李自成以及崇祯皇帝之死，等等，只不过李自成被丑化为残暴的叛贼，吴三桂却变成一位英雄的"骑士"。这两本书写的尽管好像是中国，实际上仍充满了巴洛克时期的游侠骑士小说的思想和情调，作者追求的只是冒险、艳遇、异国风情等给人以消遣的因素。

到了十七、十八世纪之交的启蒙运动时代，文学家的注意力随之转到了教化和讽喻时事方面。1721年法国启蒙运动思想家孟德斯鸠出版《波斯人信札》，在"信"中常常借中国旅行者之口对本国的弊政进行讽刺批评。由此引出了一系列诸如此类的讽喻性"旅行书简"②。在德国第一个写这种"书简"的是法斯曼(D. F. Fassmam)，此人系腓特烈·威廉一世身边讲笑话的弄臣式小官，他那长篇累牍的"书简"题名为《奉钦命周游世界的中国人》。

十分有趣的是，在众多缺少真正文学价值的"旅行书简"中，还有普鲁士国王、腓特烈·威廉一世的儿子腓特烈二世(Friedrich Ⅱ，1712—1786)的大作。腓特烈二世在德国的历史上可谓功业赫赫，世称腓特烈大帝，因此他于1760年发表的《费费胡游欧书简》也格外受人青睐。这位"大帝"崇拜法国，所以"书简"系用法文写成。"书简"共计六封，都是主人公在旅途中向中国皇帝作的观感报告，内容涉及宗教、民俗、警务、政治等诸方面，而重点在于批评讽刺罗马教廷和教会。如在第四封信中，费费胡写道："您的帝国是多么幸运啊，陛下，它有一个宽容而务实的、没有统治别人的欲望的教会！"又如在第五封信中，费费胡和一个葡萄牙朋友一起参观罗马的圣彼得大教堂，看见教皇竟然为人们用于征战的头盔和宝剑祝福，大为惊诧和不满。腓特烈二世的"书简"是匿名在科伦发表的，目的主要在于发泄对于七年战争(1756—1763)中支持他的对手奥地利的罗马教皇的不满。

与讽喻性的"旅行书简"同时盛行的还有所谓"道德小品"和"道德故事"。这类作品跟

① 转引自 Aurich：China im Spiegel der deutschen Literatur des 18. Jahrhunderts.

② 在英国，十八世纪时也出现了这样的"中国书简"，其中最有影响的为哥尔斯密著的《世界公民》。

我国旧时代街头艺人说唱的“善书”颇有些相似，都是用当时欧洲人想象中道德高尚的中国的故事或寓言，去劝喻世人提高自己的德行。

以写“道德故事”出名的作家中有一位叫菲费尔(G. K. Pfeffel)，他的代表作《寓言与故事集》是一首首短诗，宣扬的多半是儒家的孝悌伦常观念。试译其中一首《母与女》，以见一斑：

在中国，人们敬重白发，同时也
相信“黄荆棍下出好人”的道理。
一次一位八十岁的老母亲责打
女儿，一个六十岁的不成器的孩子。
女儿大声恸哭，泪如雨下。
母亲问她，为何这么痛哭流涕？
须知，我以前打得更狠、更重，
却从未听见你哭得如此悲凄。
是啊，母亲，你说得太对了，
女儿哽咽着回答，唉——！正是
见你年老体衰，胳臂没劲儿，
我心中才感到格外痛楚，哀戚。

菲费尔在诗中极力夸大中国人的孝道，同时又相信某些从中国回去的旅行者的说法：这孝是靠棍子培养成的。，

另一位写“道德故事”的作家叫塞肯道夫(F. V. Seckendorf)。他的代表作《命运之轮》(1783)写到老子和庄子，并且讲述了庄周化蝶的故事，值得引起注意。因为在此之前，人们只知道孔孟和他们的儒学，提到老庄或许以是篇为首。再者，整篇故事的说教气也不如同类作品明显，相反倒饶有诗意，这点似乎也像《庄子》。遗憾的是我们不知道《命运之轮》如何会有这些特点，以及从什么渠道了解了庄周化蝶的故事①。

如果说“道德故事”以教育老百姓为主的话，那么，同时出现的所谓“国事小说”(Staatsroman)就该是劝谏统治者了。最有名的“国事小说”作者为哈勒尔(A. V. Hailer)，他的第一部作品《乌松》(1771)写的是一个蒙古王子成长为既富有德行又勇武超群的贤明君主的过程。王子谨记中国古哲的教训，在执政后袭用了中国古代的许多好的典章制度，国力大增。晚年，乌松国王又以同样的办法培养孙子伊斯马尔，使他成为自己的继承人。在小说中，中国成了一个理想的国家。

……

(节选自杨武能：《歌德与中国》，生活·读书·新知三联书店1991年版，第3-19页。)

① 在《中国详志》里收有庄周化蝶的故事，可能为塞肯道夫所采用。

关于提高外国文学史编写质量的几个问题

（节选）

杨周翰

【导读】

杨周翰先生（1915—1989）是中国当代比较文学和世界文学研究领域著名学者，其主要译作有《埃涅阿斯纪》、《变形记》、《亨利八世》和《蓝登传》等，主要著作有《攻玉集》、《镜子与七巧板：比较文学论丛》、《十七世纪英国文学》和《忧郁的解剖》等，编有《欧洲文学史》、《莎士比亚评论汇编》和《中国比较文学年鉴》等。其著述立足于批评实践，具有高度的理论前瞻性（参见王宁《再论杨周翰的比较文学和世界文学研究》，《中国比较文学》2016年第二期，第66页）。

杨周翰先生1983年出版的《攻玉集》收集了他写于拨乱反正前后的主要针对外国文学作品研究的论文，共计十二篇，论文以一种与时俱进的态度探讨了文学批评的方法，反思了传统文学观念在新的时期存在的问题。本文是杨周翰先生1978年11月在广州全国外国文学研究工作规划会议上的发言，虽然看似针对文学史问题的探讨，但却是以文学史编写为切入点，探讨了当时比较文学研究中存在的问题，强调用实事求是、一分为二的精神来对待文学研究，注意文学史编写的历史延续性的问题；用有意识的、系统的、科学的比较方法进行研究，以获得对作家作品的深刻理解；要正确、全面地研究作家，避免传统文学研究中对作者简单化、片面化的问题；要直接进入研究对象，充分掌握材料，接触不同的观点。在文学研究和文学史的编写中，不能以主观好恶来评判，过于拔高和贬低都不能反映客观事实，对莎士比亚的评论就很少有贬词，而对资产阶级世界的文学流派的评价却一无是处，这都是不可取的。文学史不能只关注作家作品，割断历史，应该记录文学发展，总结规律。比较文学要联系社会生活，注意比较方法的使用，它可以是不同民族的文学比较，可以是文学主题、文学类型、文学潮流、批评和审美标准或诗学的比较，也可以是文学与其他文艺领域的跨学科的比较，以发现一些文学发展的共同规律。要对作家作品进行全面的研究，要掌握语言工具，直接进入到研究对象进行研究。

即使在今天中国的比较文学研究已经蓬勃发展的新阶段，回顾杨周翰先生当年所探讨的这些问题，我们无疑会惊讶于他研究视野的开阔及其前瞻性。而他正是执著于这样的信念在比较文学领域努力实践，为比较文学在中国的发展做出了巨大贡献。

（黄惠）

（一）进一步贯彻唯物辩证法，贯彻实事求是、一分为二的精神

我想一部文学史首先要求能做到一个"信"字。我国历史学的传统也历来强调"信史"、"实录"，不仅要求"其事核"，而且要求"不虚美，不隐恶"。"信"就要求符合事实，而要符合事实，就不能有片面性，也就是必须一分为二。不能只讲好的不讲坏的，也不能好的都好，坏的都坏。在选择材料问题上，要从客观实际出发，要从作家在历史上的影响出发，不能凭主观好恶而决定取舍。

反观我们编写的外国文学史，常常给人这样的印象，即客观存在的文学现象（流派、作家、作品）往往同文学史的表述之间存在矛盾。这种情况表现在把历史上进步的作家说得比原来更进步，把一些不那么进步的作家宁可说成反动。这种倾向在苏联某些文学史里已见端倪，如阿尼克斯特编的《英国文学史纲》把英国第一部史诗《贝奥武甫》中的主人公说成是"人民之父"，这样就掩盖了此诗的贵族性质，而诗中其实并未有过这样的提法；相反，在绝大多数场合都称他为"王"、"君主"。这种喜欢拔高的倾向，比比皆是。

对待莎士比亚，这种倾向也是占主导地位，从西方浪漫派评论开始，通过苏联到新中国成立后我国的文学史和评论，对莎士比亚很少有贬词。伏尔泰和托尔斯泰对莎士比亚的批评，固然是出于时代风尚不同或文学主张不同，未必全对，有时是误解，但是他们不迷信莎士比亚。

对当代资本主义世界一些文学流派的评价则反映了另一种倾向，尽量贬低，以至把它们看成一无是处。

过去我们写英国二十年代小说家乔依斯是这样写的：他的主要作品《攸利希斯》以几十万字写了广告经纪人布鲁姆及其妻和青年斯蒂芬一天的生活，写他们精神苦闷，思想肮脏腐朽，没有希望。由于阶级斗争的进一步尖锐化，中小资产阶级惶恐失望、厌世，以至仇视人类。前一时期虚伪的唯美主义和享乐主义被更为反动的对"潜意识"活动的追求所代替……

这部小说确实反映了资产阶级的没落彷徨的情绪，但是否因此就对它采取完全否定的态度呢？我觉得正是因为它反映了这种精神状态，因而有极高的认识价值。这类作家之所以能深刻地反映这种精神状态，则是因为他们对资本主义社会生活和精神生活有极深的感受，同时在表达方式上刻意寻求他们认为最好的方式（当然也有形式主义成分）。

极力贬低的倾向往往出于好意，怕对青年产生不良影响。鲁迅在《中国小说的历史的变迁》中有一段话，说得极好。他说：

> 至于说到《红楼梦》的价值，可是在中国底小说中实在是不可多得的。其要点在敢于如实描写，并无讳饰，和从前的小说叙好人完全是好，坏人完全是坏的，大不相同，所以其中所叙的人物，都是真的人物。……但是反对者却很多，以为将给青年以

不好的影响。这就因为中国人看小说，不能用赏鉴的态度去欣赏它，却自己钻入书中，硬去充一个其中的脚色。所以青年看《红楼梦》，便以宝玉，黛玉自居；而年老人看去，又多占据了贾政管束宝玉的身分，满心是利害的打算，别的什么也看不见了。①

青年主要要靠正面理想的教育，把立足点站稳，用分析批判的眼光，放眼古今中外，一切可以拿来为我所用，丰富自己的知识和智慧，毒草尚且可以肥田。消极抵挡，“封闭疗法”，自己搞得被动，得不到积极的效果。

文学史(也包括文学评论)还有一种倾向，就是对作家提出过高的要求。如对西方四十年代后期迄六十年代的存在主义文学、荒诞派戏剧、黑色幽默小说，评论者认为这些流派纵然反映了资本主义社会的荒谬、丑恶、阴暗面，但事实是资本主义社会的腐烂和丑闻已无法掩饰，以至政客们也利用彼此的荒谬丑恶互相攻讦。评论者认为这些流派的作者做些不痛不痒的嘲讽，不能损害垄断资产阶级半根毫毛，不触及本质；评论者并指责这些作家不反映劳动人民的悲惨处境和英勇斗争，却宣扬荒谬是永恒的，人类只有毁灭，因而这些都是反动流派。对历史上的批判现实主义作家也有类似的评价，说他们并不是要从根本上推翻资本主义社会，实际上却是为了维护和巩固资产阶级统治服务的。

我们评论一个作家只能就他所提供的材料来判断。据此，恩格斯称赞巴尔扎克的作品说，从中学到的东西比从经济学家和统计学家的全部著作中加起来所学到的还要多。要求一个资产阶级作家具有无产阶级先进的世界观是过高的要求。政治上的反动应当同资产阶级世界观区别开来。

……

造成文学史中以上这些现象的原因，可能是因为过去在批判客观主义、超阶级观点的倾向的同时，掩盖了另一种倾向，即忽视了科学的客观态度，甚至在文学史中造成“虚说传而不绝，实事没而不见”的现象，不能作到“文非泛论，按实而书”，或多或少陷入实用主义，而且不从实际出发，不一分为二，陷入形而上学。这些恐怕是影响文学史水平提高的根本障碍。

(二)历史连续性问题

我们过去写的外国文学史有这样一种现象，详希腊而略罗马，详文艺复兴而略中世纪，详十九世纪而略以前各时期。理由是罗马文学、中世纪文学成就不高；其次是要厚今薄古，甚至有这样的担心，现在是两千多年的文学史，再过两千年，古的都要讲怎么得了。

历史的对象本来就是过去的事，历史不讲古，古代的事由哪门学科来管？不要说文学史两千年，地质学、古生物学都以一亿年为单位。而所谓厚今薄古，不是不要古。研究古，仍是为了今。不过，这里有个用什么、如何用的问题。过去，我们的外国文学史只讲作家作品，以为这些可以借鉴，这固然是对的，但这并没有充分发挥文学史的作用。罗马文学、中世纪文学相对来说，其成就当然不及希腊、文艺复兴，但从历史角度看，把它们

① 《鲁迅全集》1957 年版第 8 卷第 350 页。

忽略过去，就总结不出什么规律性的东西来。

文学史，就其使用来说，不外两种，一种供查检，一种供通读。外国文学史只写作家作品，就变成了供查检的作家辞典，尽管略有脉络贯串，但十分单薄。供通读的文学史以脉络为主，味道应像读故事小说，但更重要的是记录文学发展，总结出规律，这样的用处要比个别作家的评价大些。这样，作为通读读物，就更具备"可读性"。

马克思主义经典作家一向告诫我们不要割断历史。恩格斯在《反杜林论》中批判杜林的政治第一性、经济第二性和政治暴力是社会发展动力的论点时，谈到奴隶制的进步意义，指出：

> 只有奴隶制才使农业和工业之间的更大规模的分工成为可能，从而为古代文化的繁荣，即为希腊文化创造了条件。没有奴隶制，就没有希腊国家，就没有希腊的艺术和科学；没有奴隶制，就没有罗马帝国。没有希腊文化和罗马帝国所奠定的基础，也就没有现代的欧洲。我们永远不应该忘记，我们的全部经济、政治和智慧的发展，是以奴隶制既为人所公认，同样又为人所必需这种状况为前提的。在这个意义上，我们有理由说：没有古代的奴隶制，就没有现代的社会主义。
>
> 用一般性的词句痛骂奴隶制和其他类似的现象，对这些可耻的现象发泄高尚的义愤，这是最容易不过的做法。可惜，这样做仅仅说出了一件人所周知的事情，这就是：这种古代的制度已经不再适合我们目前的情况和由这种情况所决定的我们的感情。但是，这种制度是怎么产生的，它为什么存在，它在历史上起了什么作用，关于这些问题，我们并没有因此而得到任何的说明。①

恩格斯把古代奴隶制一直联系到现代的欧洲，一直联系到现代的社会主义。我们的研究方法比较孤立，满足于仅仅说明希腊文学是在什么社会环境中产生的，有些什么成就，但作为具有相对独立性的文学这一上层建筑一旦产生对后来文学发展，包括现代西方文学有什么继承关系，则注意不够；特别对于同样是奴隶制产物的罗马文学注意不够。其实文艺复兴时期的作家受罗马文学影响比希腊文学可能更大些。从文艺复兴时期产生的史诗、喜剧、悲剧、抒情诗中处处可以看到罗马作家的影响。但丁为什么要维吉尔作他的向导呢？到十七世纪古典主义，甚至十八世纪诗歌、小说，都是如此。只有到浪漫主义以后，罗马文学在欧洲文学发展上，影响才逐渐减弱。即使在中世纪，一些罗马作家的作品仍为教会中人所传抄阅读。

……

西方作家是在西方文化传统的影响下创作的。我们要了解并正确评价他们，对全部西方文明不能不研究、了解。其实，学西方语言也是如此，语言本身的规律要掌握，但语言是毛，必须附在皮上，没有无内容的语言。西方作家包括科学家，他们所受的教育是西方

① 恩格斯：《反杜林论》，《马克思恩格斯选集》第3卷，第220页。

文化传统的教育，包括从古希腊、罗马直到当代资本主义、帝国主义时代的文化知识。举两个极端的例子。乔依斯的《攸利希斯》，我们从思想内容上批判是比较容易的，但要评论他的艺术技巧和匠心，就不那么容易。这部小说的结构，事件严格控制在一天之内，十八个情节严格符合荷马史诗中十八个情节。他套用荷马史诗，并不能简单地扣上一顶“形式主义”的帽子了事，也是与他的思想内容有机结合的。因此，要对乔依斯此书作出有说服力的评论，离不开对荷马的研究。

……

对历史连续性重视不够，原因很多。对厚今薄古的不恰当的理解是其一。其次是对如何古为今用、洋为中用的问题理解不一。作家作品的研究是有用的，但从大处总结一些经验，真实地再现文学的历史，在某种意义上说，借鉴作用更大。作为大学课程，过去也是讲作家作品多，讲历史发展少。主要原因是研究跟不上，因此应当大力展开研究。在这方面，我们的课题是很多的，如文学类型、主题、题材、典型、创作方法的发展，都值得我们进行系统的研究。

(三)提倡比较法

我们的文学史即使仅仅是论作家作品，也往往平铺直叙，孤立叙述，不利于加深对作家作品的理解，也不利于阐明历史的发展。没有比较就没有鉴别。马克思说，有意思的是把《农夫彼尔斯》的作者朗格兰同高雅的《坎特伯雷故事集》作者乔叟比较一下。他比较了莎士比亚和席勒，据说还比较了雪莱和拜伦。普列汉诺夫提出“对立的原理”，并据此比较了十七世纪复辟王朝英国的文学审美趣味同文艺复兴时期的差异，指出其“社会原因”，从而使两个不同时代的特点更加鲜明，给读者深刻的印象，至今读来，仍有清新的感觉。

事实上，比较是表述文学发展、评论作家作品不可避免的方法，我们在评论作家、叙述历史时，总是有意无意进行比较，我们应当提倡有意识的、系统的、科学的比较。

精辟的评论往往是从比较得来的。例如十九世纪英国批评家柯尔律治评莎士比亚有这样一段话：

> 麦辛哲(英国剧作家，1553—1640)像佛兰芒(荷兰)画家，他所描绘的对象同现实界一样，很有力，很真实，在观者心中产生同现实界对象同样的效果。但莎士比亚超乎此，他在考虑一事之时，总是用比喻和形象把过去的经验和可能的经验概括起来，使之具有普遍意义。

经过这一比较，即使我们没有看过麦辛哲的剧作，我们对莎士比亚创作的高度概括力和形象性，也有了一个鲜明而深刻的印象。而平铺直叙就很难产生这样的效果。

这里不妨约略谈谈比较文学。这门学科在欧洲十九世纪末已有开端，至二十世纪二十年代大大发展。苏联反对比较文学，因为比较文学不作阶级分析，即不探讨普列汉诺夫说的“社会原因”，主张打破民族文学的界限，表现了“世界主义倾向”。我国新中国成立前在这方面有些成就，后来在国内根本没有人提。

比较文学不联系社会生活当然是违反历史唯物主义的。但作为一种方法，可以研究。这一学科尽管有不同流派，各国也有所不同，但有些共同的基本主张。他们都认为一个民族的文学与其他民族的文学比较，才能显出其特点来；主张对文学的主题、文学类型、文学潮流、批评和审美标准或诗学进行比较研究，研究相互影响；把文学与其他文艺领域进行比较，研究其关系，在相互比较之中发现一些文学发展的共同规律。

就在从事比较文学研究的学者中也有人看到这门学科过分注意某一文学现象的渊源和影响，而忽略作家的主观取舍、作家的用意和目的、作品的客观效果的片面性，并承认比较文学只是一种辅助学科。但他们也认为如果使用得当，可以帮助我们了解作家的创作过程，扩大文学史的知识，也有助于评价；比较可以避免把文学现象看成孤立现象，他们把这种研究称为“综合”。我觉得，我们有辩证唯物主义的指导，就文学史中某些问题如文学主题、文学题材、劳动人民形象、妇女问题，在不同民族不同社会的文学中的反映作一比较，应能得出有意义的成果。

这里想着重谈谈观点的比较。我觉得我们应当在马克思主义基本原理指导下，参看国外的评论，集思广益，开拓思路，一定能够提高我们评论的水平，丰富马克思主义的基本原理。我们过去的缺点是满足于贴标签，生硬联系实际，没有能够很好地批判地继承大批优秀的评论遗产……

(四)关于作家的介绍

读者接触一部作品，实际也是读者同作者发生思想感情的接触(有意识地或无意识地同意、同感、不同意、反感，部分地同感、同意)。司马迁说：“余读孔氏书，想见其为人。”这是很自然的要求。要正确理解并评价一个西方作家和他的作品，对他的生活知之不多，是办不到的。有的作品的作者不可考，或材料不多，那也没办法。有的材料很丰富，怎样对待材料就成为主要问题。

我们现在编写文学史的做法是交代时代背景，关于作者则交代他的阶级出身、政治性的活动、作品清单。这是一种写简历、做政治鉴定的办法。其用意是好的，因为要说明作者在历史上有无进步意义以及对人民的态度。但这样做，有许多不足之处。一部文学史所有的作家都冠以资产阶级或小资产阶级的头衔，作家们面目相同。这只能说明其共性，而共性只能通过个性表现出来。其次，容易产生简单化和片面性，或则美化或则丑化。其结果反而不能正确说明他在历史中的作用和对人民的态度。

……

资产阶级著者编写的文学史不进行阶级分析，对拜伦的社会活动不感兴趣，这当然不对。但他们对作家的心理精神状态，对个人与个人之间的关系最感兴趣。我觉得这一点不应忽视。作者的思想感情和心理状态，也就是毛主席说的“作家的头脑”是同作品直接发生关系的。资产阶级文学史家掌握了比较全面的材料，看到了一些现象，这些都值得我们参考，我们如果也看到了，就不能视而不见，不予考虑。他们进一步分析这些现象时，不说完全错误吧，究竟没有分析到根本上，但恐怕也不能一概否定。

“社会生活→作家→作品”这样一个文学的生产公式，我们对作家这个环节研究不够，对作家不全面研究，对作品的分析就难免生硬，不能贴切，我们过去不甚提倡传记文学，偶然翻译一些作家传，也比较枯燥；近来传记多起来了，这是可喜的现象。作家的研究不仅是为了使文学史写得生动，有血有肉，增加其“可读性”，而且对正确评价作家、作品，如实反映文学发展历程，总结一些规律性的东西，也是必不可少的一环。

（五）直接进入研究对象，充分掌握材料，接触不同的观点

翻译外国文学作品是普及文化必不可少的手段；翻译文学对推动我国新文学的发展起过积极作用，这是人所共知的。但依靠翻译进行研究工作就有其天然的局限性；研究工作必须直接进入研究对象（原作）；翻译得再好，不能代替原作。以朱生豪译的莎士比亚剧本为例。朱译总的说来是行文流畅，词语丰富，通俗易懂，基本上正确，后来又经校订，读者对莎剧的故事情节、人物性格甚至语言风格特点，可以知其梗概。但根据朱译或任何其他译本来评论莎剧，至少是不够的。例如《李尔王》一剧，“自然”（也就是“人性”）一词，连同它的反义词、同义词，在剧中出现不下四五十次。读原著，这个词贯串全剧始终，几十次地出现，使读者不得不注意到它。在译本中，我约略统计了一下，作为正义词，有这样一些译法：“天地”、“生性”、“天性”、“本性”、“大自然”、“造化”、“上天”、“人”、“任何人”、“天伦”、“伦常纲纪”、“身体”、“生命”、“天然”、“精神”、“人情”、“仁慈”、“慈悲”、“孝道”、“身心”、“天道人伦”、“孝心”、“孝顺”；有时不译。作为反义词，有：“罪大恶极”、“违反自然”、“超乎寻常”、“什么东西”、“恶魔”、“冷酷无情”、“不孝”、“没有心肝”、“畜生”“乖离”、“冷淡”、“怠慢”、“亏待”、“没有良心”、“荒谬”、“无理”、“不近人情”、“下贱”；有时也不译。在原作中，这些都是“自然”一词和它的形容词和明显的同义词和反义词，是《李尔王》主题思想的主要组成部分，内容是两个哲学范畴：“自然”和“人性”，是我们理解莎士比亚的世界观的关键概念（在其他剧本中同样出现这个词）。从译本中，这两个范畴既然被掩盖了（至少大部分被掩盖了），我们就无法在理解和评论中着重考虑这问题，成了无的放矢。

至于语言风格，则更微妙，往往挂一漏万，甚至走样。例如：“我总是愿意贡献我的一得之愚的。殿下和夫人光临蓬荜，欢迎得很。”原文并没有这样典雅。李尔临终时对科底丽亚说：“你虐待我还有几分理由？”她连连回答两个“没有理由，没有理由”，表现出她绝对不能同意老父的意见，急于和解，并安慰他，拯救他。而译文只作“谁都没有这理由”。我们对外国文学的评论以小说、戏剧为多，很少涉及诗歌。这是一个很大的漏洞。文学同哲学、政治经济学、法学等社会科学不同，十分复杂，很难翻译，诗歌尤其如此，这方面还有很多问题，这里不是议论的场合，我只想说明直接进入研究对象的重要性。

当然，我并非非难翻译，翻译有它自己的困难，如果把上述有关“自然”的词，一律译成“自然”，根本是不可能的。译文有译文的服务对象。英国学者霍克思翻译《石头记》，在第一卷《引论》结尾时说：“我自始至终遵守一个原则，每个字都译，包括双关语。这部小说虽然是‘未完成的’小说，但是一位伟大的艺术家用他一生心血写成的。因此我认为这里面每字每句都有用意，不能忽略。我不敢说我已处处成功地做到这一点，但如果我能把我读这部小说时感到的乐趣，哪怕一小部分，传达给读者，我这一生就算没有白白度过。”翻译不可能是“再现”，只可能是“再创造”。

……

以上五个问题只是个人所见，水平有限，很肤浅，也不全面。不过我觉得实事求是、一分为二，是个很重要的问题，也是以上五个问题中最根本的问题。掌握外文也是为了更好地从实际出发。实事求是、一分为二不仅是个方法问题，也是个学风问题，学风不正，不仅不能推动研究工作，引出正确结论，总结经验，贯彻批判继承的方针，而且会影响到下一代，下两代，应当引起严重注意。

（1978 年 11 月在广州全国外国文学研究工作规划会议上的发言。原载《外国文学研究集刊》第 2 辑，1980 年；1982 年 12 月修改。

节选自杨周翰：《杨周翰作品集第六卷：〈攻玉集〉、〈镜子与七巧板〉》，上海书店出版社 2015 年版，第 1342-1354 页。）

试论欧洲十四行诗及波斯诗人莪默凯延的鲁拜体与我国唐代诗歌的可能联系

杨宪益

【导读】

杨宪益(1915—2009)，祖籍淮安盱眙(今属江苏省淮安市)鲍集镇梁集村，中国著名翻译家，外国文学研究专家，诗人。1936年，杨宪益在英国通过考试进入牛津大学学习。1952年，杨宪益应邀北上来到北京外文出版社工作和生活。

在本文中，杨宪益对唐代兴起的新体诗歌与欧洲的十四行诗以及古代波斯的鲁拜体四行诗进行比较，提出两者之间存在某种联系的假设。欧洲十四行诗的起源对于西方学者来说仍然是个尚需弄清的问题。最早可以追溯到意大利文艺复兴时期，英法等国的十四行诗是其变体。由于当时西欧文化落后于近东一带，因此意大利西西里岛流派既可能从阿拉伯传承，也可能受东罗马和大食文化的影响自己创造出十四行诗体。而中国文化居于大食文化东边，因此，十四行诗从中国——阿拉伯——西西里岛——欧洲这条流传线路也可能成立。

以李白“古风”体诗歌为例，早于西西里岛诗人维奈几百年，西方十四行诗与李白诗歌的形式相像。如此视之，李白可以算作是最早使用“十四行诗”这种诗歌体裁的鼻祖。比较一下唐代绝句体与莪默凯延的鲁拜体，鲁拜体有可能起源于民间歌谣，也有可能是由西突厥从中国传播过去的。因为鲁拜体诗不管是从形式上还是从思想内容上，都与绝句非常相似。在杨宪益看来，通过比较研读两者之间的可能联系已经超出比较文学研究的范围，属于中西交通史性质的探讨。本文得出的启示是中外文学上的“偶合现象也总是可以给以科学的解释的。”

(白阳明)

我想提出供讨论的题目是比较一下我国唐代兴起的新体诗歌和欧洲的十四行诗以及古代波斯的鲁拜体四行诗，并提出一个假设，即两者之间会不会有某种联系。我这样说，也许会使人们感觉这是毫无根据的臆测，因为中国语文不属于印度欧罗巴语系，汉文与西方语文差别很大；在诗歌形式发展上，走的是完全不同的道路；所以乍一看来，很难相信在诗歌体裁方面能够互相影响。但是我们可以提出，我国从魏晋时开始，讲究声律，创作了新体诗，早已有人说过，这是受了梵文声律的影响。虽然由于汉文的特点，齐梁以后讲究双声叠韵和四声对偶，在诗歌形式方面，有其独特的发展，然而过去中国诗歌曾受过外来影响，似乎也是一个不能忽视的事实。如果我国六朝以来兴起的新体诗歌可能受到过外来声律学的启发，我们说唐代诗歌可能影响过欧亚其他地方的诗歌形式，这个假设似乎也是可以成立的。

让我们先看看欧洲十四行诗的起源问题。西方学者一般都认为十四行诗的起源还弄不清楚。大家都知道英法等国的十四行诗体源自意大利文艺复兴时期贝特拉伽(Francesco Petrarca)等所写的十四行诗。莎士比亚的十四行诗是意大利十四行诗的一个变种，即莎士比亚的十四行诗由三个四行诗组（quatrain)加上末尾同韵的两行诗组成，而较早的意大利十四行诗则是由一个八行诗组（octave)和一个六行诗组(sestet)组成，前面的八行又可分为两个四行诗组(quatrain)，但在前八行和后六行之间，音乐上一般要有个顿挫，最后六行更加急促奔放，以结束全诗。一般西方学者认为最早的一首十四行诗是十三世纪初西西里岛的诗人披埃·德勒·维奈(Pier delle Vigne)的作品。维奈此人的名字见于但丁《神曲》地狱篇(*Inferno*)第十三章，这也是很多人都知道的。维奈约生于1190年，死于1249年；他曾是腓德烈皇帝二世的宠臣，因皇帝怀疑他不忠，被监禁备受苦刑，并被弄瞎了眼睛而自杀，根据当时基督教义，凡自杀者都要在地狱受苦，但丁把他在地狱受苦的情景写成了动人的诗句。十三世纪中除了维奈以外，还有一些别的意大利诗人用过十四行诗这一体裁，也都是属于西西里地方的这一流派。西西里岛当时还是在阿拉伯影响之下，当时西欧文化远比近东一带文化落后，很多东西都是从东罗马和大食文化传过去的，西西里岛则是接受东方文化的一个首站。当然，当时受到阿拉伯文化影响的西西里岛诗人也可能自己创造了这种诗体，但另外一个可能就是十四行诗这种体裁是从阿拉伯人方面传过去的。由于我们对中古阿拉伯诗歌知道不多，一时还没有根据来证明这个假设。可是当时阿拉伯势力横跨欧亚，在大食文化的东边就是强盛的中国文化。从历史年代和地理条件来看，如果我们在唐代诗歌里找到类似十四行诗的体裁，这个假设，即不但欧洲最早的十四行诗是从阿拉伯人方面传到西西里岛的，而且其来源还可远溯到中国，似乎也是可以成立的。

我国唐代著名诗人李白写过不少“古风”体的诗歌，其中有些从形式上来看，很像西方的十四行诗。著名的“花间一壶酒”就是很完整的一首，全诗如下：

花间一壶酒　独酌无相亲
举杯邀明月　对影成三人
月既不解饮　影徒随我身
暂伴月将影　行乐须及春
我歌月徘徊　我舞影零乱
醒时同交欢　醉后各分散
永结无情游　相期邈云汉

开头是一个八行诗组，用的是一个韵；然后是一个间隔，下面是一个六行诗组，用的是另一尾韵。

前面的八行诗组又可以分为两个四行诗组；第二个四行诗组是第一个四行诗组的延伸和发展。这和意大利尚十四行诗体的规律是完全符合的。

在李白的“古风”体诗歌中，我们还可以举出其他一些首，也都同十四行诗的形式相似，如他为当时文士的不遇慨叹的一首：

咸阳二三月　宫柳黄金枝
绿帻谁家子　卖珠轻薄儿
日暮醉酒归　白马骄且驰
意气人所仰　冶游方及时
子云不晓事　晚献长杨辞
赋达身已老　草玄鬓若丝
投阁良可叹　但为此辈嗤

头八句描写当时得宠的权贵骄纵浪游，洋洋得意，后六句以扬雄的遭遇为例，写当时文人不受重视，受到权贵们的嗤笑，也是一个八行诗组加上一个六行诗组合成的。再如他的一首游仙诗，写中原遭到战祸的悲惨情景：

西上莲花山　迢迢见明星
素手把芙蓉　虚步蹑太清
霓裳曳广带　飘幅升天行
邀我登云台　高揖卫叔卿
恍恍与之去　驾鸿凌紫冥
俯视洛阳川　茫茫走胡兵
流血涂野草　豺狼尽冠缨

头八句写登山后看见天上玉女邀请他登上云台峰，后六句写驾鸿升天，看见尘世的情景，也是一个八行诗组加上一个六行诗组合成的。我们还可以举一首嘲笑不识时务、食古不化的鲁儒的诗为例：

鲁叟谈五经　白发死章句
问以经济策　茫如坠烟雾
足著远游履　首戴方山巾
缓步从直道　未行先起尘
秦家丞相府　不重褒衣人
君非叔孙通　与我本殊伦
时事且未达　归耕汶水滨

头八句描写鲁儒形象的可笑，后六句是对鲁儒的斥责，也是一个八行诗组加上一个六行诗组合成的，前八行又可分为两个四行诗组。以上所举的例子都是五言古诗，我们还可以举一首七言古诗《行路难》为例：

金樽清酒斗十千　玉盘珍羞直万钱
停杯投箸不能食　拔剑四顾心茫然
欲渡黄河冰塞川　将登太行雪满山
闲来垂钓碧溪上　忽复乘舟梦日边
行路难　行路难　多歧路　今安在
长风破浪会有时　直挂云帆济沧海

这也是前面一个八行诗组，又可分为两个四行诗组；后面的六行诗组，虽不完全整齐，有四行是三字句，但前面的八行诗组与后面的六行诗组之间有一个顿挫，这也是同意大利的十四行诗形式完全一致的。

有人也许认为李白的古风体诗一般都是由若干四行诗组合成，其中有些偶然是六行诗组，所举各诗都是此例，只是在行数上同西方的十四行诗巧合，算不得是真正的十四行诗，但是前面所举各例都是两个四行诗组加上末尾一个六行诗组；至少这可以说明李白的古体诗常常喜欢用这个组合。李白的时代比西西里岛的披埃·德勒·维奈要早好几百年，维奈只留下一首十四行诗，而前面随便举出的李白的十四行诗则已有四五首之多，因此不管李白的诗歌影响到西方这一假设是否能成立，如果我们说李白是世界上最早使用这种诗歌体裁的鼻祖，似乎也不算过分。

下面我还想把唐代盛行的绝句体同莪默凯延的鲁拜体(Rubai)作一比较。大家都知道莪默大约生于公元1048年，死于公元1123年。他的出生地方是呼罗珊(Khurasan)省的首府尼沙波尔(Nishapur)，靠近阿姆河，在波斯(今伊朗)的东北部，也就是说，离今日的阿富汗不远。鲁拜体诗在公元十一世纪到十二世纪间盛行于波斯东北一带，这正是莪默的时代。实际上，莪默也并不是首创这种诗体的第一人，这种诗体的起源可能还要早一些。据传说，古代波斯人鲁达吉(Rudaki)在今阿富汗境内的嘎兹尼(Ghazni)城，看到小孩子们玩核桃，并唱着："滚呀，滚呀，滚到巷子那头去呀!"他就用这个调子创作了这种诗体。这当然只是民间传说，不足以证明鲁达吉就是鲁拜诗体的创始者，但至少可以说明鲁拜诗体大概起源于民间歌谣，而且早在公元十世纪就出现了，因为鲁达吉死于公元941年，还有，这种歌谣形式很可能是从阿富汗传到伊朗境内的。

鲁拜(Rubai)的原意是四行诗，在这四行中，第一行、第二行和第四行需要押韵，第三行不押韵，所以在形式上同我们唐代盛行的绝句是很像的。这种诗体在古代波斯又，被称为"塔兰涅"(Taraneh)，意思正是"断章"或"绝句"。两种诗体形式既然相似，名称又如此相同，说明两者之间很可能有某种联系。从时间和地域方面来看，如果说鲁拜体是从唐代绝句演变而来，这并不是不可能的。这个假设也并未为我首创，一位意大利学者包沙尼(Alesandro Bausani)就曾经指出，鲁拜体可能来自中亚的西突厥，而且他也认为可能与唐代的绝句同出一源。我们知道突厥人于公元1031年越过阿姆河，从东方侵入波斯境内，并在1041年占领了莪默的出生城市尼沙波尔，这正是莪默出生前八年。鲁拜体既然可能起源于民间歌谣，很可能是由西突厥从中国传播过去的。

关于莪默凯延所用的鲁拜体在中亚盛行于公元十世纪前后的问题，不少西方学者还认为这与当时在中亚流行的一种宗教派，苏菲派(Sufism)有关，这种信奉苏菲教派的人是一种在野修行的隐士，穿粗布衣裳，一说苏菲(Sufi)这个字即指粗布衣裳而言，但他们不反对耽乐饮酒，他们的人生观和世界观很类似我们唐代不得意的在野文士，吟诗饮酒，以教和道教思想寄托自己的理想。相传为莪默凯延所写的鲁拜体四行诗就反映了这种思想感情。唐代李白的不少诗篇的内容也与此非常相似，我们可以引下面的一首著名绝句为例：

问余何事栖碧山　笑而不答心自闲
桃花流水窅然去　别有天地非人间

由此可见，不但鲁拜诗体在形式上很像我国唐代的绝句，就是在思想内容上，同某些唐代文人的诗篇也是很相似的。从历史时代和地理条件来看，李白的诗歌传到中亚，影响了当地的诗歌创作，这也并不是不可能的事。

当然，以上我提出的假设，由于西方十四行诗和莪默凯延的鲁拜诗体与我国唐代诗歌的可能联系，实际上是属于中西交通史性质的探讨，已经不完全是属于比较文学研究的范围。从比较文学方面来看，我们把不同国家或地域的文学作品或现象加以比较，并不要求证明两者之间一定要有直接影响的关系。历史时代上或地域上距离很远的文学，即使两者之间不可能有任何实际联系，也可以拿来比较。但是我们中国学者们是历史唯物论者，我们认为文学艺术是人类社会活动的一种反映。在不同时代和不同地域的人，如果他们属于类似地位的社会阶层，具备类似的社会条件，经受类似的社会压迫，就可以有类似的思想感情，即使他们在时代和地域上距离很远，不可能有任何直接或间接的相互影响。相反，即使在同一地区，属于不同阶级的人，却可以具有完全不同的思想感情，这就是如鲁迅所说过的，《红楼梦》里的焦大和林妹妹，虽然都在大观园内，却并没有共同的审美观念。我们不能同意某些西方学者从人性论出发的观点，认为只要是人，就会有相同的思想感情。比较文学是一门新兴的学科，我们认为只有坚持科学的反映论，认为文学是人类社会在一定的物质条件下的产物，比较文学这个学科才能有坚实的可靠的基础。无论唐代李白的某些诗篇是否曾经直接影响过中亚和欧洲的诗歌，我们认为中外文学上这种偶合现象也总是可以给以科学的解释的。

（选自杨宪益：《试论欧洲十四行诗及波斯诗人莪攻默凯延的鲁阿体与我国唐代诗歌的可能联系》，《文艺研究》1983 年第 4 期，第 23-26 页。）

中国现代文学在日本

[日]中岛健藏

【导读】

中岛健藏(1903—1979)是日本东京人，评论家，法国文学研究家，日中文化交流协会前会长(参见裘之倬主编，《中共党史人名录》，重庆出版社1986年版，第525页)。一生中主要研究法国文学、日本现代文学、艺术社会学、新闻学和法学，作品比较丰富。他生前多次访问中国，于1979年5月任中日文化交流协会会长，是新中国成立后中日两国文化交流事业的开拓者之一。此文是中岛健藏应约于1959年创作于东京，当时中日尚未恢复邦交，中日间仅有的民间往来主要限于文化交流。由于日本在"二战"等一系列事件中给中国人民和亚洲其他国家人民带来前所未有的深重灾难，同时日本并未在亚洲范围内尤其针对受害最深的中国民众进行道歉并深刻反省战争罪行，日本与亚洲各受害国关系未走上常轨，所以中日之间的交流主要限于民间，日本方面有良知且较为开明的学者以中岛健藏为代表积极走出第一步，为中日文化交流做出了巨大贡献。

翻译学最早在西方并不从属于比较文学而是单独作为一门学科存在，中国的翻译学则早在佛教经典文学作品翻译时就已开始。媒介学的概念最早出现在法国学者梵第根(Paul van Tiegh-em)的《比较文学论》(参见梵第根:《比较文学论》，戴望舒译，吉林出版集团责任有限公司2010年版)中，探讨了媒介学研究的四个对象，即国与国之间、文学与文学之间起到桥梁作用的人或者物。随着比较文学在中国20世纪70年代的发展和兴起，翻译逐渐摆脱媒介学而进入了译介学的解释范畴。作为比较文学的翻译研究，译介学最早是在20世纪80年代由中国学者提出，在随后比较文学相关论著中关于译介学的概念也被不断界定不断完善，但是关于译介学不同于翻译学纯粹对某些语言现象的理解和表达而更是一种文学或文化研究的观点引起很大争论。

中外文学的交流可谓源远流长，中国自远古以来文化和文学经典就不断向周边国家和地区传播而形成巨大影响，在亚洲形成汉字文化圈，有的文学典籍通过传播，经过西方作家的翻译和再创作在新环境中获得新的生命力再次产生巨大影响。同时，中国也不断引入和吸收来自域外的文化和文学经典，如印度佛教文化的引入和近现代西方和日俄文学的影响，使得本国的文学在发展过程中不断得到丰富，形成自己独有的特征。中日两国是一苇可航的邻国，中日两国有记录的文化交流历史就有两千多年了，中国的思想文化最初主要通过朝鲜半岛流传到日本，最早的记录是《古事记·应神天皇》以及随后的《日本书纪》中所记录的公元三世纪日本应神天皇之子稚郎子拜和迩吉师即王仁为师学习《论语》，这也是最早有关日本接受并学习中国文献典籍的记录，《古事记》和最早的诗歌总集《万叶集》都是汉字写成，汉字既表义，又表音。古代日本文学的发展深深受到中国文学的影响，比如《源氏物语》不仅深受中国佛教文化的影响，同时大量引用了中国的典故和史实。但是要看到这种影响并非只是单纯的借鉴或者引用，而是在其美学基调"物哀"的基础上吸收了中国的文学和文化，是一种融合。事实上，每一个民族的文学在发展过程中都是选择性吸收外来文学与文化因素与本民族的审美相结合，创造出有别于"原型"而独居自身特点的文学。中日两国的文学影响并非单向，古代日本在中国的传播虽然比不上中国文学在日本的影响，但对中国文学的影响也确实有一定力度，如明万历年间李言恭等编纂的《日本考》中就收集了51首和歌的汉译文，是佛教典籍外最早的外国文学译本(参见严绍璗、中西进:《中日文化交流史》6文学卷，浙江人民出版社1996年版，第5页)。

在日本明治维新时期，其迅速成为资本主义国家，中日两国的经济、政治关系迅速发生转变。日本一方面受到西方先进科技文化影响，同时也迅速而大量学习西方文学、俄罗斯文学。中国资产阶级改良者开始学习日本的经验以寻找救治中国的道路，大批留学青年来到日本，很多西方思想文化典籍通过日本的引入，转而对中国的资产阶级民主主义革命者产生影响，一些重要的日本文学作家和作品也通过译介进入到中国，影响到中国文学的发展。

明治维新以来，日本政府逐步严格控制媒体和教育机构，镇压无政府主义者和共产主义者以控制国民思想，民族主义为主流的思想在文学界甚嚣尘上，日本进步作家集体失声。战后日本战争罪行未得到彻底清算，军国主义未彻底根除，安保体制派的保守政府对民主主义思想强力打压，通过在权力机构上设置特殊监察部门和颁布相关政策控制国民，中岛健藏本人甚至都直接受到右翼的威胁。但天皇至上的精神世界土崩瓦解让日本民众开始反思战争，尤其是进步作家希望通过文学创作来唤醒自我意识，建立民主社会。本文也反映了当时日本文学希望从中国进步作家作品中吸收养分以帮助日本建立民主社会的渴求。需要注意的是日本的"反战文学"更多的是从其作为战争受害者的角度来反思战争带来的影响，或者强调外界因素的影响，比如认为日本帝国主义带给中国人民的伤害是由于西方帝国主义和文化对日本的影响，并未真正从日本作为战争发起者和加害者的角度来剖析日本作为一整个所有国民都参与的战争机器所存在的问题并明确责任，提及日本的战争罪行和责任则模棱两可、态度暧昧，甚至压根都不提。也有大江健三郎这样的正义作家明确指出日本应该承认战争罪行，对受害国进行道歉并予以赔偿。(参见王智新:《日本"反战文学":以受害者面目出现，模糊侵略战争性质》，《文艺报》2015年8月28日第四版)。

(黄惠)

日本文学从诞生的那一天开始，就是在它的母乳中国文学的哺育下成长起来的。当然，日本民族有它独特的文化，有它自己流传下来的口头文学，但是，要把它们用文字记载和保存下来，却必须借助于汉字。日本文学的历史，本来是不能离开中国文学的历史而单独存在的，但是，这种亲密的关系。由于十九世纪中叶以后西欧文化很快的流入日本，而受到很大影响。西欧文学虽然也使日本文学产生了新的思潮，不过这已是历史的陈迹。现在，在日本翻译或研究西欧文学的风气虽然也还很盛，但为了日本文学将来的发展，日本作家必须从西方的压迫状态中解脱出来。为此，我们认为：必须从新的角度重新发掘和评价日本文学传统中的优秀成分，同时以新的眼光看待和学习中国文学。

就是在西欧文学影响很大的时期，在日本人之中，也有很多人爱好中国文学，日中两国作家的来往也曾经是频繁的。但是，这已是过去的事情。目前，我们正在完全新的意义上进行中国文学的研究工作。我自己也是最近才开始学习中国文学的，因此，我并不是最适于向中国朋友报告中国现代文学在日本的情况的人。但是，从上述的说明中，总可以了解原来是学习西洋文学的我，为什么在年过五十的时候，会产生学习中国文学的欲望。

我们对中国文学的兴趣并不单单是从艺术的角度产生的，当然，也不是出自个人爱好。现在，日本广泛深入地开展了促进和实现日本民主化的运动。但是，反对这个运动、企图保护少数特权阶级利益的反动势力，也根深蒂固地存在着，并且到处和民主力量发生冲突。有人说，日本的现状在许多方面都像中国清朝末期。当然，这是比喻，不宜就此肯定下来。但我考虑向目前的中国学习时，至少是从政治上感到目前的日本是显著地落后了，争取日本民主化的斗争，今后人必须经受严酷的考验，克服很多困难。

研究中国的现代史，会给我们日本人以极其宝贵的教训。而这种宝贵的教训，由于研究中国现代文学，就更使我们感到亲切，给我们以勇气。中国的历史和日本的历史并不相同，但是两国的关系就无法和两国各自的历史隔离开来，过去帝国主义和西欧文化同时流入日本，致使中国一直遭到日本帝国主义的很大的压迫和残害。同时，在日本国内由于国家政权的压迫，日本国民争取民主化的运动，还在萌芽时期就被扼杀了。这种体验对于我们是一种不堪忍受的痛苦记忆。但是，我认为，对于目前的日本人说来，一条最好的道路，就是受得住这种痛苦，并且认识到这种痛苦就是将来会给我们带来希望的良药。

中华人民共和国成立后的中国文学已经有了十年的历史，战后日本积极地开展中国现代文学的翻译工作，解放后的文学作品也被介绍过来。郭沫若、茅盾、老舍、赵树理等人的名字在日本读者中是很熟悉的。关于这些作家，日本读者不只是读他们解放后的作品，他们的名字是由于中华人民共和国成立前的作品而在日本人中间受到敬重。不过，他们在中华人民共和国成立前的作品，日本也多半是在战后翻译出版的。郭沫若的《中国古代社会研究》，1935年已成日文，而《屈原》却是1952年翻译的。茅盾的《子夜》、《腐蚀》和《霜叶红似二月花》，都是在战后翻译出版而被广泛阅读的。老舍的《四世同堂》和赵树理的《李家庄的变迁》，也都使战后日本的广大读者受到感动。

中国现代文学作品翻译成日文的工作，在战前，政治上受到许多限制，出版困难。当时，一般书籍的出版也没有自由，特别是对于政治方面的尖锐批评，不管其目的何在，一概都难以发表。中国现代文学里包含着许多反抗日本帝国主义和军国主义的事实，因此，当时的日本政府不欢迎其翻译出版，乃是当然的事情。在日本作家之中，也有人因为发表了描写战争的真实情况的文章而受到控告和裁判，因此，大多数日本人都为避免这种危险而保持缄默；反之，中国的作家却冒着生命的危险参加抗战。

从战前就作为广大日本读者熟悉的作家，不用说，当然是鲁迅了。直到战后的今天，我们虽然有广大人民阅读中国文学作品，但想学习中国作家生活道路的日本人，却为数不多，这对我们说来，乃是最大的憾事。现在，我们开始注意这一问题，从这一点看来，也可以说我们在开始以新的认识全面地阅读中国现代文学。

我的任务并不是开列战后介绍给日本读者的中国现代文学作品的目录。我只想回顾一下其中促使我们提出问题的一些作品。

中国文学是由毛泽东主席的《在延安文艺座谈会上的讲话》，指出了统一的方向，在日本已是众所周知的。关于"文学为什么人"的问题，也是日本从开展无产阶级文学运动以来就讨论过的，但直到现在也未得到较好的解决，日本作家尚未自觉地认识到它的意义。因为日本的政治现状恶劣，文学家常常对政治本身有所怀疑，而躲到个人主义的小天地里去；中华人民共和国成立前的中国文学的历史，正是批判这种倾向的很好的参考。我觉得，就是为了不陷入对政治绝望的不幸的深渊里去，我们也需要中国现代文学。联系到这个问题，在翻译出版黄谷柳的虾球传时，我们曾经就采用容易为人民理解的传统形式来表现有教育意义的内容的问题，展开过讨论。

日本的现实，仍然需要像清末李宝嘉的《官场现形记》那样的暴露文学。中华人民共和国成立前的中国作家是怎样暴露这种恶劣的现实和表现生活在这种恶劣的现实中的人民疾苦，怎样表现他们自己一方面有着改革社会的志愿，同时又因本身存在的矛盾而引起的苦闷和斗争，等等，也是值得当前日本文学界作为重要参考的问题之一。研究这样的中国文学，可以了解当时中国人民过的是怎样的生活，作家们是怎样感受这种生活的。

由于国内政治情况的不同，要将中华人民共和国成立后中国评价文学的标准全盘带入日本文学里来，我想那是不自然的事。但是，应该如何批判充满苦闷的日本文学的现状，那么中华人民共和国成立后的中国对之前文学的评价，显然会给我们宝贵的启示。

冈崎俊夫在1952年翻译的李广田的《引力》，使日本读者受到强烈的感动。那是在茅盾的《腐蚀》翻译出版之前，许广平的《夜记》和郭沫若的《亡命十年》等作品尚未翻译的时候，李广田的这部作品，对日本读者起了"苦口良药"的作用，那是当然的事了。

其次，不能忘记的是《高玉宝》。连文字还不大熟悉的作者高玉宝，一面在文字上请教别人，一面写成的这部作品初稿，在专业作家帮助之下，提高了质量。这一事实，也给了我们很大刺激，因为当时我们怀着一种十分强烈的愿望：除了已有的安于消费生活的作家以外，还要从工人农民中间产生民主文学的作家。

1956年，仓石武四郎编的《现代中国文学全集》第十五卷《人民文学篇》介绍的作家有张天翼、萧三、李季、田间、艾芜、康濯、马烽、胡可、马凡陀、邵子南、高玉宝等人。从前，访问日本或是在日本待过的中国作家，本来是很多的，但因为后来发生不幸的战争，两国文学的交流几乎完全断绝，因此对于日本的读者说来，关于中华人民共和国成立后的中国文学现状，很少有了解的机会，并会有过一段空白的时期。但是，很多日本读者是希望了解中国现代文学的，从这部《人民文学篇》在读者强烈要求之下发展成为全集的事实，也可以清楚地看到这一点了。

中国现代文学和日本文学的关系，从1957年11月10日在北京由中国作家协会和日本文艺家协会共同发表联合声明时起，进入了新的时期，当时，中国作家协会在联合声明上签字的是周扬、邵荃麟、臧克家、吴组缃，陈白尘、严文井、萧三。在那份联合声明中约定："两国文学工作者对于为了促进两国文化的发展，必须进一步加强文学工作者与作品的交流，取得了完全一致的意见，并愿意尽一切力量促进实现。"

在这份联合声明产生之前，我们曾经欢迎郭沫若、许广平、谢冰心、曹禺等人访问日本。由于以梅兰芳为首的京剧代表团访问日本，还开始了戏剧界的交流。早就和日本有着密切关系的欧阳予倩等人也在日本受到我们的欢迎。日本作家也有很多人被邀请前往中国访问，由于两国文学家的直接接触的刺激，我们对中国现代文学的关心，更加强烈起来。

现在的日本文学有着种种病症，而这种病症又是日本社会病症的反映。当确实感觉到这种病症而想努力克服时，作家必须改变态度。遗憾的是，大部分日本作家并不是为了这样的目的从事劳动，因此，必须根据日本的现状，发起一个新文学运动。我们现在所希望发起的文学运动，将是不会从脱离政治的文学中产生的。日本现代文学的最大病症，就是有人相信政治运动和创作活动是不能两立的。我们认为：对于这种病症的最有效的良药，就是研究中国的现代文学，从中学习更多的经验。(特约稿)

(1959.8.30 于东京)

李芒译

(选自[日]中岛健藏：《中国现代文学在日本》，《世界文学》1959 年第 9 期，第 89-93 页。)

翻译者的任务

（节选）

[德]本雅明

【导读】

瓦尔特·本雅明（Walter Benjamin，1892—1940），德国犹太裔学者，20世纪最具影响力的文学评论家和哲学家之一。本文是他为波特莱尔《巴黎风貌》的德译本的导言。

《翻译者的任务》一文表达富含哲学道理并且带有宗教神秘性，其意义晦涩难懂却又极具启发性，引起一个多世纪以来学者们的不断解读。在文中，本雅明以隐喻的方式将语言分为三个等级：上帝的语言（纯语言）、人的语言和物的语言。上帝的语言是最高级的语言，具有神性和创作力。翻译是将语言从低级（人类语言）到高级（上帝的语言）的一个跨越。翻译不但点燃了原作永恒生命和语言不断更新之火，而且翻译是从人的语言转换到神的语言的必经之路，只有翻译才能将纯语言从源语言中解放出来，进而无限接近上帝的语言。在理解上帝的纯语言之前，需要理解“样式”“意图”“亲属关系”等关键术语。理解翻译的“式样”必然要理解原作的可译性，如果翻译是一种样式，那么可译性必然是某些作品的一个本质特征。“意图”决定原作的流传和繁荣，“意图”不是任何单一的语言可以通过其自身实现的，只能通过各种语言一切互补的意图的总体来实现，而总体意图即是纯语言。“亲属关系”存在于各种语言之间，翻译能深刻而清晰地揭示语言之间的亲属关系。

翻译者的任务在于在译作语言中创造出原作，为此，他必须找到作用于这种语言的意图性。翻译直接指向语言本身和语言的总体，译作的最大主旨是将很多语言合并成一种真正的语言，译作中的各种语言本身通过各自意义的形式互相补充、交融达到和谐。翻译最了不起，也是唯一的功能是将语言从传递意义的重负中解脱出来，在语言的长流中获得纯语言，这种纯语言不再意指或表达任何东西，它依存在所有语言中间。译者的任务就是在自己的语言中将纯语言从另一种语言的魔咒中释放出来，通过再创造将囚禁于一部作品中的语言解放出来。翻译家的根本错误在于他保持了本国语言的一种偶然状态，而不是让自己的语言受到外语的强烈影响，尤其从那些同自己的语言相距很远的语言翻译的时候，他必须集中精力注意作品、意象和语调的会合点，他必须通过外语来拓宽和深化自己的语言。一切翻译所固有的最大危险是译者已经拓展、修饰了的语言之门可能会一下子关上，并将译者囚禁在沉寂之中，意义陷入一个接一个的深渊，直到在语言的无底深渊中遭遇失落的威胁为止。只有《圣经》才可能避免这样的危险，在《圣经》中，意义消失，文本和真理或教义是同一的，它本身就应该是纯语言，文本无条件地具有可译性。《圣经》的隔行对照译本是一切译作的典范和理想。

本雅明从神学和语言哲学角度提出了上帝的纯语言，纯语言似乎只能在上帝那里才能实现。然而，既然上帝讨厌人类犯的原罪，也毁灭了人类制造的巴别塔，造成了人类语言的混乱与堕落，上帝还会考虑让人类回到纯粹语言状态之中吗？这个问题的答案也许是他徘徊在某种希望和失望状态的思考，是他辩证的敏锐和才华的映射。

（潘丹丹）

翻译家的任务在于在译作语言中创造出原作，为此，他必须找到作用于这种语言的意图效果，即意向性。这就是翻译从根本上同诗人的作品区别开来的一个特征，因为后者的努力从未像翻译这样直接指向语言本身和语言的总体，而仅仅是直接指向特定的语言环境。和文学作品不同，翻译不把自身置于语言丛林的中心而是于丛林之外。眺望树木茂盛的山岭，它向丛林深处呼喊却不进人其中，全神贯注地注视着那个唯一的、在自己异质的语言中能产生原作的回声的地方。不仅仅翻译的目的与文学作品的目的不同——它指向作为整体的语言，而将另一种语言里的单一作品视为出发点——而且它也是一种全然不同于文学创作的劳作。诗人的意图是自发的、原始的、生活的；而翻译家的意图则是派生的、终极的、观念的。因为译作的最大主旨是将许多种语言合并成一种真正的语言。真正的语言是这样一种语言：其中独立的句子、文学作品、批评判断永远都不可能彼此沟通——因为他们都依赖于翻译；然而在译作里，各种语言本身却通过各自意义的形式互相补充、交融达到和谐。如果说存在着一种真理的语言，这种语言是所有思想为之奋斗的、没有冲突的终极真理的无声的宝库，那它就是真正的语言。而正是这种语言，其先见悟性，其描绘能力是一个哲学家所期望的唯一完美境界，它以一种浓缩的方式隐藏在翻译之中。既没有哲学的缪斯，也没有翻译的缪斯。尽管多愁善感的艺术家如此一口咬定，可哲学和翻译都是非实用的东西。有这样一位哲学天才，其典型特征便是渴望那种能够使用于翻译的语言出现。“各种语言的不完美之处在于其多重性，缺少一种尽善尽美的语言：思即所写，而不需要附加成分或者暗示，不朽的语词仍然保持着缄默；人世间习用语的差异性使每个人都不可能说出那些立刻使之像真理一样具体化的语词。”如果马拉美所说的这番话对于哲学家来说是完全可以理解的话，那么翻译，因为其中蕴含着这种真正的语言的基本因素，就处于诗与教义中间。虽然翻译作品的特性几乎没有得到过清楚的界定，可是它们却对历史产生了不小的影响。

如果从这种角度来看待翻译家的任务，那么解决问题的途径就更加晦暗不清、令人费解了。确实，在译作中如何使纯语言的种子成熟这一问题似乎是不可解决的。因为，如果意义的再创造不再是决定性的，难道不是就已经失去解答这一问题的基础吗？从相反的角度来看，这的确是前面所有论述的意义所在。在任何有关翻译的讨论中，传统的翻译观念都要求泽作既要忠实原文，又要不拘一格——既有再创造的自由，又须在再创造中忠实地逐字对译。对于一种意欲在翻译中寻求别的东西而不是再创造的意义的理论来说，这些观念似乎不再有什么用处。的确，传统的习惯用法使“忠实”和“自由”这些术语总是处于冲突状态。忠实难道真的对传递意义有什么用处吗？在译作中，对个别词语的忠实翻译，几乎永远不可能完全再现它们在原文中的意义。因为诗意的意蕴并非局限于字面意义，而是来自精心挑选的词语所表达的内涵。我们所说的词语都具有感情内涵。逐字逐句地对译完全摧毁了复制意义的理论，而且对可理解性造成直接威胁。19 世纪，人们将荷尔德林翻译的索福克勒斯的剧本看成是这种逐字逐句对译的怪例。它最终证明了形式上的忠实复制给传递意义带来了多大的妨碍。因此，任何逐字逐句的翻译都不能指望保留原作的意义，而拙劣译者的无节制的随意性虽然在传达意义上做得相当不错，然而对文学和语言本身则毫无益处。因此，逐字逐句直译仍然有其必要性，其正当性是显而易见的，而其合理根据则晦暗不明，必须在一个更有意义的语境中对直译加以理解。要把一个容器的碎片重新粘合成一个容器，这些碎片的形状虽然不必相似，但必须能彼此吻合。同样，译作不必与原作的意义相似，但必须煞费苦心地、从每个细节上与原作意义的形式融为一体，这样就使原文与译文都能够辨认都像是一种更高级的语言的碎片，就像它们本是一个容器的碎片。鉴于此，译作必须尽量避免想要传达什么，或是表达意义，而原作之所以对译作重要，就是因为它已经免去了译者和译作要组织和表达什么的劳累。在翻译界，“太初有言”这句话同样适用。另外，译作的语言能够——事实上必须——使自己从意义中解放出来以便再现原作的意图，这不是复制，而是一种与原作的和谐，是对原作语言的补充，从而这是译作自己的意图。所以，说翻译读起来仿佛就像是用这种语言写作的一样，并不是对它的最高褒扬，尤其是在译作刚刚问世的时代。相反，直译所确保的忠实之重要性即是译作反映出其对语言互相补充的渴望和追求。真正的翻译是透明的，它不遮盖原作，不挡住原作的光芒，而是让纯语言通过其自身的媒介而得到增强，更加充分地在原作中得以照耀。毕竟，这得依靠直译原文的句式来达到，这种直译证明：对于译者来说，最根本的因素是词语，而不是句子。因为如果说句子是矗立在原作语言面前的墙，那逐字逐句地直译便是拱廊。

翻译中的忠实与自由一向被视为是两种相互冲突的倾向。对其中一种倾向的深入阐释并不能调和两者，事实上，这似乎反而会否认另一种倾向的合理性。因为除了认为传递意义不再重要以外，自由还能意味着什么？除非把文学作品创作的意义和它所传达的信息等同起来，那些终极的、决定性的要素才变得无法传达——它们十分接近但又极其遥远，潜隐着但又是可以辨明的，支离破碎的但又是强有力的。在所有语言及其创造性作品中，除了一些可以转述的东西以外，仍然存在着不可转述的东西，即那些依赖上下文语境显露出来的东西，就是那些象征物和被象征物。前者仅仅存在于有限的语言作品中，而后者存在于诸语言自身的演变中。而在语言的演变过程中力图表现、创造自身，正是纯语言的核心所在。尽管这一核心是潜隐的和支离破碎的，可是作为被象征物自身，这是其生命的积极动力，尽管它只是以象征形式存在于语言作品之中。因为纯语言这一终极本质，在各种语言中仅仅和语言性要素及其变化紧紧相连，而在语言作品中它负载着深邃的、不同的意义。使纯语言从这种重负中解脱出来，将象征物转化为被象征物，在语言的长流中重获纯语言，是翻译最了不起的，也是唯一的功能。这种纯语言不再意指或者表达任何东西，但它作为非表现的、创造性的言语，依存在所有的语言中间，在这种纯语言中，所有的信息、意义和意图最终将碰到一个语言层，在那里，它们注定将湮灭无痕。正是这一语言层为自由的翻译提供了新的、更合适的正当理由，这一理由并非来自所要表达的意义，因为从这种意义中解放出来正是忠实翻译的任务。更确切地说，因为纯语言的缘故，意译作品是在自身语言上经受这一考验的。译者的任务就是在自己的语言中将纯语言从另外一种语言的魔咒中释放出来，是通过再创造将囚禁于一部作品中的语言解放出来。因为纯语言的缘故，他得突破自己语言衰败的障碍。路德、沃斯、荷尔德林和格奥尔格已经拓宽了德语的界域，而意义对于翻译与原作之间的关系有何重要性？为了说明问题，我们不妨打个比方，就像一条切线只在一个点上轻轻与一个圆相切，正是这一相切而不是这一个切点定下了直线沿着其笔直的路径伸向无限的法则，译作同样与原作轻轻相切，只在意义这一个无限小的切点上与原作相切，然后立即沿着根据忠实法则所确定的自己的路径在语言之流中前进。鲁道夫·潘维兹虽然没有给出明确定义或者使之具体化，却描绘了这一自由的真正重要性。他的评论收入了《欧洲文化危机》一书中，与歌德对《西东集》的评论一道，列为迄今为止在德国出版的有关翻译理论的最精当的论述。潘维兹写道：“我们的译作，甚至那些最好的译作，都是从一个错误的前提出发的。这些译作想把印地语、希腊语、英语译成德语，而不是将德语译为印地语、希腊语、英语。我们的翻译家对自己语言的惯用法的尊重远胜于对外国作品的精神的敬意。翻译家的根本错误在于他保持了本国语言的一种偶然的状态，而不是让自己的语言受到外语的强烈影响。尤其从那些同自己的语言相距很远的语言翻译的时候，他必须回到语言本身基本的要素上来，而且必须集中精力注意作品、意象和语调的会合点。他必须通过外语来拓宽和深化自己的语言。”一般说来，人们并未认识到：这种可能性究竟能达到何种程度，语言的形变又可能达到何种程度，语言与语言之间的差异和方言与方言之间的不同是多么的相似。然而，除非我们严肃地看待语言，才能认识到这最后一点的正确性。

译作在何种程度上与这种样式的本质保持一致，客观上取决于原作的可译性。原作语言的品质越低越没有特点，其传递信息的程度越大，为译作生长提供的土壤就越贫瘠，就翻译这一特殊的文字样式来说，内容绝不是一个杠杆，一旦内容具有了绝对优势，要翻译就不可能了。作品的水准越高，其可译性就越大，即使仅仅是在一瞬间触及其含意。当然这只是针对原作而言，而就译作而言，不可译并非是因为译作内在的困难，而是因为其负载意义的形式的松散。荷尔德林的译作为这一观点提供了证明，尤其是索福克勒斯的悲剧的两种译本。在他的译作中，语言之间异常和谐，语言触及意义就像风吹响了“呜呜”的竖琴。荷尔德林的译作是翻译的典范。甚至对于那些最完美的译本来说也是一样，它们是典范中的典范。只要比较一下荷尔德林和鲁道夫·波查特对品达《竞技胜利者颂之三》的不同翻译就可以证明这一点。也正因为如此，荷尔德林的译作特别容易碰到一切翻译所固有的最大危险：译者已经拓展、修饰了的语言之门可能会一下子关上，并将译者囚禁在沉寂之中。荷尔德林所译的索福克勒斯是他最后的作品。意义陷入一个接一个的深渊，直到在语言无底的深渊中遭遇失落的威胁为止。然而，这种危险也有终止的时候。只有《圣经》才可能避免这样的危险，在《圣经》中，意义不再是语言流和启示流的分水岭。在那里，文本和真理或教义是同一的，它本身就应该是纯语言，而不需要意义这一中介，这一文本无条件地具有可译性。在这种情况下，人们只是因为各种语言的不同才需要翻译。就像在《圣经》原文中，语言和启示是同一的，没有张力，所以译作和原作一定是以隔行对照的形式并存的，逐字逐句的直译和不拘一格的自由在其中是结合在一起的。就某种程度而言，所有伟大的文本在字里行间都含有一个潜在的译本。对于那些神圣作品来说，这一真实性是确定无疑的。《圣经》的隔行对照译本是一切译作的典范和理想。

（节选自沃尔特·本杰明著，乔向东译：《翻译者的任务》，《中国比较文学》1999 年第 1 期，第 78-83 页。）

中国诗的翻译

（节选）

［英］A. C. 格雷厄姆

【导读】

格雷厄姆（Angus Charles Graham，1919—1991），英国著名的汉学家之一，对中国诗歌有较深的研究。他以自由体形式翻译了《晚唐诗歌》（*Poems of the Late Tang* 1965），该书在英美两国同时出版，译本成为畅销书之一。本文是其译作《晚唐诗选》的代序言，我国学者张隆溪将其翻译成中文，并收集到其编著的《比较文学译文集》中。

诗歌流传深远的重要因素是其具体的形象，幸运的是，中国诗歌大多写得较为具体。汉英两种语言的语序虽不相同，但是由于英语诗歌中重音节的数目和中国诗歌一行中的字数很接近，将中国诗歌翻译成中文就可以取得更大的进步。然而，汉语词汇的意义及其引发的联想和英语词汇差别相当大，由此产生形象上的忠实和原诗的格律形式之间的冲突。意象派的理论确定之后，内容和形式的冲突得以成功解决，英语不仅可以表达出汉诗视觉形象的精确性、直接的感染力和含蓄的情绪，还可以表达出汉诗中自由的节奏和自然的用语。另一方面，汉字的结构不是一个简单的问题，有人以为要把汉诗的一切传达出来，就必须增加词汇，这样显然破坏了汉诗的简洁性，其英译文显得特别啰嗦。而盛唐时期的诗歌喜欢用典，译者不得不加上大量的注释，这是否可取受到质疑，至少在威利（Arthur Waley，1888—1966）那里，他喜欢翻译那些译成英语后损失最少的诗作。中国诗歌早在公元766年杜甫的诗歌中就开始趋于复杂，但是英国处于反浪漫主义运动的重要关头，对这一时期的诗，人们最不感兴趣的便是汉诗的神秘性，因此这一时期的中国诗歌翻译的都非常明朗，其直接后果是英国读者所认识的中国诗歌和20世纪20年代诗歌革新者们所见的的样子几乎没有变化。事实上，理想的译文应包含所有最复杂的含义和语言。

晚唐诗将中文的表现力发挥到极限。但由于印欧语言必须有准确的人称、数和时态，汉诗译文便遭到严重的破坏。受到《圣经》英译本的启发，洋泾浜英语（Literary Pidgin English）是保留中文复义性的解决办法之一，原因在于洋泾浜英语比标准英语更能自由地处理原文。晚唐诗中的另一个问题是用典，典故的知识（译文）读者不一定感兴趣，而且这类知识也不一定有益。一方面，读者不了解用典也能看懂诗歌，用典也不会让读者对诗歌造成深刻印象；另一方面，用典的各种注释性文字出处不一，因此本选集中(《晚唐诗选》)一般不去理会这些典故。尽管如此，晚唐诗的艰深有利于诗人的个人风格的凸显。庞德也好，威利也好，读者很容易辨别出他们的译文风格，但是却认不出他们所译的原诗作者之间千姿百态、丰富多彩的差别，读者从译文中看到的中国文明显得过于统一和单调，而晚唐诗的复杂恰好是纠正这些错误看法的机会。最后，不得不提诗歌翻译和诗歌创作之间的关系。虽然汉诗中的意象可以使英译文的韵律和词句变得生动，但是译者毕竟是用英语来想象汉语，结果可想而知，译文的词句肯定不会十分妥当和完美。因此，译成英文而取得真正诗歌的地位的很少一些外国诗，并不是依靠原文获得价值的诗作，原因可能在于原诗中可以重现在译文中的内容太少。模仿者的缺点虽然明显，但谨小慎微、学术气十足的译文也是一个错误。庞德的《中国》意味着译诗的界限，然而他完全有理由将一首改变了原诗、修改了的译文归入他的创作。

意象派受到日语俳句诗歌形式和中国象形文字的影响，提出诗歌的精髓在于意象，于是翻译中国诗的艺术成为意象派运动意想不到的重大收获。

(潘丹丹)

把中文的表现力发挥到极限的晚唐诗，如果勉强加上印欧语言不相干的准确的人称、数和时态，往往会遭到严重破坏。代词的使用便是一个例子，而且可以应用于晚唐以前的作品。中国诗人很少用“我”字，除非他自己在诗中起一定作用(如卢全的《月蚀》)，因此他的情感呈现出一种英文中很难达到的非个人性质。在李商隐描写妇女的某些诗里，究竟应该加上“我”(即从她的观点来看)还是“她”(即从诗人的观点来看)，这是一个无法回答而且难以捉摸的问题。仅仅由于英语语法要求动词要有主语而加上的“我”字，可以把一首诗完全变成抒发一种自以为是或自我怜悯的情绪。李贺是一个特别注意时光流逝的诗人，在翻译李贺诗的时候，时态、从句时态的一致等都常常造成麻烦。下面是他的《官街鼓》诗中的几行：

汉城黄柳映新帘，
柏陵飞燕埋香骨。
磓碎千年日长白，
孝武秦皇听不得。
从君翠发芦花色，
……

The willows of the Han capital shine yellow on the new blinds,
Flying Swallow's scented bones lie buried in the cypress mound;
It has pounded to pieces a thousand years of suns for ever white
Unheard by the King of Ch'in and Emperor Wu.
Your hair that glinted blue, is the color, of the blossoms on the reeds…

虽然原文里甚至在第三行也没有时间小品词，我在初稿里却译成这样：

The willows of the Han capital shone yellow on the new blinds,
When flying swallow's scented bones were buried in the cypress mound;
It has pounded to pieces a thousand years of suns for ever white
Unheard by the King of Ch'in and Emperor Wu.
Your hair that glinted blue is the color, of the blossoms on the reeds…

修改过的译文重新传达出了中文那种直接的感染力，不过却可能使读者把芦花误解为翠花而不是白花。但无论哪种译文，都能把原诗将今非昔比而为一的想象割裂开了。

保留中文复义性的一种可能的解决办法是，把译文写成一种文学洋泾滨英语(literary pidgin English)。《圣经》的英译本是一切英译文中最成功的作品，它故意把英文写得像闪族语，在句子开头用“And...”而不是希伯来语的小品词省去；为什么在译文作品中不采取类似的办法呢？这种办法之所以特别值得一试，还因为二十年代的现代派诗歌很反感逻辑的连接词，认为这类词妨碍诗人达到一种表现纯粹的感觉的语言，于是逐渐倾向于一种中文式英语(Sino-English)。有几位译者做过这一类的实验，例如威利译的汉武帝的《秋风辞》。由于种种原因，我自己做的这种实验都很不成功。本文所引的几个例子就可以证明，严格地逐字对译既能破坏英文句法，又不能使读者懂得汉语的句法；为了能让人读懂，这种译文还要求每一个中文词都是一个几乎完全对应的词，因为这种逐字对译根本不可能通过句子的调整来弥补词义的偏差。因此，洋泾滨英语的译文要能够独立存在，也许不得不比标准英语的译文更自由地处理原文。然而，自从威弗雷德·欧文(Wilfred Owen)在不和谐音韵方面做过一些实验以来，英国人的耳朵对半韵(part-rhymes)已经习惯了，把半韵和洋泾滨英语的译法结合起来，也许能取得比目前更大的成就。王文(Wong Man)的笨拙然而独特的译文在这方面很有启发性，他的某些译诗读起来很像是用英文写的汉语诗：

Grass rustle through dim Woods,
Warrior shoots into night,
Dawn finds arrow-plume
Lost in rocky heights.

Black moon geese fly high,
Tartars flee the dark,
Light horses pursue,
Sword and bow-marked.①

① 王文，《中国诗选》(香港古籍评议社)，第29页。此处所译诗为卢纶《塞下曲》。

但是这几行译诗并不比标准英语的译文更直接对应于原文，而且有点过于简单化：

林暗草惊风，
将军夜引弓，
平明寻白羽，
没在石棱中。

Woods dim, grass startled by the wind:
In the night the general draws his bow.
At dawn they seek the white feather
Loat among the corners of the stones.

月黑雁飞高，
单于夜遁逃，
欲将轻骑逐，
大血满弓刀。
Moon black, geese fly high:
The Khan flees in the night.
As they lead out the light horse in pursuit
Heavy snow covers bow and sword.

汉语诗律在历史上不止一次地发生过剧烈变化。一般认为，最早的诗纯粹以音节为基础；但到公元前1世纪时，已经出现诗行长短和韵脚位置的不规则变化，语法上的小品词在为时尚逐渐固定，表明另一种原则，也许是音节轻重强弱的原则开始起作用。在随后的6个世纪里，诗律完全是以音节为基础的，每行都是五音节，后来是七音节。这些诗律规则至今仍然存在，称为“古体”；而从7世纪开始，又出现了以中国字四声为基础的“近体”诗律。本集①中收进的杜甫、杜牧和李商隐等人的大部分作品都是近体诗，这种诗的特点有时在译文中也通过一联当中严格对应的两行表现出来。

八行的律诗中至少中间两联在句法上要讲对仗，每一个字都要和另一行中对应的字在意义上形成对比。例如，前面引用过的杜诗中的一联，“丛”字与“孤”字相对，更突出了菊花的繁茂和一叶扁舟的寂寞，“两”字和“一”字的对比似乎不那么自然，因为“一”字在这里用作副词，有“完全”的意思，但即便如此，这一对比也使人更深切地感受到年复一年时光流逝的变化，以及诗人苦苦思乡而又归去无望的苦闷心情。近体诗中加以系统化的对仗，在古体诗和散文写作中也是常用的手法之一。无需词的重复而要达到严格的对仗，在英语中显然几乎是不可能的，而有词汇重复的对仗又会很快使人感到呆板单调。但在译文中保留原诗字字对应比照这种结构上的特点，却是完全必要的。近体诗绝少用当时某些

① 指A. C. 格雷厄姆译《晚唐诗选》，本文原是这本诗选的代序言。

古风中常用的明喻；“如”字虽然不是完全不用，但却会在互相关联的具体词汇的凝练结构中造成松懈脱节的感觉。杜甫在描写雨后澄清的流水时，不说“白如天河”，而说

天河元自白，
江浦向来澄。①

进一步遇到的问题是，唐诗中越来越多地用典。注诗家对几乎每一行诗都旁征博引地加以解释，引用各种神话、历史和地理知识的标准著作，还有古人用语的例证、已经具有特别联想意义的各种意象在前人作品中的用法，等等。虽然这种逐字引注的习惯会使人觉得处处都有典故，但狭义的文学典故，即不参见某一段文字就无法看懂的地方，即便在最后的晚唐诗中也并不很多，典故的出处不止是古代经典，也常常有民间歌谣。李商隐的《锦瑟》是中国诗中最富于典故暗示性的作品之一，我为这首诗引注了各种注释性文字，但各家的注释出处不一，许多注家都否认这首诗是为前一个世纪一位作家关于诗的名言作注脚。② 除此之外，欧洲读者还需要许多别的知识，需要知道中国人的习惯——“玉”用作形容词不是“玉绿色”而是“白玉”(玉露、雪、月、玉手等)；眉毛的比喻往往和妇女把眉染成青色的风俗有关；一般译成“phoenix”的传说中的吉祥之鸟“凤”，并没有死而复活的神话传说；龙是吉祥的神物，中国人习惯于设想在每一处江河湖海的深渊里都藏着蛟龙；柏树与在西方一样，也意味着墓园和死亡；季节是按阴历计算的，所有诗人在三月里悲叹春光将逝，在七月里秋天便已来临。秋天并非“迷雾和硕果累累”的季节，③ 而是风霜高洁、天明水净，有许多西方人注意不到的迹象——咻咻的蝉鸣、吹落梧桐叶的寒风，(梧桐是一种挺拔而枝干青绿的大树，凤凰只肯在这种树上栖息)，在石砧上捶打寒衣的捣衣声、秋菊、凋零的草木，偶尔还有黄叶。

这类知识有多少是读者感兴趣的呢？同样重要的是，这类知识有多少能真正对他有益呢？20世纪初的英国诗比唐诗用的文学典故还多。我们读艾略特的诗即使不知道他用的大部分典故，也同样能深有所感，而当我们查出他用的典故时，它对于加深我们的感受所引起的作用却小得令人失望。当然，读者要读懂本文所引的第一联诗，似乎必须知道匡衡在汉元帝(公元前48—前33年在位)因日蚀和地震的凶兆而不安时，上书批评时政，受到元帝的赏识；刘向是中国第一位大目录学家，曾为皇家的图书馆收集和编辑古代典籍。然而关于他们的生平知道得再多，也很难为从上下文中已经十分明白的意思中再增添一点东西，这点意思就是诗人把他们作为政治家和学者所取得的成就与自己的失意相对比。无论如何，这联诗译成英语很难给人造成深刻印象，也许用一条注释来耽误读者的时间，还不如让它匆匆走过去为好。

另外，把一个典故解释清楚不一定就能使它在诗中发生影响。李商隐有一行诗说：

---

① 杜甫，《江边星月二首》之一。

② 这里所指作家为戴叔伦。据《困学纪闻》，司空表圣云：戴容州叔伦谓诗家之景，如蓝田日暖，良玉生烟，可望而不可置于眉睫之间也。有人认为李商隐《锦瑟》诗本此。

③ 这是英国浪漫派诗人济慈《秋颂》中描写秋天的名句。

扇戴月魄羞难言。①

一个中国人只需读到“月”字，便知道是写怨情；他也习惯了扇与月的比喻，这个比喻可以追溯到被汉成帝(公元前32—前7年在位)遗弃的班婕妤的《怨歌行》，在那首诗里，她把自己比为被人在秋凉时弃置一旁的白绸团扇：

裁成合欢扇，
团团似明月。

即便有可能逐行译出所有这类联想的意思，作抽象的解释也不能使这些联想对读者起作用；读者需要对诗中意象有一种似曾相识的朦胧意识。(顺便说一句，这并非不可能做到：庞德的《为皇上写的题扇诗》就是班婕妤诗篇的改作。)把使用同一意象的各时代诗作并列起来，编一部译成英文的中国诗选，使李商隐的诗接在班婕妤诗后，也许是颇为有用的；但按目前这种原则编的选集却最好不要去管这类典故，除非他们一再重复出现。还要一类典故其实是缩略的熟语，译者有权灵活处理，如杜牧：

楚腰肠断掌中轻。②

与其去解释楚灵王专宠细腰的美姬，班婕妤的竞争者赵飞燕身轻如燕，可以做掌中舞，还不如简单地译成：

Slim waists of ch'u broke my heart, light bodies danced into my palm.

李贺或李商隐的诗译成英文必然丧失许多东西，但这并不意味着比陶潜或白居易的平易的诗更不宜于翻译。每篇译文都有失真或歪曲原意的地方，一首简单的诗当中牺牲掉的那一小点东西，有可能正是使它成为诗的那点东西。要把白居易的诗译成英文，而不变成极平淡无味的散文，需要威利那种才华和特殊敏感。另一方面，李商隐爱情诗的意象无论有多少微妙的用典暗示，无论格律多么复杂多变，也无论历代注家怎样各说不一，却自有它强大而不会受伤害的生命力，产生于深深触动我们的一种主题，而大多数中国诗的主题都很难像它那样打动我们，它有时在英译文里几乎好像在中文原诗里那样热烈动人。

晚唐诗的艰难还有另一点重要的补偿：不断复杂化的意象使一个诗人的风格在英译文中更容易显现出来。翻译的一个十分恼人的特点，就是译者的个人风格不能不抹杀他处理的各种材料的多样性。庞德和威利都译过陶潜和李白的诗。下面这首诗是谁写的？

Swiftly the years, beyond recall,
Solemn the stillness of this fair morning.

---

① 李商隐，《无题》。
② 杜牧，《遣怀》。

I will clothe myself in spring-clothing
And visit the slopes of the Eastern Hill…
（迈迈时运，
穆穆良朝，
袭我春服，
薄言东郊。①

可以肯定，许多并不熟悉这首诗的读者也会立即认出这是威利而不是庞德的笔调，但是有谁能认出这是陶渊明的诗呢？具有1500年传统的丰富多彩的诗歌，在庞德的《中国》里互相之间区别之小，还不及他的《阿尔达弗特》（*Aitaforte*）和《休·塞尔汶·莫泊利》（*Hugh Selwyn Mauberley*）的区别。仅仅从几篇译作和几本谈艺术的书籍里去了解中国文明的欧洲人，从他站得远远的立场看去，整个中国文明都显得统一而无变化；放过纠正这种错误看法的任何机会都是可惜的。

还有一个所有诗的翻译都会遇到的难题。在一定限度之外，翻译的要求和诗的要求就很难协调一致，译者于是不得不在二者当中作一抉择。部分的一致是可以的，因为至少诗的一个因素，即意象，在另一种语言里也可以有效地起作用。但是，无论意象能使英译文的韵律和词句变得多么生动，译者毕竟还是在把对于一种语言十分自然的想象过程强加给另一种语言。结果可以是，而且也应当是诗——我们不必在此争论怎样才算是诗——但却不会给人那种最终的满足，使人觉得译诗的词句已经做到唯一妥当的、完美的安排，例如，近体诗的对仗在英译文中就成了发挥诗思的一种矫揉造作的手段；译者可以把它稍加变化，但完全不要对仗就不成其为翻译。因此，每一位诗的翻译者都必须作出决定，是在英国读者最能看到莪默·伽亚姆的真面目时就止步呢，还是像爱德华·菲茨杰拉德那样再进一步，在英国诗人的行列中去取得一席地位。②

……

（张隆溪　译）

（节选自A. C. 格雷厄姆：《中国诗的翻译》，张隆溪选编，《比较文学译文集》，北京大学出版社1982年版，第227-235页。）

① 陶渊明，《时运》。

② 英国诗人菲茨杰拉德译波斯诗人莪默·伽亚姆的《鲁拜集》，在英国文学中成为一部佳作，但从翻译角度来看，却并不忠实可靠。

诗词·翻译·文化

(节选)

许渊冲

【导读】

许渊冲，1921年生于江西南昌，北大教授，翻译家，从事翻译工作长达六十余年，主要翻译中英法文作品，被誉为“诗译英法唯一人”。1999年被提名为诺贝尔文学奖候选人，2010年许渊冲被授予“翻译文化终身成就奖”，2014年获得翻译界最高奖项之一的“北极光”杰出文学翻译奖，为第一位获此殊荣的亚洲翻译家。

许渊冲在诗歌翻译方面成就卓越，他根据自己的翻译实践，对严复的“信、达、雅”，鲁迅的直译，林语堂的美学，郭沫若的创作论，朱光潜的艺术论，傅雷的神似，钱锺书的化境等翻译理论继承和发扬，提出了“美化之艺术，创优似竞赛”的文学翻译理论。他提出翻译诗歌需要运用“三美”(音美、形美、意美)原则，就是说当诗歌进行不同语言的翻译时，要注重诗歌本身音节韵律，形式表达和诗歌本身描述意境的美，为了实现“三美”原则，需要运用“三化”(深化、等化、浅化)手法，若两种语言有相似表达，需要使用等化的处理方法，两种语言表达出现偏差时，可以诉诸深化和浅化的翻译方法。深化可以理解为翻译出深层含义如增译、语义翻译、重复等翻译手法的运用。浅化可以理解为把特殊的东西一般化，如省略、音译等翻译手法的运用，从而达到语言的转化。而美也好，化也好，最终目的是让译文读者达到“三之”(知之、好之、乐之)的目的，即理解诗歌、欣赏诗歌、赞美诗歌的目的。许渊冲认为，翻译是两种语言的竞赛，若有更好的表达，则译文应舍弃对等而求竞赛。诗歌翻译应该是艺术，为了诗歌的意象表达的“音美、形美、意美”，译文应当与原文竞赛，以求更好地表达原语诗歌内容。许渊冲独特的文学翻译理论是结合其几十年诗歌翻译经验提出来的，他的翻译观备受翻译界关注，也饱受争议和质疑，引起了多次讨论。当然，在他人争议许渊冲诗歌翻译的理论与实践的不统一时，他重申“实践第一、理论第二”，强调“忠实是译者的天职”。

正如许渊冲本人所说“实践第一、理论第二”，他的诗歌翻译有着鲜明的风格特点，自成一家，很多人情不自禁地拿他的英译本法译本作比较，欣赏研究，赞叹他方法的灵活。许渊冲在国内外出版中英法文著作六十余本，包括《诗经》、《楚辞》、《李白诗选》、《唐诗三百首》、《西厢记》、《红与黑》等中外名作，1994年，英国企鹅出版社出版了他的《中国不朽诗三百首》(1994)，在英美加澳等国同时发行，名片上印着“书销中外四十本，诗译英法唯一人”。其豪情四射，翻译成绩让人赞叹和侧目，他在2014年获得“北极光”杰出文学翻译奖的书面发言中说，“从事汉语、英语和法语文学翻译对我而言是种享受”。

（潘丹丹）

中西文化的差异不但体现在诗词中，而且显示在翻译上，简单说来，西方强调直译，体现了现代的科学精神；中国强调意译，显示了古老的艺术传统。具体说来，叶维廉是美国加州大学教授，他译的《荒原》对号入座，一个中文词对一个英文词，词序一点也不变动，可以算是代表了西方文化的求“真”精神。赵萝蕤是中国北京大学教授，她把自己译的《荒原》说成是“比较彻底的直译法”（见《当代文学翻译百家谈》609页），但和叶维廉的译文一比，可以说是不如叶译彻底。原诗说“四月是最残忍的一个月”，因为四月使生机勃勃的紫丁香长在死气沉沉的大地上，好像把鲜花插在牛粪上一样，所以说四月最残忍。但是赵译说：“荒地上长着丁香”，仿佛是在描写一个客观现象，没有说明丁香和四月的关系，这就不如叶译体现了西方文化的“真”。赵译又说：“让春雨催促那些迟钝的根芽”，“让”字用得还嫌被动，不如叶译“以春天的雨丝”。但是整个读来，赵译却比叶译更“美”，更能显示东方古老的艺术传统。这就是说，叶译虽能使人“知之”，却不能使人“好之”；赵译虽不能使人“知之”甚确，却能使人“好之”更深。

再看方重译的乔叟，不但能够使人“知之”，而且能够使人“好之”，这就比赵译更能体现艺术之“美”。最后来谈范守义的译文，每行十个字，每两行押韵，不但传达了原诗的“形美”，而且传达了原诗的“音美”；虽然不像叶译那样“对号入座”，但也不能说它“失真”，却比方译更“美”；不但使人“知之”、“好之”，而且使人“乐之”，这就可以说是“入于化境”，把英诗化为中诗，使西方文化成为中国文化，进入了翻译的最高境界，比赵译、方译都更能代表中国文化传统之“美”。综上所述，可以得出结论：叶译最能代表西方文化的科学精神，范译最能代表中国文化的艺术传统，赵译、方译却在二者之间。由此可见，翻译也能体现中西文化的异同。

以上谈的是英诗中译，中诗英译也是大同小异。美国人译的杜诗更能体现西方文化的求“真”精神，中国人的译文则更能显示东方文化的求“美”传统。但是姜词《扬州慢》今包含的文化典故太多，没有英美人的译文，只有中国人的译作。这又说明了中美文化的一个差异：中国文化更重视过去，美国文化更重视现在。包含文化典故太多的作品不容易译成外国文学，译文只能使人“知之”，很不容易使人“好之”。徐忠杰把长短句译成大体整齐的诗，每两行押韵，这是把词化诗，恐怕“化”得过分了，不能像范守义的译文那样使人“乐之”。但是，徐译还是显示了中国文化的艺术传统。

《荒原》包括的文化典故也多，它引用了三十五个不同作家的作品，但仅就这一点而言，我觉得它更像中国古代的诗词，而不能代表西方文化的主流。下面我们看看 Robert Frost 一首不包含文化典故的小诗《雪夜过深林》：

Whose woods these are I think I know, 谁家的树林？我想我知道
His house is in the village, though; 虽然他家在遥远的存郊；
He will not see me stopping here 他不会看到我呆在这里
To watch his woods fill up with snow. 看他的树林为白雪笼罩。

My little horse must think it queer 我骑的小马觉得希奇，
To stop without a farmhouse near 待在这渺无人烟的荒地，
Between the woods and frozen lake 在树林边上，结冰的湖旁，
The darkest evening of the year. 在一年中最黑暗的夜里。

He gives his harness bells a shake 我的马摇晃颈上的铃铛，
To ask if there is some mistake. 问我是不是走错了地方。
The only other sound's the sweep 微风扫落鹅毛般的雪片
Of easy wind and downy flake. 是回答他的唯一的声响。

The woods are lovely, dark and deep. 黑暗的深林真令人留恋，
But I have promises to keep, 但我有约会，有约会在先。
And miles to go before I sleep, 路还远着呢，在睡觉之前，
And miles to go before I sleep. 路还远着呢，在睡觉之前。

这首诗很容易让人联想起中唐诗人刘长卿的《逢雪宿芙蓉山主人》：

日暮苍山远，天寒白屋贫。
柴门闻犬吠，风雪夜归人。

译文：

（1）The daylight far is dawning across the purple hill.
And white the houses of the poor with winter's breathing chill.
The house dog's sudden barking, which
hears the wicket go,
Greets us at night returning through
driving gale and snow.

（Tr. W. J. B. Fletcher）

（2）Encountering a snowstorm
I Stay with the Recluse of Mount
Hibiscus
Dark hills distant in the setting sun,

Thatched hut stark under the wintry skies.
A dog barks at the brushwood gate,
As someone heads home this windy,
snowy night.

(Tr. Dell R. Hall)

(3) Seeking Shelter in Lotus Hill on a
Snowy Night
At sunset hillside village still seems far;
Cold and deserted the thatched cottages are.
At wicket gate a dog is heard to back;
With wind and snow I come when night is dark.

(Tr. X. Y. Z.)

两首诗的主题都是“风雪夜归人”，但是两位诗人的心态却不相同。中国诗人说的“日暮”，想的可能是自己已到垂暮之年；而“苍山”尚“远”，想到的可能是仕途坎坷，前路茫茫，归宿不过是“苍山”、“白屋”、“柴门”，因此心情和寒天一样凄凉，一片灰色。美国诗人写的是“一年中最黑暗的夜里”，但这“黑暗的深林却令人留恋”，到达目的地的“路还远着呢”，但因为“有约在先”，这一线希望却使漫漫的黑夜呈现出一片光明。“柴门闻犬吠”写出了山村寂寥，“犬吠”似乎并不是友好的欢迎，而是农业社会封闭自守的吠声。美国诗人的小马“摇晃颈上的铃铛”，却打破了深林的沉寂，显示了马对主人的关怀，宣告了驰骋千里、前途无限的工业社会已经来临。“风雪夜归人”，一个“归”字，写出了中国诗人对家的眷恋，反映了中国文化家庭观念的重要性。美国诗人“有约会在先”，和谁的约会呢？是树林的主人？还是树林外的情人？反正不是诗人的家人，这又反映了西方文化淡薄的家庭观念，以及四海为家、独立自主的开拓精神。在英诗中，大自然和诗人的关系不但和谐，而且友好；微风扫落雪片，似乎也是自然对小马的善意回答。在唐诗中，大自然和诗人的心情显得很和谐，但是关系并不友好，反而像是对立的。这也反映了中国文化的消极面和西方文化的积极面。

西方文化的积极性甚至在翻译中也有表现。唐诗的三种英译文，第一种的译者是英国人，第二种的是美国人，第三种的是中国人。第一种英译把“日暮”改成“日出”，把“苍山”改成“紫山”，这就把唐诗中“暮色苍茫”的灰暗情调换成了朝霞满天的紫红色彩，也就是把中国古代的文化翻成西方现代的文化了。把“夜归人”译成“我们”，这又破坏了原诗的孤寂感，“犬吠”似乎也在欢迎“我们”胜利归来，这就把意气消沉的唐诗译成意气风发的英诗了。第二种美译比第一种英译更能体现西方文化的求真精神，只是最后一行的“归”字译成“归家”，和诗题《逢雪宿芙蓉山》有矛盾，破坏了原诗的飘零感。由此可见，英美译者往往自觉不自觉地按照西方文化的精神来解释中国文化。

中国文化的孤寂飘零感，不但表现在唐诗中，也表现在宋词里，如苏东坡的《卜算子》：

缺月挂疏桐，漏断人初静。
谁见幽人独往来？缥缈孤鸿影。
惊起却回头，有恨无人省。
拣尽寒枝不肯栖，寂寞沙洲冷。

译文：

(1) Half-moon hangs on sparse wu-t'ung tree;
The water clock stops, people settle down.
Who sees the recluse passing by, all alone;
A haunting shadow of a fugitive swan.
Then, suddenly startled, it turns its head,
With a grief that no one can know.
Looking over each wintry bough, it
Settles on none;
The lonely sandbank's cold.

(Tr. Eugene Eoyang)

(2) From a sparse plane tree hangs the waning moon;
The water clock is still and hushed is man.
Who sees a hermit pacing up and down alone?
Is it the shodow of a swan?
Startled, he turns his head,
With a grief none behold.
Looking all over, he won't perch on branched dead.
But on lonely sandbank cold.

(Tr. X. Y. Z.)

这首词中孤寂飘零的，既是孤鸿，又是词人自己。第一种译文的译者是美籍华人，从中可以看出美国文化的科学精神；第二种的是中国译者，从中可以看出中国文化的艺术传统。第一行的"缺月"译成"半边月"只是客观的形象；译成"残月"却包含了词人主观的感伤情绪。第二行的"漏断"译成"漏声停止"又是客观叙述；译为"漏声静了"却包含了词人的主观感觉。第三行的“往来”，第一种译成“有往无来”，削弱了下文“无枝可依”的飘零感。第四行承上启下，第二种译成问句，巧妙地使词人与孤鸿合而为一，体现了中国文化的艺术精神，下半首的主语，在第一种译文是“它”，只指“孤鸿”；在第二种是“他”，既可指鸿，又可指人。最重要的是七、八行，画龙点睛，说明词人和孤鸿一样寂寞飘泊，无枝可依，但是不肯随波逐流，还要保持自己的清高品格。中文是一种艺术的语言，非常精简，主语、介词、连词，都可省略，但是根据上下文又可以理解字中所无、句中所有的含义，因此非常适宜于表达这种亦人亦鸿的朦胧诗意。英文却是一种科学的语言，非常精确，主语、介词、连词，都不可以或缺。简单说来，英文说一是一，说二是二；中文却可以说一是二，意在言外。美籍学者用科学的方法来译最后两句，结果看不出两句之间有什么关系；中国译者用艺术的方法来译，加上原文内容所有、形式所无的连词和介词，原诗言外之意才能和盘托出。从这两种不同的译文中，也可以看出中西文化的差异。

苏东坡的孤鸿很容易使人联想起雪莱的失伴鸟：

A widow bird sate mourning for her Love
　Upon a wintry bough;
The frozen wind crept on above,
　The freezing stream below.
There was no leaf upon the forest bare,
　No flower upon the ground,
And little motion in the air
　Except the mill-wheel's sound.

有鸟仳离枯树巅，
　哭丧其雄剧可怜；
上有冰天风入冻，
　下有积雪之河川。
森林无叶徒杈梗，
　地上更无一朵花，
空中群动皆息灭，
　只闻鸣厂有水车

（郭沫若　译）

雪莱的诗比起苏词来，似乎是客观的抒情。两首诗都写了孤鸟、寒枝，都充满了诗人对鸟的同情。雪莱的同情是从外部注入的，他先把鸟拟人，然后将心比心，以诗人之心度鸟之心，于是发出了失伴的哀鸣，不过诗人和鸟并没有合而为一。苏东坡的同情却更发自内心，看不清到底是诗人在怜悯鸟，还是鸟在怜悯诗人，二者已经难解难分了，因此比雪莱更加主观。在雪莱诗中，寒风、水车似乎都在呜咽，衬托了孤鸟的悲哀；在苏词中，缺月疏桐，寒枝沙洲，都寂突无言，却衬托出了诗人的清高。由此可见，中西文化是同中有异、异中有同的。

郭沫若是我国著名的诗人，他把这首诗译成七言古体，并且模仿李白《长相思》中的“上有青冥之高天，下有绿水之波澜”，表现了译者的文化素质。但是雪莱原诗用语平易，诗行一长一短，更接近我国的词体；郭译用词古奥，长短一律，读来更像前面徐忠杰译的《扬州慢》，而不如范守义译的乔叟。由此可见，把外国文化归化为本国文化，也有一个“度”的问题，过犹不及。有人说：诗的译者一定要是诗人，我没有读过范守义写的诗，他的知名度自然远远不如郭沫若，但是如以译诗而论，我却认为他是胜过了诗人郭沫若的。

雪莱更是世界闻名的诗人，他认为诗是不可译的；但在济慈去世时，他却把柏拉图的诗从希腊文译成英文：

Thou wert the morning star among the living,
  Ere thy fair light had fled—
Now, having died, thou art as Hesperus, giving
  New splendor to the dead.
明丽的光辉消逝以前，
  你是人间的启明，
死了，给死者新的光，
  偏似夜空的长庚。
（江枫　译）

雪莱的译诗实践否定了他的翻译理论。这四行诗有韵有调，不但使人“知之”，而且“好之”，甚至“乐之”，使希腊诗化成了英诗，使希腊文化和英国文化融合成为西方文化。而江枫的译文没有说清“明丽的光辉”是启明星清晨发出的光辉，没有反映西方文化的科学精神，而是代之以中国文化的朦胧艺术手法，结果不能使英诗归化为中诗。

雪莱哀掉济慈挽诗，容易使人联想起唐代诗人崔钰的《哭李商隐》：

虚负凌云万丈才，
一生襟抱未曾开。
鸟啼花落人何在？
竹死桐枯凤不来。
良马足因无主踠，
旧交心为绝弦哀。
九泉莫叹三光隔，
又送文星入夜台。
In vain you could have soared up to the azure sky,
Before you could fulfill your ambition you die.
The birds bewail with fallen flower: “Where are you?”

The phoenix won't alight on dead tree or bamboo.
A horse'd be crippled if not trained by riders good;
The lutist broke his lute for one who understood.
In nether world not sun or moon or star in sight,
But you're the brightest star in the eternal night.

(Tr. X. Y. Z.)

《哭李商隐》的最后一句，和雪莱的挽诗真有异曲同工之妙，这不说明千古诗人一样爱才吗？崔钰诗中有“凤栖梧”、“伯牙碎琴”等文化典故，雪莱的译诗和《阿多尼》中，引用的神话传说更多。可见诗和翻译，都“超出了个人的经验与感觉，而可以代表文化”。文化中的典故最难翻译，如果直译，即使能够存真，也往往不能存美；如果意译，即使能够存美，又往往难免失真。存真的译文可以使读者“知之”，存美的译文可以使读者“好之”，只有既不失真、又能存美的译文才能使人“乐之”。孔子说过：“知之者不如好之者，好之者不如乐之者。”所以诗词翻译应该在尽可能少失真的前提下，尽可能多保存原诗的美。存真的翻译可以介绍外国的文化，存美的翻译才能使外国文化归化为本国文化。介绍外国文化的目的似乎不是为介绍而介绍，应该是为了提高本国文化，而归化正是提高的结果。外国文化无论多好，如果不能为本国文化所吸收，也是不能提高本国文化的。归化一般说来是指进化，但有时退化也可能是进化，例如人的尾巴退化了，人不是因此而进化了吗？典故也是一样，有时七也可以退为进的，例如雪莱在译诗中把“启明星”浅化为“晨星”，不是既不失真，又能存美吗？其实，“文化”二字本身就包含了由野蛮进化为文明，由低级向高级转化的意思。最高级的文化并不一定是最高深的，而是最美的文化。

（节选自许渊冲：《诗词·翻译·文化》，《北京大学学报》(哲社版)1990年第5期，第35-41页。）

From Comparative Literature to Translation Studies

(节选)

[英]Susan Bassnett

【导读】

苏珊·巴斯奈特是英国著名的翻译理论家和比较文学家，当代翻译研究派领军人物，翻译研究“文化转向”的重要倡导者之一，著有《翻译研究》、《比较文学批评导论》等。本篇选自《比较文学批评导论》的最后一章，通过思考比较文学与翻译研究之间的关系，来为比较文学的长远发展探索新的路径，富有新意。

巴斯奈特强调了翻译史在翻译研究中的重要性，而她本人也使用历史研究方法，使其论述更具历史依据。她追溯翻译研究发展的三个阶段：第一阶段深受多元系统理论的影响，聚焦于目标系统，使传统的翻译理论话语受到直接挑战；第二阶段不再局限于对传统理论话语的批评，重点在于追溯与描绘特定历史时期翻译活动的模式，开始向后结构主义迈进；第三阶段是目前对译者使用的比喻性语言的研究。巴斯奈特大量引入女性主义的观点，来重新思考译者以及翻译的地位，表达对“原作地位高于译作”这一传统翻译观的反思，颠覆了传统的二元概念和原有的等级关系。作者还引入加拿大女性主义翻译理论代表人物西苏的“中间性”概念，即译者是一个中间性的存在。传统二元概念将原文和译文看做两极，而女性主义翻译理论则聚焦于这两极间相互作用的空间以及对这两极的性别化阐释。在该空间中，翻译是双性的，不属于男女两极中的任何一方，这就宣告了译者的主体性地位，颠覆了源文本和目标文本的权威—从属关系。此外，作者用“婚姻”比喻翻译研究与比较文学的关系，从而否定了比较文学对于翻译研究的支配地位。作者的论证还体现出解构主义的思想，她对翻译研究中原文和原作者的地位以及比较文学这一学科进行解构，既对比较文学研究提供了新思路，又对翻译活动尤其是文学翻译带来指导作用。此外，她还提出比较文学学科意义上的“死亡”，这是对比较文学学科身份的解构，但她又没有止步于此，而是对翻译活动的边缘性以及翻译研究和比较文学的彻底决裂这两种观点进行否定，对比较文学进行进一步重构，提出“应将翻译研究视为一门主要的学科，而把比较文学看做一个有价值但是辅助性的研究领域”。

本文对于翻译尤其是文学翻译具有很大指导作用。她认为，教学领域中的“忠实”及“准确性”翻译标准不能应用于文学翻译，这是因为文学翻译具有其独特性，即文学性。她批判了翻译中的源文本倾向，认为译者应充分发挥主观能动性，在多元化的背景下扩展研究范围，给目标系统注入新的活力。根据食人主义翻译观，应抹去源文本和目标文本间的界限，译者并非模仿者，而是“生产者”，从源文本中取其精华去其糟粕，将其重新创造，从而强化目标文本。巴斯奈特提出多元系统理论对文化和文学史研究提供的可能性，以及“操纵学派”的出现为翻译研究带来的多元化趋势，以强调翻译在人类文学和文化发展中所发挥的关键作用。作者揭示了比较文学的危机，但她并不是指“比较文学”这一学科的彻底消失和终结，而是指基于“二元法”的传统比较文学理念和方法的“死亡”。

（李伟荣）

The opening chapters of this book suggest that the term “comparative literature” has declined in significance in recent years, although it has also been argued that comparative practice is alive and well and thriving under other nomenclature. In contrast, however, Translation Studies has been gaining ground, and since the end of the 1970s has come to be seen as a discipline in its own right, with professional associations, journals, publishers' catalogues and a proliferation of doctoral theses.

The relationship between comparative literature and the study of translation has been a complex and problematic one. Translation has tended to be regarded as the poor relation, as an activity involving little talent and creativity, as something that could be carried out by trained hacks and financially rewarded accordingly. Hilaire Belloc's view in his 1931 Taylorian Lecture sums up a situation that is still unhappily all too recognizable in some countries:

> The art of translation is a subsidiary art and derivative. On this account it has never been granted the dignity of original work, and has suffered too much in the general judgement of letters. This natural underestimation of its value has had the bad practical effect of lowering the standard demanded, and in some periods has almost destroyed the art altogether. The corresponding misunderstanding of its character has added to its degradation: neither its importance nor its difficulty has been grasped.[1]

Belloc's lecture was polemical, in that he wanted to remind his listeners of the complexity of the translation process with a view to raising its debased status. To that end he exaggerated the issues, for it is simply not true that translation had never “been granted the dignity of original work”. The situation Belloc was referring to had developed gradually, from the seventeenth century onwards.

Certainly by the nineteenth century, the status of a translation was generally considered to he lower than that of an original and theorists of comparative literature, while acknowledging the role played by translation in their work, tended to assert the primacy of reading in original languages. Studies of comparative literature came increasingly to relegate translation to a single chapter or subsection, often placed together with terms such as "adaptation", or "imitation", all implicitly suggesting texts of a more derivative and secondary nature.

Binary comparative studies stood firmly against the idea of translation. A good comparatist, according to the binary model, would read original texts in the original languages, an infinitely superior form of reading than any which involved translation. The North American model, based on notions of universal values in literary texts, simply ignored the question of translation altogether; the processes whereby a text could be transferred from one context into another were either not regarded as a useful object of study, or seen as territory to be explored by linguists rather than literary scholars. The low status of translation was enshrined in other ways: in editorial practice of relegating translations to a separate category, often marginalized with categories such as "juvenilia" in editions of an author's works; in the poor remuneration for translation; in the ranking of translations as less than critical works when determining criteria for promotion.

In the 1970s a group of scholars began to emerge offering a different perspective on the study of translation. Led initially by Itamar Evan-Zohar from Tel Aviv, the group proposed to define their objective as "Translation Studies". In a paper entitled "Translation Theory Today", Evan-Zohar began by summarizing prevailing views on translation, before going on to propose a systematic approach that would cut through the wooliness of a great deal of thinking about the translation process:

> How many times have we been tortured by the cliches of the un-initiated, veteran or novice, that translation is never equal to the original, that languages differ from one another, that culture is "also" involved with translation procedures, that when a translation is "exact" it rends to be "literal" and hence loses the "spirit" of the original, that the "meaning" of a text means both "content" and style and so on. Not to speak of such approaches where norms are either overtly or covertly stated, i. e. where we are told how translations should look or how they should be conceived of in terms of one or another evaluative norm. [2]

The words emphasized by Kvan-Zohar are, of course, part of a discourse that prioritizes the original and sees the translation as an inferior copy, as something that loses a vital ingredient present only in that original. He draws attention to the inadequacy of such terminology, and mocks those critics he calls "uninitiated, veteran or novice" who continue to think in those terms. What this paper exposes, as does the rest of his work on translation, is the prevalence of a curiously schizophrenic position of the literary world with regard to translation. In an age when Borges has suggested that the concept of the definitive text belongs only to religion or fatigue, and post-structuralist critics have shown the fallacy of believing in a single, definitive reading, discourse on translation went on talking about "originals" and "accuracy" and continued to make use of a terminology of negativity. Translation, it is suggested, "betrays", "traduces", "diminishes", "reduces", "loses" parts of the original, translation is "derivative", "mechanical", "secondary", poetry is lost in translation, certain writers are "untranslatable".

The notion of the translation as a betrayal of the original is particularly prevalent, Lori Chamberlain, one of a growing number of feminist translation scholars, draws attention to the sexualization of this terminology, pointing out that it appears

> perhaps most familiarly in the tag "les belles infidels" like women, the adage goes, translations should be either beautiful or faithful. The tag is made possible both by the rhyme in French and by the fact that the word "traduction" is a feminine one, thus making les beaux infideles, impossible. This tag owes its longevity—it was coined in the seventeenth century—to more than phonetic similarity; what gives it the appearance of truth is that it has captured a cultural complicity between the issues of fidelity in translation and in marriage. For "les belles infidels" fidelity is defined as an implicit contract between translation (as woman) and original (as husband, father, or author). However, the infamous "double standard" operates here as it might have in traditional marriages: the "unfaithful" wife/translation is publicly tried for crimes the husband/original is by law incapable of committing. This contract, in short, makes it impossible for the original to be guilty of infidelity. Such an attitude betrays real anxiety about the problem of paternity and translation; it mimics the patrilineal kinship system where paternity—not maternity—legitimizes an offspring.[3]

Lori Chamberlain is making an important point here, stressing the cultural complicity between fidelity in translation and in marriage: it is no accident that a substantial number of feminist translation scholars such as myself, Barbara Johnson, Barbara Ciodard, Sherry Simon, Annie Brisset or Suzanne de Lotbiniere-Harwood all began using metaphors of "infidelity" or alternative marriage contract in their writings on translation in the 1980s, for all have been concerned with rethinking the view of translation that sets the original in a higher position that the text created for a new target audience.

The challenge to the original like the challenge to the canon or to the notion of correct, single reading is clearly part of a wide-ranging post-modernist strategy. Instead of reading for "truth", we now read as decoders. Barbara Johnson has suggested that the whole activity of reading and rereading reveals ever more gaps and uncertainties:

> By rereading the texts of writers and philosophers that have made a difference to Western history, it might be possible to become aware of the repressions, the elisions, the contradictions and the linguistic slippages that have functioned unnoticed and that undercut the certainties those texts have been read as upholding.[4]

The way in which translation studies began to mount an offensive against the dominance of the original and the consequent relegation of translation to a position of subservience was initially through the work of Evan-Zohar and his colleagues, most notably Gideon Toury, on polysystems theory. For Evan-Zohar went much further than simply attacking the vagueness of the language surrounding translation. He noted that although translation appeared to have played a major role in the development of national cultures, this fact was almost ignored by historians of culture and there was practically no research at all on the function of translated literature within a literary system. The Renaissance, for example, has generally been perceived as a time of intensive translation activity, yet any systematic assessment of what was translated, why, by whom and how had not taken place.

The radical implications of Evan-Zohar's polysystcmic approach to translation were immediately clear. All kinds of questions could now he asked that had previously not seemed to be of significance; why do some cultures translate more and some less? What kind of texts get translated? What is the status of those texts in the target system and how does it compare to the status of the texts in the source system? What do we know about translation conventions and norms at given moments, and how do we assess translation as an innovatory force? What is the relationship in literary history between extensive translation activity and the production of texts claimed as canonical? What image do translators have of their work and how has that image been expressed figuratively? These and countless other questions testify to the great shift in perception which has taken place, in which far from being a secondary, marginal activity, translation could be considered as a primary shaping force within literary history.

In a paper written in 1976, Evan-Zohar argues that certain conditions determine high translation activity in a culture. He identifies three major cases: when a literature is in an early stage of development; when a literature perceives itself to be peripheral or "weak" or both; when there are turning points or crises or literary vacuums.[5] Subsequent work has taken up these ideas, and developed them further through specific case studies. So, for example, Maria Tymoczko argues that translation played a central role in the great twelfth-century shift from epic to romance:

> The twelfth century marks one of the most significant transitions in Western culture: the shift from epic to romance. The change is one of poetics, of course; it represents the transition from traditional oral hero tale to written, author-innovated literature. The shift involves changes in larger literary elements such as genre and character typologies, as well as formal changes such as the development of new metres, rhetorical devices and the like. The transition is also an ideological one. It involves the turning from a warrior ethos to courtly codes and the celebration of romantic love.[6]

Tymoczko suggests that translation played a fundamental part in this shift, and points out that elements of romance can be traced in antecedent translations, and that romance emerged from a multicultural context. By focusing not only on poetics but also on the means of production, that is, by tracing the gradual move towards authored works written for named patrons, Tymoczko shows the significant role played by translation. The case of the move from epic to romance during the period that established the vulgar languages across Europe as literary languages accords with Evan-Zohar's hypothesis that translation activity is high when literatures are in an early stage of development.

Contemporary figures on translated texts as compiled from publishers lists offer a good example of the hypothesis that "peripheral" literary systems translate a great deal, in contrast to those literary systems which perceive themselves as "major". The percentage of published translations into English, for example, contrasts sharply with the percentage of published translations into Swedish or Polish or Italian. Obviously this has to do with patterns of convention, which rapidly become established, and has also to do with the technological self-sufficiency of the English speaking world as a whole and with the rise since the Second World War of English as a world language. However, the figures quoted by Lawrence Venuti in 1992 show some startling disparities. His figures for Italy in the 1980s show 26 per cent of books published annually as translations, mainly from English, with a rise to 50 per cent, 70 per cent or even 90 per cent of an individual publishers output when literary translation is considered. In sharp contrast, in the period between 1984 and 1990, translations accounted for only 3. 5 per cent of books published annually in the United States, with an even lower figure of 2. 5 per cent for Britain.[7] The steady decline in translation activity during the nineteenth century as Britain became an imperial power can be linked to changes in self-esteem and to a belief in the inherent superiority of the English literary system, as has been discussed earlier in this book.

The Czech revival in the early nineteenth century offers an example of an emergent national literature that seeks to extend its range of models through the means of translation. The Czech scholar Vladimir Macura has studied the role played by translation in the Czech revival, and points to the significance of translation as explicit cultural policy:

> Translation was not seen as passive submission to cultural impulses from abroad; on the contrary, it was viewed as an active, even aggressive act, an appropriation of foreign cultural values... translation seen as an invasion of rival territory, an invasion undertaken with the intent of capturing rich spoils of war. In his preface to his translations from Schiller, Jan Evangelista Purkeyne, the Czech writer who was to become a physiologist of world renown, tried to interpret translation as an immediate reaction against the destructive impact of foreign cultures, a literal act of revenge for the damages the Slavic world had suffered in the past: "If (to the detriment of the Slavs) the Germans, Italians, and Hungarians try to denationalize both our common people and our higher classes, let us use

a more noble way of retaliation, taking possession of anything excellent they have created in the world of the mind." [8]

Macura goes on to suggest that this expropriative function was of such importance in the Czech revival that it conditioned the choice of texts selected for translation. He reinterprets the case of Jungmann's translation of *Paradise Lost*, hotly debated by critics for decades, and argues that this translation was a conscious attempt to bring into a newly emergent literary system a text that represented an amalgam of different cultures (Christian, Jewish, pagan) united in an epic of human culture, and therefore that Milton's work had a symbolic function also as a means of stressing the universality of pan-Slavic origins.

This kind of scholarship, which often involves radical revisions of cultural and literary history, has been made possible by advances in translation studies, and by polysystems theory in particular. In a valuable essay published in 1985, the Belgian scholars Jose Lambert and Rik van Gorp endeavoured to summarize the possibilities offered by this approach. They list a number of areas of research that can be developed, which involve both detailed analysis of texts and of the means of production of those texts. Valuable areas of research, they suggest, include studying the vocabulary, style, poetical and rhetorical conventions of both source and target systems; analyzing how a translation is termed (i. e. whether it is presented as a translation, or as an "adaptation", an "imitation" or even an "original" in the target system, and its role and status in that system; mapping the history of translation theory and criticism in particular literatures at particular times; studying the emergence of groups or schools of translators and the significance of such; tracing the role of translations in the development of a literary system, with a view to establishing whether translation plays a conservative or an innovative role, etc. Significantly, Lambert and Van Gorp note that the main advantage of the scheme is that it enables us to bypass a number of deep-roofed traditional ideas concerning translational "fidelity", and even "quality" which are mainly source-oriented and inevitably normative."[9]

The essay by Lambert and van Gorp was published in 1985 in a collection of papers edited by Theo Hermans, entitled *The Manipulation of Literature*. The appearance of this collection marked another stage in the development of translation studies, for the focus of the book was on the idea of translation not only as a shaping force in literature but also as a primary manipulative textual strategy. Polysystems theory in its first stage was necessarily target system focused, principally to rebut the older notion of the primacy of the original and the secondary status of translation activity, but by the mid-1980s the first, more evangelical phase of research based on polysystems theory was becoming transformed into something else. Indeed, it is possible now to talk about three distinct stages in the development of translation studies. The first phase, heavily influenced by polysystems theory involved a series of direct challenges to the established discourse on translation. Decontextualized work in linguistics was challenged on the one hand, evaluative unsystematic work in literary studies was challenged on the other. Crucial to this stage were the often hitter debates on equivalance theory.

The traditional notion of translation, upon which the concept of the bilingual dictionary rests, is that translation between languages is possible because of the prior existence of a notional equivalence between systems. Despite the Sapir-Whorf hypothesis, which argued that

> No two languages are ever sufficiently similar to be considered as representing the same social reality. The worlds in which different societies live are distinct worlds, not merely the same world with different labels attached. [10]

generations of translators have wanted to believe in equivalence and have sought to define it in terms of sameness, sometimes arguing that that sameness could be interpreted in different ways and was open to negotiation, but nevertheless was possible. The obvious problem with a theory of equivalence as sameness is that it denies the existence of hierarchical relations between source and target texts and cultures and assumes that translation takes place on a vertical axis, between identically-placed systems. Polysystems theory, on the contrary, argues that systems are never identically positioned, and that notions of the superiority or inferiority of a text or of a literary system are always in play.

The second phase of translation studies moved beyond the challenge to previous discourses, and was principally concerned with mapping, with tracing patterns of translation activity at given moments in time. The emphasis in this phase was still predominantly on the target system, but a great deal of important historical research begin to appear. A significant development in this second stage, which marks a definite move away from the overly structuralist origins of polysystems theory and a step on the road towards post- strucruralist translation studies, has been the work carried out on the figurative language used by translators, as evidenced in their prefaces, correspondence and statements about their work generally.

The Manipulation of Literature volume also included a pioneering essay by Theo Hermans on Renaissance translators working in Dutch, English and French which categorizes their use of metaphors to describe their work and reveals clear patterns of thought.[11] Hermans shows how clusters of metaphors used by translators reflect their thinking about the role and status of translation in their own time. Predictable metaphors relating to rhetoric in general include following in footsteps, changing clothing, discovering treasure or alchemical transfer, and these metaphors also show a certain degree of ambiguity towards the source text, with the status of the text in its source system being significant in determining the attitude and strategies of the translator as well as the right of the target culture to possess it.

Mapping clusters of metaphors in use at a given point in time exposes dominant attitudes to the activity of translation. In the age that was characterized by the growth of the slave trade and by a shift in perceptions of European states towards the rest of the world, translation metaphors of the seventeenth century are very revealing. Perrot d'Ablancourt's preface to his translation of the *Annals of Tacitus*, for example, contains a statement that he has followed Tacitus "step by step" and rather as a slave than as a companion, [12] while Dryden's dedication to his *Aeneid* states that "slaves we are, and labour on another man's plantation; we dress the vineyard, but the wine is the owner's." [13]

The translator as slave, the servant of the source text, is a powerful metaphor that endures well into the nineteenth century. Implicit in this metaphor is the idea of dominance of the source text author over the subservient target text. A relatively lone voice offering a different image of the translation process was a female translator, Madame de Gournay, who suggested in 1623 that to translate was

> to engender a work anew. Engender, I say, because (the ancient writers) have to he decomposed by profound and penetrating reflection, in order to be reconstituted by a similar process; just as meat must be decomposed in our stomachs in order to form our bodies.[14]

Fidelity to an original/husband as a metaphor for translation and the loyalty of the slave to the master both reflect profound changes in reading and writing in the post-Renaissance world. The voyages of discovery were altering perspectives, and the new world waiting to be penetrated and fertilized by the powerful European colonizing originals was consistently described, as has been discussed in earlier chapters, in sexual terms. Foucault points likewise to immense changes in language: "In the sixteenth century, one asked oneself how it was possible to know that a sign did in fact designate what it signified; from the seventeenth century, one began to ask how a sign could be linked to what it signified."[15]

Notes

1. Hilarie Belloc. *On Translation*. Oxford, Clarendon Press, 1931.
2. Itamar Evan-Zohar. Translation Theory Today. *Poetics Today*, 1981, 2(4), pp. 1-7.
3. Lori Chamberlain. Gender and the Metaphorics of Translation. in Lawrence Venuti (d.). *Rethinking Translation*. London, Routledge, 1992, pp. 57-74.
4. Barbara Johnson. The Surprise of Otherness: A Note on the Wartime Writings of Paul de Man. in Peter Collier and Helga Geyer-Ryan (eds.). *Literary Theory Today*, London, Polity Press, 1990, pp. 13-23.
5. Itama Evan-Zohar. The Position of Translated Literature within the Literary Polysystem. *Papers in Historical Poetics*, Tel Aviv, 1978.
6. Maria Tymoczko. Translation as a force for literary revolution in the twelfth century: the shift from epic to romance. *New Comparison*, 1986, pp. 7-27.
7. Lawrence Venuti (ed.). *Rethinking Translation: Discourse, Subjectivity, Ideology*. London, Routledge, 1992, pp. 5-6.

8. Vladimír Macura. Culture as Translation. in Susan Bassnett and André Lefevere (eds.). *Translation, History and Culture*. London, Pinter, 1990, pp. 64-70.
9. José Lambert and Rik Van Gorp. On describing translations. in Theo Hermans (ed.). *The Manipulation of Literature*, London, Croom Helm, 1985, pp. 42-53.
10. Edward Sapir. *Culture, Language and Personality*. Berkeley, Los Angeles, University of California Press, 1956, p. 69.
11. Theo Hermans. Images of Translation: Metaphor and Imagery in the Renaissance Discourse on Translation. in *The Manipulation of Literature*, pp. 103-135.
12. Perrot d'Ablancourt. preface to the *Annals of Tacitus*, in *Lettres et Préfaces critiques*. Roger Zuber (ed.), Paris, 1972.
13. John Dryden. Dedication to The Aeneid, 1697. in *Of Dramatic Poesy and other Critical Essays*, G. Watson (ed.). 2 vols, London/New York, Dent/Dutton, 1962.
14. Madame de Gournay. *Versions de quelques piéces de Virgile*. Paris, 1619.
15. Michael Foucault. *The Order of Things*. London, Tavistock, 1970, p. 43.

（选自 Susan Bassnett. Chapter 7 of *Comparative Literature: A Critical Introduction*, Oxford UK & Cambridge USA: Blackwell, 1993, pp. 138-145.）

A New Comparative Literature

[美]Emily Apter

【导读】

在当今的全球化时代，世界各国在政治、经济、文化、科技交流日益频繁。作为一种促成跨语言交际的活动，翻译在国际交流中扮演着举足轻重的角色。艾米丽·阿普特(Emily Apter)的专著《翻译地带：一种新的比较文学》(*The Translation Zone*: *A New Comparative Literature*)力图从翻译研究的角度来重新定义比较文学这门学科。

要想厘清翻译研究和比较文学之间的关系，首先应该对两者的定义有一个清晰的认识。比较文学必须满足两个条件：一是跨越民族和语言界限；二是文学研究。翻译研究指一切与翻译活动有关的研究，包括翻译原则、翻译标准、翻译技巧、翻译理论、翻译批评、翻译家和翻译史等。作为一门跨越语言界限来进行文学研究的学科，比较文学的切入点是不同语言的文学作品，而翻译研究的切入点首先也自然是语言。但这里的语言不是纯粹语言学意义上的"语言"，而是带有特定文化霸权和意识形态色彩的"语言"。目前，比较文学早已不再停留于文学研究层面，翻译研究也早已不再停留于文本研究层面，两者都已逐步实现文化转向。

以前的比较文学要么致力于寻求两个民族或国家的文学影响与被影响的"事实联系"，要么比较两个民族或国家的文学的异同，然后从中推测它们相互间的关系。比较文学的文化转向意味着比较文学的研究者不再只关注作家与作家之间的影响与被影响的模式和途径，或是文本与文本之间的差异与相同，而是把比较文学放到一个更加广阔的文化语境中来进行研究。翻译研究的文化转向始于20世纪70年代，国际译学界一批著名的翻译理论家，像霍尔姆斯(James S. Holmes)、巴斯奈特(Susan Bassnett)、勒菲莱尔(André Lefevere)、韦努蒂(Lawrence Venuti)等，纷纷强调翻译并非在两种语言的真空中进行的，而是两种文学(和文化)传统的语境下进行的。翻译研究的文化转向意味着研究学者所关注的翻译不再是传统意义上的语言转换，而是跨文化视野下文学的翻译和接受。值得指出的是，比较文学中的翻译研究绝不是语言学派所讨论的"如何译"问题的研究，而是指从文化层面上展开的对翻译动因、翻译行为、翻译结果、翻译传播、翻译接受、翻译影响等问题的研究。换言之，这里的翻译研究是指实现了文化转向后的翻译研究。在比较文学和翻译研究双双实现文化转向之后，两个学科都开拓出了一片更为广阔的发展前景。

基于翻译研究的比较文学并不是指今后的比较文学只对翻译进行研究，而放弃传统比较文学的研究课题。事实上，实现了文化转向以后的翻译研究确实与比较文学关系密切。二者是你中有我，我中有你，既相互独立，又相互交叉，既相互利用，又相互支持的关系。从本质上来说，翻译研究为比较文学研究提供媒介和研究对象，比较文学为翻译研究提供更广阔的研究视角和方法。

（李伟荣）

In attempting to rethink critical paradigms in the humanities after 9/11, with special emphasis on language and war, the problem of creolization and the mapping of languages "in-translation", shifts in the word canon and literary markets, and the impact of enhanced technologies of information translation, I have tried to image a program for a new comparative literature using translation as fulcrum. I began with an attempt to rethink the disciplinary "invention" of comparative literature in Istanbul in the 1930s, using the work of Leo Spitzer and Erich Auerbach as figures whose names became synonymous with defining early iterations of global humanism in exile. I end with some reflections on what happens to philology when it is used to forge a literary comparatism that has no national predicate, and that in naming itself *translatio* names the action of linguistic self-cognizing, the attempt to bring-to-intelligibility that which lies beyond language ("God", Utopia, Nature, DNA, a Unified Field Theory of Expressionism).

In naming a translational process constitute of its disciplinary nomination comparative literature breaks the isomorphic fit between the name of a nation and the name of a language. As Giogio Agamben has observed (with reference to Alice Becker-Ho's determination that Gypsy *argot* failed to qualify as a language since Gypsies as a people were deemed to be without nation or fixed abode, we do not have, in fact, the slightest idea of what either a nation or a language is[1]." The Gypsy case, for Agamben, reveals the shaky ground on which language nomination rests. In affirming that "Gypsies are to people what argot is to language," Agamben unmasks standard language names as specious attempts to conceal the fact that "all people are gangs and *coquilles*, all languages are jargons and *argots*" (MWE 65, 66). For Agamben, languages that defy containment by structures of the state (as in Catalan, Basque Gaelic), or the blood and soil mythologies of peoples, might conceivably prompt the ethical experience of the pure existence of language" (MWE 68). "It is only by breaking at any point the nexus between the existence of language, grammar, people, and state that thought and praxis will be equal to the tasks at hand," Agamben concludes (MWE 69).

Samuel Weber performs a similar dissection of national/nominal language fallacies with more direct pertinence to translation, noting that,

> [I]he linguistic systems between which translation move are designated as "natural" or "national" languages. However, these terms are anything but precise or satisfactory....

> The imprecision of these terms is in direct proportion to the linguistic diversity they seek to subsume.... The difficulty of finding a generic term that would accurately designate the class to which individual languages belong is indicative of the larger problem of determining the principles that give those languages their relative unity or coherence—assuming, that is, that such principles really exsit.[2]

Comparative literature answers Weber's call for the generic term to which individual languages belong. As such, it functions as an abstract generality or universal sign on the order of Wittgenstein's *Urzeichen*, which sounds out the *forçage* of nation-subject and language-subject in the process of nomination. We hear this *forçage* in an expression like *traduit de l'américain* ("translated from the American"), which captures a non-existent language coming into being through the act of rendering it coincident with the name of a nation or people. There is, of course, no standard language with discrete grammatical rules and protocols called "American." "American" may be the name of a language referring (in nominalist terms) to a possible world of language, but it is neither a term used by North American speakers of English to refer to their idiolect, nor a legitimate nation-maker. (As Jean-Luc Godard said recently: "I would really like to find another word for 'American.' When someone says 'American' they mean someone who lives between New York and Los Angeles, and not someone who lives between Montevideo and Santiago.")[3] As the name of a language, "American" implicitly consigns Spanish to "foreign"-language status even though millions of hemispheric subjects of the Americans claim Spanish as their native tongue. A new comparative literature would acknowledge this jockeying for power and respect in the field of language. A new comparative literature seeks to be the name of language worlds characterized by linguistic multiplicity and phantom internations.

In *Poetique de la relation* Edouard Glissant authorizes the move toward linguistic internationalism when he subordinates instabilities of nomination to geopoetics, replacing the old center-periphery model with a world system comprised of multiple linguistic singularities or interlocking small worlds, each a locus of poetic opacity Glissant's paradigm of the *toutmonde*, building on the nondialectical ontological immanence of Deleuze and Gusttsri, offers a model of aporetic community in which small worlds (modeled perhaps after a deterritorialized Caribbean) connect literally through bonds of Creole and a politics of mutualism centered on resistance to debt. Looking ahead to a day when *toutmondisme* will surpass *tiermondisme*, that is to say, when the nation form gives way to the immanent, planetary totality of Creole, Glissant imagines Creole "transfigured into word of the world."[4] Building on Glissant, the authors of *Éloge de la créolité* envision *créolité* as "*the world diffracted but recomposed*, a maelstrom of signifieds in a single signifier: a Totality.... *full knowledge of Creoleness*, they argue, *will be reserved for Art*, for art absolutely."[5] As Peter Hallward has remarked: "The nation's loss is... Creole's gain."[6]

Insofar as Creole heralds a condition of linguistic postnationalism and denaturalizes monolingualization (showing it to be an artificial arrest of language transit and exchange), it may be said to emblematize a new comparative literature based on translation. Though, as I have argued in this book, Creole has emerged as an omnibus rubric, loosely applied to hybridity, *métissage*, platforms of cross-cultural encounter, or to language as a critical category of literary history; it has also emerged as a synonym for traumatic lack. Marked by the middle passage, and the coarse commands of human traffickers and plantation owners, Creole carries a history of stigma comparable to that of pidgin translation in nineteenth-century Chinese. In Huan Saussy's estimation, Chinese pidgin translation was, for the grammarians an exhibition of "incompleteness...an unequal relationship between normal speech in the target language and the halting, misarticulated, or excessive speech of the source language it represents." In Saussy's reading, Walter Benjamin's sacred, interlinear ideal of translation offers the possibility of revaluing pidgin because interlinear's word-for-word literalism authorizes a translation full of holes: "Pidgin stands for—it makes audible and visible—the incommensurability of languages. The discussion of Chinese, that 'grammarless' languages, gives pidgin its greatest representational lisence."[7] Recuperated in the guise of sacred translation, Creole, like pidgin, may be cast as a language "blessed" with the fullness of aporia.

For Derrida, the aporia, names the conceptual impasse of death lodged in the body of language. Beginning with a phrase "*il y va d'un certain pas* [It involves a certian step/not; he goes along at a certain pacel," Derrida associates the pas with a 'recumbant corpse' or limit-condition between language and that which is other to itself."[8]

A Babel "*from* and *within* itself...the stranger at home, the invited or the one who is called...this border of translation does not pass among various languages. It separates translation from itself, it separates translatability within one and the same language. A certain pragmatics thus inscribes this border *in the very inside of the so-called French language*." (A 10)

Derrida's concept of aporia-heard in the "*no*, *not*, *nicht*, *kein*" of alterity—is linked to the politics of monolingualism in *Monolingualism of the Other*: *Or the Prosthesis of Origin* (1996)[9] (A 10). The book's epigraphs from Glisant and Abdelkedir Khatibi attest to a rare engagement with *francophonie* as theoretical terrain. Derrida, with tongue in cheek, competes with Khatibi for title to the stateless status of the *Franco-Magrébin* subject. The hyphen signifies all the problems of national/linguistic unbelonging characteristic of post-Independence Algerians, including the way in which Jews, Arabs, and French were neighbored, yet separated, by the French language. "This language will never be mine," says Derrida of French, drawing from his own experience of national disenfranchisement the lesson that language is loaned to communities of speakers. "The untranslatable remains (as my law tells me) the poetic economy of the idiom" (D 56). Contrary to what one might expect, the prosthetic "other" in Derrida's title "monolingualism of the other," is not polyglottism, but an aporia within ipseity, an estrangement in language as such. For Derrida, untranslatability is the universal predicate of language names. Derrida's aporia deconstructs the nationalist nominalism of language names by locating an always-prior other within monolingual diction. The aporia loosens the national anchor from the language name, wedging a politics of the subject between the name of a nation and the name of a language. Blocking the automatic association of specified language properties with the universal set of a given nation, Derrida's aporia approximates the location's "X" i the modern nominalist formula "For any X, if X is a man, it is mortal," which disables the universal qualifier "all men are mortal" and relativizes the human status of the subject in question. X may or may not be a man in the same way that Francophone speaker X may or may not be French. The contingency of the subject sugggets here that French speakers who are French nationals constitute one possible world of French speakers among many. Once the national predicate is dislodged, no speaker maintains exclusive ownership of language properties; the right to language is distributed more freely as language is dressed as the property of X-many lease-holders.

Abolishing the divides if inside/outside, guest/host, owner/tenant, "the monolingualism of the other" names a comparatism that neighbors languages, nations, literatures, and communities of speakers. This idea of "neighboring" is borrowed from Kenneth Reinhard, specifically his Levinasian understanding of a "comparative literature otherwise than comparison...a mode of reading logically and ethically prior to similitude, a reading in which texts are not so much grouped into 'families' defined by similarity and difference, as into 'neighborhoods' determined by accidental contiguity, genealogical isolation, and ethical encounter."[10] For Reinhard, treating texts as neighbors "entails creating anamorphic disturbances in the network of perspective genealogies and intertextual relations. That is, before text can be compared, one text must be articulated as the uncanny neighbor of the other; this is an assumption of critical obligation, indebtedness, secondariness that has nothing to do with influence, Zeitgeist, or cultural context" (KS 796). Departing from philological tradition, which argues for textual relation based on shared etymology, tropes, aesthetic tastes, and historical trajectories, Reinhard proposes in their stead a theory of "traumatic proximity"; "How [he asks] can we re-approach the traumatic proximity of a text, before or beyond comparison and contextualization? Asymmetrical substitution implies that there is no original common ground for textual comparison, but only the trauma of originary nonrelationship, of a gap between the theory and practice of reading that is only retroactively visible" (KS 804). Reinhard's notion of "otherwise than comparison" shifts the problematic from language nomination to the ethics of traumatic proximity.

"Neighboring" describes the traumatic proximity of violence and love, manifest as explodes holes in language and translation gaps. Such spaces of nonrelation can be condemned as sigh of profanation, but they are also susceptible to being venerated as sighs of sacred incommensurability. These aporias are directly relevant to the problem of how a language names itself because they disrupt predication, the process by which verbal attributes coalesce in a proper name or noun.

The difficult process of depredication, otherwise known as secular criticism, is one of the premier tasks of philology, as conceived by Edward Said in his final writings. In a chapter of Humanism and Democratic Criticism devoted to "The Return of Philology," Said wrote:

> Philology is, literally the love of words, but as a discipline it acquires a quasi-scientific intellectual and spiritual prestige at various periods a quasi-scientific intellectual and spiritual prestige at various periods in all of the major cultural traditions, including the Western and the Arabic-Islamic traditions that have framed my own development. Suffice it to recall briefly that in the Islamic tradition, knowledge is premised upon a philological attention to language beginning with the Koran, the uncreated word of God (and indeed the word "Koran" itself means reading), and continuing through the emergence of scientific grammar in Khalil ibn Ahmad and Sibawayh to the rise of jurisprudence (*fiqh*) and *ijtihad* and *ta'wil*, jurisprudential hermeneutics and interpretation, respectively.[11]

Saidmakes a sweeping pass through systems of humanistic education based on philology in Arab universities of southern Europe and North Africa in the twelfth century, Judaic tradition in Andalusia, North Africa, the Levant, and Mesopotamia, then on to Vico and Nietzsche. He extols a humanism of reading and interpretation "grounded in the shapes of words as bearers of reality, a reality hidden, misleading, resistant, and difficult. The science of reading, in order words, is paramount for humanistic knowledge" (HDC 58).

Just as *Humanism and Democratic Criticism* openly engages Leo Spitzer's philological legacy (Spitzer rather than Auerbach for once!), so too does the 2002 essay "living in Arabic," which invites being read in tandem with Spitzer's "learning Turkish." Spitzer with Said plays off the epistemological modalities of "living" and "learning" a language.[12] Where Spitzer fastened on the ontological implications of sequencing in Turkish, and emphasized how the consecutive unfolding ("one by one") of an action mimics the nature of experience, thereby enlivening narration in a uniquely "human and subjective way," Said gleaned significance from the relational gaps of word-by-word analysis, Spitzer was drawn to modes of expression that seemed wreathed in scare-quotes, that somehow marked "what is happening" as things happen. Interrogative enunciations in Turkish such as "He saw me, or did he not?" or "Did he or did he not open the door?" epitomized for Spitzer a habit of self-questioning that initiated an othering of self within subjectivity. The term *gibi* he suggested, whether attached to verb forms or just thrown out at random, indexed the speaker's loss of conviction in his own words. "Words no longer signify a definite event but carry the ambiguity of comparison within them." *Gibi*, then, was interpreted as a part of speech tailored for the philologist, for it called attention to how each word internalizes comparability. Similarly, in his conclusion to "The return to Philology," Said fixed on the "space of words" as the aporia of comparison,

Humanism, he maintained,

> is the means, perhaps the consciousness we have for providing that kind of finally antinomian or oppositional analysis between the space of words and their various origins and developments in physical and social place, from text to actualized site of either appropriation or resistance, to transmission, to reading and interpretation, from private to public, from silence to explication and utterance, and back again, as we encounter our own silence and mortality—all of it occurring in the world, on the ground of daily life and history and hopes, and the search for knowledge and justice, and then perhaps also for liberation. (HDC 83).

As if anticipating Said's lifelong commitment to a lexicon of exile affording existential humanism, Spitzer delighted in the way in which the grammar of mitigation—the generous sprinkling of equivalent terms for "buts" and "howevers" through Turkish speech—afforded felicitous relief "to the thinking man from the pressures of this difficult life." "In this decreasing voice," Spitzer asserted, "I see our humility. For an instant, the human spirit descends to pessimism to rid itself of numbness, triumphing over difficulty through reasons. Thus a small word like 'but', or 'yet,' through a mere grammatical tool of negation, becomes an emotional manifestation loaded with the weight of life. In these small words, we see humanity deal with adversity." Spitzer traveled down to the micrological stratum of speech particles to observe "life" swimming against the current of "death." Grammatical markers of doubt or negation were cast as valves that released the pressure that builds up in the course of fighting to stay alive, rallying the subject's determination to go on. For Said, these particles comprise a syntax of traumatic incommensurability; they contour the aporias of militant love. Said and Spitzer seem to have entered into stichomythia in their common regard for word spacing as the "program" of life and death, the grammar of grounding and unhoming. Saidian-Spitzerian philology portends the advent of a translational humanism that assumes the disciplinary challenges posed by Turkish and Arabic in their respective circumstances of institutional exile. Turkish and Arabic name, for each of them, a crisis of theo-poetics in secular time.

In his considerations on the status of Arabic language, which one can only speculate might have been the subject of a book-in-the-making, Said experimented with using philology to re-articulate the sacred otherwise. It was as if he were aware of Kenneth Reinhard's conviction that the uncouscious—like divine language—comes through in the desire to "respeak or repunctuate" a language that comes from the outside, bearing "the marks of its strange desires and cruel imperatives."[13] Rather than dodge the issue of how a secular language copes with the mandate of neighboring a sacred tongue, Said took up the problem of "living in Arabic," a task complicated in everyday life by the split between classical (*fus-ha*) and demotic ('*amiya*).[14]

Though one of Said's clear intentions in the essay was to reform Arabic so that it could better deal with classical expression in quotidian speech, his greatest concern, it would seem, was to use philology to de-translate the "fundamentalist" attribution of Arabic. To this end, he recalled the term *al-qua'ida* to its philological function (as the word for "grammar," or "base" of language), just as in *Humanism and Democratic Criticism*, he reclaimed *jihad* for secular usage, contextualizing it as commitment to "isnad" or hermeneutical community:[15]

> Since in Islam the Koran is the Word of God, it is therefore impossible ever fully to grasp, though it must repeatedly be read. But the fact that it is in language already makes it incumbent on reader first of all to try to understand its literal meaning, with a profound awareness that others before them have attempted the same daunting task. So the presence of others is given as a community of witnesses whose availability to the contemporary reader is retained in the form of a chain, each witness depending to some degree on an earlier one. This system of interdependent readings id retained in the form of a chain, each witness depending readings is called "isnad." The common goal is to try to approach the ground of the text, its principal or *usul*, although there must always be a component of personal commitment and extraordinary effort, called "*ijtihad*" in Arabic. (Without a knowledge of Arabic, it is difficult to know that "*ijtihad*" derives from the same root as the now notorious word jihad, which does not on behalf of the truth.) It is not surprising that since the fourteenth century there has been a robust struggle going on about whether *ijtihad* is permissible, to what degree, and within what limits. (HDC 68-69)

As this passage affirms, Said was committed to extracting the predicate "terror" from Arabic as the name of a language. But in seeking to secularize the sacred word, Said wandered into the nominalist quandary of how to name languages otherwise. The need to disrupt the deep structural laws by which language are named after nations, peoples, and God-terms complemented Said's concern to posit a philological humanism no longer hobbled by neoimperialist jingoism, no longer shy of facing off against the autocracy of theocratic speech-acts, and yet, also no longer able to deny the idea of "life" as an untranslatable singularity, a "cognition of paradise" that assumes tangible guise in Babel or the "afterlife" of tranlation.[16] Linguistic monotheism (inherent in Derrida's "monolingualism of the other"), Said's paradigm of "Living in Arabic" (the set that excludes itself, the logic of one sacred language constituted as two—*fus-ha* and '*amiya*), and Spitzer's paradigm of "Learning Turkish" (which activates standing reserves of nontranslaiton) together push the limits of how language thinks itself, thereby regrounding the prospects for a new comparative literature in the problem of translation.

Notes

1. Giorgio Agamben. *Means without Ends*: *Notes on Politics*. trans. Vincenzo Binetti and

Cesare Casarino (Minneapolis: University of Minnesota Press, 2000), p. 64. Further references to this work will appear in the text abbreviated MWE.

2 Samuel Weber. A Touch of Translation: On Walter Benjamin's "Task of the Translator" in *The Ethics of Translation*, eds. Sandra Bermann and Michael Wood (Princeton: Princeton Unviersity Press, 2005), p. 66.

3. Jean-Luc Godard in interview with Manohla Dargis. Godard's Metaphysics of the Movies. *New York Times*, 2004(21), Arts and Leisure, p. 22.

4. Edouard Glissant. *Poétique de la Relation* (Paris: Gallimard, 1990), p. 88.

5 Jean Bernabé, Patrick Chamoiseau, Raphaël Confiant. *Éloge de la créolité* Edition bilingue français/anglais. trans. M. B. Teleb-Khyar (Paris: Gallimard, 1989), pp. 88-90. Emphasis in italics as appears in the original.

6. Peter Hallward. Edourard Glissant between the Singular and the Specific. in *The Yale Journal of Criticism*, 1998, 11. 2, p. 455.

7. Haun Saussy. *The Great Wall of Discourse and Other Adventures in Cultural China.* (Cambridge, Mass.: Harvard East Asian Monographs/Harvard University Press, 2001, pp. 78 and 79.

8. Jacques Derrida. *Aporias.* trans. Thomas Dutoit (Stanford: Stanford University Press, 1993), p. 6. Further references to this work will appear in the text abbreviated A.

9. The Word *négritude* offers a good example of a "prosthesis of the origin" since it was coined by Aimé Césaire in Martinique, a place that had no single African language on which to ground it.

10. Kenneth Reinhard. Kant with Sade, Lacan with Levinas. *Modern Language Notes* 1995, 110. 4, p. 785.

11. Edward Said. *Humanism and Democratic Criticism.* New YorK: Columbia Unvierstiy Press, 2003, p. 58. Further references to this work will appear in the text abbreviated HDC.

12. Leo Spitzer. Learning Turkish in *Varlik*, Translation by Tülay Atak.

13. The unconscious is like a text without punctuation written in familiar characters and a foreign language, a sacred or *revealed* text, moreover, in the sense that the discourse it speaks comes from the outside, from the Other, and bears the marks of its strange desires and cruel imperatives. The interpretive work of analysis is not to translate it so much as to *rearticulate* it, to respeak and repunctuate its components: here a stop or blockage separating two morphemes or phonemes is elided, there an associative connection is severed; or perhaps as isolated and intransigent signifier in the unconcious stream, the pole star of a discursive constellation or "complex", is put into significative motion, and another falls out of circulation, as a newly fixed and unspeakable center of gravitation.

Kenneth Reinhard, "Lacan and Monotheism: Psychoanalysis and the Traversal of Cultural Fantasy", in *Jouvert*, vol. 3, no. 12 (1999), p. 7. http: //social. chass. ncsu. edu/ jouvet/v3i12/reinha. htm.

14. On the issue of two Arabic languages in one, see Iman Humaydan Younes, "Thinking *Fussha*, Feeling 'Amiya: Between Classical and Colloquial Arabic", *Bidoun: Arts and Culture from the Middle East*, issue 02, vol. 01, Fall (2004): 66-67.
15. "In a few years I felt I had no alternative but to commit myself to a reeducation in Arabic philology and grammar. (Incidentally, the word for grammar is the plural *qawa'id*, whose singular form is thte by now familiar *al-qua'ida*, also the word for a military base, as well as a rule, in the grammatical sense.)" Edward Said, "Living in Arabic", *Raritan*, Spring 2002, Vol. 21, no. 4, p. 229.
16. The phrase "cognition of Paradise", close to the concept of "imparadising" that I developed in my chapter on Saidian humanism, was used by Martin Vialon in an unpublished essay on the Arcadian paitings of Traugott Fuchs, another German émigré who made his career in Istanbul under the mentorship of Spitzer and Auerbach. See "The Scars of Exile: Paralipomena concerning the Relationship between History, Literature and Politics—Demonstrated in the Examples of Erich Auerbach, Traugott Fuchs and Their Circle in Istanbul". I am grateful to Martin Vialon for his rich, ongoing research on Auerbach's Istanbul exile, and for his williingness to share work in progress.

（选自 Emily Apter, Chapter 16 of *The Translation Zone: A New Comparative Literature*, Princeton and Oxford: Princeton University Press, 2006, pp. 243-251.）

试论文学形象学的研究史及方法论

（节选）

[法]让·马克·莫哈

【导读】

《试论文学形象学的研究史及方法论》原载法国《比较文学杂志》1992年第3期，《文艺研究》中所载孟华汉译版本为192-199页，仅节选形象学学科发展史部分。让·马克·莫哈，法国比较文学教授，对在法语世界中引入后殖民理论作出了决定性的贡献，与达尼埃尔·亨利·巴柔等被视为当代形象学的创始人。让·马克·莫哈认为文学形象学研究方向之一是“游记这些原始材料”，并将“文学形象视为一个幻影、一种意识形态、一个乌托邦的迹象”。

本文概述形象学学科的发生和发展史，然后指明其理论特质。开篇莫哈提出文学形象学研究的两个主要方向，一是研究“游记这些原始材料”，另一个也是主要的研究方向是“文学作品”。形象学起源于对异国形象的描绘，与人类社会的形成具有同样悠久的历史。“异国”通过把什么拒之门外标示社会的界限，反映社会真实，说明“异国”的本质。“异国形象”超越文学本来的意义，在此背景之下，必须采取跨学科的方法进行形象学研究。因为形象学全面思考和研究其它民族的文化，为了规避民族主义的危险，形象学研究需要学会应对多学科交汇的局面。由于“创始者”们的共同努力，文学形象学对社会与文学的联系加以肯定，法国比较文学从而有了新的研究视角。形象学在两个方面显示其特征，一是“跨学科性”，二是“使用诸多新文学理论，特别是符号学和接受美学。这使我们可以明确形象学的研究方法”。由此提出了形象学的基本原则。

在文中，莫哈认为：“文学形象学所研究的一切形象，都是三重意义上的某个形象：它是异国的形象，是出自一个民族(社会、文化)的形象，最后，是由一个作家特殊感受所创作出的形象。”从三个方面对形象学工作研究的核心问题“对他者形象的定义”予以说明。“1/定义形象自身”，需要排除两个问题，一是类比问题，二是光学词汇的运用问题。“2/在形象与社会集体想象物中的关系中来定义它”，研究的主要困难存在于找到“想象他者”时需要遵循的规律、原则和惯例。“3/按照能在具体文本中分析形象的适当方法来定义它”，强调“由具体的文学和(或)精神生活的形式，以及当时社会整体想象物的形式来决定”采用形象分析的方法。

（白阳明）

大家知道，文学形象学的定义是研究文学作品中所表现的异国。它有两个主要的研究方向：一是研究“游记这些原始材料”；但主要还是研究“文学作品。这些作品或直接描绘异国，或涉及到或多或少模式化了的对一个异国的总体认识”。① 由于近期涌现出了大量的研究工作，形象学取得了引人瞩目的、持续的发展。对此，我们有必要加以总结：首先概述这一学科的发生、发展史，然后指明其理论特质。

一、学　科　史

早在人类最古老的表现艺术中就已有了对异国形象的描绘，其历史可能与人类社会的形成同样悠久。“异国”标示出了一个社会的界限，反映了这个社会的真实情况：它将什么拒之门外，从而也就说明了它本质上是什么。这样，形象学首先就令文学史家们生疑。异国形象属于对一种文学或一个社会的想象，它在各方面都超出了文学本来意义上的范畴，而成为人类学或史学的研究对象。正因为文学作品是在这个广阔的背景上形成的，形象学研究就必须按照跨学科的方法来进行，这总是要令文学纯粹主义者不满的。此外，提出异国往往只是民族主义的一种策略，而形象学又是对描写其它民族(或文化)的民族(或文化)进行总体的思考和研究，因而就会被怀疑为是中了民族主义的圈套(有时这种怀疑是有道理的)。这就是比较学者在这一研究领域内所面临的两大危险：不正规的跨学科性和民族主义，甚至是那些未被承认的民族的心理学。考察该领域内已进行的研究可以证明，这些危险不仅已经逐渐被避免，且如总体文学与比较文学的全局一样，形象学研究已学会利用这种多学科交汇的局面。

19 世纪，法国首创了比较文学的系统教育。她从 18 世纪继承了文化史编纂学的传统，这一传统可以用博纳尔的一句名言来概括：“文学是社会的表现。”②从斯达尔夫人③到伊波利特·泰纳——他将文学作品减化为作家的主要才能和三要素间④的相互影响——我们已对这句话印象深刻，它过分强调了民族心理学和民族主义的重要性。当然，我们可以如同乌茨森·M. 波斯奈特所做的那样，从广义上去运用这个公式。波斯奈特在比较文学“教科书”中将文学的表现形式同产生文学的社会形式结合起来。⑤ 但在他的书中，无论是严谨的分析还是比较主义，都不占主要地位。恰如梵蒂根所指出的，这位英国学者的书，其内容与题目所标示的相去甚远，是一本“重被置于人类历史中的文学史综合论文集”。⑥

① Y. 谢夫莱尔：《比较文学》，法国大学出版社 1989 年版，第 25-26 页。

② 《法兰西水星》，1802。

③ 特别是她 1800 年以醒目的题目出版的著述《论文学与社会制度的关系》。

④ 这些要素为种族、阶级和时代(见《英国文学史导言》，1863)。

⑤ 文学依照下列顺序而发展：“社会生活是由部落而城邦，由城邦而国家渐次扩展的，再从这后两者进入人类大同的世界。”(《比较文学》，1886，第 86 页)

⑥ 《比较文学》，A. 高兰出版社 1931 年版，第 5 页。

由于那些被蒙菲德·S. 费歇准确地称之为形象学"创始者"们的努力①，特别是在让·玛丽·卡雷起决定作用的宣传鼓动下，文学形象学后来进一步肯定了这种社会与文学的联系。② 卡雷将形象学定义为"各民族间的、各种游记、想象间的相互诠释"。③ 这样，他就对博纳尔那句全景式的名言做出了"形象学的解释"。这解释虽有局限，却更精确了。文学至少是社会的表现，因为通过文学，可以破译出一个社会在他者那里产生的幻象。从那时起，让·玛丽·卡雷的工作，特别是那本《法国作家与德国幻象，1800—1940》④，就将法国的比较文学引向了一种全新的研究视角。他的高徒 M. F. 基亚对此做了如下概述："不再追踪研究使人产生错觉的一般影响，而是力求更好地理解在个人和集体意识中，那些主要的民族神话是怎样被制作出来，又是怎样生存的。"⑤如果说当时尚未明确使用"形象学"这个词，那么，这一研究的基本原则已经被提出来了。⑥

当时尚待明确的问题是：在文学和关于异国的集体神话间存在着一种什么样的关系：同时，形象学在总体文学与比较文学研究中的地位也有待确定，以免使其沦为不敢直报家门的民族心理学，或成为被法朗索瓦·诺斯特称为"文化自足性"⑦的那种东西的材料来源。尽管形象学被轮流疑为实证主义或虚妄的百科全书主义⑧，它毕竟还是得到了发展，且形成了自己特殊的概念，这使它后来能在下述两个方向上显示其特征：

——跨学科性：形象学研究处于"文学史、政治史和民族心理学几个领域的交叉口上"⑨。因此，它就与史学家及社会学家们的工作相交了。⑩ 当形象学研究考察某一文学形象是如何加入(或不加入)到能够触及整个社会阶层的更宽泛的作品总体中时，这种研究就属于社会批评范畴了。在这方面，有"文学感觉的社会学"(非常接近于历史学和一般

---

① M. S. 费歇：《作为比较文学的民族形象》。尤请参阅巴尔登斯贝格：《文学：创 作、成就、期限》，巴黎，1913。

② 在 1931 年出版的著述中，P. 梵蒂根在"比较文学的方法及成果"一节中甚至未提及形象学。当时是用"机运"、"成就"、"影响"、"模仿"这些词来定义国际文学关系的。

③ 见 M. F. 基亚《比较文学》一书序，法国大学出版社 1951 年版，第 6 页。

④ 巴黎，布瓦文出版公司 1947 年版。

⑤ 见基亚书，第 111 页。

⑥ M. F. 基亚将他著述中有关形象学的章节命名为"人们所看到的异国"。

⑦ 由此，F. 诺斯特便攻击了 J. M. 卡雷的比较文学观。他指出，卡雷所设计的国际文学关系有强化民族文学观念的危险，这恰与比较学者们的目标相反。(《比较文学论文集》，弗莱堡大学出版社，1968，第 331 页)

⑧ 参阅 R. 雷马克：《比较文学的危机》，载《第二届国际比协年会论文集》，1958。另请参阅艾田伯《比较不是理由》，伽里玛出版社 1963 年版，第 79-79 页)。艾田伯在其新作(《中国之欧洲》，伽里玛出版社，2 卷，1988—1989)中研究了法国及欧洲描写的中国。难道这不就是一个未敢直报家门的形象学研究？

⑨ M. 克斯泰格：《比较文学为何存在？》，载《文学研究》第 3 期，洛桑，1974。

⑩ 如乔治·杜比的"心态"史或乔纳斯·哈斯一海的舆论史及其社会学(如，《在外国评论中的联邦德国三十年》，慕尼黑，C. H. 贝克出版社，1979)，或芒弗莱德·柯赫-希勒布莱希特《当代德国形象，心理学史》，慕尼黑，C. H. 贝克出版社，1977。

社会学)与“创作社会学”(等同于社会批评)之别。①

——使用诸多新文学理论，特别是符号学和接受美学。② 这使我们可以明确形象学的研究方法。③

1951年，M.F. 基亚在他那本综述性的书中，按时代(自15世纪至20世纪)和地理位置(德、英、意、西、俄)对法国的形象学研究做了概述。④ 毫无疑义，这样一种划分方式今天已不具什么意义了。我们只需看看从那时至今已发表的最著名的研究工作及与形象学有关的重要的理论贡献即可明白此点。⑤ 在这方面，我们可试着列出一份简表(可惜是不完全的)。首先是J.M. 卡雷那些几乎是开拓性的工作，之后，我们还应列出：

1966 雨果·迪斯林克：《关于形象和幻象的问题及其在比较文学范畴内的检验》，载《阿卡迪亚》杂志，1期；

1971 芒费莱德·施坦格：《关于比较文学的概念和研究》，见芒·施坦格等著《比较文学理论》，柏林—纽约；

1976 阿列克桑德鲁·杜图：《模式、形象、比较》，载《综合》杂志，Ⅲ(此杂志中载有多篇有关论文)，布加勒斯特；彼得·别尔纳：《作为文学研究对象的异国形象》，载《当代技术语言》杂志，柏林，H. 56；

1980《文学形象学——在文学中民族模式的形式及功能》，载《比较文学手册》，2卷，拜罗伊特大学；

1981 D.H. 巴柔：《一种比较文学的研究角度：文学形象》，载《综合》杂志，Ⅷ，布加勒斯特；M.S. 费歌：《关于比较文学形象学的产生，民族形象——比较文学史的研究对象》，波恩，布维耶出版社；

1982 H. 迪斯林克：《在内在作品与超验作品之外的比较文学形象学》，载《综合》杂志，IX，布加勒斯特；

1983 M. 卡多：《形象研究》，载《总体与比较文学研究》，法国总体与比较文学学会主编，巴黎；D.H. 巴柔：《文化形象：从比较文学到文化人类学》，载《综合》杂志，X，布加勒斯特；

1988《爱尔维修研讨会》，7期，《形象学：文学再现问题》；H. 迪斯林克，K.V. 辛德朗：《欧洲和民族的自我理解》，波恩，布维耶出版社；

1989 D.H. 巴柔：《从文化形象到总体想象物》，载《比较文学概论》，P. 布律耐尔、

① 见克斯泰格书。

② 参阅D.H. 巴柔《一个比较文学研究的视角：文化形象》，载《综合》杂志，Ⅷ，布加勒斯特，1981。

③ 在研究一国形象时，对一个作者或一部作品的接受可成为其中最重要的部分。

④ 见上引书，126页。

⑤ 为了不使书目过长，我们此处只论及与法国有关的研究。[译者注：作者在此注中列举了1932—1989年间出版的13部著作及5部博士论文，因与本文内容无密切关联，恕不一一译出。其中与东方有关的题目为：J.C. 拜歌：《东方之旅》，拉封出版社，1985；G. 瑟加尔：《20世纪最初25年间德国游记中的远东形象》(博士论文)，里尔三大，1981；J.J. 莫哈：《1969—1980年间法国小说中的第三世界形象》(博士论文)，巴黎三大，1987。]

Y. 谢夫莱尔主编，巴黎，法国大学出版社。

以上是一些综述性论文和著述。这些工作描绘了形象学方法论的演化过程，其中最新的贡献是 D. H. 巴柔的文章。自该文发表起，形象学的基本原则就被明确提出了。这些工作研究的核心问题是对他者形象的定义。为了简要而忠实地说明问题，我们可将此定义具体为：1/定义形象自身，2/在形象与社会总体想象物的关系中来定义它，3/按照能在具体文本中分析形象的适当方法来定义它。下面我们逐一予以说明：

1/形象被理解为"在文学化但同时也是社会化的过程中得到的对异国的总体认识"，① 最典型的例子是有关异国的固定模式，它是"一种文化的象征性表现"，② 即使是在文学文本中，这种固定模式也与大量的意识形态问题相联。

有两个问题不在此列，需要排除。首先是类比问题(一个形象不是更像或更不像什么的问题，它与先存于作品的一种思想或一个价值体系直接相关)；其次是光学词汇(如感觉、注视、棱镜、视觉……)的运用问题，这些词会使人误以为形象是现实的反映或误译。事实上，研究一个形象时，真正的关键在于揭示其内在"逻辑"、"真实情况"，③ 而非核实它是否与现实相符。说到底，正是这样，人们才使"再现"(representation)一词摆脱了认识论哲学传统赋予它的意义。我们知道，认识论实际上将再现建立在戏剧表演(形象使我们面对着什么)和外交手段(再现被理解为替代物，它是现实事物的某种复制品)的双重隐喻之上。④ 对认识论来说，再现就是将事实上的、直接的和间接的、经媒体转介的两类存在重叠在一起。形象学拒绝将文学形象看作是对一个先存于文本的异国的表现或一个异国现实的复制品。它将文学形象主要视为一个幻影、一种意识形态、一个乌托邦的迹象，而这些都是主观向往相异性所特有的。因此形象是"对一种文化现实的再现，通过这种再现，创作了它(或赞同、宣传它)的个人或群体揭示出和说明了他们生活于其中的那个意识形态和文化的空间"。⑤

2/这一形象"源自一个宽泛且复杂的总体：整体想象物。更确切地说，是社会整体想象物"。⑥ 而社会整体想象物是"全社会对一个集体、一个社会文化整体所作的阐释，是双级性(同一性/相异性)的阐释"。它显然部分地"与事件、政治、社会意义上的历史"⑦ 相联。形象学研究的主要困难在于找到"想象他者"时所特有的规律、原则和惯例。就像人们所说的，这种想象在一定程度上是与历史铰接在一起的，但它并非历史的"代用品"，⑧ 更非历史的影象。

3/分析形象采用的方法依托于形象与社会整体想象物的关系。由于每一具体问题与历

① 《比较文学概论》，135 页。

② 《一个比较文学研究的视角：文化形象》，173 页。另请参阅雅诺斯·列兹《论无处不在的民族和人种固有模式》，载《比较文学手册》，2 期，1980。

③ 见《比较文学概论》，137 页。

④ 见《通用百科全书》"再现"条目。(J. 拉德里耶撰)

⑤ D. H. 巴柔，上引书，135 页。

⑥ 同上。

⑦ 同上，135、154 页。

⑧ 同上，154 页。

史语境铰接的方式不同，因而就不可能硬性规约使用的方法。譬如，阿莱克·G. 哈格瑞夫就很正确地指出：对于一部如同彼也尔·洛蒂那样表面上自夸和“冷漠”的作品，应首先将其置于当时达到顶峰的法国殖民扩张的历史语境中去理解它。① 然而很明显，得出这一结论的分析方法与一部直接与殖民主义有关的作品所要求的方法是全然不同的，后者如卢蒂亚·吉卜林的作品。采用何种方法分析形象，每一次都要由具体的文学和(或)精神生活的形式，以及当时社会整体想象物的形式来决定。但是就总体而言，我们仍可指出分析文学作品的三个主要(和非常传统的)阶段：文本主要结构的定位(它们经常是对立的)、大的主题单位、最后是词汇层面(通过这些词汇来描写相异性)。由此，我们便可按照克洛德·列维—斯特劳斯结构人类学原理②的步骤，推知“文本的总体结构”和“主要的叙事或推论策略”。这样，我们就得出了一个有关异国形象的具体、但非强制性的概念，这一概念毫无疑义具有一定的跨学科性。当然，以上这些理论结果尚有待补充。与形象关系密切的哲学传统(特别是保尔·利科的阐释学)将使我们能够同时指出这些理论的局限性和使用范围。

(孟华　译)

（选自让·马克·莫哈(Jean-Marc Moura)：《试论文学形象学的研究史及方法论》，孟华译，《文艺研究》1983 年第 4 期，第 192-199 页。）

① 《在法国文学作品中的殖民经验》，麦克米伦出版社，1981。

② 尤请参阅《文化形象》(第 83 页)。需要指出的是，并非所有的形象学理论家都 同意使用结构主义原理。我们甚至可质疑，文学理论与这些人类学观念的分手，是否更有利于文学的发展。

比较文学意义上的形象学[①]

（节选）

［法］巴柔

【导读】

本文原标题为《形象》，是巴柔教授所著《比较文学与总体文学》一书中的第四章。巴柔教授是法国著名学者，曾任巴黎第三大学总体与比较文学系系主任。巴柔教授的主要研究领域为形象学、比较文学方法论和法西文学关系研究。自20世纪80年代以来，巴柔教授对传统的形象研究进行了重大革新，提出了一整套理论与方法论并使之体系化，因而被公认为是当代形象学的领军人物。他的代表性著作有：《法国文学中的西班牙形象，1700—1755》(1971)，《总体与比较文学》(1994)，《词汇之翼：对创作的文学与诗学批评》(1994)，《小说的诞生》(1996)，《阅读历险记——〈堂·吉诃德〉五论》(2005)等，另有其他专著及译作十余部，论文数百篇。

在本文中，巴柔教授首先确定比较文学意义上形象的概念，形象是为两种类型文化现实间的差距所作的文学的或非文学且能说明符指关系的表述。换言之，形象就是对一个文化现实的描述。对比较文学学者而言，异国形象属于社会整体社会总体想象物的范畴。社会总体想象物具有双极性：同一性和相异性，两者既对立又互补。形象学所研究的绝不是形象真伪的程度，它研究的是形形色色的形象如何构成了某一历史时期对异国的特定描述；研究那些支配了一个社会及其文学体系、社会总体想象物的动力线。接下来，巴柔教授重点分析了套话，套话如何在自然属性和文化间造成混淆；某一特定时期某种特定文化中的词汇如何构成形象，等等。套话如何以隐含的方式提出一个恒定的等级制度，一种对世界和对一切文化的两分法。巴柔还分析了主体对待他者的三种基本态度：狂热、憎恶、亲善；此外可能还有第四种情况：一个已经消失的整体重新组建起来，如泛拉丁主义，泛日耳曼主义等。巴柔还探讨了形象学与身份认同，形象学与异国情调等问题。最后巴柔强调：文化之间应该平等地对话和交流，不应把对方看作自己的附属品，而应成为对方的客人。

（霍晓珊）

---

① 此标题为译者所加，原标题《形象》，是巴柔教授所著《总体文学与比较文学》(高兰出版社，1994)一书中的第四章。

比较文学意义上的形象

要确定比较文学意义上的形象的概念，就需先下一个定义，或者更确切地说，需要先设定一个研究范围。对此，我们或可作如下表述：一切形象都源于对自我与“他者”，本土与“异域”关系的自觉意识之中，即使这种意识是十分微弱的。因此，形象即为对两种类型文化现实间的差距所作的文学的或非文学，且能说明符指关系的表述。而使用了“差距”这个概念，我们就又回到了异国的层面，这是一切比较文学思考的基础。在社会学领域，这个差距将表现为各种社会阶级的差别，或各人种、各地缘文化区域(地区或首都)的差别。在人类学方面，它将是书写与历史的社会与那些所谓“原始”社会间的对立。

描述和差距

因此，形象就是对一个文化现实的描述，通过这种描述，制造了(或赞同，宣传)这个形象的个人或群体，显示或表达出他们乐于置身其间的那个社会的、文化的、意识形态的、虚构的空间。这个我们所设定的研究空间是一个剧场，是以形象化的方式(当然要承认文字游戏仅是表面的)，即用形象、描述等方式，表达各种范式的场所。按照这些范式，一个社会在审视和想象着“他者”的同时，也进行着自我审视和反思。毫无疑义，异国形象事实上同样能够说出对本土文化(审视者文化)有时难于感受、表述、想象到的某些东西。因而异国形象(被审视者文化)就能将未被明确说出、定义的，因此也就隶属于“意识形态”的各个“国别”的现实，置换为一种隐喻的形式。但在更宽泛的意义上，对比较学者而言，异国形象属于社会总体想象物的范畴。后者具有双极性：同一性和相异性，这两个词既对立又互补。

因此，形象学所研究的绝不是形象真伪的程度，这个层面的研究当然也还可以继续进行下去(因为形象描述了某些“事实”，是用词语来表述后者的，就此而言，所有的形象必然都是虚假的)；形象学也绝不仅限于研究对简称为“现实”的东西所做的文学置换。它应该研究的是形形色色的形象如何构成了某一历史时期对异国的特定描述；研究那些支配了一个社会及其文学体系、社会总体想象物的动力线。即使受到用语的限制，比较学者不得不借用某些光学词汇(感觉，注视，阅读，看法，幻觉……)，我们仍然要确认：形象是描述，是对一个作家、一个集体思想中的在场成分的描述。这些在场成分置换了一个缺席的原型(异国)，替代了它，也置换了一种情感和思想的混合物，对这种混合物，必须了解其在感情和意识形态层面上的反映，了解其内在逻辑，也就是说想象所产生的偏离。比较文学意义上的形象，并非现实的复制品(或相似物)；它是按照注视者文化中的模式、程序而重组、重写的，这些模式和程式均先存于形象。在一定程度上说，形象是一种语言，一种次要语言，它平行于“我”说的那种语言，与之同在，并在某种意义上复制了它，以便说出他者，说出其他的事物来。

……

套　话

套话在信息交流中的意义很明显：它释放出信息的一个最小形式，以便进行最大限度、尽可能广泛的信息交流，无论如何，它以普及化为终极目标。显然，套话是对一种文化的概括，它是这种文化标志的缩影(如陈词滥调，福楼拜常说的“被普遍接受的思想”等)。套话就是在一个社会和一个被简化了的文化表述之间建立起一致性关系的东西：次要部分、表语被提高到了本质的部位，这就要求社会——文化要尽可能广泛地取得一致。

作为他者定义的载体，套话是陈述集体知识的一个最小单位，它希望在任何历史时刻都有效。套话不是多义的，相反，它却具有高度的多语境性，任何时刻都可使用。还需补充一点，如果说意识形态是以(道德、社会的)规范和话语间的混淆为其特点，那么，套话代表的就是一种成功的、因而也就是有效的混淆。

实际上，套话以隐含的方式提出了一个恒定的等级制度，一种对世界和对一切文化的真正的两分法。比如，说法国人爱喝葡萄酒，这是一个套话。但若此话出自一个法国人之口，这就是一个自我套话。那么，这个自我定义就以首要和基本的方式对立于英国人爱喝茶或德国人爱喝啤酒。而这种对立的目的，其实就是要在法国文化内部制定出一个有利于法国人的等级制度。若认为这个例子过于简单化，那就是忘记了诸如“复仇”时代法国散文大家莫里斯·巴雷斯那样的一些作品：他的小说《科莱特·博多士》，曾取得过巨大成就。在这部作品中，法国文化自始至终对立于普鲁士文化，也就是说拉丁文化(就是作家本人和他为之写作的公众观念中的文明)自始至终对立于日耳曼文化，即野蛮文化。

这样，套话一经提出就是对立的，而它是以它陈述的唯一事实来对立，甚至在陈述的同时它就证实了这一点。套话是对精神和推理的惊人省略，是一种恒定的预期理由：它显示出(并证明了)的是它原本应该证明的。它不仅是一个凝固文化的标志，还揭示出了一个重言、重复的文化，一切批评尝试此后都被排除在这个文化之外，以有利于对某些本质化和歧视类型的确定。

自然属性和文化间的混淆

还应该看一看以套话作为载体的定义是怎样制作出来的。定义在两类不同但互补的事实(自然和文化，存在和行为)间生成混淆。在这里，人们对生理词汇所具有的重要性将不会感到惊讶，这些词汇是用来描述和生产套话的，如犹太人的鹰勾鼻，黑人一笑即露出的白齿等。自然属性是对一种文化情境的说明和担保：鹰勾鼻：这就是为什么“他们”会拿我们的钱；大娃娃笑脸上露出的白齿：所以在管理有方的殖民统治中，就要对这些人严加管束。这是他者的自然属性解释了他者的文化，他的存在解释了他的行为(低级的)和作为叙述者的我的行为(高级的)。在描述性语言(即“什么民族是……”的话语)和起规范作用的用语(即规范，如我们所说的“什么民族不知道……”“不能……”)间的这种意识形态的典型混淆，通过套话就被经久地保持下去了。于是，描述性语言(生理属性)就混入了规范性范畴(某个民族、某种文化的低下)之中。而多种多样殖民主义意识形态正是建立在这种对他者生理、精神低下或(与一个被认为是高级的叙事者提出的标准相比)不正常性的错误证明之上的。

显然，对套话的这些思考更得益于人文科学，而非文学。它们以某种方式参与到总体文学(套话如同文学或副文学表述与社会间的关系)和比较文学的理论探讨中来。但文学形象研究，或最好是说文化形象研究，其价值所在，就是把文学思考重新引回到社会和文化问题方面，而恰在被称为总体文学的研究中，这些问题都占有一席之地。

从词汇到形象

在某一特定时期，某种特定文化中都或多或少存储了一批能够直接或间接传播他者形象的词汇。作为形象的原始构成成分，我们要对这样一批词汇进行鉴别。

为了举例说明，并探讨一下西班牙在法国的形象，我们随便就可举出："骄傲"、"高贵"、"荣誉"、"热情"、"嫉妒"、"懒惰"等词。几个世纪以来，这些词就是用来形容在法国文化中法国人对西班牙人的看法的。这样一张词汇表可以引发出一种历时(史学家们称之为长时段)研究，它可上溯至17世纪，且毫无疑问，还可追溯至更久远的过去，它可提供关于西班牙人的在场、自然属性及其作用的精确情况，而这是一个被想象、具象了的，即在数百年法国人想象中以词汇来表述的西班牙。但在16至18世纪间所使用的词汇则是"爱吹牛"、"充好汉"、"胡言乱语"、"浪漫"等。

鉴别这样一些词汇，把它们与各种词汇网中的其他词重新组合，并以此为出发点来构成一些可能的同位词，这些同样需要深入到社会总体想象物——我们思考的对象中去。当涉及一些未被翻译的词汇时，调查内容就更丰富了(且更具有比较文学的意义)。这些词未被翻译，那就是不可译的，因为这些词传递(它们就是这样被感知的)和表示了一个绝对的外国现实，相异性的一个不变成分。

我们可看到从词汇出发进行研究所能获得的全部益处，这一研究从某些操作观念(如同位)中，以普遍的方式从一切能由一个系列过渡到另一系列的比较类别中，从所有可能的等价中都能获得益处。这个"等价"问题是我们在研究翻译时曾探讨过的。形象就是一种对他者的翻译，同时也是一种自我翻译。

基本态度或象征模式

第一种基本态度：狂热

一个作家或团体把异国现实看作绝对优于注视者文化、优于本土文化的东西。这种优越性使被注视的异国文化形态全部或部分地表现出来。它所引起的后果就是作家或团体把本土文化看成是低级的。与提高异国身价相对应的，就是对本土文化的否定和贬抑。有了"狂热"的态度，对异国的描述更多地就属于一种"幻象"，而非形象。启蒙时代法国思想家们极度赞美英国，对这种态度大致可做如下解释：他们意识到了英国制度的优越和法国的落后，甚至缺陷(较少自由和宽容)。当时人们对俄国的某种"狂热"也基于同样的原因，它源于片面提高了一些形象的价值，如彼得大帝，叶卡捷琳娜二世等。

第二种基本态度：憎恶

这是第一种态度的反面：与优越的本土文化相比，异国现实被视为是落后的。有"憎恶"之感时，幻象就会呈现出本土文化的形态。法国人对日耳曼的憎恶，其必然结果就是对拉丁文化的"幻象"，它与日耳曼的粗野相对立。然而弱小毕竟是事实，因为法国战败了，领土亦被吞并。这种做法就是不顾描述逻辑，把用来帮助想象物(或相反)的意识形态工作计算在内，以构成一个对普鲁士而言正面的法国形象，这个形象优先占有了被表现出，且被先验地确定为本质上优越的价值，正如在莫里斯·巴莱斯的小说中所描述的那样。

第三种基本态度：亲善

异国现实被看成、被认为是正面的，它纳入了注视者文化，而后者也被视为是正面的，且是对被注视者文化的补充。"亲善"是唯一能真正实现双向交流的态度，大家都知道，重要的是不要把它与"狂热"相混淆。后者依靠对外来语的借用(它涉及到的是思想或服饰，如"dandy(花花公子)"对英国的狂热，"花花公子"一词未被确切译出，因为在被视为负面的、低级的文化，如法国文化中无法找到相对应的词)，而前者(亲善)靠的则是互相了解和承认，批评交流和平等对话。与"狂热"所要求的机械的文化适应相对立的，是通过"亲善"而发展起来的真正的"文化对话"。"憎恶"以对他者的排除和象征死亡为前提，而"亲善"则力图使人不得不采用一种困难的要求很高的方法，它要求承认存在于"我"旁边，与"我"相对，既不高于"我"，也不低于"我"的"他者"，这个"他者"是独特的不可替换的。倘若联想到哲学家埃马纽埃尔·勒维纳斯有关道德的思考，那么用"亲善"的态度就会注意到他者，并会发现他有一张"面孔"。毫无疑问，这是因为注视别人的目光也会返回到自我身上，而投射到自我身上的目光并未忘记绕经别人那里。"亲善"的他者恰是"别人"，这是一个只能用伦理术语思考的"他者"。

有第四种可能吗?

可能还有第四种情况，例如：交流、对话等现象都被取消了，而代之以新的正在统一的整体，或将已消失的整体重新组建起来：如泛拉丁主义，泛日耳曼主义，泛斯拉夫主义，当然还有形形色色的世界主义和国际主义，我们似乎很难在这些主义中区分出正面或负面来。对那些正在统一的整体来说，在同语种的兄弟姐妹间的关系(日耳曼、斯拉夫民族间的兄弟关系，使用拉丁语各民族间的姐妹关系……)显然是正面的。但使用拉丁语各民族姐妹间之所以相互视为"正面"，恰是为了更好地反对被视为负面的日耳曼人。大家都知道如何看待30年代的泛日耳曼主义。这样，"憎恶"的态度就在比一个国家更宽泛的范围内重新形成了。

形象学与身份认同

某些研究领域，还有某些待调查的问题都可从形象学研究中获益。如有关身份认同的问题，这中间就涉及对他者地位及形象的讨论。所有对自身身份依据进行思考的文学，甚至通过虚构作品来思考的文学，都传播了一个或多个他者的形象，以便进行自我结构和自我言说：对他者的思辩就变成了自我思辩。殖民地国家的文学，美洲和非洲的文学都直接或间接地涉及这些问题：美洲对应于欧洲，"新世界"对应于旧世界，旧殖民地对应于欧洲大都会，西属、葡属殖民地的"克里奥尔"白种人面对着大都会里的欧洲人，西化了的土著人面对着殖民者，最后还有欧洲人面对着所有的“善良”和“恶毒”的野蛮人。

“为了理解他者，不应将对方当作自己的附属品，而应成为对方的客人。”这是形象学研究应遵循的至理名言，这些铿锵有力的话语今天仍然对我们具有指导意义。

（孟华 译）

（节选自巴柔：《比较文学意义上的形象学》，《中国比较文学》1998 年第 4 期，第 79-90 页。）

论“文化语境”与“变异体”以及文学的发生学

（节选）

严绍璗

【导读】

严绍璗，北京大学教授，北大古文献研究所副所长，北京大学比较文学研究所副所长，北大日本研究中心委员会委员、中国中日文学关系史学会副会长。严先生在古典文献、东亚文学、海外中国学、思想史等方面都有很高成就。他的突出贡献在于在原典实证的基础上，系统地揭示了东亚文化的历史联系和各自的民族特征，阐明了构成各种联系的文化的内在机制，建立了理解东亚文化本质的“变异体”理论。他把对东亚文化的“双边关系研究”提升为以“文化语境”为生存环境的“发生学研究”。

文学的发生学是关于文学生成的理论，它关注的是文学内在运行的机制，从而阐明每一种文学文本之所以成为一种独特的文学样式的内在逻辑。本文以文学的发生学为基点，详细地讨论了构成文学的发生学的文化语境的三个层面，并指出文本的变异机制是文学的发生学的重要内容，而文明社会中的文学文本的大多数都是变异体文学。

文化语境是文学文本生成的本源。文化语境指的是在特定的时空中，由特定的文化积累与文化现状构成的文化场。文化语境实际上存在着三个层面，第一层面是显现本民族文化沉积与文化特征的文化语境，第二层面是显现与异民族文化相抗衡、相融合的文化语境，第三层面是显现人类思维与认知的共性的文化语境。几乎所有的东亚文学都是在这样的文化语境中生成的。在文化语境中还原文学文本，便可凸显文学文本内含的真正的美的意识特征，并阐明文学文本的实际的成因。

从文学发生的立场上观察文学文本，可以说，在文明社会中，他们中大多数都是变异体文学。例如日本的和歌在面临中国大陆汉诗的冲击与挑战中，逐渐形成了自身的格律化，并衍生出了俳句等形式。文学的变异中所形成的新的文学样式，都是本土文学传统的延伸和在另一层面中的继承。而影响文学的本质，正是在于从文本的立场上探索文学的成因。因此文学的发生学是跨文化研究中具有重要意义的成员。

（霍晓珊）

文学的发生学，是关于“文学”生成的理论。我国人文科学领域内对文学的研究，大多数学者都是在国别文学史的系统内加以展开的，即是对已经生成的“文学文本”在民族文化的范畴中进行阐述。(这里使用的是广泛意义上的“文本”概念，包括文学样式、文学创作和文学理论等，下同。)文学的发生学，更加关注文学内在运行的机制，从而阐明每一种文学文本之所以成为一种独特的文学样式的内在逻辑。

从文学研究的广谱上加以考察，“比较文学研究”确立了对文学研究的新的视角，这一学术与其说是提供了研究的方法论，不如说它是确立了突破狭隘陈说，从而重新构建文学研究的新理念。正是基于比较文学研究的这一基本学术特征，本来在传统的国别文学史的范畴内事实上无法解决的“文学的发生学”问题，终于被提到了“比较文学研究”领域中来了，从而使比较文学在研究趋向与研究结论方面，更接近于触摸到”文学”的本质实际。

文学的发生学，即探明文学文本之所以形成现在已经显现的面貌的内在成因。它与文学的诠释学不同，其学术意义并不在于“诠释”文学——在“诠释”的领域内，诠释的立场则是每一个诠释者的独特思想立场。由于每一个诠释者的时代不同、文化底蕴不同、美学趣味不同，当然也由于诠释者本人的生存价值不同和生存取向不同，等等，一个文学“文本”可以有而且也必然会有多种多样的“诠释”。但是，作为文学的发生学研究的有价值的成果，在关于“文学生成”的阐述上，其答案应该是唯一的。当然，这种探索“唯一”的过程可以是多样的，但真正符合科学意义的结论是不二的。在某种意义上，它可能多少与生命科学领域内关于探索“人之所以成为人”的命题在思维逻辑和实证推导方面有些类似。

现在，从我们对东亚文学发生的研究体验说来，或许有把握提出关于“文学的发生学”的范畴，解析其路径，并尽可能提供操作的程序。

在“文化语境”中“还原”文学文本

“文化语境”(Culture Context)是文学文本生成的本源。

从文学的发生学的立场上说，“文化语境”指的是在特定的时空中由特定的文化积累与文化现状构成的“文化场”(The Field of Culture)。这一范畴应当具有两个层面的内容。其第一层面的意义，指的是与文学文本相关联的特定的文化形态，包括生存状态、生活习俗、心理形态、伦理价值等组合成的特定的“文化氛围”；其第二层面的意义，指的是文学文本的创作者(有意识或无意识的创作者、个体或群体的创作者)在这一特定的“文化场”中的生存方式、生存取向、认知能力、认知途径与认知心理，以及由此而达到的认知程度，此即是文学的创作者们的“认知形态”。事实上，各类文学“文本”都是在这样的“文化语境”中生成的。因此，揭示文学的发生学的轨迹，首先应该借助“文化语境”的解析，即在“文化语境”中“还原”文学文本。

构成“文学的发生学”的“文化语境”，实际上存在着三个层面。第一层面是“显现本民族文化沉积与文化特征的文化语境”；第二层面是“显现与异民族文化相抗衡与相融合的文化语境”；第三层面是“显现人类思维与认知的共性的文化语境”。每一层“文化语境”都是有多元的组合。目前的研究可以证明，几乎所有的东亚文学都是在这样的文化语境中生成的。

一般说来，所谓“文学”，可以说是在精神形态中以艺术形式显现的“人”的美意识。这里说的“艺术形式”，是作者在自己生存的“文化场”中对它所关注的生活，以他或他们自身的“认知形态”加以虚构、象征、隐喻，并以编纂成意象、情节、人物、故事等手段来表现作者作为“人”的美意识特征。因而，在“文化语境”中“还原”文学，便是在一定的“文化语境”的层面中，透过组合成”文学”的各个“装置”，如意象、情节、人物、故事等，对其内含的各种虚构、象征、隐喻等进行“实在意义”上的解析，这样便可凸显”文学文本”内含的真正的美意识特征，并阐明”文学文本”的实际的成因。

例如从比较文学研究的立场上观察日本古代的文学，我们常常会感到“文学史”给予我们的知识的匮乏——目前几乎所有的《日本文学史》(包括篇幅更加巨大的《东方文学史》)，都无力揭开深藏在日本文学文本之中的使各个“文本”之所以成为“如此形态”的秘密，例如，……为什么神话创造了一个“太阳女神”而不是“男神”呢？为什么太阳女神委派她的“孙子”而不是她的“儿子”再次下降大地，组织起对人间的统治呢？……由文本所提供的疑问实在是很多的，这些疑问如果思考下去，就必然会涉及日本古代文学中关于“发生学”的一系列具有根本意义的问题。如果我们能够把这些“疑问”放置于生成这些“疑问”的特定的“文化语境”中加以解析，其内含的各种虚构、象征、隐喻等便可以显彰其真实的意义。

日本当代具有权威意义的学者梅原猛教授，构筑起了庞大的“梅原古代学”。在关于日本“记纪神话”的解读方面，梅原教授认为，以《古事记》为核心的日本“记纪神话”，实际上是公元8世纪时代日本皇室为安排政权接替而特意创作的作品，因为当时执政的元明女天皇正在依照她的婆婆持统女天皇，安排她自己的孙子接任天皇位，因而，《古事记》便特地把“太阳神”描述为“女性”，并且安排了“天孙降临”的场面。[①]

这是很典型的“Euhmerization”(欧赫美尔主义)解密论！[②]梅原先生对《古事记》的发生的阐述，由于在事实上脱离了相应的“文化语境”，因而对这一特定的“文学文本”中的虚构、象征、隐喻等的解析，步入了重大的误区，终于使神话失去了民族的灵光，而沦落为政治的僵尸。

如果我们把《古事记》放置于与它相关联的“文化语境”中解析，便有可能从本体上把握它的一系列的虚构、隐喻、象征等的真正意义。例如，在日本“记纪神话”中，太阳神为什么是女性神而不像希腊神话、中国神话那样是男性神呢？这应该从以《古事记》形成时代为中心的“显现本民族文化沉积与文化特征的文化语境”中加以探索。这一层面的“文化语境”，向研究者提供了日本古代居住民把太阳神定格为“女神”，并进而把这位女神幻化为日本皇谱的“皇祖”的丰厚的民族文化资源，即日本古代社会中长期持续而且深刻化的“女性崇拜”的心理特征，它构成为特定时空中日本人普遍性的人生观与世界观，并且表现为一种社会时尚。[③]

……

一般说来，在这样三层文化语境中解析文本，就有可能揭示文本中原先通过情节、人物、故事等而内含着的虚构、象征、隐喻、符号等所具有的真实意义，显现了各个文本所生成的“文化场”的基本特征，阐明了各个文本之所以具有“个性”的基本内因。[7]

文学的“变异体”与文学的发生学

从文学发生的立场上观察文学文本，则可以说，在“文明社会”中，它们中的大多数皆是“变异体”文学。[8]

在人类文明发展的过程中，一个脱离了“野蛮”的民族，多少总会有与外部世界相接触的机会，在文化活动的层面上，——无论主动还是被动，此种活动一定会形成“新”的文化语境。这种状况不一定只是在“弱势文化”中存在，就是在“强势文化”中也是普遍存在的。即使像在古代汉字文化圈内的各个民族，在它们吸纳汉文化的同时，也仍然以各种不同的方式在不同的层面上把他们自己的文化渗透于处于“强势”状态的大陆汉文化之中；18世纪末至20世纪初期是欧洲殖民主义文化冲击世界的时代，然而，正是在这个时代，各“弱势民族”的文化，在世界文化的若干领域中成就着最伟大和最杰出的业绩，像“进化论”、“文化人类学”等这些影响着后来社会历史进程的学说，以及像达尔文、摩尔根和泰勒等这样一些近代文化杰出的创造者，他们的“文化”中事实上留存有大剂量的“弱势民族”的文化成分。

当年，当比较文学研究从“法国学派”发展为所谓的“美国学派”的时候，据说是因为一些学者不屑于做“文学的输出输入”的买卖，这当然有其历史的必然性和学术的功绩。但事实上，这一观念的背后，多少也表露出从事比较文学研究的一部分学者十分地缺少像文化史学、文化人类学、考古学、文献学、民族学和民俗学的理论和知识。今天当我们回过头来读一读这些相关的著作的时候，应该说，这是一个不争的事实。

文化现象清楚地表明，在世界大多数民族中，几乎都存在着本民族文化与“异文化相抗衡与相融合的文化语境”。当我们从这一文化语境的视角操作还原文学文本的时候，注意到了原来在这一层面的“文化语境”中，文学文本存在着显示其内在运动的重大的特征，此即文本发生的“变异”活动，并最终形成为文学的“变异体”。

文本的“变异”机制，是文学发生学的重要内容。

那么，什么是文学的“变异”呢？

人类早期的“文化”(包括文学)，都是在古代居住民生存的特定的自然环境与人文环境中形成的，由此而在文化中孕育的气质，是文化内具的最早的“民族特性”。任何文化的“民族特性”一旦形成，就具有了“壁垒性”特征。其实，“文化”与“文化运动”，从本质上说，应该是没有文化学家们所津津乐道的所谓“开放的文化”还是“闭锁的文化”之分的。这种由文化的“民族性”特征而必然生成的文化的“壁垒性”，是普遍范围内各民族文化冲突的最根本的内在根源(这里是在排除了文明社会中经济对文化的制约和政治权力对文化的控制等各种因素而言的)。文化冲突并不一定是一件坏事(这里的“冲突”，指的是在广泛的意义上发生的由接触而生的撞击现象)，从文化运行的内在机制来说，文化冲突能够激活冲突双方文化的内在的因子，使之在一定的条件中进入亢奋状态。无论是欲求扩展自身的文化，还是希冀保守自身的文化，文化机制内部都会发生一系列的“变异”。

……

从文本的解析中揭发这一具有决定意义的“文学发生学”现象，并从实践上与理论上加以确认，将对文学文本的发生学研究，具有相当实际的意义。

……

“文学的发生学”这一学术范畴本身所显示的基本特征，以及对它的解析所显示的路径与操作程序等，表明这一学术是“跨文化(文学)”研究中具有重要意义的成员，尽管它在学术范畴的界定方面可能还不完整，在具体的研究路径的提示方面还有不清晰的地方，但是，我以为比较文学的研究只有在对作为“研究基础”的各类“文本”的发生有了准确的把握之后，才有可能得出各种各样的见解、论说和理论，才能显示出这一学术的稳定的科学意义。

注：

① 参见梅原猛撰：《诸神流窜——论日本〈古事记〉》(中文版)，经济日报出版社 1999 年第 1 版(日文原文请参见日本集英社刊，1982 年第 1 版)。

② Euhmerus(前 4 世纪—前 3 世纪初)，古希腊美塞尼亚哲学家。其名著 *Sacred Writing* 提出了关于希腊神话中诸神起源的理论。他认为神话中的诸神，都是被“神化了的”氏族或部落的酋长或帝王。例如，他指宙斯原本就是克里特岛国的国王等。

③ 参见严绍璗撰：《确立解读文学文本的文化意识》，北京大学外国语学院《日本语言文化论集》北京出版社 2000 年版。

⑦ 发生学研究中对文本“个性”的解读，与文本创作者关于文本的自我表述不一定是一致的，这好比是“人”对自我的认知与科学家对“这个人”的例如“生物学”的“解剖学”的以及基因结构的认识不一定是相同的同理。

⑧ 这里说的“文明社会”，是文化人类学的概念，指的是以金属生产工具的出现、文字的形成等为标志的社会形态。关于“变异体”文学的特征，本文著者自 1985 年在《中国比较文学》(第 1 期)上刊出《日本“记纪神话”变异体的模式和形态及其与中国文化的关联》以来，零零散散有所阐发，张哲俊博士在今年《中国比较文学》第 2 期的“人物志”上发表《踏实的学风，实在的研究》一文，对“变异体”理论的概述至为妥切，有兴趣的读者请参见作者相关的论著和张哲俊博士的文章。

(节选自严绍璗：《“文化语境”与“变异体”以及文学的发生学》，《中国比较文学》2000 年第 3 期，第1-14页。)

比较文学导论

（节选）

[奥]彼得·冯·齐玛

【导读】

奥地利学者彼得·冯·齐玛的《比较文学导论》是一本关于比较文学理论研究的著述。齐玛具有深刻的反思和批判意识，用德国批判理论反观比较文学研究的方法论，提出比较文学研究应该同其他学科相关联，从而不断发展、完善自身的理论建构。同时，他以自己所生活地区以德语为主的多民族语言的驳杂性来反思世界，也具有独具一格的研究视角。在该著作中，齐玛首先回顾了比较文学的学科史，主张以批判理论的意识形态立场建构对话理论的比较文学研究，从而探索类型学和发生学比较的方法论及意义，强调意识形态批判对文学接受、文学翻译、文学分期和文体史的作用，还从地区角度探讨多民族语言的复调性和对话性，为比较文学研究拓宽了思路。导论部分浓缩了书中的核心观点，主要从以下四个方面来讨论如何建构比较文学。

一是比较文学和美学。齐玛首先一针见血地指出了比较文学研究中存在的普遍性问题，许多学者把这一学科当做艺术的比较研究，但却忽视了把比较文学同哲学美学相比较的问题。美学是哲学的一个分支，黑格尔认为美学，其实当名为“艺术哲学”。文学和艺术之间的共栖现象就决定了文学同美学的相关性，因此，比较文学研究中的美学问题是无论如何也绕不过去的。在齐玛看来，海德格尔的本体论哲学割裂了哲学与科学之间的联系，波珀的批判理性主义则醉心于片面追求“自然科学潜在意识的发展”，而阿多诺、霍克海默的批判理论坚持理论研究对社会现实的批判性。为此，他认为可以借鉴批判理论的方法进行比较文学研究，把文学研究同美学相结合，批判性地反映社会学、符号学、心理学等。

二是比较文学与总体文学研究。齐玛认为“比较文学是比较文艺的科学”，因此，作为一种文学理论，比较文学隶属总体文学研究中。但在这种嵌入关系中，齐玛指出了比较文学同梵·第根设计的“总体文学”是相区别的。梵·第根认为比较文学囿于两个因子之间的二元比较，存在严重缺陷，所以提出“总体文学”的构想，从而研究各国文学之间共同存在的事实。他的这种提法遭到美国学派的尖锐抨击，同时也受到乔玛的批判。乔玛认为梵·第根固守专业范围，无视题材、理论与方法间的密切联系，而比较文学的学科性质就决定了要进行二元比较，但是否进行多种文学或所有文学流派的研究并非问题的重点，问题的关键是用什么理论和方法开展比较文学研究。为此，乔玛认为总体文学研究应该在理论层面被理解为“比较文学研究理论和方法的全部”。

三是比较文学与社会科学。比较文学不仅是一门关于文学艺术的科学，同时与其他诸多社会科学存在着千丝万缕的联系。齐玛认为如果没有社会科学的存在，比较文学研究的方法论讨论则无异于空中楼阁，可谓皮之不存毛将焉附。在方法论层面，比较文学同比较社会学研究、比较政治学研究、比较语言研究等有着非常密切的联系。因此，文学社会学、文学符号学、文学心理学等才应运而生。另外，齐玛还肯定了法国的实证主义比较文学研究，因为它曾试图寻求文学与其它学科之间的对话。

四是比较文学与民族语文学。齐玛发现民族语文学研究和比较文学研究之间存在很大区别，这主要是由于研究工作的不同分工造成的。民族语文学研究固守民族文学的专门化研究，而比较文学研究则要跳脱民族文学的束缚，以来自不同语言地区和不同文化的作品为研究对象，争取在国际文化范围内进行比较。他还引述布什豪斯的观点“比较文学的不可避免性”来论证比较文学在比较中才能发掘不同文学之间的同一性和异质性。因此，齐玛认为在比较文学和民族语文学研究工作中，民族和国际意识应相互渗透、互为补充。

（马礼霞）

一、比较文学与美学

比较文学领域中的某些代表人物把这一学科想象为一种艺术的比较研究，但是却忽视了把比较文学的种种问题与同样是以各种艺术形式为研究对象的哲学美学的问题相比较，这是令人遗憾的。黑格尔（G. W. P. Hegel）（1770—1831）的《美学讲话》（Vorlesung, 1832—1842），不仅详细论述了19世纪上半叶众所周知的艺术形式，也论及了从早期古希腊罗马文化到新时期艺术发展的各个阶段。因此，把他的《美学讲话》看作是对这种美学的神化，是不无道理的。

在黑格尔的青年信徒中（福伊尔巴赫、马克思），与经济、社会、政治、法律、宗教和艺术脱离的黑格尔庞大体系已瓦解，不仅如此，黑格尔信徒魏舍尔（F. T. Vischer 1807—1887）所研究和更新的美学也已经成为探讨学科分工的牺牲品。因为作为哲学的一部分的美学参与了它的转变和对抗。个别哲学家虽然对语言学、美学、政治学和经济学问题感兴趣，但他们不可能在某个单一学科和思想体系内解决这个问题。因为专业学科研究（社会学、语言学、心理学）的迅速发展，使哲学的权威性陷入一种窘境。

……

海德格尔假设了哲学与科学之间有分裂，与其相反，像波珀（Karl. R. Popper）这样的批判理性主义者和维也纳圈子①的其他继承人则把哲学至科学理论的转变引导到这样一

① 由文件纲要“科学世界观——维也纳圈子”（Wis：enschltlche Weltauffasung-der Wiener Kreis）（1929）的作者施里克（Moritz Schlick）建立的，维也纳圈子努力以形式逻辑和经验为基础的科学思维克服形而上学。卡纳普（Rudolf Carnap）、莱辛巴赫（Hans Reichenbach）、波珀（Karl. R. Popper）等人属于此团体。

条道路上：对他们来说，哲学变成了探索完善并解释科学发展的辅助学科(ancilla sciontiae)。与此同时，实证论者科姆特(Comte)和辩证论者马克思(Marx)所提出的，必须批判性反映限制科学发展的社会现实这一要求，在他们那里遭到了拒绝。其中波珀表现得尤为明显，他几乎只追求自然科学潜在意识的发展。

与批判理性主义和海德格尔的存在哲学相反，批判理论的代表人物阿德诺(Theodor W. Adorno)，霍克海默(Max. Horkheimer)陷入了一种矛盾的、似是而非的状态。这是因为他们抛弃了黑格尔的整体思维体系，但却不愿放弃具体地理解并批判社会现象和社会进程的总和这一要求。阿德诺说："哲学作为整体，作为体系而提出，也许会成为空想。如果哲学放弃对整体的要求，那么她由自身发展为应该是真理的整体则不需要很长时间，那么她就会与其全部传统产生剧烈的冲突。"①

批判理论提出的解决问题的办法，也正是贯穿本书的理论导向，是一种使社会科学研究方法与哲学反映相联系、对社会科学的发展进行评论的探索。就文学研究而言，则意味着文学必须与哲学——美学基础理论相关联，批判性地反映其社会学、记号学或者心理学的方法②。对比较文学则补充提出了进行理论研究，以及对其进行科学评论的意义。

……

鉴于这种片面性及美学理论中的缺憾，比较文学应该转向早期批判理论纲领，并同时探索社会科学方法论与哲学反映论的结合。基于这一原因，不仅比较文学要努力把总体文学研究的方法论拿来为已用，同时，比较文学对于文学研究，科学研究的重要意义也必须得到共识。

二、比较文学与总体文学研究

比较文学总是一再与超越文学范畴的学科领域相关联，这是因为文学与音乐，文学与电影或者绘画是非常紧密地交织在一起的。另一方面，鉴于现代科学研究工作的分工，比较文学不能完全继承哲学美学观点并使之转变为文艺比较理论，这一点必须明确。比较文学就是比较文艺的科学，因此与口头文学有关。作为文学理论，它已经嵌入总体文学研究中，包括杜撰文学作品及其发展各种不同的思维观念。

在这种关系中，比较文学与梵·第根(Paul Van. Tieghem)设计的"总体文学"(Littèrature gènerale)无共同之处。两者的定义截然相反。比较文学的题材研究是要进行二元比较的，如"莎士比亚与歌德(Shakespeare und Gvethe)"；"陀斯妥耶夫斯基与尼采(Dostoevskij und Nietsche)"，而总体文学却包括更多的文学甚至全部文学流派，如"欧洲古典文学"、"欧洲浪漫主义"等。

像其它比较文学家一样，梵·第根过分地固守其专业范围而对题材、理论和方法之间

① Th. W. 阿德诺，"哲学的目的是什么"(Wozu noch Philosophie)，出处：同一著作，"啮合"(Eingriff)，《九种评论模式》(Neun kritischc Mcdelle)，法兰克福，苏尔卡姆，1963，第13页。

② 参阅：Vt.《文学美学，文学研究的方法与模式》(Literarische Ästhetik Methoden und Modelle der Lileraturwissenschafl, Tübigon, Francke (UTB), 1991.

的充满活力的联系视而不见，也就是说，他忽略了如何借助某种方法构成某种理论范畴并研究某一题材的问题。比较文学是否研究两种或多种文学、全部文学流派或者非口头文学作品(绘画、电影)，并非是关键问题；用何种理论和方法着手解决比较文学问题才是问题的实质。毫无疑问，客观范畴和要探讨的疑难问题共同确定了研究方法的选择。谁对拍成电影拷贝的卡莫斯(Albert Camus)的《陌生人》(*L'Etronger*)加以评论，则将通过电影记号学的补充,① 进一步探索一定的记号学文本(Textsemiotik)叙述体(Narrativik)。

基于这种看法，总体文学研究可以定义为是比较文学研究理论与方法的全部。比较文学研究者可以在总体文学范围内，借助于总体文学，抉择用何种理论以及用何种方式划定和探讨比较文学的研究课题。在这种情况下，比较文学工作者应该考虑到，理论和方法的每次抉择同时也是思想艺术与美学的抉择。如果我自己站在理论评论的角度，像现在这种情况，那么我将得出不同于以往倾向于布拉格(Prager)结构主义者的康德主义理论或者卢西恩·戈迪曼(Lucien-Golimann)马克思主义-结构主义的另一种社会论断。这样，总体文学的全部理论将作为另一种思想意识范畴出现，并且此范畴不仅被视为纯方法的，(此理论的作用是什么?)而且被视为评论一对话。(此理论道出何种论断和利害关系?)

文学社会学、文学心理学、记号学和篇章语言学的理论与方法如何使文学的比较具体化和精细入微，这个问题必然是焦点。在这种相关性方面，以洛特曼(Jurij Lotman)的文学记号学和作品记号学为例，受益匪浅。因为他指出，在各种不同的文化中，不仅各种不同的文学概念占优势，而且各种不同的作品概念也占主导地位。当某种类型文化只能通过口头文学来实现作品的功能时，在另一种文化中则只有书面作品才能被理解并得到承认："'他是位真正的诗人，受到压制'，'他是位真正的诗人，人们没有压制他'，这两种表达方式均可行。"②如果洛特曼注释一系列古典和中世纪文化以书写文学方式描述了授以圣职的宗教仪式(像允许阅读相应作品一样)，例如在喇嘛佛教中；但在更古老的文化中，授以圣职的仪式起到文学意义的口头传达作用，如在《奥义书》(*Upanischaden*)中。③ 这种解释在其他文章中同时得到发展并具体化。

……

洛特曼的叙述表明以下两点：其一，进行比较的题材不是关键，只有进行比较的全部理论思维观念才是主要的；其二，包括比较文学在内的每一文学科学的研究均与社会科学有着密不可分的关系，它扎根于社会科学之中，与语言学研究、人类学和社会学紧密相连。

……

三、比较文学与社会科学

洛特曼提出的有关书面语言的社会功能问题已经超出了比较文学研究的范围，因为它

① 参阅麦茨(Ch. Metz)：《电影记号学》(Semiologie des Films)，慕尼黑(Fnik)，1968。

② J. M. 洛特曼(lotman)：《作品与功能》(Text und Funktion). 齐玛 (P. V. Zima)《作为思想评论的作品记号学》(Textsemiotik als Ideologie kr'tik)，法兰克福，Suhrkamp，1977，第152页。

③ 《讽刺诗》，(同上)第150-151页。

涉及社会制度、作品种类和社会交流的功能化等诸方面。这个问题使人们认识到比较文学研究与社会科学的密切关系。没有社会科学的存在，60 年代和 70 年代有关比较文学研究方法论的讨论是完全不可能的。像文学社会学、文学心理学或者文学记号学，统统属于社会科学范畴。离开社会科学，上述学科均不可能发展。洛特曼的文学记号学理论就是最好的例子，他是综合人类学和语言学术语和原理而得到这一理论的。①

比较文学不仅是作为一门文艺科学，同时也是作为文学比较的理论与社会科学交织在一起。这种文学比较理论与比较教育研究、比较语言研究、比较社会学研究及政治学、经济学的比较研究有着亲缘关系。而其中与教育比较研究的关系尤为密切。教育比较研究不仅探讨了文学课程的重要地位，而且还研究了在不同国家的教育体制中，语言课程所起的作用。② 文学课程是教育体制的关键，因为文学作品（同报纸、杂志和电影一样）展现的异国风情和异族文化特色，直接对儿童和青年起教育作用。基于这一缘故，比较文学和比较教育是相互认同，互为补充的。尤其是作为意象学者和从事意象研究（Imagologe und Image-Forscher）③的比较文学学者，不仅想了解异国文化在某种文学中是如何表达的，而且还探讨文学在一定机构中（学校、高等院校）对集体观点是如何起作用的。

显然，在方法论方面，比较文学和比较政治学都为自己设立了相同的目标。④ 举例来说，为了解因缺少书面成文宪法，使得大不列颠政治体制受到何种影响，采用对比方法为上策。类似情况还有：荷兰文学发展过程中缺少先锋派运动（未来主义、超现实主义）导致了何种后果？大不列颠公众与已适应书面宪法的法国人对于合乎宪法的行为的理解是否有所不同？与法国人、比利时人和意大利人不同，荷兰公众在本国文学领域内尚未接触到值得一提的先锋派运动，实验作家沃格勒（J. F. Vogelaar）的先锋派小说（arantgardisder Roman）《魏卓特·杰拉德》（Vijaud Gerraagd）（1967）是否因此而遭到了荷兰公众的不解和非议呢？

比较文学和比较政治学的这些共同问题不仅使人们认识到两者共同具有的艰巨性（及对照比较的意义），而且也表明，两个学科均以社会科学为指导。为了能够探讨大不列颠公民和法国公民如何理解宪法及合乎宪法的行为，我必须采用一定的经验社会学方法（Methoden der enpirischen Soziologie），如果这种方法同样适用于比较荷兰公众与比利时或法国公众对先锋派大胆尝试的不同反应，那么这种方法也会被读者社会学

---

① 参阅：洛特曼（Y. M. Lotman），乌斯彭斯基（B. A. Ouspenski），塔图学派（Ecole de Tartu）：《记号学的规范系统》（Trayaux sur les systemes de signes）. Bruxelles, Ed. Complexe, 1976.

② 参阅：康德尔（I. L. Kandel）《比较教育学》（Comparative Education）Westpert（Conn）Greenwood Press, 1933, 1970, 第 8 章，汉斯，（N. Hans）; London Reutfledge and Kegau Paul., 1949, S. 46-47.

③ "关于比较文学研究范畴的意象学"，参阅杜泽林克（H. Dyserinck）《比较文学，导论》（第二版）（Komparatistik Eine Einführung），波恩，Bouvier. 1981，第 4 章。

④ 参阅：巴第耶（B. Badie），海尔默特（G. Hermet），《政治比较学》（Poitigue Comparee），PUF, 1990。

(Lesersoziologie)或者接受社会学(Rezeptionssoziologie)所采用。①

……

曾受到大量毁谤的法国实证主义比较文学，至少还有一点功绩，就是在它发展的初期阶段就已经尝试寻求与其他学科进行对话。过去，实证主义受到的指责是合理的。它对科学发展的关注在这里以新的思维观念现实化：因为传统的比较文学不仅在实证主义下受损害，而且在其精神史的变态反映中也是反对社会科学演泽的(sozialwissehschaftlich)。

四、比较文学与民族语文学

正像雨果·杜泽林克(Hugu Dyserink)指出的那样，比较文学与民族语文学之间的大量讨论在处于世纪之初的德国引发了比较文学与德国文学之间的剧烈冲突。② 与此相联系，研究两者之间的争执，从中得到有益启发的诱惑是巨大的。事实也许可以证实，诸如日耳曼人可以不固守其民族文学范畴，因为研究题材本身迫使它突破民族框框而进行比较。在不考虑特罗伊斯(Chretien de Troyes)影响的情况下，③ 仅仅谈论沃尔夫拉姆·封埃申巴赫著作的本身，至少不能令人满意。这是中世纪(Mediäristik)人们所共知的真理。同样，在介绍乔治(Stefan George)的唯美主义理论时，如果只字不提马拉梅斯(Stephane Mallarmes)和鲍德莱斯(Charles Baudlaires)对其本人以及理论的影响，也是不完善的，并且不能令人满意。

在这点上，布什豪斯(Ulrich Schutz-Buschhaus)的观点也许是正确的。他对"比较文学的不可避免性"(Unvermeidlichkeit dsr Komparatistik)发表了如下见解："如果文学史的理念知识不想损害自己，那么它们的比较将双倍地不可避免。因为一方面它可以从单一语种的文学特点中获取共同之处；另一方面又可以证实单一语种文学的特点，当然，只有从以共同点存在为前提进行的差异对比中才能勾画出来。"④换句话说，德国和荷兰文学的特点只有在对照比较中才看得出，并且只有这种比较才能使各种不同的欧洲浪漫主义、象征主义、先锋派显示出共同的同一性。

谁证实了比较文学的不可避免性，就不应该再附加提出垄断权的要求，而应该探索展现其他对立面，并谅解地提出：在此不应否定民族文学存在的合理性，而应该只进行具体化地比较。因为正如存在只有在比较文学范畴内才能理解的现象与结果一样，必须在民族文学思维观念中作基本解释的事件也是存在的。尽管在塞万提斯的《堂吉诃德》(*Cervantes*

---

① "关于读者社会学或接受社会学"(vergleichende Leser-oder Rezepliosso-ziologie)，参阅莱茵哈特(J. Leenhardt)，约萨(P. Jozsa)《作品阅读》(Lire la lecture)巴黎 Leyscomore，1992。在本书中法国和匈牙利读者对一部成功的法国和匈牙利小说进行了分析。

② 参阅：H·杜泽林：《比较文学》(Kamparatistik) op. cit，第 34 页。

③ 参阅科勒(E. Köhler)"骑士文学中的理想与现实"(Ideal und Wirklichkeit in der höfischen Epik)，Tübingen，Niemeyer，1970，第 188 页，第 243 页。

④ 布什豪斯(U. Schulz-Buscbhaus)："比较文学的不可避免性，单语种文学状况和比较文学研究"(Die Unvermeidlichkeit der Kamparatistik) zum Verhältnis von einzelsprachlichen literatur und Vergleichender Literaturwissenschaft)，Arcadia Nr. 14. 1979，第 235 页。

Don Ouijote）中可以证实其受到古典文学的大量影响，但是，阅读时首先必须明确，他的小说是对西班牙骑士小说讽刺性的模仿，即在卡斯提尔（Kastilisch）——西班牙文学进化的范畴内理解。同样，德国的狂飙突进运动（Sturm-und-Drang-Bewegung）虽然从现实角度解释莎士比亚作品，并且向僵化的法国古典主义提出挑战，但首先应该理解为是与德国肩蒙运动（Aufklarung）对立而言的文学运动。最后一例来自法语区域：如果没有弗尔克内尔（Faulkners）、卡夫卡（Kafka）、约瑟斯（Joces）和贝凯特（Beckett）的试验，"新小说"（Nouvean Roman），古典的西蒙斯（Buters Simons）和葛利兹（Alain Robbe-Grillets）大概会丧失发展的可能性。此外，对葛利兹的《未来小说的道路》（*Pour un nouvean Roman*，1963）和里卡多斯（Jean Richardous）的《关于新小说理论》（1971）（*Paur une tlieorie du nouvean roman*，1971）进行的理论阐释明确表明，这种新的小说形式原则上可以理解为是对存在主义者萨特（Satre）和卡姆斯（Camus）写作方式的挑战，是与布鲁斯特（Marcel Proust）势不两立的表现。因此，民族和国际的思维观念相互渗透，而不应相互隔离。

这就是为什么比较文学与民族语文学在研究工作中应该互为补充和相互支持的原因所在。只要作为经济学、社会学和政治学的合法客观的形式结构（Legitime Objekte Objektkonstruktion）的民族社会存在，那么从民族的（而非民族主义的）角度看待文学则是合情合理的。正如法国和德国的政治机构在内在体制上大相径庭（前者为中央集权主义，后者则为联邦主义），法国的文学机构（诸如法国科学院）与德国、荷兰或英国的也不相同。在社会科学脉络中出现集中探索民族语文学的现象是有益的，但是，这种脉络却不得不依靠比较、类比和对照而存在。如果科学家们对赋予他们的这种比较的可能性置若罔闻的话，他们注定将无所作为。

（节选自彼得·冯·齐玛：《比较文学导论》，马宝珠、刘介民译，李媛校译，《中国比较文学》1994年第2期，第169-177页。）

中西长篇小说文类之比较

（节选）

[美]浦安迪

【导读】

浦安迪(Andrew H. Plaks)，1945年生于美国纽约，1973年获普林斯顿大学博士学位，现为普林斯顿大学东亚系和比较文学系荣休教授，以色列希伯来大学东亚系教授。浦安迪教授通晓十几种语言，尤其精通汉语、日语、俄语、法语和希伯来语。他主要研究中国古典文学、叙事学、中国传统思想文化、中西文学文化比较等。重要著作有《〈红楼梦〉中的原型和寓意》(*Archetype and Allegory in the Dream of the Red Chamber*)，《明代小说四大奇书》(*The Four Masterworks of the Ming Novel*: *Ssu ta chishu*, 1987)，《中国叙事文：批评与理论文汇》(*Chinese Narrative*: *Critical and Theoretical Essays*)。浦安迪教授主持的重译中国古代思想名著系列的项目，对中国文化的海外传播具有重大意义。

《中西长篇小说文类之比较》属于文类学研究。浦安迪指出，尽管中西的长篇小说在结构组织、人物塑造以及文学发展史上都有显著的差别，但它们仍然可以划归同一文类之下。原因如下：一是，中西长篇小说的产生都与现代以前的整个社会经济环境有直接联系。二是，中西长篇小说皆植根于现实主义的表现基础。写实是此文类的最重要特性，即使是在一个假想的构架上，作者也努力创造出一个与读者的思想历史及个人经验相符的完整的世界。例如卡夫卡的小说和科幻小说。长篇小说的第二个特性是，长篇小说虽然根基于现实，却往往要跃进一个假想的非现实层次里去探索有关生命、潜意识等比较抽象的问题。西方长篇小说大半围绕着个人追寻自我，力求一己之个性与外在环境中得到肯定等主题来发展。爱是整个西方文学传统的核心主题，而中国文学传统的核心是文人的修心修身之道。长篇小说的第三个特性是作者常采用反语修辞的叙事手法。长篇小说的反语修辞手法，不单是针对作品里的人物，它的锋刃更刺向作者本人。从中世纪稳定的世界观到现代小说中那种荒唐无意义的价值观，西方长篇小说的发展不但忠实地反映出几个世纪以来西方文化传统价值的动荡，而且还显出小说家渐能把握问题中内涵的关乎自我意识的问题了。中国的长篇小说家惯用反语笔法，基本上也是因为他们对作家所创的"世界"的本质有所疑惑。最后长篇小说重心不断的内移是和个体对自我本质的质疑、以及整个文化和世界观基层的崩溃，相辅相成合为一事。三是，无论在中国还是欧洲，长篇小说的兴起都与当时流行的批判精神相关。不仅长篇小说的创作艺术与批评理论之间维系着紧密的关系，而且许多小说家本身也是一流的文艺理论家。

（霍晓珊）

就文学史的观点而言，我们固然不可将长篇小说看作一种“凭空而出”、“无中生有”的新文体，而认为它的目的即在反映现代文明发端期中一些前所未见的现实。相反，我们得正视中西长篇小说这两种文类与其个别文学的发展和文体的血统之间纵横相交的关系。不过虽然如此，我们仍可看出长篇小说和以前的长篇叙事文体（西方的史诗和 romance 文学，中国的史书和民间故事）有根本的差别。西方学者发现，要在纯形式的基础上分辨长篇小说和其他长篇叙事的文体，的确十分困难；他们于是退而求其次，依据内容上的特色以辨定长篇小说为一独立的叙事文体。举例来说，许多十八世纪的作家，包括小说家菲尔丁、理查生及批评家克莱拉·里夫（Clara Reeve）等，都强调长篇小说是忠于“现实生活”的，因此它显然与 romance 文学之引人奇想大相径庭。此外，晚近的批评家弗莱在提到中古传奇文体中之所“内心热情之灵光”时，则用人物塑造之因素作为辨别中古传奇文体与长篇小说之主要基础。

此一理论之最具说服力者，则立论时必先断然以结构组织、人物塑造、内容之虚实等作为识别文类之基础，然后设法从十七至十九世纪之间（即西方长篇小说的形成时期）的欧洲社会思想背景着手，阐明长篇小说的文类特性。例如卢卡契即曾设想长篇小说为一篇歌咏“末世为上帝所弃”的史诗；此处卢氏不但假定长篇小说和史诗为本质相通的文类，并且还暗中指出居于两者间的一条意识形态的鸿沟，它把长篇小说和史诗中的昔往“英雄时代”隔分两岸。诚然，中西长篇小说各有不同的思想背景；但有趣的是，我们在深入文类探究其背后之思想史时，却猛然发现两个迥异的传统竟有不少显著的共通处。我们到此始能问心无愧地以西洋“长篇小说”这术语来指称中国的作品，而毋需斤斤计较于结构、人物等其他方面的差异。

长篇小说诞生之背景，自有其超乎文学范畴以外的一面。诸如都市化、商业化、工业大革命、教育之普及、印刷术之面世等各种因素，在当时整个欧洲社会经济的历史背景中纵横交错，互相影响互相推进着，最后结合起来，巩固了近代西方世界的中产阶级文化。一如伊恩·瓦特在他那部《长篇小说之兴起》里所说，这种社会与文化上的历史因素，正是导致欧洲长篇小说产生的原因。我们再回顾十六至十八世纪的中国社会背景，也同样发现许多与瓦特所说相差无几的因素；更有趣的是，一种新的散文叙事体竟也伴同此类因素而于中国诞生。当时，中国的社会与经济因素，如急促的都市化，以洋银为基础的新货币制度，拓展海运所带来的贸易机会，以及印刷业的兴旺，等等，都确实与白话小说的世界息息相关。这种情况在江南以及东南沿岸的大城市一带（即当日小说印行之总基地）尤其显著。此类因素，既然不独在欧洲的社会里出现，并且在中国的社会里亦会出现，瓦特的假设也就显得更富说服力了，瓦氏推论，长篇小说之形成不独基于文学的内在因素，它同时是在各种超乎文学范畴以外的因素上扎根而起的。……

瓦特的研究固然有其价值，他所提出的论说——社会史与文学史之间系有必定的关系——也应当可以成立。不过，问题是学者们(包括瓦特本人)仿佛都要从中而联想出某种不正确的结论来。他们设法从社会经济各方面的发展中，洞悉某种共存的因素，以解释都市文化渗透民间的现象；可惜无论他们用什么“资本主义的萌芽”、“中产阶级的思想心态”之类的讲法，结果都一样引起大家普遍的误解，以为长篇小说基本上是属于“通俗文化”的。不少学者在研究西方叙事文体时即揭示出他们这种假想。回顾中国的情况，自从二十世纪的文学革命家纷纷“重新发现”这个道理，断定白话小说为通俗传统的产品之后，几乎所有研习中国小说的学者都奉之为金科玉律。由于白话小说的文体逐渐演变成首要的叙述媒介，而小说的内容又多围绕着发迹商户、绿林侠士、浪人贼盗等各类饱受剥削的群众而发展，加上小说家在下笔之际还套用了市井说书的修辞技巧为标准的叙事模式，故此历代的读者自然容易得出结论，认为小说的确是完全属于“广大群众”的文学(至少是属于新兴中产阶级的文学)，而不像古诗古文那样为高高在上的文士阶级所垄断。此外，传统道统派对小说时加轻视，反而加强了本来的论据，关于这点我们容后再谈。

就中国的长篇小说而论，这样的看法也是无可厚非的。明末的白话小说之所以能够迅速发展，实有赖于坊间印刷术的普及和读者群众的扩增；而另一方面，读者之能够有多余的时间和充足的资金来好好地欣赏文学，也实在与经济贸易不断的发展有关。事虽如此，我们却仍须申明一点：我们不愿以本文所讨论的中国长篇小说归属于某种非正统的变风文化；相反，我们该把它视为明清文士界主流之下的一批极其重要的作品，这样大家才能得到其中最深切有力的诠释。(此处我们的大前提是：任何文类的理论工作都必须建基于此文类最优秀的作品以为研究的对象，因为只有深具影响力的著作，才能代表一文类之基本概念和建立它本身特有的规范典则。)

中西的小说都采用了一种比较自由的语文媒体。但此事本身并不证明小说与社会阶级之间必定存有任何特殊的关系。原因之一即在于中国长篇小说实际采用的语文媒体，有别于日常生活中的口语，是小说家糅合传统文言和市井俗话而成的一种新的文学媒体。我们因此不难理解为何许多一流的明清小说家同时也是其他古典文体的名家；这跟西方的情形一样，薄伽丘、但丁、弥尔顿以及欧洲各个语文叙事体的其他先进作家，也都是拉丁文的名家。所以，如果小说里仍保留着说书人的一批套语，那并不证明它的作者、读者和书中的人物全是出身低微的俗人，因为它其实是小说家有意选择的艺术手法，务使在处理那种题材时制造特殊的反语效果。整个问题与作者和读者“群众”之间的阶级结合，鲜有关联。

中国传统对白话“小说”时加轻视，仿佛定要使它归为一种普遍通俗的文体。但此处我们须要强调，实际情况并不像几十世纪文学史家所说的严重；那种偏见，大概只是清代特有的现象，在十六七世纪的文坛上并不十分普遍。既然当日不少文坛的要角(他们可能是作家、出版家、批评家或读者)都加入了白话文学的行列，我们不妨直接指出，此一新“文类”在他们心目中已成为整个载道文学传统中不可缺少的成分。我们目睹序跋题署、笔记条目一类的文章将《三国演义》、《西游记》等作品同其他的古典名著并排而列，对于此说即更能了解。有趣的是，大家一方面对新兴的文体随意批评谴责，另一方面却又热心积极地投入它的行列。这种双重的态度，竟同样道出欧洲文坛对长篇小说的兴起所作的反应(法国的情形尤其显著，当时长篇小说遭受的抨击颇多，但身负大才的作家仍不断地涌现）。

我们要把中国长篇小说纯粹看成一种“通俗”小说，所面临的最大困难，不是起源的问题，而是思想内容上的问题，即如何透过人世间生活的描绘来推展作品内涵的意义。我们并不否认，中西长篇小说崛起与两个文化的扩散流播有关；扩散面越大，读者群众自然越多。可是细看之下，我们又发现其中重要的作品都含有一种知人知事的深奥的哲理，显示它与民间智慧有别，而实际与上层文士的艺术传统更有渊源。此处再要重申：我们这里所谈的是长篇的“大作”——诚然，中西文学里都出现过无数的长篇小说，但其中有不少的著作，都未必能培养出这种思想内涵方面的深度；此类作品，若非被视为文类中比较次要的产品，则需根本被摒诸文类的范畴之外。

大家时常认定长篇小说始终要受到广大读者群众的支配，此即该文类主要特性之一。无论中西的读者，都对长篇小说抱有一种艺术的期望，认为它对人类生活的经验必可作“写实性”的披露。此种艺术期望非常重要，许多学者甚至因而界定“写实主义”为长篇小说文类之首要特性。诚然，由描绘社会的风俗礼节及经济现状，到塑造人物的内心世界，我们可看出写实主义各种不同的着眼点。不过一般读者心目中所期望的长篇小说，却是在人类生存的某种层面上，以可信的客观形式对日常生活作出比较忠实的反映。接纳此种定义的批评家，在处理一些题材超越日常生活的作品时，若不予以归划到其他文类去（中古传奇、寓言文学 allegory、志怪文体 fantastic，等等），则或容忍其非现实之叙事架构，而将着眼处置于它所传达的某种“真实”的历史和哲学性道理上。就中国传统的实例而言，学者则当以深具历史阔度如《三国演义》等作品作为 romance 的例子，以《西游记》一类作品归于寓言的范畴之下，而把长篇小说这名称留给《金瓶梅》、《红楼梦》那种所谓“人情小说”（domestic fictions）。

然而，“写实主义”实在是个含义很复杂的专用名词，大家时常随意用它来指称许多不同的观念。为求探索其中不同层面的意义，我们在此先辨识“写实主义”的两大领域：一是作品所描绘的事物本身的性质，二是作者描绘事物时所用的手法。……先从描绘对象的性质来讲，我们对某某小说产生“写实”的印象，常常是因为我们在作品中读到许多“熟悉”的经验——我们看到的、听到的、嗅到的，全是大家在日常生活里所能经验到的。有时候，小说的布景会移置于某些地理与历史背景皆十分奇异的地方（例如在夏多布里昂、麦尔维尔等小说家的作品里即是）；有时候，作品所描写的社会阶层极高或极低，一般读者都不太熟悉。但尽管如此，小说家仍可在一个相当陌生的环境之中，突出某些大家都熟悉的平凡的场面，加以具体细节的描写，而使读者依然对作品产生“现实感”。……

就描绘事物的手法而言，小说家也运用了各种技巧来突出作品的现实感。例如留意事物的细节，控制故事发展的时间律度，维持前后一贯的视线（即所谓“叙事观点”），以及加强事态动机与人物个性之说服力等等即是。当然，小说家绝对有权用写实的方法来描绘虚构的事物，他更可以在处理现实的题材时，采用印象主义、超现实主义，或者近代其他美学运动所鼓吹的虚幻式表现手法。纵使反写实主义的浪潮已成为当代小说创作之主流，但它无需改变我们对长篇小说文类基本概念之理解。适得其反，反现实潮流本身即可证明写实传统的各种准则在长篇小说的黄金时期，确实占有核心的地位。

无论把着眼点放在内容题材或者叙事手法上，我们都可以归结一点作为此文题之基本特性：长篇小说总是力求在一个假想的架构上，创造出与读者之思想、历史及个人经验相符的完整的"世界"。这个小说世界，即使脱离了大家日常所熟悉的生活，却仍可透过扎实的逻辑结构(以别于纯形式上的结构)，来加强自身的说服力，让读者纵使接触到一些超乎常人经验范畴以外的事物，也能体会出连串逻辑因果的关系来(许多卡夫卡的长篇小说以及一流的科学幻想小说皆属此例)。

长篇小说虽然根基于现实，却往往要跃进一个假想的"非现实"层次里去，这可说是此文类的第二个基本特性。小说家(至少其中最伟大者)在力求忠实地表现(或捏造)一个满布可信的细节、深具说服力的完整世界时，必然要面临现实世界里一些比较深入的、本质上的难题。……

如上所说，西方长篇小说大半环绕着个人追寻自我、力求一己之个性于外在环境中得到肯定等主题来发展。这种披露意识成长过程的主题，可说在所谓"启蒙小说"里表现得最为突出，某些理论家即因而提出"启蒙小说"为长篇小说文类之典范模式。……

从叙事的对象回到叙事的手法，我们又发现长篇小说在人物塑造上的一大特色：以反语修辞为其惯用的、典型的叙事手法；此亦我们界定该文类的另一准则。换句话说，长篇小说家越来越意识到他笔下所有英雄人物的矛盾本质，而此种态度则难免要驱使他运用曲笔反语法来反映他一手所创的矛盾人事。……

长篇小说以曲笔反语为修辞的利刃，不但是针对作品里的人物而发，它的刃锋有时更刺向作者本人。最后，小说家甚至要对自己以种种模仿手法所创出的整个小说境界，提出疑问。但矛盾是小说家越想在处理行文期间所遭遇的困难时，自由地施展他个人的意志，他就越得面对小说创作的基本准则：长篇小说的内容形式，总不能脱离现实主义的固有局限。……

最后，我们要从长篇小说文类的基本特性，从两个传统在这方面的一些显著的共通点出发，来试谈一两点结论。长篇小说在中西文化少有交通的情况之下，从两个不同的传统中崛起，这实在容易使我们妄下判断，认定散文体的写实小说即为人类文化发展过程中必然成分之一，以为不管历史条件如何不同，它都可于任何文化传统中出现。持此论说的学者，与研究史诗的学者犯了同一错误，以为既然不同的文化可产生同一文类，则该文类必为文学创作过程中之必然现象。

……

就思想发展史而言，长篇小说可说是显出了现代社会急切追求一个文化综合体的倾向，急切需要大家对历史文化作全面的检讨和重新的评价，使其更能切合新时代的新需求。

最终的一个可能性，即将责任推卸到西欧文化的身上。我们可以辩称，中国文化根基于万物一体的世界观，根基于中国的文人长久以来主张人性善恶难定的态度。因此，一个适合长篇小说发展的思想环境，至少在宋代新儒家体系成立以后，已酝酿成熟。再回顾西方的发展，那种奠基于批评现实反映时局的小说文类，一直要到十六七世纪思想界发生基层变化之后，才有条件形成雏体。当然，我们此番推论是否合用、是否有意义，仍待大家研究讨论。但有一点已是十分清楚的：要找出长篇小说的基本文类特性与形成的因素，我们最好从该文化的思想史着手研究，这样，才能得到最结实的成果。

（节选自浦安迪：《中西长篇小说文类之比较》，李达三、罗钢主编，《中外比较文学的里程碑》，人民文学出版社 1997 年版，第 316-332 页。）

中国小说的历史的变迁

（节选）

鲁　迅

【导读】

“中国小说的历史的变迁”是鲁迅1924年7月在西安讲学时的记录稿，修订后收入西北大学出版部1925年3月印刷的《国立西北大学、陕西教育厅合办署期学校讲演集》(二)。在《鲁迅全集》第9卷中在附录中列出，本书节选其第一讲“从神话到神仙传”和第二讲“六朝时之志怪与志人”，311-322页。鲁迅(1881—1936)中国现代伟大的文学家和翻译家和新文学运动的奠基人。原名周树人，字豫才，浙江绍兴人，出身于破落的封建家庭。青年时代受进化论思想影响。鲁迅的一生，对中国的文化事业做出了巨大的贡献。

鲁迅“从倒行的杂乱的作品里寻出一条进行的线索来”，有意识地总结中国小说的发展规律和经验教训。中国小说的历史变迁如人类历史一样是进化的，但也具备中国的特色，一是新旧反复，二是新旧羼杂。第一讲“从神话到神仙传”，从小说的起源谈起。小说起源于神话，先是口传的“传说”，经过演进，正事归类到史，而逸史则归类到小说。诗歌在小说的前面出现。作为韵文的诗歌是从劳动时发生的，而作为散文的小说则是从休息时发生的。在古代印度、埃及、希腊及至中国，不管是小说还是诗歌，均离不开神话。从《山海经》至《列仙传》，当时并不是有意当做小说写的，但是以现在的眼光看去，可以当做小说来看。第二讲“六朝时之志怪与志人”是对第一讲进行总结，认为神话是文艺的萌芽，而现存汉人的小说多半是假的，然后探讨了六朝时的小说。六朝承接以前巫鬼之说，志怪之类的书特别多。而印度思想的输入也使得六朝人志怪思想特别发达，所以六朝的志怪小说与印度相关。六朝人写志怪小说，并不是有意当做小说写作，与如今的新闻相似。六朝时志怪与志人的文章“当作记事实”，都比较简短，一般放在历史的传记一类，直至宋朝欧阳修才开始将其归入小说的类别。

（白阳明）

我所讲的是中国小说的历史的变迁。许多历史家说，人类的历史是进化的，那么，中国当然不会在例外。但看中国进化的情形，却有两种很特别的现象：一种是新的来了好久之后而旧的又回复过来，即是反复；一种是新的来了好久之后而旧的并不废去，即是羼杂。然而就并不进化么？那也不然，只是比较的慢，使我们性急的人，有一日三秋之感罢了。文艺，文艺之一的小说，自然也如此。例如虽至今日，而许多作品里面，唐宋的，甚而至于原始人民的思想手段的糟粕都还在。今天所讲，就想不理会这些糟粕——虽然它还很受社会欢迎——而从倒行的杂乱的作品里寻出一条进行的线索来，一共分为六讲。

第一讲　从神话到神仙传

考小说之名，最古是见于庄子所说的“饰小说以干县令”。“县”是高，言高名；“令”是美，言美誉。但这是指他所谓琐屑之言，不关道术的而说，和后来所谓的小说并不同。

因为如孔子，杨子①，墨子②各家的学员，从庄子看来，都可以谓之小说；反之，别家对庄子，也可称他的著作为小说。至于《汉书·艺文志》上说：“小说者，街谈巷语之说也。”这才近似现在的所谓小说了，但也不过古时稗官采集一般小民所谈的小话，借以考察国之民情，风俗而已；并无现在所谓小说之价值。

小说是如何起源的呢？据《汉书·艺文志》上说：“小说家者流，盖出于稗官。”稗官采集小说的有无，是另一问题；即使真有，也不过是小说书之起源，不是小说之起源。至于现在一班研究文学史者，却多认小说起源于神话。因为原始民族，穴居野处，见天地万物，变化不常——如风；雨，地震等——有非人力所可捉摸抵抗，很为惊怪，以为必有个主宰万物者在，因之拟名为神；并想像神的生活，动作，如中国有盘古氏开天辟地之说，这便成功了“神话”。从神话演进，故事渐近于人性，出现的大抵是“半神”，如说古来建大功的英雄，其才能在凡人以上，由于天授的就是。例如简狄吞燕卵而生商，尧时“十日并出”，尧使羿射之的话，都是和凡人不同的。这些口传，今人谓之“传说”。由此再演进，则正事归为史；逸史即变为小说了。

我想，在文艺作品发生的次序中，恐怕是诗歌在先，小说在后的。诗歌起于劳动和宗教。其一，因劳动时，一面工作，一面唱歌，可以忘却劳苦，所以从单纯的呼叫发展开去，直到发挥自己的心意和感情，并偕有自然的韵调；其二，是因为原始民族对于神明，渐因畏惧而生敬仰，于是歌颂其威灵，赞叹其功烈，也就成了诗歌的起源。至于小说，我以为倒是起于休息的。人在劳动时，既用歌吟以自娱，借它忘却劳苦了，则到休息时，亦必要寻一种事情以消遣闲暇。这种事情，就是彼此谈论故事，而这谈论故事，正就是小说的起源。——所以诗歌是韵文，从劳动时发生的；小说是散文，从休息时发生的。

但在古代，不问小说或诗歌，其要素总离不开神话。印度，埃及，希腊都如此，中国亦然。只是中国并无含有神话的大著作；其零星的神话，现在也还没有集录为专书的。我

① 杨子：即杨朱，战国初期魏国人。主张“贵生重己”，“全性葆真，不以物累形”的“为我”思想。其言论事迹，散见《孟子》、《庄子》、《韩非子》、《吕氏春秋》等书。《列子》中虽有《杨朱》篇，但系后人伪托。

② 墨子（约前468—前376）：名翟，春秋战国之际鲁国人。曾任宋国大夫，墨家学派创始者。他主张“爱无差等”的“兼爱”思想。现存《墨子》五十三篇。

们要寻求，只可从古书上得到一点，而这种古书最重要的，便推《山海经》。不过这书也是无系统的，其中最要的，和后来有关系的记述，有西王母的故事，现在举一条出来：

“玉山，是西王母所居也。西王母其状如人，豹尾虎齿而善啸，蓬发戴胜，是司天之厉及五残。”

如此之类还不少。这个古典，一直流行到唐朝，才被骊山老母夺了位置去。此外还有一种《穆天子传》，讲的是周穆王驾八骏西征的故事，是汲郡古冢中杂书之一篇。——总之中国古代的神话材料很少，所有者，只是些断片的，没有长篇的，而且似乎也并非后来散亡，是本来的少有。我们在此要推求其原因，我以为最要的有两种：

一、太劳苦。因为中华民族先居在黄河流域，自然界底情形并不佳，为谋生起见，生活非常勤苦，因之重实际，轻玄想，故神话就不能发达以及流传下来。劳动虽说是发生文艺的一个源头，但也有条件，就是要不过度。劳逸均适，或者小觉劳苦，才能发生种种的诗歌，略有余暇，就讲小说。假使劳动太多，休息时少，没有恢复疲劳的余裕，则眠食尚且不暇，更不必提什么文艺了。

二、易于忘却。因为中国古时天神，地祇，人，鬼，往往殽杂，则原始的信仰存于传说者，日出不穷，于是旧者僵死，后人无从而知。如神荼，郁垒，为古之大神，传说上是手执一种苇索，以缚虎，且御凶魅的，所以古代将他们当作门神。但到后来又将门神改为秦琼，尉迟敬德，并引说种种事实，以为佐证，于是后人单知道秦琼和尉迟敬德为门神，而不复知神荼，郁垒，更不消说造作他们的故事了。此外这样的还很不少。

中国的神话既没有什么长篇的，现在我们就再来看《汉书·艺文志》上所载的小说：《汉书·艺文志》上所载的许多小说目录，现在一样都没有了，但只有些遗文，还可以看见。如《大戴礼·保傅篇》中所引《青史子》说：

“古者年八岁而出就外舍，学小艺焉，履小节焉；束发而就大学，学大艺焉，履大节焉。居则习礼文，行则鸣佩玉，升车则闻和鸾之声，是以非僻之心无自入也。……”

《青史子》这种话，就是古代的小说；但就我们看去，同《礼记》所说是一样的，不知何以当作小说？或者因其中还有许多思想和儒家的不同之故吧。至于现在所有的所谓汉代小说，却有称东方朔所做的两种：一、《神异经》，二、《十洲记》。班固做的，也有两种：一、《汉武故事》；二、《汉武帝内传》。此外还有郭宪做的《洞冥记》，刘歆做的《西京杂记》。《神异经》的文章，是仿《山海经》的，其中所说的多怪诞之事。现在举一条出来：

“西南荒山中出讹兽，其状若菟，人面能言，常欺人，言东而西，言恶而善。其肉美，食之，言不真矣。”(《西南荒经》)

《十洲记》是记汉武帝闻十洲于西王母之事，也仿《山海经》的，不过比较《神异经》稍微庄重些。《汉武故事》和《汉武帝内传》，都是记武帝初生以至崩葬的事情。《洞冥记》是说神仙道术及远方怪异的事情。《西京杂记》则杂记人间琐事。

然而《神异经》，《十洲记》，为《汉书·艺文志》上所不载，可知不是东方朔做的，乃是后人假造的。《汉武故事》，《汉武帝内传》则与班固别的文章，笔调不类，且中间夹杂佛家语，——彼时佛教尚不盛行，且汉人从来不喜说佛语——可知也是假的。至于《洞冥记》，《西京杂记》又已经为人考出是六朝人做的。——所以上举的六种小说，全是假的。

惟此外有刘向的《列仙传》①是真的。晋的葛洪又作《神仙传》②，唐宋更多，于后来的思想及小说，很有影响。但刘向的《列仙传》，在当时并非有意作小说，乃是当作真实事情做的，不，到现在还多拿它做儿童读物的材料。现在常有一问题发生：即此种神话，可否拿它做儿童的读物？我们顺便也说一说。在反对一方面的人说：以这种神话教儿童，只能养成迷信，是非常有害的；而赞成一方面的人说：以这种神话教儿童，正合儿童的天性，很感趣味，没有什么害处的。在我以为，这要看社会上教育的状况怎样，如果儿童能继续更受良好的教育，则将来一学科学，自然会明白，不至迷信，所以当然没有害的；但如果儿童不能继续受稍深的教育，学识不再进步，则在幼小时所教的神话，将永信以为真，所以也许是有害的。

第二讲　六朝时之志怪与志人

上次讲过：一、神话是文艺的萌芽。二、中国的神话很少。三、所有的神话，没有长篇的。四、《汉书·艺文志》上载的小说都不存在了。五、现存汉人的小说，多是假的。现在我们再看六朝时的小说怎样。中国本来信鬼神的，而鬼神与人乃是隔离的，因欲人与鬼神交通，于是乎就有巫出来。巫到后来分为两派：一为方士；一仍为巫。巫多说鬼，方士多谈炼金及求仙，秦汉以来，其风日盛，到六朝并没有息，所以志怪之书特多，像《博物志》上说：

"燕太子丹质于秦，……欲归，请于秦王。王不听，谬言曰，'令乌头白，马生角，乃可。'丹仰而叹，乌即头白，俯而嗟，马生角。秦王不得已而遣之……"(卷八《史补》)

这全是怪诞之说，是受了方士思想的影响。再如刘敬叔的《异苑》上说：

"义熙中，东海徐氏婢兰忽患羸黄，而拂拭异常，共伺察之，见扫帚从壁角来趋婢床，乃取而焚之，婢即平复。"(卷八)

这可见六朝人视一切东西，都可成妖怪，这正就是巫底思想，即所谓"万有神教"。此种思想，到了现在，依然留存，像：

常见在树上挂着"有求必应"的匾，便足以证明社会上还将树木当神，正如六朝人一样的迷信。其实这种思想，本来是无论何国，古时候都有的，不过后来渐渐地没有罢了。但中国还很盛。

六朝志怪的小说，除上举《博物志》、《异苑》而外，还有干宝的《搜神记》，陶潜的《搜神后记》。但《搜神记》多已佚失，现在所存的，乃是明人辑各书引用的话，再加别的志怪书而成，是一部半真半假的书籍。至于《搜神后记》，亦记灵异变化之事，但陶潜旷达，未必作此，大约也是别人的托名。

此外还有一种助六朝人志怪思想发达的，便是印度思想之输入。因为晋，宋，齐，梁四朝，佛教大行，当时所译的佛经很多，而同时鬼神奇异之谈也杂出，所以当时合中，印两国底鬼怪到小说里，使它更加发达起来，如阳羡鹅笼的故事，就是：

---

① 《列仙传》：《隋书·经籍志》著录二卷，题刘向撰。叙写赤松子等七十一个仙人的故事。

② 《神仙传》：《隋书·经籍志》著录十卷，题葛洪撰。叙写许由、巢父等八十四人名列仙班的故事。

“阳羡许彦于绥安山行，遇一书生……卧路侧，云脚痛，求寄鹅笼中。彦以为戏言，书生便入笼……宛然与双鹅并坐，鹅亦不惊。彦负笼而去，都不觉重。前行息树下，书生乃出笼谓彦曰：‘欲为君薄设。’彦曰：‘善。’乃口中吐出一铜奁子，中具肴馔。……酒数行，谓彦曰：‘向将一妇人自随，今欲暂邀之。’……又于口中吐一女子……共坐宴。俄而书生醉卧，此女谓彦曰：‘……向亦窃得一男子同行……暂唤之……’……女子于口中吐出一男子……”

此种思想，不是中国所故有的，乃完全受了印度思想的影响。就此也可知六朝的志怪小说，和印度怎样相关的大概了。但须知六朝人之志怪，却大抵一如今日之记新闻，在当时并非有意做小说。

六朝时志怪的小说，既如上述，现在我们再讲志人的小说。六朝志人的小说，也非常简单，同志怪的差不多，这有宋刘义庆做的《世说新语》，可以做代表。现在待我举出一两条来看：

“阮光禄在剡，曾有好车，借者无不皆给。有人葬母，意欲借而不敢言。阮后闻之，叹曰：‘吾有车而使人不敢借，何以车为？’遂焚之。”（卷上《德行篇》）

“刘伶恒纵酒放达，或脱衣裸形在屋中。人见讥之，伶曰：‘我以天地为栋宇，屋室为裈衣，诸君何为入我裈中？’”（卷下《任诞篇》）

这就是所谓晋人底风度。以我们现在的眼光看去，阮光禄之烧车，刘伶之放达，是觉得有些奇怪的，但在晋人却并不以为奇怪，因为那时所贵的是奇特的举动和玄妙的清谈。这种清谈，本从汉之清议而来。汉末政治黑暗，一般名士议论政事，其初在社会上很有势力，后来遭执政者之嫉视，渐渐被害，如孔融、祢衡等都被曹操设法害死①，所以到了晋代底名士，就不敢再议论政事，而一变为专谈玄理；清议而不谈政事，这就成了所谓清谈了。但这种清谈的名士，当时在社会上却仍旧很有势力，若不能玄谈的，好似不够名士底资格；而《世说》这部书，差不多就可以看做一部名士底教科书。

前乎《世说》尚有《语林》、《郭子》，不过现在都没有了。而《世说》乃是纂辑自后汉至东晋底旧文而成的。后来有刘孝标给《世说》作注，注中所引的古书多至四百余种，而今又不多存在了；所以后人对于《世说》看得更贵重，到现在还很通行。

此外还有一种魏邯郸淳做的《笑林》，也比《世说》早。它的文章，较《世说》质朴些，现在也没有了，不过在唐宋人的类书上所引的遗文，还可以看见一点，我现在把它也举一条出来：

“甲父母在，出学三年而归，舅氏问其学何所得，并序别父久。乃答曰：‘渭阳之思，过于秦康。’（秦康父母已死）既而父数之，‘尔学奚益。’答曰：‘少失过庭之训，故学无益。’”（《广记》二百六十二）就此可知《笑林》中所说，大概不外俳谐之谈。

上举《笑林》，《世说》两种书，到后来都没有什么发达，因为只有模仿，没有发展。如社会上最通行的《笑林广记》，当然是《笑林》的支派，但是《笑林》所说的多是知识上的

① 孔融（153—208）：字文举，东汉末鲁国（今山东曲阜）人。曾任北海相，后因反对曹操，为曹操所杀。祢衡（173—198）：字正平，东汉末平原般（今山尔临邑）人。因反对曹操被送至刘表处，刘表又将他送至黄祖处，终为黄祖所杀。

滑稽；而到了《笑林广记》①，则落于形体上的滑稽，专以鄙言就形体上谑人，涉于轻薄，所以滑稽的趣味，就降低多了。

至于《世说》，后来模仿的更多，从刘孝标的《续世说》——见《唐志》——一直到清之王晫所做的《今世说》，现在易宗夔所做的《新世说》等，都是仿《世说》的书。但是晋朝和现代社会底情状，完全不同，到今日还模仿那时底小说，是很可笑的。因为我们知道从汉末到六朝为篡夺时代，四海骚然，人多抱厌世主义；加以佛道二教盛行一时，皆讲超脱现世，晋人先受其影响，于是有一派人去修仙，想飞升，所以喜服药；有一派人欲永游醉乡，不问世事，所以好饮酒。服药者——晋人所服之药，我们知道的有五石散，是用五种石料做的，其性燥烈——身上常发炎，适于穿旧衣——因新衣容易擦坏皮肤——又常不洗，虱子生得极多，所以说："扪虱而谈。"饮酒者，放浪形骸之外，醉生梦死。——这就是晋时社会底情状。而生在现代底人，生活情形完全不同了，却要去模仿那时社会背景所产生的小说，岂非笑话？

我在上面说过：六朝人并非有意作小说，因为他们看鬼事和人事，是一样的，统当作事实；所以《旧唐书》《艺文志》，把那种志怪的书，并不放在小说里，而归入历史的传记一类，一直到了宋欧阳修才把它归到小说里。可是志人底一部，在六朝时看得比志怪底一部更重要，因为这和成名很有关系；像当时乡间学者想要成名，他们必须去找名士，这在晋朝，就得去拜访王导，谢安一流人物，正所谓"一登龙门，则身价十倍"。但要和这流名士谈话，必须要能够合他们的脾胃，而要合他们的脾胃，则非看《世说》、《语林》这一类的书不可。例如：当时阮宣子见太尉王夷甫，夷甫问老庄之异同，宣子答说："将毋同。"夷甫就非常佩服他，给他官做，即世所谓"三语掾"。但"将毋同"三字，究竟怎样讲？有人说是"殆不同"的意思；有人说是"岂不同"的意思——总之是一种两可、飘渺恍惚之谈罢了。要学这一种飘渺之谈，就非看《世说》不可。

（节选自鲁迅：《中国小说的历史的变迁》，《鲁迅全集》第9卷，人民文学出版社2005年版，第311-350页。）

① 《笑林广记》：清游戏主人辑。笑话集，四卷，分古艳、腐流、形体、闺风等十二类。

比较文学导论

（节选）

［德］胡戈·狄泽林克

【导读】

胡戈·狄泽林克（Hugo Dyserinck），德国著名比较文学学者，主要著作有《凯瑟林伯爵与法国》、《比较文学导论》、《比较文学与欧洲研究》（主编）等。《比较文学导论》作为一部在西方具有“教科书”般意义的比较文学著作，初版完成于1977年，历经两次再版，其思想对当今比较文学研究仍然是有意义的。“总体文学”是比较文学研究中一个传统论题，其间虽然经过一段时间的沉寂，但是一直没有完全被忘记，尤其是21世纪以来，随着“世界文学”研究热潮的兴起，再回头去清理其学术历程，是很有必要的。

狄泽林克在本文中致力于厘清总体文学与比较文学、国别文学的关系，纠正人们认识上的一些偏颇之处。他首先对“总体文学”做出界定：“‘总体文学’指的只能是这样一种文学理论的研究分支，它同国别文学研究相反，要求其涉猎的问题和追求的答案，具有普遍意义而不是单一文学的效用。”（148页）这里有两个关键词，即“研究分支”、“普遍意义”，下文主要就是对这两方面的阐述。所谓“研究分支”，首先指的是“文学研究整体的一部分”，从类属上来说，仍然属于文学研究，而非与文学有关的其他学科。其次，它有自己特有的研究对象与方法，是与国别文学相区别的独立学科。这就指出了总体文学概念上与“文学研究”、“国别文学”的逻辑关系。所谓“普遍意义”，首先是说总体文学研究的对象不是单一语言文学（这里狄泽林克单纯以语言作为国别文学的分类标准有一定局限性），而是超越国界的文学总体；同时，总体文学所要解决的理论及系统问题带有普遍性意义，可用于解释各国别文学所共有的问题。国别文学在文学史研究以外，也探讨文学原理问题，但是以本国文学为研究对象所得出的结论并不具有普遍性，不能用于解释其他国家的文学现象。

狄泽林克指出“总体文学”的特性就是“超国界立场与多国研究对象的结合”（149页），相当于英语中的“比较文学理论”（comparative literary theory）和“比较批评”（comparative criticism），即是说总体文学属于比较文学中文学理论和文学批评这一部分。他又指出韦勒克和沃伦、马克斯·魏尔利等人在超国界基础上进行文学理论与方法学的探讨，有其代表性意义。作者肯定了总体文学的独特价值，“只有超国界进行的文学研究才能回答具有普遍意义的系统—理论问题(例如‘文学的本质’、‘文学与社会的关系’、‘文学与其他艺术的关系’),只有超国界进行的文学研究才能系统地、历史地把握和分析各种不同的方法”。接下来,狄泽林克通过历来对文学与社会关系问题的研究的梳理,具体展示了总体文学的研究路径及成果,强调了只有不受语言或国家的局限,在跨国界立场上进行探究,才有可能解答带有普遍意义的问题,创建有价值的理论。本文第二部分追溯了总体文学的发展历程。第三部分狄泽林克指出将“总体文学”作为一个独特的专业术语,并无多大必要,同样的研究也可采用其他类似称呼。他最后批评了用“总体文学”统辖整个比较文学研究的观点,认为“比较文学”这一术语已经在国际学术界得到认可,应该保留下去。这意味着从逻辑关系来说“总体文学”不应该完全等同于“比较文学”。

关于总体文学的概念与学科性质,历来众说纷纭,难成定论,狄泽林克对此问题的论述把握住“超国界”与“普遍意义”两个要素,把它作为比较文学中一个重要的研究分支,可谓得其要领,至今仍是经得起推敲的。

(常芳)

第二章　第一节　总体文学与比较文学的关系

什么是“总体文学”?它的追求是什么?它的职能又是什么?关于这些问题有许多不同的观点,其中的不少看法是互相抵牾的。然而,就其大旨而言,有一点看来可以毫无问题地保留着:“总体文学”指的只能是这样一种文学理论的研究分支,它同国别文学研究相反,要求其涉猎的问题和追求的答案,具有普遍意义而不是单一文学的效用。

一方面,这里所说的研究分支完全可以理解为文学研究整体的一部分,而不是在别的领域运用文学材料,以获取特别有利于那个领域的知识。作为哲学分支的美学便是很典型的例子,它能随意涉猎文学材料,而且也完全有助于文学研究。另一方面,这里所说的研究分支,既以自己独特的研究对象,又通过自己的考察方法,明显地区别于国别文学研究。这一点是我们必须特别强调的。

我们确实不可忘记,除了所有单一语言文学的基础研究以外,还有一种专门的、超国界的文学研究。它所探讨的理论和系统问题是许多国别文学所共有的,解释这些问题对许多国别文学都很重要,而且也只有在超国界范围内才能完成这个任务。我们在此运用“总体文学”这一名称,指的仅仅是这门学科——不错,我们的立场是,只要谈到“总体文学”,只能是指这样一门学科。

事实上,每一门单一文学学科除了掌握历史问题以外,也完全了解理论问题,如同它对自己的方法也要进行批判性思考一样。还有,几乎所有单一语言文学研究今天都试图更好地认识自我,并(鉴于教学和研究的新发展)采用改进了的新的研究方法。另外,还有一个显而易见的事实是,国别文学研究在基础研究方面所做的一些工作,同其姊妹学科的有关理论研究相近,不错,它们甚至还有重叠和吻合的部分。尽管如此,假如把国别文学研究的文学理论和原理研究（或者它们的混杂物）与“总体文学”相提并论，那是一个很大的误会。其原因绝不只在于，罗曼语文学史家、英美文学史家或斯拉夫文学史家，他们在文学理论和方法上的一切研究成果，并不一定适用于德语文学史。

对不管何种文学确实都很重要的原理，只有通过坚持不懈的超国界探讨才能取得。

可称做“总体文学”的这一比较文学分支的特性，就是（如同比较文学史编撰一样）超国界立场与多国研究对象的结合。比较文学中的这个部分，在英语术语中被称为“比较文学理论”（comparative literary theory）和“比较批评”（comparative criticism），在法国比较文学中也有这种研究，虽然在过去的半个世纪中比在美国少得多。

这种超国界基础上的理论和方法学探讨，正是沃伦和韦勒克的《文学理论》的特征。这本书虽然在内容上有很多方面现已陈旧，但依然堪称“总体文学”方面的一部代表性著作。具有这一特征的还有马克斯·魏尔利于1951年出版的专业论著，书中把“总体文学”诠释为“关于文学艺术的本质、起源、表现形态和生存关系的学科……狭义上说，它是一门特殊的、关于文学研究学术原则和方法的学科”[1]。

在以往的这种研究和类似研究中，我们能够清晰地看到所要把握的要点：

只有超国界进行的文学研究才能回答具有普遍意义的系统—理论问题（例如“文学的本质”、“文学与社会的关系”、“文学与其他艺术的关系”），只有超国界进行的文学研究才能系统地、历史地把握和分析各种不同的方法。这些方法是在对文学研究的国际发展具有重要意义的语区中发展起来的。

可以由任意一种国别文学来承担这类任务的设想简直是悖谬的。一种单一文学试图提出“普遍的”亦即对所有或至少不同文学都有意义的理论，最终必然失败。A文学中所探讨的现象同B文学中名称相似或情形相似的现象，在理论层面上可能是大相径庭的，而且在许多情况下也确实如此。

近来人们越来越感兴趣的一个问题，即文学的存在形式和功用问题，是一个典型的例子，它能够简要地说明这一点：文学与社会的关系问题，多半是考察文学在多大程度上是社会的表现，以及文学怎样作用于社会。

当然，人们能在国别文学的框架内提出这些问题，比如某个国家在特定时期的文学与社会的关系是怎样的？考察这个问题能得到什么结论？这类问题见之于埃里希·奥尔巴赫对《十七世纪的法国读者》的研究，还有布鲁福特对歌德时期社会基础的探讨。[2]可想而知，这些研究涉及的是法国文学史或德国文学史，它们虽然在某些方面具有“普遍”意义，但从严格的科学意义上来说，必须把它们看做罗曼语文学史或者日耳曼文学史的研究，而且是对特定时期完全特定的单一文学现象的历史研究。

对文学与社会之关系的兴趣，一旦显示出确实的“一般文学研究的”意义，那么，就应在“总体的”亦即超国界的层面上探讨这个问题。这时，很容易看到我们应该采用的方法。

众所周知，相关理论大体上可以追溯到不多的几个主要来源。例如泰纳的环境理论，尤其是他在《英国文学史》（1864）的序言中所发展的理论，认为文学（以及所有艺术和文化）是由“种族、环境、时代”（race, milieu, moment）决定的。另外还有卡尔·马克思在《〈政治经济学批判〉序言》（1857）中的著名论断，即不是人们的意识决定人们的存在，相反，是存在（尤其是社会存在）决定人们的意识。这一理论（虽然产生于泰纳的环境理论之前）确实如同实证主义环境学说的延续和深化，无论如何是一种"更现代的"说法。

这两种理论以及比它们更早的思想，导引出一系列不同的理论和观点，直到今天还时常引起极为激烈的争辩，并提供了一幅（就整体而言）相当完整的画面，呈现出文学与社会"基础"之间的可能存在和确实存在的联系。大家知道，泰纳的观点是以今天依然值得重视的一些前辈的理论为基础的。例如，路易·德·波纳德在18世纪与19世纪之交①，根据布丰的"风格即人"的名言②，给文学这个颇有成就的词打上了"社会的表现"的印记。另外还有斯达尔夫人，她在《论文学》(1800)中的理论，鼓吹欧洲"北部"和"南部"文学的差异，认为它们受到社会和意识形态的影响，基至部分地受到气候的制约；斯达尔夫人还接过了夏尔·德·维莱尔的部分思想。③ 同样众所周知的是，泰纳的理论发表以后不断成为人们讨论的话题，其环境决定论在世纪之交的时候一再在世界上遭到否定。人们谴责他鼓吹没有事实根据的空想，因时代局限而过高地评价了"物质的"影响，不科学地玩弄"种族"概念，尤其是低估了历史因素。然而，他却一直吸引着那些把探讨文化和文学生活的渊源看做自己的科学使命的人。

马克思的理论则导致一场更加长久的争论，因其政治内涵而远远超出了文学和审美范畴。引起争论的是马克思所运用的概念的含义及其后果，尤其是后来很著名的"基础决定上层建筑"这一模式的作用范围。讨论的表现形式是多种多样的：对基础和上层建筑之间可能的相互作用问题的讨论（恩格斯、斯大林），对二者之间可能的中间环节问题的讨论（普列汉诺夫）④，对文学作为上层建筑如何反映基础的讨论（列宁），等等。换言之，从马克思的原初表述到乔治·卢卡契的观点⑤，组成了一个论点和论证的色彩斑斓的整体，而且论题还没有完全穷尽。卢卡契的观点联系整个历史发展，认为马克思主义立场的结晶是：在"历史发展的全过程"和"复杂的相互作用的整体"中，经济因素不过是第一性的因素而已。[3]

除了这些模式之外，还有很多庞杂的理论也得到了发展，试图用其他推动力量——从表述含糊的"人的本体"（substrat humain）[4]，到宗教性的各种思潮[5]——来代替"决定性的"经济或物质基础。它们都可视为持马克思主义观点的唯物主义一派与某些追随泰纳的常常强调生物学的一派以外的"理想主义"派别。如果人们同样注意到了这些派别，便能很容易地发现，所有发展迄今的关于文学与社会之关系的理论，不仅组成了一个其单一成分直接要求人们对之进行比较的整体系统，而且这个整体的主要内容完全是多国来源的。

---

① 波纳德（1754—1840），法国哲学家，法国大革命的坚定反对者。他是法国第一个明确提出具有文学社会学意义之命题的人。我们今天讨论文学与社会的关系，通常是以波纳德的"文学是社会表现"（La littérature est l'expression de Ia société）这句话为起点的。

② 布丰（1707—1788），法国启蒙运动时期卓越的思想家、博物学家和文学家。

③ 维莱尔（1765—1815），流亡德国的法国军官，哥廷根大学哲学教授。他同斯达尔夫人有私交，并在很大程度上影响了她的德国形象。

④ 普列汉诺夫（1856—1918），俄国哲学家、政论家、历史学家、文学批评家、文学理论家，俄国和国际社会主义运动的活动家。

⑤ 卢卡契（1885—1971），匈牙利文学理论家、美学家、哲学家。

如果说这些跨国立场能够说明社会对文学的产生所具有的影响，那么，它也适用于另外一种观点，即文学对社会也有影响，或曰社会和读者对文学的接受也会产生影响。这都明晰地体现于近期的所谓“接受研究”，即接受美学所发展的文学社会学：历史上的文学社会学主要从事创作美学，直到20世纪50年代，它在国际范围内逐渐转变方向，开始把注意力集中于文学对社会的影响，进而干脆集中于文学的接受。波尔多大学的比较文学家罗伯特·埃斯卡庇是最重要的倡导者之一，他立足于法国比较文学学派的思维方式并步其后尘，于1958年在《文学社会学》中提出了他的新设想。60年代下半期，推崇研究文学接受的“经验主义”模式得到不少人的认可，最后也在德语区(主要以康斯坦茨大学罗曼语文学史家姚斯为首)获得突破。

不言而喻，只有不断查考不同语区的文学作品，这些理论才得以创建。同样，要使这些理论进一步完善，也只有不受语言或国别的拘囿，在多国层面上探究各种典型事例，才是可以想象的。倘若要在总体文学的意义上回答诸如文学与社会的关系这类问题，而却局限于一个语区的作品，那确实是很荒唐的。斯达尔夫人对“北方文学”(Littérature du Nord)和“南方文学”(Littérature du Midi)的分析，至少需要探讨近代德国文学和法国文学；从较大的意义上说，这里当然也包括其他日耳曼语和罗曼语的文学。伊波里特·泰纳的环境决定论，不仅需要推究英国文学(例如他的《英国文学史》)，而且还涉及非语言创作中的一系列独特事例，比如他在《艺术哲学》中所阐述的那样。卡尔·马克思的学说甚至最终通向对古典文学的接受问题的研究。乔治·卢卡契的浪漫主义和现实主义理论，迫使人们既要研究德国的浪漫主义和现实主义文学，又要探讨法国的浪漫主义以及巴尔扎克和福楼拜等。① 他在《理性的毁灭》中所发展的关于浪漫派思想之保守性和反动性的理论，分明是受到德国文学发展的影响才产生的。这一理论再好不过地说明了比较文学研究的必要性。我们有必要把德国浪漫派同法国浪漫派的发展进行对比：法国浪漫派的革命性质，确实明显地区别于德国浪漫派的政治思潮。我们还能罗列许多这方面的事例，一直说到埃斯卡庇关于功能和接受的经验主义研究模式。不管人们试图探索哪一方面的内容，如下结论必然随处可得：要解答带有普遍意义之文学研究的问题，最终只有在比较文学专业范围内才是可能的。

确实，如果一个研究者真想获得不仅适用于某一种文学、而且适用于其他更多文学的认识，那么他就不得不进行比较。而且，这种比较不是所有文学研究中常见的那种，即借助文本的比较得出某种结论。这里说的是确切的比较文学意义上的比较，即跨国的、不受国别文学立场拘囿的比较。

注：

[1]魏尔利：《总体文学》——M. Wehrli, *Allgemeine Literaturwissenschaft*, Bern 1951, 2.

① 巴尔扎克(1799—1850)，19世纪法国伟大的批判现实主义作家，欧洲批判现实主义文学的奠基人和杰出代表。他创作的《人间喜剧》被称为法国社会的“百科全书”，共91部小说，展示了19世纪上半叶的法国社会生活。福楼拜(1821—1880)，19世纪中叶法国重要的批判现实主义作家。主要作品有《包法利夫人》、《萨朗波》和《情感教育》等。

Aufl. 1969，4 页。

[2]布鲁福特：《古典魏玛的文化与社会(1775—1806)》——W. H. Bruford, *Culture and society in classical Weimar* 1775—1806, Cambridge 1962 (Dt.: *Kultur und Gesellschaft im klassischen Weimar* 1775—1806, Göttingen 1966).

[3]卢卡契：《马克思恩格斯美学论文引论》，206 页。——G. Lukács, *Einführung in die ästhetischen Schriften von Marx und Engels* (1945), in: ders., Probleme der Ästhetik, Neuwied/Berlin 1969 (Werke, Bd. 10).

[4]参见居维利埃：《社会学引论》——A. Cuvillier, *Introdution à la sociologie*, Paris 1936, 4. Aufl. 1949. (尤其是第六章"社会学的主要设想")

[5]参见舍夫勒和许京具有典范意义的研究。舍夫勒：《耶稣教与文学——通向 18 世纪英国文学的新途径》——H. Schöffler, *Protestanismus und Literatur. Neue Wege zur englischen Literatur des achtzehnten Jahrhunderts*, Leipzig 1922, 2. Aufl. Göttingen 1958; 许京：《清教主义中的家庭》——L. L. Schücking, *Die Familie im Puritanismus*, Bern/München 1929; 2. Verb. Aufl. u. d. T.: *Die puritanische Familie in literar¯soziologischer Sicht*, Bern/München 1964.

(节选自胡戈·狄泽林克著：《比较文学导论》，方维规译，北京师范大学出版社 2009 年版，第 148-153 页。)

异质同伦与影响变异

——中日德《灰阑》故事比较谈

（节选）

姚玉光

【导读】

姚玉光，汉族，山西洪洞人，1950年生。山西师范大学文学院教授，研究方向为宋元明清文学。主持完成国家项目"元代'平阳戏剧圈'的综合考察与研究"和"《昆曲大典》之《寻亲记》研究"。出版《黄花怜瘦影——李清照传》、《荆钗记评注》等专著。

姚教授的《灰阑故事比较谈》是一篇典型的影响研究论文。在本文中，姚教授首先梳理了学界对"灰阑"断案故事根源的几种假说：主要有赵景深先生的印度说、外来说、中国说和敦煌壁画说。这几种假说探究的主要问题是元代李行道《灰阑记》的题材来源问题。姚教授详细分析了这几种假说在论证上的得失，最后得出结论：李行道独创了灰阑断子的情节，但整个故事应该受到汉代"黄霸断子"和佛教"药王断子"的影响。"黄霸断子"、"药王断子"、"所罗门断子"三个断子故事是在各自独立的文化环境中产生的，它们之间惊人的相似之处是人类处理同类事件采用相同原则的体现，姚教授称之为"异质同伦"。而日本和德国的《灰阑》故事是在李行道《灰阑记》的基础上再次变异。日本江户时代的《大冈政谈》中"二母争一女"的故事应该是受到了黄霸断子故事和李行道《灰阑记》的双重影响，并发生了变异。大冈系列故事和中国包青天系列故事非常类似。"二妇争子"的故事在细节上虽有变异，但故事意蕴基本没有变化，都是真战胜假、善战胜恶。德国作家布莱希特在李行道《灰阑记》的基础上创作了一系列灰阑作品，其中最著名的是《高加索灰阑记》。当然，布莱希特肯定也很熟悉所罗门断子的故事。布莱希特的《高加索灰阑记》表面上虽然以假为真，实则本质上还是以善为真、善战胜恶。在民族文化传承和各国文化交流中，故事虽然会发生变异，但人类的智慧和伦理都是相似的。中外《灰阑》故事非常典型呈现了文化和文学的"异质同伦"与影响变异。

（霍晓珊）

山西绛州李行道，是元代平阳戏剧圈的重要作家，他的《灰阑记》不仅是元代包公戏中的佼佼者，也是最早传入日本、欧洲的作品之一。在研究过程中学术界存在着看法不一甚至观点相左的情况。主要表现在：(一)“灰阑断案”故事的根源在印度，在以色列，还是在中国？(二)中、日、德这些类似的故事属于异质变化？还是影响交融的结果？本文对这两个问题谈谈自己的看法，以就教于大方之家。

关于“灰阑断案”故事的根源有几种代表性的观点。

1. 印度说。前辈文学史家赵景深先生，早在1932年《所罗门与包拯》的考证中，就列出了九种相关的记载：(1)犹太人的《旧约全书列王记》；(2)中国的《包待制智赚灰阑记》；(3)中国西藏的《聪明的国王》；(4)印度的《诞生为大药王》；(5)希腊的《贝布立阿斯》；(6)希腊的《飞德拉斯》；(7)中国的出自谭勒《中国民俗学》中的故事；(8)希腊的《巴兰与约瑟菲》；(9)罗马的《罗马人的行迹》。① 赵先生是主张影响说的。……赵先生是非常渊博的，考证也大都在理。至今有许多支持者，认为“《灰阑记》的源头是来自印度佛教《大藏经》内《贤愚因缘经 · 檀腻鞨品》中的一则短小故事”②。也有人说《贤愚经》“二妇争子”型戏剧故事从印度以及我国西域传入中原地区后，又通过东西方文化交流复传入国外。

2. 外来说。这种观点在佛教与犹太教谁影响谁的问题上不置可否，却都认为中国的同类故事受到了外来文化的影响。“不论源于《圣经》还是印度本土，这个佛经故事都于5世纪中叶流传到中国西藏和内陆。数百年后，元杂剧作家李行道以它为基础，写出包公断案曲本《包待制智赚灰阑记》”③；李行道的《灰阑记》“无疑受到三个宗教故事的影响”④，即所罗门智断两妓女争子故事，《古兰经》中先知素莱曼判断两妇人争子故事，以及《贤愚经》中药王判断人鬼争子故事。

3. 中国说。有的学者力排外来说，认为：“从李行道的身份，他对中国典籍和外国宗教熟悉的程度，从元代杂剧作家创作的风气着眼，更重要的是从《灰阑记》的故事情节、题旨与《风俗通义》中所载黄霸断子的情节、题旨的相同着眼，我认为若说李行道写《灰阑记》是从《风俗通义》中取材，似乎更确切一些，更可信一些。因此可以断定，李行道的《包待制智赚灰阑记》是中国文化的家生子，不是外洋文化的混血儿。”⑤

4. 敦煌壁画说。有的先生认为：“《灰阑记》杂剧的直接源头显然是敦煌壁画中的《贤愚经》，当然李潜夫在改编杂剧时作了艺术上的加工，并把这一故事与包公断案相联系，使主题从歌颂母爱演变为赞扬清官。”⑥

在我看来，这个问题其实是互相区别又互相联系的三个问题。第一，中国汉代“黄霸断子”是否受到了外来影响？第二，元代李行道的《灰阑记》受到了什么影响？有何变异？

---

① 赵景深：《中国小说丛考》，齐鲁书社1983年版，第501-511页。

② 冯君豪：《元曲〈灰阑记〉西传纪略》，《中外文化交流》1995年第4期。

③ 梁工：《所罗门断案故事在东西方的流变》，《中州学刊》2000年第5期。

④ 朱炳荪：《〈灰阑记〉纵横谈》，《社会科学战线》1983年第1期。

⑤ 曲德来：《关于元杂剧〈灰阑记〉的来源问题》，《古籍整理与研究学刊》2002年第3期。

⑥ 朱建明：《敦煌壁画与〈灰阑记〉杂剧》，《上海艺术家》2000年第6期。

第三，日本的《审问生母与继母之事》，德国布莱希特的系列灰阑作品，是受到什么影响产生的？有何变异？学术界目前没有在“黄霸断子”上得出受影响与否的结论，在李行道《灰阑记》之题材来源上又存在较大分歧。

……

应劭的《风俗通义》，学术界大都以为成书于194—204年间，书中所记的黄霸断子应是一个真实的历史事件。黄霸，字次公，淮阳阳夏人，主要为政于汉武帝至汉宣帝年间。据《汉书》本传记载，黄霸曾两次在颍川担任太守。……本传中虽然没有断子记载，然而多次强调黄霸是一个处议得法，吏民爱敬的官。断子故事当是黄霸颍川担任太守时所为，“垂相”之称，乃后人追记时的尊称，时间应在前65—前55年之间。

佛教传入中国，最早可能在汉哀帝元寿元年(前2)，一般的说法是东汉明帝永丰八年，佛经的翻译始于桓帝建和元年(147)，大量翻译佛经是魏晋南北朝的事了。佛教中药王断子故事在中国的流传，最早可能在魏晋南北朝时期。《贤愚经》最早译成汉文是北魏的凉州僧人慧觉。藏文《贤愚经》更晚，是唐文宗时的吐蕃族翻译家管·法成。

所罗门断子故事，若从以色列人进入中国算起则是北宋时的事。12世纪初，流移到印度孟买的犹太人移居到了中国的开封，他们还建立了“一赐乐业教”，俗称“挑筋教”，并设立了会堂。我很怀疑“一赐乐业”就是“以色列”的音译。据说，现在开封的经教胡同曾是犹太人的聚集地，DNA检测的结果是，开封犹太人源于伊拉克两河流域的犹太人。而且经教胡同的三通相关石碑还保存在开封市博物馆。

伊斯兰教在7世纪初由穆汗默德创立，传入中国，影响我国回、维、哈萨克、塔吉克等民族也是7世纪中叶以后的事了，影响汉人则自然更晚。因此，理论上讲不可能影响“黄霸断子”故事。

犹太教对基督教的影响要更直接一些，时间在1、2世纪的罗马帝国时期，所罗门断子案可能于此时在欧洲传播。

综上所述，汉族的黄霸断子，佛教的药王断子，犹太的所罗门断子，这三个断子故事是在各自独立的文化环境中产生的，然而却有惊人的相似之处，这是人类智慧的相似性的体现，更是人类处理同类事件采用相同原则的体现，我把这种情况称为异质同伦。异质是指文化形态的各不相同，同伦是指相同或基本相同的处事原则。汉族、释迦族、犹太族，在文化上原本是各自独立的，属于异质文化。但在断子上把握的原则是相同的，这就是真的总归是真的，假的总归是假的，真善美战胜假丑恶，是人们的共同愿望，也是“神”的意志。正所谓人同此心，心同此理。

当然，这种异质同伦也是需要一定条件的，其中的一个重要条件，就是异质文化间相对微弱的辐射能力。这种异质文化间的封闭状，随着人类科技力量的进步，必然会被打破，这时异质文化间交融的力度就会逐渐增大，并且在相互影响中产生变异。李行道的《灰阑记》，日本大冈故事中的《审问生母与继母事》以及德国布莱希特的系列灰阑之作，就是这种影响变异的有力证明。

关于李行道《灰阑记》所受的影响，我们首先来看“敦煌壁画说”。第一，《贤愚经》卷十一之五十三品之《国王判案》，并不是一个完全独立的故事，更不是本事的源头，无论从审案者、告状者、所审之事，还是以判案方式及结局上，与印度的“药王断子”、《西藏故事集》中的《聪明的国王》，都没有区别。第二，作者无法证明李行道确实看过这幅壁画。为此，它不能成立。

“外来说”并没有区分三种外部文化对中国影响的先后，也没有否定“印度说”。这种观点的缺陷，一是只从时间的角度，看到所罗门、药王、素莱曼所生活的年代比李行道早得多，而没有用确凿的事实证明这些故事完全有可能对李行道产生影响，而且是唯一的影响。二是没有找到中国本地的同质故事对李行道的影响，特别是东汉应劭《风俗通义》中的争子故事，断语下得有点偏颇。

“中国说”的观点颇有可取之处，但在论证过程中也有疏漏欠严谨的地方。首先，似乎不清楚赵景深先生1933年写的《包公传说》，因此，涉及“印度说”的许多论述自然有失公允；其次，以为“现今为止，在元杂剧中，还见不到有一种是从外国宗教故事取材的”，“元代不少杂剧作家，是从流传的历史的故事和以往的笔记以及唐宋传奇、志怪小说、话本、民间故事中取材来结构自己的杂剧作品的”。其实，中国的笔记、传奇、志怪小说、话本和民间故事，有的已经受到外来文化特别是佛教的影响。佛教在汉代传入中国后，影响逐渐深入而广泛，从官方到民间都相当笃信，并形成了中国式的佛教。元杂剧中也有直接取材于佛教故事的，如《来生债》、《忍字记》、《度柳翠》、《猿听经》、《东坡梦》、《度黄龙》等，间接受到影响的如《张生煮海》、《柳毅传书》、《西天取经》、《齐天大圣》、《锁魔镜》等。陈洪先生在《文学评论》撰文专门探讨了这方面的问题；第三，以为李行道是个隐士，《风俗通义》中黄霸断子的故事，被马总的《意林》、虞世南的《北堂书钞》、李昉的《太平御览》、郑克的《折狱龟鉴》、桂万荣的《棠阴比事》等广泛引录，这些书都是宋元时社会上所见的，李行道“读这些笔记是完全可能的”，“他并不是佛教徒，当然更不是伊斯兰教和景教信徒。在平阳这个传统文化盛行的地方，他读那些宗教经书的可能性是很小的”[11]。其实，佛教在元代民间的影响非常大，一个作家受佛教影响，可以直接受之于佛经，也可以受之于变文、俗讲和勾栏瓦肆中的民间文学艺术中的佛教故事。平阳地区传统文化的积淀虽然非常丰厚，但佛教已经成了传统的一部分，新绛县中就有很多座唐、宋、金、元时的佛寺。……在如此浓厚的佛教文化的氛围中，如果说李行道就没有受到外来文化的影响，是不可能的。要找到“药王断子”对李行道影响的直接证据肯定是难事，但他受佛教文化影响，却是一个不争的事实。

……

综上所述，《灰阑记》中，灰阑断子的情节完全是李行道的创造；创造中受到了前人同类故事的启发，汉代“黄霸断子”的影响是主要的，也可能有佛教药王断子的影响。

需要特别指出的是，说赵景深先生没有找到《风俗通义》中的这则故事是不符合事实的。赵先生不但找到了这则故事，而且是最早找到的人之一。早在1933年5月10日，赵先生的《包公传说》，就遗憾自己在《所罗门与包拯》中“惜未举出我国比元曲更古的故事”，并全文引述了应劭《风俗通义》中黄霸断子的原文，只是没有明确说《灰阑记》到底是受了谁的影响。这说明赵先生已经肯定了《灰阑记》吸收了黄霸断子的素材，只是没有回答在中外同类故事中，《灰阑记》到底吸收了谁，或者在多大程度上吸收了谁的问题，把这个问题留给了后人。

将《风俗通义》中的争子故事与《灰阑记》的故事进行比较，可以看到，在四个方面中国故事有内在的血缘联系，明显比外国同类故事相似。(1)争子双方的身份：《风俗通义》中是妯娌，《灰阑记》中是妻妾，所罗门故事中是没有血缘关系的妓女，药王故事是亲娘与鬼；(2)争子的目的：两个中国故事都是继承财产，而所罗门故事是为了孩子本身，药王故事中的鬼则是为了吃掉孩子；(3)判案者的身份：两个中国故事都是朝廷官吏，而外国故事都是先知神佛。……

从黄霸断子到灰阑断子，中国故事的继承和变异是比较清楚的：争夺的对象和目的基本相同，都是男孩，都是为了占有孩子并获得巨额遗产；但争夺双方由妯娌变成了妻妾，由平等变成了家庭地位尊卑有异，势力强弱有别，道德善恶分明。黄霸断子中兄、嫂之恶与弟、媳之善只是在争子情节中表现的，对日常生活中的善恶表现并无涉及。《灰阑记》将笔触拓向更加鲜明的日常生活，妓女出身的张海棠心地善良、诚实勤俭、不谙世事在情节中有充分的展示；而马大娘子阴险、毒辣、世故的描写也非常充分，她与赵令史通奸并伙同奸夫杀死丈夫。断案的手段更加科学、公正、合理，更具有公正性和观赏性，这也是由生活向艺术转化过程的质的飞跃。在中外同类的断子故事中，灰阑的确是一个艺术的创新；思想意蕴方面除了主要表现惩恶扬善之外，对贪官污吏的鞭挞，对人性冷暖的褒贬，都达到了入木三分的效果。正是："律意虽远，人情可推。视其所以，观其所由。本为家私赖子孙，灰阑辨出假和真，外相温柔心毒狠，亲者原来则是亲。"①

日本江户时代(1603—1868)出现的《大冈政谈》中，也有"二母争一女"的故事，这故事显然受到中国"黄霸断子"和《灰阑记》的双重影响，并发生了变异。

……

《灰阑记》对德国的影响更加巨大。《灰阑记》传播到欧洲后，先后出现了法文译本和德文译本，接着出现了改编本和启发创新本。

改编本是德国作家克拉本特的《灰阑记》，把四折的元杂剧改编为五幕剧，剧名、人名、主题都没有变化，情节方面只增加了一些爱情的成分。改编后曾于1925年在柏林演出，获得了很大的成功。

……

1944年，流亡到美国的布莱希特创作了史诗剧《高加索灰阑记》，剧作围绕战后一个山谷归属于牧民农庄还是果农农庄的问题展开，用传说故事进行启发以求得问题的解决。布氏公开宣称"一个非常古老的传说。它叫《灰阑记》，从中国来的，当然，我们的演出在形式方面做了更动"。相对于李行道的杂剧和布氏自己的小说，《高加索灰阑记》的继承和变异主要是：第一，争子双方还是主妇与主仆，只是主妇由商人之妇变成了总督夫人，抨击的对象由奸商变成了赃官；而格鲁雪相对于安娜，对生命的爱护更主动更自觉，付出的艰辛更大，经历了包括生死在内的种种考验，阿兹达克的性格更加复杂而鲜明，他威严又诙谐，放浪形骸又头脑清醒，对富人公开受贿，滥定罪名，对穷人却故意袒护。第二，在灰阑断案中，情节与《灰阑记》更接近，只把孩子放在圈内，两个女人在圈外拉。第三，断子的结局与《灰阑记》相反，与《奥格斯堡灰阑记》相同，让养母取得胜利，让生母败诉，目的是"一切归善于对待的，比如说孩子归慈爱的母亲，为了成才成器；车辆归好车夫，

① 李行道：《灰阑记》，《全元戏曲》第三卷，人民文学出版社1999年版，第596页。

开起来顺利；山谷归灌溉的人，好让它开花结果”①。第四，表面上看中国灰阑系列故事是以真为真，布氏阑系列故事是以假为真，在本质上都是一样的，因为中国故事中的善在生母一方，而布氏故事中的善在养母一方，都是“善”获得了最后的胜利。

事实再次证明，人同此心，心同此理。尽管中、日、德灰阑故事，在文化传承和影响中发生了许多变异，但人类的智慧和伦理都是相似的。

（节选自姚玉光：《异质同伦与影响变异——中日德〈灰阑〉故事比较谈》，《中华戏曲》2007年第5期，第276-287页。）

① 布莱希特：《布莱希特戏剧选》，人民文学出版社1980年版，第359页。

中西复仇文学主题比较

（节选）

王　立

【导读】

王立，大连大学教授，文学博士，东北师范大学博士研究生导师。在比较文学、文学主题学、古代文学与文化等方面研究成果丰富。

原始人复仇的三个阶段，第一阶段，复仇不怕过火，世代世仇，直到对方死亡；第二阶段，同态复仇；第三阶段，赎金代替复仇。《荷马史诗》、《左传》等都有相关和传说故事记载。以暴抗暴、敢于向篡位国君或暴君复仇，是中西方上古复仇文学共同的可贵之点。虽然仇怨起因与复仇者意志是为了维护尊严和伦理道德，但是复仇主体的动机和维持复仇的意志力中西方文学侧重不同。在西方文化精神中强调的是个体的价值、个人权利、荣誉、尊严。古代中国复仇文学的主体复仇的动机则突出为他人报仇，他人多数为主体的恩人、好朋友、亲属报仇，受传统文化尽忠尽孝和江湖义气影响。西方文学中复仇主体的情仇将自身之恨与社会不公正联系起来，突出个体性；古代中国则强调了复仇的群体性，多是士为知己者死。西方复仇主体意志磨炼的多是以悲剧表现，古代中国复仇主体多是被突显于伦理实现动机的果决。

至于复仇的方式、手段和目的，既包含精神摧毁，也包含肉体毁灭。相对于古代中国的较为稳定复仇手法、目的，西方复仇文学主题分为古希腊、文艺复兴后及十八世纪后三个阶段。古代中国复仇文学主题思维定势就是“被复仇者必定是坏人”，这在实现复仇时一个突出的表现就是不择手段，直到达到复仇目的。古希腊时期复仇文学主题和古代中国较为相似，文艺复兴后人们普遍接受了平等、正义思想，复仇手段变得更加复杂。复仇者充分借助习俗和文化模式进行复仇，运用金钱和法律的威力实现复仇。十八世纪后，复仇主体为了实现让仇主更加痛苦，不直接果断地置对方于死地，而是从精神上让仇主更加痛苦。这与古代中国以亲手诛、杀急不可待的复仇手段和目的有所不同。

中西方的复仇与爱情婚姻的存在密切关系。西方复仇文学的复仇主题往往突出了复仇者陷于情仇之间的矛盾。中国复仇文学复仇主题在婚姻、爱情、女子交织中多倾向于复仇，为了复仇可以以身相许接近仇人，这是复仇中常见手法。二者手段的差别的根本原因源于中西伦理文化传统之差异。西方文化中将增进个体幸福称之为善，中国古代复仇时是为了维护血缘伦理纲常，维护封建等级与封建礼教，牺牲个人的幸福微不足道。

对复仇的褒贬和总体评价中，中西复仇主题文学的价值流向、形态不同。中国复仇文学一以贯之，几乎一致赞美复仇，复仇是个体人格品位评定的重要风标。西方复仇文学的评价呈现动态发展，显示出文明演变轨迹，复仇不全是正义的，因此褒奖复仇逐渐弱化。西方文学描写复仇多从人物内心矛盾展开，而中国写复仇较偏重人物实施报复的行动过程及社会反响。

（潘丹丹）

二、尊严维护与伦理实现——仇怨起因及复仇者意志

作为主题表现的首要问题，仇怨起因牵涉到主体的复仇动机及维持此动机的意志力，对此中西方文学各有侧重。

源自古希腊的西方文化精神较为重视个体价值、崇尚个人权利、荣誉与尊严，像波塞冬、阿波罗，以及赫拉、雅典娜同特洛亚城结仇，均因尊严受到轻亵。经罗马角斗精神中转为中世纪的“骑士精神”，倡扬孤注一掷的冒险无畏、不惜代价。像史诗《罗兰之歌》写他面对强敌仍不愿求援，耻于显示懦弱。这与西方复仇每每因个体自身名誉、尊严受损而起，有内在相通之处。莎士比亚笔下的伊阿古阴谋得逞，正是利用了奥瑟罗自感尊严受损的情绪冲动，而骑士精神正是将女性之爱、理想荣誉视为生命；麦尔维尔写亚人船长向白鲸复仇，也因莫比·狄克不仅直接致残他的肢体，更严重的是造成了他精神上难于愈合的创伤：“假如太阳侮辱了我，我也要戳穿它。”对人性威严的珍视，在《基督山伯爵》、《呼啸山庄》中展示为主体报虐待、陷害和情敌夺爱之恨；事实上，这与西方“决斗”之风长期盛行亦密切联系，决斗即往往因一方或双方名誉利益受侵害而起。

究其中西之别的深层原因，即古巴比伦《汉穆拉比法典》“同态复仇”规定所影响下的西方复仇观，较为讲究复仇的对等性质，而两汉后的中原人扩大化复仇则受族诛酷刑熏染而长期持续。弗雷泽曾指出以酬金赎罪以免遭复仇，是一种历史的进步；而精确计算人体哪怕一个最小（拇指、小指）部位所受伤害的偿金，① 也与西方复仇偏重摧折人的精神而非偏重肉体毁灭有关。只有在较强的法制观念支配下，赎金制体现的讲究复仇分寸，才具有理性的意义。

古代中国的复仇文学则偏爱传扬为他人报仇，即主体的恩主、挚友与血亲故旧。体现侠之自尊而为己雪恨的虽非绝无，毕竟较前者是为数甚少。尽孝尽忠，归结为恪尽人伦义务和社会使命，社会对复仇者特定的角色期待使其不得不然。较有突破性的是《水浒传》中的林冲、宋江、杨志、石秀等人行事，然而这种维护自尊的杀人越轨，却多为江湖豪侠的禁脔。传统文化所讲求的恕道宽仁，往往在压抑个体为自尊遭亵雪恨时体现出来；至于其尽义务为他人报怨时则鼓励有加。

---

① 《人类学——人及其文化研究》，七海文艺出版社 1993 年版，第 390 页。

西方文学较多地描写复仇主体的情仇，此与西方文化肯定个人情欲有关。主体又往往将自身的夺爱之恨同对社会不平的愤懑联系起来，毕竟偏重社会性中的个体性；古代中国多血亲复仇、士报知己描写，主体常将报亲仇雪友(主)恨同个体价值实现于社会系于一处，在偏重家族伦理中突出复仇的群体性，一雪私怨也恰恰在正教化、敦人伦、美风俗，诸鬼灵雪怨也在个别性中宣示着惩恶扬善的普遍教化之旨。

西方文学在侧重表现复仇主体意志磨炼过程时，常热衷于写其精神苦痛折磨甚至困惑，像哈姆莱特的一再"延宕"；而邓蒂斯在度过14年囚役生活，行将复仇时，作者也着意描绘了他在漫长且艰辛的精神历炼后气质性情的变化，从而绝好地揭示了复仇者意志的愈挫愈奋。因此，西方复仇之作多采用悲剧、小说体裁，此为细致曲折刻画人物性格提供了施展作者才情的较多机缘。而惜墨如金的写作积习与重情节的史传传统，使中国的复仇英雄们被突显于伦理实现动机的果决。

三、精神摧残与肉体毁灭——复仇的方式、手段及目的

与古代中国较稳定、几乎一成不变的复仇手法、目的不同，西方复仇文学主题可分古希腊、文艺复兴后以及18世纪后三阶段，而以后两阶段尤其最后阶段为定型期，亦最能看出西方文化特征及中西方复仇观念差异，尽管这三阶段互有联系，不能截然分开。

虽则像奥德修还乡后的复仇也充满了血腥气，但对复仇手段的限制在西方萌芽较早，最终发展到对复仇失当乃至复仇本身的否定。塔西佗《历史》中即谴责过那些对罗马皇帝尸体"加以卑鄙的蹂躏"的民众，而这位皇帝面对威胁敢于维护自尊，还引起了作者的钦赞。并不象古代中国将被复仇对象说得丝毫不值得悯惜。听说仇人波吕尼刻斯战死，克瑞翁下令不得收尸，死者的妹妹冒死犯禁得到了公众的同情，年老的预言家也劝克瑞翁收回成命："荼毒已死的人，这算什么光荣呢?"克瑞翁终受严惩：安提戈涅自缢，引得克瑞翁之子海蒙殉情，克瑞翁之妻也伤心自杀。这一切惨重代价皆因复仇失当而来。

伍子胥鞭尸楚平王雪父兄大怨，并未受到责难。史书写董卓、侯景等被刑尸满泄愤，反映了"食肉寝皮"的民俗心理。众多类似故事在主题系统中被充分渲染，说明中国古人更重视复仇目的的实现。对丧悼礼俗的尊尚及相关禁忌，也每多对亡灵本身的敬畏，缺少有关向死者泄愤是否符合正义的反思①。这当然与复仇伦理化阐释、被复仇者必定是坏人的主题模式有关。因对坏人人格的蔑视，阴阳对举正邪不两立的思维模式就判定：可以不择手段地加以损害侮辱。

文艺复兴后平等、正义等观念被普遍接受，西方复仇方式、手段的表现随之更为复杂。哈姆雷特即将个人复仇同拯救社会责任一并考虑，审慎地思索更适合的时机、更准确的途径实现目标，如黑格尔《美学》里说的："他所犹豫的不是应该做什么，而是应该怎样去做。"痛苦地意识到使命的艰巨性，又清醒地意识到恶势力强大而自感孤立无援，便不得已采取了远非上策的手段。哈姆莱特的复仇悲剧，至少从复仇使命的艰巨复杂性和复仇主体实现正义目标应具备的条件这两个重要角度，为主题开拓了新的视野，西方文学遂呼

① 参见拙文：《丧悼文化与中国古代复仇文学主题》，《社会科学战线》1994年第3期。

唤着更具备主体条件的复仇英雄。

到了两个生卒年相仿佛的法国作家——梅里美与大仲马，主题又有了新的开拓。《高龙巴》所写的科西嘉少女之年龄似乎与她的复仇智慧不成比例，因为由家长复仇的习俗不容许她下手，就千方百计鼓动前来探家的哥哥雪报父耻，竟至暗将自家的马耳朵割碎以移祸仇凶。高斯习俗认为伤敌仇之马表示挑战、恐吓对方，是一种严重的侮辱。随后高龙巴愤愤地嚷叫："我们还不回手吗？你们还能算人吗？"如果说，高龙巴洞察到习俗的力量而有效地借用，那么，邓蒂斯的复仇手段实施也是充分地利用了所处社会的文化模式，为了向三个仇人雪恨他运用金钱与法律的威力。巧遇拥有巨大财富的狱友和14年中容貌的改变，使他有条件智取仇人，他要的不是让其短时间内死去，而是饱受精神折磨。对富翁马瑟夫是将其卖主丑史公开，使其迫于舆论而自杀；对检查官维尔福是利用其夫人争夺遗产贪欲，透露制毒秘方使之在阴谋败露后母子双亡，仇主惊而发疯；对银行家邓格拉司则诱以假信息，使其公债投机失败，同时揭露其妻阴私，妻女离去，仇主成了穷人。金钱使邓蒂斯博得仇人信任，介入仇人家族矛盾中，法律地运用更能使他将仇人弄得声名狼藉。尤其是对贝尼台多的"指控和供认"，完全是在合乎法律程序下，利用法律效力进行的。当年初闻狱友说起宝藏时，邓蒂斯就想，在当今时代"一个人拥有一千三百万到一千四百万财富，能给仇人带去多大的灾难"。洞悉金钱社会的本质，他处心积虑行使复仇权利才一再马到成功。

基督山伯爵从精神上摧折仇主，又绝好地体现了西方复仇文学第三阶段的特点。

17世纪欧洲兴起的宗教改革运动尤其是法国宗教改革家加尔文的学说，很大程度上影响了此后西方复仇观念。加尔文《基督教原理》认为，人们在世间是接受着上帝预先给定的命运，社会、法律体现的是上帝意志，基督徒贯彻上帝法律不是消极盲从，而是运用之以体现上帝的意志。像邓蒂斯看到维尔福夫人、儿子尸体时，"脸色变得惨白；他明白，他刚才已经把报仇的权利用过了；他明白他已经不能再说说这句话了：'天主是站在我的一边的，他和我同在'"。得悉无法将孩子复生与仇人发疯，邓蒂斯也深感恐惧、悲伤和内疚，决定停止报复："天主希望我别做得太过分了！"复仇在一种体现上帝意志的正义范围之内进行，这种有分寸的合乎人世与天主双重法律的复仇，其目标也就制约了手段与方法，而手段实施也一定要考虑目标的适度，超出限度并非基督山伯爵的初衷。

相关的习俗风尚制约复仇目标手段的选择，后者又反馈于主体对复仇雪恨的进一步思考。西方式复仇所费时日、周折较多，像邓蒂斯就觉得不能太便宜了仇人，"觉得再可怕的刑罚也太轻，尤其对这些人也太短暂，因为施刑后就是死亡，而死亡意味着安息"，这与古代中国"虎吏和暴君"们发明了酷刑，而复仇者却非大奸大恶之人才慢慢折磨之以泄愤，是有很大区别的。迫于舆论急于实现伦理使命，中国古人往往以亲手诛杀仇凶为最佳雪怨方式，急不可待地摧毁仇命，历览绝大部分相关描述，此当与农业民族之天性有关：

……内向克制，彬彬有礼，心理稳定，在任何灾难面前都表现出淡然怡乐、泰然处之气度；但另一方面，却在狂热地信仰中表现出一种极其迷醉的冲动，甚至表现出一种潜藏极深的欲望的驱力甚至是刻毒、自私的攻击性。这种近乎"二律背反"式的现象竟和谐地交汇在一个民族甚至一个人的心灵中。①

基于主静守尚沉稳的民族积习，因其农耕生产方式带来的种种弱点，使国人在不断抵御草原文化的游牧民族侵袭过程中，产生并强固了“弱者复仇心态”：讲求后发制人，但若出手便期置仇于死地；微怨小耻的忍耐宽恕遮掩着“动如脱兔”一发毙仇的酷烈刚猛；受到伤害后创伤很难平复，必以最严厉、最极端化的报复来泄愤雪恨，不给仇人留下存活肆虐的任何机会。

可见中西方复仇文学主题昭示着：西方较为偏重复仇行使时主体灵魂世界的冲突，偏重复仇实施尤其是精神摧残的过程描绘；中国则较关注复仇的结局，包括复仇者成功后的命运。西方写复仇注重个体人格的完善，中国写复仇偏好伦理目标的实现，从而往往省略了必要的心灵冲突与过程描绘，以期让结局尽快展露，让人如饮醇醪。西方复仇之作常引发人对个体与命运抗争的悲壮感，中国复仇之作常激起善必胜恶的愉悦感。

四、纠葛难分与主从分明——复仇与爱情婚姻的关系

西方文学中的复仇主题，常常与复仇主体或其亲属的情爱交织，复仇与爱情间矛盾冲突激烈，二者孰重纠葛难分，乃至普遍存在着一个绵长久远的“仇人子女相爱”母题。

在高乃依悲剧《熙德》中，罗德里克与施曼娜这对情侣的父辈失和，为报父辱罗德里克经过激烈的思想斗争杀死了施蒂娜之父，而施蒂娜也恪守义务要求处死凶手；正当罗德里克准备死于决斗成全恋人复仇决心时，施蒂娜反用爱情激励他获胜。复仇成为家庭利益和个体爱情理想间矛盾的聚焦。面对悖论的罗德里克曾有激烈的心理斗争：

> 要成全爱情就得牺牲我的荣誉，
> 要替父亲报仇，就得放弃我的爱人。
> 一方面是高尚而严厉的责任，
> 一方面是可爱而专横的爱情。
> 复仇会引起她的怨恨和愤怒，不复仇会引起她的蔑视。
> 复仇会使我失去我最甜蜜的希望，
> 不复仇又会使我不配爱她

复仇是有限的，这一点很重要，由此其作为封建贵族的荣誉义务，既可否定爱情；经过个人幸福理想陶冶，又可激励爱情，在肯定复仇理性的同时，爱情也得到了肯定。

爱与仇间的纠葛在西方文学中较多地与悲剧性的命运母题联系着，仿佛两个相爱男女总受着命运之神的摆布，他们力图冲出命运的羁绊只会加速毁灭。17 至 18 世纪间德国戏剧家克莱斯特的悲剧《施罗芬施泰因家族》也描写两家因争夺遗产敌对，误会而仇深，奥托卡爱上了仇人之女阿格纳斯，两人幽会时被发现，奥托卡为掩护女友被误刺死，随后阿格纳斯也无端被误杀。仇怨使当事人变得偏执，它带给人们无法摆脱的血腥祸患，竟使爱

① 葛兆光：《道教与中国文化》，上海人民出版社 1987 年版，第 362 页。

情这一最为美好而神圣的事情，也构成仇杀的契机和催化剂。换来两个家族悔恨的代价未免太沉重了。

稍早些的法国悲剧《安德洛玛克》则探索了女性利用爱情进行复仇，以及冲突构成的连锁反应。庇吕斯以杀死遗孤要挟，让赫克托耳的遗孀嫁给自己，在保存儿子和屈从仇敌之间，安德洛玛克选择了暂且允诺，婚礼完毕自杀一途。但早已同庇吕斯订婚的爱尔米奥娜妒恨交加，唆使情人俄瑞斯忒杀死了庇吕斯，而后自杀。杀夫之仇便这样曲折地通过相关人物情欲作用而得以报雪，事态发展并非复仇主体所料，但安德洛玛克忠于爱情的意志行为毕竟导致了复仇实现的结局。

……

（节选自王立：《中西复仇文学主题比较》，《外国文学研究》1996 第 3 期，第 104-107 页。）

摩罗诗力说

（节选）

鲁　迅

【导读】

《摩罗诗力说》是鲁迅(1881—1936)于1907年留学日本期间用文言文所创作的一篇文论，是他早期文艺思想的代表作。当时国内思潮正经历以孙中山为首的资产阶级革命派和康有为为首的资产阶级改良派的论战，而鲁迅站在革命派这一边，所以该文响应资产阶级民族民主革命应时而作，对以拜伦为代表的英、俄、波、匈等国的浪漫派进行了开拓性的研究，对旧传统和旧文化进行批判，是当时中国思想界成就最高的作品，也代表我国现代比较文学研究的开始。

“摩罗”是梵语音译，意为“魔鬼”，与基督教的魔鬼“撒旦”(Satan)意义较接近，“摩罗诗力说”意思就是“论恶魔派诗歌的力量”，当时人们以此来称呼离经叛道的浪漫派诗人拜伦，而“摩罗诗派”是指以拜伦为代表的浪漫主义诗派。在西方，“摩罗诗派”的正式名称应该为“Poets of Romanticism”，因此有学者认为鲁迅假“摩罗”一词引入“摩罗诗派”多半因为国人熟悉佛教远胜于基督教。拜伦被看作是反抗强权和压迫的英雄式人物，被鲁迅称为“性解”(genius 天才)，“摩罗”即代表着这样一种崇高的力量，他们蔑视虚伪、舍命抗争，具有强烈反抗精神和爱国热情，能创作出触动人们心灵的作品，也象征着鲁迅所呼吁的中国的“精神界之战士”。

《摩罗诗力说》开篇引用了尼采的名言：“求古源尽者将求方来之泉，将求新源。嗟我昆弟，新生之作，新泉之涌于渊深，其非远矣。”其大意是：探求古老的源泉已经穷尽了，将要去寻找未来的源泉，新的起源。兄弟们啊，新生命的兴起，新的源泉从深渊中喷涌而出，那日子不会遥远了。鲁迅以他特有的方式，在篇首引用此段文字，开宗明义点明其主题，表达了他对中国旧传统和旧文化的失望，对“新声”的向往。节选的第一篇谈到了文学与国家命运的关系，鲁迅列举了印度、希伯来、伊朗和埃及这些在古代曾一度辉煌而后来运势衰败的国家，它们的文学和艺术与国运相伴随。而俄国和意大利都有着自己享誉世界的文学巨匠，民族必将振兴。野蛮也可以孕育文明的光辉，但中国沉湎于曾经的辉煌而缺乏进取的精神。摩罗诗派不随波逐流，放声呐喊，与世抗争，他们的精神能打动后世人们的心灵。后文继续评介拜伦、雪莱、莱蒙托夫、密茨凯维奇、佩多芬等人的思想和创作，赞扬他们的战斗精神具有唤醒被压迫人民的民主主义思想。

严复所作《天演论》以及尼采、康德等西方思想家的观点对鲁迅创作《摩罗诗力说》产生了重要影响。有学者认为鲁迅所受到西方思想的影响，多是通过日本学者对西方各种思潮的引进，因为当时鲁迅在日本留学期间西方思想和文化在日本的影响日盛，这也为从事比较文学研究的学者研究摩罗诗力说和中国文学运动与其他国家的文学运动的联系提供了一定参考。

（黄惠）

求古源尽者将求方来之泉，将求新源。嗟我昆弟，新生之作，新泉之涌于渊深，其非远矣。

——尼佉

一

人有读古国文化史者，循代而下，至于卷末，必凄以有所觉，如脱春温而入于秋肃，勾萌绝朕，枯槁在前，吾无以名，姑谓之萧条而止。盖人文之留遗后世者，最有力莫如心声。古民神思，接天然之閟宫，冥契万有，与之灵会，道其能道，爰为诗歌。其声度时劫而入人心，不与缄口同绝；且益曼衍，视其种人。递文事式微，则种人之运命亦尽，群生辍响，荣华收光；读史者萧条之感，即以怒起，而此文明史记，亦渐临末页矣。凡负令誉于史初，开文化之曙色，而今日转为影国者，无不如斯。使举国人所习闻，最适莫如天竺。天竺古有《韦陀》四种，瑰丽幽夐，称世界大文；其《摩诃波罗多》暨《罗摩衍那》二赋，亦至美妙。厥后有诗人加黎陀萨（Kalidasa）者出，以传奇鸣世，间染抒情之篇；日耳曼诗宗瞿提（W. von Goethe），至崇为两间之绝唱。降及种人失力，而文事亦共零夷，至大之声，渐不生于彼国民之灵府，流转异域，如亡人也。次为希伯来，虽多涉信仰教诫，而文章以幽邃庄严胜，教宗文术，此其源泉，灌溉人心，迄今兹未艾。特在以色列族，则止耶利米（Jeremiah）之声；列王荒矣，帝怒以赫，耶路撒冷遂隳，而种人之舌亦默。当彼流离异地，虽不遽忘其宗邦，方言正信，拳拳未释，然《哀歌》而下，无赓响矣。复次为伊兰埃及，皆中道废弛，有如断绠，灿烂于古，萧瑟于今。若震旦而逸斯列，则人生大戬，无逾于此。何以故？英人加勒尔（Th. Carlyle）曰，得昭明之声，洋洋乎歌心意而生者，为国民之首义。意太利分崩矣，然实一统也，彼生但丁（Dante Alighieri），彼有意语。大俄罗斯之札尔，有兵刃炮火，政治之上，能辖大区，行大业。然奈何无声？中或有大物，而其为大也喑。（中略）迨兵刃炮火，无不腐蚀，而但丁之声依然。有但丁者统一，而无声兆之俄人，终支离而已。

尼佉（Fr. Nietzsche）不恶野人，谓中有新力，言亦确凿不可移。盖文明之朕，固孕于蛮荒，野人狉獉其形，而隐曜即伏于内。文明如华，蛮野如蕾，文明如实，蛮野如华，上征在是，希望亦在是。惟文化已止之古民不然：发展既央，隳败随起，况久席古宗祖之光荣，尝首出周围之下国，暮气之作，每不自知，自用而愚，污如死海。其煌煌居历史之首，而终匿形于卷末者，殆以此欤？俄之无声，激响在焉。俄如孺子，而非喑人；俄如伏流，而非古井。十九世纪前叶，果有鄂戈理(N. Gogol)者起，以不可见之泪痕悲色，振其邦人，或以拟英之狭斯丕尔(W. Shakespeare)，即加勒尔所赞扬崇拜者也。顾瞻人间，新声争起，无不以殊特雄丽之言，自振其精神而绍介其伟美于世界；若渊默而无动者，独前举天竺以下数古国而已。嗟夫，古民之心声手泽，非不庄严，非不崇大，然呼吸不通于今，则取以供览古之人，使摩挲咏叹而外，更何物及其子孙？否亦仅自语其前此光荣，即以形迹来之寂寞，反不如新起之邦，纵文化未昌，而大有望于方来之足致敬也。故所谓古文明国者，悲凉之语耳，嘲讽之辞耳！中落之胄，故家荒矣，则喋喋语人，谓厥祖在时，其为智慧武怒者何似，尝有闳宇崇楼，珠玉犬马，尊显胜于凡人。有闻其言，孰不腾笑？夫国民发展，功虽有在于怀古，然其怀也，思理朗然，如鉴明镜，时时上征，时时反顾，时时进光明之长途，时时念辉煌之旧有，故其新者日新，而其古亦不死。若不知所以然，漫夸耀以自悦，则长夜之始，即在斯时。今试履中国之大衢，当有见军人蹀躞而过市者，张口作军歌，痛斥印度波阑之奴性；有漫为国歌者亦然。盖中国今日，亦颇思历举前有之耿光，特未能言，则姑曰左邻已奴，右邻且死，择亡国而较量之，冀自显其佳胜。夫二国与震旦究孰劣，今姑弗言；若云颂美之什，国民之声，则天下之咏者虽多，固未见有此作法矣。诗人绝迹，事若甚微，而萧条之感，辄以来袭。意者欲扬宗邦之真大，首在审己，亦必知人，比较既周，爰生自觉。自觉之声发，每响必中于人心，清晰昭明，不同凡响。非然者，口舌一结，众语俱沦，沉默之来，倍于前此。盖魂意方梦，何能有言？即震于外缘，强自扬厉，不惟不大，徒增欷耳。故曰国民精神发扬，与世界识见之广博有所属。

今且置古事不道，别求新声于异邦，而其因即动于怀古。新声之别，不可究详；至力足以振人，且语之较有深趣者，实莫如摩罗诗派。摩罗之言，假自天竺，此云天魔，欧人谓之撒但，人本以目裴伦(G. Byron)。今则举一切诗人中，凡立意在反抗，指归在动作，而为世所不甚愉悦者悉入之，为传其言行思惟，流别影响，始宗主裴伦，终以摩迦(匈加利)文士。凡是群人，外状至异，各禀自国之特色，发为光华；而要其大归，则趣于一：大都不为顺世和乐之音，动吭一呼，闻者兴起，争天拒俗，而精神复深感后世人心，绵延至于无已。虽未生以前，解脱而后，或以其声为不足听；若其生活两间，居天然之掌握，辗转而未得脱者，则使之闻之，固声之最雄桀伟美者矣。然以语平和之民，则言者滋惧。

……

（节选自鲁迅：《摩罗诗力说》，载《坟》，人民文学出版社1980年版，第56-59页。）

文学的历史动向

闻一多

【导读】

闻一多先生是20世纪饮誉中国现代诗坛的诗人，早年热衷于新诗创作，两部代表诗集《红烛》和《死水》开创了新的诗风，组诗《七子之歌》在澳门回归时曾经响彻中华大地。同时，他也是一位满腔爱国热忱的民主斗士，最后却倒在了反动派的枪子下，为国家的民主进步事业奉献了宝贵的生命。他更是一位研究中国古代文化和文学史的知名学者，尤其在唐诗领域的研究造诣深厚，甚至上溯古代神话、《周易》、《诗经》、《楚辞》、《庄子》等方面的论述也很精到，对推动中国现代学术的发展做出了巨大的贡献，因此他在中国现代学术发展史上享有崇高的声望。他的这篇学术论文以历史发展的眼光和比较文学研究的方法，把中国文学放在世界文学的视野下进行考察，其目的在于探寻中国文学的特质及其发展规律，其研究成果体现了比较文学性质，呈现了中国文学的发展趋势。

其一，探讨中国文学，以世界文学为参照，开展平行研究。本文一开始就以宏阔的视野把中国的古老文化同其他三个不存在事实联系但有价值联系的古老民族的文化放置一起进行比较审视。在人类文明的发展史上，大约在纪元前一千年左右，中国的《诗经》、印度的《梨俱吠陀》、希伯来《旧约》中最古老的诗篇、希腊的《伊利亚特》和《奥德赛》都相继以歌的形式诞生并被记录于文字，泽被后世。可见，四个古老民族的文化都发端于文学，但闻一多先生通过平行对照探究出了彼此的异同，印度和希腊的歌在性质上近乎小说戏剧，而中国和以色列则是以歌咏人生为主的抒情诗。同时，这四种古老文化在历史的长河中最初都沿着各自的路线衍化，但并非永远平行发展没有交集。随着各自文化势力的扩张，都开始互相交流、融合。因此，四种文化的特性逐渐削弱，而呈现出世界文化的发展态势。在闻一多先生看来，文学史也是人类历史的一个有机组成部分，这是势不可挡的人类历史发展潮流。

其二，用影响研究的方法分析了中国文学史经历了一个从诗歌到小说戏剧发展的历史演变过程。首先，闻一多先生认为中国是一个诗歌的国度，从西周到宋代，诗歌在漫长的中国文学史上占据了长久的主导地位。最古老的《诗三百》一开始就奠定了中国文学发展的基调，抒情诗就成了中国文学的正统类型，并广泛地渗透在其他文学形式以及人们生活的诸多领域之中。同时，诗歌在中国文化中还承载着强大的社会功能，体现了宗教、政治、教育、社交等文化元素，支配着中国封建社会中人们的主流思维方式和价值取向，甚至影响至今。中国古诗发展到唐朝，迎来了繁荣鼎盛时期，到了南宋时期则走向衰落，中国文学史的发展轨迹自此偏离了诗歌路线，而迎来了小说戏剧时代。那么，为什么小说戏剧得以萌芽并茁壮成长？在闻一多先生看来，中国之前不是没有本土故事，只是没有发展壮大，但在佛典的译介影响下，催生了中国的小说戏剧。他看到了中国文学艺术形式的嬗变受到了异国形式的影响，同时，在思想内容方面仍然在很大程度上受到了佛教因果论的影响，从唐传奇，到宋元话本，再到明清小说，它们大多教诲人们弃恶从善，以获得人生的圆满。

其三，以发展的眼光看待中国文学发展的趋势。未来的中国文学将走向何方？闻一多先生认为中国文学将沿着明清小说的方向继续深化发展，而且“待写的一页文学史，必然又是一段小说戏剧史”。在小说日益发达，并屡将小说搬上银幕的今天，闻一多先生在20世纪预言的热闹景象无疑得到了很好的印证。至于诗歌的发展前景，他认为在一个小说戏剧占主导地位的时代，如果死守传统意识，将会难逃被时代抛弃的厄运，只有利用小说戏剧的技巧，让诗歌的形式“完全洗心革面”，才能获得广大读者的青睐。此外，为什么世界上四个古老的文化大约同时出发，到最后只剩下中国文化免于没落的劫运？他揭示了中国文化发展的成功经验，也即找到了一个具有普遍性的规律，因为中国文化拥有博大的胸怀，敢于“受”，勇于“受”，从而取长补短，相得益彰，才有可持续的长足发展。

20世纪的中国文学是在中西文化交融的历史背景下发展演变的，闻一多先生凭借自身扎实的古典文学的修养，以历史发展的眼光、世界文学的学术视野和比较文学的治学之道照亮了中国文学史的研究，在学术研究上富有开拓创新的意义。

（马礼霞）

人类在进化的途程中蹒跚了多少万年，忽然这对近世文明影响最大最深的四个古老民族——中国、印度、以色列、希腊——都在差不多同时猛抬头，迈开了大步。约当纪元前一千年左右，在这四个国度里，人们都歌唱起来，并将他们的歌纪录在文字里，给流传到后代。在中国，《三百篇》里最古部分——《周颂》和《大雅》，印度的《黎俱吠陀》(Rig-Veda,)《旧约》里最早的《希伯来诗篇》，希腊的《伊利亚特》(Iliad)和《奥德赛》(Odyssey)——都约略同时产生。再过几百年，在四处思想都醒觉了，跟着比较可靠的历史记载的出现，从此，四个文化，在悠久的年代里，起先是沿着各自的路线，分途发展，不相闻问，然后，慢慢地随着文化势力的扩张，一个个地胳臂碰上了胳臂，于是吃惊，点头，招手，交谈，日子久了，也就交换了观念思想与习惯。最后，四个文化慢慢地都起着变化，互相吸收，融合，以至总有那么一天，四个的个别性渐渐消失，于是文化只有一个世界的文化。这是人类历史发展的必然路线，谁都不能改变，也不必改变。

上文说过，四个文化猛进的开端都表现在文学上，四个国度里同时迸出歌声。但那歌的性质并非一致的。印度、希腊，是在歌中讲着故事，他们那歌是比较近乎小说戏剧性质的，而且篇幅都很长，而中国、以色列则都唱着以人生与宗教为主题的较短的抒情诗。中国与以色列许是偶同，印度与希腊都是雅利安种人，说着同一系统的语言，他们唱着性质比较类似的歌，倒也不足怪。

中国，和其余那三个民族一样，在他开宗第一声歌里，便预告了他以后数千年间文学发展的路线。《三百篇》的时代，确乎是一个伟大的时代，我们的文化大体上是从这一刚开端的时期就定型了。文化定型了，文学也定型了，从此以后二千年间，诗——抒情诗，始终是我们文学的正统的类型，甚至除散文外，它是惟一的类型，赋、词、曲，是诗的支流，一部分散文，如赠序、碑志等，是诗的副产品，而小说和戏剧又往往以各自不同的方式夹杂些诗。诗，不但支配了整个文学领域，还影响了造型艺术，它同化了绘画，又装饰了建筑(如楹联、春帖等)和许多工艺美术品。

诗似乎也没有在第二个国度里，像它在这里发挥过的那样大的社会功能。在我们这里，一出世，它就是宗教，是政治，是教育，是社交，它是全面的生活。维系封建精神的是礼乐，阐发礼乐意义的是诗，所以诗支持了那整个封建时代的文化。此后，在不变的主流中，文化随着时代的进行，在细节上曾多少发生过一些不同的花样。诗，它一面对主流尽着传统的呵护的职责，一方面仍给那些新花样忠心的服务。最显著的例是唐朝。那是一个诗最发达的时期，也是诗与生活拉拢得最紧的一个时期。

从西周到春秋中期，从建安到盛唐，这中国文学史上两个最光荣的时期，都是诗的时期。两个时期各各拖着一条姿势稍异，但同样灿烂的尾巴，前者是《楚辞》、《汉赋》，后者是五代宋词，而这辞赋与词还是诗的支流。然则从西周到宋，我们这大半部文学史，实质上只是一部诗史。但是诗的发展到北宋实际也就完了。南宋的词已经是强弩之末。就诗本身说，连尤杨范陆和稍后的元遗山似乎都是多余的、重复的，以后的更不必提了。我们只觉得明清两代关于诗的那许多运动和争论都是无谓的挣扎。每一度挣扎的失败，无非重新证实一遍那挣扎的徒劳无益而已。本来从西周唱到北宋，足足两千年的工夫也够长的了，可能的调子都已唱完了。到此，中国文学史可能不必再写，假如不是两种外来的文艺形式——小说与戏剧，早在旁边静候着，准备届时上前来“接力”。是的，中国文学史的路线南宋起便转向了，从此以后是小说戏剧的时代。

故事与雏形的歌舞剧，以前在中国本土不是没有，但从未发展成为文学的部门。对于讲故事，听故事，我们似乎一向就不大热心。不是教诲的寓言，就是纪实的历史，我们从未养成单纯地为故事而讲故事、听故事的兴趣。我们至少可说，是那充满故事兴味的佛典之翻译与宣讲，唤醒了本土的故事兴趣的萌芽，使它与那较进步的外来形式相结合，而产生了我们的小说与戏剧。故事本是民间的产物，不用讳言，它的本质是低级的。(便在小说戏剧里，过多的故事成分不也当悬为戒条吗?)正如从故事发展出来的小说戏剧，其本质是平民的，诗的本质是贵族的，要晓得它们之间距离很大，而距离是会孕育恨的。所以我们的文学传统既是诗，就不但是非小说戏剧的，而且推到极端，可能还是反小说戏剧的。若非宗教势力带进来那点新鲜刺激，而且自己的歌实在也唱到无可再唱的了，我们可能还继续产生些《韩非·说储》，或《燕子丹》一类的故事和《九歌》一类的雏形歌舞剧，但是，元剧和章回小说绝不会有。然而本土形式的花开到极盛，必归于衰谢，那是一切生命的规律，而两个文化波轮由扩大而接触而交织，以致新的异国形式必然要闯进来，也是早经历史命运注定了的。异国形式也许早就来到了，早到起码是汉朝佛教初输入的时候，你可以在几百年中不注意它，等到注意了之后，还可以延宕，踌躇个又一度几百年；直到最后，万不得已的，这才死心塌地，接受了吧！但那只是迟早问题。反正自己的花无法再开，那命数你得承认。新的种子从外面来到，给你一个再生的机会，那是你的福分。你有勇气接受它，是你的聪明，肯细心培植它，是有出息，结果居然开出很不寒伧的花朵来，更足以使你自豪！

第一度外来影响刚刚扎根，现在又来了第二度的。第一度佛教带来的印度影响是小说戏剧，第二度基督教带来的欧洲影响又是小说戏剧(小说戏剧是欧洲文学的主干，至少是特色)，你说这是碰巧吗？

不然。欧洲文化正如它的鼻祖希腊文化一样，和印度文化往大处看，还不是一家？这样说来，在这两度异乡文化东渐的阵容中，印度不过是欧洲的头，欧洲是印度的尾而已。就文化接触的全盘局势来看，头已进来，尾的迟早必须来到，应该也是早已料到的事。第一度外来影响，已经由扎根而开花了，但还不算开到最茂盛的地步，而本土的旧形式，自从枯萎后，还不见再荣的迹象，也实在没有再荣的理由。现在第二度外来影响，又与第一度同一种类，毫无问题，未来的中国文学还要继续那些伟大的元明清人的方向，在小说戏剧的园地上发展。待写的一页文学史，必然又是一段小说戏剧史，而且较向前的一段，更为热闹，更为充实。

但在这新时代的文学动向中，最值得揣摩的，是新诗的前途。你说，旧诗的生命诚然早已结束，但新诗——这几乎是完全重新再做起的新诗，也没有生命吗？对了，除非它真能放弃传统意识，完全洗心革面，重新做起。但那差不多等于说，要把诗做得不像诗了。也对。说得更确点，不像诗，而像小说戏剧，至少让它多像点小说戏剧，少像点诗。太多"诗"的诗，和所谓"纯诗"者，将来恐怕只能以一种类似解嘲与抱歉的姿态，为极少数人存在着。在一个小说戏剧的时代，诗得尽量采取小说戏剧的态度，利用小说戏剧的技巧，才能获得广大的读众。这样做法并不是不可能的。在历史上多少人已经做过，只是不大彻底罢了。新诗所用的语言更是向小说戏剧跨近了一大步，这是新诗之所以为"新"的第一个也是最主要的理由。其他在态度上，在技术上的种种进一步的试验，也正在进行着。请放心，历史上常常有人把诗写得不像诗，如阮籍、陈子昂、孟郊，如华茨渥斯(Wordsworth)、惠特曼(Whitman)，而转瞬间便是最真实的诗了。诗这东西的长处就在它有无限度的弹性，变得出无穷的花样，装得进无限的内容。只有固执与狭隘才是诗的致命伤，纵没有时代的威胁，它也难立足。

每一时代有一时代的主潮，小的波澜总得跟着主潮的方向推进，跟不上的只好留在港汊里干死完事。战国秦汉时代的主潮是散文。一部分诗服从了时代的意志，散文化了，便成就了《楚辞》和初期的《汉赋》，成就了《铙歌》，这些都是那时代的光荣。另一部分诗，如《郊祀歌》、《安世房中歌》、韦孟《讽谏诗》之类，跟不上潮流，便成了港汊中的泥淖。

明代的主潮是小说，《先妣事略》、《寒花葬志》和《项脊轩记》的作者归有光，采取了小说的以寻常人物的日常生活为描写对象的态度和刻画景物的技巧，总算是黏上了点时代潮流的边儿(他自己以为是读《史记》读来了的，那是自欺欺人的话)，所以是散文家中欧公以来惟一顶天立地的人物。其他同时代的散文家，依照各人小说化的程度的比例，也多多少少有些成就，至于那般诗人们只忙于复古，没有理会时代，无疑那将被未来的时代忘掉。以上两个历史的教训，是值得我们的新诗人书绅的。

四个文化同时出发，三个文化都转了手，有的转给近亲，有的转给外人，主人自己却都没落了，那许是因为他们都只勇于“予”而怯于“受”。中国是勇于“予”而不太怯于“受”的，所以还是自己的文化的主人，然而也只仅免于没落的劫运而已。为文化的主人自己打算，“取”不比“予”还重要吗？所以仅仅不怯于“受”是不够的，要真正勇于“受”。让我们的文学更彻底地向小说戏剧发展，等于说要我们死心塌地走人家的路。这是一个“受”的勇气的测验，也是我们能否继续自己文化的主人的测验。

过去记录里有未来的风色。历史已给我们指示了方向——“受”的方向，如今要的只是勇气，更多的勇气啊！

一九四三年十二月

（节选自闻一多：《闻一多选集》第一卷，四川文艺出版社 1987 年版，第 363-369 页。）

东西比较文学中“模子”的运用

（节选）

[美]叶维廉

【导读】

近年来，叶维廉的“模子寻根理论”在比较文学界得到越来越多的关注和讨论，并被不少学者认定为比较文学中国学派的典型方法。叶先生之所以提出这一方案，乃在于他聪慧地认识到，欧美各国文学的民族性虽然有差异，但是它们基本的思维模式、语言结构、修辞方式却是同源的。法国学派乃至后来的美国学派都不曾面临的一个问题是，伴随着比较文学的拓展，文学的比较开始在不同的文化甚至文明体系之间进行。当两种文化本源不同的文学进行比较时，问题就变得复杂甚至尖锐，这恰如维斯坦因察觉到的：“我不否认……比较风格的研究有其意义，但对于不同文化中的类比，则颇值得商榷。因为照我看来，只有在同一文化系统中才能找到那些大家有意无意共同支持着的一些共同的元素……（欧美国家内作家之间的比较）从比较文学的立场来说，比在西方诗与中东或远东诗之间找寻相似性的研究来得合理多了。”这一论述对异质文化间的文学比较持怀疑态度，这也恰恰折射了法国学派和美国学派的局限和问题，亦即它们在研究非同源文化之间的文学对话时的无力和失效。亨廷顿所言的“文明的冲突”既是这一事实的表征，也是西方部分学人面对文明共存且时有碰撞时的理论应对。但是，在“全球化”乃至“地球村”的背景下，在学界以及政界精英们重建“世界秩序”的吁求中，在学人们凭靠的有超脱文化异质限制的“基本形式和结构行为”的“相信”里，对话、沟通、求同以共存就成为一种必需，甚至可以说，这也是比较文学面临的新使命。正如叶先生所言：“‘模子’的寻根探固的比较和对比，正可解决法国派和美国派的争执，因为‘模子’的讨论正好兼顾了历史的衍生态和美学结构行为两个方面。”不难看出，“模子寻根理论”的提出既体现出一种知难而上的勇气和“寻根探源”的智慧，同时也是中华学人敢于担当的思想呈现。

“模子寻根理论”认为，“模子”是任何文化形态中的人们心智活动的起点。在史前时代，初民如同未接受文化枷锁的孩童，有一段时间是活在质朴的和谐里，尚没有受到任何由文化活动塑造的“模子”的约束。但文化的本质即包含着人为建构并指导实践行为的意图，是人为地将世界纳入设计和规范的努力，而这种规划下的社群结构、行为模式即构成文化模子的雏形。叶先生通过“青蛙和鱼”的寓言指明了在人们的心智活动中“模子”的存在及其重要性，而后续的有关中国人象形文字和西方字母文字差别的论述，以及中国诗的英译中存在的问题则将忽视"模子"存在的后果展现出来。叶先生的"模子"论断与卡尔·雅斯贝尔斯的"轴心时代"概念有相通之处。它们表述的均是社群的思维习惯、行为方式在某一时期得以确立并在相当长的时间里相对固定的事实。"模子"存在，但其呈现形态却是多样纷繁的，有生活方式的模子，如儒家之君子之道、犹太人之十诫、穆斯林的伦理原则、佛教徒的"八正道"和众多戒规等；有观念的模子，如宇宙论、自然观等；有语言的模子，如语言的构成、语法的变化等；有诗学的模子，如文类、文体、修辞等。

哪怕个体有意跨越或者遗忘或者隐瞒自身的文化身份，以尽可能地在研究或者言说时保持中立，但其必然还是归属于某种文化体系，(归属的体系未必是其成长时处身的体系)亦即其从事智性活动时必定要依照某种模子。在同一文化体系内部，比如欧美文化体系，文化的同源决定了它们在模子上的相通，但是，在欧美体系和以中国为代表的东方体系之间，儒家文明体系和伊斯兰文明体系之间，基督教文明和伊斯兰文明之间，这些跨越不同文明体系的文化，其源头处的文化形态是不同的，甚至是截然相异的。在这些文化或者文学之间进行比较和研究时就必须考虑其根源处的差异。按照叶维廉的说法："思维模子或者语言模子决定了，要寻求共相，我们就必须放弃死守一种模子的固执。我们必须寻根探固，必须从其本身的文化立场去看，然后加以比较加以对比，始可得到两者的面貌。"也就是说，要对跨越两种文化的文学现象或者理论进行比较，必须要先将二者各自还原到它们所在的本源处，即两个模子中，然后对这两个模子进行比较，找出它们的重合和歧异之处。重合处是相似的地方，歧异处则是相异的地方。一般认为，研究是为了找到相同之处，亦即两种模子重合的地方，但这种研究的独特之处恰在于其更为看重二者的差异。因为差异使我们更清楚地看到研究对象的本相，明白了两者之间的差别，对二者的相似才能有更深的认识。比如对杜甫和犹太先知思想的比较，如果单从表象上看出二者都在作品或者言辞中表现了对自身所处群体前途的忧虑，对民众贫苦遭际的同情，而仅得出他们均是心忧天下、心怀大爱之人的结论，这样的研究便毫无意义。或许更有研究者胆大心大，肆意想象，甚至得出杜甫受到唐代传入中国的景教的影响的结论。这样的研究实为作恶，甚或可视作犯罪。依照模子寻根理论，我们首先应看到杜甫所受儒家思想的影响，"士"和"君子"对中国读书人的道德修为及行为方式的要求，应看到先知背后的上帝以及先知传统对先知职责的限定。在行为伦理上，他们确有相通之处，但相同之处也仅到此为止，他们背后的儒家义理和犹太教律法恰是二者的差异所在，如果再寻根溯源的话，儒家对"天"的悬而不论和犹太教上帝的时刻临在才是两者差别的根本缘由。当研究一直"寻根"到模子中时，我们才可能为研究找到比较的契合点，并才有得出有益有效结论的可能性。

叶维廉还深刻地看到："在对模子作寻根探固的了解时，我们不应认为，一个模子一旦建立以后便是一成不变的，模子可能在不断地变化不断地生长。"叶先生确是位"懂史"的严谨学者。他认识到在思想史中，一些概念和观念虽然在一定时期内有其相对固定的意思，但超逾时限，它们的内涵却可能发生同以前截然相异的变化。比如，在柏拉图思想体系当中，诗人(作家)因鼓动人柔弱的、不虔敬的情感而在城邦中处于被批判的弱势地位，这一思想对后世影响深远。而到了启蒙时代之后，诗人（文字工作者）已经俨然取代了传统礼法中的立法者和教士而成了时代的“精神导师”。也就是说，在同一文化体系之内，也存在着泾渭分明的古今之别。我们要对中西的诗人或者诗学进行比较，不能不对此细心甄别。

（陈会亮）

让我们从故事或事件中学起：

……青蛙无意中跳出水面……看到了许多新鲜的事物……决意……向他的好友鱼报告一切。……青蛙又说，有鸟，可展翼在空中飞翔；此时，在鱼的头脑中便出现了一条腾空而飞的鱼。青蛙又说，有车，带着四个轮子滚动向前；此时，在鱼的头脑中便出现了一条带着四个圆轮子的鱼……

这个寓言告诉我们：……所有的心智活动，不论在其创作上或是在学理的推演上以及最终的决定和判断，都有意无意地必以某一种“模子”为起点。鱼，没有见过人，必须依赖它本身的“模子”……去构思人。可见，“模子”是结构行为的一种力量，使用者可以把新的素材来拼配一个形式，这种行为在文学中最显著的，莫过于“文类”（Genre）在诗人及批评家所发挥的作用。……所以，桂伦氏在其“文类的应用”中说：“文类引发构形……文类同时向前及向后看。……文类是一个引发结构的‘模子’”。

但“模子”的选择及选择以后应用的方式及其所持的态度，在一个批评家的手中，也可以引发出相当狭隘的错误的结果。我们都知道……鱼只局限于鱼的“模子”，它不知道鱼的“模子”以外人的“模子”是不同的……跳出自己的“模子”的局限而从对方本身的“模子”去构思，显然是最基本最急迫的事。

证诸文学，大家的第一反应很可能是：文学是人为的，……我们眼前的成品乃根据人的“模子”而来……只要抓住这一个基本不变的“模子”及其结构行为的要素，便可放诸四海而皆准。……事实上并不那么干净利落。首先，我们不知道所谓“基本不变的模子”怎样建立才合理；其次，我们深知人们经常地使用着许许多多各有历史来由、各不相同，甚至互相抵触的“模子”去进行结构、组合、判断。……文化模子的歧异以及由之而起的文学模子的歧异，我们必须先予正视……（有些人认为）英文字母（印欧语系字母）那种抽象的、率意独断的符号才是最基本的语言符号……只以一个（他们认为是绝对优越的）“模子”为最终的依归！（却没有认识到）象形文字代表了另一种异于抽象字母的思维系统……二者各具所长，各异其趣。缺乏了对“模子”的寻根的认识，便会产生多种不幸的歪曲。或说，以上二人，像鱼一样，因未熟识另一个“模子”，所以无辜。但对于近百年来汉诗的英译者呢（……）？他们……对中国这个“模子”的忽视，以及硬加西方“模子”所产生的歪曲，必须由东西的比较文学学者作重新寻根的探讨始可得其真貌。

类似的歪曲现象同时发生在别的学术领域中……譬如初期的考古人类学家和社会学者，在探究原始民族的文化模式时，往往就依赖一个西方的科学统计学加上西方历史中归纳出来的文化观念与价值，来判定非洲某族某族是野蛮、落后、没有文化，而不知道……

这些民族有另外的一套宇宙观，另外一种精神价值，而它们正是西方社会所缺乏的，甚至是最需要的。……我提出这个现象，不外提出“模子”误用所产生的破坏性。

“模子”的寻根认识既然如此重要，我们应该如何去进行呢？况且，“模子”所采取的方式繁多，有观念的“模子”，如宇宙观、自然观，有美感经验形态与语言模式略如上面所述，有创作过程中的文类、体制、主题、母题、修辞规律、人物典范。各个“模子”有其可能性及限制性，我们如何将其轮廓勾出应用？寓言告诉我们，甲“模子”不一定适用于乙“模子”。这个事实连带提出了另一个问题来，那便是批评家所极力追求的所谓“共相”，柏拉图之所谓 ideal forms，亚里士多德所谓 universal logical structures，这个“共相”能否建立？在两个或三个或四个不同的文化系统中，我们能否找出一组共同的构思方式？要找这一个“共相”时，我们应该从亚里士多德以来的逻辑思维系统出发吗？我们现在都深知古希腊哲人的思维方式虽伟大，却有其限制性，不可完全依赖。……

让·杜布菲的“反文化立场”(其正代表着文化立场的换位，即弃西方的“模子”而肯定其他文化的“模子”之意)……以及查尔斯·奥尔森和罗伯特·邓肯……这些反理性主义的批评容或过于激烈，但柏氏与亚氏极力从全面经验(包括直觉感性经验及理知经验)中只划分出一部分而将之视为典范，这一个“模子”所发挥的可靠性便很可疑。所以当结构主义者之一列维·斯特劳斯追求各种制度各种习俗各种文化下意识中共分的结构时，我们对其提供的方式便不得不存疑……列维·斯特劳斯所面临的困难，我们可以用海德格尔有关语言及思维之间的相克相生的困扰来说明……语言的“模子”和思维的系统是息息相关的、不可分离的。列维·斯特劳斯用科学方法从神话中分出来的一间一间的“屋”，也就未必能在其中交通。更重要的是，电脑所能分析的，往往还是知性理性活动的成品，不易于处理感性的直觉的经验幅度……结构主义者最成功的文学探讨，泰半在以意义层次结构为中心而带较多知性活动的叙事文学(叙事诗、神话、寓言、戏剧)，而对超脱知性的诗还没有令人满意的表现，其原因之一，便是诗中确有所谓“神来之笔”的机遇元素(Chance elements)。……由此我们便可知列维·斯特劳斯所应用的“模子”中隐藏的危机。

……

由沃尔夫氏的说明我们可以了解到，一个思维“模子”或语言“模子”的决定力，要寻求“共相”，我们必须放弃一个“模子”的固执。我们必须要从两个“模子”同时进行，而且必须寻根探固，必须从其本身的文化立场去看，然后加以比较加以对比，始可得到两者的面貌。

设若我们用两个圆来说明，A 圆代表一模子，B 圆代表另一模子，两个模子只有一部分相似，这二者交叠的地方 C，C 或许才是我们建立基本模子的地方，我们不可以用 A 圆中全部的结构行为用诸 B 圆上。而往往，不交叠的地方——即是歧异之处的探讨和对比更能使我们透视二者的固有面貌，必须先明了二者操作上的基本差异性，我们才可以进入“基本相似性”的建立。我毫不怀疑雅各布逊所说的有关语言行为的话：选择与组合。但不同的文化决定了不同的选择方式和不同的组合方式。……

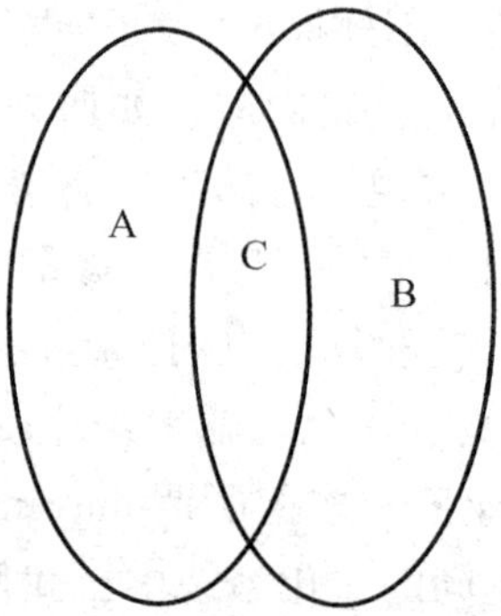

在对“模子”作寻根探固的了解时，我们不应以为，一个“模子”一旦建立以后便是一成不变的。“模子”不断地变化，不断地生长。“模子”建立后会激发诗人或批评家去追寻新的形态。在他们创作或研究时，他们增改衍化……因而，在为一个“模子”下定义时，我们也必须同时顾及该“模子”形成的历史，所谓文学的外在的因素及文学史的领域都必须重新引进来构成一个明晰的轮廓，我们始可以找出适当的重点加以比较和研究。

“模子”的问题，在早期以欧美文学为核心的比较文学里是不甚注意的……

“模子”问题的尖锐化，是近百年间由于两个三个不同文化的正面冲击而引起的……必须有待西方人跳出其自己的“模子”，接触一个有相当程度相异的“模子”以后……才不敢乱说放诸四海而皆准。……

……文化的交流正是要开拓更大的视野，互相调整，互相包容，文化交流不是以一个既定的形态去征服另一个文化的形态，而是在互相尊重的态度下，对双方本身的形态作寻根的了解。……新批评派在强调“自身具足的美学结构”时，却把其间结构行为的历史因素摒诸门外……但……新批评派把美学问题作了极端有效的提升，是故后来的历史批评(包括社会文化批评、心理批评等)都扩大其领域而兼及美学结构的考虑。

……“模子”的寻根探固的比较和对比，正可解决了法国派和美国派之争，因为“模子”的讨论正好兼及了历史的衍生态和美学结构行为两个方面。譬如我们举立体派画和中国山水画中的透视及时间观念来说……

“模子”的自觉在东西比较文学的实践上是非常迫切的需要，尤其是在两方的文化未曾扩展至溶合对方的结构之前。我们经常看见如下的尝试：“浪漫主义者李白”，“从西方浪漫的传统看屈原”。……

我们不能借助浪漫主义的范畴……把表面的相似性看作另一个系统的全部。……而要借助“模子”的自觉……找到更重要更合理的出发点。

……

既然这个问题是起自两个文化未接触未融合前的文学作品(中国古典文学与西方文学作品)，我们不能不说，新文学，如“五四”以来的文学，既然接受了西方的“模子”，我们便不会受到“模子”的困扰吗？这句话只有某一个程度的真实性。(可举刘邵铭先生的《曹禺所受的西方文学的影响》一书为例)首先文化及其产生的美感感受并不因外来的“模子”

而消失，许多时候，作者们在表面上是接受了外来的形式、题材、思想，但下意识中传统的美感范畴仍然左右着他对于外来“模子”的取舍。……

“模子”的自觉还可以有效地应用在另一种文学情景上。譬如，当一个新的文学运动，就说欧美的现代主义吧，当其打破传统的思维模子，反对亚里士多德的推理方式时，他们是预期着或慢慢地衍化着一种新的“模子”——一种对还在传统模子影响下的读者而言，尚无法认可的新的模子，我们此时把另一个文化下的“模子”介入，譬如相异于西方的初民的诗，或非洲民族，或东方的诗，这个介入的对比及比较便可以使他们更清楚他们传统“模子”的强处和弱点，而同时了解正在成形中还未能命名的新的美感范式，及此新的范式所提供的领域如何可以补传统“模子”之不足。

（节选自叶维廉：《东西比较文学中“模子”的运用》，李达三、罗钢主编：《中外比较文学的里程碑》，人民文学出版社 1997 年版，第 44-64 页。）

刘勰的譬喻说与歌德的意蕴说

王元化

【导读】

王元化(1920—2008)，我国著名文论家，《文心雕龙》研究学者。主要著作有《文心雕龙创作论》(1979)、《向着真实》(1982)、《文学风格论》(1983)、《王元化文学评论集》(1983)、《文学沉思录》(1983)、《传统与反传统》(1990)。本文收录于王元化先生的论著《文心雕龙创作论》。要了解该文的写作目的与用意，首先要对《文心雕龙创作论》有一定的认识。《文心雕龙创作论》成书于1979年，后分别有三次再版。全书分为上下两篇，《刘勰的譬喻说与歌德的意蕴说》一文位于下篇，乃《文心雕龙》创作论八说之第四说附录二。《文心雕龙创作论》最大的特色在于采用了中西文论附录的方法。此附录法以论述一种文化体系中的文学为主，在阐释某种理论话题时，将世界各国文论观点用“附录”形式加以比较，并在比较中展开细致辨析。通过“附录法”，中西诗学理论两相呈现，进而达到拓展诗学研究视野，求得共同诗心的目的。“附录法”的运用，能保证论者在研讨诗学问题时既条清理顺，又行文活跃，以便读者深入领会其要义。

《刘勰的譬喻说与歌德的意蕴说》一文附录于“创作论八说”第四说“释《比兴篇》拟容取心说——关于意象：表象与概念的综合”之后，起到补充与说明的作用。“释《比兴篇》拟容取心说——关于意象：表象与概念的综合”着重阐明刘勰在《比兴篇》中所论及的“诗人比兴，拟容取心”观。论者指出，《比兴篇》是刘勰分析艺术形象话题的专论，其中的“诗人比兴，拟容取心”正是其艺术形象观的高度凝练。王元化先生在分析“拟容取心”之“容”与“心”时，以为这二字代表了同一艺术形象的两面，即外者和内者。由此他借用歌德的“意蕴说”加以比较，总结出了二者在艺术形象观点上的异同性。在论证过程中，论者推导出，歌德“意蕴说”由于不受唯心主义思想制约，较“譬喻说”更能真正揭示客观真理。随后，论者又通过刘勰与歌德的比较，深入探讨艺术创作中主观与客观、一般与个别的关系。在将刘勰与歌德的观点进行比较分析之余，王元化先生得出结论，艺术创作中的一般与个别、主观与客观同时存在，不可分割。

作为一则附录文，本文完成于1979年。此时正值“文革”结束，改革开放实行之时。中国比较文学迎来了复苏的春天，《管锥编》、《美学散步》、《中印文化史论文集》、《攻玉集》等一大批中外比较文学专著的涌现，深深地影响了王元化先生。“其中大多数问题是长期被忽视、甚至被摒弃的，这种活跃的学术空气带来的清新气息，不仅给人鼓舞，也使人的头脑从僵滞狭窄的状态变得开豁起来。它打开我的思路，使我想在《文心雕龙》的研究方面做些新的尝试。"①而本文便是王元化先生蓄势待发之作。

（曾小月）

在艺术形象问题上，歌德的"意蕴说"也包含着内外两个方面。外在方面是艺术作品直接呈现出来的形状，内在方面是灌注生气于外在形状的意蕴。他认为，内在意蕴显现于外在形状，外在形状指引到内在意蕴。歌德在《自然的单纯模仿·作风·风格》一文中，曾经把"艺术所能企及的最高境界"说成是"奠基在最深刻的知识原则上面，奠基在事物的本性上面，而这种事物的本性应该是我们可以在看得见触得到的形式中去认识的"（据古柏英译本迻译）。歌德把艺术形象分为外在形状和内在意蕴，似乎和刘勰的"拟容取心"说有着某种类似之处，不过，它们又不尽相同，其间最大区别就在于对个别与一般关系的不同理解上。

《比兴篇》："称名也小，取类也大。"这一说法本之《周易》。《系辞下》："其称名也小，其取类也大，其旨远，其辞文，其言曲而中。"韩康伯《注》云："托象以明义，因小以喻大。"孔颖达《正义》云："其旨远者，近道此事，远明彼事。……其辞文者，不直言所论之事，乃以义理明之，是其辞文饰也……其言曲而中者，变化无恒，不可为体例，其言随物屈曲，而各中其理也。"从这里可以看出，前人大抵把《系辞下》这句话理解为一种"譬喻"的意义，这种看法和刘勰把比类当作"明喻"、"隐喻"看待是有相通之处的。（首先把《系辞下》这句话运用于文学领域的是司马迁，他评述《离骚》说："其称文小而其旨大，举类迩而见义远。"这一说法也给予刘勰以一定影响。）

刘勰的形象论可以说是一神"譬喻说"。《比兴篇》"称名也小，取类也大"，《物色篇》"以少总多，情貌无遗"，是两个互为补充的命题。"名"和"类"或"少"和"多"都蕴涵了个别与一般的关系。刘勰提出的拟容切象和取心示义，都是针对客观审美对象而言，要求作家既摹拟现实的表象，也揭示现实的意蕴，从而通过个别去表现一般。然而，这里应该看到，刘勰对个别与一般关系的理解不能不受到他的思想体系的制约，以致使他的形象论本来可以向着正确方向发展的内容受到了窒息。由于他认为天地之心和圣人之心是同一的，因此，按照他的思想体系推断，自然万物的自身意义无不合于圣人的"恒久之至道"。这样，作家在取心示义的时候，只要恪守传统的儒家思想就可以完全揭示自然万物的内在意义了。自然，刘勰的创作论并不是完全依据这种观点来立论的。当他背离了这种观点时，他提出了一些正确的看法。可是他的拟容取心说却并没有完全摆脱这种观点的拘囿，其中就夹杂着一些这类糟粕。例如，《比兴篇》开头标明"诗文弘奥，包韫六义"，接着又特别举出："《关雎》有别，故后妃方德。尸鸠贞一，故夫人象义"作为取心示义的典范。（《金针诗格》也同样本之儒家诗教，把"内意"说成是"美刺箴诲"之类的"义理"。）从这里我们

① 王元化：《文心雕龙创作论》，上海古籍出版社1983年版，第310-311页。

可以看出，尽管刘勰在理论上以自然界作为取心示义的对象，但是他的儒家偏见必然会在实践意义方面导致相反的结果。因为在儒家思想束缚下，作家往往会把自己的主观信条当作现实事物的本质。因此，很容易导致这种情况：作家不是通过现实的个别事物去表现从它们自身揭示出来的一般意义，而是依据先入为主的成见，用现实的个别事物去附会儒家的一般义理，把现实事物当作美刺箴诲的譬喻。因而，这里所反映出来的个别与一般的关系，也就变成一种譬喻的关系了。(例如：《诗小序》说"关雎，后妃之德也。鹊巢，夫人之德也"，就是这方面的一个典型例证。)

歌德的"意蕴说"并不像刘勰的"譬喻说"那样夹杂着主观色彩。他曾经这样说："在一个探索个别以求一般的诗人和一个在个别中看出一般的诗人之间，是有很大差别的。一个产生出譬喻文学，在这里个别只是作为一般的一个例证或例子，另一个才是诗歌的真正本性，即是说，只表达个别而毫不想到或者提到一般。一个人只要生动地掌握了个别，他也就掌握了一般，只不过他当时没有意识到这一点罢了，或者他可能在很久之后才会发现。"(《歌德文学语录》第十二节)歌德这些话很可以用来作为对于"譬喻说"的批判。歌德反对把"个别只是作为一般的一个例证或例子"的譬喻文学，强调作家首先要掌握个别，而不要用个别去附会一般，表现了对现实生活的尊重态度。这一看法是深刻的，对于文学创作来说也是有重要意义的。事实上，一般只能从个别中间抽象出来。作家只有首先认识了许多个别事物的特殊本质，才能进而认识这些个别事物的共同本质。就这个意义来说，歌德要求作家从个别出发，是可以避免"譬喻说"以作家主观去附会现实这种错误的。

不过，我们同时也应该看到，歌德的"意蕴说"是存在着过去现实主义理论多半具有的共同缺陷的。他对于个别与一般关系的理解带有一定的片面性。在作家的认识活动中，他只注意到由个别到一般这一方面，而根本不提还有由一般到个别这一过程。人类的认识活动，由特殊到一般，又由一般到特殊，是互相联接的两个过程。人类的认识总是这样循环往复地进行。歌德恰恰是把这两个互相联接的过程分割开来。他在上面的引文中赞许"只表达个别而毫不想到或者提到一般"的诗人，以为这样的诗人在掌握个别的时候，没有意识到一般，或者可能在很久以后才会发现一般。但是，由个别到一般，又由一般到个别，这两个互相联接的过程是不可分割的。事实上，完全排除一般到个别这一过程的认识活动是并不存在的。作家不是抽象的人，他在掌握个别的时候，他的头脑并不是一张白纸，相反，那里已经具有一般的烙印了。在作家的具体认识活动中，这一阶段由个别到一般的过程，往往是紧接着上一阶段由个别到一般的过程。在这种情况下，不论作家自觉或不自觉，他必然会以他在上一阶段所掌握到的一般，作为这一阶段认识活动的指导。因此，这一阶段由个别到一般的过程，也就和由一般到个别的过程互相联接在一起了。作家的认识活动总是由个别到一般，又由一般到个别这两个互相连接的过程，循环往复地进行着。只有这样，他的认识活动才可能由上一阶段过渡到这一阶段，再由这一阶段过渡到下一阶段，形成不断深化运动。

事实上，作家的创作活动同样不能缺少由一般到个别的过程。作家的创作活动是把他在认识活动中所取得的成果进行艺术的表现。他在动笔之前，已经有了酝酿成熟的艺术构思，确立了一定的创作意图。因此，他的全部创作活动都是使原来存在于自己头脑中的创作意图逐步具现。创作意图是普泛的、一般的东西，体现在作品中的人物和事件是具体的、个别的东西。任何作家的创作活动，都不可能像歌德所说的那样“只表达个别而毫不想到或者提到一般”。作家总是自觉地根据自己的创作意图去进行创作的。人类劳动并不像蜜蜂造蜂房那样，只是一种本能的表现，而是自觉的、有目的的、能动的行为。作家的创作活动也具有同样的性质。否认作家的创作活动是根据自己的创作意图出发，就会否定作家的创作活动的自觉性和目的性。

艺术和科学在掌握世界的方式上是各有其不同的特点的。艺术家不像科学家那样从个别中抽象出一般，而是通过个别去体现一般。科学家是以一般的概念去统摄特殊的个体，艺术家则是通过特殊的个体去显现它的一般意蕴。艺术形象应该是具体的，科学概念也应该是具体的，科学家在作出抽象规定的思维进程中必须导致具体的再现，正像《政治经济学批判导言》所说的，由抽象上升到具体的方法是唯一正确的科学方法。不过，这里所说的具体是指通过逻辑范畴以概念形态所表述出来的具有许多规定和关系的综合。科学家把混沌的表象和直观加工，在抽出具体的一般概念之后，就排除了特殊个体的感性形态。而艺术家的想象活动则是以形象为材料，始终围绕着形象来进行。艺术作品所呈现的一般必须呈现于感性观照，因此，艺术家对现实生活进行艺术加工，去揭示事物的本质，并不是把事物的现象形态抛弃掉，而是透过加工以后的现象形态去显示它们的内在联系。不过，在艺术作品中所表现的现象形态已不同于原来生活中的现象形态，因为前者已经使直观中彼此相外、互相独立的杂多转化为具有内在联系的多样性统一。这就是由个别到一般与由一般到个别这一认识规律体现在艺术思维中的特殊形态。艺术形象的具体性就在于它既是一般意义的典型，同时又是特殊的个体。它保持了现实生活的细节真实性，典型性即由生活细节真实性中显现出来，变成可以直接感觉到的对象。在这里，由个别到一般，再由一般到个别，这两个认识过程不是并列的。作家的认识活动只能从作为个别感性事物的形象出发。在全部创作过程中，并不存在一个游离于形象之外从概念出发进行构思的阶段。因此，由一般到个别的认识功能，不是孤立地单独出现，而是渗透在由个别到一般的过程之中，它成为指导作家认识个别的引线或指针。对于由个别到一般、再由一般到个别这一认识规律，可以有两种不同的理解：一种理解是把它们截然分割为孤立排他的两个互不相干的独立过程。例如，所谓表象—概念—表象的公式，就是意味着在艺术创作过程中存在着一个摈弃形象的抽象思维阶段，而艺术创造就在于把经过抽象思维所获得的概念化为形象。这可以说是一种“形象图解论”，它是反对形象思维的。另一种理解则相反，认为由个别到一般，再由一般到个别，不是孤立排他的，而是互相联接、互相渗透的。后一种理解才是辩证的观点。

（选自王元化：《刘勰的譬喻说与歌德的意蕴说》，《文心雕龙创作论》，上海古籍出版社 1979 年版，第 142-147 页。）

中西诗在情趣上的比较

（节选）

朱光潜

【导读】

朱光潜(1897—1986)，安徽桐城人，现当代著名美学家、文艺理论家、教育家和翻译家。他的主要著作有《悲剧心理学》、《文艺心理学》、《西方美学史》、《谈美》等。朱光潜先生学贯中西，在比较文学研究领域具有重大影响。在平行研究中，美国学者偏重类同研究，而中国学者偏爱异同比较。因为通过对相异之处的比较辨析，能使中国文学的文化传统和文学个性更加鲜明地凸显出来。本文选自朱光潜先生的《诗论》。朱先生开篇就强调：进行中西诗歌的比较研究，不是为了一较高下比个优劣，而是为了凸显各自的民族特色。

文章主要从中西诗歌共同表现的人伦、自然、宗教哲学三个重要题材出发，通过比较辨析，探讨中西不同的文化传统。在有关人伦的诗歌中西方以恋爱为中心，中国以忠君爱国为中心。西方人擅长写“慕”，对于恋人的思慕往往上升到对神的敬仰，因此爱情诗中往往表达出哲学和宗教情操。中国诗人热衷表现“怨”，“盛年独处，忧伤终老”的闺怨诗往往是文人失意的委婉表达。在自然诗歌中，中国诗人强调人与自然的默契相安，而西方诗人则在自然中体悟神秘主义和宗教情感。为何中国诗人在爱情中只能见到爱情，在自然中只能见到自然，而不能有深一层的澈悟？朱先生通过分析儒家老庄和佛教对中国诗歌的影响，指出即使是深受老庄影响的游仙派诗人，骨子里仍带有浓厚的儒家入世思想。他们在超越世俗的渴望和淑世济民的理想之间徘徊，终不能战胜这种矛盾和痛苦得到安顿。受佛教思想影响的诗人们虽然有意参禅但无心证佛，他们的诗有禅趣但无禅理。中国人好信教但不求甚解，宗教上的兼容并蓄到了逻辑混乱的地步，这既是中国文化的优点也是缺点。宗教哲学是诗歌生长发展的根基，所以朱先生认为中国哲学的平易和宗教情感的淡薄，使得中国诗歌虽然神韵微妙、格调高雅，但不如西方诗歌深广伟大。

朱先生对于中西诗情趣上的比较，重点是对本民族文化的反思和批判意识。这种对传统文化和文学的反思，是“五四”以来现代学人所禀有的一种基本思路：即文学的比较研究是为了更深入地认识本民族的传统文化，批判地继承本国优良的文化传统。

（霍晓珊）

诗的情趣随时随地而异，各民族各时代的诗都各有它的特色，拿它们来参观互较是一种很有趣味的研究。我们姑且拿中国诗和西方诗来说，它们在情趣上就有许多的有趣的同点和异点。西方诗和中国诗的情趣都集中于几种普泛的题材，其中最重要者有(一)人伦(二)自然(三)宗教和哲学几种。我们现在就依着这个层次来说：

(一)先说人伦

西方关于人伦的诗大半以恋爱为中心。中国诗言爱情的虽然很多，但是没有让爱情把其他人伦抹煞。朋友的交情和君臣的恩谊在西方诗中不甚重要，而在中国诗中则几与爱情占同等位置。把屈原、杜甫、陆游诸人的忠君爱国爱民的情感拿去，他们诗的精华便已剥丧大半。从前注诗注词的人往往在爱情诗上贴上忠君爱国的徽帜，例如毛苌注《诗经》把许多男女相悦的诗看成讽刺时事的。张惠言说温飞卿的《菩萨蛮》十四章为“感士不遇之作”。这种办法固然有些牵强附会。近来人却又另走极端把真正忠君爱国的诗也贴上爱情的徽帜，例如《离骚》、《远游》一类的著作竟有人认为爱情诗。我以为这也未免失之牵强附会。看过西方诗的学者见到爱情在西方诗中那样重要，以为它在中国诗中也应该很重要。他们不知道中西社会情形和伦理思想本来不同，恋爱在从前的中国实在没有现代中国人所想的那样重要。中国叙人伦的诗，通盘计算，关于友朋交谊的比关于男女恋爱的还要多，在许多诗人的集中，赠答酬唱的作品，往往占其大半。建安七子，李杜，韩孟，苏黄、纳兰成德与顾贞观诸人的交谊古今传为美谈，在西方诗人中为歌德和席勒，华兹华斯与柯尔律治，济慈和雪莱，魏尔兰与兰波诸人虽亦以交谊著称，而他们的集中叙友朋乐趣的诗却极少。

恋爱在中国诗中不如在西方诗中重要，有几层原因。第一，西方社会表面上虽以国家为基础，骨子里却侧重个人主义。爱情在个人生命中最关痛痒，所以尽量发展，以至掩盖其他人与人的关系。说尽一个诗人的恋爱史往往就已说尽他的生命史，在近代尤其如此。中国社会表面上虽以家庭为基础，骨子里却侧重兼善主义。文人往往费大半生的光阴于仕宦羁旅，“老妻寄异县”是常事。他们朝夕所接触的不是妇女而是同僚与文友。

第二，西方受中世纪骑士风的影响，女子地位较高，教育也比较完善，在中国得于友朋的乐趣，在西方往往可以得之于妇人女子。中国受儒家思想的影响，女子的地位较低。夫妇恩爱常起于伦理观念，在实际上志同道合的乐趣颇不易得。实际上志同道合的乐趣颇不易得。加以中国社会理想侧重功名事业，“随着四婆裙”在儒家看是一件耻事。

第三，东西恋爱观相差也甚远。西方人重视恋爱。中国人重视婚姻而轻视恋爱。潦倒无聊，悲观厌世的人才肯公然寄情于声色，隋炀帝李后主几位风流天子都为世所垢病。我们可以说，西方诗人要在恋爱中实现人生，中国诗人往往只求在恋爱中消遣人生。中国诗人脚踏实地，爱情只是爱情；西方诗人比较能高瞻远瞩，爱情之中都有几分人生哲学和宗教情操。

这并非说中国诗人不能深于情。西方爱情诗大半写于婚媾之前，所以称赞容貌诉申爱慕者最多；中国爱情诗大半写于婚媾之后，所以最佳者往往是惜别悼亡。西方爱情诗最长于“慕”，莎士比亚的十四行体诗，雪莱和布朗宁诸人的短诗是“慕”的胜境；中国爱情诗最善于“怨”，《卷耳》、《柏舟》、《迢迢牵牛星》，曹丕的《燕歌行》，梁玄帝的《荡妇秋思赋》以及李白的《长相思》、《怨情》、《春思》诸作是“怨”的胜境。总观全体，我们可以说，西诗以直率胜，中诗以委婉胜；西诗以深刻胜，中诗以微妙胜；西诗以铺陈胜，中诗以简隽胜。

(二)次说自然

在中国和在西方一样，诗人对于自然的爱好都比较晚起。最初的诗都偏重人事，纵使偶尔涉及自然，也不过如最初的画家用山水为人物画的背景，兴趣中心却不在自然本身。《诗经》是最好的例子。“关关雎鸠，在河之洲”只是作“窈窕淑女，君子好逑”的陪衬。“蒹葭苍苍，白露为霜”只是作“所谓伊人，在水一方”的陪衬。自然比较人事广大，兴趣由人也因之得到较深广的意蕴。所以自然情趣的兴起是诗的发达史中一件大事。这件大事在中国起于晋宋之交约当公历纪元后 5 世纪左右；在西方则起于浪漫运动的初期，在公历纪元后 18 世纪左右。所以中国自然诗的发生比西方的要早一千三百年的光景。一般说诗的人颇鄙视六朝，我以为这是一个最大的误解。六朝是中国自然诗发轫的时期，也是中国诗脱离音乐而在文字本身求音乐的时期。从六朝起，中国诗才有音律的专门研究，才创新形式，才寻新情趣，才吸收哲理来扩大诗的内容。就这几层说，六朝可以说是中国诗的浪漫时期，它对于中国诗的重要亦正不让于浪漫运动之于西方诗。

中国自然诗和西方自然诗相比，也像爱情诗一样，一个以委婉、微妙、简隽胜，一个以直率、深刻、铺陈胜。本来自然美有两种，一种是刚性美，一种是柔性美。刚性美如高山、大海、狂风、暴雨、沉寂的夜和无垠的沙漠，柔性美如清风皓月，暗香、疏影、青螺似的山光和媚眼似的湖水。昔人诗有“骏马秋风冀北，杏花春雨江南”两句可以包括这两种美的胜境。艺术美也有刚柔的分别。诗如李杜，词如苏辛，是刚性美的代表，诗如王孟，词如温李，是柔性美的代表。中国诗自身已有刚柔的分别，但是如果拿它来比较西方诗，则又西诗偏于刚，而中诗偏于柔。西方诗人所爱好的自然是大海，是狂风暴雨，是峭崖荒谷，是日景；中国诗人所爱好的自然是明溪疏柳，是微风细雨，是湖光山色，是月景。这当然只就其大概说。西方未尝没有柔性美的诗，中国也未尝没有刚性美的诗，但西方诗的柔和中国诗的刚都不是它们的本色特长。

诗人对于自然的爱好可分三种。最粗浅的是“感官主义”，爱微风以其凉爽，爱花以其气香色美，爱鸟声泉水声以其对于听官愉快，爱青天碧水以其对于视觉愉快。这是健全人所本有的倾向，凡是诗人都不免带有几分“感官主义”。近代西方有一派诗人，叫做“颓废派”的，专重这种感官主义，在诗中尽量铺陈声色臭味。这种嗜好往往出于个人的怪癖，不能算诗的上乘。诗人对于自然爱好的第二种起于情趣的默契忻合。“相看两不厌，惟有敬亭山”，“平畴交远风，良苗亦怀新”，“万物静观皆自得，四时佳兴与人同”。诸诗所表现的态度都属于这一类。这是多数中国诗人对于自然的态度。第三种是泛神主义，把大自然全体看作神灵的表现，在其中看出不可思议的妙谛，觉得超于人而时时在支配人的力量。自然的崇拜于是成为一种宗教，它含有极原始的迷信和极神秘的哲学。……这是多数西方诗人对于自然的态度，中国诗人很少有达到这种境界的。中国诗人在自然中只能听见自然，西方诗人在自然中往往能见出一种神秘的巨大的力量。

(三)哲学和宗教

中国诗人何以在爱情中只能见到爱情，在自然中只能见到自然，而不能有深一层的澈悟呢？这就不能不归咎于哲学思想的平易和宗教情操的淡薄了。诗虽不是讨论哲学和宣传宗教的工具，但是它的后面如果没有宗教和哲学，就不易达到深广的境界。诗好比一株花，哲学和宗教好比土壤，土壤不肥沃，根就不能深，花就不能茂。西方诗比中国诗深广，就因为它有较深广的哲学和宗教在培养它的根干。没有柏拉图和斯宾诺莎就没有歌德、华兹华斯和雪莱诸人所表现的理想主义和泛神主义；没有宗教就没有希腊的悲剧，但丁的《神曲》和弥尔顿的《失乐园》。中国诗在荒瘦的土壤中居然现出奇葩异彩，固然是一种可惊喜的成绩，但是比较西方诗，终嫌美中有不足。我爱中国诗，我觉得在神韵微妙、格调高雅方面往往非西诗所能及，但是说到深广伟大，我终无法为它护短。

就民族性说，中国人颇类似古罗马人，处处都脚踏实地走，偏重实际而不务玄想，所以就哲学说，伦理的信条最发达，而有系统的玄学则寂然无闻；就文学说，关于人事及社会问题的作品最发达，而凭虚结构的作品则寥若晨星。中国民族性是最“实用的”，最“人道的”。它的长处在此，它的短处也在此。它的长处在此，因为以人为本位说，人与人的关系最重要，中国儒家思想偏重人事，涣散的社会居然能享到二千余年的稳定，未始不是它的功劳。它的短处在此，因为它过重人本主义和现世主义，不能向较高的地方发空想，所以不能向高远处有所企求。社会既稳定之后，始则不能前进，继则因其不能前进而失其固有的稳定。

我说中国哲学思想平易，也未尝忘记老庄一派的哲学。但是老庄比较儒家固较玄邃，比较西方哲学家，仍是偏重人事。他们很少离开人事而穷究思想的本质和宇宙的来源。他们对于中国诗的影响虽很大，但是因为两层原因，这种影响不完全是可满意的。第一，在哲学上有方法和系统的分析易传授，而主观的妙悟不易传授。老庄哲学都全凭主观的妙悟，未尝如西方哲学家用明了有系统的分析为浅人说法，所以他们的思想传给后人的只是糟粕。老学流为道家言。第二，老庄哲学尚虚无而轻视努力，但是无论是诗或哲学，如果没有西方人所重视的“坚持的努力”(sustained effort)都不能鞭辟入里。老庄两人自己所造虽深而承其教者却有安于浅的倾向。

我们只要把老庄影响的诗研究一番，就可以见出这个道理。中国诗人大半是儒家出身，陶潜和杜甫是著例。但是有四位大诗人受老庄的影响最深，替儒教化的中国诗特辟一种异境。这就是《离骚》、《远游》中的屈原(假定作者是屈原)，《咏怀诗》中阮籍，《游仙诗》中的郭璞，以及《日出入行》、《古有所思》和《古风》五十九首中的李白。我们可以把他们统称为“游仙派诗人”。他们所表现的思想如何呢？……都是想由厌世主义走到超世主义。他们厌世的原因都不外看待世相的无常和人寿的短促。他们超世的方法都是揣摩道家炼丹延年驾鹤升仙的传说。但是这只是一种想望，他们都没有实现仙境，没有享受到他们所想望的极乐。……

他们都是不满意于现世而有所渴求于另一世界。这种渴求颇类西方的宗教情操，照理应该能产生一个很华严灿烂的理想世界来，但是他们的理想都终于“流产”。他们对于现世的悲苦虽然都看得极清楚，而对于另一世界的想象却很模糊。超世而不能超欲，这是游仙派诗人的矛盾。……

中国游仙诗人何以止于徘徊呢？这要归咎于我们在上文所说过的哲学思想的平易和宗教情操的淡薄。哲学思想平易，所以无法在冲突中寻出调和，不能造成一个可以寄托心灵的理想世界。宗教情操淡薄，所以缺乏“坚持的努力”，苟安于现世而无心在理想世界求寄托，求安慰。屈原、阮籍、李白诸人在中国诗人中是比较能抬头向高远处张望的，他们都曾经向中国诗人所不常去的境界去探险，但是民族性的牵累太重，他们刚飞到半天空就落下地。所以在西方诗人心中的另一世界的渴求能产生《天国》、《失乐园》、《浮士德》诸杰作，而在中国诗人心中的另一世界的渴求只能产生《远游》、《咏怀》、《游仙诗》和《古风》一些简单零碎的短诗。

……

老庄和道家学说之外，佛学对于中国诗的影响也很深。可惜这种影响未曾有人仔细研究过。我们首先应注意的一点就是：受佛教影响的中国诗大半只有“禅趣”而无“佛理”。“佛理”是真正的佛家哲学，“禅趣”是和尚们静坐山寺参悟佛理的趣味。晋人中以天分论，陶潜最易于学佛。……陶潜以后，中国诗人受佛教影响最深而成就最大的要推谢灵运、王维和苏轼三人。他们的诗专说佛理的极少，但处处都流露一种禅趣。我们细玩他们的全集，才可以得到这么一个总印象。如摘句为例，则谢灵运的“白云抱幽石，绿筱媚清涟”，“虚馆绝诤讼，空庭来乌鹊”，王维的“兴阑啼鸟散，坐久落花多”，“倚杖柴门外，临风听暮蝉”和苏轼的“舟行无人岸自移，我卧读书牛不知”，“敲门都不应，倚杖听江声”诸句的境界都是我所谓“禅趣”。

他们所以有“禅趣”而无“佛理”者，固然由于诗本来不宜说理，同时也由于他们所羡慕的不是佛教而是佛教徒。晋以后中国诗人大半都有“方外交”。中国诗人大半都有“方外交”，谢灵运有远公，王维有瑗公和操禅师，苏轼有佛印。他们很羡慕这班高僧的言论文采，常偷“浮生半日闲”到寺里去领略“参禅”的滋味，或是同禅师交换几句趣语。诗境与禅境本来相通，所以诗人和禅师常能默然相契。中国诗人对于自然的嗜好比西方诗要早一千几百年，究其原因，也和佛教有关系。魏晋的僧侣已有择山水胜境筑寺观的风气，最早见到自然美的是僧侣。（中国僧侣对于自然的嗜好或受印度僧侣的影响，印度古婆罗门教徒便有隐居山水胜境的风气，《沙恭达罗》剧可以为证）。僧侣首先见到自然美，诗人则从他们的“方外交”学得这种新趣味。“禅趣”中最大的成分便是静中所得于自然的妙悟。中国诗人所最得力于佛教者就在此一点。但是他们虽有意“参禅”，却无心“证佛”，要在佛理中求消遣，并不要信奉佛教求彻底了悟，彻底解脱；入山参禅，出山仍然做他们的官，吃他们的酒肉，眷恋他们的妻子。本来佛教的妙义在“不立文字，见性成佛”，诗歌到底仍不免是一种尘障。

佛教只扩大了中国诗的情趣的根底，并没有扩大它的哲理的根底。中国诗的哲理的根底始终不外儒道两家。佛学为外来哲学，所以能合中国诗人口胃者正因其与道家言在表面上有若干类似。晋以后一般人尝把释道并为一事，以为升仙就是成佛。孙绰的《游天台山赋》和李白的《赠僧崖公诗》都以为佛老原来可以相通，韩愈辟“异端邪说”，也把佛老并为一说。老子虽尚虚无而却未明言寂灭。他是一个彻底的个人主义者，《道德经》中大部分是老于世故者的经验之谈所以后来流为申韩刑名法律的学问。佛则以普济众生为旨。老子主张人类回到原始时代的愚昧，佛教人明心见性，衡以老子的“绝圣弃智”的主旨，则佛亦当在绝弃之列。从此可知老与佛根本不能相容。晋唐人合佛于老，也犹如他们合道于老一样，绝对没有想到这种凑合的矛盾。尤其奇怪的是儒家诗人也往往同时信佛。白居易和元稹本来都是彻底的儒者，而白有“吾学空门不学仙，归则须归兜率天”的话，元在《遣病》诗里也说“况我早师佛，屋宅此身形”。中国原来有“好信教不求甚解”的习惯，这种马虎妥协的精神本也有它的优点，但是与深邃的哲理和有宗教性的热烈的企求都不相容。中国诗达到幽美的境界而没有达到伟大的境界，也正由于此。

（节选自朱光潜：《中西诗在情趣上的比较》，《中国比较文学》1984 年第 1 期，第 37-48 页。）

李渔论戏剧结构

（节选）

杨　绛

【导读】

我们在对中西戏剧进行比较时，偶尔会陷入中国是否有悲剧、中西戏剧的结局比较等问题中，杨绛先生的《李渔论戏剧结构》另辟蹊径地从“戏剧结构”这一内部研究、形式研究的角度对李渔的戏剧理论进行深入分析，并得出了令人信服的结论。她的很多观点对我们的研究确具有醍醐灌顶、指点迷津的功效。

本文首先从“所应有者”和“当然或必然”之事的角度，指出李渔和亚里士多德都强调了故事的真实性问题；从李渔说的对话要表现人物的个性，到亚里士多德认为的模仿人物性格要切合人物身份；从李渔的故事要新奇但不荒唐，到古典派的故事要神奇但似真；它们都指向了一个事实：李渔的理论和西方戏剧理论有相似或相同的地方。比较文学既要寻求研究对象之间的“同”，更要看到它们之间的“异”，并进而分析这种差异背后的原因以及意义。杨先生认为，李渔在戏剧结构上的观点概括起来就是要“一人一事”，“承上接下，血脉相连”（完整的有机体），这似乎和亚里士多德《诗学》中的观点“故事的整一性”是一致的。但这种一致仅仅是表面上的，“表面上看似相同的理论，所讲的却是性质不同的两种结构。”亚里士多德结合古希腊悲剧家们的创作实践，认为一部悲剧只演一个完整而统一的故事，但是由于故事的紧凑和集中，所谓故事的整一，实际包含着时间和地点的限制。支持这种观点的剧作家确实不少，17世纪的古典主义剧作家及理论家更是据此提出了著名的“三一律”，这本身表明了限定时间、地点的合理性，所以在戏剧理论上“结构紧密派”向有拥趸。与这种要求相悖的，认为故事不应受到时间和地域限定、情节可以很长、结构无需紧凑的是史诗的结构。这一点亚里士多德亦有论及。而这一点倒应和着中国戏剧创作实践的事实。我们的戏剧没有地点的限制，可以移步换景，一桩事件的方方面面都可以在舞台上展现出来，戏剧时间也可以根据故事编织的需要，来随意延长。这使得我国传统戏剧的结构虽不合亚氏所谓戏剧的结构，倒是类似他说的史诗的结构。

杨先生这些观点深入到戏剧理论的内部，对中西戏剧的构成要素做了细致的比较分析，因此，其观点“因为史诗结构不是戏剧结构，一部史诗不能改编为一个悲剧，一本我国传统的戏也不能不经剪裁而改编为一个话剧”就特有说服力，它其实很好地揭示了中西戏剧差别甚大的原因。

当然，在对杨先生论证过程及观点叹服之时，我们也要看到，对中西戏剧进行比较，不能仅仅停留于戏剧结构这个形式因素，对戏剧所要模仿的“行为”进行分析，并对行为背后的“思想”(剧作家的写作意图)进行剖析、比较，才能找出中西戏剧的本质差别何在。

(陈会亮)

我国古代论戏曲的著作往往着重“曲”而忽略“戏”。……清代李渔《闲情偶寄》的“词曲部”和“演习部”，才是有系统地从“戏”的角度来讨论编写和排演的技巧。他注重故事的结构，提倡宾白的功用，也谈到人物的个性。他把词采贬到次要地位，并且不是讲究雕章琢句，而要求叙出故事,① 描写人物,② 并且着重要使观众了解。③ 李渔的这部书代表我国戏曲理论史上的一个新发展。

李渔的戏剧理论里，许多地方跟西方的戏剧理论相似。例如，……就故事真实性的问题，他提出的“所应有者”就是亚里士多德所谓“当然或必然”的事。……又如李渔谈到人物，不但指出“生旦有生旦之体，净丑有净丑之腔”④，还谈到，对话表达人物的个性。作者先得创造人物，然后设身处地，代他道出心中的话来，什么样的人说什么样的话，要口角毕肖，把细微曲折的心思都很自然地表达出来。这就是亚里士多德论描摹人物性格当切合身份之说(appropriateness)⑤。又如李渔要故事新奇，又要不涉荒唐，也正是分开古典派理论家所讲究的“神奇”(le merveilleux)而“似真”(la vraisemblance)。⑥

李渔的理论与西方戏剧理论相似或相同的地方……本文不想探讨那些东西，而想指出我国和西方在理论上很相似而实践上不大相同的一点——戏剧结构。

论戏曲讲究结构，并不从李渔开始。凌闲初的《谭曲杂札》、王骥德《曲律》都曾提到戏剧的结构。

李渔论戏剧结构，和《曲律》所论略有相同之处……但《曲律》所论侧重形式，以为“修辞当自炼格始”,⑦ 目的在修辞。李渔却是侧重内容，以为“有奇事方有奇文”,⑧ 所以他接着就仔细讨论戏文里所表演的故事。

他以为一本戏应该只表演一个人的一桩事，所谓“立主脑”……又说，“头绪繁多，传奇之大病也”。他称赞有些剧本“一线到底，并无旁见、侧出之情”，“始终无二事，贯串只一人”。⑨ 这一件事又必须前后贯穿：顾前者，欲其照应；顾后者，便于埋伏。照应、

① 见中国戏曲研究院编《中国古典戏曲论著集成》第7册，第24-25页。

② 见中国戏曲研究院编《中国古典戏曲论著集成》第7册，第26-27页。

③ 见中国戏曲研究院编《中国古典戏曲论著集成》第7册，第28页。

④ 见中国戏曲研究院编《中国古典戏曲论著集成》第7册，第20页。

⑤ 《诗学》15，1454a。

⑥ 见《古典主义的形成》，第233页。

⑦ 《中国古典戏曲论著集成》，第4册123页。

⑧ 《中国古典戏曲论著集成》，第7册10页。

⑨ 《中国古典戏曲论著集成》，第7册18页。

埋伏，不止关照一人，埋伏一事，凡是此剧中有名之人，关涉之事，与前此、后此所说之话，节节俱要想到。① 各部分不能有“断续痕”，到收煞时，又不可有“包括之痕”。全剧收场，剧中人物“会合之故”——须要自然而然。水到渠成，非由车戽。② ……

概而言之，李渔对结构完好的戏剧有以下两点要求：(1)一本戏只演一个人的一桩事，不是一个人一生的事；(2)这一桩故事像一个完整的有机体，是“具五官百骸”的全形，通体“承上接下，血脉相连”，全剧的结局是前面各情节的后果，“自然而然，水到渠成”，没一点牵强凑合。

这套理论跟亚里士多德《诗学》所论悲剧的“故事的整一性”(unity of action)非常相近。亚里士多德认为悲剧最要紧的是结构。悲剧摹拟一桩完整而具有相当广度的事件。……悲剧结尾，主角从顺境转入逆境，隐情一一暴露。

亚里士多德也是说：悲剧演一个人的一桩事，不是演一个人一生的事；这桩事件像完整的有机体，开头、中段和结尾前后承接，各部分有当然或必然的关系，结局是以前种种情节造成的后果。

李渔对于戏剧结构的要求，跟《诗学》所论悲剧结构的整一性几乎相同，只是没有提到《诗学》所说的广度。……但李渔的理论和这点并无抵触。因为按他的主张，决不容许故事在半途中收场，也不会要求一个戏由悲而欢、由离而合之后，再来一番离合悲欢。他主张一本戏演一个故事，不是半个故事或两个故事。

所以单从理论的表面看来，李渔论戏剧结构时提出的各点，正就是亚里士多德论戏剧结构时所提出的故事整一性。可实际上李渔讲究的戏剧结构的整一，并不是亚里士多德《诗学》讲究的戏剧结构的整一。一个是根据我国的戏剧传统总结经验，一个是根据古希腊的戏剧传统总结经验。表面上看似相同的理论，所讲的却是性质不同的两种结构。

希腊悲剧不分幕，悲剧里的合唱队从戏开场到收场一直站在戏台上。戏里的地点是不变的。戏台上所表演的只是一桩事件的一个方面——就是在戏台上所代表的那一个地点上所发生的事情。至于其他方面……只好由剧中人(包括合唱队)对话里叙述。

希腊悲剧的故事又限于短短的一段时间以内。故事的焦点就是悲剧的结局；悲剧的开始紧挨着这个焦点。悲剧故事既然集中在一个焦点上，结构就非常紧密，戏里一个个情节因果相关，导致末尾的结局，好比一浪推一浪，把故事推到最高潮。这样一个紧凑而集中的故事，如果把地点分散，时间延长，就会影响它的整一性。

按《诗学》，史诗的结构和悲剧相同，不过有以下的差别：

总的来说，戏剧集中在较短的时间，较小的地域，穿插的情节短，整个的故事约束得很紧密。悲剧不能把一桩事件同时发生的许多方面都表演出来，只能表演戏台上演出的一面，而且只限于关涉到台上角色的事。……情节单调容易使人厌倦，演出悲剧往往因此失败。③ 但悲剧能在较短的时间内达到模仿的目的……效果愈集中，愈多快感。④

① 《中国古典戏曲论著集成》，第7册，第16页。

② 《中国古典戏曲论著集成》，第7册，第69页。

③ 《诗学》，24，1459b。

④ 《诗学》，26，1462b。

而史诗，故事没有时间和地域的限制，穿插的情节长，结构不那么紧密。史诗采用叙述体，可以把同时发生的许多情节一一描述。……这是史诗的方便。① 史诗的整一性较差……一部史诗包含许多事情，例如《伊利亚特》和《奥德赛》包含许多事，每件事都相当长。② 此外，史诗时间拉得长，快感就会冲淡。③

十六、十七世纪，意大利和法国文艺理论家根据亚里士多德所提出的故事的整一性，以及“悲剧的时间不超过一天”那句话，生发出时间限于一天的规律，又从而生发出地点限于一个场面的规律，形成所谓的“三一律”。……④小仲马、斯克利布、易卜生都属于这个结构紧密的一派。

反对“三一律”的剧作家，对亚里士多德所说故事的整一性这一点，向例并无异议，⑤并且也承认戏剧的时间和地点应该集中。如西班牙的洛贝・台・维加、英国的德莱登、歌德、雨果等结构宽阔的一派。可是就像莎士比亚的戏那么不合规律，还比我国的传统戏剧拘束一些，因为莎士比亚的戏，至少是在一个景里，地点限于一处，时间限于一段。……

在我国传统的戏剧里，地点是流动的，像电影里的景。……如《窦娥冤》第一折，台上先是城外赛卢医的药铺，又变为野外无人处，又变为蔡婆家里。李渔的戏里也是一样，戏里的角色只在台上迈几步，就走过许多地方。⑥ ……因为没有地点的限制，一桩事件同时发生的许多方面，都可以在台上表演出来，不必借助于剧中人的叙述。我国传统的戏剧……像一个转动的立体，每一面都可以转向观众。史诗只可以把一桩事件同时发生的许多情节一一描叙，我国的传统戏剧却能把这许多情节一一表演。我国传统戏剧里的叙述，不是向观众叙述戏台以外所发生的事，而是剧中人向其他不知情的角色叙述台上已经演过的事。

在我国传统的戏剧里，并没有必要把戏的起点挨近结局，因而把许多情节挤到戏剧故事以外，成为叙述的部分。我国传统戏剧里时间的长短，只凭故事需要，并没有规定的限度。因为没有时间的限制，故事不必挤在一个点上，幅度不妨宽阔，步骤就从容不迫，绰绰有余地穿插一些较长的情节。

李渔说，“戏之好者必长”,⑦ 又怕贵人没闲暇从开场看到终场，就想出个“缩长为短”的办法，去掉几折，上下加几语叙述。⑧ 按亚里士多德的理论，这些可去的情节就不是整体中的有机部分；结构整一的戏剧容纳不下这些无关紧要的情节。此外，有相当长度的情节，《诗学》所讲究的戏剧结构里也是容纳不下的。

法国古典派理论家在解释《诗学》所论戏剧故事的整一性时指出，故事到收场，就不容穿插任何情节。可在我国传统的戏剧里，故事收场时并不急转直下，还有余闲添些转

① 《诗学》，24，1459b。
② 《诗学》，26，1426b。
③ 《诗学》，26，1462b。
④ 见《法国古典主义的形成》，第 253-285 页。
⑤ 见《法国古典主义的形成》，第 245 页。
⑥ 例如《比目鱼》第二出，又《蜃中楼》第二出。
⑦ 见《中国古典戏曲论著集成》第 7 册，第 77 页。
⑧ 见《中国古典戏曲论著集成》第 7 册，第 77 页。

折，李渔所谓求“团圆之趣”该有“临去秋波那一转”。……李渔所著十种曲，每本收场都有一番波折。……

……李渔关于戏剧结构的理论，表面上、或脱离了他自己的实践看来，尽管和《诗学》所说相似相同，实质上他所讲的戏剧结构，不同于西洋传统的戏剧结构，而是史诗的结构——所谓比较差的结构。……

西洋小说往往采用戏剧式的紧密结构，把故事尽量集中在较小的地域，较短的时间。如奥斯汀的小说就称为“戏剧式的小说”(Drammatie novel)。① 我国的传统戏剧却采用了幅度广而密度松的史诗结构。希莱格尔说：“但丁的《神曲》是一部小说”，“莎士比亚的悲剧是古典悲剧和小说的混合产物”。② 那么，我国的传统戏剧可称为“小说式的戏剧”。现代欧洲提倡的“史诗剧”(epic theatre)尽管和我国的传统戏剧并非一回事，可是提倡者布莱希特(Brecht)显然深受中国传统戏剧的影响。他赞扬“史诗剧”，也因为它有松懈的结构，可以反映宽阔的社会背景。他说：“现在对一个人应该从他整个社会关系来掌握他。戏剧家惟有用史诗的形式，方才能反映世界全貌”。③

戏剧的结构和史诗的结构虽然都须有整一性，但整一性在程度上的差别造成性质上的不同。戏剧理论家为了打破“三一律”的束缚，反对时间和地点的规律，往往说，亚里士多德《诗学》只提出故事整一的要求，并未有时间和地点的规定。可是，他们如果把时间和地点的约束全盘否定，那么，亚里士多德所论的戏剧结构就等同于李渔所论的戏剧结构——也就是说，不成为戏剧结构，而成了史诗结构。

（节选自杨绛：《李渔论戏剧结构》，《杨绛全集 5 戏剧 · 文论卷》，人民文学出版社 2014 年版，第 332-348 页。）

---

① 见缪尔《小说的结构》(*The Structure of the Novel*)，第 42-47、58-59 页。

② 见《文学笔记》(*Literary Notebooks*)，艾希纳编注本，第 76、86 则。据说这是浪漫主义文评的常谈。

③ 见转引自般特立《剧作家兼小说家》，第 218 页。

道与逻各斯：中西文化与文论分道扬镳的起点

（节选）

曹顺庆

【导读】

曹顺庆(1954—)，四川大学文学与新闻学院院长、教授、博士生导师，曾先后在复旦大学中文系和四川大学中文系学习，后留四川大学任教。本文倡导从文化生成规律和学术运作规则入手，来理清中国文化和文论话语体系。文章认为，古老的两个术语“道”和“logos”在中西文化和文论构成中占据重要问题，作者梳理，钱锺书和海德格尔之所以将其相提并论是因为他们看到了二者的相同之处。其一，二者都是“永恒”的，是“常”的。赫拉克利特和老子都认可在千变万化的宇宙中存在永恒之物，它是万物的本原，是万物之“母”。其二，二者都有“言谈”之意。从词源上说，“logos”的第一个意义是“言语”、“谈论”的意思，而“道”也有“说出来”，“用言辞表达”之意。其三，二者都与规律或理性相关。“道”是万物之“所以然”的规律，是万理之所用，而赫氏认为“logos”是最高之宇宙规则，包含了理性、艺术、智慧以及各种关系。然而，对比二者的相通是为了寻找二者的差异，为什么“道”和“logos”作为中西文化的起点，有如此多的相似，却引发了中西文化的分道扬镳？比较文学的价值不仅仅在求同，更在于求同的基础上寻找相异性。

二者的根本不同在于，老子的“道”倾向于“无”，而赫氏的“logos”更倾向于“有”。“道”是产生天地万物之本原，而本原自身是“无”，“道”即是无物之“物”。赫氏则认为，只有少数智慧的人(包含他本人)可以看得见或听得见“logos”，可以分别事物的本性，表明事物的实质。从二者第一层区别意义来看，“道”的“虚无”具有“空灵”“象外之象”的特征，引导中国文学艺术及文论偏向心的感知和言外之意，而“logos”的“有”显示了西方文论“求知—观察—追问原因—总结规律”的基本学术话语，其更注重内在逻辑和外在结构。第二点不同在于，老子开篇“道可道非常道”，因此“道”是不能言说的，但老子却希望用言语领悟无言之道，进而超越语言，认识道之本意；相反，“logos”目的是寻求智慧、探寻万物规律，推崇理智的说话方式，因此，西方传统上将其归纳为“逻辑”，倾向于可以言说的理性、规律和逻辑。文章进一步指出，海德格尔从中国“道”的“虚无”和“不可言说”出发，批评了西方的逻各斯中心主义。海德格尔认为，西方观念中思想以逻辑为本质与logos的逻辑和思想差别巨大，logos不是逻辑法则。他指出“大道”(Ereignis)才是不可言说的道之本真。

同时作者也指出，海德格尔对“逻各斯中心论”的解构是依据科学理性的逻辑话语分析的，再次陷入了西方话语言说方式的套路之中。

从中国老子的“道”和西方赫拉克利特的“logos”出发，寻找他们对中西文化和文论的根源性影响，在求同的基础上研究各自的异质性，到底是“道的西方化”还是“logos的中国化”，进一步探究这一问题，我们还需要深入研究曹庆顺教授近几年的变异学理论和“他国化”问题。

（潘丹丹）

“道”与“逻各斯”的不同之处，大致可以分为“有与无”、“可言者与不可言”、“分析与体悟”这样三个方面。而这三个方面恰恰是与上述三个相同或相似方面相对应的，这种“二律背反”现象确是意味深长的。限于篇幅，我们只比较论述前两个方面。

我们前面说过，“道”与“逻各斯”都是“永恒”的、“恒常”的，同时又都是万物之本原，是产生一切的东西，是万物之“母”。不过，就在这相似之中蕴含着极为不同之处，那就是老子的“道”更倾向于“无”，而赫拉克利特的“逻各斯”更倾向于“有”。也正是这一基本倾向，从起点上确定了中西方文化与文论的话语的基本方向和路径。

老子的“道”，其根本是“无”。《老子》云：“道可道，非常道，名可名，非常名，无名，天地之始，有名，万物之母。”（《老子》1章）王弼注曰：“凡有，皆始于无。故未形无名之时，则为万物之始；及其有形有名之时，则长之育之，亭之毒之。为其母也，言道也无形无名始成万物。”也就是说，虽然道是产生天地万物之本原，是万物之“母”，但这个本原自身却是“无”。正如老子明确指出：“天下万物生于有，有生于无”。（《老子》40章）王弼注曰：“天下之物，皆以有为生，有之所始，以无为本；将欲全有，必反于无也。”在这里，老子对于“道”的根本特征——“无”已表述得很明确、很充分了。这种“无”，并非虚无，并非真正的空空如也的“无”，而是一种无在之“在”，是一种以“无”为本的“无物之物”。老子这样描述这种“无”的情态：“有物混成，先天地生，寂兮寥兮，独立而不改，周行而不殆。可以为天下母，吾不知其名，强字之曰道，强为之名曰大。”（《老子》25章）显然，这种以“无”为本的“道”，仍然是一种“物”（“有物混成”），只不过它不是具体的物，而是宇宙间“有”的本原，是万物的来源。这个本原之“无”，是看不见、摸不着、听不见的；“视之不见，名曰夷；听之不闻，名曰希；搏之不得，名曰微。此三者不可致诘，故混而为一。其上不皦，其下不昧，绳绳不可名，复归于无物。是谓无状之状，无物之象，是谓惚恍。迎之不见其首，随之不见其后。”（《老子》14章）老子的“道”就是这样一种以“无”为特征的无物之“象”，无物之“物”。

从某种意义上说，赫拉克利特的“逻各斯”也具有某些“视之不见”、“听之不闻”的特征。赫氏常常把“逻各斯”描述得似乎有些“近之不见其首，随之不见其后”的意味，他指出：“这个‘逻各斯’，虽然永恒地存在着，但是人们在听见人说到它以前，以及在初次听见人说到它以后，都不能了解它。虽然万物都根据这个“逻各斯”而产生，但是我在分别每一事物的本性并表明其实质时所说出的那些话语和事实，人们在加以体会时却显得毫无经验。另外一些人则不知道他们醒时所作的事，就像忘自己睡梦中所作的事一样。”不过，只要我们仔细体会一下这段文字，便不难见出赫拉克利特与老子的不一样之处。老子从根本上就认为“道”就是一种“无”，所以无论谁都看不见、听不着。而赫拉克利特则并非认为“逻各斯”本身是“无”，只是人们理解力不高，不能懂得它、了解它。所以赫拉克利特说：“我在分别每一事物的本性并表明其实质时所说出的那些话语和事实，人们在加以体会时却显得毫无经验。”请注意赫氏这句话中提到的是“事物的本性”、“实质”，这个“本性”与“实质”，绝不是“无”，而是“有”，是一种存在之物，是万物的“实质”与“本性”，人们听不懂的正是事物的“本性”与“实质”，而表明“实质”与“本性”的，正是赫拉克利特本人，即此段文字中的“我”。这说明至少赫氏本人是看见了或听见了“逻各斯”的，如此他才可以“分别”事物的“本性”，“表明”事物的“实质”。这就是赫氏“逻各斯”与老子“道”的一个根本区别。所以说，“逻各斯”的根本特征是“有”(或存在)。赫拉克利特进一步指出：“因此，应当遵从那人人共有的东西。可是，‘逻各斯’虽是人人共有的，多数人却不加理会地生活。”赫拉克利特明确指出“逻各斯”是人人共有的，只是人们不加以理会，或没有能力去理解它、听从它，因为“自然喜欢躲藏起来”。因此，赫氏主张去爱智慧，去寻求听从和遵循“逻各斯”。他说：“智慧只在于一件事，就是认识那善于驾驭一切的思想。”“如果你不听从我本人而听从我的‘逻各斯’，承认一切是一，那就是智慧的。”听从“逻各斯”，实际上就是遵循万物的规律，认识那驾驭一切的思想，寻求事物生灭变化的规律与本质。沿着这条思路走下去，必然会走向“有”，而不会走向“无”。在亚里士多德看来，赫拉克利特曾摇摆于“有”与“无”之间，他说：“任何人都不能设想同一事物既存在又不存在，像有些人认为赫拉克利特所主张的那样。”(《形而上学》第4卷第5章)的确，赫氏常常具有辩证的相对论观点：“不死的就是有死的，有死的就是不死的。”“善与恶是一回事。”这与老子的看法何其相似。但赫拉克利特最终走向了“有”，走上了从“有”寻求万物原因和规律之途，并把这个“有”陈述为实实在在的东西——“火”。赫氏认为，万物是由“火”构成，他说：“这个世界对一切存在物都是同一的，它不是任何神所创造的，也不是任何人所创造的；它的过去、现在和未来永远是一团永恒的活火，在一定的分寸上燃烧，在一定的分寸上熄灭。”这“火”绝不是“无”，绝不是老子所谓视之不见，听之不闻的“无物之象”，而是“有”，是实实在在之物，是一团永恒的“活火”。正如邬昆如指出：存在的追求是赫拉克利特哲学的目的。若用“太初”的问题来衡量赫拉克利特，则“逻各斯”是实体，“火”是表象，那么“太初是火”或“太初是逻各斯”，有同一意义。这里的哲学方法是：抓紧逻各斯，以逻各斯为出发点，通过“思想”达到哲学追求的对象——存在。赫拉克利特终于从“逻各斯”走向了物质实体“火”，即从“求智慧”中观察万物，从观察万物中追问原因，寻求规律，“爱智慧的人应当熟悉很多的事物”，“智慧只在于一件事，就是认识那驾驭一切的思想”。而这条由求知—观察—追问原因—总结规律的链条组成的哲学话语规则和路径，正是西方文化与文论的基本学术话语特征。哲学大师亚里士多德，正是在对“有”，对“存在”的研究追问之中，建立起了西方科学理性话语和确立逻辑分析推论的意义生成方式的。而这种话语系统，正是当代海德格尔与德里达(Jacques Derrida)等人所激烈批判的“逻各斯中心主义”。从某种意义上也可以说，这种“逻各斯中心主义”，是从赫拉克利特使“逻各斯”偏向“有”而肇其端的。海德格尔认为，传统哲学正是固执于“言谈所及的东西”，才把“逻各斯”解释为理性、判断、定义、根据等，也即把“逻各斯”归约为逻辑了。正因为总是以外在的“有”，即现成存在者为取向，古希腊哲学家们(如亚里士多德)在分析“逻各斯”时就不可避免地“误入歧途”，将西方文化导向一种外在的“判断理论”——逻辑主义或逻各斯中心主义。海德格尔指出：“古代存在论在论述生长于其上的方法基础时不够原始。逻各斯被经验为现成的东西，被阐释为现成的东西；同样，逻各斯所展示的存在者也具有现成性的意义。”因而，传统存在论的迷误就是“逻各斯”的不幸，此不幸即是：“逻各斯”沦为现存事物的逻辑了。于是乎海德格尔便力图重新审视赫拉克利特的“逻各斯”的本源意义，企图克服和改造传统以“有”为核心的存在论，站在全新的生存论存在论的基点上来理解语言现象，“把语法从逻辑中解放出来”，从而拯救“逻各斯”。无论海德格尔能否拯救“逻各斯”，我们都可以从中发现西方文化执着(或拘执)于“有”的特征。同时也可以发现中西方文化中“道”与“逻各斯”这种“无”与“有”的特征，或许还可以发现“道”与“逻各斯”互释互补的价值。

老子“道”的崇尚“无”与赫拉克利特“逻各斯”的偏向“有”，都对中西文化与文论产生了巨大而深远的影响。中国文学艺术及文论中的“虚实相生”论，“虚静”论等，显然与老子的“尚无”密切相关，“无中生有”(天下万物生于有，有生于无)的话语方式，使中国文学与文论更注重“不着一字，尽得风流”的空灵和“象外之象”、“味外之旨”的隽永深长。

同样，“逻各斯”对“有”的探索、追问与分析，也使得西方文化与文论显得更加严密而系统，更注重逻辑因果、注重情节结构。老子的重“无”，将中国文论引向了重神遗形，而赫拉克利特的偏“有”，将西方文论引向了注重对现实事物的摹仿，注重外在的比例、对称美、注重外在形式美的文论路径。

老子的“道”是不可道，不可言的，所谓“道可道，非常道，名可名，非常名。”已经非常清楚地表述了这一点。但是“道”虽不可以道，不可以言说，然如果完全不用语言文字，就根本无法论述道；而老子既然著书立说，肯定又非用语言文字来言说不可，这样就形成了一个无法回避的悖论。刘勰《文心雕龙·情采》指出：“老子疾伪，故称‘美言不信’，而五千精妙，则非弃美矣。”钱锺书说：“道不可说、无能名，固须卷舌缄口，不著一字，顾又滋生横说竖说，千名万号。”具有“大智”的老子，实际上是认识到了这一两难悖论的，他清楚地知晓，“道”是不可以言说的，但他要著书论道，却又必须以语言来表述这不可言之道，以名号来名不可名之名。老子于是迫不得已走向了“强为之名”、强为之言之途，“吾不知其名，强字之曰道，强为之名曰大”。(《老子》25章)这种“强为之名”，实际上必然造成“道”之本真的失落。王弼注曰：“吾所以字之曰道者，取其可言之称最大也，责其字定之所由，则系于大，大有系则必有分，有分则失其极矣。故曰‘强为之名’。”显然，这种“强为之名”，是“失其极”的，老子之所以曰“强为之名”，实是不得已。不过，在这不得已之中，老子实际上闯出了一条“以言去言”之路，即通过有言，教人去认识、去领悟那无言之道，从而超越语言，直达“道”之本真。魏源《老子本义》说：“圣人知有名者之不可常，是故终日为而未尝为，终日言而来尝言，岂自知其为美为善哉！斯则观徼而得妙也。若然者，万物之来，虽亦未尝不因应，而生不有，为不恃，终不居其名矣。”(《老子本义》第2章)魏源的解说是准确的，老子正是以言达到无言，以名寻求无名，从语言描述之中令人捕捉那微妙之道，去体悟那纯真之道。正如熊十力先生所说：“体不可以言说显，而又不得不以言说显。则亦无妨于无可建立处而假有设施，即于非名言安立处而强设名言……体不可名，而假为之名以彰之。”所以老子说：“是以圣人处无为之事，行不言之教。”这种“不言之教”，正是以“有言”来加以导引的，于是乎，语言便成为了桥梁与津渡，引导着人们通向“道”之本真。老子这样为我们描述那纯真之“道”：“道之为物，惟恍惟惚，惚兮恍兮，其中有象；恍兮惚兮，其中有物；窈兮冥兮，其中有精，其精甚真，其中有信，自古及今，其名不去。”(《老子》21 章)王弼注曰：“至真之极，不可得名，无名则是其名也。”这就是无名之名，无言之言。“不自见故明，不自是故彰”。(《老子》22 章)在通过有言来达到无言的津渡中，老子处处提醒人们，不要拘执于言，而要追求超越语言的“无言”；这就是后人强调的“不落言筌”，“不要死在言下”，“不着一字，尽得风流”之意。老子指出：“道常无为而无不为，侯王若能守之，万物将自化，化而欲作，吾将镇之以无名之朴，无名之朴，夫亦将无欲，不欲以静，天下将自定。”(《老子》37 章)道虽无名、无象、无言，但却是本真，是大音、大象，“大音希声，大象无形，道隐无名。”(《老子》41 章)从“无名”到“有名”，最终还是要回到“无名”，回到“道”之本真。这就是老子“道”“不可言”的特征，这种特征是言无言，以不言言之，或者说通过言说使人明白道不可言说。对这一点，庄子表述得更为明确，“悲夫，世人以形色名声为足以得彼之情。夫形色名声果不足以得彼之情，则知者不言，言者不知。”(《庄子·外物》)所以庄子说：“终身言，未尝言。”(《庄子·寓言》)言说的关键是直指“道”本身，而不必拘执于语言，这样就可以超越语言之拘囿，这就是庄子著名的“得意忘言”说，“筌者所以在鱼，得鱼而忘筌；蹄者所以在兔，得兔而忘蹄；言者所以在意，得意而忘言，吾安得夫忘言之人而与之言哉！”(《庄子·外物》)

……

(节选自曹顺庆：《道和逻各斯：中西文化与文论分道扬镳的起点》，《文艺研究》1997 年第 6 期，第 54-60 页。)

美国诗人如何看待中国诗学

（节选）

[美]钟　玲

【导读】

影响研究是比较文学学科中一个重要的研究方法，主要通过实证主义的方法来考察两国文学间或多国文学之间所存在的因果事实联系。钟玲女士的《美国诗与中国梦——美国现代诗里的中国文化模式》，从副标题就可以看出其研究旨向，即中国文化、中国文学对美国现代诗歌的影响研究。她试图通过跨文化的双向影响研究来透视中西文化、中西文学之间存在的事实联系和依据，主要从美国现代诗中所表现的几种中国文化，如中国思想、中国诗学、多元艺术观和人物模式，来研究美国现代诗如何融入中国文化元素以及中西文化融合过程中所呈现的文化和美学意义。在第一章美国现代诗和中国文化中，钟玲分析了美国诗人如何看待中国诗学。有些美国现代诗人认为中国诗学对美国诗歌的影响和冲击力很大，那么他们为什么持这种看法呢？中国诗学又是如何影响他们的诗艺观和诗歌创作呢？对此，钟玲选取了有代表性的美国诗人进行深入分析。首先，钟玲引述了诗人雷克思罗斯和雷文的观点，并认为他们都夸大了中国诗学对美国现代诗歌的影响。雷克思罗斯认为中国诗歌和日本诗歌对20世纪的整个西方诗坛都产生了深远的影响，尤其是远东的诗歌论述方式影响了欧美三代诗人。雷克思罗斯所谓的远东论述方式与意象主义类似，钟玲对此表示认同，并举杜甫的《旅夜书怀》和华兹华斯的《当我看见了，我的心挑起》及庞德的《在地铁站》来证明他的观点。但在钟玲看来，雷克思罗斯夸大了东方的影响，因为远东诗歌的论述方式实质是20世纪的一种文学成俗，它会受到多种源流的影响，比如文化思想层面、宗教思想层面以及文化自身内部的因素影响。同时，这与雷克思罗斯本人喜爱远东文化也密切相关。因此钟玲认为他的问题在于没有考虑其他因素对美国诗歌的影响，比如詹姆斯·弗雷泽有关神话和仪式，弗洛伊德的精神分析等其实都成为了美国现代诗歌充分汲取的养分。另外，钟玲在“中国诗歌与美国想象力”的学术会议上注意到诗人莫文在大会发言中竟然把中国诗歌的影响力拔高到了与詹姆斯国王钦定本《圣经》的英译本同等重要的高度，并且认为中国诗歌已然成为美国诗歌传统本身的一部分，而他本人的诗歌中并没有明显的中国诗学的论述方式存在。因此，钟玲认为莫文也夸大了中国诗歌的影响力。其次，钟玲考量了雷克思罗斯和雷文把作为边缘文化的远东诗歌纳入美国诗歌体系的中心位置的动机。一方面，他们是否有帝国主义或欧洲中心主义的动机？从美国的大众文化到庞德的《诗篇》分析来看，钟玲认为他们或许有这种上国意识，但认为庞德吸纳中国的古典文化又更多地体现了他的个人风格。另一方面，由于他们觉察到了自己所属的西方文化危机，所以向远东文化寻求自救之道。比如，庞德吸收儒家思想来拯救日益腐败的西方文明，雷克思罗斯模仿元稹悼亡诗中的意念和论述方式创作了《王河谷》来排遣心中的丧妻之痛。

“美国诗人如何看待中国诗学”这一研究的切入点令人耳目一新，这不是建立在钟玲女士本人如何看待中国文化对美国现代诗的影响基础之上，而是从接受者美国诗人如何看待这个问题来进行论述，从而克服了本位主义研究可能会导致的有失偏颇的主观学术论断，因而她的研究从客观的立场并以严谨的治学态度来分析，其研究结论也必然更具说服力。

（马礼霞）

姑且先不论美国现代诗到底受了多少中国诗学论述的冲击，事实上，有几位美国诗人的确抱持着一种特别的看法，他们认为中国诗学对美国诗歌的冲击非常巨大。那么，他们认为美国诗歌采取了哪些中国诗学论述呢？他们的这种看法，在一般美国文学史作者的眼中大概是颇为极端的。那么，他们的看法究竟在多大程度上为自己的主观因素所左右呢？本节将探讨何以这些美国诗人会认为中国诗学对美国诗歌的冲击那么巨大。此外，他们既然认为中国诗学的冲击甚巨，中国诗学在他们自己的诗观及诗歌创作方面自然可能会有相当的影响，这种影响又是怎样的呢？至于美国诗歌受了哪些中国诗学的冲击，将留待后面的章节讨论。

诗人雷克思罗斯在1965年以前就大胆地主张，中国诗歌与日本诗歌对20世纪的整个西方诗坛都产生了无可比拟的影响，影响所及包括英、美、德、法、意、俄诸国的诗歌。他说：“继波德莱尔之后，对西方诗歌影响最大的可能来自外面，来自中国与日本诗歌的译文。”①他认为远东诗歌的影响及于欧美三代诗人：第一代是第一次世界大战前正值年轻的一些诗人，如庞德、里尔克（R. M. Rilke）、阿波里奈尔（G. Apollinaire）、玄姆（F. Jammes）、马拉美（S. Mallarme）、巴斯特钠（B. Pasternak）、马恰度（A. Machado）等，这些诗人的诗风或多或少都受远东诗歌之影响。第二代，即“一战”后崛起的诗人，已然接纳远东诗歌，并将其视为“他们诗艺固有的一部分”（as the very matter of fact of their art, *Classics Revisited* 131）。雷克思罗斯没有列举第二代诗人的名字，他所指的我想应该是他自己、杜丽特、康敏斯（E. E. Cummings）等。第三代是指在20世纪30、40年代写作的诗人，如丹尼斯·勒弗朵夫（Denise Levertov）、罗伯特·克利里（Robert Creeley）、罗伯特·邓肯、劳伦斯·弗林格第、金斯伯格、史奈德，他们继承了前一代诗人已采用的远东诗歌的“论述方式”。那么雷克思罗斯所谓的远东诗歌的论述方式是指什么呢？他解释如下：暗喻及各种象征皆非由意象推出的结论，它们是意象本身彼此具体的关系。就是这种诉说

① “Possibly the greatest single influence on the poetry of the West since Baudelaire has come form outside: the Chinese and Japanese poetry in translation.”（*Classical Revisited* 131）

手法的直接性，令中国诗歌的译文在大多数西方诗人那里受到如此的欢迎①。

雷克思罗斯所谓的论述方式的确是中国及日本的诗歌常用到的表现手法。这里，我试举例说明他的上述看法。以杜甫《旅夜书怀》中的句子"星随平野阔"为例，此句中"星随"及"平野阔"两个意象，并非着重指涉意象背后的象征主义，而是令读者联想这两个意象本身之间的具体关系，即因为平野非常辽阔，坐在舟上的诗人在视觉上会觉得天边的星星一直在跟随着他，因此这意象本身所表现的大平原星夜的辽阔气象会直接打动读者②。至于西方诗歌的论述方式，我们试以威廉·华兹华斯(William Wordsworth)的一首短诗《当我看见了，我的心跳起》("My Heart Leaps When I Behold")为例作一说明。诗中的叙述者说他由小到大一见到彩虹就心跳，但此诗并非以"彩虹"为其重点，而是有"彩虹"推出"孩子是人类之父亲"(The Child is Father of Man)，并以"自然的虔敬"(Natural Piety)等意义为重点。以此二例为证，我想雷克思罗斯对东西方诗歌论述方式的理解基本是对的。他也举例说明其论点，他举的远东诗人包括杜甫及日本17世纪的大诗人柿本人磨。他所提到的这种论述方式实际上与意象主义的主张也有想通之处，后者也注重意象之明晰与精确。王新甫(音译，David Hsin-F. Wand)就认为很多美国诗人创作时也很重视意象主义所推崇的意象，他们包括路易斯·祖科夫斯基(Louis Zukofsky)、华伦、勃莱、莫文(W. S. Merwin)、詹姆斯·赖特、史奈德、勒弗朵夫及西维娅·普拉丝(Sylvia Plath)等。

然而西方诗歌真的受了远东诗歌如此大的影响吗？程度或许没有雷克思罗斯所说的那么深，但20世纪的西方诗歌的确显现了这种论述方式，如法国的象征主义诗歌、超现实主义诗歌，美国的意象主义诗歌都使用了这类论述方式，庞德的名诗《在地铁站》("In the Station of Metro")及马拉美的《繁花》("Les Fleurs")皆是很明显的例子。但雷克思罗斯却未能区分影响(influence)与文学成俗(convention)二者的不同。在此我们可以参考克劳迪欧·纪严(Claudio Guillen)关于成俗与影响有别的观点：

> 成俗(就整体而言)是广泛的，而影响(源流的影响及个别的影响)则是强而有力的……当多种影响散布开来，且混合起来，当它们变成惯常的前提或用法——变成作家们在同一时刻呼吸的同样的空气——的时候，那么就该称它们为成俗或者此类名称……文学的成俗不仅只是技巧上的先决条件，也是更广大的场域制度，有早期多种单一的源流影响所形成的场域制度③。

---

① "The metaphor, the symbols are not conclusions drawn from the images; they are the images themselves in concrete relationship. It is this immediacy of utterance that has made Chinese poetry in translation so popular with most western poets."(*Classical Revisited* 130)

② 另一读法为"星垂平野阔"，见《全唐诗》第7册，卷229，页2489。本人采"随"字乃因此诗应是叙述者身在舟中，故由视觉上而言，星星跟着船走比较合理。

③ "Where convention (systematically speaking) are extensive, influences (genetic and individual) are intense... When influences spread and amalgamate, when they become common premises or usages—the common air that writers breathe at the same moment—then they ought to be called something like conventions... literary conventions are not only technical prerequisites but broader fields of systems resulting from earlier, singular genetic influence."(Guillen 60-61)

我要说的是，雷克思罗斯其实夸大了东方的影响，他所为的远东诗歌的论述方式，其实是一种20世纪诗歌的文学成俗，它的确已成为西方“作家们在同一时刻呼吸的同样的空气”，但这种成俗之形成不全赖东方的影响，而是“有早期多种单一的源流影响所形成的场域制度”，远东诗歌的论述方式不过是其中一个单一的源流影响而已。造成这种论述方式的还有其他各种源流影响，例如：就文化思想的层面而言，西方原来比较注重自我的主观意识，19世纪浪漫主义诗歌中主观意识会笼罩外在的客观事物，就是一个明显的例子；到了20世纪，这种主体意识逐渐瓦解，外在的、客观的事物便慢慢受到重视。这个文化思想上的大趋势也是形成以意象为主的论述方式的一种源流影响。就宗教思想层面而言，在基督教的理念中，自然万物是上帝创造来供人类主宰和利用的：“上帝就赐福给他们，又对他们说：‘要生养众多，遍满地面，治理这地；也要管理海里的鱼、空中的鸟和地上各样的活物。’上帝说：‘看哪，我将遍地上一切结种子的菜蔬和一切树上所结有核的果子，全赐给你们作食物。’”(《创世记》第一章，28-29)当20世纪基督教的势力开始衰退之时，西方人开始反省自己的地位，甚至颠覆人类自己的主宰地位，对大自然本身的关注也开始普遍起来，大自然的地位开始上升了。这种在宗教思想上关注重点的转移也是形成以自然意象为主的论述方式的另一源流。我要说的是，当一种新的文学论述方式形成之际，外来的冲击与影响固然应该加以重视和研讨，文化自身内部的因素更应该受到关注。文化内部的因素如尚未成熟，外来影响是很难扎下根的。

雷克思罗斯如此偏重远东诗歌与他自己的爱好有关。自童年起，他就倾心于远东文学艺术，如日本的能剧及歌舞伎、中国书法、中国山水画及人物画、中国瓷器、中日文学、乃至广东大戏(钟玲《热爱中国文化的王红公》，27-28页)。由此可以想见，个人的偏好可能是影响最大的因素，此立论之问题在于，他没有拿其他的影响因素来作对比。其实，20世纪诗歌的论述方式杂多并陈，以意象为主的方式固然重要，也只是其中之一。比如，詹姆斯·弗雷泽(James Frazer)有关神话与仪式的著作《金枝》(*The Golden Bough*)就对20世纪的的美国诗歌产生了很大的冲击，此单一的源流影响所及者，不仅是诗歌的内容，还有诗歌的论述方式，即诗人以仪式颂歌的方式来呈现诗歌，也企图以诗歌本身来达到净化人心、再造生命的目的。在艾略特的《荒原》、詹姆斯·狄奇(James Dickey)的《雪橇葬礼，梦的典礼(“Sled Burial, Dream Ceremony》)，及嘉璐莲·凯莎的《再造的瑟米勒女神》(“Semele Recycled”)等诗中，《金枝》对其论述方式之影响很是明显。又如弗洛伊德的精神分析法，直接催生了20世纪50年代及60年代的告解式诗歌(confessional poetry)的产生，成为一重要的诗歌论述方式，其代表诗人罗伯特·洛威尔(Robert Lowell)、约翰·贝里曼(John Berryman)、西维娅·普拉丝、安妮·塞克斯顿(Anne Sexton)等皆刻意在诗中挖掘潜意识的情结，以诗为媒介，呈现被压抑的苦闷。此外，法国的超现实主义诗歌、女性主义的观点，都成为美国诗歌吸收的论述方式。相比之下，很难说雷克思罗斯所谓的远东诗歌的论述方式一定会比其他论述的影响更普遍或更重要。

1977年4月23日至27日，美国诗人学会(the Academy of American Poets)在纽约市

举办了一个"中国诗歌与美国想象力会议"(Chinese Poetry and American Imagination Conference)①。应邀参加会议的共有13人，其中包括七位在美国诗坛居一席地位的诗人，如雷克思罗斯、史奈德、勃莱、孔尼兹、詹姆斯·赖特、莫文等诗人，另有学者与译者共六位，包括叶维廉(William Yip)、乔纳森·查维斯(Jonathan Chaves)、汉斯·弗兰克尔(Hans Frankel)、大卫·拉提莫(David Lattimore)与笔者。有趣的是，在会议中，这七位诗人都异口同声地说他们喜爱中国诗歌——当然大多数是读中国诗的英译本——而且还有些诗人说他们自己写诗很受这些译文的影响。在莫文自己的诗歌创作之中，实在是搜索不到什么中国诗学的论述方式，但是他却在会议中发言说：

> ……我们对当今整体的中国诗歌译文负欠，我们深受这些译文对我们的诗歌的持续影响，对这一种总是难以捉摸的艺术[钟玲按：指中国诗歌英译文不能准确地表达原文的意思]，这些都是我们最乐于负担的债务之一……这种债，至少在种类上说，可以比拟在我们这个时代，我们对詹姆斯国王钦定本《圣经》的翻译者所负欠的……它已经扩充了我们语言的范畴与能力，扩充了我们自己艺术及感性的范畴与能力。到了现在，我们甚至难以想象，没有这种影响美国诗歌会是什么样子，这影响已经成为美国诗歌传统本身的一部分了②。

莫文竟把中国诗歌之影响力与最重要的的《圣经》英文译本相比拟，并且说中国诗歌已成为美国诗歌传统必不可缺的一部分！雷克思罗斯在此会议上甚至说，远东诗歌对现代美国诗歌的影响大于19世纪至20世纪法国诗歌的影响，而且远大于自己传统的影响，即19世纪英美诗歌的影响；他还说有些美国诗人"如果用中国或日本习语之外的任何其他的方式来思考，就会有问题了"③。中国诗歌对美国现代诗的影响真有如莫文与雷克思罗斯所讲的那么大吗？他们为什么提出这种似乎是夸张的说法呢？当然，这个会议本身的性质就影响了他们的发言方式。会议主持方面当然会邀请诗中多少呈现了中国诗风的美国诗人，或对中国诗歌有很浓的兴趣的诗人。会议的主题既然是"中国诗歌与美国想象力"。总而言之，由于讨论主题受到特别关注，中国诗歌的影响力则自然被凸显且被夸大了，不过这影响的存在确实不争的事实。在第三章中，我们将讨论参加这次会议的诗人自身的创作究竟吸纳了什么中国诗学。

然而，另一个值得思考的问题是，雷克思罗斯与莫文这种急于把一种边缘文化，即远东诗歌，纳入美国诗歌的中心位置，是基于一种什么样的心态呢？有没有帝国主义或欧洲中心主义的动机呢？我想这种动机可以说有，也可以说没有。也许我这种答案本身，这种

---

① 此次会议发言的记录全部刊于《铁树》(*Ironwood*)第17期。

② "...What we owe to the present corpus of Chinese poetry in translation, and its continuing influence on our own poetry is one of our great happy debts to this perennially improbable art. A debt, in our time, comparable in kind at least, to that owed to the makers of the King James Version... It has extended the range and capacity of our own speech, our own art and sensibility. By now American poetry is unimaginable without this influence, which has become part of its own tradition." (Orr 18)

③ "...have difficulty in thinking in any other idiom than Chinese or Japanese."

思维方式，就是中国式的，是一种相对的思维方式。美国在20世纪50年代和60年代是世界第一强国，对外的经济援助、军事援助，甚至宗教文化的交流都很频繁，在美国方面多少都有点上国的意识，有点沙文主义倾向，且有把对方纳为己有的倾向。最明显的例子反映在大众文化中，譬如好莱坞的电影模式。在那个年代拍的电影如《樱花恋》(*Sayonara Goodbye*, 1957)及《苏丝黄的世界》(*The World of Susie Wong*, 1960)，其主题都是高大英俊的美国男子征服、拥有了东方女子娇小的身躯及无悔的感情①。当庞德在他的《诗篇》(*The Cantos*)把中国文字、历史及思想都纳入他的思想体系中的时候，或许多少也是有上国意识的：那个无所不包的文艺复兴时代的心灵竟包容了异国情调的东方古中国呢！在这一段中英文并列的诗中，庞德以诗为工具，把古典中国的历史、五行学说和文字都纳入他的系统之中。

皋陶
丰饶。
后来皇后怀着少康逃亡。
伏羲乃木德；
神农火德；皇帝以土德治天下，
青帝以金德。
颛顼乃帝王，即水德。
舜，治之
禹，养之
表面上是不足够的，在上帝前无所遁形。②
……

但是，从另外一个方面来说，诗人对自身所属之文化的变迁和匮乏是比较敏感的。在

① 两部影片中的男主角皆是当时最红的英俊男明星。《樱花恋》的男主角是马龙·白兰度(Marlon Brando)，他虽不十分高，但站在日本女主角Muko Taka旁边则显得很魁梧。《苏丝黄的世界》威廉·荷顿是当红的中生，高大而自信，女主角关家倩(Nancy Kwan)仅五英尺二英寸高。

② **皋陶**
abundance.
Then an Empress fled with Chao Kang in her belly,
Fou-hi by virtue of wood;
Chin-nong, of fire; Hoang Ti ruled by the earth,
Chan by metal,
Tehuen was lord, as is water,
CHUN, govern
Yu, cultivate
The surface is not enough,
From Chang Ti nothing is hidden.
(*The Cantos* Ⅷ 264)

1950 年，美国诗人感觉西方的思想、宗教信仰和生活方式已经不足以让他们安身立命了，他们向东方寻求自求之道。在这一点上则不能给他们贴上帝国主义的标签。这毋宁说是一种诗人感到文化面临危机时的自救之道。中国在五四运动时期为了要救民族，为了追上世界潮流，不也曾大量吸收西方文化吗？庞德采纳中国文明入诗亦可作如是观：他认为西方的商业文明腐败已极，故要用儒家的思想，用古中国圣王精神等来拯救西方。在雷克思罗斯作于 1950 年追悼他的亡妻的诗《王河谷》(“King's River Canyon”, *Collected Shorter Poems*, 191-192) 中，他谈到元稹悼亡诗动人的力量，你能说这也是帝国主义思想吗？

……

（节选自钟玲：《美国诗与中国梦：美国现代诗里的中国文化模式》，广西师范大学出版社 2003 年版，第 16-24 页。）

王国维及其文学批评

（节选）

[加]叶嘉莹

【导读】

叶嘉莹（1924— ）先生生于北京书香世家，自幼师从名师研习古典诗词，1945年以优异成绩毕业于北京辅仁大学，五十年代曾执教台湾大学、辅仁大学和淡江大学，六十年代赴美任密歇根大学及哈佛大学客座教授，1969年迁居加拿大温哥华，受聘不列颠哥伦比亚大学终身教授。1979年开始每年利用假期在中国讲学，1991年当选加拿大皇家学会首位中国古典文学院士，2013年正式回到中国定居，住在南开大学。叶先生教学生涯长达半个多世纪，遍历海峡两岸，大洋东西，培养海内外人才无数。她在诗词方面的著述非常丰富，不仅写有大量诗词，同时把前人理论结合自身创作和研究，开创了诗词研究领域的新篇章。她的研究还涉及文学评论，理论阐释和作品批注等。她以自己的生命历程作注脚，充分阐释了"以无生的彻悟，来做有生的事业"，"以悲观的彻悟，乐观地去工作去生活"的深刻含义。

叶嘉莹先生的《王国维及其文学批评》以其开阔的视野、深厚的西学和国学底蕴，对王国维的治学特点进行了较为翔实的分析和探讨，并高度评价了其在中国文学史上的地位。一方面尝试"有不为政治私见所拘束的客观的态度"从王国维生平尤其是其个性为人，其持守的理想和道德之价值标准来探讨一代学者一生治学之途径为何从早期西方哲学及文学研究忽而转向古文字、古器物、古史地考证研究，又如何在盛年之时自沉于湖，这是世人仍未解答之困惑；另一方面通过对王国维在文学批评上的成就来评价他在中国文学史上的地位。而其文学批评成就主要体现在两组著述，一组是《王观堂先生全集》，包括《静安文集》及《静安文集续篇》，是他早期的一些杂文及一些作品，属于"启蒙时期的一些没有完整体系的琐杂概念而已"，有较为浓厚的西方文论色彩，体现了他早期对西方哲学和文学的研究。其中又以《〈红楼梦〉评论》为其文论主要代表，在中国文论史上属开天辟地之作，因为该文运用西方的哲学和文艺理论来分析中国的古典文学作品，这种大胆的尝试在中国文学史上是第一次。另一组是《人间词话》六十四则，形式上采用了中国古代文论的诗话词话，表面看起来王国维退回到了传统，而事实上因其深受西方思想洗礼，对于中国的旧诗词的理解注入了现代文论的内核，实现了中西融合的批评模式。

（黄惠）

第二编　王国维的文学批评

第一章　绪　论

……

二、中国文学批评之传统及其需要外来之刺激为拓展的必然性

如我们在前一节之所叙述，静安先生在文学批评方面的成就，既然主要乃是在于他能够把西方之新观念带进中国之旧传统，要想了解这一点对于中国文学批评之拓展的重要性，我们就不得不先对中国批评之旧传统是否有待于外来之思想理论以为拓展的问题作一检讨。

一般说来，中国的文学批评乃是发生得极早却发展得极慢的一门学问。如果远究其原始，则早自群经诸子之中，我们便已可以见到不少零碎片段的论文论诗的言语了。及至魏晋南北朝之世，中国的作者们更开始对于文学有了极广泛的反省和自觉，于是有关文学批评的专门著述乃不断相继出现，自魏文帝的《典论·论文》、陆机的《文赋》，以迄于刘勰的《文心雕龙》和钟嵘的《诗品》，更加之以沈约诸人的声病之说。在这一时期中，中国的文学批评无论在质的方面或量的方面，可以说都有着极为可观的成就。如果仅就此一初度反省与自觉之时代所留下的著述而言，则中国的文学批评经过以后千余年来的发展，实在应当有较之今日所能见的更伟大更具体的批评相继出现。可是自唐代以后，则在创作一方面虽然是名家辈出盛极一时，可是在批评一方面则除了散见于各大家诗文中的一些单篇述作外，其余一些表面看来属于文学批评之专著如皎然之《诗式》与司空图之《诗品》等，则其实不过只是一些泛论诗之品式或对诗之风格加以主观品第的作品而已，它们都不曾对批评理论方面有什么更具体的建树。至于宋代，则因为受了当时流行的佛教之语录体的影响，诗话之作乃开始盛行一时，而又因五代以来词之兴起，于是除了诗话以外，又开始有了词话之作。明清以来相因成风，于是诗话及词话遂尔络绎争出。此外，在一般诗人文士的书牍论说之中当然也不乏谈文论诗的述作，可是却大多零星散乱，并没有什么具备理论体系的专门述作。在从周代以讫于明清直至静安先生以前的文学批评作品中，其所触及的方面可以说极为广泛。论及内容的，则自《尚书》便已有“诗言志”[12]之语；论及功用的，则自《论语》孔子谈诗便已有“兴观群怨”、“事父”、“事君”[13]之言；论及作法的，则自《毛诗·大序》便已有“赋比兴”[14]之说；论及作者之时代背景的，则自《孟子》便已有“知人论世”[15]之主张；论及声律的，则自司马相如《答盛问作赋》便已有“一宫一商”[16]的辨别；论及体制的，则自魏文帝《典论·论文》便已有“奏议宜雅，书论宜理，铭诔尚实，诗赋欲丽”[17]的区分；论及源流和品第的，则自钟嵘之《诗品》便已曾溯源别流地把诗人衡定为上中下三品。至其综合大成，对于文学之源流体式创作与鉴赏都曾有所论及的，则前有陆机之《文赋》，后有刘勰之《文心雕龙》。不过陆机以赋体论文遂为对偶声韵之形式所拘限，因此乃不免于“巧面碎乱”[18]之讥。而刘勰则采取专门论著的方式，对于源流、名义、文

类、文体以及写作与鉴赏之各方面，都曾各立专题分别加以探讨和论析。所以在中国文学批评史上，如果要说到集大成而且有体系的作品，则自当推刘勰之《文心雕龙》为一大巨著。至于唐宋以来历代之诗话词话及诸家评论诗文之单篇述作中，当然也有不少极为可贵的精论要义，然而却可惜体例驳杂，都不是理论精严的专著。写到这里，我们就不得不一加反省：中国之文学批评既然发生得如此之早，注意的方面也如此之广，对于文学之内含与形式也曾经有过很精微的体认与辨别，那么为什么我们始终未曾发展成一套体系精严的批评理论，而除了刘勰一部《文心雕龙》略具规模纲领以外，自刘氏以后一千多年以来，竟也没有一部更像样的具有理论体系的专门著作出现。这在我们一向以文学历史之悠久及文学遗产之丰富自豪的中国人来说，当然乃是一件极值得自我检讨的问题。

关于此一问题可以分为以下几方面来加以探讨。第一，我们所要提到的乃是不同的民族各有其不同的特质，中国的民族似乎一向就不长于西方之科学推理的思辨方式。这样说虽似乎有些武断，可是我们只要对中国语言的特征一加反省，便可知道这话乃是可信的，因为语言的组合方式也便是民族思维方式的具体表现。中国语言的组合在文法上乃是极为自由的，没有过去、现在与未来的时态的区分，没有主动与被动的语气，也没有阳性与阴性及单数与复数的区分，而且对于一些结合字句的词语，如前置词、接续词、关系代名词等，也都不加重视，一切都有着绝大的自由，因此在组成一句话时，主语、述语与宾语以及形容词或副词等都可以互相颠倒或竟而完全省略，而且在行文时也一向没有精密的标点符号。具有这种语言特征的民族，其不适于作严密的科学推理式的思考岂不乃是一件显而易见的事。再则中国的思维方式还有一个特征，那便是重视个别的具象的事物而忽略抽象的普遍的法则。中国人喜欢从个别的事例来观察思索，而不喜欢从多数个别者之间去观察其秩序与关系以建立抽象的法则，所以中国的诗话词话便大多乃是对于一个诗人的一首诗或一句诗甚至一个字的品评，或者竟然只是一些与作品无关的对诗人之轶事琐闻的记述，而从来不愿将所有作品中的个别的现象归纳出一个抽象的理论或法则，甚至在触及极抽象的问题时也仍然只予以具体的形象化的说明，如司空图《诗品》把诗分为二十四种不同的风格。风格本是抽象的东西，司空图对于何以形成如此不同之风格的因素，如风格与内容，修辞以及作者之性情、人格、时代之背景等种种关系竟完全未加理论的说明，而但举出一些如“采采流水，蓬蓬远春”、“落花无言，人淡如菊”[19]等具象的比喻。如果不取此具象的比喻，则中国人对于抽象的风格便只剩下了“高古”、“典雅”、“清奇”、“飘逸”等一些极难以掌握其义界之确限的模糊的概念了。总之中国人忽视客观的抽象法则之建立，乃是中国文学批评缺乏理论精严之著述的一个重要原因。其次则中国人的思想乃是以儒家思想为根本的，重视实践的道德，也重视文学的实用价值。这种思想影响及于文学批评，所以衡定作品既往往以其经世致用的价值为准，而发言立论也往往喜欢尊崇往古依托圣贤以自重。这种崇古载道的文学观，无疑地乃是限制了中国文学批评理论之发展的另一个原因。而且除去儒家思想以外，另外还有两种思想也曾给予中国文学批评以极大之影响的，那就是老庄的道家思想和佛教的禅宗思想。如我们在前面所言，中国民族的思维特色原就比较偏重于具象及直观的方式，而老庄的思想则更重在爱好自然而弃绝人为，因此中国人对于文学乃形成了一种想要超越寻常智虑而纵情直观的欣赏态度。至于印度的佛学，则虽然有其因明学一派严密的理论，可是这种思辨方式与中国的民族性并不相合，所以佛学传入中国以后，给予中国影响最大的乃并非因明之学而是禅宗之学。禅宗之学自灵山会上世尊拈花迦叶微笑的传法方式开始，所倡示的乃是“不立文字”、“见性成佛”。[20]这种“直指本心”的妙悟方式，融会了道家的弃绝智虑的直观态度，于是乃形成了中国偏重主观直觉一派的印象式的批评。更加之以中国文士们对于富于诗意的简洁优美之文字的偏爱，所以在文学批评中也往往不喜欢详尽的说理，而但以寥寥几个诗意的字来把握一个诗人或一篇作品的灵魂精华之所在。这种直观印象式之批评的风习和偏爱，乃是使中国文学批评不易发展成为体系精严之论著的另一个重要的原因。

综合上面几点来看，中国文学批评的特色乃是印象的而不是思辨的，是直觉的而不是理论的，是诗歌的而不是散文的，是重点式的而不是整体式的，因此像齐梁之间刘勰的体大思精的巨制《文心雕龙》之出现，在中国文学批评史的发展上来说，实在乃是一种意外的收获。虽然一向谈文学批评的人往往把钟嵘的《诗品》与刘勰的《文心雕龙》相提并论，可是《诗品》在理论方面的建立较之《文心雕龙》乃是迥然不可同日而语的。《诗品》的品评乃是完全中国传统式的直觉的、主观的赏鉴式的批评，与沈约的《棋品》及庾肩吾的《书品》等[21]，应该同是东汉魏晋以来九品论人之风气下的产物，并没有什么谨严精密之理论建树，而《文心雕龙》则不然了。《文心雕龙》全书五十章共分上下两篇。上篇推源本末分别为有韵之文与无韵之文，标举出源流体制的重要纲领，是所谓文体论。下篇讲文章之风格与修辞谋篇等写作时所当注意之各种创作的方法，以及批评时所可资为衡量的各种标准，是所谓文术论。而以最后一章《序志》总述全书要旨，是一本具有相当理论体系的文学批评专著。郭绍虞在《中国文学批评史》中就曾经说：

《诗品》用的旧方法，只以较正确的赏鉴式批评代替那不正确的赏鉴式批评，而《文心雕龙》则提出了有关批评的理论，所以能在批评界中立一正确的标准，这是《文心雕龙》正确的地方，我们要在这方面认识《文心雕龙》。[22]

所以《文心雕龙》的出现，在中国的文学批评史上说起来乃是一部并无先例的空前巨著。而且不仅如此，在《文心雕龙》以后历唐宋以迄明清，也更无一部如此体大思精的文学批评作品可为继响，这才是一个真正值得我们反省思考的问题。关于这一点有一个近在目前却一向未被人提出的答案，那就是《文心雕龙》之所以能有如此特殊的建树，成为中国文学批评史上不仅空前而且绝后的一部巨著，乃是因为《文心雕龙》的作者刘勰，在立论的方式上，曾经自中国旧有的传统以外接受了一份外来之影响的缘故。据《梁书》卷五十《刘勰传》载云：

勰早孤，笃志好学，家贫，不婚娶，依沙门僧佑与之居处，积十余年，遂博通经论，因区别部类录而序之，今定林寺经藏，勰所定也。[23]

又云：

勰为文长于佛理，京师寺塔及名僧碑志，必请勰制文。[24]

这两段叙述乃是极可注意的，因为印度佛经中既原有其因明学一派的论理思辨的方式，刘勰又博通经典，则其思想方式之曾受此种论理思辨之影响，当然乃是极为可能的一件事。再则刘勰曾经从事于佛经的区分部类的工作，这对他立论时之整理归纳的方法当然也可能有相当的影响。这一点写中国文学批评史的人们也曾注意及之，朱东润在其《中国文学批评史大纲》中就曾经说："勰究心佛典，故长于持论。"[25]朱氏此语不能说不是有见之言，只是朱氏未曾因此而注意到外来的影响对于中国文学批评之发展上的重要性，因此朱氏所说的"究心佛典长于持论"的话也就成了只是对刘氏个人的一句批评，而忽略了其"究心佛典"之影响对于建立中国文学批评之理论的整体的重要性。而历来写文学批评史的人，也没有一个人曾经提出过中国文学批评要想建立理论体系，必须有待于外来之影响的此一严重之问题。可是事实俱在，刘勰之值得注意的成就乃是因为受了外来佛典之影响，而刘勰以后一千多年以来的中国文学批评，都只能在单篇零简的诗文书牍，及琐屑驳杂的诗话中打圈子，虽有精义却始终不能发展组织为有理论体系的著述，便也正是因为缺少了这种外来刺激之助力的缘故。了解了此一事实，则静安先生在晚清之世，因受西方思想影响而写作的文学批评，对于中国文学批评之新发展的重要性就可以想见了。

不过必须要接受外来的推理思辨方面的助力虽属事实，可是怎样去接受，如何才可以取长补短，则仍是一个极值得反省思考的问题。刘勰所受的影响毕竟仅是得自印度佛典而已，并非得自外来的某一文学批评的理论体系，所以他之胜过旧传统的一点拓展，便也只是比较有纲目条理的体系观念而已。至于谈到文学批评本身，则从现代观点来看，就会觉得他在观念方面仍有一些不尽细密明确之处。第一是专门术语的义界不够明确，因为如本文在前面所言，中国的民族性乃是重具象直觉而不重分析推理的民族，因此对于较抽象的事物，并不能如西方之从推理的思考来界定它的名义，而往往喜欢用一些意念模糊的批评术语，因而在中国文学批评述作中，便往往充满了像"道"、"性"、"气"、"风"、"骨"、"神"等一些颇具神秘性的字样来作为批评的准则。《文心雕龙》所用的批评术语便正复如此。而当其使用时，又往往因其上下行文口气之不同，而在含义方面可以发生很多不同的差别。陆侃如在其《文心雕龙术语用法举列》一文中便曾经说，"文心雕龙中有些常见的字如道、性、气、风、骨之类大都带有专门术语的性质，对于这些字的解释在学术界中曾引起不少的争论"[26]，那便正因为这些字眼都过于神秘化，在推理的思考上其意义不够明确的缘故。第二则在行文方面刘勰也和中国的一般文士一样有着对文字之美的过分的偏爱，因而遂妨碍了说理的明确。因为如本文在前面所言，中国语文的特征乃是独体单音而且疏于文法，因此在组织排列方面虽适于作声律对偶的唯美的安排，而并不适于作曲折详尽的说理，尤其因为刘勰正生当于唯美主义盛行的齐梁之际，因此在他的作品中便充满了美丽的对偶字句，有时为了字句的整齐，甚至不惜牺牲内容的完整。最明显的一个例证就是在《文心雕龙》卷四《史传篇》当他谈到《史记》一书的五种体例时，竟然为了要写成四个整齐的句子，便只写了"故本纪以述皇王，列传以总侯伯，八书以铺政体，十表以谱年爵"[27]四句极概略的叙述，一方面既把"世家"一种体例完全略而不提，而另一方面则"列传"所记的人物又本不尽属侯伯，而侯伯实在该是属于"世家"的一部分，于今刘勰乃竟只说了一句"列传以总侯伯"，便把"列传"与"世家"二体一并不求甚解地一笔带过，这在有"旧学修养”的读者而言，原可一望而知其意旨之所在，因为这原是中国文人在写作时所常用的一种手法。可是这种手法虽可用之于文学创作，却实在不宜用之于文学批评，因为创作可以求“美”为目的，所以有时不免因为要求在文字方面表现对偶整齐之美而对原来的意思有所剪裁牺牲，可是批评却实在当以求“真”为目的，一定要交待得条理明晰、观念正确。刘勰的《文心雕龙》虽然为我们留下了一个颇为宏大的体系规模，可是在文学批评的理论方面则无疑地仍有着许多不够细密精确之处，因此要想使中国文学批评在理论方面有更进一步的发展，则我们正还有待于另一次新的外来的刺激与另一条新途径的开拓，这是从中国文学批评的传统中足可得到证明的。

……

注释：

⑫ 见《尚书·舜典》，《十三经注疏》第1册，第46页。
⑬ 见《论语·阳货》，《十三经注疏》第8册，第156页。
⑭ 见《毛诗·大序》，《十三经注疏》第2册，第15页。
⑮ 见《孟子·万章下》，《十三经注疏》第8册，第188页。
⑯ 见《两汉三国文汇》，第1846页，台湾《中华丛书》1960年版。
⑰ 见《汉魏六朝百三家集·魏文帝集》，第789页，台北新兴书局1968年版《四部集要》。
⑱ 见《文心雕龙·序志》，第726页，台北明伦出版社1970年版。
⑲ 司空图：《诗品》，第24页，台北艺文印书馆《历代诗话》，全一册，1971年2月第3版。
⑳ 见《六祖法宝坛经》，第1-33页，香港商务印书馆1954年版。
㉑ 沈约《棋品》今佚，《全梁文》存《棋品序》一卷，见《全梁文》卷三十，第3123-3124页。庾肩吾《书品》见《全梁文》卷六十六，第3343-3345页，中华书局1965年版。
㉒ 郭绍虞：《中国文学批评史》，第51页，新文艺出版社1955年版。
㉓《梁书》卷五十《文学传·刘勰传》，第8-9页，毛氏汲古阁本。
㉔ 同上。
㉕ 朱东润：《中国文学批评史大纲》，第51页，台湾开明书店1968年版。
㉖ 陆侃如：《文心雕龙术语用法举例》，《文学评论》第2期，第17页。
㉗ 见《文心雕龙·史传》，第284页，台北明伦出版社1970年版。

（节选自叶嘉莹：《王国维及其文学批评》，河北教育出版社1997年版，第113-120页。）

中西诗画中所表现的空间意识

（节选）

宗白华

【导读】

“中西诗画中所表现的空间意识”是宗白华极具代表性的一篇文章，写于新中国成立前夕，后被收入《美学散步》。宗白华（1897—1986）曾用名宗之櫆，字白华、伯华，籍贯为江苏常熟虞山镇，祖籍浙江义乌。1916年8月受聘上海《时事新报》副刊《学灯》，任编辑、主编。将哲学、美学和新文艺的新鲜血液注入《学灯》，使之成为“五四”时期著名四大副刊之一。

宗白华通过“中西诗画中所表现的空间意识”，展示其美学研究的基本思路。在文章开头，宗白华陈述德国现代哲学家斯宾格勒的名著《西方之衰落》所阐明的观点，并以其为切入点来考察中国艺术，尤其是画与诗中所表现的空间意识。在文中，宗白华以西方文化艺术为参照，通过比较西方绘画中的空间意识和中国传统诗画中所蕴藏和表现出来的空间意识，凸现出中国绘画艺术中空间的独特性。从14世纪初期开始，西洋画家采用科学与数学的眼光来看待世界，在绘画时采用透视法，通过画面将空间表现出来。直到18世纪，中国开始了解西洋的透视画法，大多数中国画家对这种写实的画法并不认可，认为西方透视法原理注重写实，精确科学计算，然而没有笔法，只是一种技巧，是机械的照相，只见片面，不见全面，与真正的绘画艺术没有关系。中国画家虽然知晓西方透视画法，但是中国画推崇“以大观小之法”，由画中节奏与表情支配画面上的空间组织，构成“气韵生动、有节奏有和谐的艺术画面”。中国画家笔下的自然是“节奏化了的自然”，“有势有情的自然”，是“有声的自然”，表现出一个“音乐化的空间境界”。中国画家追求无穷空间，并“饮吸无穷于自我之中”，使得透视法至今在中国画中很难得到体现。中国画家和诗人希望达到的是“时空合一体”的艺术境界，即“一个充满音乐情趣的宇宙”。

宗白华著有《宗白华全集》及美学论文集《美学散步》、《艺境》等，在20世纪中国美学研究中，具有其原创性、深邃性和示范性，是我国现代美学的先行者和开拓者，被誉为“融贯中西艺术理论的一代美学大师”。

（白阳明）

现代德国哲学家斯宾格勒(O. Spengler)在他的名著《西方之衰落》里面曾经阐明每一种独立的文化都有它的基本象征物，具体地表象它的基本精神。在埃及是“路”，在希腊是“立体”，在近代欧洲文化是“无尽的空间”。这三种基本象征都是取之于空间境界，而它们最具体的表现是在艺术里面。埃及金字塔里的甬道、希腊的雕像、近代欧洲的最大油画家伦勃朗(Rembrandt)的风景，是我们领悟这三种文化的最深的灵魂之媒介。

我们若用这个观点来考察中国艺术，尤其是画与诗中所表现的空间意识，再拿来同别种文化作比较，是一极有趣味的事。我不揣浅陋作了以下的尝试。

西洋十四世纪文艺复兴初期油画家梵埃格(Van Eyck)的画极注重写实、精细地描写人体、画面上表现屋宇内的空间，画家用科学及数学的眼光看世界。于是透视法的知识被发挥出来，而用之于绘画。意大利的建筑家勃鲁纳莱西(Brunellec)在十五世纪的初年已经深通透视法。阿卜柏蒂在他一四三六年出版的《画论》里第一次把透视的理论发挥出来。

中国十八世纪雍正、乾隆时，名画家邹一桂对于西洋透视画法表示惊异而持不同情的态度，他说：“西洋人善勾股法，故其绘画于阴阳远近，不差锱黍，所画人物、屋树，皆有日影。其所用颜色与笔，与中华绝异。布影由阔而狭，以三角量之。画宫室于墙壁，令人几欲走进。学者能参用一二，亦其醒法。但笔法全无，虽工亦匠，故不入画品。”

邹一桂认为西洋的透视的写实的画法“笔法全无，虽工亦匠”，只是一种技巧，与真正的绘画艺术没有关系，所以“不入画品”。而能够入画品的画，即能“成画”的画，应是不采取西洋透视法的立场，而采沈括所说的“以大观小之法”。

早在宋代一位博学家沈括在他名著《梦溪笔谈》里就曾讥评大画家李成采用透视立场“仰画飞檐”，而主张“以大观小之法”。他说：“李成画山上亭馆不应见中庭及巷中事。若人在东立，则山西便合是远境。人在西立，则山东却合是远境。似此如何成画？李君盖不知以大观小之法，其间折高、折远，自有妙理，岂在掀屋角也？”

沈括以为画家画山水，并非如常人站在平地上在一个固定的地点，仰首看山；而是用心灵的眼，笼罩全景，从全体来看部分，“以大观小”。把全部景界组织成一幅气韵生动、有节奏有和谐的艺术画面，不是机械的照相。这画面上的空间组织，是受着画中全部节奏及表情所支配。“其间折高折远，自有妙理”。这就是说须服从艺术上的构图原理，而不是服从科学上算学的透视法原理。他并且以为那种依据透视法的看法只能看见片面，看不到全面，所以不能成画。他说“似此如何成画”？他若是生在今日，简直会不承认西洋传统的画是画，岂不有趣？

这正可以拿奥国近代艺术学者芮格(Riegl)所主张的“艺术意志说”来解释。中国画家并不是不晓得透视的看法，而是他的“艺术意志”不愿在画面上表现透视看法，只摄取一个角度，而采取了“以大观小”的看法，从全面节奏来决定各部分、组织各部分。中国画法六法上所说的“经营位置”，不是依据透视原理，而是“折高折远自有妙理”。全幅画面所表现的空间意识，是大自然的全面节奏与和谐。画家的眼睛不是从固定角度集中于一个透视的焦点，而是流动着飘瞥上下四方，一目千里，把握全境的阴阳开阖、高下起伏的节奏。中国最大诗人杜甫有两句诗表出这空、时意识说：“乾坤万里眼，时序百年心。”《中庸》上也曾说：“诗云鸢飞戾天，鱼跃于渊，言其上下察也。”

中国最早的山水画家六朝刘宋时的宗炳(公元五世纪)曾在他的《画山水序》里说山水画家的事务是:

身所盘桓,目所绸缪。
以形写形,以色貌色。

画家以流盼的眼光绸缪于身所盘桓的形形色色。所看的不是一个透视的焦点,所采的不是一个固定的立场,所画出来的是具有音乐的节奏与和谐的境界。所以宗炳把他画的山水悬在壁上,对着弹琴,他说:

抚琴动操,欲令众山皆响!

山水对他表现一个音乐的境界,就如他的同时的前辈那位大诗人音乐家嵇康,也是拿音乐的心灵去领悟宇宙、领悟"道"。嵇康有名句云:

目送归鸿,手挥五弦。
俯仰自得,游心太玄。

中国诗人、画家确是用"俯仰自得"的精神来欣赏宇宙,而跃入大自然的节奏里去"游心太玄"。晋代大诗人陶渊明也有诗云:"俯仰终宇宙,不乐复何如!"

用心灵的俯仰的眼睛来看空间万象,我们的诗和画中所表现的空间意识,不是像那代表希腊空间感觉的有轮廓的立体雕像,不是像那表现埃及空间感的墓中的直线甬道,也不是那代表近代欧洲精神的伦勃朗的油画中渺茫无际追寻无着的深空,而是"俯仰自得"的节奏化的音乐化了的中国人的宇宙感。

《易经》上说:"无往不复,天地际也。"这正是中国人的空间意识!

这种空间意识是音乐性的(不是科学的算学的建筑性的)。它不是用几何、三角测算来的,而是由音乐舞蹈体验来的。中国古代的所渭"乐",是包括着舞的。所以唐代大画家吴道子请裴将军舞剑以助壮气。

宋郭若虚《图画见闻志》上说:

唐开元中,将军裴旻居丧,诣吴道子,请于东都天宫寺画神鬼数壁,以资冥助。道子答曰:"吾画笔久废,若将军有意,为吾缠结,舞剑一曲,庶因猛厉,以通幽冥!"旻于是脱去缞服,若常时装束,走马如飞,左旋右转,掷剑入云,高数十丈,若电光下射。旻引手执鞘承之,剑透室而入。观者数千人,无不惊栗。遭子于是援毫图壁,飒然风起,为天下之壮观。道子平生绘事,得意无出于此。

与吴道于同时的大书家张旭也因观公孙大娘的剑器舞而书法大进。宋朝书家雷简夫因听着嘉陵江的涛声而引起写字的灵感。雷简夫说:"余偶昼卧,闻江涨瀑声。想波涛翻翻，迅駃掀撞，高下蹙逐奔去之状，无物可寄其情，遽起作书，则心中之想尽在笔下矣！”

节奏化了的自然，可以由中国书法艺术表达出来，就同音乐舞蹈一样。而中国画家所画的自然也就是这音乐境界。他的空间意识和空间表现就是“无往不复的天地之际”。不是由几何、三角所构成的西洋的透视学的空间，而是阴阳明暗高下起伏所构成的节奏化了的空间。董其昌说：“远山一起一伏则有势，疏林或高或下则有情，此画之诀也。”

有势有情的自然是有声的自然。中国古代哲人曾以音乐的十二律配合一年十二月节季的循环。《吕氏春秋·大乐》篇说：“万物所出，造于太一，化于阴阳。萌芽始震，凝寒以形。形体有处，莫不有声。声出于和，和出于适。和适，先王定乐，由此而生。”唐代诗人韦应物有诗云：

万物自生听，大空恒寂寥。

唐诗人沈佺期的《范山人画山水歌》云(见佩文斋书画谱)：“山峥嵘，水泓澄。漫漫汗汗一笔耕。一草一木栖神明。忽如空中有物，物中有声。复如远道望乡客，梦绕山川身不行！”这是赞美范山人所画的山水好像空中的乐奏，表现一个音乐化的空间境界。宋代大批评家严羽在他的《沧浪诗话》里说唐诗人的诗中境界：“如空中之音，相中之色，水中之月，镜中之像，言有尽而意无穷。”西人约柏特(Joubert)也说：“佳诗如物之有香，空之有音，纯乎气息。”又说：“诗中妙境，每字能如弦上之音，空外余波，袅袅不绝。”(据钱锺书译)

这种诗境界，中国画家则表之于山水画中。苏东坡论唐代大画家兼诗人王维说：“味摩诘之诗，诗中有画。观摩诘之画，画中有诗。”

王维的画我们现在不容易看到(传世的有两三幅)。我们可以从诗中看他画境，却发现他里面的空间表现与后来中国山水画的特点一致！

王维的辋川诗有一绝句云：

北垞湖水北，杂树映朱栏，
逶迤南川水，明灭青林端。

在西洋画上有画大树参天者，则树外人家及远山流水必在地平线上缩短缩小，合乎透视 法。而此处南川水却明灭于青林之端，不向下而向上，不向远而向近。和青林朱栏构成一片平面。而中国山水画家却取此同样的看法写之于画面。使西人诧中国画家不识透视法。然而这种看法是中国诗中的通例，如：

“暗水流花径，春星带草堂。”
“卷帘唯白水，隐几亦青山。”
“白波吹粉壁，青嶂插雕梁。”
——以上[唐]杜甫

"天回北斗挂西楼。"

"檐飞宛溪水，窗落敬亭云。"

——以上[唐]李白

"水国舟中市，山桥树杪行。"

——[唐]王维

"窗影摇群动，墙阴载一峰。"

——[唐]岑参

"秋景墙头数点山。"

——[唐]刘禹锡

"窗前远岫悬生碧，帘外残霞挂熟红。"

——[唐] 罗虬

"树杪玉堂悬。"

——[唐]杜审言

"江上晴楼翠霭开，满帘春水满窗山。"

——[唐]李群玉

"碧松梢外挂青天。"

——[唐]杜牧

玉堂坚重而悬之于树杪，这是画境的平面化。青天悠远而挂之于松梢，这已经不止于世界的平面化，而是移远就近了。这不是西洋精神的追求无穷，而是饮吸无穷于自我之中！孟子曰："万物皆备于我矣，反身而诚，乐莫大焉。"宋代哲学家邵雍于所居作便坐，曰安乐窝，两旁开窗曰日月牖。正如杜甫诗云：

山河扶绣户，日月近雕梁。

深广无穷的宇宙来亲近我，扶持我，无庸我去争取那无穷的空间，像浮士德那样野心勃勃，彷徨不安。

中国人对无穷空间这种特异的态度，阻碍中国人去发明透视法。而且使中国画至今避用透视法。我们再在中国诗中征引那饮吸无穷空时于自我，网罗山川大地于门户的例证：

"云生梁栋间，风出窗户里。"

——[东晋] 郭璞

"绣甍结飞霞，璇题纳明月。"

——[六朝] 鲍照

"窗中列远岫，庭际俯乔林。"

——[六朝] 谢朓

"栋里归白云，窗外落晖红。"

——[六朝] 阴铿

"画栋朝飞南浦云，珠帘暮卷西山雨。"

——[初唐] 王勃

"窗含西岭千秋雪，门泊东吴万里船。"

——[唐] 杜甫

"天入沧浪一钓舟。"

——[唐] 杜甫

"欲回天地入扁舟。"

——[唐] 李商隐

"大壑随阶转，群山入户登。"

——[唐] 王维

"隔窗云雾生衣上，卷幔山泉入镜中。"

——[唐] 王维

"山月临窗近，天河入户低。"

——[唐] 沈佺期

"山翠万重当槛出，水光千里抱城来。"

——[唐] 许浑

"三峡江声流笔底，六朝帆影落樽前。"

"山随宴坐图画出，水作夜窗风雨来。"

——[宋]米芾

"一水护田将绿绕，两山排闼送青来。"

——[宋]王安石

"满眼长江水，苍然何郡山？"

"向来万里急，今在一窗间。"

——[宋]陈简斋

"江山重复争供眼，风雨纵横乱入楼。"

——[宋]陆放翁

"水光山色与人亲。"

——[宋]李清照

"帆影多从窗隙过，溪光合向镜中看。"

——[清]叶令仪

"云随一磬出林杪，窗放群山到榻前。"

——[清]谭嗣同

而明朝诗人陈眉公的含晖楼诗(咏日光)云："朝挂扶桑枝，暮浴咸池水，灵光满大千，半在小楼里。"更能写出万物皆备于我的光明俊伟的气象。但早在这些诗人以前，晋宋的大诗人谢灵运(他是中国第一个写纯山水诗的)已经在他的《山居赋》里写出这网罗天地于门户，饮吸山川于胸怀的空间意识。中国诗人多爱从窗户庭阶，词人尤爱从帘、屏、栏干、镜以吐纳世界景物。我们有"天地为庐"的宇宙观。老子曰："不出户，知天下。不窥牖，见天道。”庄子曰：“瞻彼阙者，虚室生白。”孔子曰：“谁能出不由户，何莫由斯道也”？中国这种移远就近，由近知远的空间意识，已经成为我们宇宙观的特色了。谢灵运《山居赋》里说：

> 抗北顶以葺馆，瞰南峰以启轩，
> 罗曾崖于户里，列镜澜于窗前。
> 因丹霞以赪楣，附碧云以翠椽。
>
> ——《宋书·谢灵运传》

六朝刘义庆的《世说新语》载：

> 简文帝(东晋)入华林园，顾谓左右曰：“会心处不必在远，翳然林木，便自有濠濮间想也。觉鸟兽禽鱼，自来亲人！”

晋代是中国山水情绪开始与发达时代。阮籍登临山水，尽日忘归。王羲之既去官，游名山，泛沧海，叹曰：“我卒当以乐死！”山水诗有了极高的造诣(谢灵运、陶渊明、谢朓等)，山水画开始奠基。但是顾恺之、宗炳、王微已经显示出中国空间意识的特质了。宗炳主张“身所盘桓，目所绸缪，以形写形，以色貌色。”王微主张“以一管之笔拟太虚之体”。而人们遂能“以大观小”又能“小中见大”。人们把大自然吸收到庭户内。庭园艺术发达极高。庭园中罗列峰峦湖沼，俨然一个小天地。后来宋僧道灿的重阳诗句：“天地一东篱，万古一重久。”正写出这境界。而唐诗人孟郊更歌唱这天地反映到我的胸中，艺术的形象是由我裁成的，他唱道：

> 天地入胸臆，吁嗟生风雷。
> 文章得其微，物象由我裁！

东晋陶渊明则从他的庭园悠然窥见大宇宙的生气与节奏而证悟到忘言之境。他的《饮酒》诗云：

> 结庐在人境，而无车马喧。
> 问君何能尔，心远地自偏。
> 采菊东篱下，悠然见南山。
> 山气日夕佳，飞鸟相与还。
> 此中有真味，欲辨已忘言！

中国人的宇宙概念本与庐舍有关。“宇”是屋宇，“宙”是由“宇”中出入往来。中国古代农人的农舍就是他的世界。他们从屋宇得到空间观念。从“日出而作，日入而息”(击壤歌)，由宇中出入而得到时间观念。空间、时间合成他的宇宙而安顿着他的生活。他的生活是从容的，是有节奏的。对于他空间与时间是不能分割的。春夏秋冬配合着东南西北。这个意识表现在秦汉的哲学思想里。时间的节奏(一岁十二月二十四节)率领着空间方位(东南西北等)以构成我们的宇宙。所以我们的空间感觉随着我们的时间感觉而节奏化了、音乐化了！画家在画面所欲表现的不只是一个建筑意味的空间“宇”而须同时具有音乐意味的时间节奏“宙”。一个充满音乐情趣的宇宙(时空合一体)是中国画家、诗人的艺术境界。画家、诗人对这个宇宙的态度是象宗炳所说的“身所盘桓，目所绸缪，以形写形，以色貌色。”六朝刘勰在他的名著《文心雕龙》里也说到诗人对于万物是：

“目既往还，心亦吐纳。……情往似赠，兴味如答。”

“目所绸缪”的空间景是不采取西洋透视看法集合于一个焦点，而采取数层视点以构成节奏化的空间。这就是中国画家的“三远”之说。“目既往还”的空间景是《易经》所说“无往不复，天地际也。”我们再分别论之。

……

(节选自宗白华：《中西诗画中所表现的空间意识》,《宗白华全集》(第2卷)，安徽教育出版社1994年版，第420-441页。)

中国诗与中国画

（节选）

钱锺书

【导读】

钱锺书先生这篇关于中国诗和中国画的长文最开始完成于1939年，只有九千多字，而到1983年被收入《七缀集》时，经过反复修改，已经有两万多字。文章开宗明义表明其宗旨是厘清中国传统文艺批评中关于中国诗和中国画有失偏颇的认识，从追溯其知识产生的渊源到其形成状况及问题所在均采用大量例证来一一说明，旁征博引，逻辑严谨，其科学的研究方法和严谨的治学态度为从事文艺批评的学者树立了榜样。

中国诗和中国画长久以来被认为是“诗原如画”、“诗画本一律”，且无论是国内还是国外，“无声诗”即“有形诗”，“有声画”即“无形画”，两者的对比和西洋传统的诗、画对比用意都是相似的，“诗、画是孪生姊妹”的说法是西方文艺理论千余年来的奠基石。旧传统有惰性，它成为习惯而把常然作为当然和必然，所以新传统的批评家就应该对旧传统的作品有全面的认识，中国旧诗和旧画并非如我们常说的那样融和无间，而是有矛盾的。

文章以中国传统文艺批评中的旧诗和旧画的正统——“南北宗”的讨论作为切入点，指出中国传统文艺批评中对旧诗和旧画的评价标准是不一样的。传统观点认为正宗中国旧诗和中国旧画都属“南宗”，这种说法非常牵强，类似于把莎翁名剧和伦勃朗画作同归类于巴罗克艺术一样。中国画史上最具有代表性的流派属“南宗文人画”的画作，这一点董其昌的《容台别集》就已提到，但夏敬观先生从南人北人作者籍贯着手质疑画作南北之分。把南北两个地域和两种思想方法和学风联系早从六朝起就已有了，禅宗分南北之说，唐朝不过延承了这一说法，“南宗画”代表一种简约的风格，绘画笔墨“从简”、“用减”，与“南人学问”的“清通简要”是一致的，对“南宗画”的定义超越了画家籍贯，揭示了画风的本质，并非“无所取义”。

而旧诗里的“南宗”——“神韵”派却不能代表中国旧诗作风。虽然西洋批评家认为中国的古诗“空灵”、“清淡”，含蓄简约，这种评价并不中肯，中国古诗在他们看来多大同小异。而事实上，中国旧诗并非“灰黯诗歌”，神韵诗在中国旧诗传统中并不如“南宗画派”在中国旧画中的地位，不占有统治地位。南宗画派的创始人王维也是神韵诗的大师，但与他在旧画传统中排第一的画作相比较，他的诗作却不能算第一。神韵诗虽然在明末陆时雍的宣传和清初王士祯的鼓动下形成一定风气，但持续时间较短。所以中国传统文艺批评对诗和画有不同的标准；评画时赏识王世贞所谓"虚"以及与此相联系的风格，而评诗时却赏识"实"以及与此相联系的风格。这种分歧需要我们承认，并且去认真探讨其原因。

（黄惠）

一

这不是一篇文艺批评，而是文艺批评史上一个问题的澄清。它并不对中国旧诗和旧画试作任何评价，而只是阐明中国传统批评对于诗和画的比较估价。

当然，文艺批评史很可能成为一门自给自足的学问，学者们要集中心力，保卫专题研究的纯粹性，把批评史上涉及的文艺作品，也作为干扰物而排除，不去理会，也不能鉴别。不过，批评史的研究，归根到底，还是为了批评。我们要了解和评判一个作者，也该知道他那时代对于他那一类作品的意见，这些意见就是后世文艺批评史的材料，也是当时一种文艺风气的表示。一个艺术家总在某些社会条件下创作，也总在某种文艺风气里创作。这个风气影响到他对题材、体裁、风格的去取，给予他以机会，同时也限制了他的范围。就是抗拒或背弃这个风气的人也受到它负面的支配，因为他不得不另出手眼来逃避或矫正他所厌恶的风气。正像列许登堡所说，模仿有正有负，"反其道以行也是一种模仿"(Grade das Gegenthiel tun ist auch eine nachahmung)；圣佩韦也说，尽管一个人要推开自己所处的时代，仍然和他接触，而且接触得很着实(on touché encore a son temps, et tres fort, meme quand on le repousse)①。所以，风气是创作里的潜势力，是作品的背景，而从作品本身不一定看得清楚。我们阅读当时人所信奉的理论，看他们对具体作品的褒贬好恶，树立什么标准，提出什么要求，就容易了解作者周遭的风气究竟怎么一回事，好比从飞沙、麦浪、波纹里看出了风的姿态。

一时期的风气经过长时期而能持续，没有根本的变动，那就是传统。传统有惰性，不肯变，而事物的演化又迫使它以变应变，于是产生了一个相反相成的现象。传统不肯变，因此惰性形成习惯，习惯升为规律，把常然作为当然和必然。传统也有弹性，因而不得不变，不断的相机破例，实际上做出种种妥协，来迁就演变的事物。批评史上这类权宜应变的现象，有人曾嘲笑为"文艺里的两面派假正经"(ipocrsia letteraria)②，表示传统并不呆板，而具有相当灵活的机会主义。它一方面把规律定得严，抑遏新风气的产生；而另一方

---

① 列许登堡(C. C. Lichtenberg)《隽语·散文·书信》(*Aphorismen · Essays · Bricfe*)，巴德(K. Batt)编本70页。圣佩韦(Sainte-Beuve)《我的毒素》(*Mes Poisons*)，季洛(V. Giraud)编本197页；他这几句话也在《月曜日文谈》开卷第一篇里早就说过(causeries du Iundi, t. I, "M. Saint-Mare Girardin", PP: 15-6)。

② 克罗齐(Croce)《美学》(*Estetica*)，第10版，495页。

面把规律解释得宽，可以收容新风气，免于因对抗而地位摇动。它也颇有外交老手的“富于弹性的坚定”(elastic or flexible rigidity)那种味道。传统愈悠久，妥协愈多，愈不肯变，变的需要愈迫切。于是不再能委屈求全，旧传统和新风气破裂而被它破坏，新风气的代兴也常有一个相反相成的表现。它一方面强调自己是崭新的东西，和不相容的原有传统立异；而另一方面更要表示自己大有来头，非同小可，向古代也找一个传统作为渊源所自。例如西方十七、八世纪批评家要把新兴的长篇散文小说遥承古希腊、罗马的史诗①；圣佩韦认为当时法国的浪漫诗派蜕变于法国十六世纪的诗歌。中国也常有相类似的努力。明清批评家把《水浒》、《儒林外史》等白话小说和《史记》挂钩；我们自己学生时代就看到提倡“中国文学改良”的学者煞费心机写了上溯古代的《中国白话文学史》，又看到白话散文家在讲《新闻学源流》时，远追明代“公安”、“竟陵”两派。这种事后追认先驱(préfiguration rétro active)的事例②，仿佛野孩子认父母，暴发户造家谱，或封建皇朝的大官僚诰赠三代祖宗，在文学史上数见不鲜。它会影响创作，使新作品从自发的天真转为自觉的有教养、有师法；它也改造传统，使旧作品产生新意义，沾上新气息，增添新价值。

一个传统破坏了，新风气成为新传统，新传统里的批评家对与旧传统的作品能有比较全面的认识，作比较客观地估计；因为他具有局外人的冷静和超脱，所谓“当局称迷，傍观见审”(元行冲《释疑》)，而旧传统里的批评家就像“不识庐山真面目，只缘身在此山中”(苏轼《题西林壁》)。除旧布新也促进了人类的集体健忘，一种健康的遗忘，千头万绪简化为二三大事，留存在记忆中，节省了不少心力。旧传统里若干复杂问题，新的批评家也许并非不屑注意，而是根本就没想到它们一度存在过。他的眼界空阔，没有枝节凌乱的障碍物来扰乱视线；比起他这样高瞰远瞩，旧的批评家未免见树不见林了。不过，无独必有偶，另一个偏差是见林不见树。局外人也就是门外汉，他的意见，仿佛清官判断家务事，有条有理，而对于委屈私情，终不能体贴入微。一个社会、一个时代各有语言天地，各行各业以至于一家一户也都有它的语言天地，所谓“此中人语”。譬如乡亲叙旧、老友谈往、两口子讲体己、同业公议、专家讨论等等，圈外人或外行人听来，往往不甚了了。缘故是：在这种谈话里，不仅有术语、私房话以至“黑话”，而且由于同伙们相知深切，

① 梅(G. May)《小说在十八世纪的困境》(*Le Dilemme du roman au 18e sieècle*)，18-9 页，33 页。

② 这是柏格森论古典主义文学是否有浪漫主义成分所用名词，见《思想与流动》(*La Pensee et le mouvant*)，23-4 页。参看尼采论后起的艺术大师不由自主地(un willkürlich)改变了前人艺术作品的评价和意义(Mons chliches, Allzumenschliches, II. i. P147, Werke, hrsg. K. Sehlechta, Bd I, S. 793)，艾略脱论新起作品能改换(alter)传统作品的位置(T. S. Eliot: “Tradition and Indidvidual Talent”, Selected Prose. ed. J. Hayward, Penguin, P. 23)。艾略脱那节话是一般人引用惯的，但不如柏格森讲得透彻。博尔赫斯论卡夫卡的“先驱者”时说：“事实上，每个作家都创造他的先驱者“(Elhecho es que cada escritor crea a sus Precursores”, —J. L. Borges: “Kafka y sus precursores”, Otras Inquisiciones, Alianza Emece, 1979, p. 109)，正是柏格森的用意。博尔赫斯列举卡夫卡的“先驱者”，第二名是作《获麟解》的韩愈；这和卡奈蒂(Elias canetti)《另一审判》(*Der andere Prozess*)里赞美卡夫卡是唯一具有中国精神的近代西方作家，都未必是咱们乐意听的好消息，然而必将成为研究者捕风捉影的好题目。

还隐伏着许多中世纪经院哲学所谓彼此不言而喻的“假定”(suppositio)①，旁人难于意会。释诛宏《竹窗随笔》论禅宗问答：“譬之二同邑人，千里久别，忽然邂逅，相对作乡语隐语，旁人听之，无义无味。”这其实是生活里的平常情况，只是“听之无意无味”的程度随人随事不同。批评家对旧传统或风气不很认识，就可能“说外行话”，曲解附会。举一个文评史上的惯例罢。

我们常听说中国古代文评里有对立的两派，一派要“载道”，一派要“言志”。事实上，在中国旧传统里，“文以载道”和“诗以言志”主要是规定个别文体的职能，并非概括“文学”的界说。“文”常指散文或“古文”而言，以区别于“诗”、“词”。这两句话看来针锋相对，实则水米无干，好比说“他去北京”、“她回上海”，或者羽翼相辅，好比说“早点是稀饭”、“午餐是面”。因此，同一个作家可以“文载道”，以“诗言志”，以“诗余”的词来“言”诗里说不出口的“志”。这些文体仿佛台阶或梯级，是平行而不平等的，“文”的等级最高。西方文艺理论常识输入以后，我们很容易把“文”一律理解为广义上的“文学”，把“诗”认为文学创作精华的同义词。于是那两句老话仿佛“顿顿都喝稀饭”和“一日三餐全吃面”，或“两口都上北京”和“双双同去上海”，变成相互排除的命题了。传统文评里有它的矛盾，但是这两句不能算是矛盾的口号。对传统不够理解，就发生了这个矛盾的错觉。当然，相反的，也会发生统一的错觉，譬如我们常听说中国诗和中国画是融合一致的。

二

诗和画号称姊妹艺术。有人进一步认为它们不但是姊妹，还是孪生姊妹。唐人只说：“书画异名而同体。”(张彦远《历代名画记》卷一《叙画之源流》)。自宋以后，大家都把诗和画说成仿佛是异体而同貌。郭熙《林泉高致》第二篇《画意》：“更如前人言：‘诗是无形画，画是有形诗。’哲人多谈此言，吾人所师。”冯应榴《苏诗合注》卷五十《韩干马》：“少陵翰墨无形画，韩干丹青不语诗。”孔武仲《宗伯集》卷一《东坡居士画怪石赋》：“文者无形之画，画者有形之文，二者异迹而同趣。”张舜民《画墁集》卷一《跋百之诗话》：“诗是无形画，画是有形诗。”释德洪觉范《石门文字禅》卷八：《宋迪作八景绝妙，人谓之“无声句”。演上人戏余曰：“道人能作‘有声画’乎？因为之各赋一首”。岳珂《宝真斋法书赞》卷一三《薛道祖百石潭诗帖》：“‘画’以‘有声’著，‘诗’以‘无声’名。‘有声’者、道祖之所已知，‘无声’者，道祖之所欲为而未能者也。”《宋诗纪事》卷五九钱鍪《次袁尚书巫山诗》：“终朝诵公有声画，却来看此无声诗”；《全宋词》三四五三页陈德武《望海潮》：“对无声诗，哦有声画，仪行已见端倪。”这两处的“有声画”指诗，而“无声诗”指景物，由画引申，指入画的真山真水。两者只举一端，像黄庭坚《次韵子瞻，子由题憩寂图》：“李侯有句不肯吐，潜墨写作无声诗。”米友仁《自题山水》：“古人作语咏不得，我寓无声缣楮间。”周孚《题所画梅竹》：“东坡戏作有声画，叹息何人为赏音。”例子更多。舒岳祥《阆风集》卷六《和正仲送达善归钱塘》：“好诗甚似无形画，昏眼羞同没字碑。”求对仗的平仄匀

① 艾尔德曼(K. O. Erdmann)《文字的意义》(*Die Bedeutung des Wortes*)，第3版，66-9(ein Kapitel Scholastik)。

称，换“有”字为“无”字，出了毛病。“碑”照例有“字”，“没字碑”是自身矛盾语，恰好用作比喻，去嘲笑目不识丁；“画”压根儿“无声”，说“好诗似画”，词义具足，所添“无声”两字就不免修辞学所谓“赘余的形容”(redundant epithet)了①。南宋孙绍远搜罗唐以来的题画诗，编为《声画集》；宋末名画家杨公远自编诗集《野趣有声画》，诗人吴龙翰作序，说：“画难画之景，以诗凑成；吟难吟之诗，以画补足。”(曹庭栋《宋百家诗存卷一九》)从那两部书中，可以推想这两部书的流行。

“无声诗”即“有形诗”和“有声画”即“无形画”的对比，和西洋传统的诗画对比，用意差不多。古希腊诗人(Simonides of Ceos)早说：“画为不语诗，诗是能言画。”②嫁名于西塞罗的一部修辞学里，论“互换句法”(commutatio)第四例就是：“正如诗是说话的画，画该是静默的诗。”(Item poema loquens pictura，pictura tacitum poema debet esse)③达·芬奇干脆说画是，“嘴巴哑的诗”(una poesia muta)，而诗是“眼睛瞎的画”(una pittura cieca)④。莱辛在他反对“诗画一律”的名著里，引了“那个希腊伏尔太的使人眼花缭乱的对照”(die blendende Antithese des griechischen Voltaire)，也正是那句希腊古诗，顺手又把它所敌视的伏尔太扫上一笔⑤。“不语诗”、“能言画”是同一回事，因为“声”在这里不指音响，而指说话，就像旧小说、旧戏曲里“不则(作)声”、“禁(噤)声！”的那个“声”字。古罗马诗人霍拉斯的名句：“诗亦犹画”(ut pictura poesis erit)，经后人断章取义，理解作“诗原通画”⑥，仿佛苏轼《书鄢陵王主簿折枝》所谓：“诗画本一律。”诗、画作为孪生姊妹是西方古代文艺理论的一块奠基石，也就是莱辛所要扫除的一块绊脚石，因为由他看来，诗、画各有各的面貌衣饰，是“绝不争风吃醋的姊妹”(keine eifersüchtige Schwester)⑦。

诗和画既然同是艺术，应该有共同性；它们并非同一门艺术，又应该各具特殊性。它们的性能和领域的异同，是美学上的重要理论问题。我想探讨的，只是历史上具体的文艺鉴赏和评判。我们常听人有声有势地说：中国旧诗和中国旧画有同样的风格，体现同样的艺术境界。那句话是什么意思？这个意思能不能在文艺批评史里证实？

---

① 参看昆体良(Quintilian)《修词原理》(*Institutio Oratoria*)第8卷第6章第40节，《罗勃(Loeb)古典丛书》本第3册324页。

② 艾德门茨(J. M. Edmonds)《希腊抒情诗》(*Lyra Graeca*)，罗勃本第2册258页。参看哈格斯特勒姆(Jean H. Hagatrum)《姊妹艺术》(*The Sister Arts*)10又58页。

③ 西塞罗《修词学》(*Rhetoriea ad Herennium*)第4卷第28章，罗勃本326页。

④ 达·芬奇《画论》(*Trattato dellla Pittura*)第16章，米兰奈西(G. Milanesi)编本12页。近代一个意大利作家对这句话承而又转：“这些画家的绘画不但是无言语的诗歌而且是无声响的音乐”(La lor Pittura non e soitan to una Poesia muta, ma e anche una musica muta. —D' Annunzio, HFuoco, ed. Fratelli Treves, P. 107)。这也透露，浪漫主义运动以来，音乐在艺术里的地位高升在诗歌之上了。参看纪德(A. Gide)1926年5月说批评家(l' abbé Brémond 把“诗如画”(ut Pictura Poesis)的标准变为“诗如乐”(ut musica Poesis)，《日记、回忆》(*Journal. Souvenirs*)，《七星丛书》(*Ie Pleiade*)本1004页。

⑤ 莱辛《拉奥孔》(*Laokoon*)《前言》(*Vorrede*)，李拉(P. Rilla)编《莱辛集》第5册10页。

⑥ 霍拉斯《论诗代简》(*Ars poetica*)361行，参看《姊妹艺术》26，37，59-61页。

⑦ 《拉奥孔》第8章，82页。

三

那句在国会展览会上、国画史等著作里说惯、听惯、看惯的话，和“诗原通画”、“诗画一律”，意义大不相同。“诗原通画”、“诗画一律”是树立一条原理，而那句话只是叙述一个事实。前者认为：诗和画的根本性质是一样的；后者认为：在中国传统里，最标准的诗风和最标准的画风是一致的。假使前者成立，也许可以解释后者这个事实；假使后者成立，却还不够证明前者那条原理。对于前者，要求它言之成理，免于牵强理论；对于后者，要求它言之有物，免于歪曲历史。说破了，那句客套话的意思就是：中国旧诗和中国旧画同属于所谓的“南宗”，正好比西洋文艺史家说，莎士比亚的戏剧和鲁本斯德(Rubens)、雷姆勃朗德(Rembrandt)的绘画同属于“奇崛派”(Barock)①。

中国画史上最具有代表性、最主要的流派是“南宗”。董其昌《容台别集》卷四有一节讲得极清楚：“禅家有南北二宗，唐时始分。画之南北二宗，亦唐时分也，但其人非南北耳。北宗则李思训父子着色山水，流传而为宋之赵干、赵伯驹、伯骕以至马、夏辈。南宗则王摩诘始用渲淡，一变钩斫之法，其传为张璪、荆、关、董巨、郭忠恕、米家父子以至元之四大家；亦如六祖之后，有马驹、云门、临济儿孙之盛，而北宗微矣。要之摩诘所谓‘云峰石迹，迥出天机，笔意纵横，参乎造化’者，东坡赞吴道子、王维画壁亦云：‘吾于维也无间然’，知言哉！”(参看同卷《文人画自王维始》一条，叙述更详)。董氏同乡书画家莫是龙《画说》十五条里有一条，字句全通；董氏同乡好友陈继儒《偃曝余谈》卷下有论旨相类的一条，坦白地把李思训、王维分别比为“禅家”北宗的神秀和南宗的惠能。南、北画家的区别，也可用陈氏推尊的王世贞的话来概括，《弇州四部稿》卷一五四《艺苑卮言·附录》卷三：“吴、李以前画家，实而尽俗；荆、关以后画家，雅而太虚。今雅道尚存，实德则病。”这是明人鉴赏的常谈，清人承袭了，例如厉鹗说：“尝以词譬之画，画家以南宗胜北宗。稼轩、后村诸人，词之北宗；清真、白石诸人，词之南宗也”(《樊榭山房文集》卷四《张今涪红螺词序》)。清人论书法，把南、北宗的概念来判别流派，而且应用到董其昌本人身上：“太仆[归有光]文章宗伯[董]字，正如得髓自南宗”(姚鼐《惜抱轩诗集》卷八《论书绝句》三)；“尝与钱梅溪(泳)论书，画派分南、北宗，书家亦分南、北。如颜、柳一派，类推至于吾家文敏[张照]，是为北宗；褚、虞一派，类推至于香光，是为南宗”(张祥河《关陇舆中偶忆编》)。近年来有人反对董其昌的分类，夏敬观先生《忍古楼画说》就批评说：“余考宋元以前论画书，未见有‘南、北宗’之说。夫南北画派诚有别，然必剿袭禅宗之名以名之，而‘南’、‘北’字均无所取义，盖非通人所为。李思训父子为唐宗室，王维太原祁人，均北人也。只张璪唐人，余皆宋人，安见唐时亦分南北乎？”

画派分南北和画家是南人、北人的疑问，不难回答。某一地域的专称引申而为某一属性的通称，是语言里的惯常现象。譬如汉、魏的“齐气”，六朝的“楚子”，宋的“胡言”，明的“苏意”；“齐气”、“楚子”不限于“齐”人、“楚”人，苏州以外的人也常有“苏意”，汉族并非不许或不会“胡说”、“胡闹”。杨万里说：“诗‘江西’也，非人皆江西也”(《诚斋

① 沃尔则尔(O. Walzel)《各门艺术的相互阐发》(*Wechselseitige Erhellung der Kunste*)95页。

集》卷七九《〈江西宗派诗序〉》)；家铉翁说："奋乎齐鲁汴洛之间者，固中州人物也。亦有生于四方，奋与遐外，而道学文章为世所宗工，德业被于海内，虽谓之中州人物可也"(《元文类》卷三八家铉翁《题中州诗集后》，四库辑本《则堂集》漏收)；更是文学流派名称的好例子。拘泥着地图、郡县志，太死心眼儿了。画派在"唐时"虽然未"分南北"，但唐人诗文评早借用了"南北宗"的概念。遍照金刚《文镜秘府论》南卷《论文意》："荀孟传与司马迁，司马迁传于贾谊……乃知司马迁为北宗，贾生为南宗，从此分焉。"这位日本和尚居然讲司马迁而连《史记》都没看，不知道有《屈原贾生列传》，但他也显然道听途说，拣得了唐人的一些谈屑。伪托贾岛撰的《二南密旨》，据《四库全书总目》卷一九七的提要："以《召南》'林又朴遬，野有死鹿'句，及鲍照'申黜褒女进，班去赵姬升'句，钱起'竹怜新雨后，山爱夕阳时'，句，为南宗。以《卫风》'我心匪石，不可转也'句，左思'吾爱段干木，偃息藩魏君'句，卢纶诗'谁知樵子径，得到葛洪家'句，为北宗。"论画"剿袭禅宗之名"，或许"无所取义"，也还可以说有所借鉴。不过，真是"无所取义"么?

把"南"、"北"两个地域和两种思想方法或学风联系，早已见于六朝，唐代禅宗区别南、北，恰恰符合或沿承了六朝古说①。事实上，《礼记·中庸》说"南方之强"息事宁人，"不报无道"，不同于"北方之强"好勇斗狠，"死而不厌"，也就是把退敛和肆纵分别为"南"和"北"的特征。《世说·文学》第四记褚季野云："北人学问，渊综广博"，孙安国答："南人学问，清通简要"，支道林曰："圣贤固所忘言。自中人以还，北人看书如显处视月，南人看书如牖中窥日。"历来引用的人只知道"牖中窥日"仿佛"管中窥豹"，误解支道林为褒北贬南；而刘峻在这一节的注释里又褒南贬北，说什么北人"学广则难周，难周则识暗"，南人"学寡则易覈，易覈则知明"。支道林是仲裁者讲公道话。孙、褚分举南、北"学问"各有长处，支承认这些长处，而指出它们也各有流弊，长处就此成为缺点(le défaut de la qualité)。我国有关"性格类型"(Personality types)的最早专著、三国时刘劭《人物志·八观》里第七观是："观其所短，以知其所长"，支道林可以说是"观其所长，以知其所短"。"中人以还"的"中"不是《论语·雍也》"中人以下，中人以上"的"中"，而是《中庸》"中庸其至矣乎"的"中"，不指平常凑货、不出众，而指恰如其分、无偏差，就是《人物志·体性》所说："中庸之德……抗者过之而拘者不逮，抗拘违中。""中人"以下追求广博，则流为浅泛，追求精简，则流为寡陋；浮光掠影和一孔片面都是毛病，尽管病情不同，但都是《人物志·材能》所称"偏材之人"。《隋书·儒林传》叙述经学说："大抵南人约简，得其英华，北学深芜，穷其枝叶。"这简直像唐后对南、北禅宗的惯评了。看来，南、北"学问"的分歧，和宋、明儒家有关"博观"与"约取"、"多闻"与"一贯"、"道问学"与"尊德性"的争论，属于同一典型。巴斯楷尔区分两类有才知的人(deux sortes d'esprit)：一类"坚强而狭隘"，一类"广阔而软弱"(l'esprit pouvant être fort et étroit, et pouvant être ample et faible)②。康德曾分析"理性"里有两种基本的倾向：一种按照万殊的原则，喜欢繁多(das Interesse der Mannigfaltigkeit, nach dem Princip der Specification)；另

---

① 据文廷式《纯常子枝语》卷9、卷27所引道士著作，宋后道家也分"南北宗"。原则是否和禅宗的分派相近，我没有去考究。

② 帕斯卡尔(Pascal)《思辩录》(*Pensées*)第1篇第2节，季洛(V. Giraud)编本50页。

一种按照合并的原则喜欢一贯（das Interesse der Einheit, nach dem Princip der Aggregation）①。禅宗判别南北，可以说是两类才智或两种理性倾向在佛教思想里的一个表现。

南宗禅把“念经”、“功课”全鄙弃为无事忙，要把学问简至无可再简、约至不能更约，说什么“微妙法门，不立文字，教外别传”，“经诵三千部，曹溪一句亡”，“广学知解，被知解境风之所漂溺”（《五灯会元》卷一释迦牟尼章次、卷二惠能章次、卷三怀海章次）。李昌符《赠供奉僧玄观》：“自得曹溪法，诸经更不看。”张乔《宿齐山僧舍》：“若言不得南宗要，长在禅床事更多。”都是说南宗禅事省“事”，不看经卷，不坐禅床。南宗画的原则也是简约，以经济的笔墨获取丰富的艺术效果，以减削迹象来增加意境（less is more）。张彦远讲“疏体画”用笔不同于“密体画”，早说出这个理想：“笔才一二，像已应焉。离披点画，时见缺落，此虽笔不周而意周也。”（《历代名画记》卷二《论顾陆张吴用笔》）“周”是“周密”、“周到”、“周备”的“周”。他在本节里强调“书画用笔同”，我们不妨挪借另一个唐人论书法的话作为注解：“损谓有余。……谓趣长笔短，常使意势有余，点画若不足”（《全唐文》卷三三七颜真卿《张长史十二意笔法记》）。“损”就是见“缺落”，“若不足”就是“不周”。当代卓越的美术史家论“印象派”（Impressionism）含蓄不露（suggestion）的手法，说，观画者不是无所用心，而是“更有事可做”（the artist gives the beholder inceasingly “more to do”），参与了作者画的创造（making, creation），在心目中幻出（“conjured up” in our minds）那些未落迹象的景色（the inarticulate and unexpressed）②，也不外乎这个原则。休谟可能是首先揭示这种心理活动的哲学家，虽然他泛论人生经验，并未联系到文艺。他认为情感受“想象”的支配，“把对象的一部分隐藏不露，最能强烈地激发情感”（Nothing more powerfully excites any affection than to conceal some part of its object）；对象蔽亏不明（by throwing it in to a kind of shade），欠缺不全，就留下余地，让想象“有事可做”，（leaves some work for the imagination），而想象为了“完足”那个观念所作的努力又能增添情感的力量（the effort which the fancy makes to complete the idea gives an additional force to the passion）③。把休谟的大理论和我们的小题目拍合，对象“蔽亏”正是“笔不周”，在想象里“完足”正是“意周”，“complete”可算是“周”字的贴切英译。和石溪并称的“二溪”程正揆反复申明这一点。他的《青溪遗稿》似乎三百年来无人过问，不妨多引一些。卷一五《山庄题画》六首之三：“铁干银钩老笔翻。力能从简意能繁；临风自许同倪瓒，入骨谁评到董源。”卷二二《题卧游图后》：“论文字者谓参一分见不如增一分识，识愈高则愈淡。予谓画亦然。多一笔不如少一笔，意高则笔减。何也？意在笔先，不到处皆笔［‘不’字直贯

① 《纯理性批判》（*Kritik der reinen Vernunft*），艾尔德曼（B. Erdmann）校本，格鲁依德（W. de Gruyter）版500页，参看495页。当代心理学有关“性格型”的基本分类：“外向”（extrovert）和“内注”（introvert）、“发散”（diverger）和“收聚”（converger），也相发明。

② 贡布里支（E. H. Gombrich）《艺术与错觉》（*Art and Illusion*）第5版（1977）169页。

③ 休谟《情感论》（*Dissertation on the Passions*）第6节6条，见《道德、政治、文学论文集》（*Essays Moral, Political, and Literary*），格林（T. H. Green）与格罗士（T. H. Grose）编本第2册164页。休谟的话很像后来莱辛《拉奥孔》第3章讲绘画该挑选富有生发余地的景象，好“让想象力自由游戏”（was der Eindildungskraft freies Spiel lasst）。

全句，等于‘非到处皆笔’]繁皱浓染，刻划形似，生气漓矣。”卷二四《龚半千画册》：“画有繁简，乃论笔墨，非论境界也。北宋人千丘万壑，无疑比不減，元人枯枝瘦石，无一笔不繁。予曾有诗云云[即‘铁干银钩’那一首]。同卷《题石公画卷》：“予告石溪曰：‘画不难为繁，难于用减，减之力更大于繁。非以境减，减以笔’。所谓‘弄一车兵器，不若寸铁杀人’者也。”卷二六《杂著》一：“画贵减不贵繁，乃论笔墨，非论境界也。宋人千丘万壑，无一笔不减；倪元镇疏林瘦石，无一笔不繁。”翁方纲《复初斋诗集》卷一二《程清溪〈江山卧游图〉》：“枯木瘦石乃繁重，千岩万壑翻轻灵”；就地取材，正用程氏自己的话来题他的画。吴雯《莲洋集》卷六《题云林〈秋山图〉》：“岂但秾华谢桃李，空林黄叶亦无多”，也是赞叹倪瓒的“力能从简”。值得注意的是，程氏借禅宗的“话头”来比喻画法。“弄一车兵器，不是杀人手段，我有寸铁，便可杀人”，那是宋代禅师宗杲的名言，儒家的道学先生都欣赏它的。例如朱熹《朱子语类》卷八就引用了，卷一一五教训门徒，又“因举禅语云：寸铁可杀人；无杀人手段，则载一车刀枪，逐件弄过，毕竟无益”。南宗禅提倡“单刀直入”(《五灯会元》卷一一守廓章次、旻德章次)，不屑拈枪弄棒，所谓“只要单刀直入，不要广参”(《宗镜录》卷四一)，嘲笑“博览古今”的“百会”为“一尚不会”(《五灯会元》卷七洛京南院和尚章次)。那和“南人学问”的“清通简要”、“约简得英华”，只是程度上的差异。体现在造型艺术里，这个趋向就是绘画的笔墨“从简”、“用减”、“笔不到”。“南宗画”的定名超出了画家的籍贯，揭示了画风的特色，难道完全是“无所取义”的么？

那末，能不能说南宗画的作风也就相当于中国旧诗里正统的作风呢？

……

（节选自中国社会科学院文学研究所《中国文学研究年鉴》编辑委员会：《中国文学研究年鉴 1986》，中国文联出版公司 1988 年版，第 307-320 页。）

文学与思想史

（节选）

[美]牛顿·P. 斯托尔克奈特

【导读】

牛顿·P. 斯托尔克奈特(Newton Phelps Stallknecht)，美国比较文学学者，美学家。主要著作有：*Spirit of Western Philosophy*（1950），*Compass of Philosophy*：*An Essay in Intellectual Orientation*（1954），*Wordsworth and Philosophy*：*Suggestions Concerning the Source of the Poet's Doctrines and the Nature of His Mystical Experience*（2010）等。

斯托尔克奈特的《文学与思想史》是一篇关于比较文学跨学科研究的经典文章，主要讨论文学和哲学之间的关系，并对研究方法提出具体的指导性意见。作者首先阐明研究文学作品中的思想问题的必要性，指出正是思想性使文学和哲学之间拉近了距离，文学的思想性主要体现在对人性及其相关问题的思考。对文学作品思想性的认识是有一定的方法可循的，比如考察其是否从思想上代表了自己的时代，是否包含着过去时代的思想，等等。在对思想的历史发展过程的梳理中，可探知文学与其他学科之间相互影响的模式及其连续性，文学是思想史研究中的重要对象，而不仅仅是补充或附庸。

文章主要讨论了文学与思想这种跨学科研究的具体方法及应该注意的问题。(1)思想在发展中往往会从一个领域转至另一个领域，对文学作品的思想的研究必须考虑到这些变化。这一洞见意味着文学与思想的问题不仅涉及到哲学，还涉及到其他更多的学科，其跨学科性具有更为广泛的意义。在研究思想的发展变化模式的时候，要注意与作家的生活事件相关联的那些"影响"真正发生的特殊时刻。斯托尔克奈特认为文学与哲学的关系是相互的，不但哲学会影响文学，诗人也会影响哲学家甚至科学家。(2)思想是微妙复杂的，绝不能做简单化处理。文学思想的传达具有如下特点：思想是用词语来表达的，而对词语的理解要结合上下文语境；思想的存在状态是交流对话式的，必须维持交流中的平等互换关系才可保持活力，这意味着思想是一种潜在的意义，需要人们在交往对话关系中去掌握，这与接受美学的观念不谋而合。此外，思想的存在是过渡性的，它会不断转化，也会经常被重述、重释，这就需要进行细致入微的分析辨别，注意其动态流变的过程。最后，通过对"单位思想"的检讨，作者指出在不同时代以各不相同的方式表现出来的思想只是一种"意象"、"倾向"或"趋势”，满足于对单一思想的流变转移轨迹进行研究，不免有简单化之嫌。(3)思想的发展是一个不断被重述、重释和转化的过程，具有历史延续性和影响关系的思想观点不可能会以相类似的方式在不同地方同时存在。作者强调这一点的目的在于提醒人们注意避免过于轻率地做出结论，以证明不同文化具有相似性。比较文学跨学科研究最常犯的错误就是容易被表面的相似性迷惑，匆匆得出似是而非的结论，这是值得引起注意的。(4)思想在流传转化的过程中，其结构、方向和接受方式都会发生较为剧烈的变化，尤其是从思想家传向艺术家时更是如此，这和文学家与思想家传达思想的方式有密切的关系。文学家以想象、象征、比喻等艺术手法呈现思想，其目的在于展示和“欣赏”；思想家以推理论证的方式提出观点，得出结论，其目的在于让人信服，这种巨大的差异导致作家所传达的思想与他所继承来的思想有了天然的鸿沟。如果轻率地寻找二者的一致性，就有可能得出错误的结论。作者用“历史距离”一词来指称时间在事物上、思想上留下的印记，提醒人们注意历史的差距，避免“把思想变成反复出现的陈规旧套”。作者通过文学实例详尽地分析证明“历史距离”的存在及其对于研究者的意义，这构成文章后半部分的主要内容。

最后作者指出这些例子有助于学者们找到合理的方法，以了解不同时期的各种思想及其组合对比关系。斯托尔克奈特在文章结尾特别说明思想对于确立文学作品价值的重要性，这也再次确认了文学与思想之间关系的研究是有着重大意义的。

（常芳）

已故哲学家 R. G. 柯林伍德(Collingwood)的著作使许多文学研究者受到裨益。他曾写道：

> “我们大家(尽管我们中的许多人附庸风雅而想否认这一点)对乔叟、西马布亚(Cimabue)甚至莎士比亚和提香(Titian)的作品远没有对音乐厅和电影院的艺术熟悉。通过一种历史的同感，我们能够感受遥远的古代艺术或异族的现代艺术，能够欣赏洞穴人的壁画和日本的彩色版画。然而，这种努力的可能性是和历史观念的发展(过去两个世纪里我们的文明的最伟大的成就)密切相关的。不了解这种发展的人是决不能做到这一点的。自然的和基本的审美态度表现为：欣赏当代艺术，轻视和厌恶最近的过去时代的艺术，而对任何其他的东西则全然予以漠视。”①

人们会争辩说，文学研究的最终目的是纠正这种自发的偏狭，因为它会模糊一般大众、报纸评论家，甚至有创造性的艺术家本人的视线。由此便可产生一种不只着眼于当代作品的文学研究。这种研究可以有多种形式。而研究文学作品所表达的思想则是其中的一种。当然，研究思想的学者完全没有理由漠视当代的情况，他将经常观察这种情况。他会发现过去和现在之间的连续性、差别和相同点是无穷尽的，而且，对其中一个的了解经常

① R. G. 柯林伍德，《艺术哲学纲要》，伦敦，1925，pp. 98-99。

是通过了解另一个来实现的。

肯定这种研究的价值，意味着恪守一项重要的假定。大多数文学研究者，不管他们是学者还是评论家，都认为理解文学作品和欣赏文学作品一样是可能的。许多人会进而讲道，理解能够提高我们的欣赏能力。当然这种理解本身可以有多种形式。其中的某些形式，尤其是那些使比较文学研究者最感兴趣的形式，本质上是历史的。然而，文学史家不必只注意传记以及象形式、“结构”或技巧等文体方面的问题。他也不妨考虑一下思想方面的问题。的确，对风格和思想的这种区分经常接近于武断，因为我们最终必须承认风格和内容经常相互影响或渗透，有时则是同样洞察力的表现。然而，一般说来，研究者可着重研究两者之中的任何一个方面。

至此，给思想下一个可用的定义是适宜的，尽管随着探讨的深入它还有待臻于完善。‘思想’这个术语指的是我们头脑里和感觉或情感经验的直接性相对的那种更富思考、更具启发性的意识。正是通过这种思考文学才接近于哲学。我们不妨说，思想可被粗略地解释为我们的思考所涉及的主题或题目。在这篇文章里，我们和大多数史学家一样，对更普遍或范围更广的思想感到兴趣。它们在文学史里反复出现，可以说被“写熟”了。其中最突出的是关于人性本身的思想观点，包括许多世纪以来人们为之所下的许多定义；它还包括诸如人的完善、人的堕落和人的尊严等派生的观念。人们确实可以争辩说，思想史既然包括文学，就必须集中描述人性的特点。文学史上的各个重大时期可依据其对人性的描述而彼此区别开来。

当然，这些思想不见得存在于每一篇文学作品里。尽管我们头脑里的那种思想必须随时为想象服务，但它在含义上仍较大多数诗歌的或文学的意象笼统，尤其是要比试图捕捉个人瞬间感受的抒情诗里的意象笼统得多。因此，彭斯的“我的爱人像一朵红红的玫瑰花”，和霍普金斯①的“霹雳般紫红色的海滩，装点着霹雳般的紫红色”，就很难说表达出了我们这里所讨论的那类思想，尽管它们在内容上明白易懂。而阿诺尔德②的“未被探测的、咸味的、陌生的大海”，从上下文来看，无疑就表达了那类思想。

对一件艺术品的理解必定包括对它所反映或体现的思想的认识。因此，文学研究者有时会发现下述做法是有益的：把一首诗或一篇文章进行分类，看其是否从思想上或虚构的内容上或主题上代表了产生它的那个时代。另外，他会发现蕴含在它的结构里已在别处、别的时代用不同的方法表达了的主题或思想。要理解作品，我们很可能要了解对上述两个方面的解释与说明。同时，我们也很可能要认识到，我们正在阅读的作品反映了或者属于被称之为某种“流派”或“主义”的思想方式，亦即同时出现而又有足够的共同特征可被辨认出来的思想的“综合体”。因此，像“神恩”、“灵魂拯救”和“天意”之类的概念，在传统的基督教里是群聚一起的。学习过的作品通常都是我们所讨论的思想的一种特殊的甚至是带有个人特色的表达或论述。这样，研究者就感到有必要对一种“主义”或思想方式的几种表达方法进行细致的区分。因此，我们可以谈论雪莱诗歌所特有的柏拉图主义或谈论亨

① 霍普金斯(1844—1889)，英国诗人。

② 阿诺尔德(1822—1888)，英国批评家和诗人。

利(Henley)①在《未被征服的人》里表现的那种斯多葛哲学。我们会发现，描述这种柏拉图主义或斯多葛哲学以及把同一态度或思想方式的一种表达方式和其他表达方式进行比较，是一件困难和带有挑战性质的工作。然而，雪莱毕竟不是一个“正统”的或古希腊的柏拉图主义者，甚至他的“浪漫的”柏拉图主义也和他的同代人的浪漫的柏拉图主义有着明显的区别。另外，亨利的蔑视一切的态度给其自我控制的理想增加了特色，但它远不具有像马科斯·奥勒留斯②那样的斯多葛派哲学家的特征。后者那种高雅的默认一切的态度几乎是基督教式的，堪与弥尔顿在其论自己失明的十四行诗里所表现的那种忍耐相比。

近年来，我们越来越认识到思想是有其历史发展过程的。而且，并非是这部历史的最不重要的章节才和文学与艺术的主题与观念方面有关，尽管这些方面应和哲学史、宗教史和科学史一起来研究。当我们通览这些领域时，我们会发现它们彼此关系的重要模式。这些模式表明了它们相互之间的巨大影响以及思想和表达的连续性。这种连续性包括许多传统，主要是文学的、宗教的和哲学的传统，但也经常包括与美术、甚至在某种程度上与科学的联系。

这里，我们可以说，至少有一种现代的历史哲学是建立在思想是史学家研究的首要对象这样一种假定上的。让我们再引一段柯林伍德的话吧：③

> “历史是与人的行动密切相关的……从外部看来，一个行动是发生在物质世界里的一个或一系列事件；从内部看来，它是把某种思想付诸实践……史学家的任务是深入到他论述的行动的内部去，重建，或者更确切地说，重新思考产生这些行动的思想。思想的一个特征是……在重新思考的过程中，我们以此而逐渐理解到它们当时为什么会被这样考虑。”

尽管这种理解必须具有同感，但它并非是一种直觉的产物。

> “历史和所有其他科学的共同点是：史学家不能把任何知识视为自己的发明，除非他能首先对自己，其次对其他既能够、又愿意理解他的论证的人指出他这样做的正当理由。这就是我们为什么把历史描述为推论性的意义所在。一个人成为历史学家所必备的知识是一种他用什么样的证据来证实某些事件的知识。”

很明显，在研究某一特定时期的思想如何激发了人们行为的过程中，史学家会发现那个时代的文学和艺术也是他主要关心的一个问题，而决不仅仅是卓有成效的历史研究的一种补充或附属品。

研究思想及其历史地位的学者总会涉及转变的、同时又是改革的模式。依据这些模式思想从活动的一个领域转至另一个领域。我们不妨权且通览一下现代思想的发展——从注

---

① 亨利(1849—1903)，英国作家和编辑。

② 马科斯·奥勒留斯(121—180)，罗马皇帝(161—180在位)和哲学家。

③ R. G. 柯林伍德，《历史的概念》，伦敦，1948，pp. 252。

意了解宗教改革运动到其后革命性的浪漫主义运动，直至详细研讨最近几十年的情况。这样我们就会发现，个人意志自由的观点最初表现在宗教活动里和反映在神学上，之后又出现在实用政治和政治理论中，最后则在文学、艺术领域里体现了出来。最后，我们注意到，这种观点也出现在教育理论里，并在其中产生着广泛的影响。不可否认，如此巨大的发展变化具有极大的内在价值。因此，对文学作品的思想的研究必须经常联系这些发展变化；否则，这种研究就是极不完全的。但我们必须牢记，如果不考虑神学、哲学、政治思想和文学等各个领域之间相互影响的许多特殊的范例，我们就不能正确地进行这类概括。彼此影响的实际时刻是至关重要的。这些时刻是各个作家生活里的历史事件。比较文学研究者必须经常考虑这些历史事件。

《旧约》和《新约》可能一度对西方文学产生着最强大、最经常的影响。对过去十六七个世纪里西方文明的任何时期的精神和文化生活的评论必然涉及那一时期的领导者如何理解和解释《圣经》。这种理解以及由此而产生的评论便构成了影响。把圣·奥古斯丁、约翰·班扬和托马斯·杰弗逊(他们都通过研究《圣经》而找到了启蒙思想的真正来源)对《圣经》的理解做一比较，我们就能深入了解这三个人以及他们每人所代表的、并自觉地予以表达的时代。以同样的方式，我们认识到莎士比亚对普鲁塔克和蒙田的作品的熟谙、雪莱研究柏拉园对话录以及柯勒律治热诚借鉴从柏拉图到谢林、威廉·葛德文历代哲学家和神学家的作品的重大意义。借此，大量抽象的观念才引起了英国作家的注意。

我们也能看到诗人影响了哲学家甚至间接地影响了科学家的例子。英国哲学家撒缪尔·亚历山大受益于华滋华斯和梅瑞狄斯就是一个有趣的近代例子。A. N. 怀特赫德①(Whitehead)对英国浪漫主义诗人，主要是对华滋华斯和雪莱的诗歌的理解则是另外一例。黑格尔对古希腊悲剧家的洞察力的深深仰慕，表明了古典主义对十九世纪哲学产生的广泛影响。此外，研究生物进化的学者会在卢克莱修(他看来是借用了哲学家恩庇道克勒斯②的观点)的作品里发现一种十分有趣的、虽然对我们来说也许是怪诞的现象——他对偶然变异和自然淘汰学说的预知。

这里，给以认真的告诫是适宜的。我们必须避免这样的看法(这已在上述的例子里向一些人做了暗示)，即在某种意义上把思想比做象硬币或柜台那样的“整体单位”,③ 能原封不动地从一部分人手中转到另一部分人手中，甚至能从一个人手中转到另一个人手中。对思想影响的描述总是一个微妙、复杂的问题，因此决不能过分简单化。思想通常要用词

---

① A. N. 怀特赫德(1861—1947)，英国数学家及哲学家。

② 恩庇道克勒斯，公元前5世纪希腊哲学家及政治家。

③ 研究者会在像 R. O. 洛弗乔伊和乔治·博厄斯(George Boas)这些作家的作品里看到他们对单位思想的理论所作的充分论述。特别要参看洛弗乔伊的《存在的巨大链条》(剑桥，马萨诸塞，1936，pp. 3-24)。虽然我不能接受他们的理论，但我们乐于承认，他们的研究并未因其不足而经常受到影响。然而，“单位思想”这一术语是危险的，它的含义常会使研究者误入歧途。尽管如此，洛弗乔伊的《存在的巨大链条》一书在其领域里仍是一部杰作。任何对思想史和对哲学与文艺之间的关系感兴趣的人都应把它作为整体来读。从事这种研究的人还应阅读一些较少技术性的有关哲学史的补充读物。关于包括这类书籍的附有说明的参考书目，可参阅 N. P. 斯托尔克奈特和 R. S. 布兰柏(Brumbaugh)合著的《西方哲学实质》(纽约，1950，pp. 511-530)；此外，还可参看韦勒克和华伦合著的《文学论》一书的第十章。

来表达。和音乐、美术不同，文学作品的思想也必须用词来表达。词不仅要人听见或读及，而且必须依据上下文被解释出来。只有对词进行解释，思想才引起我们的注意。但思想不是以现成商品的形式存在，而主要是(这里我们必须超出我们所下定义的范围)以隐伏在人类交流里的“意义”的形式存在。它们不是我们通常所说的那种“主观的”或“客观的”，而是“相互主观的”，交流的或对话式的。一旦离开实际交流里的平等互换关系，思想也就失去了它的活力。它们真实的存在方式是过渡性的，不断从一种环境转向另一种环境。即使在一个单独的个人的头脑里，思想要拥有活力或保持真正的意义，也必须经常被重述，实际上也是不断地被解释。一个固定的公式只不过仅有记忆的价值。只有在那些最基本的教科书里，它才是适宜的。

因此，“单位思想”这个术语很难被用来指任何公认的整体，因而也就更谈不上对文学研究者有用了。当然，我们可以和洛弗乔伊(A. O. Lovejoy)一起把它重新解释为某些人所表现出的那种倾向，即喜欢听某些像“真实的就是‘一个’”或“世界上充满了一部分事物”之类的主张。这样，我们就把哲学上的“一元论”和“多元论”看做单位思想。然而，在这种认识水平上，我们如果不把“单位思想”这一术语甚至用做一种比喻，效果也许会更好一些。如前所述，它的含义经常产生不好的效果。我们还是应该满足于使用“意向”、“倾向”或“思想或感情”的“趋势”之类更为直接的表达方式。这些倾向可用各种因时代而迥异的方式表现出来。然而，把一个单位思想解释为不断重复出现或作家之间、时代之间的转移，则常常是一种过分简单化的麦现。

思想和感情的这些倾向在从作家到作家、时代到时代的传递中，经历了不断被重述、被重新解释和转化的过程。思想史实质上是对这个过程所作的一部评论。这种评论是形成思想而又通过思想意识到自身及其环境的人类精神的具体体现。正如黑格尔在他的第一部巨著《精神现象学》里所竭力表明的那样，思想史可被看做自我意识增长的一个标志。依据这个标志，人类中的个体不断解释他们在社会中和世界上的位置。不言而喻，这个自我意识的出现改造了个人的生活，影响了他的社会关系并极大地改变了他对自然的态度。这种认识的改变以记录的形式出现时，便构成了历史的首要主题。因此，史学家必须考虑思想领域里的所有变化，这样才能把人类生活的一个阶段和先前的、后继的阶段区分开来。他也会认识到，任何包含实际影响和联系的历史延续性的观点不可能在相同和类似之中得到发展。如果我们把中国道学家的著作，特别是老子本人的著作，和欧洲浪漫主义作家的作品，比如华滋华斯的《早春》，做一比较，这种有趣的联系就显而易见了。上述两者的作品都可与新柏拉图主义哲学家普洛丁的作品中的某些段落进行比较。一些学者看到了这些相同点的重要性，并试图通过它们勾勒出远古文化发展的相似方面。这些推测(例如奥斯瓦尔德·斯潘格勒所作的那些推测。他把远古的斯多葛哲学和现代的社会主义“等同”起来，把毕达哥拉斯、穆罕默德和克伦威尔看成“同代人”或历史上的相似者)几乎总是有趣的和富有启发性，有时还开拓了重要的探求途径。然而，像所有基于直观相似上的推理一样，这种论点也必须非常谨慎地予以估价。在没有进行更为一般的仔细研究之前，绝不能把它看做是带有结论性的。

(节选自牛顿·P. 斯托尔克奈特：《文学与思想史》，冯国忠译，载张隆溪选编《比较文学译文集》，北京大学出版社 1982 年版，第 87-94 页。)

文学与艺术的关系研究

张汉良

【导读】

张汉良《文学与艺术的关系研究》一文原刊1981年4月《人与社会》第8卷第1期。文章伊始，作者提出一个问题，即文学与艺术的关系研究到底应该属于何种学科范畴。作者指出，传统学者把这个课题划归为美学范畴，但是目前它已被多数学者认可为合法的比较文学课题。法国比较文学学者以文学关系史为依归，自然排斥文学史料之外的研究。不过，对法国学者持反对态度的美国比较文学学者也多半不认可这种艺术科际整合研究。他们反对的论点大致可分为两类。第一类与他们反对法国学者的比较文学历史性研究立场一致，即文学与艺术的关系研究是外缘研究(extrinsic study)，无助于吾人对文学本身的了解，即内涵研究(intrinsic study)。第二类反对论据则从比较文学的定义出发。既然比较文学划分文学畛域的依据是语言文字，一旦我们再让媒介、表达方式殊异的其他艺术形式介入其中，则比较文学的界限益发难以确定与厘清。作者认为，文学与其他艺术的关系研究，大致可以归纳为三类：(一)形式主义研究(formalistic approach)；(二)历史研究(historical approach)；(三)人类学与心理学研究(anthropological and psychological approach)。

关于形式主义研究，作者首先讨论了Ecphrasis这种文学类型，即以文字写出(或说出)某件想象中的或真实的艺术作品。西方第一个发声的造型艺术作品，便是荷马在史诗《伊里亚德》十八书中的阿契力士之盾。但是，荷马的Ecphrasis很难引起形式上的讨论，原因之一是他状写的对象是虚拟的造型。一个更适当的，在美学史上引起更大争论与影响的例子便是罗马诗人维吉尔(Virgil)的状写《拉奥孔》(*Laocoon*)。雷辛对拉奥孔的分析导致(或基于)他对媒介的新认识：造型艺术是空间艺术，诗(文学)是时间艺术。由于文学具有时间性的特性，有人便认为文学是空间的造型艺术和美术与时间的音乐之间的介中媒人，兼具两者之长。某些形式主义者如雅可布逊希望能作些更系统性的综合性研究。不过，雅氏的语言学模式只不过是一个比喻，因为事实上，我们很难将“造型”艺术与美术的媒介或基本单位，简化或更换为语言单位。与形式主义有关，但企图不同的另一种研究，是从事实用批评的学者，在诠释个别作品时，涉及到两种以上的艺术形式。他们固然讨论到多种艺术，但其兴趣是经验性的，描述性的，而非演绎性或预示性的，甚至还是操之在人的。

关于历史研究，作者指出主题学或题材学应划归于历史研究的范畴，其认知基础便是文学与其他艺术的摹拟性，即指某些艺术作品的指涉性与某件文学作品的指涉性有谱系关系。不过，作者也指出，追溯这些渊源时，必然要摒弃艺术作品本身而不顾，这是形式主义者绝对无法容忍的事；这种探澜索源的追索工夫，是纯粹的历史研究，它除了理论基础薄弱外，极易流入主观与印象式。另外一种历史研究，其兴趣不在追溯渊源与际遇，而系希望了解时代的风格，进而作为断代的依据或观察文艺史的演化现象。此类学者是形式主义者(相信构成风格的体制与典式)兼历史主义者，相信摹拟，即风格能反映时代精神。从人类学与心理学角度，作者指出，摹拟并非真正复制外在物体或内心的思想，而系以艺术传统与体制中的形象，取代外物或内在思想。

作者最后指出，文学与艺术的关系研究，是比较文学的新课题，但它几乎涉及比较文学所有的问题，包括历史研究(文学与艺术史)、断代问题、主题学、影响研究、文类研究，以及类比研究。

(李伟荣)

一

……文学与艺术的关系研究到底应该属于何种学科范畴?

传统学者把这个课题划归为美学范畴，但是目前它已被多数学者认可为合法的比较文学课题，本文也是从后者立场来讨论。

法国比较文学学者以文学关系史为依归，很自然地排斥了文学史料之外的研究。令人诧异的是，对法国学者持反动态度的美国比较文学学者也泰半不认可这种艺术科际整合研究。他们反对的论点大致可分为两类。第一类与他们反对法国学者的比较文学历史性研究立场一致，即文学与艺术的关系研究是外缘研究(extrinsic study)，无助于吾人对文学本身的了解，即内涵研究(intrinsic study)。由于文学与其他艺术的表达方式以及传统有本质上的差异，它们的沟通显然有困难；在我们充分了解文学作品的存在模式与其时代典式(norm)之前，我们无法冒然把它与另外一种艺术的存在模式与时代典式合而为一。例如巴镂刻建筑与巴镂刻音乐无法相提并论。

第二类反对论据则从比较文学的定义出发。既然比较文学划分文学畛域的依据是语言文字，一旦我们再让媒介、表达方式殊异的其他艺术形式介入其中，则比较文学的界限益发难以确定与厘清。例如莫札特的歌剧和德国文学的关系研究，属于德文学者研究的范畴；但他与意大利文学的关系，便不再属于德文学者的内务，而涉及到比较文学的领域了。到底我们应该如何划定界限呢?如何决定莫札特研究的哪一部分属于德文学者，哪一部分属于比较文学学者，哪一部分属于音乐学者的研究范围呢?

严格说来，文学与其他艺术(乃至其他学科)，都是文化系统中的支系统，彼此密切排列组合，而这个文化系统并非形而上的、抽象的、同时性的，必须是特定的、具体的、历史性的。反对法国比较文学研究的美国学者的口实是外缘研究，这个口实使他们也反对文学与相关艺术的研究，但是令人好笑的是，法国学者的排斥文学与艺术研究，其口实也无非是文学外缘的(extra-literary)。唯一不同的是，美国学者把法国人的文学内涵的(intra-literary)或文学之间的(inter-literary)也视为外缘的罢。总之，我们无法严格划分内涵的与外缘的，甚至文学的与非文学的。在这个前提之下，文学与其他艺术的并置研究便是合法的。但是我们要声明，这种并置研究不等于科际整合，因为后者意味着它们彼此相通，无论在创作动机上、“本质”上，或效果上。我们也不用俗成的姊妹艺术(sister arts)这个名词，因为它暗示“家族相似关系”(family resemblance)与“文化圈”(culture circle)，两者皆基于似是而非的生物学的类比。

文学与其他艺术的关系研究，大致可以归纳为三类：(一)形式主义研究(formalistic approach)；(二)历史研究(historical approach)；(三)人类学与心理学研究(anthropological and psychological approach)。以下分别讨论。

二

首先我们要讨论形式主义研究。有人把文学与艺术的关系研究分为形式与内容两种。这种二分法久已为人摒弃，因为无论作品的内容或作者欲传达的旨意为何，它都需要以媒介来表达，换言之，形式驾驭了内容。如果我们坚持以内容为定位，唯一的贡献便是主题学研究，而此处主题学可能还需要把母题排除在外，因为文学的母题与造型艺术、音乐等的母题不同，尤其后者，更是非摹拟性的(non-mimetic, non-referential)。换言之，主题学研究仅限于题材(subject matter)或素材(raw material)的排比，如追溯赤壁为题材的诗文与造型或美术作品(但这又流入第二项历史研究范围了)，或相同的主题(如玫瑰花)，以不同的媒介表现(但这又非涉及形式讨论不可)。因此，笔者认为在形式主义研究中，主题是不存在的，它应归入第二、三两类。

虽然如此，让我们仍然以同一题材开始形式主义的讨论。首先要谈到 Ecphrasis 这种文学类型，即以文字写出(或说出)某件想象中的或真实的艺术作品，这个希腊字的原意是“说出”(speaking out)，因为艺术作品是哑然的，诗人以语言使它发声。我们立刻会想到杜甫的题画诗，典型的例子便是《奉先刘少府新画山水障歌》中的句子：“悄然坐我天姥下，耳边已是闻清猿；反思前夜风雨急，乃是蒲城鬼神入。元气淋漓障犹湿，真宰上诉天应泣。”(卷三)透过杜甫的语言——尤其是听觉意象语——这幅立轴等于发出了声音。

西方第一个发声的造型艺术作品，便是荷马在史诗《伊里亚德》十八书中的阿契力士之盾。荷马在描绘此神器时，想象中有件艺术作品，然后将它“说出”来。至于后来 20 世纪英国诗人奥登(W. R. Auden)再写“The Shield of Achilles”，便是纯粹的文学影响，而非 Ecphrasis 了。研究荷马与奥登的作品的关系，应属主题学或影响研究范畴，但研究荷马的创作勉可算是本文课题。

荷马的 Ecphrasis 很难引起形式上的讨论，原因之一是他状写的对象是虚拟的造型。一个更适当的，在美学史上引起更大争论与影响的例子便是罗马诗人维吉尔(Virgil)的状写《拉奥孔》(*Laocoon*)，虽然迄今没有凭据证明诗人确实看过这个作品(按《拉奥孔》大致成于纪元前 2 世纪，维吉尔史诗写于纪元前 1 世纪，前者 1502 年在罗马出土)。维吉尔史诗《伊尼懿德》(*The Aeneid*)第二书中，有一段生动的文字，描写拉奥孔和其子被巨蟒勒死的经过。即便我们不敢大胆假设维吉尔见过这雕刻，然后“说出”来，使得这个 Ecphrasis 成为历史悬案；至少批评家有两件不同的艺术作品并列眼前，可以自如地讨论媒介与表现问题。

18 世纪的德国艺术史家温克曼(Winckelmann)分析《拉奥孔》时，提出一个问题，为何拉奥孔临死哀号时，嘴是微张的，而不像维吉尔所写的“他的吼号震动了周遭的空气”？温克曼等人的解释是：美是希腊艺术的第一义，情感抑制则为道德理想，为了求美，雕刻家只得把丑掩盖，把强烈的情绪舒缓，因此拉奥孔的“呐喊”(screams)被减弱为“喟叹”(sighs)。雷辛(Lessing)批驳温氏的解释，他认为由于雕刻家无法像诗人一样作持续的描写，因此只能选择一个最具潜力(pregnant)的瞬间，来暗示前因后果。造型艺术家局限于空间性(spatiality)，仅能表现物象(object)；但诗的性质是时间性(temporality)的，我们读诗时，可见到持续的行动(action)，因此，除了为了服膺希腊艺术的美与合宜原则外，拉奥孔的雕刻家选择的刹那是主人翁尚未张口大叫的一刻，以物象暗示出持续的行动。正如诗人以行动暗示物象一样。雷辛对拉奥孔的分析导致(或基于)他对媒介的新认识：造型艺术是空间艺术，诗(文学)是时间艺术。

由于文学具有时间性的特性，有人便把它和音乐扯上关系，认为文学是空间的造型艺术和美术与时间的音乐之间的介中媒人，兼具两者之长。例如我们欣赏音乐“时”，聆听一连串音符的持续，而朗诵或聆听诗时，情况大致相同。观赏一件艺术作品，我们会得到瞬间的整体空间印象，正如“看”诗(尤其是图形诗)也会得到整个的空间印象。

《拉奥孔》所揭示出来的问题，到今天仍然有人讨论。新批评家法兰克(Joseph Frank)提出反证，认为现代文学，尤其是叙述文学(小说)，在表现方式上是空间性的，而非时间性的。乔埃斯、普鲁斯特(Proust)等利用心理时间，而非机械时间，以及并置、交错等技巧，打破叙述的时间连续性。庞德、艾略特的用典，也产生了同时感的效果。叶维廉倡言“出位之思”(Anders-streben)，认为现代艺术跳脱自己的“位”，而与其他的艺术相结合。他除了一再证明中国古典诗(与现代英美诗)强调空间性外，甚至响应法兰克的说法，指出中国现代小说的风貌，就是切断时间上的连续，而在空间中求发展。雷辛与法兰克等人皆由表现方法与媒介的认知——不论他们的认知是否正确——来界定文学及其他艺术之间的关系。雷辛的基本观念是摹拟说的。法兰克对媒介与形式的探讨相当空泛，甚至流于抒情式、印象式的暗喻。暗喻，正是讨论文学、艺术关系的学者常犯的毛病，但除非不谈这个问题，否则暗喻似乎是“必然的邪恶”。

某些形式主义者希望能作些更系统性的综合性研究，雅可布逊是一个显例，他的理论基础(也正是他的漏洞基础)是语言学。雅氏认为所有的(?)语言都有两大原则：暗喻式(metaphorical)与换喻式(metonymical)，前者是空间的置换过程，后者是时间接续过程。例如请人以 hut 这个字造句，可能的句子有两类：(A)The hut is a small house.(B)The hut was burnt down.(A)句是一种代换过程，属暗喻结构(small house = hut)，在时间上是停滞的，而其语义空间则因并置而扩张；(B)句则是一个句构的连贯过程，属换喻结构。如果有所谓衍生诗学(generative poetics)的话，(B)句便具有小说的潜力，因为它强调水平轴上持绩的行动。

雅可布逊认为儿童的失语症不外乎这两种情形，而诗人或文学家的语言，也是根据这两个原则而运用的。当然这是极大胆的假设，雅氏的二分法也有问题，此地，笔者只是指出有人用这种方法来研究文学与姊妹艺术的关系。雅氏指出诗歌，尤其浪漫主义与象征主义的诗，其基本语言作即属暗喻的替换原则，因此诗的时间性句构有限，而往空间性的语义层次发展。写实主义的小说则不然，虽然作家有时会离开叙述主线，去描绘情景或人物，而不得不把暗喻原则投射到换喻原则上，但大体上小说是遵循换喻原则的。

更令人惊讶的是，雅可布逊认为这两个语言原则，不仅现诸于文学作品，在其他艺术上亦然。立体主义绘画的多重透视与分割构图，正是换喻(部份代全体喻)的运用，每个切割的细部和全体是连续的关系。超现实主义绘画则很明显地采用暗喻的替代原则。有趣的是，如果我们把焦距凝聚在一九一〇年代立体派绘画(尤其毕卡索与布拉克)盛行的时候，看看艾略特当时写的诗，如《序曲》，会发现整首诗最突出的喻词竟然是部分代全体的换喻，我们仿佛从多重透视上看到割裂的现代人形象(手、腿、脚丫子)。

与形式主义有关，但企图不同的另一种研究，是从事实用批评的学者，在诠释个别作品时，涉及到两种以上的艺术形式。他们固然讨论到多种艺术，但其兴趣是经验性的，描述性的，而非演绎性或预示性的，甚至还是操之在人的，譬如他们研究的作者运用了一个结构上的典，他们便不得不援用其他艺术坐标作为诠释的工具。如海伦·迦登娜(Helen Gardener)以音乐的形式与术语为工具，诠释或分析艾略特的《四个四重奏》(*The Four Quartets*)。在这种情形之下，我们便不把这类学者列入讨论的范围。至于实际创作的作家，如艾略特，则更非我们后设批评的对象了。这是必须要说明的。

三

其次要谈到历史研究。我们在前面曾指出主题学，或更确切地说，题材学，应划归于历史研究的范畴。其脆弱的认知基础便是文学与其他艺术的摹拟性，也唯有在这个薄弱的基础上才能谈主题学。质言之，某些艺术作品的指涉性(referentiality)与某件文学作品的指涉性有谱系关系(myth of filiation)，如罗马诗人奥维德(Ovid)写伊卡拉斯(Icarus)之畔，布鲁格根据前人的描述绘 Icarus，奥登在布鲁塞尔美术馆见到这幅画，又写出一首近似 Ecphrasis 的诗。追溯这些渊源时，吾人必然要摒弃艺术作品本身而不顾，这是形式主义者绝对无法容忍的事。这种探澜索源的追猎工夫，是纯粹的历史研究，它除了理论基础薄弱外，极易流入主观与印象式。

另外一种历史研究，其兴趣不在追溯渊源与际遇，而系希望了解时代的风格(style)，进而作为断代的依据或观察文艺史的演化现象。此类学者必须综合历史研究与形式主义研究始能为功，因为所谓风格，不是史实，而是体制、典式，而风格的形成或被确认又复取决于创作者与观者(读者、批评家、史家)的视境。就这层意义上而言，他们是形式主义者(相信构成风格的体制与典式)兼历史主义者，相信摹拟(mimesis)，即风格能反映时代精神(Zeitgeist)。这派学者的开山祖之一是本世纪初的德国艺术史家吴尔夫林(Heinrich Wolfflin)，他认为文艺复兴与巴镂刻的风格反映出不同的观物心态。构成这两个时期风格的体制有五：(一)形象本身，(二)空间的安排，(三)作品部分与全体的关系，(四)结构，（五）整体印象。继他而起的有德国艺术史家瓦尔查尔（Oskar Walzel）与美国学者赛佛（Wylie Sypher），发扬光大了此类研究。赛佛相信一个时代的风格是该时代意识的句构（形式），会呈现在任何一首诗、一幅绘画、一件雕塑或一座建筑上，因此对任何一件艺术作品的观察与体认，都有助于吾人对文学经验结构的了解。赛佛规模吴尔夫林的秩序，加以敷衍发挥，定出了十四项鉴定文艺复兴四阶段风格的二元对立标准。大体上说来，他的作法属于文学与艺术的类比研究（analogy 而非 parallel）。我们抽样举两项来看。第一个二元标准是“线条式的——绘画式的”（linear-painterly），前者轮廓清晰、局部突出，可称轮廓艺术，如波底且利（Botticelli）的画和史宾塞（Spenser）的十四行诗；后者界限模糊，轮廓与物象溶合，产生似幻似真，不可即之感，可称为色彩艺术，如林布兰特（Rembrandt）的画和弥尔顿（Milton）的《沉思的人》（*Il Penseroso*）。第二个二元标准是“平面式的-后退式的”（plane-recessional），与前一标准互相发明。线条式的形式其透视是水平的，物件或构图在一明确的平面上，呈现出二度空间，如早期文艺复兴宫殿的正面，以及上述波底且利与史宾塞；在后退的形式中，平面被打破，甚或完全消逝，所具之象有深度，造成距离的幻觉，如巴镂刻时期教堂的正面，层次深浅对照分明，又如弥尔顿《失乐园》的塑型与空间效果强烈。

赛佛虽然有时失诸武断，但颇多有趣的发现，譬如他指出弥尔顿与鲁本斯（Reubens）代表着巴镂刻的想象力，见证著文艺复兴人文主义的英雄传统；又如哥瑞柯（EL Greco）与顿约翰（John Donne）二人代表著文艺复兴瓦解期矫揉形式主义（mannerism）的风格等等，虽非一针见血之论，却也颇能发人深省。值得注意的是，赛佛所举出的风格判断标准，实为形式主义者的典式，根据这些典式才能界定文学与其他艺术的关系，唯有重建典式，才能建立艺术的系统——虽然威立克等人会怀疑各种艺术是否可能有共同的典式，虽然他们会讥讽所谓时代精神或风格是“形而上的玩意儿”（metaphysical entities）。但话说回来，任何系统的建立必经融合同时性研究与历史性研究，否则便落入“普遍形式”或“普遍人性”的陷阱。后者正是心理学与人类学研究的大弊。

四

吴尔夫林与赛佛对风格的界说，大致基于摹拟说，这也是所有艺术“史”学者无法避免的“邪恶”。赛佛的摹拟说还可进一步讨论。他认为艺术家的感性有如一张银幕，他所摹拟（具象）的事物便反映在上面。艺术便是吾人现实经验的成形（Configuration Gestalt）。赛佛接受格氏塔（Gestalt）的观念，使他接近心理学与人类学的研究。但是此地我们要指出，心理分析学者如容（Jung）所揭示的诸般潜意识原型，或者我们思想的格氏塔，本身不是艺术作品，虽然它们会透过不同的媒介或表达方式“成形”。如果我们以原型解释一切艺术现象，那便犯了创作简化主义的弊病。赫伯特·瑞德（Herbt Read）在《现代艺术哲学》（*The Philosophy of Modern Art*，1953）中，应用弗洛伊德心理分析解释并沟通超现实主义绘画与诗。充其极，他只能说明潜在内容的思想会转化为明显内容中的感觉意象，但忽略了潜意识中的思想具象成艺术时，体制扮演着重要的角色。

艺术批评家冈不列希（Gombrich）对这点发挥得很好。摹拟并非真正复制外在物体或内心的思想，而系以艺术传统与体制中的形象，取代外物或内在思想。我们受惠的不是自然，而是其他无数的，我们曾经见过的图画。

文学与艺术的关系研究，是比较文学的新课题，但它几乎涉及比较文学所有的问题，包括历史研究(文学与艺术史)、断代问题、主题学、影响研究、文类研究，以及类比研究，尤其是后者，因为这门学问的出发点与依归，无非都是基于一个形式或媒介的暗喻。

(选自张汉良：《比较文学理论与实践》，东大图书公司 1986 年版，第 292-304 页。)

弗洛伊德与文学

（节选）

[美]莱昂内尔·特里林

【导读】

弗洛伊德是奥地利的一位精神病医生和心理学家，是精神分析学说之父。他创立的精神分析由于对人格理论提出了极富创见性的观点，不仅在心理学领域产生了深远的影响，而且在文学批评、人类学研究及文化艺术研究等领域被广泛运用。美国的文学评论家特里林教授就“弗洛伊德与文学”作出过精辟的论述，他从弗洛伊德与文学之间的关系出发，批判了弗洛伊德的艺术观，同时客观地分析了弗洛伊德关于艺术在生活中的地位的观点以及精神分析在文学阐释中的功用，最后他对弗洛伊德精神分析的艺术贡献作出了中肯的评价。

特里林认为，弗洛伊德与文学的亲缘关系不是单向度的，而是双向的，二者之间相互影响，弗洛伊德影响文学，文学也同样影响弗洛伊德。第一，特里林认为文学是弗洛伊德学术思想发展的沃土。他从弗洛伊德赞许的《拉摩的侄儿》中就看出了这二者之间亲缘关系的端倪，并从华兹华斯等浪漫主义诗人身上看到了潜藏的和无意识的精神成分对文学创作的重要作用，同时其他的诗人、小说家、哲学家对性的疾呼，对死亡欲望的关注，对恐怖的魅惑的描绘，对梦的兴趣都说明了文学是弗洛伊德学说成长的重要养料。第二，特里林认为弗洛伊德对文学的影响不仅是普遍的而且是巨大的。虽然普鲁斯特未曾读过弗洛伊德的作品，但他小说中的睡眠、性欲、隐喻和联想的大量使用，都表明了弗洛伊德的影响是明显的。同时，具有弗洛伊德气质的作家也非常多，如卡夫卡、乔伊斯等，足见弗洛伊德对文学影响的广度和深度。

虽然弗洛伊德的思想同浪漫主义传统有着亲缘关系，但特里林认为他的思想体系中仍然存在理想主义的成分。首先，他否定了托马斯·曼认为弗洛伊德的精神分析中的理性成分处于第二位甚至偶然的观点，并对此予以了矫正，认为弗洛伊德是个实证主义者，理性成分在精神分析中是首要的。其次，特里林论述了弗洛伊德的艺术观。虽然弗洛伊德赞赏文学家在情感方面的洞察，但他对艺术的态度却有些轻佻，因为弗洛伊德提出过艺术“是一种替代性满足”，同时，“是与现实对立的幻象”。究其原因，特里林认为是由于弗洛伊德没有正确的哲学思想的引导，其批判的突破口则是弗洛伊德行医过程中与幻象对立的实在的存在。此外，弗洛伊德还提出了艺术家、诗人与神经病人的区别。前者能主动控制自己的幻想，而后者却沉湎其中无法自拔。

特里林认为，弗洛伊德的艺术观是有瑕疵的，同时批判了弗洛伊德关于精神分析的两个功用。第一，对于阐释文学作品的“内在意义”，特里林认为任何艺术作品的意义都不是封闭，也不是唯一的，正如有一千个人阅读《哈姆莱特》，就有一千个哈姆莱特。第二，对于解释艺术家的个人气质，特里林认为我们研究艺术作品，考察艺术家的身份是可行的，但探索他们的无意识就行不通。因为离开艺术作品去探索艺术家的死亡本能、性欲、梦幻等，那么得到的东西是不完整的，也不能确定作品的意义。

虽然特里林发现了弗洛伊德的艺术观和精神分析功用的不足之处，但他最后依然肯定了弗洛伊德对艺术的理解和艺术实践的贡献，他的贡献不在于弗洛伊德的艺术论断，而蕴含在整个精神观念之中。因此，弗洛伊德的精神分析从一个新的切入点提出了极富洞见的文学审美思想，丰富和拓展了文学研究的方法和路径。

（马礼霞）

一

弗洛伊德心理学精湛深刻、生动感人，是对人类精神唯一的系统说明，可与多少个世纪以来文学作品中所积累的五花八门的心理学见解相媲美。放下一部文学名著，转而读一篇心理学中的人性，却正是诗人创作时始终在运用的材料。由此看来，精神分析学说对文学影响之重大也就不足为奇了。不过影响是相互的，弗洛伊德影响文学。文学也以同样的力量影响弗洛伊德。在庆祝弗洛伊德七十诞辰的仪式上，有人恭维他是“无意识的发现者”。他当即纠正这种说法，辞谢了这一荣誉。他说：“在我之前的诗人们和哲学家们就已发现了无意识，我发现的是研究无意识的科学方法。”

……

在说明弗洛伊德与浪漫主义传统的联系时，很难确定从何处开始讨论，不过将这一传统追溯至起源之前，一直回溯到1762年狄德罗的《拉摩的侄儿》可能是适当的。这毕竟是19世纪思想界的某些核心人物认为了不起的一本小书，有非凡的重要性。歌德将它译成德文。马克思称赞它，并写信告诉恩格斯说他将这本书作为礼物赠送给他，还提醒恩格斯，当年黑格尔赞扬并且详细地解释过这本书。肖伯纳颇受这本书的影响。弗洛伊德本人则喜悦而赞许地读了它，这一点我们是从他的《初级讲义》的一句引言中得知的。

……

从拉摩的自我暴露到卢梭对自己童年的记叙，这一步跨得并不太大。社会尽可无视或否认“好人”生涯的一开端就隐藏着“不道德”的观念，正如对于布莱克社会尽可表示厌恶，因为他挖空心思力图阐释一种包含潜藏在一般社会的人礼节下面诸种力量的心理学。但是关于潜藏之物的观念继续发展，终于成了时代的占统治地位的观念之一。潜藏的成分采取多种表现形式，并不一定就是“黑暗的”和“坏的”；在布莱克看来，“坏的”就是好的，而华滋华斯和伯克则认为潜藏的和无意识的东西正是不受意识的理智制约而发挥作用的智慧和力量。

……

我们很难继续这方面的考证，因为我们探究得越深入，就会发现越来越多的弗洛伊德的文学亲缘关系，即使只限于开列书目，至多也只能挂一漏万。不过我们必须提到雪莱、写《露辛德》的希勒格尔，以及乔治·桑等人大声疾呼的性的革命，还有后来易卜生的更加尖锐的见解；我们还应提到蒂克坦率直言以及叔本华隐晦含蓄的关于艺术起源于性爱的观点；还有斯汤达尔关于性欲失调的研究，他对性爱激情的见解在我们看来带有明显的弗洛伊德色彩。

但是，我们或许应该在此搁笔问一问，由于这些都是弗洛伊德本人得以从中发展起来的时代精神的成分，我们究竟可不可以说弗洛伊德在文学上造成了普遍性的影响？弗洛伊德对于文学趋向本身之发展有何必不可少的独特贡献？假如我们要找一个显示了弗洛伊德影响的作家，普鲁斯特是我们或许会首先想到的。他的作品，同他作品的标题(法语原文标题尤甚于英语标题)一样，都表明他在致力于精神分析——研究睡眠、变态性欲、联想方式、对于暗喻的近乎强迫性的兴趣，在这些方面及其他许多方面，弗洛伊德的影响也许有所显露，但是我相信普鲁斯特并没有读过弗洛伊德的著作。

虽然如此，弗洛伊德对文学的影响仍是十分巨大的，其中大部分内容影响之广甚难估计，它往往以反常的或歪曲的简化形式在不知不觉中渗入我们的生活，成了我们文化的一部分。……

二

相当明显，弗洛伊德思想与浪漫主义传统中的反理性成分很有几分亲缘关系。但我们也应同样清楚地看到，他的体系中并不缺少激进的理性主义。托马斯·曼在他第一篇论述弗洛伊德的文章中使人觉得精神分析的“阿波罗”方面亦即理性方面纵然也很重要和确实值得赞许，却似乎是第二位的和甚至是偶然的，他的观点不正确。他给我们造成的印象是弗洛伊德只注意生活的隐秘的和黑暗的方面。事实完全不是这样。弗洛伊德的理性主义成分是首要的；他首先是个实证主义者。

……

弗洛伊德的理性实证主义既造成他的大部分优点，也造成他所有的不足之处。优点包括他的精细、明确而坚定的积极性目标、治疗的目的、使人类享受足够现世欢乐的心愿。但是作为其早期思想的特点的往往是幼稚肤浅的一些科学原则(后来得到了相当的修正)也得归咎于理性主义，这些原则主要就是声称他的理论与外界实在完全相符。而对于赞赏弗洛伊德，尤其是一板一眼地接受他的艺术观的人，这一点造成了极大的麻烦。

……

不过，归根到底，我们不得不将弗洛伊德讨论艺术时所取的态度称之为轻蔑。他说，艺术是“一种替代性的满足”，因而是“与现实对立的幻象”。然而，这一幻象不同于一般的幻象，艺术“几乎总是无害而有益的”，因为“它仅仅是个幻象而已，并不追求成为别的什么。除了一小部分所谓对艺术入了魔的人，这一幻象从不敢攻击现实领域”。幻象的主要功能之一是起“麻醉剂”的作用。它具有与梦相同的特点，弗洛伊德称其中歪曲的成分为“某种内心的不诚实”。至于艺术家，这些人实际上与神经病患者是一流人物。弗洛伊德在议论一部小说的主角时说：“想象和智力既被这样割裂，他就注定要成为诗人，要不就是变成神经病，他属于那类不生活于现实世界的人物。”

精神分析思想的本身逻辑并没让弗洛伊德非抱这种观点不可。但是在精神分析疗法的实行过程中有大量事实使人们明白弗洛伊德是由于缺乏一种适当的哲学而采取了他那种态度的。分析治疗跟幻象打交道。病人来找医生治疗，故且就算患的是不敢上街行走的恐惧症吧。这种恐惧相当真实，就这点而论，这儿不存在什么幻象；另外，还由此而引起确确实实的恐惧的一切身体症状：手心出汗、心悸、呼吸急促。但是病人知道自己的恐惧是无端的，或者用他的话说：“没有实在的原因。”街上并没有机关枪、陷阱或老虎。不过，医生知道，恐惧背后的确有实在的原因，虽然这原因与街上有或没有什么东西毫不相干。原因是在病人心中，治疗过程就是要一步步发现这个实在的原因，使病人摆脱它的影响。

……

对于作为精神分析临床医师的弗洛伊德来说，存在着我们不妨称之为两个相对极端的东西——实在与幻象。实在是一个褒词，意思就是存在的东西；幻象是个贬词，指的是对于并不存在的东西的反应。一个精神分析疗程的说教性质无疑要求在作出这种区别的时候具有某种大胆的粗略；但它的目的毕竟不在于精细的理论分类，而是追求实际效果。两个极端就是切切实实的实在的和神经错乱的幻象，后者受前者的判断。情况无疑就应该是这样；我们不是在给病人讲授形而上学和认识论。

……

弗洛伊德当然也知道必须将艺术家与神经病人区别开來。他说艺术家与神经病人的不同点在于他懂得如何从想象的世界中找到一条路回到现实世界。不过，照他的意思看来，似乎艺术家只有在中止艺术活动时才去对付实在。至少有一次，当他在讨论艺术对付实在时，他的真意是指成功的艺术家所能获得的酬劳。他并不否认艺术的功能和用途；它在减轻心理的紧张方面具有疗效；它作为“替代性的满足”可以使人们甘心情愿地为文化做出牺牲，从而起到文化方面的作用；它有助于让社会全体成员共享价值巨大的感情经验；它使人们时刻记住自己的文化理想。我们中有些人会发现艺术的功效还不止于此，但作为一种麻醉能起这么些作用已是很了不起的了。

三

我一开头就说过弗洛伊德的学说能为我们提供一些关于艺术的见解，但到此为止我所做的仅仅是表明弗洛伊德的艺术观是不恰当的。那么，它的启发意义或许就在于将分析方法应用于专门艺术作品或艺术家本人？我看不是这样，而且说句公道话，弗洛伊德本人确实曾经意识到精神分析运用于艺术方面的限度及局限性，尽管他在实践中并非始终一贯地服从前者并承认后者。

……

那么，弗洛伊德认为分析方法能做些什么呢？两件事：一是解释艺术作品的“内在意义”，二是解释艺术家作为人的气质。

分析方法的一个著名例子就是试图解答《汉姆雷特》的那个“问题”，这是由弗洛伊德提议，由他早期的著名追随者欧内斯特·琼斯博士执笔写成的。琼斯博士的论文堪称旁征博引、独具匠心的大作。这一研究不仅试图揭示汉姆雷特性格之谜，而且要发现“莎士比亚许多思想深处活动的线索”。这儿所谓的谜，当然首先就是为什么汉姆雷特在显然下定决心之后，并没有为父亲之死向可恶的叔父讨还血债。

但剧本还有另一个谜，就是弗洛伊德称之为“剧本影响之迷”，即剧本所以能吸引这么大的兴趣靠的是何种神奇的魅力。他没有忘记多少人曾企图解决这个剧本的魅力之谜，结果都失败了。因此他怀疑我们最终是否将不得不认为“它的神奇的魅力纯粹有赖于剧中动人的思想和美妙的语言”。弗洛伊德认为我们总还能找到除此以外的某种魅力的来源。

我们记得弗洛伊德说过梦的意义在于其意向，所以我们不妨假定一出戏的意义也在于其意向。琼斯的研究论文就致力于探讨关于汉姆雷特莎士比亚想说些什么。琼斯发现作者将其意图包裹在一片梦幻般的朦胧晦暗之中，因为这种意图深深触及了他的私生活和社会的道德生活。莎士比亚想说的是哈姆雷特被他那种因无意识爱恋母亲而感到的内疚束缚得失去了行动的能力。依我看，对于《汉姆雷特》中存在着恋母情境的说法是没什么可讨论的了。如果精神分析确实给这剧本增加了使人感兴趣的地方，那也就是提高了剧本的声誉①。

这里涉及的并不是证据是否站得住脚的问题，尽管这个问题自然很重要。更重要的是，我们必须反对弗洛伊德和琼斯博士的结论，理由就在于这两位的追随者们对于何谓艺术意义并没有恰当的观点。任何艺术作品都不是只有唯一的一层意义——这样说是正确的，不只是因为这个说法比较有利，亦即这么一说，艺术会变得更为丰富一点，也还因为历史经验和个人经验都已证明其正确性。历史背景和个人心绪的变动会改变艺术作品的意义，从而表明艺术上的理解不是事实的问题，而是一个价值的问题。作者的意向是不能够精确肯定的，而即使能够做到这一点，艺术作品的意义也不仅仅在于作者的意向，还必须由该作品所产生的效果所决定。简言之，观众部分地决定了作品的意义。弗洛伊德似乎多少认识到这一点，因为他说我们除了作者的意向，还应考虑到《汉姆雷特》效果之谜。但他接下去说的话使人觉得《汉姆雷特》问世以来好象只有唯一的效果，而这一效果又是完全由我们在无意识之中对之反应强烈的恋母动机的“魅力”造成的。

我认为我指出弗洛伊德解释方法的不足之处，并未限制我们讨论研究艺术作品的种种方法。培根说过，实验可以把自然绑在刑具上扭绞折磨，逼它供出秘密；而为了发现作品的意义，批判可以对一件艺术作品使用任何工具。艺术的要素并不只限制在艺术的天地里，它们渗入生活，而不管我们对于这些要素所得的知识是怎样的琐细而无

① 然而，A. C. 布拉德莱在讨论《汉姆雷特》(莎士比亚的悲剧)时明确指出汉姆雷特强烈的性欲方面的厌恶感，认为这有助于说明他的犹豫不决。隆宁在布拉德莱之前已有同样说法。不久以前多弗·威尔逊重申了众所周知的一点：在现代观众眼中，汉姆雷特的母亲丈夫一死忙不迭嫁给克劳地厄王仅仅是鄙俗，而在伊利莎白时代观众的眼中她的婚姻还属于通奸性质，因为小叔属于禁止通婚的近亲。

关宏旨，例如考证某艺术作品的历史背景，这些知识都可以加强我们对作品本身的感受，甚至理所当然地渗入这种感受。另外，我们关于艺术家本人的任何了解也都是正当的，并有增进知识的作用。但是探索艺术家的头脑是完全无法实行的，不管这种探索在理论上说来是多么适当。这种探索就是要离开作品本身来探讨艺术家的无意识意向。评论界认识到艺术家关于自己有意识意向的说明尽管有时是有用的，但不能最终确定作品的意义。那么离开了整个作品，仅以无意识意向为根据就更只能得到支离破碎的知识，其中绝没有多少可靠和科学的东西。因为正如弗洛伊德本人指出过的那样，我们无从盘问艺术家本人，而是只能对于他所使用的象征使用分析梦的手法。不过，弗洛伊德也愤愤不平地说过，有些人以为可以不通过做梦人对梦中种种细节的自由联想去解释梦，这些人不懂他的学说。

……

四

所以说，如果我们既反对弗洛伊德关于艺术在生活中的地位的观点，又反对他的分析方法的功用，那么他对于我们对艺术的理解和艺术实践又有些什么贡献呢？我认为，他的贡献大大超过他的错误；贡献是最主要的。贡献并不在于他关于艺术的某些具体言论，而是蕴涵在关于精神的整个观念中。

因为在所有研究精神的体系中，弗洛伊德心理学是唯一主张诗歌是精神体制所固有的。弗洛伊德本人甚至认为精神从主要倾向来看恰恰就是创作诗歌的器官。当然，这有些言过其实，因为这样似乎就把无意识精神的作用与诗歌本身等同了，忘记了在无意识精神与完工的诗歌之间还有社会意向和有意识精神的形式的控制两者在起作用。不过这一说法至少还有与相反观点起抗衡作用的好处，一般人总是公开声言或者暗示诗歌是精神某种有益的偏离正轨的现象。

弗洛伊德不仅还诗歌以自然面目，他还发现诗歌就像一个先驱者，他把诗歌看作一种思想方法。他几次三番力图证明作为一种思想方法，在征服现实方面诗歌是不可靠和无效的。但是在建造他本人的学说时，他又不得不使用它。在讨论精神的配位时，他带着几分挑战的意味道歉说，他使用的关于空间关系的隐喻实在是极不确切的，因为对于精神根本没有什么空间可言。然而不靠隐喻又无从构想这一困难的概念。早在18世纪维科①就谈到过文明最初阶段的隐喻和形象的语言；有待于弗洛伊德来探讨的就是在一个科学时代，我们怎么会仍旧使用譬喻形式来感觉和思想，怎么会创立精神分析这样一种转义、隐喻及其变异形式——提喻和换喻的学说。

弗洛伊德还说明了精神的某一部分的作用可以如何不受逻辑制约，不过还是受着目的的指引和意向的控制，而我们或许可以认为逻辑正是产生于这种指引和控制的。无意识精神可以离开句法联词而起作用，而句法联词恰恰就是逻辑的根本。无意识精神不承认什么“因为”、“所以”、“但是”。相似、一致、共同之类的概念是通过压缩各成分成为统一整

① 维科(Giovanni Battista Vico) 1668—1744，意大利哲学家。

体而在梦中形象地表现的。无意识精神在与意识的斗争中总是从一般转向具体，总是发现可触知的细微末节比高度的抽象来得称心些。弗洛伊德在精神的组织中找到了艺术得以造成其效果的机制，如意义的压缩、重点的转移，等等。

……

任何人在读弗洛伊德的著作时，总感到他的思想中厌世冷嘲的成分确实微乎其微。他满腔热望的就是人要富于人性，他的学说也只是奉献给这一目标的。艺术家的人生观不能保证其作品的质量，但是弗洛伊德学说的诗意显然与古典悲剧的现实主义完全合拍，从而表明这一学说并未使艺术家眼中的人世显得狭小和单调，相反倒是开阔并丰富了这一天地。

（节选自莱昂内尔·特里林：《弗洛伊德与文学》，陆谷孙、曾道中译，《文艺理论研究》1981年第3期，第155-166页。）

文学与艺术

（节选）

［美］玛丽·盖塞

【导读】

即使做主观的判断，我们也会认为文学和艺术是相关的，但是一旦将这种关系纳入学术审视的范围，人们马上就意识到这并不容易。我们面临的第一个挑战就是术语的不通约，比如诗歌和音乐对“节奏”和“主题”的界定，戏剧和绘画对“表现”的定义，等等。不过要说的是，它们之间的关系是切实存在的。学界对二者关系进行研究的途径大致有三种：形式与内容的关系、影响及综合。

就第一种路径而言，我们先悬置形式与内容的学理探究式的定义辨析，而着眼于现象，不难发现，在纷繁复杂的作品背后，共通的是作者们的心灵。当我们把一些诗歌和一些绘画作品并置时，往往会有这样的体验。这方面的代表性著作首推《拉奥孔》。莱辛看到，同样的主题，既可以在诗中表达，也可以通过绘画呈现。他更注意到，同样的题材，在文学和造型艺术之间的表现是有差异的。诗歌能够将动态的过程描述下来，而雕塑只能传达瞬间的感受。这种差别基于它们各自主题传达可凭借的手段和媒介。可以说，正是这些材料质素决定着文学和艺术描绘的具体内容。比如，画家用色彩和线条来表现空间中的物体，而作家用词语描述时间中的活动或行为。也就是说，绘画的赏鉴必须借助空间关系，而文学的阅读则需凭靠时间序列。一般而论，莱辛的见解是正确的适用的。但是，现代文学的一些作家的创作实践似乎印证着时间（文学）、空间（造型艺术）关系的可交融性。T. S. 艾略特、庞德、普鲁斯特以及乔伊斯等人的叙事都给人以很强的空间感，他们的创作似乎印证着文学与艺术的紧密关联。注意文学和艺术之间的相互关系，有助于我们更好地理解所要研究的作品。借助于音乐，我们能更好地理解艾略特的诗歌；借助绘画，我们能更好地解读赫伯特·里德的诗作。

对于影响，我们能够注意到的是文学和艺术因处于相同时期或空间而存在的对应关系，也就是说，它们因接受同样的影响而表现出某种相似。这样的例子很多，夏多布里昂的描写和画家的作品可以相互参照，库尔贝的画作《奥南的葬礼》和福楼拜《包法利夫人》中爱玛的入葬亦可类比。研究文学和艺术间的影响还可聚焦于它们之间的相互借鉴。文学家在创作时会从音乐中汲取灵感，音乐家也会从文学家那里获取主题要素。

有些学者尝试将艺术史原理运用到文学史研究中，他们的成果变相证实着文学和艺术关系紧密，但却更属于彼此相异的两个领域。这其实也提醒我们对文学和艺术进行综合、归纳的危险及困难。但学术道路上从来不缺有勇气的学人，他们已经在这个领域做出了有益的探索。我们或许要看到他们的成绩，而尤要留心他们这样做的弊端，因为这可能是一个陷阱。

（陈会亮）

文学与艺术的比较研究是一个相当麻烦的领域。……研究者……绝不可穿凿附会，为比较而比较。

……进行文学与艺术的比较研究似乎有三种基本途径：形式和内容的关系、影响以及综合。这三者当然可以有重合之处，不过强调重点的不同就能有所区别。下面我想通过一些出色的研究来说明这些途径。

……形式和内容这两个术语充其量也只能不甚精确地描述包括风格、技巧、叙述及思想等广阔范围内的各种问题。绝大部分研究都无疑属于形式及构成形式的所有成分的广大范畴。甚至研究相隔数代独立存在的两种艺术的关系，把这种研究作为帮助我们分别去鉴赏这两种艺术的一种办法，也完全有理由被看成属于形式研究的范畴。……《赛斯的新来者》……这本书出版时同时印有六十幅保罗・克勒①的自然风景素描，但不是作为书的插图，而是与文字平行的。……诗画并置可以使意义明朗，奥登②的诗《美术博物馆》……里要人们注意勃吕盖尔③画的构图，以此来测定人类对于苦难的态度。……这两例都证明了各门艺术之间存在着非常明显的关系。……

18世纪德国批评家莱辛……在《拉奥孔》中试图明确划分诗和造型艺术的界限，认为有的主题更适于绘画，有的主题则更适于诗。……

莱辛承认，每一个艺术家在解释他的题材时都受到他那一门艺术的局限。……艺术家或诗人如果认识不到自己那门艺术所遵循的规律，就不能创造出从审美角度看来能给人快感的艺术形式。

莱辛之所以把诗和造型艺术加以分别，是基于两方面的考虑：即艺术形式和我们自己的感觉方式。莱辛认为时间是诗的因素，空间是造型艺术的因素（第91页）。……如果最终的目的是要传达出一个有意义的整体，那么在正确选择题材这一点上，画家比诗人承担的责任更大。画家因此而必须选取行动当中“最具包孕性的片刻”来描绘。他应当能暗示出下一刻的行动，但他能做的也仅止于此——暗示。画家的作品的空间形式本身必然限制他只能描绘“实体的美”。……

艺术家能够描绘的内容受到空间关系的限制，诗人在选材上较为自由，但在手段上也

---

① 瑞士画家，现代派艺术的先驱之一。

② 英国诗人，20世纪文学重要的代表人物之一。

③ 尼德兰画家，作品多反映乡村生活和社会风俗。《伊卡露斯》则以希腊神话为题材，描绘蜡粘着羽毛做翅膀的伊卡露斯，因飞得太高，被太阳将蜡晒化而坠入海中死亡。

受到局限。画家用色彩和线条在空间中表现的东西，用词句在时间中就较难表现。于是诗人不去描绘人或物，往往宁可去描绘这人或物产生的作用(例如，荷马描写海伦的美貌所起的作用，而不直接描绘她的美貌)。……对莱辛来说，造型艺术的领域局限于空间中的物体，而诗的领域则包括了时间中的运动。

在大部分现代写作和绘画当中，莱辛讨论过的审美感觉原理仍然是适用的，但有一些现代作家使用意识流技巧，在创造一种新的叙述形式时认识到了空间感觉的原理。……约瑟夫·弗朗克(Joseph Frank)在研究现代文学中的空间形式时说："……读者大多在一个时间片刻里从空间观念上去理解他们的作品，而不是把作品视为一个序列。"感觉的方法和莱辛描述的造型艺术中的方法一样，但感觉的对象却不同了。

弗朗克先生指出，读者……是靠"反射式参照"(reflexive reference)的办法，即读者在把作品读完的时候，把作品中提到的各个东西拼合起来，对诗人或小说家通过空间形式完成的东西获得一个完整的画面。尤其是现代诗歌"以空间逻辑为基础，这种逻辑要求读者全面重新调整自己对语言的态度"。读者必须把表面上孤立的片断和一组组词汇与诗中一个暗示的、集中的情境联系起来，组成一个整体。……

(举例玖娜·巴恩斯(Djuna Barnes)的《夜林》、弗吉尼亚·伍尔芙(Viginia Woolf)的《达洛威夫人》。)

各门艺术之间的相互关系常常可以帮助批评家更深刻地理解他所研究的作品。但我们也可以进一步地说：艺术家本身也可以通过这样的类比获得好处。T. S. 艾略特在论《诗的音乐》这篇文章里，明确地论述了研究音乐可以给诗歌带来什么好处：

> 我相信，音乐当中与诗人最有关系的性质是节奏感知结构感。……使用再现的主题对于诗象对于音乐一样自然。诗句变化的可能性有点象用不同的几组乐器来发展一个主题；一首诗当中也有转调的各种可能，好比交响乐或四重奏当中不同的几个乐章；题材也可以作各种对位的安排。

(海伦·伽德纳小姐(Miss Helen Gardner)对艾略特的《四个四重奏》这组诗的形式与相应的音乐形式作了一个比较。具体比较内容略。)

……

伽德纳小姐不仅要求我们注意这组诗明显依照音乐形式原则的结构，而且指出了意象、象征和某些辞句的重复使之获得一种更深的、扩展的意义。艾略特本人也描述了这种"意义的音乐"……

> 词的音乐可以说是在一个交叉点上：它的产生首先来自它与前后各个词的关系，与它的内容其余部分的关系；而且还来自另一种关系，即在那特定上下文中这个词的直接意义与它在别的上下文中所有的其他的意义之间的关系……一首"音乐性的诗"就是这首诗具有音乐型的声音。构成这首诗的词汇具有音乐型的第二层意义，而这两种音乐型是统一不可分割的。

伽德纳小姐在考察了《四个四重奏》的音乐结构和主题材料的处理之后，在艾略特的意象的处理中又发现了另一个与音乐类似的因素，这些意象“在它们的上下文中或在与其他反复出现的意象的联合当中，不断以变化的形式反复再现，正如音乐中一个乐句以变化的形式反复再现一样”。第一次接触时，它们似乎很普通、明显而且平常。但是，“在它们重新出现时就发生了变化……”

再举一个“文学与绘画”的例子。赫伯特·里德爵士(Sir Herbert Read)在他写的一首诗里探索梦的形成与诗的形成之间的对应关系。……他把……超现实主义的诗，描述为“梦幻内容的显现，梦幻潜伏的思想被转变成感性形象或可见的场景；也就是说，抽象的东西重新融入它所从来的具体形式当中去”。

到此为止，我们一直讨论的是各门艺术的关系而没有谈到时代或文化影响的共同特性。……现在来看看文学与艺术由于处于同一时期而存在的对应关系。在这里很难绕过影响问题，也很难避免这样的暗示，即同一时期不同的艺术形式是在同样的影响下发展的。

赫尔穆特·哈兹菲尔德(Helmut Hatzfeld)的《从艺术看文学》……把研究局限于……考察相同因素条件下的两种艺术，从而更容易揭示出互相反映的关系……他考察文学与艺术的基本理论，就是认为把同一文化时期内不同的艺术形式并列起来，必然会增加可能的解释。……不过，这种比较研究强调的是“时代的文化类型”。

哈兹菲尔德……从文化与艺术表现相互关系的广泛研究中得出的结论是，对于任何特定历史时期的文学与艺术，都可从七个范畴去加以研究：1. 用图画阐释作品本文的细节，2. 用作品本文说明图画的细部，3. 用构图艺术说明文学的概念和主旨，4. 通过文学阐释绘画作品的主旨，5. 和 6. 文学艺术中的文学语言形式和文学文体的表现，7. 文学与艺术的交界。

……哈兹菲尔德的研究也许在定义和选择例子上有些不尽正确的地方，甚至可以批评这一研究的理论基础，……但是，这种研究却的确有助于加深对文学与艺术的认识，的确提示了采用语言分析方法的可能性。

研究文学与艺术的关系的另一种方法见于喀尔文·布朗(Calvin Brown)的《音乐与文学》。布朗不是去探讨从文化和语言分析观点进行的类比，而是把文学与音乐的关系的研究基于这两者的共同因素、它们互相协作的情形(从民间叙事诗到歌剧)以及作家影响音乐家、音乐家影响作家的实例。……布朗没有考虑历史发展或任何共同文化背景的反映——在这一研究中他把全部音乐和全部文学作为自己的研究范围。……

艺术史是对文学和艺术的比较研究产生影响的领域之一。亨利希·沃尔夫林(Heinrich Wolffllin)的《艺术史原理》(1915)提出了艺术是在看待和感受事物的方式的基础上进行创造的理论。……其原理的重要意义在于对文学史家的影响，为文学史家们提供了解释文体风格的类似手法。……

把艺术史原理应用于文学史这类尝试的意义在于，可以由此发现不能把一种艺术媒介的基本概念简单地借过来……尽管这两种艺术形式可能含有某些共同因素。因此，形式和风格不会有完全对应的发展，解释某一艺术形式的原则必须是来自作品的性质本身。注意同一时期的同一种艺术形式无疑可以启发解释另一种艺术形式的概念，但却不能简单地转移过来。

通过艺术风格和艺术批评来描述和解释文学的一次较近的尝试，是怀里·塞弗尔(Wylie Sypher)的《文艺复兴风格的四个阶段》。……其方法完全以风格为基础。他不谈各门艺术风格之间的对应，而宁可用风格之间的“类似”(analogy)这个术语来描述艺术反映社会变化的种种方式，每一个风格都有它“本身的进化、演变和最终的消亡”。在这些风格开始形成出现的时候，常常有各门艺术之间技巧的“交换”，这时一种艺术的技巧向另一种艺术渗透……也就是塞弗尔所谓风格的“转换”……

塞弗尔就这样研究了三个世纪的文学、绘画、雕塑、建筑……然而，这些风格并不是在每一个国家里都同时期发展变化的。一国与另一国，一种艺术与另一种艺术，都有“时差”。……

现在可以来分辨一下这一研究领域里的不同派别。对过去的成就和现在的努力表示极度怀疑的一派，在韦勒克和沃伦的《文学理论》中得到了权威性的表现。韦勒克在该书的第十一章“文学与其他艺术”……结束时提出一个严厉的警告：不要过早地进行综合。……

但是，纯理论家的审慎态度并不是大多数在这个领域里从事研究的人的态度。……一九一四年创办的《美学与艺术批评杂志》……充满了生动的争论，但它所代表的团体，即美国美学学会，却一直努力进行综合，不管这种综合是多么暂时的和试验性的。……

对理论不那么感兴趣，却更注重文学观点的是现代语言学会的“文学与其他艺术”讨论小组。……其往往论述一个作家与姊妹艺术的关系。……

这种研究以全部艺术为领域，从单个艺术品之间的偶然联系直到整个文化时期文学艺术作品互相渗透的极为复杂的情形……严肃的艺术家和批评家都随时意识到，文学与艺术间存在着“天然的姻缘”……而这种姻缘本身就包含着构成比较分析之基础的对应、影响和互相借鉴。有时候，艺术家本人就意识到自己的主题、布局技巧、形式安排和思想的发展方式其实属于另一门艺术的范畴。……

（张隆溪　译）

（节选自[美]玛丽·盖塞：《文学与艺术》，张隆溪选编，《比较文学译文集》，北京大学出版社 1982 年版，第 120-136 页。）

说不尽的莎士比亚

（节选）

[德]歌　德

【导读】

英国戏剧大师莎士比亚一生创作了37部戏剧、两首长诗和一百多首十四行诗，代表了欧洲文艺复兴时期最卓著的成就，为后人留下了宝贵的文学财富。至今在世界范围内早已形成了蓬勃发展的莎士比亚研究产业，即使在歌德所处的时代，莎士比亚研究也蔚为大观。歌德是德国最杰出的作家之一，既是小说家、戏剧家，还是诗人，他为莎士比亚这位旷世奇才深深折服，惊叹于莎剧的博大精深，不禁赞叹"说不尽的莎士比亚!"歌德以散文随笔的方式，从以下三方面对莎士比亚进行了考察：一是把莎士比亚作为一般意义上的作家来分析；二是把他与古人和今人进行对比分析；三是把他作为剧作家来分析。他娓娓道来，趣味盎然，不乏真知灼见，这是一篇视角独特的莎士比亚研究文献。

首先，作为一般意义上的莎士比亚是什么样的呢？歌德认为莎士比亚把人们错综复杂的世界写得非常通透，把美丽与丑陋，高尚与卑劣，情感与理性，欲望与道德都体现得淋漓尽致。那么，莎士比亚又是如何实现这样的艺术效果呢？在歌德看来，他有一枝生花的妙笔，用能激发读者感官的语言，表达人类的精神，尤其是充满想象力的语言可以把潜藏在人们内心世界中最隐秘的东西发掘出来，从而使人们获得人生的真谛。其次，歌德试图发现莎士比亚与古人和今人之间的区别与联系。由于莎剧中的写实成分明显，人们普遍认为莎士比亚不属于现代作家，更应属于古代作家。然而，歌德认为莎士比亚同古代作家还有一段很长的距离，所以更确切地说他还是一个现代作家。因为在古代文学中主要是应当同现实之间的矛盾，在现代文学中则是愿望同现实之间的矛盾，应当是外在强加于人的事情，而愿望则是人主观赋予的东西，因此事件的执行过程和后果在人物内心造成的影响也是完全不一样的。而实际上，莎士比亚是力图把古代与现代巧妙地糅合起来，从而使应当、愿望与现实之间达到一种平衡。最后，歌德把莎士比亚当作剧作家进行考察，发现了以下两方面的特点：一是莎士比亚对剧本的改动和剪裁是最独具匠心的。在剧本的创作过程中，莎士比亚非常擅长对他人的小说和戏剧进行改编。他对史料的提炼非常严谨，在历史剧系列中，他触及了篡权、废黜、战争等社会政治历史问题，对当时的王朝内政都有不同程度的影射，如《哈姆莱特》、《理查二世》。对于趣闻轶事，莎士比亚则要轻率得多，根据剧情他可以随意加入一些插科打诨的角色，如《罗密欧与朱丽叶》。二是莎士比亚的剧本创作与舞台艺术是不合拍的。歌德发现如果把莎剧原原本本搬上舞台，是十分荒谬的做法，无论在英国还是德国都不会收到好的效果。为此，歌德赞成施罗德的做法，即选择莎剧中能产生舞台效果的素材，而抛弃会破坏民族精神及时代特色的剧情。

为什么莎士比亚及其作品历久弥新？为什么莎剧能在不同时空拓展？歌德认为是莎士比亚的精神特性激励着一代又一代人的精神，他不只属于某一个国家，也不只属于某一个时代，因为莎士比亚精神是超越时空限制的。因此，在歌德时代有说不尽的莎士比亚，至今仍不断在世界文学界产生广泛而深远的影响，并具有重要的现代意义。

（马礼霞）

关于莎士比亚已经论述过很多，看来似乎再没有什么可说的了。然而精神的特性就在于它永远在启发精神。这一回我要从几个方面考察莎士比亚，首先把他作为一般意义上的作家，然后把他与古人和现代人相比较，最后把他作为真正的剧作家加以考察。我想试图阐明，他的那种模仿对我们曾产生过什么影响，以及它到底能发生什么影响。对于已经发表过的观点，同意的部分，我就再把它重复一下，不同意的部分，我要简要地，正面地表示不同意，但不进行反驳，也不与之争论。现在先谈第一点。

一、莎士比亚作为一般意义上的作家

人所能达到的最高境地，就是他明确地意识到他自己的信念和思想，认识到自己并且由此开始也深切地认识到别人的思想感情。有些人生来就有这种天赋，并且通过经验发展这种天赋，以实现实际的目的。这样就产生了一种能力，使人能在社会上以及在各种活动中获得更高意义上的成功。作家也是生来就有这种天赋，不过他发展这种天赋不是为了直接的，人世的目的，而是为了更高的、普遍的精神目的。如果我们称莎士比亚是最伟大的作家之一，我们就必须同时承认，并不是轻而易举地就能找到一个人，他能像莎士比亚那样洞察世界，也并不是轻而易举地就能找到一个人，他能像莎士比亚那样说出自己内心深处的见解，并且让读者跟他一起在更高的程度上领悟世界。我们读了莎士比亚的作品，世界剧变得完全透明，我们突然发现，我们对美德与陋习，伟大与渺小，高贵与卑贱都非常熟悉，而且这一切，甚至还不只这一切，都是用最简单的方式实现的。但是，若要问这都是些什么方法，回答看上去好像是这样：莎士比亚是为我们的眼睛写作；然而，这是我们的幻觉，莎士比亚的著作并不是为肉眼写的。这一点我想解释一下。

眼睛也许可以称作是最明亮的感官，通过眼睛可以最容易地传情达意。但是内在的感官比眼睛更明亮，通过语言可以把一切事物最完美地，最迅速地传达给它，因为语言才是真正能开花结果的东西，而我们的眼睛所看见的东西本身却是外在的，对我们不会产生深刻的影响。莎士比亚完全是对着我们的内在感官说话，通过内在感官想象力所编织的图像世界立即有了生命，像活的一样；于是就产生了一种完整的效应，对于这种效应，我们不知道如何解释。这也正是所以有那种以为一切都是在我们眼睛前面发生的错觉的根源。但是，如果我们自行观察一下莎士比亚的剧本，我们会发现，其中诉诸感性的行为要比表达精神的词句少得多。他让一些容易想象的事，甚至一些最好通过想象而不是通过视觉来把握的事发生在他的剧本中。《哈姆雷特》的鬼魂，《麦康白》的女巫以及一些残暴行为都是通过一些想象的力量才获得它们的价值，而那各种各样的小插曲就更得依靠这种想象的力量了。这一切在阅读时顺利地、理所当然地从我们眼前掠过，而在表演时则显得累赘障事，甚至令人厌恶。

莎士比亚是通过有生命力的词句发生影响。而诵读是传达词句的最好方式，听众的注意力很集中，无论表演恰当还是拙劣都不影响他们。闭目倾听自然正确声调的诵读，而不是像演员那样朗诵莎士比亚的作品，这是再高不过，再纯粹不过的享受。人们跟随一根线索，听他讲各种事件。虽然听了对性格的描述之后，我们也可以想象出某些人物的形象，但只有通过一系列的词语和言谈我们才能知道这些人物的内心活动，而所有的人物好像事先都已经约好，不让我们有一点不清楚或是怀疑的地方。在这一点上英雄和小卒，主人和奴仆，王公和差役是同谋，甚至于次要的角色往往比主要角色更为活跃。在大的世界性事件发生时把空气吹得飒飒作响的一切，在巨大事件发生的瞬间人们心灵中隐藏的一切，都被说了出来。一切在心灵深处被胆怯地封存着的，隐藏着的东西，在这里被自由而通畅地采掘出来；我们获知生命的真谛，然而却不知道是怎样获得的。

莎士比亚与世界精神①结伴，他也像世界的精神一样看透了这个世界，什么都不能瞒过他。不过，如果说世界精神的职务是在行动前，甚至常常是在行动之后保守秘密的话，那么作家的旨意则是将秘密吐露出来，让我们在行动之前，或是就在行动过程中相互了解。为非作歹的人和静观世界的人，他们都把自己的心事袒露出来，常常没有一点含混，各个都很能言善谈。总之，秘密一定得吐露，就是石头也得吐露秘密。因此没有生命的东西也蜂拥而至，要吐露秘密，一切次要的附属物都跟着说话，大自然的各种因素，天上，地面和海洋的现象，雷，电，野兽都在大声呼喊，它们往往看上去是一种比喻，但每一次都参加进来一起行动。

但是，文明世界也必须献出它的珍品。科学与艺术，手工业与各种工艺行当都解囊奉献，莎士比亚的著作是一个广大的，活跃的市场，然而他有这样的财富应归功于他的祖国。

英格兰无处不在，它四面环海，云雾笼罩，它把活动的足迹伸向了世界各地。作家生活在一个值得尊敬的重要的时代，他把这个时代的文化教养，甚至是不良的教养极其清楚地展现给我们。可以说，假如他不是跟他生活的时代溶为一体的话，他就不会对我们发生那么大的影响。再也没有人比他更轻视物质的行为了，他很了解人的灵魂行为，在这一方面所有的人都没有区别。有人说，他对罗马人的描写好极了，我以为不然，那是彻头彻尾的英国人。当然，他们都是人，地地道道的人，因此罗马人的长袍他们穿着也合身。如果我们是立足于这一点的话，那么就会发现，莎士比亚的这种时代差错，才使他的作品具有如此的生命力。

……

① 歌德所说的“世界精神”指使世界有了生命的一种精神。

二、莎士比亚与古代和今人之比较

世界是莎士比亚的兴趣所在，正是这种兴趣使他的伟大思想富有生气。因为虽然像预言和疯癫、梦魇、预感、异兆、仙女和精灵、鬼魂、恶魔和巫师这样一些神秘魔幻的要素，适当的时候在他的作品中也会出现，但这些虚幻的形象绝不是他著作中的主要成份，而真实的生活和精干的生命才是他的著作立足的伟大基础，因此出自他笔下的一切我们都觉得是那么纯真和实在。因此人们已经认识到，他不属于现代作家，即所谓的浪漫的①作家，他更应归属于朴素类作家，因为他的价值是以现实为基础的，他极少柔情脉脉，甚至可以说，只是在最极端的情况下才有一点渴望的味道。

然而尽管如此，如果仔细地观察一下，他还是一个真正的现代作家，他与古人之间隔着一道鸿沟；而且这不是就其外在形式而言，这种外在形式的差别完全可以撇开不管，而是指最内在的深层涵义。

……

一个人所能遭受到的最大和最多的痛苦，产生于每个人胸中存在着的应当与愿望之间的，还有应当与现实，愿望与现实之间的不协调关系，正是这些不协调关系时常使人在生命的过程陷入窘境。由不期而然地，毫无损失地就能加以克服的轻微错误而引发的最微不足道的窘境，是造成可笑情景的基础；相反，无法解决的，或者还没有解决的最厉害的窘境带给我们的则是悲剧因素。

古代文学作品中占统治地位的是应当与现实之间的不协调，在近代文学作品中则是愿望与现实之间的不协调。我们暂且把这一根本性的区别跟其他的对比放在一起，看看这样做是否有好处。我刚才说，在这两个不同的时代中，时而这一面，时而那一面占统治地位，可是因为应当与愿望在一个人的身上不能截然分开，因此这两个侧面总是同时存在，虽然其中一个占优势，另一个处于从属地位。应当是强加给人的东西，必须是一颗苦果，愿望是人自己加给自己的东西，人的意志是人的天国。不容变通的应当让人厌烦，无法实现的行动使人害怕，坚毅顽强的愿望使人愉快，而坚定不移的意志甚至可以使人忘却行动上的无能而感到宽慰。

古代的悲剧是以不可避免的应当为基础的，愿望竭力抵御应当，但这只是使它更加严酷，来得更加迅速。神谕宣示所是一切可怕事物的所在地，在这个区域里《俄狄浦斯》首屈一指。在《安提戈涅》中应当作为义务似乎显得温和一些，但不是也转变成许许多多其他形式而出现吗？不过，只要是应当就是专横的，不管它是属于理性范畴，如道德法则、城市法则，还是属于自然范畴，如生成、发展和消亡的法则以及生与死的法则。面对这些法则我们感到胆战心惊，而没有想到，只有它们才能造福于整体。愿望的情况正好相反，它是自由的，看上去是自由的，而且对于个体有利。因此愿望靠阿谀奉承讨人喜欢，人们一旦与它相识，就要被它缠住。它是近代之神，我们对它俯首帖耳，唯恐有什么东西与之

① 这里“浪漫的”一词是席勒所说的“感伤”的别称，因而与“朴素的”相对。席勒所说的“朴素的”与“感伤的”之间的对立，也包含“古代”与“现代”想对立的意思，歌德正是在这个意义上用这两个词的。

对抗。这就是为什么我们的艺术和我们的感知方式与古典艺术和古典感知方式永远相隔的原因。应当使悲剧宏伟有力，愿望使悲剧渺小软弱。在后一种情况下，产生了所谓的戏剧，因为我们用愿望代替应当这一庞然大物。不过，正因为愿望在我们软弱的时候帮助了我们，使我们在痛苦的期待之后最终还得到少许慰藉，所以我们很受感动。

……

在我们作了这些评述之后再来读莎士比亚的时候，我希望我的读者们能够自己去进行比较和实用。莎士比亚热情洋溢地将古与今结合起来，在这一方面他是独一无二的。在他的剧作中，他竭力使愿望与应当达到平衡，二者进行强烈的抗争，然而，最终总是愿望处于劣势。

对个人性格中愿望与应当的最初的伟大衔接没有谁比他描绘得更为出色了。单个的人，从性格方面看，应当意味着：他是有限的，是个特殊。但是，这个单个的人作为人又怀有愿望，因此他是无限的，要求一般。这样就已经产生了一种内在的冲突，而莎士比亚让这一冲突处于突出的地位，使它比其他一切充实更显著。不过，此外还有一种外在冲突，这种外在的冲突常常会更趋尖锐，因为一个难以实现的愿望由于某些机缘会上升为不可避免的应当。过去我曾就《哈姆莱特》一剧证明过这一原则①，但是，这一原则在莎士比亚的其他作品中也同样出现。正如哈姆莱特由于鬼魂而陷入他无法应付的困境一样，麦克白是由于女巫和黑刻提以及超级女巫即他的夫人，勃鲁托斯是由于他的朋友而陷入同样的困境。甚至在《科里奥兰纳斯》也能找到类似的情况。总之，一种超越个人力量的愿望是近代才有的。但是，莎士比亚不是让这种愿望从内部蹦出，而是通过外在的机缘把它激发出来，因而愿望就变成了某种应当，这就跟古代文学差不多。……

三、莎士比亚作为剧作家

……

一个得到普遍认可的有才能的人也可能对他的能力使用不当。出类拔萃的人做的事并不件件都是最好的。莎士比亚属于文学史，这是必然的，他在舞台戏剧史当中的出现却是偶然的。如果说，他在文学史当中受到人们无条件的崇敬，那么在舞台戏剧史当中人们就必须考虑他所顺应的那些条件，不能把这些条件当作优点或是典范来颂扬。

我们要把那些渊源相近，在用活泼生动的方式处理时常常汇合在一起的文学种类区分开来，这些文学种类是：史诗，对话，戏剧和舞台剧。史诗要求由一个人向群众做口头传述；对话是在一定范围内的谈话，当然群众也可以在场旁听；戏剧史在行动中进行的对话，即使这种对话只是靠想象力进行的；舞台剧是前三者的结合，它使视觉也参预工作，而且人们可以在有确定的地点和出场人物的条件下去理解它。

在这种意义上，莎士比亚的著作是最富有戏剧性的；他把最内在的生活开掘出来，通过这种处理方法去赢得读者，舞台的要求在他看来是无足轻重的，他对这些要求很随便，于是人们在思想上对他也很随便。我们跟着他从一个地点调到另一个地点，中间被他省略

① 歌德在他的小说《维廉麦斯特的学习时代》第四部第十三章中论述过莎士比亚的《哈姆莱特》。

的情节要由我们用想象力来填补。我们甚至得感谢他，因为他是以这样一种高尚的方式激励我们的思维能力。……

莎士比亚的整个创作方法与真正的舞台是有抵触的，他具有的是一位概括者的伟大才能，而且因为一般意义上的作家总是以大自然的概括者的身份出现，所以我们也必须承认他在这方面的伟大功绩。我们只是认为，舞台并不是与他的天才相称的空间，而且我们是为了尊敬他才这样认为的，因为正是舞台的局限性使他自己受到限制。但在这方面，他也不是像其他作家那样，为每部作品选择特定的题材，而是以一个概念为中心，把世界和宇宙同这个概念联系起来。当他对古代和近代历史进行压缩提炼时，他可以利用每一部编年史的材料，而且往往甚至是严格到一字不变。他对待趣闻轶事就不那么严谨，这一点我们以《哈姆莱特》为证。《罗密欧和朱丽叶》比较忠实于原来的传说，然而由于加进了两个滑稽角色迈立西奥和保姆，原来传说中的悲剧内容几乎全部被破坏了。……

不过，莎士比亚最引人注目的地方是他对已有剧本的改动和剪裁。我们可以拿《约翰王》和《李尔王》做这种比较，因为原来的剧本都保留了下来。但就是作为一般意义上的作家而不是作为剧作家进行工作的。

……

施罗德把莎士比亚的剧本搬上德国舞台，他能获得这一伟大功绩，不正是因为他对莎士比亚这一概括者又做了一番概括吗！施罗德看重的仅仅是那些能产生效果的东西，其余的一切他一概抛弃，如果他觉得，这些情节破坏了剧本对他的民族，对他的时代应产生的影响。譬如说他删去《李尔王》一剧的最初的一场。

但是多年来德国流行一种偏见，认为莎士比亚在德国舞台上必须逐字逐句一点不错地演出，即使演员和观众会因此感到窒息也应如此。由于精彩而又准确的翻译①而引起的这类尝试从未获得成功，魏玛剧院的那些真诚的反复不断的努力为此提供了最好的证据。所以，如果想要观看莎士比亚的剧本的话，那就必须再度采用施罗德的改编法。但是，有人坚持即使是演出莎士比亚的剧本也不能改动一个字，尽管这种看法十分荒谬，但却一再出现。如果这种看法的维护者占了上风，那么几年内莎士比亚就会从德国舞台上完全被排挤出去。不过这也并不是什么坏事，因为这样一来不论是喜欢独自一人还是喜欢大家一起阅读的读者，在阅读莎士比亚作品时感到的快活都更加纯洁。

……

（安书祉　译）

（节选自歌德：《论文学艺术》，范大灿、安书祉、黄燎宇等译，人民文学出版社 1999 年版，第 234-241 页。）

---

① 1797 年到 1810 年奥古斯特施莱格尔主持翻译了莎士比亚的十四部剧本，从 1826 年起又在蒂克主持下把莎士比亚其余的剧本译成德文。

The Concept of Baroque in Literary Scholarship

（节选）

［美］René Wellek

【导读】

雷内·韦勒克(1903—1995)被普遍认为是当代文学研究领域的大师。他能使用几种语言进行阅读和创作，他的研究领域覆盖了文学理论、比较文学、艺术理论、社会学、心理学、哲学和宗教等领域，是建树颇高的文学评论家和文艺理论家，也是资深的翻译家、教育家和编辑。韦勒克生于维也纳，从小就学会了德语和捷克语，后又学习了拉丁语、希腊语和英语。他和兄弟两人都酷爱读书，渴望吸收各种知识。在布拉格查理大学，他有幸师从马泰休斯，研究莎士比亚。后在父亲资助下到英国继续学习。1930年他回到布拉格在查理大学工作，并写出第一本书，关于康德，并成为著名的布拉格语言学派的活跃分子。1935年，在捷克政府资助下到伦敦用捷克语讲授文学，此间他接触到奥斯丁渥伦并与之合作开始写作文学领域内的巨著《文学理论》。1946年他来到耶鲁大学成为斯拉夫语和比较文学教授。1949年《文学理论》完成。他一生著作颇丰，著作包括1949年出版的与奥斯丁沃伦合作的《文学理论》，1941年出版《英国文学史起源》，1955年开始出版、1992年最终出版完《近代文学史八卷本》，1963年出版的《批评的概念》，1969年出版的《文学理论和布拉格学派的美学》，1981年出版的《四位批评家：克罗齐、瓦里莱、卢卡契、英加登》等。

韦勒克是新批评学派后期主要人物，他与沃伦合著的《文学理论》对文学的研究产生很大影响，该书先后被译成多种文字，并促使很多国家对文学研究的方法和理论进行改革。该书分为四个部分："定义区分"，"初步工作"，"文学的外部研究"和"文学的内部研究"。其中提出了一个非常有影响力的观点，认为文学研究分为"外部研究"和"内部研究"，前者涉及到作家的创作心理、创作过程和所处的社会环境等作品以外的因素，后者研究的是"文学艺术作品的存在方式"，即把文学作品作为一种符号结构加以研究，相对于"外部研究"这种因果式的研究方法，"内部研究"更关注文学作品本身，即文学的"文学性"，这也是新批评派的主要观点。

巴罗克作为一个文学批评术语，在国外曾经引发热烈讨论，争议颇多，而国内的研究远远落后于国外对巴罗克的研究。在上个世纪国内对于巴罗克的研究主要处于介绍阶段，译介过来的作品较为有限，这方面的研究较少，也有少量的评述和系列的论文，但远未形成规模，比较有影响力的有杨周翰先生的一篇文章《巴罗克的涵义、表现和应用》，学者叶廷芳也对巴罗克有过较系统的研究，尝试为巴罗克在中国扎根进行过努力。进入新世纪以来，国内对巴罗克的研究逐渐深入，形成一定影响。韦勒克在这篇文章中非常详细地探讨了巴罗克概念含义，其演变史及其如何被运用到文学的过程，采用了大量来自各国的文献进行论证，因此文中有大量较为生僻的名称。节选第一章首先从语源的角度探讨了巴罗克的涵义，涉及到西班牙语、葡萄牙语、法语和意大利语等几种语源(此处韦勒克自己在该书1962年附录中对错误做了修改，认为主要是葡萄牙语和法语两种语源)。巴罗克作为一种艺术领域内的术语是如何被使用的，作为一种反宗教改革时期的建筑艺术风格，是"奢华的"、"怪诞的"，其涵义与"哥特式"与"罗可可"很难区别，它也被运用在雕刻、音乐和绘画中，被认为是文艺复兴时期后的一个新的艺术阶段。随后描述了这个概念如何从艺术到文学的转移和扩展，沃尔弗林被认为是第一个把巴罗克运用在文学评论中的学者(在1962年的附录中也进行了更正，事实上，有相当一部分学者已经在文学领域使用巴罗克这个概念)，其后德国学者大量使用巴罗克的概念，一战后，对巴罗克的推崇在德国达到巅峰。德国学者不仅适用巴罗克评价本民族文学艺术，同时也适用这一概念作为标准来评价欧洲其他国家文艺作品。随后这个概念也被荷兰、意大利、西班牙和法国学者所采用，而英美两国学者对巴罗克的接受则晚于其他国家。

(黄惠)

All students of English will realize that the use of the term "baroque" in literature is a recent importation from the continent of Europe. A full-scale history of the term, which has never been attempted, [1] would be of considerable interest, even though I do not believe that the history of any term needs to be decisive for its present-day use, and though I realize that a term cannot be returned to any of its original meanings; least, of course, by the dictum of one man.

"Baroque" as Karl Borinski and Benedetto Croce have shown by convincing quotations, [2] is derived from *baroco*, the name for the fourth mode of the second figure in the scholastic nomenclature of syllogisms. It is a syllogism of the type: "Every P is M; some S are not M, hence some S are not P"; or to give Croce's example: "Every fool is stubborn; some people are not stubborn, hence some people are not fools." This type of argument was felt to be sophistical and far-fetched as early as 1519 when Luis Vives ridiculed the Parisian professors as "sophists in *baroco* and *baralipton*."[3] Croce gives several examples of the use of such phrases as "ragioni barrochi" from 1570 on. The etymology found in the *New English Dictionary* and elsewhere which would derive the term from the Spanish *barrueco*, an oddly-shaped pearl, must apparently be abandoned. In the eighteenth century, the term emerges with the meaning of "extravagant", "bizarre." In 1739, it is used thus by the President de Brosses, and in the sense of "decorative, playfully free" by J. J. Winckelmann in 1755.[4] In Quatremere de Quincy's *Dictionnaire historique de l'architecture* (1795-1825), it is called "une nuance du bizarre" and Guarino Guarini is considered the master of the baroque.[5] Jakob Burckhardt seems to have stabilized its meaning in art-history as referring to what he considered the decadence of the High Renaissance in the florid architecture of the Counter-Reformation in Italy, Germany and Spain. In 1843, he had used the term *rococo* in exactly the same sense as he later used baroque, and suggested that every style has its *rococo*: a late, florid, decadent stage.[6] This suggestion of Burckhardt's of an extension of the term was taken up by Willamowitz-Moellendorf, the famous classical philologist, who in 1881 wrote about "ancient baroque," i. e., Hellenistic art. L. von Sybel, in his *Weltgeschichte der Kunst* (1888)[7] has a chapter on ancient Roman Baroque. The same year is the date of Heinrich Wölfflin's *Renaissance und Barock*, a detailed monograph chiefly concerned with the development of architecture in Rome. Wölfflin's work is highly important not only because it gave a first reliable technical analysis of the development of the style in Rome in appreciative terms, but because it also contains a few pages on the possibility of applying baroque to literature and music. With Wölfflin's began the revaluation of baroque art, soon taken up by other German art-historians such as Gurlitt, Riegl, and Dehio, and soon to be followed in Italy by Giulio Magni and Corrado Ricci, and in England by Martin S. Briggs and Geoffrey Scott. The latter wrote a fervent defence, oddly enough called *The Architecture of Humanism* (1914).[8] After the first World War, admiration and sympathy for even the most grotesque and tortured forms of baroque art reached its peak in Germany; there were a good many individual enthusiasts in other countries, such as Eugenio d'Ors in Spain, Jean Cassou in France, and Sacheverell Sitwell in England.[9] In art history, today, baroque is recognized as the next stage of European art after the Renaissance. The term is used not only in architecture, but also in sculpture and painting, and covers not only Tintoretto and El Greco but also Rubens and Rembrandt.

Baroque is also fully established as a term in the history of music. It was apparently well-known in the eighteenth century, as *Rousseau's Dictionnaire de Musique* (1764) lists it as a term for music with "confused harmony" and other vices.[10] But the Czech music historian, August W. Ambros, seems to have been the first to use it as a period term, in 1878.[11] Today it is the current label for seventeenth century music and seems to be applied widely to Schütz, Buxtehude, Lully, Rameau, and even Bach and Handel.[12] There are now also baroque philosophers: Spinoza has been called baroque and I have seen the term applied to Leibniz, Comenius, and even Berkeley.[13] Spengler spoke of baroque painting, music, philosophy, and even psychology, mathematics, and physics. Baroque is now used in general cultural history for practically all manifestations of seventeenth century civilization.[14]

So far as I know, Wölfflin was the first to transfer the term baroque to literature. In a remarkable page of *Renaissance und Barock* (1888)[15] he suggests that the contrast between Ariosto's *Orlando Furioso* (1516) and Tasso's *Gerusalemme liberata* (1584) could be compared to the distinction between Renaissance and baroque. In Tasso, he observes a heightening, an emphasis, a striving for great conceptions absent in Ariosto, and he finds the same tendency in Berni's reworking of Bojardo's *Orlando inamorato*. The images are more unified, more sublime; there is less visual imagination (*Anschauung*), but more mood (Stimmung). Wblfflin's suggestions do not seem to have been taken up for a long time. A search through a large number of writings on marinism, gongorism, euphuism, *preciosite* and German *Schwulst* has failed to produce more than one or two passages where a literary work or movement is actually called baroque before 1914, though baroque art was discussed as a parallel phenomenon under that name.[16] This seems to be true of the writings of Benedetto Croce before the first World War. In *Saggi sulla letteratura italiana del Seicento* (1910), the literature is never called baroque, though Croce discusses the parallel with baroque in the arts and even warns against the "exaggeration" in the appreciation of seventeenth century literature "to which the present fashion which in the plastic arts has returned to the baroque could easily seduce us."[17]

In 1914, however, a Danish scholar, Valdemar Vedel, published a paper "Den digteriske Barokstil omkring aar 1600".[18] He draws there a close parallel between Rubens and French and English poetic style between 1550 and 1650. Literature is, like the art of Rubens, decorative, colorful, emphatic. Vedel lists favorite themes and words in literature which he considers applicable to the art of Rubens: grand, high, flourish, red, flame, horses, hunt, war, gold, the love of show, swelling bombast, bragging blank-verse. But Vedel's article, possibly because it was in Danish, was, I think, completely ignored. The radiating point for the spread of the term was Germany and especially Munich where Wölfflin, a Swiss by birth, was professor. His colleague in German literature, Karl Borinski, wrote a long book, *Die Antike in Poetik und Kunst-theorie* (1914), with the subtitle for Volume I, *Mittelalter*, *Renaissance und Barock*, where he discusses especially the conceptist theories of Gracian and sketches the history of the term in a learned and substantially accurate note.[19]

In 1915, Wölfflin published a new book, *Kunstgeschichtliche Grundbegriffe*,[20] where Renaissance and Baroque are contrasted as the two main types of style, and criteria for their distinction are worked out very concretely. This book made a tremendous impression on several German literary historians struggling with the problem of style. It seemed to invite imitation and possibly transfer to literary history. In 1916, without mentioning Wblfflin, Fritz Strich gave a stylistic analysis of German seventeenth century lyrical poetry which he called "baroque".[21] Oscar Walzel, in the same year, followed with a paper which claimed Shakespeare as belonging to the baroque.[22] In 1917, Max Wolff rejected Walzel's claim but admitted baroque in Shakespeare's *Venus and Adonis*, in the *Rape of Lucrece* and in Lyly. 23 In 1918, Josef Nadler published the third volume edition of his *Literaturgeschichte der deutschen Stdmme und Landschaften*,[24] an original attempt to write the history of German literature "from below", from the local literature of the German cities and provinces. Nadler, whose orientation was then strongly Austrian and Roman Catholic, used the term baroque very prominently to describe the Jesuit Counter-Reformation literature of Southern Germany.

But all these items I have described up till now are comparatively isolated. The enormous vogue of baroque as a literary term arose in Germany only about 1921-1922. In 1921, Rudolf von Delius published an anthology of German baroque poetry and in the next year no fewer than four such anthologies were issued.[25] Joseph Gregor wrote a book on the Vienna Baroque theater[26] and Arthur Htibscher started the long line of philosophers on the baroque with a piece, "Barock als Gestaltung antithetischen Lebensgeftihls".[27] Herbert Cysarz, one of the most prolific and pretentious of the German writers on literary baroque, published his first large, boldly conceived book, *Deutsche Barockdichtung*, in 1924.[28] Since then, interest in the German seventeenth century has risen by leaps and bounds and produced a large literature permeated by the term baroque. I would be hesitant to dogmatize about the exact reasons for this revival of German baroque poetry; part of it may be due to Spengler who had used the term vaguely in the *Decline of the West*, [29] and part is due, I think, to a misunderstanding: baroque poetry was felt to be similar to the most recent German expressionism, to its turbulent, tense, torn diction and tragic view of the induced by the aftermath of the war; part was a genuine change of taste, a sudden comprehension for an art despised before because of its conventions, its supposedly tasteless metaphors, its violent contrasts and antitheses.

German scholars soon applied their newly found criterion to other European literatures. Theophil Spoerri was, in 1923, I believe, the first to carry out Wölfflin's suggestions as to the difference between Ariosto and Tasso.[30] Ariosto is shown by Wölfflin's criteria to be Renaissance; Tasso, baroque. Marino and the marinists appeared baroque. Spain was also easily assimilable, since gongorism and conceptism presented clearly parallel phenomena which had but to be christened baroque. But all other Spanish literature, from Guevara in the early sixteenth century to Calderon in the late seventeenth century, was soon claimed as baroque. Wilhelm Michels in a paper on "Barockstil in Shakespeare und Calderon" (1929)[31] used the acknowledged baroque characteristics of Caleron to argue that Shakespeare also shows the same stylistic tendencies. There seems to be only some disagreement among the German writers as to the status of Cervantes: Helmut Hatzfeld, as early as 1927, had spoken of Cervantes as "Jesuitaenbarock"[32] and had argued that his world-view is that of the Counter-Reformation. In a later paper, "El predominio del espiritu espafiol en las literaturas del siglo XVII", [33] Hatzfeld tried to show that Spain is eternally, basically baroque and that it was historically the radiating center of the baroque spirit in Europe. The permanently Spanish features which are also those of baroque were only temporarily overlaid by the Renaissance. Ludwig Pfandl, however, who wrote the fullest history of Spanish literature during the Golden Age, [34] limits baroque to the seventeenth century and expressly exempts Cervantes. Both Vossler and Spitzer, however, consider even Lope de Vega baroque (in spite of his objections to Góngora).[35]

French literature was also described by German scholars in terms of the baroque. Neubert and Schürr [36] talked, at first somewhat hesitatingly, of baroque undercurrents and features in seventeenth century France. Schürr claimed Rabelais as early baroque and described the *précieux*, the writers of the sprawling courtly novels and of burlesques, as baroque, a style which was defeated by the new classicism of Boileau, Moliere, LaFontaine and Racine. Others advocated the view that these French classics themselves are baroque. Apparently Erich Auerbach, in 1929, was the first to voice this view.[37] Leo Spitzer endorses it with some qualifications. In a brilliant analysis of the style of Racine,[38] he has shown how Racine always tones down baroque features, how Racine's baroque is tame, subdued, classical. Though Hatzfeld does not completely deny the obviously striking distinctions of French classicism, he is the one scholar who most insistently claims all French classicism as baroque. In an early paper[39] he discusses the French religious poetry of the seventeenth century, showing its similarity to Spanish mysticism and its stylistic similarities to general baroque. In a long piece in a Dutch review,[40] he has accumulated many observations to show that French classicism is only a variant of baroque. French classicism has the same typically baroque tension of sensuality and religion, the same morbidity, the same pathos as Spanish baroque. Its form is similarly paradoxical and antithetical, "open" in Wölfflin's sense. The discipline of French classicism is simply a universal characteristic of the "rule over the passions", recommended by the Counter-Reformation everywhere.

English literature, even outside of the attempts to claim Shakespeare as baroque, was also soon brought in line. As far as I know, *Friedrich Brie's Englische Rokokoepik* (1927) is the first attempt of this sort.[41] There *Pope's Rape of the Lock* is analyzed as rococo, but in passing a contrast to the baroque Garth and Boileau is drawn. *Fritz Putzer in Prediger des englischen Barocks stilistisch untersucht* (1929) then claimed almost all English pulpit oratory from Latimer to Jeremy Taylor as baroque.[42] F. W. Schirmer in several articles and in his *Geschichte der englischen Literatur*[43] uses the term for the metaphysicals, Browne, Dryden, Otway and Lee, excluding Milton from the baroque expressly. This was also the conclusion of Friedrich Wild[44] who called even Ben Jonson, Massinger, Ford and Phineas Fletcher baroque. The idea of an antithesis of sensualism and spiritualism in English seventeenth century poetry was, in the mean time, carried out, in a rather mechanical fashion, by Werner P. Friederich,[45] a work which was accepted as a Harvard Ph. D. thesis under J. L. Lowes. There are a good many other German theses on English literary baroque: Jünemann[46] has compared Dryden's Fables with their sources to show how Dryden translated, e. g., Chaucer into a baroquestyle; Wolfgang Mann[47] has examined Dryden's heroic tragedies as an expression of courtly baroque culture. A recent piece by Elisabeth Haller[48] analyses the baroque style of Thomas Burnet's *Theory of the Earth* in comparison with its Latin and German translations. The view that all English seventeenth century civilization is baroque has been pushed farthest by Paul Meissner,[49] who includes also Milton and who has devised a whole scheme of contraries covering all activities and stages of the English seventeenth century. In a piece which stresses the Spanish influence in England, Hatzfeld goes so far as to call Milton "the most hispanized poet of the age, who to the foreigner appears the most baroque."[50] Bernhard Fehr finally has extended the frontiers of English baroque by finding it in Thomson and Mallet and even tracing it in the verse-form of

Wordsworth.[51] Thus all literatures of Europe in the seventeenth century (and in part of the sixteenth century) are conceived of by German scholars as a unified movement. E. g., in Schnürer's bulky volume, *Katholische Kirche und Kultur der Barockzeit* (1937), [52] Spain, Portugal with Camoens, Italy, France, Germany, Austria, but also Poland, Hungary and Yugoslavia are treated as baroque. It is a coherent view which needs discussion, acceptance, refutation or modification.

I have reviewed the Germans first because they were the originators and instigators of the movement (if one ignores the isolated Dane, Vedel). But the idea was taken up soon by scholars of other nationalities. In 1919, the term made its first conquest outside Germany. F. Schmidt-Degener published a piece on "Rembrandt en Vondel" in *De Gids*[53] where Rembrandt is made out an opponent of baroque taste, while the poet Vondel, Flemish by descent and a convert to Catholicism, is drawn as the typical representative of the European baroque. The author looks with distinct disfavor on the baroque, its sensual mysticism, its externality, its verbalism in contrast to the truly Dutch and at the same time universal art of Rembrandt. To judge from a little book by Heinz Haerten, *Vondel und der deutsche Barock* (1934)[54] the revaluation of baroque has also triumphed in Holland. There Vondel is claimed as the very summit of Northern, Teutonic baroque. In general, seventeenth century Dutch liter- ature seems by the Dutch themselves to be now described as baroque.

…

Notes

1. J. Isaacs, "Baroque and Rococo: A History of Two Concepts," in *Bulletin of the International Committee of the Hitorical Sciences* IX (1937), 347-48, is only a very brief abstract of an unpublished lecture.
2. Karl Borinski, *Die Antike in Poetik und Kunsttheorie* Vol. I. [Leipzig. 1914], 199, 303. Benedetto Croce, *Storia delta Età barocca in Italia*, Bari, 1929, 20ff.
3. Quoted in Gustav Schnürer, *Katholische Kirche und Kultur in der Barockzeit*, Paderborn, 1937, 68, from *In pseudodialeticos*.
4. Charles de Brosses, *Le President de Brosses en Italie*, ed. R. Colomb. Paris, 1885, Vol. II, 15, quoted by W. Weisbach, note 117. J. J. Winckelmann, *Sendschreiben* (1744), 113, quoted by Borinski, *loc. cit.* 303 and *Gedanken über die Nachahmung der grieschischen Werke*, Dresden, 1756, 87.
5. Quoted by Heinrich Wolfflin, *Renaissance und Barock*, Munich, 1888, 10.
6. Wölfflin, *loc. cit.* refers to Burckhardt's "Über die vorgotischen Kirchen am Nieder- rhein," in Lerschs *Niederrheinisches Jahrbuch* (1843).
7. See Note 5.
8. Cornelius Gurlitt, *Geschichte des Barockstils in Italien*, Stuttgart, 1887. *Geschichte des Barockstiles und des Rococo in Deutschland*, Stuttgart, 1889. Alois Riegl, *Barockhunst in*

Rom, Vienna, 1908. Magni, Guilio, *Il Baroco a Roma*, 3 vols. Turin, 1911-13. Corrado Ricci, *Baroque Architecture and Sculpture in Italy*, London, 1912. Martin Shaw Briggs, *Baroque Architecture*, London, 1913. Geoffrey Scott, *The Architecture of Humanism*, London, 1914 (Second ed. New York, 1924).

9. Eugenio d' Ors, *Du Baroque*, Paris, 1935. Sacheverell Sitwell, *Southern Baroque Art*, London, 1931; *Spanish Baroque Art*, London, 1931; *German Baroque Sculpture*, London, 1938. Jean Cassou, "Apologie de l' art baroque" in *L' Amour de l' Art*, September, October 1927.
10. Amsterdam, 1769. Vol. I, 62 (First ed. 1764).
11. *Loc. cit.* 85-86.
12. Thus e. g. in Oscar Thompson's *Dictionary of Music and Musicians*, New York, 1943. Leichtentritt, Paul LAng, McKinney and Anderson and apparently most other current histories of music have sections on the baroque. W. August Ambros, *Geschichte der Musik*, Vol. IV, Breslau, 1878. Cf. also Robert Haas, *Die Musik des Barocks*, Potsdam-Wildpark, 1929.
13. Carl Gebhardt, " Rembrandt und Spinoza, Stilgeschichtliche Betrachtungen zum Barockproblem", in *Kant-studien* XXXII (1927), 161-181, argues that Rembrandt and Spinoza are both baroque and closely similar. Karl Jöel's *Wandlungen der Weltanschauung* (Vol. I Tubingen, 1938) has a chapter on baroque philosophy. See Hermann Schmalenbach, *Leibniz*, Munich, 1921, especially 11-18. Dietrich Mahnke, " Der Barock-Universalis-mus des Comenius" in *Zeitschrift fur Geschichte der Erziehung*, XXI (1931), 97-128, and XXII (1932) 61-90. "Der Zeitgeist des Barock und seine Verewigung in Leibnizens Gedankenwelt", *Zeitschrift fur deutsche Kulturphilosophie* II (1936), 95-126.
14. Oswald Spengler, *Der Untergang des Abendlandes*, Munich 1923, Vol. I, 400 (First ed. 1918). Egon Friedell, *Kulturgeschichte der Neuzeit*, Munich, 1929, Vol. II. Willi Flemming, *Deutsche Kultur im Zeitalter des Barocks*, Potsdam, 1937. Schnurer in Note 3.
15. *Loc. cit.* 83-85.
16. Corrado Ricci, *Baroque Architecture and Sculpture in Italy*, New York, 1912, calls Marino "the Baroque poet *par excellence*". (p. 1). This would be the first use of the term applied to literature known in English.
17. Bari, 1910, cf. XIX, XX, 404 etc.
18. In *Edda* II (Kristiana, 1914), 17-40.
19. See Note 2.
20. Munich, 1915. 7th ed. 1929. English translation: *Principles of Art History* by M. D. Hottinger, New York, 1932.
21. " Der lyrische Stil des 17. Jahrhunderts", in *Abhandlungen zur deutschen Literaturgeschichte*, *Festschrift für Franz Muncker*, Munich, 1916, 21-53.
22. " Shakespeares dramatische Baukunst," in *Jahrbuch der Shakespearegesellschaft* LII

(1916), 3-35, reprinted in *Das Wortkunstwerk*, *Mittel seiner Erforschung*, Leipzig, 1926, 302-25.

23. "Shakespeare als Künstler des Barocks", in *Internationale Monatsschrift* XI (1917), 995-1021.

24. Regensburg, 1918. Vol. III.

25. *Die deutsche Barocklyrik*, Stuttgart, 1921. Pirker, Max, *Das deutsche Liebeslied in Barock und Rokoko*, Zurich, 1922. Fritz Strich, "Die deutsche Barocklyrik" in *Genius* (Munich) Vol. III. (1922). W. Unus, *Die deutsche Lyrik des Barock*, Berlin, 1922. R. Wiener, *Pallas und Cupido. Deutsche Lyrik der Barockzeit*, Vienna, 1922.

26. *Das Wiener Barocktheater*, Vienna, 1922.

27. "Grundlegung einer Phaseologie der Geistesgeschichte" in *Euphorion*, XXIV, (1922), 15. Ergänzungsheft, 517-62; 759-805.

28. Leipzig, 1924; see his earlier article, "Vom Geist des deutschen Literaturbarocks", in *Deutsche Vierteljahrschrift fur Literaturwissenschaft und Geistesgeschichte* I (1923) 243-368.

29. *Der Untergang des Abendlandes*, Munich, 1923, 236, 308, 399-400, etc.

30. *Renaissance und Barock bei Ariost und Tasso. Versuch einer Anwendung Wölfflin'scher Kunstbetrachtung*, Bern, 1922.

31. *Revue Hispanique* LXXXV (1929), 370-458.

32. *Don Quixote als Sprachkunstwerk*, Leipzig, 1927, 287.

33. *Geschichte der spanischen Nationalliteratur in ihrer Blütezeit*, Freiburg im Breisgau, 1929, 289.

34. In *Revista de Filologia Hispánica* III (1941) 9-23.

35. Karl Vossler, *Lope de Vega und sein Zeitalter*, Munich, 1932, especially 89-105. Leo Spitzer, *Die Literarisierung des Lebens in Lopes Dorotea*, Bonn, 1932.

36. V. Klemperer, H. Hatzfeld, F. Neubert, *Die romanischen Literaturen von der Renaissance bis zur franzosichen Revolution*, Wildpark-Potsdam, 1928. Friedrich Schürr, *Barock*, *Klassizismus und Rokoko in der franzosischen Literatur. Eine prinzipielle Stilbetrachtung*, Leipzig, 1928.

37. Reported by Leo Spitzer, "Klassische Dampfung in Racines Stil", in *Romanische Stilund Literaturstudien*, Marburg, 1931. I, 256.

38. Cf. Note 27. The paper appeared first in *Archivum Romanicum* XII (1928), 361-472.

39. "Der Barockstil der religiosen klassischen Lyrik in Frankreich", in *Literaturwissenschaftliches Jahrbuch der Görresgesellschaft* IV (1929), 30-60.

40. "Die französiche Klassik in neuer Sicht. Klassik als Barock", in *Tijdschrift voor Taalen Letteren* XXIII (1935), 213-281.

41. Munich, 1927.

42. Diss. Bonn, 1929.

43. "Die geistesgeschichtlichen Grundlagen der englischen Barockliteratur", in *Germanisch-romanische Monatsschrift* XIX (1931), 273-84. "Das Problem des religiösen Epos im siebzehnten Jahrhundert in England", in *Deutsche Vierteljahrschrift für Literaturwissenschaft und Geistesgeschichte* XIV (1936), 60-74. *Geschichte der englischen Literatur*, Halle, 1937.
44. "Zum Problem des Barocks in der englischen Dichtung", in *Anglia* LIX (1935), 414-22.
45. *Spiritualismus und Sensualismus in der englischen Barocklyrik. Wiener Beiträge*, Vol. 57, Vienna, 1932.
46. *Drydens Fabeln und ihre Quellen*, *Britannica*, No. 5. Hamburg, 1932.
47. *Drydens heroische Tragödien als Ausdruck höfischer Barockkultur*, 1932. Diss. Tübingen.
48. *Die barocken Stilmerkmale in der englischen, lateinischen und deutschen Fassung von Dr. Thomas Burnets Theory of the Earth*, *Swiss Studies in English* IX, Bern, 1940. See a review by this writer in Philological Quarterly XXI (1942), 199-200.
49. *Die geisteswissenschaftlichen Grundlagen des englischen Literaturbarocks*, Munich, 1934.
50. *Loc. cit.* in Note 34, page 22.
51. "The Antagonism of Forms in the Eighteenth Century", in *English Studies* XVIII (1936) 115-21, 193-205 and XIX (1937), 1-13, 49-57.
52. See Note 3.
53. LXXXIII (1919), 222-275. A German translation by Alfred Pauli was published as *Rembrandt und der holldndische Barock*, *Studien der Bibliothek Warburg*, No. 9, Leipzig, 1928.
54. *Disquisitiones Carolinae. Fontes et Acta Philologica et Historica*, ed. Th. Baader, Vol. VI, Nijmegen, 1934.

（节选自 The Journal of Aesthetics & Art Criticism, Vol. V, No. 2, December, 1946, pp. 77-84.）

文明的冲突与世界秩序的重建

（节选）

[美]亨廷顿

【导读】

塞缪尔·亨廷顿(Huntington Samuel P.，1927—2008)美国哈佛大学教授，政治学家，《外交政策》杂志发起人。1993年夏，亨廷顿在美国《外交》季刊发表《文明的冲突?》认为新世界的冲突根源不再是意识形态和经济发展，文化是引起冲突的主要根源，提出了“文明冲突论”，引起了国际学术界的普遍关注和争论。为了回答各种观点的质疑，亨氏1996年将此文扩展为专著《文明的冲突与世界秩序的重构》，系统阐述了“文明冲突论”的观点。

当前的世界存在着5个主要文明：中华文明、日本文明、印度文明、伊斯兰文明、西方文明，或许还应该加上拉丁美洲文明和非洲文明，这样就形成了7~8个主要的文明，文明的核心国家形成当前的国际关系。西方文化的传播正在日益形成一种普世文明，并从语言、宗教等方面论述了西方消费模式和大众文化对人们的影响。拒绝主义、基马尔主义和改良主义是当前回应西方化的三种主要方式。现代化并不意味着西方化，非西方国家现代化的进程加强了历史文化的多元性。由此，世界文明的中心及影响力正在转移，西方文明的影响范围正在缩小，伴随着的是伊斯兰文明等文明的崛起，本土化文化已经成为非西方国家的发展日程。国内民族运动进一步推动了非西方文化的本土化。非西方国家反对受过西方教育的精英执政理念，这在穆斯林国家中表现得更加明显。西方的价值观在拜占庭人、阿拉伯人、中国人、土耳其人、蒙古人、俄罗斯人、伊朗人中遭到不同方式的反对，由西方国家所主导的意识形态已经结束，全球正在跨入不同文明相互影响、合作的时代。中国、日本等亚洲国家重新树立自己本土文化的自信，甚至在有的亚洲国家形成了狭隘的亚洲普世主义文化，穆斯林国家形成了伊斯兰文化的复兴运动，中国文明、伊斯兰文明和印度文明的影响人数超越了西方。

全球政治正在沿着文化线重构，文化相似的民族和国家走在了一起，以往的以意识形态和大国关系确定的同盟让位于文化和文明的结盟，文化共同体取代了冷战阵营，文化断层线成为冲突的界限，文化共性存进人们之间的合作，反之，文化差异加剧了冲突。虽然通过谈判可以解决国家、民族间物质利益的分歧，但解决不了文化的冲突。主要文明的核心国家正取代冷战时期的超级大国，世界秩序要建立在文明的基础上，文明的核心国家是内部秩序的源泉，文化的共性使核心国家对成员国及其他外部国家的领导合法化。一个以文明(文化认同)为基础的世界新秩序逐步形成。

文明的冲突有两种形式。在地区或者微观层面上，断层线冲突发生在不同文明的邻国、一国不同文明集团之间；在全球或者宏观层面，冲突主要发生在不同文明的国家之间。这些冲突问题根源主要包括：对全球发展的相对影响力；相对的军事权力；经济权力和福利；人民；价值观观念和文化冲突；领土问题。亨廷顿认为，核心国家地区集团间断层线冲突不断升级和文明间全球均势变化可能会导致战争。断层线冲突是属于不同文明的国家或集团的冲突，最终发展为战争，能够结束断层线战争主要取决于世界主要文明的核心国家的利益和行动。

西方文明开创了世界范围内现代化和工业化的进程，通过伊斯兰复兴运动和亚洲经济的发展势头表明，其他非西方文明对西方文明构成了潜在的威胁。要避免文明间战争，文明核心国家应遵守“避免原则”和“共同调解原则”，避免干涉其他文明，通过相互谈判来制止文明国家或集团间的断层线战争。

（潘丹丹）

首先，在单一文明和多元文明的看法之间存在着分歧。文明的观点是由18世纪法国思想家相对于“野蛮状态”提出的。文明社会不同于原始社会，因为它是定居的、城市的和识字的。文明化的是好的，非文明化的是坏的。文明的概念提供了一个判断社会的标准；而且19世纪期间，欧洲人把许多思想能量、外交能量和政治能量投入于详细阐述一个标准，根据它来判断非欧洲人的社会是否充分“文明化”到可以被接受为欧洲人所支配的国际体系的成员。然而同时，人们越来越多地谈论多元文明。这意味着“放弃把一个文明解释为一种理想，或毋宁说是唯一的理想”，并意味着放弃一个假定：只存在一个单一的标准来判断什么是文明化的，这个标准用布罗代尔的话说即是，“仅限于少数特权民族或集团，即人类的‘精英’”。相反，存在着许多文明，它们每一个都以自己的方式文明化了。简而言之，单一文明的论点“丧失了其某些威望”，而一个单一意义上的文明事实上可能在多元意义上是相当非文明化的。

多元文明是本书所关注的，但单一文明和多元文明之间的分歧仍然与本书有关。单一文明的观点已重现在关于存在着一个普遍的世界文明的争论中。这一争论不可能持久，但探索各文明是否将变得更加文明化是有用的，这正是本书最后一章所做的。

第二，在德国之外，文明被看作是一个文化实体。19世纪德国的思想家描述了文明和文化之间的明显区别，前者包括技巧、技术和物质的因素，后者包括价值、理想和一个社会更高级的思想艺术性、道德性。这一区分在德国的思想中保持了下来，但在其他地方并没有被接受。一些人类学家甚至颠倒了这一关系，把原始的、一成不变的、非城市的社会设想为代表了文化，而更复杂的、发达的、城市的和动态的社会是文明。然而，这些区分文化和文明的努力从未被人们所理解，而且在德国之外，绝大多数人赞成布罗代尔的观点，即：“想要用德国的方式把文化分离于其基础——文明，是虚妄的。”

文明和文化都涉及一个民族全面的生活方式，文明是放大了的文化。它们都包括“价值、规则、体制和在一个既定社会中历代人赋予了头等重要性的思维模式”。对于布罗代尔来说，文明是“一个空间，一个‘文化领域’”，是“文化特征和现象的一个集合”。沃勒斯坦把文明定义为“世界观、习俗、结构和文化(物质文化和高层文化)的特殊连结。它形成了某种历史总和，并与这一现象的其他变种(即使不总是同时)共存”。根据道森的看法，文明“是一个特定民族发挥其文化创造力的一个特定的原始过程”的产物，而对于德克海姆和毛斯来说，它是“一种包围着一定数量的民族的道德环境，每一个民族文化都只是整体的一个特殊形式”。在斯宾格勒看来，文明是“文化不可避免的命运……是一种发达的人类能够达到的一些最外部的和人为的状态……是一个从形成到成熟的结局”。文化实际上是所有文明定义的共同主题。

当雅典人向斯巴达人重新保证自己不会向波斯人出卖斯巴达克人时，他们用古典的形式提出了界定文明的文化核心因素：

> 因为即使我们倾向于此，也有许多强有力的考虑禁止我们这样做。首要的是，众神的形象和住所被焚烧和夷为平地，我们必须竭尽全力为此雪耻，而不是同那些犯下如此罪行的人达成协议。其次，希腊种族具有同样的血统和同样的语言，有相同的神庙和献祭；以及我们相似的习俗；雅典人如果背叛这些将不会有好结果。

血统、语言、宗教、生活方式是希腊人共有的东西，也是使他们区别于波斯人和非希腊人的东西。然而，正如雅典人所强调的，在所有界定文明的客观因素中，最重要的通常是宗教。人类历史上的主要文明在很大程度上被基本等同于世界上的伟大宗教；那些具有共同的种族和语言，但在宗教上相异的人们可能相互屠杀，就像在黎巴嫩、前南斯拉夫和南亚次大陆所发生的那样。

根据文化特征把人们划分为不同的文明与根据身体特征把人们划分为不同的种族，其结果有相当大的重合。然而文明与种族并不等同。同种族的人可能因文明而产生深刻的分裂；不同种族的人可能因文明而趋向统一。伟大的负有使命感的宗教基督教和伊斯兰教，尤其包含了来自各种种族的社会。人类群体之间的关键差别是他们的价值、信仰、体制和社会结构，而不是他们的体形、头形和肤色。

第三，文明是包容广泛的，即，如果不涉及全面的文明，它们的任何构成单位都不能被充分理解。汤因比认为，文明“包含着不被其他文明所理解的东西”。文明是一个“整体”。梅尔科继续说，文明具有一定程度的整合。文明各个部分之间的关系和它们同整体之间的关系规定了它们的各个部分。如果文明是由一些国家组成的，这些国家彼此之间的关系将多于它们同该文明之外的国家的关系。它们可能更多地相互打仗和更经常地建立外交关系，在经济上将更加相互依赖，会存在普遍的美学潮流和哲学潮流。

一个文明是一个最广泛的文化实体。乡村、宗教、种族群体、民族、宗教群体都在文化异质性的不同层次上具有独特的文化。意大利南部的村落文化可能不同于意大利北部的村落文化，但它们具有使自己区别于德国村落的共同的意大利文化。欧洲社区也具有使自己区别于中国社区或印度社区的文化特征。然而，中国人、印度人和西方人都不是任何更大的文明实体的一部分。他们构成了一些文明。因此，文明是对人最高的文化归类，是人们文化认同的最广范围，人类以此与其他物种相区别。文明既根据一些共同的客观因素来界定，如语言、历史、宗教、习俗、体制，也根据人们主观的自我认同来界定。人们的认同有各种层面：一个罗马居民可能以不同的强度把自己界定为罗马人、意大利人、天主教徒。基督教徒、欧洲人、西方人。他所属的文明是他与之强烈认同的最大的认同范围。文明是最大的“我们”，在其中我们在文化上感到安适，因为它使我们区别于所有在它之外的“各种他们”。文明可能包含大量的人，如中国文明，也可能包含很少的人，如讲英语的加勒比文明。纵观整个历史，一直存在着许多小的人类群体，它们具有独特的文化，但缺乏更大范围的文化认同。人们一直根据规模和重要性来区分主要的文明和边缘的文明(巴格比)，或者区分主要的文明和被征服的或流产的文明(汤因比)。本书所关心的是，一般来说是什么决定了人类历史上的主要文明。

文明没有明确的边界，也没有精确的起点和终点。人们可能而且确实重新界定过它们的认同，结果，文明的内涵和外延会随着时间的变化而变化。各民族的文化既相互作用又相互重合。各种文明的文化彼此相似或相异的程度也发生着相当大的变化。然而，文明是有意义的实体，尽管它们之间的界限难得清晰，但这些界限却是真实的。

第四，文明终有终结，但又生存得非常长久；它们演变着，调整着，而且是人类最持久的结合，是“极其长久的现实”。它们的“独特性和特殊性”是“它们长期的历史延续性。事实上，文明是所有史话中最长的史话”。帝国兴起又衰落，政府上台又下台，但文明依旧，它“历经政治的、经济的、社会的、甚至意识形态的动荡而幸存下来”。博兹曼总结说，“世界历史正确地证明了下述论点：政治制度是文明表面转瞬即逝的权宜手段，每一个在语言上和道德上统一的社会的命运，都最终依赖于某些基本的建构思想的幸存，历代人围绕着它们结合在一起，因此，它们标志着社会的延续性”。实际上，20 世纪世界上的所有主要文明都已经存在了一千年之久，或者像拉丁美洲的文化一样，是另一个长期生存的文明的直接后代。

文明虽然是持久的，但它们也在演变。文明是动态的；它们兴起又衰落；合并又分裂；而且正如所有历史研究者所了解的，它们也会消失，掩埋在时间的沙丘之中。它们的演变阶段可以用各种方式来详细说明。奎格利认为文明的运动经历了七个阶段：混合、孕育、扩张、冲突时代、普遍帝国、衰败和被入侵。梅尔科总结出了一个变化模式：从一个定型的封建制度演变到一个定型的国家制度，再从一个定型的国家制度演变到一个定型的帝国制度。汤因比把文明的兴起看作是对挑战的回应，在其发展过程中，富于创造性的少数人所造成的文明环境日益得到控制，接下来便是动乱时期，普遍国家兴起，然后崩溃。虽然所有这些理论之间存在着重大差别，但它们都认为文明经过动乱或冲突时期演变到普遍国家，再到衰败和崩溃。

第五，既然文明是文化实体而不是政治实体，它们本身并不维持秩序，建立公正，征缴税收，进行战争，谈判条约，或者做政府所做的任何其他事情。文明的政治组成在文明之间各不相同，在一个文明之内也随着时间而变化。一个文明可能包含一个或多个政治单位。这些单位可以是城市国家、帝国、联邦、邦联、民族国家。多民族国家，所有这些单位都可以有不同的政府形式。当一个文明演变时，其政治构成单位的数量和性质一般也会发生变化。在一个极端上，文明和政治实体可能恰好重合。卢西思·派伊曾评论说，中国

“自命是一个国家的文明”。日本既是一个国家又是一个文明。然而，大多数文明包含一个以上的国家或其他政治实体。在现代世界，大多数文明包含两个或两个以上的国家。

最后，学者们一般在确认历史上的主要文明和在现代世界存在的文明上意见一致。然而，对于历史上曾经存在的文明总数，他们常常各执一词。奎格利认为，历史上有16个明显的文明案例，很可能还有另外8个。汤因比起先列出了20个文明，然后是23个；斯宾格勒详举了8个主要文化。麦克尼尔分析了全部历史上的9个文明。巴格比也认为有9个文明，或者11个，如果把日本文明和东正教文明从中国文明和西方文明中区分出来的话。布劳代尔识别了9个文明，罗斯托万内指出了7个主要的当代文明。这些差别部分取决于是否把像中国人和印度人这样的文化群体看作在整个历史上曾有一个单一的文明，或者有两个或两个以上密切相关的文明，其中一个是另一个的后代。尽管存在着这些差别，人们对主要文明的身份都没有争议。正如梅尔科在考察文献之后所得出的结论，人们至少在下述看法上存在着合理的共识：至少有12个主要文明，其中7个文明已不复存在(美索不达米亚文明、埃及文明、克里特文明、古典文明、拜占庭文明、中美洲文明、安第斯文明)，5个仍然存在(中国文明、日本文明、印度文明、伊斯兰文明和西方文明)。一些学者还加上了东正教文明，作为区别于其母文明拜占庭文明和西方基督教文明的独立文明。鉴于我们认识当代世界的目的，除这6个文明之外，或许还应加上拉丁美洲文明，可能还有非洲文明。

这样，当代的主要文明可以列举如下：

中华(Sinic)文明。所有学者都承认存在着一个单一的独特的中国文明，它可以追溯到至少公元前1500年，也许还可以再往前追溯一千年；或者存在着两个中国文明，其中一个在公元最初的世纪中继承了另一个。我在发表在《外交》季刊的文章中，把这个文用称为儒教文明。然而，使用“中华(Sinic)文明”一词更为精确。虽然儒教是中国文明的重要组成部分，但中国文明却不仅是儒教，而且它也超越了作为一个政治实体的中国。许多学者所使用的“中华”(Sinic)一词，恰当地描述了中国和中国以外的东南亚以及其他地方华人群体的共同文化，以及越南和朝鲜的相关文化。

日本文明。一些学者在一个单一的远东文明的称呼下把日本文明和中国文明合并在一起。然而，大多数学者不这样看，而是承认日本文明是一个独特的文明，它是中国文明的后代，出现于公元100-400年之间。

印度(Hindu)文明。人们普遍认为至少自公元前1500年以来，在南亚次大陆存在着一个或一个以上的相继的文明。这些文明一般被称为Indian、Indic或Hindu文明，人们更喜欢用后者来称呼最近的那个文明。自公元前2000年以来，印度教一直以这样或那样的形式成为南亚次大陆文化的中心。它“不止是一个宗教或一个社会制度；它是印度文明的核心”。它经过现时代继续起着这种作用，即使印度本身有重要的穆斯林社区以及一些更小的少数文化。像“中华”一词一样，Hindu一词也把文明的名称与它的核心国家分离开来，因为在这些情况下，当该文明的文化超越了那个国家时，这样做是合乎需要的。

伊斯兰文明。所有重要学者都承认存在着独特的伊斯兰文明。伊斯兰教起源于公元7世纪的阿拉伯半岛，然后迅速传播，跨越北非和伊比利亚半岛，并向东伸展到中亚、南亚次大陆和东南亚。结果，许多独特的文化或次文明存在于伊斯兰文明之中，包括阿拉伯、土耳其、波斯和马来文化。

西方文明。西方文明的出现通常被追溯到公元700—800年。学者们一般认为它有三大组成部分，分布于欧洲、北美和拉丁美洲。

拉丁美洲文明。然而，拉丁美洲有区别于西方的独特认同。虽然拉丁美洲文明是欧洲文明的后代，但它却是沿着非常不同于欧洲和北美的道路演进的。它具有社团主义的、独裁主义的文化，而这种文化在欧洲的程度要小得多，在北美则则根本不存在。欧洲和北美都感受到宗教改革的影响，并且把天主教和新教文化结合在一起。从历史上看，虽然可能会有所变化，但拉丁美洲一直仅仅是天主教的世界。拉丁美洲文明结合了一些本土文化，这些文化不曾存在于欧洲，在北美也已被有效地消灭，而在以墨西哥、中美、秘鲁和玻利维亚为一方和以阿根廷和智利为一方两者之间有重大的不同。拉丁美洲的政治演变和经济发展与流行于北大西洋国家的模式大相径庭。从主观上说，拉丁美洲人在他们的自我认同上存在着分歧。一些人说，“是的，我们是西方的一部分。”另一些人则声明，“不，我们有自己独特的文化”，拉丁美洲人和北美人的大量文学作品详细描述了他们的文化差别。拉丁美洲可以被看作西方文明中的次文明，或者被看作是与西方有紧密联系、但在它是否属于西方的问题上有分歧的独立文明，对于把注意力放在文明的国际政治含义(包括以拉丁美洲为一方和以北美洲和欧洲为一方两者之间的关系)的研究来说，后者是更恰当的和有用的称呼。

……

非洲文明(可能存在的)。除了布罗代尔之外，大多数研究文明的学者都不承认存在着一个独特的非洲文明。非洲大陆的北部及非洲的东海岸属于伊斯兰文明。历史上，埃塞俄比亚构成了自己的文明。在其他地方，欧洲的帝国主义和殖民活动带去了西方文明的因素。在南非，荷兰、法国，然后是英国的殖民者创造了一个多板块式的欧洲文化。最重要的是，欧洲的帝国主义把基督教带到了萨哈拉沙漠以南的大部分大陆。在整个非洲，部落认同普遍而强烈，但非洲人的非洲认同感也在日益发展，可以想象，由于南非可能成为撒哈拉以南非洲的核心国家，这个地区可能会粘合成为一个独特的文明。

……

（节选自亨廷顿：《文明的冲突与世界秩序的重建》，周琪等译，新华出版社1998年版，第23-32页。）

对话的文学理论
——误差、激活、融化与创新
（节选）

钱中文

【导读】

钱中文《对话的文学理论——误差、激活、融化与创新》一文就如何正确对待东西方文学理论的交流与碰撞提出了一个“对话模式”，并对其进行了逻辑严密的详尽论述。全文可分四部分。首先通过我国的近现代文学理论发展史引出东西方文化交流的目的就是在文化上互通有无，形成文化互补，其深层意义在于引进外国文化中的有用部分，用以激活本土文化，从而进入创新，推动整个文化的发展。最后落脚点就是提出文化的“异质性”的概念，并提出要利用文化“异质性”。接下来的一部分列举我国接收者在处理中外文化文学理论交流碰撞问题时出现的两种错误，一种是简单的排斥，另一种是不加区分的全盘接受。并借用结构主义理论来观察说明文化交流中的两种情况，并辅以近现代世界上出现的文化交流错误例证。提出错误之后，就是提出到底应当如何正确处理本土文学理论与外来文学理论之间的相互关系。在这部分，作者引入了本文的主旨理论——“对话的批评”，重要的是形成东西方“对话”的文学理论批评，重视“同一”和“异质”，这有两个具体的步骤，其一是阅读西方文学理论文本，要理解其价值所在，不能用单一的文学观去衡量；其二在交流中，要把多种外国文论看成是激活本国文学理论传统的重要手段。将“移入”变成“创造”，使交流推动传统的创新。最后一部分，作者向我们具体论述了激活发生的内部机制。首先要确保文化交流的双方有被借鉴的价值，即他们之间存在一定的同一性和异质性；其次文化交流中的一方要在能看到对方独特的理论或研究方法，承认对方的价值时，也要不卑不亢，不能只满足于认同，一味颂扬，过分迁就；最后我们要明白在理论的对话中，出现“误差”是必然的，也是必要的。并通过举例向我们展示对话机制的建立对文化交流与发展的必要性，当然，作者也提出了现阶段要建立平等的对话机制所存在的障碍和问题，并提出了美好的希冀。

公允而论，本文有如下优点：作者提出文化的“异质性”是促进本土文化创新发展至为重要的因素；作者借用结构主义来观察说明文化交流中的两种极端的情况也很有说服力；充分肯定每一种理论的价值；从而提出任何一种文学理论传统，都是在一定历史时期中形成的，都是与创作实践相结合。当然，本文也存在一些缺陷，例如作者认为，对话的文学理论的建立，最大障碍在于本土传统思维方式的定势，不同文化的现实差异以及由此产生的自我感觉良好的优越感。诚然，这些都是文学理论在对话中的巨大障碍，但是这些均非关键原因，真正的障碍在于文学理论的双方首先必须站在平等的平台上，这样才会有对话进行的可能性，而现实差异以及自我优越感只是关系到对话能否获得良好结果的因素。在跨文化对话中，最困难的就是要形成一种不完全属于任何一方又能相互理解的话语。

（李伟荣）

……在近百年来中国文化的现代化过程中，各种形态的文化冲突从未中断过。双重的误读，对西方文学理论的全面认同，往往导致对本土文学理论的全面否定。

那末，如何协调本土文学理论与外来文学理论之间的相互关系？文学理论接受的境界是什么？在前面，我讲到东西文化交流的目的在于互通有无，形成文化互补，而其深层意义，在于通过外国文化对本土文化的激活，进入创新。对于文学理论来说也是如此。茨维坦·托多洛夫根据米·巴赫金的一个理论观点——对话，提出了“对话的批评”①，显示了他在结构主义道路上的转折，从而从单一的执着，趋向更为宽阔与丰富。我想我们可以根据巴赫金的对话理论，② 使东西方文学理论的交流，变为东西方文学理论的对话，逐渐形成对话的文学理论批评。

文学理论作为一种文化现象，是其作者艺术思想的体现，在不同国家，由于其产生的历史、社会、文化条件、价值观念的不同，而显得形态殊异。它们都各有自己的出发点，有的企图从总体上来把握文学现象，有的可能只从一个方面如本文、结构、符号、叙述等来阐释文学问题，从而形成了各自的价值取向。各种不同方式的理论探索，其价值有高低上下之分。我们现在可以这样说，在充分估计到理论的社会倾向性的条件下，还未发现一种绝对无用的文学理论形态，虽然在10多年前，不少西方文学理论在被冠以资产阶级、唯心主义的帽子下曾经遭到全盘否定。资产阶级是存在的，唯心主义也是有的，但是这类简单的定性，并未使它们失去程度不同的价值。我们见到，非资产阶级的、非唯心主义的文学理论，实际上并未全面阐明过文学现象。意识形态论的文学观抓住了文学现象的一个重要方面，但在几十年来的文学过程中，它被推向极端，对不少文学现象作了庸俗化的解释。有多样的文学理论形态，就会出现多种的理论差异。即使是处于对立语境中的差异，它们不同的价值都应给以肯定，在理论的整体中形成互补。自然，外国文论中的价值与偏颇是互见的，这种现象我们见得很多。承认文学理论的多样，自然要看到它们之中的同一与差异。东西文论中的差异，往往表现为一种难以对应的差异，它们为一种文论所特有，而为另一种文论所不具，如一些具有特定含义的范畴、观念甚至理论系统，同时由于文化传统的不同，而表现出价值的差异来。此外还有一种差异，这就是同一中的差异。作为一种探讨文学现象的共同形态，必然因文学现象的共性而表现出同一性来，但同时这种同一

① 茨维坦·托多洛夫：《批评的批评》，三联书店版，第169-183页。
② 巴赫金：《陀思妥耶夫斯基诗学问题》，三联书店1988年版。

都是在差异中显示出来的。差异与同一相辅相成，它们成为东西文学比较研究的广阔场所。

在谈到同一与差异时，应提到佛克马教授的“文化相对主义”。这一很有意义的观点，大致有如下内容：一、不要用一种统一的文学观去对待别国的文学现象。二、要研究具有不同文化背景的读者所阅读的本文，在阅读中复原它的价值系统。三、在了解它们后，与本土文学的价值系统进行比较，发现各自的差异与相似点，从而显示出本土文学价值系统的相对性。① 这一观点相当符合东西文学理论交流的实际需要。阐读西方的文学理论本文，要理解其价值所在，不能用单一的文学观去衡量。单一的、统一的文学理论往往会用自己的一套观念排斥不同见解，以为自己说的都是真理。它不能容忍第二个声音，更不能容许别的声音的分辩。它只能让人听它一个声音，一种往往是嘲弄与压制的声音。它表现的是理论的独白，而不是探讨真理的对话。

其次，在交流中，要把多种外国文论看成是激活本国文学理论传统的重要手段。东西文学理论交流中的互通有无，还只是一种移入，并不能代替创造，所以还要使交流推动传统的更新。任何一种文学理论传统，都是在一定历史时期中形成的，都是与创作实践相结合、排除不适应的理论因素而逐渐丰富，形成体系的。传统一旦形成，就会获得极大的稳固性。如果人们是站在时代潮流之上来看待传统，那末自然会认识到，传统既需要保护，又需要不断更新。更新的传统保持了原有的精神，但又汲取了人类心智所创造的新知识，使自己不断丰富而永葆青春。如满足于把原有理论变为传统，满足于它的不可动摇性、固定不变，把其它理论都视为异已的思维现象，那就会使这种传统产生排它性，就会原地踏步，停滞不前，固步自封，变为文化发展中的惰力。我国古代文论有漫长的历史传统，它的某些阶段发生的重大变革，是与外来文化思想如佛家思想以及西方文论的影响密切相关的。至于20、30年代自日本、苏联引进的马克思主义文论，与我国的文艺实践结合了起来，对我国原有的文论传统以及介绍过来的欧美文论思想冲击甚大。用马克思主义文学理论观察文学现象，加深了人们对文学的认识，促使人们从总体上去把握纷繁的文学问题，从而推动了我国40、50年代的文学创作，产生了一批优秀作品，进而形成了一种传统。但也要注意到，由于当时的社会、历史条件，以及材料的有限和介绍者认识水平，这一理论形态常常夹杂着简单化倾向。到了50年代，这一文学理论据以为出发点的阶级斗争观点和意识形态论，往往被推向极端，代之以“阶级斗争为纲”，意识形态被截然对立化，形成一切都是阶级斗争的庸俗化理解，使文学成为政治附庸，出现了强烈的排它性。一些人把自己从未见过或不同意的种种外国文论，统统说成是反动的资产阶级文学理论，不仅自身停滞不前，同时使文学理论走向专断。80年代初，原有的文学理论观念及其传统，再现了其原有的生命力。但是如前所说，生活之树常青，在创作与理论的新的要求面前，它同样必须进行更新。我们看到，在80年代，外国文学理论对传统文学理论的冲击与激活，几乎是全方位的。

那么，再次，这个激活是如何发生的？要激活异国文化传统，自然应具备自己的理论品格，即它本身具有一定的真理与价值，提供有用的理论成分，或者在方法上可供借鉴，

① 佛克马·布思：《二十世纪文学理论》，三联书店1988年版，第8页。

给异国文论以启迪。外国文论中有哪些成分可激活我们的理论传统的呢？前面我提到东西文化中的同一与差异，在同一中是存在着有价值的成分的。两种文论对某些文学现象形成的见解，往往十分相似，两者加以比较，能使人们扩大视野，以致豁然开朗，总结出某些规律性的理论观点。这对本国文论自然是一种丰富，以致可以使传统活跃起来。但是一种理论激活另一种理论，真正起作用的是它的异质性部分。在政治、社会学的理论中，截然对立是一种普遍现象，而在文艺理论中，对立现象也时有发生，但在一般情况下，理论的异质性部分的冲突与功能，大体采取下面两种方式应变。一种情况是，异质性成分的理论前提是错误的，但在这一理论的具体运作中，其异质性部分可以被改造，转变其方向，而导致新理论的产生。如马克思主义文学理论与黑格尔、歌德等人的文艺思想的关系。又如胡塞尔的现象学，不少理论家认为是先验的唯心主义，其学说被英加登所接受。英加登“希望确立独立于意识的实在世界的存在”,① 于是在对作品进行现象学的研究中，建立起了相当有影响的不再是唯心主义的文学作品构架的理论。另一种情况是，这异质性的成分是某一文化所拓展了的学术领域或新理论的建构，它为我国文论所不具或未有完整理论形态的东西，一旦被介绍过来，可以起到发聋振聩的作用；如果进一步被改造吸收，则可以对传统起到激活的作用，使其获得丰富，或者引出新的理论。如20、30年代传入我国的马列文论，如近10年来吸引了我国不少学者注意的文艺心理学、文艺符号学、叙述学、文学本体论、原型批评、文学接受理论等等，它们既充实了我国传统理论，又拓宽了文学理论研究的道路。我国古代文论的研究，同样受到新观念、新方法的激活而使其深邃内涵得到多方面的发展。比较文艺学、交叉学科研究的兴起，为传统理论的更新、酝酿新的理论而推波助澜。

激活以何种方式进行？对于对方独特的理论或研究方式视而不见，把异质性成分绝对化，不愿承认对方价值；在探讨问题时习惯于独白、独断的方式，不容他人争辩，显然，这种方式已经陈旧。自然，只满足于认同，一味颂扬，对外国文论中的异质性成分过分迁就，也难以使它生根于中国土壤。在这里，我以为采用对话方式是最适用于文化交流的。前面指出，巴赫金提出过对话复调的理论来研究陀思妥耶夫斯基的小说。把这一理论应用于文论的研究，那就是接受者站在平等的地位上，充分肯定对方的价值方面，择优而取，在诘难对方中发现不足，予以扬弃；用宏放的目光看待外国文论中的异质性部分，显示其自身价值，尊重其在理论整体中的积累，同时也不忌讳接受一方——对话者的价值判断与观点。接受者的观点，不是从固定不变的教条出发，他的价值判断不是理论宗派的判断，而是建立在对中外文学经验的感悟之上的判断，对中外文学理论有着深切理解之上的判断，建立在总体文艺学与比较文艺学知识之上的判断。自然，这与虚无主义和全面认同都是断然有别的。在中外文学理论的对话、交流中，可以揭示双方各自的理论品格的高低上下，各自在理论的总体格局中所处的层次与地位。

在理论的对话中，出现“误差”是必然的，也是必要的。误差不同于误读。如前所说，误读一开始就认为要误读本文，找出本文中的次要部分，给以强化，使之成为解构主义者的主要研究对象；或是从本文中找出矛盾，一块能够松动整座大厦之砖，使之倾倒于瞬

① 英加登：《对文学的艺术作品的认识》的英译者前言，中国文联出版社1988年版。

间、颠覆对方的本文。颠覆就是消解对方，解体对方，使对方理论变成无价值。语词、本文固然多义，但无论语词还是本文，在特定的语境中才有意义，并显示其核心意义。本文中的语词或本文本身，不是一部辞典中词的多义陈列、多义解释。读者无目的阅读，可以了解词的多种意义；而读者有目的的阅读。则只能根据语境择取其中之一，而不能选择任何词意。所以在我看来，误读是避开本文本意，在不甚理解本文的基础上的一种阅读操作。误读理论对传统影响焦虑提出了挑战，它的基本倾向是不信任传统并力图超越传统，自有其积极一面。但它对传统与当代创作之间的关系的解释，并不符合当代文学、当代诗人与其一脉相承的文学与作家间的相互关系，因为这一关系实在要复杂得多。我在这里所说的"误差"，则是对话中的相互探讨真理的结果，是尊重对方理论异质性部分的价值的表现，是在对话中受到异质性观念的提示、启迪而形成的新观点；或是对同一现象所作出的不同反应、不同见解；或是在对话中通过比较而了解到自己和对方的长处与短处，由此而形成的见解、理论上差异。误差是理解的结果，是在比较研究之后形成的一种独立见解，独立的理论价值与理论判断。我在《误解要避免，"误差"却是必要的》一文中说："任何一种有价值的理论，都是在它所处的特定范围内的文学传统与反传统(不是虚无主义的反传统)、社会与文学思潮的基础上形成的。所以适用于美国、法国的，未必就可搬到我国直接使用，何况，即使在产生它的故土，也往往是充满争论的。一种文学理论一旦被引入另一国家的文学进程，就必然会给以鉴别，科学地判断它的得失，确定它的价值取向。有鉴别，就有真伪的辨析与判断；有分析，就有偏颇与创新的识别；有取舍，就有侧重与扬弃；有创新，就要有不同程度的改造，就要有必要的'误差'。"①误差通过顺应与融化建立新理论。理论的误差只是一种新的认识，尚不能改变已有的理论格局。只有通过接受者——对话者的自我调节才能促使原有格局的变化。"从发生认识论的角度看，调节即顺应，是指个体受到刺激或环境的作用和原有格局(即图式)的变化和创新以适应外界环境的过程。适应包括同化与顺应这种作用与机能，通过这一过程，使整个结构发生变化。当它形成新的平衡，建立新的理论的时机也就成熟了。

20世纪中国各种获得成就的文学理论，大体是通过对话方式而获得发展的，这就是，在发现东西文论差异之后，用外国文论中有用的异质性部分激活我国文论，然后使之融入自己进入创新。例如王国维的纯文艺思想，就是吸收了康德、席勒、叔本华等人的美学思想而形成的；他的游戏说、悲剧观、意境论，都显示了西方美学思想的影子。五四时期出现过各种文学主张，那时搬用欧洲文艺思想的情况很多，但是那些不切当时中国实际的文艺思想，其对话性就很薄弱，而对话性很强的主张，则在新文学中扎了根，如"文学为人生"的主张。后来发展起来的马克思主义文艺思想，无疑在被改造之后才适应了中国新文学的需要，后来不再对话，部分观念就被发展到极端。80年代，我国文学理论学说繁多，出现了新的照搬西方文论与一边倒现象，但由于缺乏真正的对话关系，所以只是热闹一时。而那种根本不与西方文论对话的文学理论，也即继续进行独白的理论，则基本停滞不前，无所进展。倒是发现本土文论与西方文论误差，并使它们对话，有所比较，用西方文论中的有用成分激活本国的文论，进而使之融化一体，进行对话探索的文论，显出了理论

① 见拙文《误解要避免，"误差"却是必要的》，《外国文学评论》1989年第4期。

的生机，而有所更新、前进，为本国文论的繁荣和文学理论不同学派的出现开辟了良性发展的前景。我本人是对话方式的受益者，我既肯定传统文论中的有生命力的因素，也广泛吸取西方文论中的种种长处。我得出的一些文学观念，既有传统因素，但也融进了西方文论。所以它们既不是原来的文论，但也非西方文论的照搬，而是另一种文学理论形态。

对话的文学理论的建立是一个十分困难的过程。主要障碍在于本土传统思维方式的定势，不同文化的现实差异以及由此而产生的自我感觉良好的优越感。在各种文化的传统中，有对话思维，但独白式的理论思维已习以为常。不仅我国如此，欧洲国家文化中的传统思维也是如此。例如一种文学理论的兴起，往往不是对话的结果，而是不容对方分辩、颠覆对方的结果。这能否可以成为文学理论进展的唯一道路？同时在东西方文化交流中，就目前情况来说，东方人的求知欲望、了解西方的愿望，要比西方人强烈得多，这可以从文化交流中的不平衡状态看得出来，东方人熟悉西方文化远较西方人了解东方文化广泛得多，深入得多。但是西方的有识之士早已看到东西方文化是可以互补的。罗素把希望寄托于中国，他说如果中国变来变去变得与西方一样，那世界就没有希望了。西方物质文明高度发展，但由此也出现了精力过剩症，一部分文化富于侵略性，在精神上不断出现危机。东方文化特别是具有深邃内涵的东方哲学与伦理思想，经过对话改造，也许可以充实西方人的精神生活，减弱他们对世界发展前途未卜的消沉心理。自然，要使他们像现代中国人渴望了解西方那样来了解东方，还为时过早，那是需要中国的物质文明的发展和精神文明的进一步建设为基础的。不过即便如此，我们已经有了许多西方朋友。到下一世纪，东西文化交流中人为的异质性会大大削弱，对话性的程度会大大加强，而东西文化在不断相互激活中也会更趋繁荣。

（节选自钱中文：《对话的文学理论——误差、激活、融化与创新》，《中国社会科学院研究生院学报》1993 年第 5 期，第 4-10 页。）

从比较文学到比较文化

——“后文学时代”的文学研究展望

(节选)

叶舒宪

【导读】

叶舒宪教授是中国比较文学学会常务理事，中国文学人类学研究会副会长，并兼任《20世纪国外文艺学丛书》等多种丛书主编。叶教授在比较文学、文学人类学研究等方面的研究处于国内领先地位。《从比较文学到比较文化》这篇论文在比较文学学科界限日渐模糊化的时候明确提出，比较文学学科发展的方向就是比较文化。比较文学处于多种语言文化和学科交汇的重要位置，因此它总是处于学科探索变异的前沿。近年来比较文学发展中出现的文化化现象，不仅是比较文学学科的未来发展方向，也是整个文艺学的一种导向。

有学者认为，比较文学研究的文化是一次危机，是被文化研究淹没。这种危机意识完全是学科本位主义的产物。“淹没”的实质是文学研究的深化。文化绝不只是文学背景，也是文学构成的整合性要素。比较本身并不构成比较文学学科存在的理由和目的，而文化整合作用机制的发现和认识应成为比较文学的核心任务之一。从比较文学到比较文化是自然而然顺理成章的，它符合学术发展自身的累进逻辑。

纵观20世纪文学研究史，内向派与外向派始终是相互对立彼此消长。比较文学具有外向型的天性。它的文化化，是它顺应时代变革，引导新世纪的科技整合大趋势的先锋预兆。

后文学时代的全球性主流话语是“文化”。除了“文化”概念以外，尚未有任何一个其他范畴能够使人们更有效的从总体上观照和把握人与社会、历史与现实之间的种种现象及其相互关联。只有“文化”范畴能够容摄并整合各学科领域的视角、观点和方法。大众传媒与市场化社会进程使后文学时代不可避免地到来。文学与非文学的传统界限正在一步步地消解着。文学研究的传统格局面临釜底抽薪的威胁，分化或重新定位势在必行。

文化研究是21世纪人文研究的新取向。“文化”概念因其出入文、史、哲，纵贯人与社会的独特整合效应，势必成为破学科之利器及人文研究中最具吸引力和涵盖力的核心范畴。比较文学的文化化应理解为它的新生契机，而不是危机。

(霍晓珊)

比较文学作为文学研究总阵营中最为敏锐求新也最为活跃多变的一翼，由于它处于多种语言文化和学科交汇要津的位置，接受来自各方面的理论信息较快也较易，它往往能够先于一般的研究而走在学科探索变异的前沿，早一步预示出文学研究总体的某种变革前兆和发展趋向；从另一方面看，比较文学本身也常常充当跨越传统藩篱、探闯学术禁区的先锋角色。正因为如此，近年来比较文学发展中日益显露出的“文化化”迹象就足以引起我们的注意，从见微知著或窥斑见豹的意义上为整个文艺学乃至人文学者提供某种有益的启迪。

一、比较文学与比较文化：“淹没”还是“深化”？

第 14 届国际比较文学学会年会(1994，加拿大)给人最深的总体印象就是文学研究被文化研究所“淹没”。似乎前不久因概念的定义界说而引发的“比较文学的危机”，现在又以新的形式第二次悄然降临了。所不同的是前一次“危机”是由个别学者大胆质疑而人为地引发的，此次“危机”却似乎在不知不觉之间铺天盖地而来，越来越多的学者对“文化”的兴趣超过了对文学本身的兴趣，以致使人产生一种“城头变幻大王旗”的感觉。不仅热衷于理论的美国派学者大力提倡综合性的文化研究视角，就连一贯侧重于文学史的实证性研究的法国派学者也表现出对文化问题的浓厚兴趣。……

如何看待比较文学的二次“危机”呢？如果说前一次“危机”只是比较文学自身面临的问题，那么这二次“文化淹没危机”从更一般的意义上也可视为整个文学学科所面临的“危机”吧。过去，比较文学曾被固守学科专业界域的庄重守成者视为咄咄逼人的入侵者；现在这个入侵者自己尚未确认的领域也被大举入侵了。反击与捍卫自然是本能的反应方式。

多年以前，韦勒克就在他的著名论文《比较文学的危机》中告诫人们说：应该划清文学研究与思想史、宗教和政治观念史以及情感史的研究的界限。这种坚决捍卫文学研究自身特性的要求至今似乎已成了老生常谈，尽管还有相当数量的拥护者，但却无法阻挡研究者们的浓厚兴趣和广泛尝试，正所谓“青山遮不住，毕竟东流去”。第 14 届国际比协大会的主题就定为“多元文化语境中的文学”，堂而皇之地让文学与文化攀亲结缘了。再看看下设的六个分议题，几乎都是在同韦勒克当年的谆谆告诫唱对台戏，如“文学的民族个性”，实指文学的文化特性；“外国与本土的相互影响”，正相当于文化人类学所说的文化传播(diffusion)与文化涵化(acculturation)问题；“文学类型、语言和文化”、“文学与其它文化表现形式”、“区域研究”、“比较文学与多元文化的方法及范式”等，无一不可作为标准的比较文化课题。难怪会有人感到“淹没”，并由此而担忧新一轮的“危机”。继往开来的捍卫者自然不乏其人。加拿大学者瓦尔特·莫泽使以《文学研究与文化研究：重新定位的问题》为题发表报告，重提保持文学研究独立性以防止学科淹没消失的话题。不过无论从哪方面看，都已显得温和、宽容了许多。捍卫的立场也从文学的独立性退到“相对的”独立性了。

假如我们转换一下立足点，真正站到相对化的立场上，或许不难悟出：比较文学研究者的“危机”意识完全是学科本位主义的产物。“淹没”表象背后的实质是文学研究的深化。文化绝不只是文学背景或“语境”，也是文学构成的整合性要素。如果说“比较”本身并不构成比较文学存在的理由和目的，那么，文化整合作用机制的发现和认识似应成为比较文学的核心任务之一。

不少从事比较研究的人似乎都经历过这样一种体验：在着手“比较”之前总是胸怀大志，似乎会有重大发现在等待着你；但在“比较”做完之后方才意识到并没有什么惊人的结果。造成这种皮尔·金特剥洋葱式喜剧现象的原因在于，比较的视界仅仅停留在“文学”本身，未能深入到文化整合要素中去，因而也就不能升华到比较文化的透视高度。不识“文学”真面目，只因身在“文学”牢笼之中。“文化”视角的引入是解放学科本位主义囚徒的有效途径，使研究者站得更高，看得更远，因而是利而非弊，它带来的将是新的“契机”而非新的“危机”。从某种意义上甚至可以这样说：比较文化研究未必是比较文学，但有深度有“洞见”的比较文学研究自然是比较文化。换言之，比较文学研究若能得出具有文化意义的结论，那将是其学术深度的最好证明，应视为比较文学之大幸，而非不幸。

从另一角度去观照这个问题，我们还可意识到，比较方法的运用，不论在平行研究中还是在影响研究中，其最直接的目标总是指向“异”和“同”的。文学上的“异”和“同”的认识固然十分重要，但毕竟还停留在“知其然”的层面上，至于为什么“异”或为什么“同”的追问则往往不是在文学的自身界域中所能解决的，这势必将比较文学学者引向更深一层的“所以然”的层面以求得理性的阐释。列维-斯特劳斯认为这种深层的东西正是文化人类学家所关注的“文化”——它是构成我们社会生活的无意识基础。① 也有学者将此种文化的深层解释称为“文化哲学”。

从事实的观点辨别出各文化表现的差异与相似之处，这是一切文化研究共同的必要的起点，它们是基础的工作，但并不是我们唯一可以着手研究的对象。

如果比较文学不愿意停留在它的起点——对超越国界的文学现象中表层的异同事实的认识，那么它也责无旁贷地面对着文化人类学和文化哲学所面对的深层解释的课题。

所以说，从比较文学到比较文化是自然而然、顺理成章的，它符合学术发展自身的累进逻辑。如果不是出于职业饭碗的考虑，我们大可不必为文学研究的拓展性变革而担忧，与其那样，不如以宽容而坦然的心境去静观其变，进而调整自已的思维习惯和观念定势，以求有效地适应我们这个日新月异的时代的发展和变革。

二、文学研究：“内转”还是“外转”？

纵观20世纪的文学研究史，有两种相互对立的倾向彼此消长变化：“向内转”和“向外转”，或可称为内向派与外向派、向心倾向与离心倾向，等等。内向一派的立场是：明确和捍卫文学之所以为文学的特殊属性，让文学研究成为具有自身独立存在的一门学科，它应专注于文学文本的审美形式方面；外向派的立场则是：文学与社会、历史、意识形态等等其它方面有不可分割的联系，因而不能脱离这种活生生的联系去孤立地研究文学作品。

大致看来，作为对外向研究占主导地位的19世纪文学批评传统(泰纳“种族、环境、

① 列维-斯特劳斯：《结构人类学》，雅各布逊英译本，纽约，基础图书公司1963年版，第18页。

时代”模式、圣·佩夫的作家人格说、勃兰兑斯的时代精神说、阿诺德的文化教化理想等)的反拨，20世纪前半叶是文学研究向内转，内向派崛起并成为主流的时期，20年代兴盛一时的俄国形式主义和30、40年代风靡欧美学坛的新批评派为显著标志。内向派的明显优势可以从40年代末向世的、影响深远的文学研究的理论教科书——韦勒克、沃伦《文学理论》中看到一个缩影。该书虽试图从一个不偏不倚的公允立场明确划分出“文学的外部研究”和“文学的内部研究”两大阵营，分别加以对待和说明，但由于时代风气所濡染，两位作者还是明显地偏向于“内部研究”一面，这从该书的章节安排重心便可看出。一种旨在切入文本内部的近距离的“细读，成为大学文学专业课堂中普遍的训练方式，其余波至今仍在延续。然而，物极必反。20世纪50年代出现了以原型批评为先兆的外向派复兴。弗莱在其里程碑式的文学理论著作《批评的解剖》中公开向“新批评派”的一统天下挑战，倡导一种与“细读”相对的“向后站”①的研究立场，并以“原型”概念去恢复从神话宗教到文学的有机联系，使作品与外部世界的关系重新成为批评所关注的焦点。在他看来，并不存在纯而又纯的孤立的文学，“文学只是人们称为通才教育、文化或人文学研究的那种东西的一个组成部分。”②

无独有偶，20世纪后半叶众多的理论和批评流派虽然对原型批评看法不一，但是在强调文学的外部联系方面却与之相伴，促成了文学研究又一次向外转向的国际性潮流。尤其是精神分析批评、读者反应批评和接受美学理论，以及最近的从后结构主义、解构主义到新历史主义的重要转变，都从不同的角度凸显出与文学文本同等重要的语境或背景对于理解和阐释的决定意义。

……

与阐释学密切相关的解构主义或许是自新批评派以来最关注文本的批评流派，但该派代表人物对文本的分析也同样显示了由内向外的重要转变。阿瑟·C. 丹特在评价法国解构主义大师们的历史功绩时，将他们同文艺复兴时代的佛罗伦萨艺术相提并论。他说：“他们都详尽地阐述文本的概念以结合历史、文化、心理学以及变革狭义上的文学阐读。……如果精神的关联犹如雅克·拉康所坚决主张的那样，如果文化的关联犹如克洛德·列维-斯特劳斯所提出的那样，如果历史的关联犹如米歇尔·福柯或费尔南·布劳德尔的所表达的那样，那么，即使文本并不照按雅克·德里达所假定的方式组合，休漠实际上仍是现存的形而上学的牺牲品，这是持原子说者的另一名称，而且文本理论的范围总体上说是拓宽了，对学术蓝图的重新划分业已就绪。因而批评是一种范例人类科学。”③从拘谨狭隘的“内部研究”到通向“人类科学”的广义的文学研究，这种几乎是一百八十度的逆反变革在短短几十年内便悄无声息地完成了。甚至连亲身经历这一过程的“过来人”也会觉得不可思议。于是有人将这场变革解释为批评之前的旧有研究范式的复归。……

现代文学批评史上出现了类似黑格尔在哲学史中、弗莱在西方文学史中洞见的那种圆

① 弗莱：《批评的解剖》，普林斯顿大学出版社1971年版，第140页。

② 弗莱：《批评的解剖》，普林斯顿大学出版社1971年版，第3页。

③ 阿瑟·丹特：《美的科学与批评的未来》，见拉尔夫·科恩主编《文学理论的未来》，程锡麟等译，中国社会科学出版社1993年版，第411页。

圈式的循环运动。不过，无论是黑格尔还是弗莱都不曾把这种运动简单化地理解为单纯的复旧或者回归，而是理解为螺旋上升式的发展。文学研究由外转内又由内转外的往复变动亦如此。只要把斯蒂芬·葛林伯雷或海登·怀特的著述同阿诺德或李维斯时代的批评著作加以对照，新旧历史主义之间的天差地别就会一目了然。虽然这一流派并没有统一的纲领和严格的界线，但多数人确认的解读原则还是相当明确的：把文学文本与非文学文本都视为历史话语的构成部分；历史话语既处于文本之中又外在于文本；在文学与文化系统的关系中探讨话语、权力和主体间的相互作用；强调批评中的政治和意识形态作用，等等。

……

以上借助于弗莱所倡导的“向后站”的原则，从20世纪以来文学批评和文学研究的宏观变化中为比较文学的“文化化”倾向寻找背景和线索，便可使局限在比较文学自身的近距离视野中不易看清、使人困惑乃至诱发“危机”感的问题得到理解。如果用“内部研究”和“外部研究”的二元对立尺度来判断，那就可以说比较文学从它诞生时候起便具有“外向型”的天性。一旦“跨学科”研究率先在这一领域中获得合法性并得到研究者的普遍认同，一种被学科壁垒压抑已久的离心冲动便化为巨大的能量一发而不可收了。我们还可以简略回顾一下前几届国际比协年会的情形：1988年第十二届大会（慕尼黑）的主题“文学的时间与空间”，1991年第十三届大会（东京）的主题“欲望与幻想”，其实均可视为比较文化或人类学的课题，只是字面上没有出现“文化”字样而已。1994年大会终于到了“满园春色关不住”的时机，“多元文化语境中的文学”这个主题已使“文化”由潜台词变为显台词，成了大有喧宾夺主之嫌的一枝“出墙红杏”。再放眼瞻望一下本次会议为1997年大会（荷兰莱顿）预设的主题“作为文化记忆的文学”，此种反客为主的印象一定会更加强烈吧？不过站在“向后站”的全景立场上，谁还能够说出比较文学拥抱“文化”的超前冲动是盲目的或是误入歧途的呢？难道不该把它视为顺应时代变革、引导新世纪的科际整合大趋势的先锋预兆吗？

三、“后文学时代”的全球性主流话语——文化

我们已从文学研究的世纪性变革这一角度解说了比较文学趋向于比较文化的现象。接踵而来的更深一层的问题是：文学研究本身的这场大变革为什么会发生？倘若我们不把这种显而易见的变化简单地归结为循环回归或人为炒热的暂时性现象，那么应该如何理解推动文学批评走向泛文化批评的必然性呢？其内在动力因素又是什么？

……

在这种强烈自觉的跨学科意向的背后，我们还可以找到一个更为根本也更为有力的因素，那就是现代化进程本身已经打破了固有的文学观念，使一种前所未闻的“后文学”时代不期而来，只有从此种既突兀又实在的现实变革中方可深切体会在文学创作和文学研究领域所发生和将发生的一切。

……

四、结语：21世纪人文研究的新取向

学科的划分不是从来就有的，也不会永远不变。20世纪来自各学科内部的“跨学科”呼声日益高涨，这决不能视为偶然之巧合。“文化”概念因其出入文史哲，纵贯人与社会的独特的整合效应，势必成为破学科之利器及人文研究中最具吸引力和涵盖力的核心范畴。由此看来，比较文学向比较文化的靠拢，应理解为它的新生契机而不是危机。

（节选自叶舒宪：《从比较文学到比较文化——“后文学时代”的文学研究展望》，《东方丛刊》1995年9月，第114-126页。）

“美美与共”和人类文明

（节选）

费孝通

【导读】

费孝通(1910. 11—2005. 04)，江苏吴江人，伦敦大学经济政治学院院士，曾获联合国大英百科全书奖。费孝通是中国社会学和人类学的主要奠基人，也是第七、八届全国人大常委会副委员长，政协第六届全国委员会副主席。费孝通先生一生经历了中国社会的重大变迁。终其一生，他都致力于推动中国与世界的交流与联系。他的努力不仅让世界重新认识中国特殊的社会结构和中国特殊的生产方式，也推动了包括浦东、黄河上游、南方丝绸之路在内的多个区域经济的布局和发展。费孝通先生提出的“中华民族多元一体格局”已经成为政府和学术界定义中国民族关系史的核心理论框架。北大校长周其凤盛赞费先生的“文化自觉”理念、全球化时代中国国际地位的战略思考，以及他的“美美与共、天下大同”的和谐世界设想，都将指引着我们坚实地走向中华民族的伟大复兴。

费孝通先生对中国的现代化进程具有重要影响。费先生师从英国社会人类学家、功能主义的创始人马林诺思基，终其一生他都坚持其导师实证主义的价值观，亲自深入农村进行实地调查。马林诺思基提倡田野工作，要求人类学者要到那些不够为“人”的原始社会去体验、观察。费先生认为马老师使这些化外之民恢复了“人”的地位和尊严。只有对“异文化”抱有尊重和开放的心态，才可能真正平等的进行对话和交流。因此在跨文化交流的时候，一定要培养社会工作者具有跨越文化偏见的心态、抛弃自我中心主义，这样才能做到费孝通先生提倡的“各美其美，美人之美，美美与共，天下大同”。“各美其美，美人之美，美美与共”就是要做到不仅欣赏本民族的文化，也能够欣赏异民族的文化，而且不能以自己的标准去评判异民族文化的“优劣”。中国历史上一再出现“盲目崇拜”和“闭关排外”的现象，究其原因，是国人未能达到“各美其美”与“美人之美”的境界。历史上日本善于“美人之美”，向中国学习，因此获得了很多文化资源。这不仅使日本得到了巨大进步，对中国文化也有一定的促进作用，可以说达到了“双赢”的结果。

“全球化”的渊源是19世纪西方主导的世界各地不同文化之间的广泛接触和交往。在此过程中，各文化之间互相交融、彼此吸收，各文明中都出现了一些新的外来的内容。今日之世界文明，已非昔日历史上的那种“纯粹”的传统文明。各文明几乎无一例外是以“多元一体”这样一个基本形态构建而成，文化的“纯正性”只是民粹主义编织的神话。但在探讨文化问题时，很容易掺杂进情感和心理因素，甚至制造民粹运动为所谓的“国家利益”服务，激化不同文明之间的误解和矛盾。因此费先生强调，要以“美美与共”的心态，博采众家之长，建立一个“和而不同”的美好社会。毕竟，我们的古人正是以“和而不同”的价值观，包容众多族群和不同文化，建立了大一统的中华文明。

（霍晓珊）

文明的话题

探讨全球化和不同文明之间的关系，不是一个新话题，也不是一个新现象。今天我们经常说的“全球化”，其渊源可以追溯到19世纪西方(主要是英国)主导的世界各地不同文化之间的广泛接触和交往。对这种广义的全球化趋势的关注与研究，也是从19世纪开始的，比如卡尔·马克思就关注过资本主义全球扩张和原始积累的过程。关于这方面问题的探索，一直是社会学、人类学、民族学等诸多社会科学研究的重要领域。

……

近年来，在讨论全球化这个话题的时候，我多次提到“和而不同”的概念。这个概念不是我发明的，它是中国传统文化中的一个重要核心。这种“和而不同”的状态，是一种非常高的境界，它是人们的理想。但是要让地球上的各种文明，各个民族、族群的亿万民众，都能认同和贯彻这个理想，绝不是一件轻而易举的事。为此，我们还有很长的路要走，还要付出沉重的代价。

我还提出了“文化自觉”。什么是文化自觉？简单地说，就是每个文明中的人对自己的文明进行反省，做到有“自知之明”。这样，人们就会更理智一些，从而摆脱各种无意义的冲动和盲目的举动。

后来，我又进一步提出“各美其美，美人之美，美美与共，天下大同”的设想。这几句话表达了我对未来的理想，同时也说出了要实现这一理想的手段。我认为，如果人们真的做到“美美与共”，也就是在欣赏本民族文明的同时，也能欣赏、尊重其他民族的文明，那么，地球上不同文化、不同民族、不同国家之间就达到了一种和谐，就会出现持久而稳定的“和而不同”。

经验性研究(empirical study)

研究文化和文明问题，可以有多种不同的视角和方法，不同的视角和方法之间可以互相支持和取长补短。作为一名从事实地调查研究的社会工作者，我想借此机会，谈一谈我在对全球化和文化、文明的关系的研究中所采用的方法和体会。

我的学术生涯，大约是70年前从广西大瑶山开始的，那次人类学和民族学的田野调查的研究方法(用今天的话说，就是“理论和实际相结合”的方法)，对我一生学术研究产生了决定性的影响，成了我后来学术研究的基本手段。

我提出这个问题，是想提醒大家在关注探讨全球化和文明的问题时，如何拓展我们的研究方法。今天，世界上发生了许多新的问题和现象，这些问题和现象，都是由于不同文化的相互接触、碰撞、融合而产生的，没有现成的答案可以解决。也就是说，用原有的思维逻辑，原有的研究方法来解决现在的问题已经不行了。要想找到解决问题的方法，就是回到现实社会生活中去，扎扎实实地做实地调查。要超越旧的各种刻板的印象(stereotype)和判断，搞清楚各种文明中的人们的社会生活，并以此为基础(而不是以某种意识形态体系为基础)来构建人类跨文明的共同的理念。这种研究的难点，在于研究者必须摆脱各种成见，敞开胸怀，以开阔的视角，超越自己文化固有的思维模式，来深入观察和领悟其他族群的文化、文明。在跨文化的交流和沟通中，构建起新的更广博的知识体系。

为什么必须要到现实生活中去调查呢？因为人类社会是复杂的、多样性的；又是多变的、富于创造性的，它绝不是只有单一文化背景和有限知识和经验的研究者能够想像和包容得了的。所以，研究者必须深入到你要了解的“他人”的生活中去观察、研究。从某种意义上说，这种实地调查的方法，也反映出研究者的一种心态，就是你是不是真正要去理解、接受“他人”的文化、文明，这种心态正是今天不同文明之间交流的一个关键。深入到“异文化”中去做调查，努力了解“他人”的语言、传统，做到设身处地地用当地人的眼光来看待周围的事物……这本身就是对“异文化”的尊重和对“异文化”开放的心态。如果连这种最基本的平等态度都没有，还谈什么交流和沟通。

……

心态和价值观

……

要进行跨文化的观察体验，还必须具有一种跨越文化偏见的心态。由某一种文化教化出来的人，因为对“他文化”不习惯，出现这样那样的误解、曲解，对“他文化”产生偏见(prejudice)，应该说是一种正常的现象。但作为一个研究者，则必须具备更高的见识、更强的领悟力，能够抛弃这种偏见。我特别提到一个“悟”字，这个字在跨文化的研究中显得特别重要，它不仅要求研究者全身心地投入到被研究者的生活当中，乃至他们的思想中，能设身处地地像他们一样思考；同时，又要求研究者能冷静、超然地去观察周围发生的一切。在一种“进得去，出得来”的心态下，去真正体验我们要了解的“跨文化”的感受。我认为，在讨论全球化和不同文明之间的关系时，具体的研究方法等技术因素，并不是最重要的，最要紧的还是研究者的心态。

……

培养这种良好的跨文化交流心态，是提高每个社会工作者人文修养的一门必修课，应该把这方面素质的提高，作为对社会学专业学生的基本要求。如果再扩大一些，我们能在一般民众中也推行这方面的宣传教育，其结果，必然能够增进不同文明中普通成员之间的良好沟通、交流和理解。如果这种沟通、交流和理解能够有广泛的群众基础，那么，今天世界上诸多民族和文明之间的矛盾、偏见、冲突以及冤冤相报、以暴制暴等等就有了化解和消除的希望。

交融中的文明

近几百年来，西方文化一直处于强势地位，造成了其社会中某些势力的自我膨胀，产生了殖民主义、种族主义、极端民族主义、文化沙文主义、单线进化论等形形色色的自我中心主义的思潮。但与此同时，在西方学术界，也出现了像马林诺斯基这样的，对西方文化中自我中心主义思潮进行反思和反制的学术流派。这种反思，可以说就是“文化自觉”的一个表现。然而直到今天，西方社会中各种势力和学术界各派别之间，仍然存在着巨大的分歧和激烈的较量。从另一方面看，非西方的各种文明，在经历了几百年的殖民主义、世界大战、冷战、民族解放运动等等磨练后，其社会成员的思想和心理都起了十分复杂的变化，产生了多种多样的社会思潮，其中不乏与“西方至上主义”相对立甚至相对抗的思潮。这个状况，被一些人称作是“文明的冲突”，这种冲突已经影响到了今天的世界局势。目前所谓的“恐怖主义”和“反恐斗争”，就是这种“冲突”的表现之一。

几百年来，主导世界的西方文化大量地传播到其他文明中，随着时间推移，世界已经越来越紧密地联系在一起，这种传播也变得越来越快了。然而，文化交流是双向的，在西方文化快速传播的同时，西方社会也大量地汲取了其他文明的文化，而且这种文化上的交融，每时每刻都在发生着。这些被吸收的“异文化”，经过“消化”、“改造”之后，成了各自文明中新的、属于自己的内容，并从宗教、政治和意识形态等方面反映出来。可以说，今天世界上不同文明之间已经是“你中有我，我中有你”。今日之世界文明，已非昔日历史文献、经典书籍中所描绘的那种“纯粹”的传统文明了。因此，我们必须改变过去概念化的、抽象的、刻板的思维方式，以一种动态的、综合的、多层面的眼光，来看待当今世界上不同文化和文明之间的关系。

中华文明的启迪

…… 在辽、金、元、清的时候，统治者在不同民族、不同族群的地区，实行不同的行政制度，因地制宜，顺应当地民众的传统文化、信仰和习俗来进行统治。但是，这种“顺应”又都统一在更高一层的“国”的框架之内。

这些例子，说明中华文明的结构和机制，在漫长的岁月中，经过一代代先人在实践中的不断探索、积累、完善，已经形成了一套相当成熟的协调模式。它充分体现了古人高度的政治智慧和中华民族深厚的文化底蕴。时至今日，在我们的生活实践中实施的“民族区域自治”、“一国两制”等政治制度，无不缘于厚重的中华传统文化。

中华文明有着悠久的历史和深厚的内涵，也有与“异文化”交流的丰富经验。我相信，在今后中国越来越广泛、深入地融入到世界的过程中，一定能为重构全球化和不同文明之间的关系做出应有的贡献。

跨文化研究的人文属性

人们常常把世界上不同文明之间如何相处的问题，看成是国与国、民族与民族之间政治、军事、综合国力等方面的比较，像是在做一种“力学”关系的分析。这样的分析不能说没有道理，但是不全面，因为文明、文化都是关于“人”的事情，所以要搞清楚还得从“人”入手。

……

从总体上说，人类文明的多样性，是各个文明得以“不朽”的最可靠的保证。一种文明、文化，只有融入更为丰富、更为多样的世界文明中，才能保证自己的生存。人们常说，“只有民族的，才是世界的”，这是不错的；反过来说，只有世界的，才是民族的，才能使这个民族的文化长盛不衰，也很有道理。所以，文化上的唯我独尊、固步自封，对其他文明视而不见，都不是文明的生存之道。只有交流、理解、共享、融合，才是世界文明共存共荣的根本出路。不论是“强势文明”还是“弱势文明”，这是唯一的出路。

探讨文明和文化问题，不可避免地要涉及价值观和信仰，而这些又极容易转变成感情和心理因素，然而在科学研究中，一旦掺杂了这些因素，就会产生巨大的阻力，这是我们从事族群、民族、宗教研究的社会科学工作者都遇到过的问题，因此，必须构建一种超越常规的理念。我们不提倡用某一种文明的意识形态、价值观念来解决不同文明之间的问题，因为用一种文明的“标准”去评判另一种文明，不管这种做法“对不对”，实际上会让人感觉到这样做“好不好”。由于不同文明之间人们的认知体系有差别，所以不同文明的人，对同一个问题的看法，常常会变得不是“是”与“非”而成了“好”与“坏”了。我觉得，不管出于什么动机，强迫别人接受一种本来不属于他们的价值观，这种做法，本身就含有欺压和侮辱人的性质。

……

当前世界上某些人，常常有意无意地把不同文明、文化之间的关系，直接与国家或民族利益挂钩，这是一种加大，甚至是激化不同文明之间误解和矛盾的做法。这些人在大谈“国家利益”的时候，手里不断挥舞着文明、文化的大旗，把赤裸裸的为“一国谋利益”的做法，装扮成捍卫“某某文明”的“义举”；把具体的国家利益之争，混淆成不同文明之间的争斗。当然，从广义上讲，文化价值也包含在“利益”之中，但它们并不是简单地连接在一起的，这种随意的联系，是不成熟、不理智、不准确、不负责任的表现。犹如我们不能把美国的国家利益，等同于基督教文明的利益；也不能把中国的国家利益，说成是儒家文明的利益。

我们认为，国家利益可以“一事一议”，好像谈生意那样，通过理性的协商来解决。如果把这种事情上升到文明、文化的层次里，就会变成充满感情和心理因素的、非理性的问题。

一个国家不能自命为某一种文明的代表或化身，说成是某文明的卫士；各种政治集团也不该盗用文明、文化的名义，制造民粹运动来为自己的政治利益服务。这种夹杂着经济和政治目的的“国家利益”，会大大歪曲不同文明之间关系的本质，造成恶劣的结果。

美美与共

从历史和现实中可以看到，要想处理好不同文明之间的关系，首要的条件应该是各自能够保持一种平和、谦逊的心态，就是中国古人所谓的“君子之风”。

前几年，我提出了“各美其美、美人之美、美美与共、天下大同”的设想，这是我的心愿。要想实现这几句话，还要走很长的路，甚至要付出沉重的代价。比如要做到“各美其美、美人之美”，也就是各种文明教化的人，不仅欣赏本民族的文化，还要发自内心地欣赏异民族的文化；做到不以本民族文化的标准，去评判异民族文化的“优劣”，断定什么是“糟粕”，什么是“精华”。

……

为了人类能够生活在一个“和而不同”的世界上，从现在起就必须提倡在审美的、人文的层次上，在人们的社会活动中树立起一个“美美与共”的文化心态，这是人们思想观念上的一场深刻大变革，它可能与当前世界上很多人习惯的思维模式和行为方式相抵触。在这场变革中，一定会因为不被理解而引起一些人的非议甚至抵制，特别是当触动到某些集团的利益的时候，可能还会受到猛烈的攻击。但是，当我们看到人类前进的步伐已经迈上全球化、信息化的道路；已经到了一个必须尽快解决全球化和人类不同文明如何相得益彰、共同繁荣的紧要关头，这些抵制和攻击又算得了什么。

博采众家之长

当我们探讨和研究不同文明如何相处的时候，必须充分了解和借鉴世界上各种文明，做到博采众长、开阔胸怀、拓宽思路、启迪灵感。中国的社会科学工作者在探讨、研究中华文明的时候，也要认真地理解和研究世界上其他文明的文化，要“美人之美”。

……

作为人类学社会学工作者，我们应该以严肃、认真的态度，不带任何偏见地深入研究本民族的历史文化，同时也应该下功夫研究其他国家、民族的历史文化，以扩展我们的视野，增强我们的想像力和创新能力，为当今世界经济迅速“全球化”的同时，建设一个“和而不同”的美好社会贡献力量。

（本文是作者2004年8月在“北京论坛”上所作的书面发言，《群言》分两期刊载。节选自费孝通：《“美美与共”和人类文明》，《群言》2005年第01期，第17-20页，2005年第02期，第13-16页。）

东方和西方：文化的多元化标准

[荷]佛克马

【导读】

杜威·佛克马(Douwe W. Fokkema, 1931—2011, 又译佛克玛), 荷兰著名的比较文学学者和文学理论家、汉学家。其独撰或合著的著作主要有:《中国的文学教义及苏联影响》(1965),《20 世纪文学理论》(1978),《总体文学和比较文学论题》(1987),《知识和专注: 文学研究的问题与方法》(2000)等。《东方和西方: 文化的多元化标准》一文是佛克马多元文化主义(multiculturalism)思想的简短精练的阐述。他首先指出原教旨主义会导致种族净化与政治的同一性, 在宗教、经济、科技等方面亦有影响。与此相对, 他提出世界主义。此处还只是说"某种新世界主义的可能性", 在 1998 年北京的"全球化与人文科学的未来"国际研讨会发言中, 他已经开始明确呼吁"走向新世界主义"。

人性的同一性是世界主义的前提, 但是提出"文化的多元化标准", 并非是要强调同一性, 而是要承认并尊重差异性。这一观点是基于以下几个方面的认识。

首先, 在种族上和文化上具有独特品质的族群在长期的共同生活中, 会形成某些共同遵守的行为准则, 即文化惯例, 或曰成规(convention)。佛克马认为成规是一种文化的基本单位, 生活于其中的个体可以通过后天学习获得关于文化惯例方面的知识。其次, 学习是人类普遍具有的能力, 人们不但具有学习本族群的文化惯例的能力, 也具有学习另一种文化惯例并付诸实践的能力, 这就有助于克服文化障碍, 达到更好的沟通, 这是世界主义的基础。他指出, 这样的观念对于比较文学系而言是有价值的。再次, 承认不同文化传统之间存在着根本差异, 并不是所谓的分离主义, 并不意味着要强调隔阂, 否认对话和沟通。他指出文化代码的转换不仅可能, 而且往往有着极强的吸引力。但是, 已转换的代码并不等同于原代码, 也不是"纯"代码, 文化往往是相互影响相互交流的结果。提出文化多元化标准的目的"是要探寻文化识别的可能性","探寻"这一行为本身的意义并不亚于探寻的对象。不同文化之间不断的碰撞与交融, 是促使文化发展的重要因素, 跨文化交流的目的不在于作出孰优孰劣的价值判断, 而在于互相认识, 互相了解, 认识和了解就是对文化识别的可能性的探寻。多元文化主义承认文化差异, 尊重不同的价值观、道德行为和生活模式, 批判主流意识形态, 而世界文学正是各种不同的艺术形式、文化观念的载体, 对不同文化圈的文学文本的阅读是文化参与和文化观察的重要途径, 也是克服文化障碍的有效手段。最后，佛克马贯彻了他的多元文化主义思想，希望每个比较文学系能够从自身出发，制订阅读书目，在人性同一性的前提下，比较不同文化之间的差异性与共同点。

佛克马对文化的多元化的强调，对文化差异的尊重，与他自己所受的汉学教育及对中国文学的长期关注是有密切关系的，这使他的思维能够超越一般西方学者的局限，自觉地以跨文化的眼界探讨备受争议的热点问题，并且发表自己独特的见解，这些观点是富有启发意义的。

（常芳）

这个世界遭致原教旨主义的种种威胁：从种族净化、同一性政治到宗教、经济和科技观念。因此，我们需要一种有助于读者打破意识形态壁垒，并解除原教旨主义的信仰的文学。我的政治信仰中包括了一种世界主义的观点，它可以与任何一种同一性政治相提并论。这一讨论已进行了多年，不仅斯卡佩塔的《世界主义的颂歌》(1981)，托多洛夫的《历史的风尚》(1991)，而且马克思主义的作家们也都涉及这个问题——人类有某种共同的东西使之与动物区别开来。也许这种共同因素正是与动物相区别的愿望以及对这一愿望的思索。实际上，这一愿望并非完全依赖于自然的、生物的以及其他的条件。这种愿望导致伦理和人权的产生。某种新世界主义的可能性可使我们避免文化战争的衍生，“文化战争”一词最近在美国广为流行，令人尬尴，例如哈佛大学非洲裔美国学系系主任小亨利·路易斯·盖茨就写了一本名为《松散的标准：文化战争笔录》的书。

然而，盖茨选择的是和平地适应于文化本体的战壕之中。他的理由是人们学习另一文化惯例的能力是无限的：“任何人，只要有足够的好奇心和驱使力，就能完全掌握另外一种无论看似多么陌生的文化。”(1993：XV)这一点恰恰与我关于教育的准则不谋而合。有许多人获得了另一文化惯例的有关知识，并能付之于实践，这方面例子很多。例如众多的北美移民还有那些政治家，如尼赫鲁，他在牛津和剑桥期间如同呆在自己家里一般悠闲自得。对于比较文学系而言，树立不同的文化惯例是可以传播和学习的观念，是一个有价值的目标。然而，许多学者都强调诸如中国与欧洲传统之间的根本差异，将此作为强烈对比的例子，这种对比也许可以作为其他文化差异的一个范例。刘若愚(James J. Liu)是中国传统与欧美传统之间最成功的调停人之一，他在一本遗著中表达了这样一种观念：“只有通过来自两种不同传统的文本的并列，我们才能突出各自传统中真正独特的东西。……这种并列将使我们意识到那些难以表述的先决条件，即有关构成各种传统的语言、诗歌、政治和阐释本质的先决条件，这就为真正的比较诗学扫清了障碍，得以超越欧洲中心主义或中国中心主义。”(摘自 Idema 1989：279)

承认文化传统之间的根本差异，如中国与欧洲相去甚远，并不意味文化代码不能转换。刘若愚本人的生活和著作已表明了这种可能性。这种文化代码的转换不仅可能，而且对那些尝试者们有极强的吸引力。这种转换并不意味已转换的代码可以等同于原代码，或还是“纯”代码。实际上，正如爱德华·赛义德在《文化与帝国主义》中所指出的那样：“一切文化都相互影响；没有哪一种是孤立的、纯粹的，一切文化都是混合物。”(1993：XXIX) 尽管这些混合物之间仍存在着差异。

至此，我所赞同的标准得以形成的轴线开始明朗。这个标准将是动态的，其目的不是去强调总是已经建构的同一性，而是探寻文化识别的可能性。对这种标准的寻求实际上是一种卓越的文化行为，而这种寻求本身至少与其寻求的对象同等重要。在这一点上，我同意沃尔特·米格罗洛关于文化的定义："文化指导行动和行为的方式，而不是文化得以衡量和评估的累积性成果或成就。"(1995：179)

于是我所赞同的标准就将受到代码转换可能性的影响，这与同一性政治完全相反，它将集中于不同的价值观，传统的差异，对主流意识形态的批判，以及道德行为和个人生活的多种模式上。它将包容世界各主要文化圈的复杂文学的各种文本，不仅是当代的文本，还有古代的、近现代的文本，其假定是尽力理解难的文本比想当然地去理解简单的文本更有意义。然而，我在解构上下文的方式上，自己对呈现意义(上下文重构)属性的把握上，将与自己的同行们持不同的观点，因此我所赞同的标准也与他们的不一样。所以，没有必要将我所偏好的文本罗列出来，正如某个比较文学系采用的文本总是一种折衷产物，是由多种信条支配，由我们身处的特定文化和当时的条件(如书的来源是否方便)所决定的。

倘若我提倡的是一种理想的世界主义，那么这并不意味着由各个比较文学系设计世界文学的一切标准在全世界都是同样的，而是说每一个比较文学系须从自身的角度出发，制订一个阅读目录(最好不止一个)，而这一书目除了其他因素之外，应基于人性是同一的这一观念，尽管语言、民族、种族、宗教、性别以及文化的差别仍然存在。对东西方关于世界主义标准的种种概念——当然仍与文化密切相关——进行比较，并体验二者的差异与共同点，是最有趣不过的事。

(沈小茜　译　王晓路　校)

(选自佛克马：《东方和西方：文化的多元化标准》，沈小茜译，《中外文化与文论》1996年第1期，第94-96页。)

文化相对主义与“和而不同”原则

乐黛云

【导读】

北京大学乐黛云教授是我国著名的比较文学理论家，为我国比较文学事业的开拓和发展作出了巨大贡献。在长期的比较文学理论研究过程中，乐黛云教授非常关注的一点，就是如何保护文化多元主义，反对文化霸权主义。《文化相对主义与“和而不同”原则》是她1996年发表在《中国比较文学》杂志上的一篇文章，这篇文章着重阐述了中国传统文化中“和而不同”的原则是如何弥补文化相对主义之不足的。

“西方文化相对主义”是西方学者为了和平共处，针对“西方文化中心主义”而提出的一个概念，这一概念提倡承认文化多样性，反对用一种文化去阐释、判断或是吞并另一种文化。如今，西方和东方文化自觉使全球文化发展呈现多元化趋势，这一概念的提出相对于“西方文化中心主义”无疑是一个巨大进步。但这一概念也有着自身固有的弱点，例如，如果文化相对主义发展到极端境地，很可能使得一个民族对自身文化抱有优越感，进而盲目排斥其他民族的优秀文化，导致不同文化之间的孤立和隔绝。针对这一弱点，乐黛云教授仔细思考之后提出，中国传统文化中的精华是可以对其进行弥补的，具体来说就是，“‘和而不同’原则以其‘最少侵犯不同文化群体的利益，最大容忍不同文化群体特点’为解决这一悖论提供了重要价值的文化资源”。

“和而不同”的理论源自《左传》，是中华民族智慧的结晶，简单来说就是统筹事物内部各个不同的要素，使它们达成和谐，进而共同发展。“和而不同”的“和”有着特定的内涵。首先，不同的事物不能离开相互关系而独立存在，“和”就是要探讨这些差异如何共存；其次，“和”就是要协调诸多不同而达成和谐，产生新的事物，新事物本身又与其他事物构成新的不同；再次，“和”的主要内容是“适度”。中国传统文化的核心之一是“中庸”，追求节制、均衡之美。比如文学作品追求“乐而不淫，哀而不伤”；建筑追求对称、均齐……所谓“执两用中”，就是要在“过”和“不及”之间找到一个合适的点。最后，“适度”的标准是什么？道家认为顺应自然规律就是“适度”，自然万物只有遵循自然规律才能生长，而人类社会也只有遵循普遍的法则才能正常运行，达到和谐的目的。可见，所谓的和谐，并不是要抹杀不同要素的差异，使它们完全相同，而是尊重这种差异，帮助它们在整体中找到各自的位置，最终达到共同的进步，产生新的事物。

“和而不同”固然可以弥补“西方文化相对主义”的缺陷，但它缺乏一定的可操作性。比如，“和而不同”的实现要求遵循人类共同认可的某些原则，那么这些原则如何产生？如何使不同群体中的人接受这些原则？这些问题都有待解决。德国哲学家哈伯马斯曾试图解决同样的问题。他提出“正义原则”和“团结原则”，既保障对个人尊重的平等权利，也要求个人尊重和包容他人。为了实现这些原则，他进一步提出了交往、商谈、互为主体等途径。

在文化多元发展的今天，古老的中国传统文化是可以重新焕发生机，和西方文化一起，为不同文化的和平共作出贡献的。这就要求我们充分把握自己文化的特点，并用现代思想对其加以创造性诠释，增强中国传统文化的适应性，使它更能理解和包容其他文化，这样才能促成文化多元共存格局的形成。

（潘丹丹）

今天世界的纷争虽不完全是由文化冲突引起，但也绝非与文化冲突无关。因此，关于文化冲突与文化共处的讨论正在世界范围内展开。是增强不同文化间相互理解和宽容而引向和平，还是因为文化隔离和冲突而导致战争，决定着21世纪人类的命运。自从二战之后，由于殖民体系的瓦解，文化上的“西方中心论”也逐渐随之消退，世界文化呈现出多元发展的趋势。近半个世纪以来，世界经济贸易、信息传递的发展，使民族与民族，国家与国家，地域与地域之间文化上的交往越来越频繁，世界日益成为一个不可分割的整体。目前，世界文化发展中，出现了两股不同方向的文化潮流：某些西方国家的理论家从维护自身的传统利益或传统习惯出发，仍然坚持“西方中心论”，与此同时，许多取得独立或复兴的民族，抱着珍惜自身文化的情怀，形成了一种返本归根，固守本土文化的民族主义和回归传统的保守主义，甚至某些东方学者鉴于两个世纪以来西方文化对世界造成的灾难和自身所曾受到的欺压，而提出文化上的“东方中心论”。如何使这两股相悖的潮流不致发展成为大规模对抗，并得以消解，实是当前一大问题。

19世纪与20世纪两百年的历史已经证明，用某种文化来“吞并”或“统一”另一种文化都不太可能，或者其结果是灾难性的。西方文化终于不能同化东方文化，也不能综合各种文化，造成新的“世界文化”。我们面临的是一个文化多元共生的现实。我们只能承认这个现实。承认这个现实，就有一个在不同文化之间，如何相处的问题。为了能和平相处，有的西方学者提出了文化相对主义。

西方的文化相对主义比西方中心主义显然进了很大一步，它承认不同文化存在的合理性，反对用自身判断是非善恶的标准去判断另一种文化，反对用一己的诠释框架去套用或解释其它文化现象。但文化相对主义也有它自身的弱点，例如它可能导致一种排他性，只尊重自身文化的优越，甚至为维护本民族文化的认同，而牺牲部分成员变异求新的要求，采取封闭、隔绝的孤立政策。另一方面，完全认同文化相对主义就不能不容忍某些已经对，或即将对人类共同生活带来重大危害的文化现象，如日本法西斯、德国纳粹，显然都有他们自身的文化根源，属于某种既定的文化。

看来在文化多元的现实社会，既要承认文化的相对性，又要有不同文化之间的交往和商谈，从中达成某种标准和共识，同时还要重视本民族文化的变异、更新和发展。中国传统文化中的“和而不同”原则或者可以为我们提供某些有正面价值的资源。

“和而不同”的理论出自两千多年前《左传》所记载的一段故事。那时齐国的大臣晏婴和齐侯曾经有过一段很有意思的对话。齐侯对晏婴说：“唯据与我和。”“据”指的是齐侯侍臣，姓梁，名丘据。晏婴说：“梁丘据不过是求同而已哪里谈得上和呢?”齐侯问：“和与同，难道还有甚么不一样吗?”这引出晏婴的一大篇议论。他认为“不同”是事物组成和发展的最根本的条件。例如做菜，油盐酱醋，必须“不同”，才能成其为菜肴；又如音乐，必须有“短长疾徐”、“哀乐刚柔”等“不同”，才能“相济相成”。晏子说，像梁丘据那样的人，你说对，他也说对，你说不对，他也说不对，有什么用呢?

此后，“和而不同”成了中国传统文化的核心观念之一。孔子说：“君子和而不同，小人同而不和”；郑子产说：“和宜生物，同则不济”(《国语·郑语》)。首先要承认不同，没有不同就不会发展，但不同并不是互不相关，各种不同因素之间，必须有“和”，“和”就是事物之间和谐有益的相互关系。唯有“和”，才能产生新的事物，才能发展。“同”或相互隔绝的“不同”都是不可能发展的。如果按照这样的“和而不同”的原则来处理一种文化内部或不同文化之间的关系，也许会得出一些很有益的结论。

首先，承认“不同”是普遍存在的。在同一文化内部，个人有说“是”或“否”的权利，也就是有与别人不同的权利。承认在一种文化传统内，可以有不同的传统，如中国的儒家、道家和佛教，以及其他民间文化传统，它们“相生相济”，共同发展。今天的文化多元论者也可以把文化一元论看作多元中的一元，承认其不同的存在。在不同文化之间，则要承认他种文化存在的权利，包括某些自己一时还难于理解和接受的方面。总之，坚持“不同”，就要使自己的存在形式相对化，能够站在一定距离之外，或站在他种文化立场，从不同角度来审视自己，十分小心地注意绝不轻易使自己认同的原则普遍化，并强加于人。

“和”，按照中国传统的解释，应包含四方面的意思：

第一，事物虽各不相同，但决不可能离开相互的关系而孤立存在，“和”的本义就是要探讨诸多不同因素在不同的关系网络中如何共处。儒家立论的基础是人和人的关系，道家立论的基础是人与自然的关系都说明了这一问题。

第二，“和”的精神，就是要协调“不同”，达到新的和谐统一，产生新的事物，这一事物又与其他事物构成新的不同。例如不同的原料构成一道菜，这道菜又与其他许多道菜一起，构成一桌筵席。最后，所有的不同并不消失，而是构成了更大，更完美的和谐。文化发展也是如此，中国的儒家要求“制礼作乐”，即要求“有为”，以维持社会的和谐；道家则要求“顺应自然”，即要求“无为”，以保持社会的安宁(也是和谐)。这本是两种不同的思想流派，后来，经过近千年的发展，西晋的哲学家郭象提出儒家的“制礼作乐”，本来就是顺应自然的，并不需要有所作为去让别人接受，因此也是一种“无为”。这个说法儒家和道家都可以接受，但它又不全然是原来的道家和儒家了，这就达到了新的和谐。中国传统文化的最高理想是：“万物并育而不相害，道并行而不相悖”(《中庸》第三十章)。“万物并育”和“道并行”是“不同”，“不相害”，“不相悖”则是“和”。

第三，“和”的主要内容是“适度”，“适度”就是“致中和”，既不是“过”，也不是“不及”，恰到好处，因适度而达到各方面的和谐。公元前3世纪，一位中国诗人描写一位美女说：“增一分则太高，减一分又太矮；再加粉则太白，再加胭脂又太红，”(《登徒子好色赋》)总之是身材容颜，恰好适度，达到了各方面的和谐，这就是“中和”。

第四，怎样才算“适度”呢？道家认为顺应自然就是“适度”。庄子指出，在大自然中，天在上，地在下，在一年之内，春夏在先，秋冬在后。无论是天地还是春夏秋冬，都不会因过度或不及而影响相互之间的顺序和发展。天道已有这样的盛衰次序，人道社会也应有一些大家都会自然遵循的普遍原则。他说：“顺之以天理，行之以五德，应之以自然”就可以“太和万物”，使世界达到最圆满的和谐。作为儒家学说核心的道德伦常观念，强调“父慈子孝”、“兄友弟恭”、“君义臣忠”等双方面的行为规范，力图找到两者之间关系的和谐和适度。所以说：“礼之用，和为贵”，“礼”是共同遵守的原则和规范，它必须在和谐、适度的前提下才能真正实现。

从以上的论述，可以看到“和而不同”原则在某些方面弥补了文化相对主义的不足，但仍有一个重要问题尚需解决，那就是处理人类相互关系，需要遵循人类共同认可的某些普遍原则。只有这样，才能真正实现“和而不同”。然而，这些原则如何产生呢？如何使这些原则最少侵犯不同群体的利益，最大容忍不同群体的特点？如何使不同群体的人们能认同并自愿接受这些原则？无论是认为普遍原则出自“圣人之言”的儒家，还是认为普遍原则出自“自然”的道家，都未曾正面回答这些问题。

德国哲学家哈伯马斯从当代西方文化的趋势出发，也提出了，并力图解决同样问题。他在最近的著作中所思考的一个中心问题也就是如何才能找到社会的共识，找到某些普遍原则，作为社会合作的道德基础。他的基本出发点之一就是任何人都必须通过社会，其特点才能得以实现，但一旦嵌入社会的网络，就必须臣服于这一网络的普遍原则，使个人特点和意愿受到压制，乃至异化。哈伯马斯提出“正义原则”，保障对个人尊重的平等权利，同时提出“团结原则”，要求个人有同情和尊重他人的义务，使宽容的空间不断变得更大。如果可以说前者讨论的是“不同”，那么，后者讨论的就是“和”。为了实现这些原则，哈伯马斯提出了交往、商谈、互为主体等重要途径。哈伯马斯还强调这些原则可以在不同层面展开。可以限于制定互利互惠规则的功利层面；可以用于共同探求一种更好生活的伦理层面，也适用于一些更为抽象的层面。这一切对于中国传统文化中长期追求的“和而不同”原则的实现都具有十分重要的启迪和实际意义。

从历史发展来看，通过交往和商谈达到“和而不同”，也不是始于今日，而是已有一些成功的先例。这些交往和商谈有几种不同的情形。一种情形是甲文化并不具有乙文化的某些观念，但这些观念与甲文化的其它观念并非不能相容，例如在中国文化中本来没有印度佛教关于“顿悟”的观念，但到宋明时代，程朱理学和陆王心学都接受了这一观念，并将其融汇在他们的体系之中，促成了他们的思想的新发展。另一种情形是发现乙文化的某些观念与甲文化的某些观念实相抵触，但这些观念对于甲文化的发展具有重大意义，甲文化按照自己的需要，吸收并改造了这些观念，成为自身文化的组成部分，因而得到发展。例如中国传统文化中以民众为治理对象，重视民众只是为巩固自己的统治，因而有“民可使由之，不可使知之”之类的说法。这与西方的民主思想大不相同。中国文化要容纳西方的民主，就不能不批判原来传统中的某些观念。20 世纪以来，中国文化对于西方文化中民主思想的改造和吸收，对中国政治的改善起了很大的作用。还有一种情形是在文化的交往和商谈中，发现双方都未曾有过，然而十分有用的新观念，它本身就是交谈的产物。例如“文化多元共处”的原则之于西方中心论和东方中心论者。

这种通过交往和商谈达到的“和而不同”原则，可以在最低的功利层面上进行，例如两个完全不同的国家可以在互不侵犯领土这一点上，只因互利而达到“和”。交往和商谈也可以在很抽象的层面进行。例如基督教讲“博爱”，佛教讲“慈悲”，儒家讲“泛爱众”，其内涵并不相同，但从抽象的层面来看，都是讲“人类之爱”。“爱”就可以成为不同文化传统都可接受的普遍原则，同时，“博爱”，“慈悲”，“泛爱众”仍然保留其各自的不同。

事实上，人类文化就是在这样不断的交往、商谈，达到新的“和而不同”的过程中进步发展的。英国哲学家罗素在他1922年所写的《中西文化比较》一文中曾说：“不同文化之间的交流过去已被多次证明是人类文明发展的里程碑。希腊学习埃及，罗马借鉴希腊，阿拉伯参照罗马帝国，中世纪的欧洲又模仿阿拉伯，而文艺复兴时期的欧洲则仿效拜占庭帝国”。欧洲文化在其自身发展的过程中，吸收了各种各样外来文化的因素，但它不仅未失去其欧洲文化传统，而且还大大丰富了自身文化的内涵。各种文化“并育而不相害”，“并行而不相悖”，这就是“和而不同”的表现。

然而，在过去的历史上，无论是“和而不同”原则，还是商谈、交往等行为，都还不是自觉地，有意识地实现的。中国传统文化在其数千年的发展历史中，创造过许多非常精采和有意义的思想原则，但由于各种社会原因和它本身往往缺乏必要的可操作性，很少能真正付诸实行；“和而不同”原则也是其中之一。哈伯马斯在他的商谈伦理学中努力建构的一方面接受多元，另一方面坚持通过商谈取得共识的普遍理论，特别是他关于后形而上学时代的思考和他对人类命运的关切，也许可以和中国古老的“和而不同”原则一起，为21世纪不同文化的和平共处与共同发展，作出有益的贡献。

（选自乐黛云：《文化相对主义与“和而不同”原则》，《中国比较文学》1996年第1期，第22-28页。）

世界文学

（节选）

［印］泰戈尔

【导读】

泰戈尔（Rabindranath Tagore，1861—1941），印度诗人、哲学家和社会活动家。主要作品有《故事诗集》（1900）、《吉檀迦利》（1910）、《园丁集》（1913）、《新月集》（1913）、《飞鸟集》（1916）等。1913年凭借抒情诗集《吉檀迦利》获得诺贝尔文学奖，成为首位获得该奖的亚洲人。1924年访问中国，其创作对中国现代诗人郭沫若、冰心、王统照、徐志摩等都有重要影响。泰戈尔《世界文学》一文发表于1907年，后由斯瓦潘·查卡拉瓦蒂（Swapan Chakravorty）翻译成英文。在本文中，泰戈尔从普遍人性出发，层层递进，最终完成了对比较文学和世界文学的独特理解。他先是指出在此世界中，我们与真理的关系有三种：理性关系、实用关系和享乐关系。理性关系如同我们的学校，实用关系如同我们的工作场所，享乐关系如同我们的家园，人们唯有在家园中才能身心放松，恣意展现自我。享乐关系就是了解他人如同了解自身，了解自身如同了解他人。人类的灵魂具有了解自身的天性，寻求个别的人性与人类普遍人性之间的联系也是人类灵魂的本性，此中亦有快乐。当人性的光辉穿越重重障碍得到充分展示时，我们就倍感欢欣，我们所发现的东西就是不断延伸的自我。那些外部世界得以充分呈现的东西，不论是日出的光辉、高贵的灵魂还是我们的激情——那些使我们心潮澎湃的一切——心灵都会以其创造物相互交织，融为一体，此时，心灵就会以某种独特的方式表达自己。

泰戈尔进而指出，人类在此世界中的自我表达方式可分为两大类——实践和文学，这两种方式并行不悖。人类使其自身投入实践的创造和思想的表达之中，它们相得益彰。我们必须通过阅读历史与文学作品来领悟二者所展示的人性。换言之，就世界本身而言，我们发现两种活动在发挥作用：实践的表达与思想的表达。在人类世界，知识的力量在于实际应用，而欢乐的力量在于创造情味。实践中我们力求自保，情味中我们力求自我表达。自保是必需的，但自我表达超越了需要。因而在一个有物质需要的世界中，人类一直致力于构建一个远离物质需要的文学王国。在文学中，人类通过情味乐于感受自己的本性，他们也能看到没有牵绊的自我。在文学世界中没有义务，只有欢乐；没有种种约束，自己就是国王。

基于此，泰戈尔表明了自己对比较文学与世界文学的理解：若文学仅囿于特定的时空，它就不能凸显其真正的价值。若我们意识到文学作品中所展示的是普遍的人性，我们就能在其中发现有价值的东西。若文学仅囿于作者本身，文学就会消亡。只有当作者的内心意识到人类的思想并在作品中表达人性的痛苦时，其作品方能被置于文学的殿堂。泰戈尔将世界文学比喻为一座神殿，它是在具有世界意识的作家的领导下修建的，不同民族、不同时代的作家在其指挥下劳作，没有人能设计出整座建筑的蓝图，但有瑕疵的部分被不断拆除，每位建设者都发挥其才能将其创作融入整体设计中，竭力符合那张蓝图的设计要求。换言之，世界文学中真正有价值的东西是通过文学表达人类快乐的方式，也是借助表达的丰富性来揭示人类灵魂显现自身的那些亘古不变的艺术形式。

泰戈尔对世界文学的理解与歌德和马克思的主张是基本一致的，在今天依然具有强烈的现实意义，也应该是比较文学和世界文学所追求终极目标、终极理想。

（李卫华）

我们内心的许多想法，只是为了同所有人建立关系而存在的，我们就是通过这种关系揭示自己存在的真实性，获得真理。如果没有这种关系，我们的存在和其他事物的存在就毫无意义。

在世上，我们与真实存在着三种关系，即理性关系、实用关系和享乐关系。其中理性关系可以被称做一种竞争。这种关系好像猎人与猎物之间的关系。这种关系仿佛把真实当作被告，逼它一点一点吐出自己的隐私。所以，理性对真实来说是十分傲慢的。理性对真实了解得越多，就越强烈地感受到自己的力量，理性关系之后，是实用关系。在实现这个实用目的或在满足需要关系里，我们的力量与真实结合起来。由于这种需要的满足，真实更加接近我们，但我们同它的距离依然无法消除。英国商人曾经在印度贵族面前低头哈腰、奉献礼品，从而达到自己的目的，取得统治地位。同样，我们把真实与实践相结合，由此实现了自己的目的，最后我们自认为自己已成为世界的主宰。到那时，我们说，大自然是我们的奴隶，水、火和空气是我们的义务仆人。

实用关系之后是享乐关系。因为有了美或享乐关系，所有的距离都消失了。那时，没有任何形式的高傲，我们与低贱和懦弱的人相处不会感到难堪，在那里默吐拉的大神化身黑天与牧区的女子一块玩耍，不顾自己大神的尊严。有享乐关系的存在，我们就不会感到自己的理性力量，只感到没有任何障碍或距离阻碍认识自己。

简而言之，理性与真实的关系好比是我们的学校，实用与真实的关系好比是我们的办公室，而享乐与真实的关系则是我们的家庭。我们不会完全待在学校里，也不会完全待在办公室里，只有在家里我们才无拘无束、自由自在。学校是不加装饰的，办公室也是不加装饰的，但家里却装饰得十全十美。

这种享乐关系究竟是什么呢？就是把别人看做自己，把自己看做别人。当我们这样理解时，任何问题都能迎刃而解。我们从未想过，我们为什么爱自己？我们往往就在自己经验中感受快乐，但当我们在别人身上也体验到自己的这种感受时，那时提出我们为什么爱自己或爱他们的这个问题就毫无意义了。

……

所以，在文学里，自我表现对人来说不存在任何障碍，私利远离着它。在文学中，痛苦不对我们的心灵产生影响，只使我们流泪，它并不干预我们的世俗的事务；恐惧使我们心灵颤抖，但它不对我们身体产生任何影响；幸福使我们的心灵感到喜悦，但不唤起贪婪。这样，人就在自己需要的世界的旁边，建立起一个超脱需要的文学世界。它对人毫无损害。人通过种种情味和形象感受着自己的本性而获得快乐，并且无阻碍地观察着自己。文学中没有责任，没有快乐，没有卫兵，自己就是帝王。

通过文学，我们认识了什么？认识了人的丰富感情，认识了具有神性的人，认识了超脱需要的人，认识了在世界内部永不消逝的事物。

我曾经在一篇文章中写道：虽然男女老少都能品尝食品的味道，但这件事在文学里除了闹剧外，不会取得特殊的位置，原因是，它没有超过满足食物的需求。倘若吃饱了肚子，我们像猴子般叫了声“啊”！付了钱扬长而去，我们就不会邀请它进入文学的王宫大门。然而，丝毫不沾我们餐具储藏室边的事物，却带着全部情味，如潺潺流水般渗入我们的文学之中。人不能在自己种种需要里消灭它，而在文学里用充满自己心灵的激情表现它。

这样，人就在丰富感情里表现着自己。人是喜爱食物的，这无疑是真实的，但人是英雄，这是最真实的。谁能够阻挡住人的这个真实潮流呢？这潮流像帕基勒梯一样开山劈岭，骑在因陀罗的神像上，消除了城镇乡村的干渴，归入大海。人的英雄气概完成了人类世界的所有事业，超越了世界。

因此，人无法在自己日常事务中消灭自己身上的天然的伟大的永恒的东西，相反，人的文学表现着这些东西，使它们成为人的巨大形象。

还有一个原因，我们在世上所看到的东西都是不完全的。我们或是从这一方面或是从另一方面观察它，或是从上面或是从下面观察它，或是从前面或是从后面观察它。但在文学里不是这样观察事物的。文学对所要表现的东西进行全面的阐述，除这个东西以外，文学不让看到其他任何东西，运用各种艺术手段为它建立惟有它才能放出异彩的地位。

在这种情况下，在如此严格的独立性和如此灿烂的光芒里，如果某种东西显得不好，那么，我们自然而然地不会让它占有那种地位。如果把一个庸碌之辈放在这种地位上，那等于是羞辱他。世界上有的是穿着五光十色的衣服的饕餮者，一般说来，他们不会引起我们的注意。但当我们在文学的舞台的聚光灯下看到他们时，我们会忍俊不禁的。只要人所表现出来的不是低贱的形象，只要是人的心认为能够在痛苦或豪气中，在恐怖和力量中代表自己，只要是能够在艺术技巧的扶持下站住，又能昂起头忍受时代的凝视的东西，人总会在文学里赋予它们以一席之地。否则，它们的不恰当地位会使我们心灵遭受折磨。如果我们看到他人而不是皇帝坐在宝座上，我们心中会觉得不是滋味。

但是，不是所有人的思想和理智都是伟大的，也不是所有社会都是伟大的。有的，也会出现这种情况：人迷恋上稍纵即逝和低劣卑微的东西而变得渺小。那时，在那不幸的的时代的哈哈镜里渺小的东西会变得伟大；在那种时代的文学里，人把自己微不足道的东西加以夸大，竞相夸耀自己的污斑。那时技巧代替了艺术，高傲代替了荣誉，吉卜林代替了丁尼生。

但是，时间是无情的，它筛选着一切事物。经过它的筛选，那些低劣卑微和缺乏生命的东西被淘汰，化成尘埃。只有所有人能够从中看到自己的东西，方能在不同时代和不同人身上立于不败之地。经过这番筛选后，存留下的东西成为一切国家和一切人的财富。

这样，经过淘汰和提炼，文学确立起关于人的本性和人的表达的一个永恒的理想。这双理想的手，掌握着新时代文学的航舵。如果我们根据这个理想来研究文学，那么我们就不得不依赖整个人类的思想智慧。

现在，言归正传。只限于时间、地点和人物来观察文学的方法不是观察文学的真正方法。如果我们懂得，人类正是在文学里表现自己，那我们就能够在文学里发现值得观赏的东西。如果在某文学作品里作家本身成为惟一描写的目标，那个文学作品就会湮灭，一个作家在自己的作品里用自己的感情体验人类的感情，体验整个人类的痛苦，这样他的作品在文学里就占有一定的地位。我们应该如此去理解文学。全人类犹同世上的泥瓦匠，他们在建造文学神庙，不同时代和不同国家的作家则是他们的帮工。整个建筑的设计蓝图是什么样子，谁也不知道。在建造过程中，哪儿出了差错，就一次又一次地再造。每一个帮工应该充分发挥自己的天生才华，配合其他人造出与那个看不见的蓝图相符合的构件。在这个过程中一个作家的才华得到了了解，因此，他不拿普通工人的工资，而像一个师傅那样受到尊敬。

本文所评论的内容，在英语中称为Comparative literature(比较文学)，印度语叫“世界文学”。

人类通过实践反映什么？他们的目的是什么？他们的努力是怎样的一种努力？如果我们想知道这些问题，那么我们就得在全部历史中探索人的目标。如果仅是分别地了解阿克巴大帝的统治、古吉拉特的历史或伊丽莎白女王的传略，那只能满足了解新闻的好奇性。假如一个人懂得对阿克巴大帝或伊丽莎白女王的描写只是次要目的；如果懂得，人通过全部历史，经历各种实践、各种挫折、各种纠正来达到自己庄严的目的而坚持不懈地奋斗；如果懂得，人为了在所有实践里以饱满情感同一切结合，从而取得解放而努力；如果知道，自由使自己在君主制内站住脚，君主制要使自己压倒共和制而进行艰巨努力；如果懂得，人为在世界人类之中反映自己，个别为在整体之中谋取一席之地而锲而不舍地努力，那么，这个人就会力图在人类历史中了解永恒人的永恒奋斗目的，而不是想要看到某个具体人的特殊目标；这个人也不会仅仅看到个别香客就回转，而是要看到来自各个方向的、渴望瞻仰大神的众多香客之后才踏上归路。

人在文学里如何表达自己的快乐，以及人的心灵在这种表达的绚丽多彩的形象里想显示自己的某种永恒的本质，这才是文学中值得一看的东西。人是怎样喜欢把自己描绘成病夫、享乐者或是瑜伽僧的呢？世界上人的亲近感在何种程度上成为真实，也就是说真实在何种程度上会变成人自己的呢？我们正是为了了解这一切而进入文学世界的。不能把这个文学世界理解为人为的虚假世界。这是如此一个世界，其真实性不是依附于某一个人的，这个世界像物质世界一样也被创造着，在这无穷无尽的创造的尽头，存在着一个终极的理想。

太阳内部的物质，通过各种方式变成流动的液体和坚硬的固体。我们看不到这些物质，但它们四周的光圈向全世界显示着太阳。就在这世界上，惟独太阳奉献出自己，融合于一切之中。如果我们能用这种全面的眼光来观察人的话，那么我们也会像太阳一样观察他。那时，我们会看到，他内部的各种物质在各种不同程度上，渐渐地形成起来，其周围的光束射向四方，从而取得欢乐。请看一看作为散发在人的周围那个用语言构成的文学光束吧！在这里，光的风暴骤然而起，光的源泉喷涌而出，光的雨倾盆如注。

我们漫步在市场上时会发现，人忙得没有闲工夫：粮商忙着招徕顾客；铁匠忙着打铁；工人忙着搬运重物；高利贷者忙着算账。但是与此同时，我们却没有看到另一样东西。如果我们神情专注地再次观察一番，那就会看到：在道路两旁的家家户户，在商店市场，在大街小巷里，情味的激流变成细流，通过无数途径涓涓流于污秽、狭隘和贫困之上。《罗摩衍那》、《摩诃婆罗多》、《往世书》和颂神诗把世界人类之心灵的情感日夜不停地分给每个人。罗摩和罗什曼那超脱在凡人小事之上；黑暗的小屋里飘溢着颂诗的混有同情的香风；人的心灵的创造及其表达，用戴上美和善的手镯的双手，掩饰人的实践领域里遇到的艰难困苦。我们应该再次悉心观察人的周围，观察整个文学。应该看到，人通过感情的力量扩充了自己的实际力量。在他的四周有不可胜数的歌的雨，诗的雨，《云使》和维德亚伯迪。维德亚伯迪把自己家中的喜怒哀乐倾注在王公的喜怒哀乐的故事里，并加以夸大。湿婆神的同情永远和他的普天下儿女同存，他把自己贫困的痛楚融合在盖拉斯山的巨大贫困的庄严里。这样，人不断在自己周围进行创造扩展，通过这种创造和扩展，人似乎在扩展着自己。限于环境而变得狭隘的人，通过自己的感情的创造在创造自己的扩展力，也就是在这世界的周围，创造着另一个世界，那就是文学。

你们切不可以认为，我将成为你们在世界文学领域里的带路人。我们应该根据各自的力量，在这条道路上前进。我只是想强调指出，大地不是我的、你的或他的大地，把大地分成你的我的的做法是极其无知的。同样，文学也不是我的、你的或他的创作。然而，我们往往如此无知地看待文学。我们的目的是，去掉那些无知和狭隘，从世界文学中观察世界的人。我们要在每一作家的作品里看到整体，要在这种整体里看到整个人类为表现自己所做的努力，现在是立下这样的决心的时候了。

（节选自泰戈尔：《世界文学》，《泰戈尔全集》（第22卷），河北教育出版社2000年版，第84-99页。）

Crossing Borders

[美]Gayatri C. Spivak

【导读】

《跨界》(Crossing Borders) 是佳亚特里·斯皮瓦克的专著《一门学科之死》(*Death of A Discipline*) 的第一章。该书标题看似骇人听闻，实则为斯皮瓦克运用吊诡的手法，展现了比较文学亟待由内向外进行革新的现状。为此，斯皮瓦克在《跨界》中提出了一种"无所不包的"、"去政治化的"比较文学。要实现这份蓝图，她认为应当结合区域研究并强调跨界的互动。然而，跨界存在的"有限渗透性"等问题，使得比较文学的革新道阻且长。如何使跨界由边缘国出发，改变以往宗主国的主导地位，使边界"渗透"真正意义上实现"双向平等"？斯皮瓦克提出了这样一个关键问题。而这个问题将在本书的后几章中得到进一步阐释并提出解决方案。

作为后殖民主义的代表人物，斯皮瓦克在《一门学科之死》中充分展现了她既深谙西方理论，又熟知第三世界的历史与社会现状的博学之姿，一改以往囿于文学和美学等角度的分析，运用解构主义对比较文学的发展进行了重新解读，对西方传统比较文学观发起了猛攻。在这一章中，作者对于她所倡导的区域研究合作进行了深入探讨。她提出："没有人文学科的支持，区域研究只能以跨越边界的名目来侵越界线；没有经过改造的区域研究的支撑，比较文学将会禁锢在自己的边境内，永远无法逾越出去"。然而，现在的区域研究在斯皮瓦克看来，仅仅是从宗主国，即欧美国家出发，向其边界进行渗透。无论是从语言、文化背景，还是政治层面上看，欧美国家持有话语权的现状毋庸置疑且难以改变。这种有限渗透性问题的实质，便是"世界庶民文化内部存在巨大的差异，而且彼此间缺乏交流"。对此，斯皮瓦克提出要"展开区域研究间的合作，并对其实施改革"。尽管她一再强调这种研究的"去政治化"，但从文中的字里行间无不透露着斯皮瓦克的政治观。然而，也正是由于这种批判宗主国在比较文学上的主导地位，为庶民文化发声的政治观，使得她的观点得到了世界的广泛关注，并获得了众多拥趸。

斯皮瓦克在《越界》中对比较文学的探讨，理论上确实有助于瓦解欧美国家在比较文学上宗主国地位的现状，然而在论述的过程中仍略显不足。首先，对于比较文学的界定，斯皮瓦克显示出不自信。她提到，"对于这门学科，其出路似乎在于承认一种明确的、未来的前在性(anteriority)，一种'将要来临'(to come-ness)的状态，还有那种'将是已经发生'(will have happened)的性质"。换句话说，她认为比较文学这个学科目前尚不存在，只是一个未来明确学科的前身。其次，她没有明确界定区域研究，即何为区域研究，区域研究所包含的范围如何等。最后，其意图"去政治化"的政治观也是矛盾难解的。

然而，瑕不掩瑜，斯皮瓦克关于比较文学跨越边界的提出，极具个人特色，十分大胆却合情合理，在思考比较文学现状的同时，对其未来也提出了展望并给出了建议。这也进一步奠定了斯皮瓦克在比较文学和后殖民主义研究方面的学术地位。

（李伟荣）

Since 1992, three years after the fall of the Berlin Wall, the discipline of comparative literature has been looking to renovate itself. This is presumably in response to the rising tide of multiculturalism and cultural studies. The first pages of Charles Bernheimer's *Comparative Literature in the Age of Multiculturalism* tell a story that those with experience of national-level professional organizations at work can flesh out in the imagination into a version of the Quarrel of the Ancients and the Moderns:

> In the summer of 1992... [the] president of the American Comparative Literature Association (ACLA), asked me to appoint and chair a committee charged to write a so-called Report on Standards for submission to the association. The bylaws of the ACLA... mandated that such a report be prepared every ten years. The first report was submitted in 1965 by a committee chaired by my thesis director, Harry Levin; the second was submitted in 1975 by a committee chaired by Tom Greene. A third report was written ten years thereafter, but...the chair of that committee was so dissatisfied with the document that he exercised a pocket veto and never submitted it. The first two reports... are impressively strong articulations of a view of comparative literature which, in my view, no longer applies to actual practices in the field. ... A diverse group of top scholars from diverse institutions...felt uneasy about being asked to establish "standards" and decided to give more importance to our ideas about the intellectual mission of the discipline than to spelling out requirements (... the report [was renamed] the Report on the State of the Discipline).[1]

This is an account of the transformation of comparative literary studies. Comparative social studies, as represented by Area Studies, were undergoing their own transformation. This is well represented by a recent influential pamphlet by Toby Volkman, written while she was Program Officer at the Ford Foundation, from which I have taken my chapter title: "Crossing Borders":

> Recent developments have challenged some of the premises of area studies itself. The notion, for example, that the world can be divided into knowable, self- contained "areas"

> has come into question as more attention has been paid to movements between areas. Demographic shifts, diasporas, labor migrations, the movements of global capital and media, and processes of cultural circulation and hybridization have encouraged a more subtle and sensitive reading of areas' identity and composition.[2]

The rest of Volkman's pamphlet contains actual descriptions of institutional projects under six headings: Reconceptualization of "Area"; Borders and Diasporas; Border-Crossing Seminars and Workshops; Curricular Transformation and Integration; Collaborations with Nongovernmental Organizations, Activists, and the Media; and Rethinking Scientific Areas. There are a few examples of Ethnic Studies and Area Studies pulling together, but the only one that may touch traditional comparative literature is the project at Middlebury College, building on its already considerable resources of European language teaching. Indeed, although "popular culture" is an item often included, literature does not seem particularly important in this venture of, as Volkman's subtitle suggests, "Revitalizing Area Studies."[3]

If this is what may be called the current situation, the recent past of these two institutional enterprises can perhaps be recounted as follows. Area Studies were established to secure U. S. power in the Cold War. Comparative Literature was a result of European intellectuals fleeing "totalitarian" regimes. Cultural and Postcolonial Studies relate to the 500 percent increase in Asian immigration in the wake of Lyndon Johnson's reform of the Immigration Act of 1965. Whatever our view of what we do, we are made by the forces of people moving about the world.

How can we respond to the changes brought about by the end of the Cold War, as both the Bernheimer report and the Volkman pamphlet implicitly ask? A simple splicing of Comp. Lit. and Cultural Studies/multiculturalism will not work or will work only too well; same difference. A combination of Ethnic Studies and Area Studies bypasses the literary and the linguistic. What I am proposing is not a politicization of the discipline. We are *in* politics. I am proposing an attempt to depoliticize in order to move away from a politics of hostility, fear, and half solutions. Why, for example, as in the fairly representative passage below, appropriate Brecht to trash Ethnic Studies and Cultural Studies in order to praise a friend's book in the pages of a journal that was established in 1949, in the full flush of Area Studies development, "at a time when the strengthening of good international relations [was] of paramount importance"?

> In the face of the wholesale selling-off of the German intellectual tradition by current "German Studies" and the shallowing of philosophically-informed literary theory by the conversion of comparative literature into cultural studies, Premises brings to mind Brecht's 1941 comment on Benjamin's "Theses on the Philosophy of History": "one thinks with horror of how small the number is of those who are ready even to misunderstand something like this."[4]

Compared to such an outburst, my ideas for an inclusive comparative literature are so depoliticized as to have, unlike the Bernheimer report or the Volkman pamphlet, little to do with the times. I thought Comparative Literature should be world embracing at the beginning of my career. And I continue to believe that the politics of the production of knowledge in area studies (and also anthropology and the other "human sciences") can be touched by a new Comparative Literature, whose hall- mark remains a care for language and idiom.

In 1973, when I was an associate professor, I invited Claudio Guillén to the University of Iowa to give a minicourse. Guillén was moved by my idealism about a global Comparative Literature. He put me on the Executive Committee of the International Comparative Literature Association. I went to Visegrad the following year. I wish I could regale the reader with the symptomatology of that meeting, but must confine myself to one detail.

The association was putting together new scholarly volumes on the periods of European literary history. We discussed the production details of the volume on the Renaissance, if memory serves. I offered to get contacts for scholars in the Indian languages so that we could enlarge the scope of the series. I offered to be active in setting up committees for such investigations in the other comparative clusters of the world: Korean-Chinese-Japanese; Arabic-Persian; the languages of Southeast Asia; African languages. A foolish notion, no doubt. M. Voisine of the Sorbonne, a senior member of the committee, quelled me with a glance: "My friend René Etiemble tells me," he said, "that there is a perfectly acceptable scholarly history of literatures in Chinese."

Memory has no doubt sharpened the exchange. And one person's caustic remark cannot represent an entire discipline. What the exchange does vouch for, however, is my long-standing sense that the logical consequences of our loosely defined discipline were, surely, to include the open-ended possibility of studying all literatures, with linguistic rigor and historical savvy. A level playing field, so to speak.

As it happened, I had also been speaking of what was not yet called Cultural Studies teaming up with Area Studies for some time. Selecting one example among many, I quote myself, admonishing, in 1988: "As we in the margins try to shore up our defenses, we tend to leave untouched the politics of the specialists of the margin—area studies, anthropology, and the like."[5]

Even from a restricted U. S. perspective, it seems obvious that the sources of literary agency have expanded beyond the old European national literatures. For the discipline, the way out seems to be to acknowledge a definitive future anteriority, a "to come"-ness, a "will have happened" quality. This is a protection from self-destructive competition for dwindling resources. It is also a protection from losing the best of the old Comparative Literature: the skill of reading closely in the original. Such a philosophy of planning welcomes nonexhaustive taxonomies, provisional system making, but discourages map- making literary criticism as an end in itself because diagnostic cartography does not keep the door open to the "to come." It is in the acknowledgment of such an open future that we need to consider the resources of Area Studies, specifically geared for what lies beyond the Euro-U. S.

In spite of all the noise about "these times," if the 145 departments or programs listed in the bulletin of the ACLA form a representative sample, the general model in Comparative Literature seemed still, in 2000 when these lectures were delivered, to be Europe and the extracurricular Orient. Ten Comp. Lit. units in the United States seem to have some arrangement with either the social sciences or multiculturalism, and only two of these mention Area Studies. I have no doubt that this is now changing, but cannot keep up with the pace of that change.

Area Studies were founded in the wake of the Cold War and funded by federal grants, backed up by the great foundations, especially Ford.

> To meet the demands of war, scholars of diverse disciplines were forced to pool their knowledge in frantic attempts to advise administrators and policy makers...The war also showed the need for trained personnel for most foreign areas... In these Army Specialized Training Programs and Civil Affairs Training Schools many professors had their first experience with curricula organized by area rather than by discipline, and many students made a real beginning in the study of foreign areas and in their languages, ...

says the introduction to the "national conference on the study of world areas, which was held in New York on November 28-30, 1947."[6] Language and Area Centers between 1959 and 1968 were authorized by Public Law 85-864, the National Defense Education Act of 1958 (as amended), Title VI.

Without the support of the humanities, Area Studies can still only transgress frontiers, in the name of crossing borders; and, without a transformed Area Studies, Comparative Literature remains imprisoned within the borders it will not cross. Area studies have resources but also built-in, restricted, but real interdisciplinarity. If one goes down the list of Comparative Literature programs and departments, the interdisciplinarity with music, philosophy, art history, and media remains less persuasive and exceptional. And, whatever we think about the relationship between Comparative Literature and Area Studies, the polarity between Area Studies and Cultural Studies is clear.

Area Studies exhibit quality and rigor (those elusive traits), combined with openly conservative or "no" politics. They are tied to the politics of power, and their connections to the power elite in the countries studied are still strong; the quality of the language learning is generally excellent, though just as generally confined to the needs of social science fieldwork; and the data processing is sophisticated, extensive, and intensive. Academic "Cultural Studies", as a metropolitan phenomenon originating on the radical fringes of national language departments, opposes this with no more than metropolitan language-based presentist and personalist political convictions, often with visibly foregone conclusions that cannot match the implicit political cunning of Area Studies at their best; and earns itself a reputation for "lack of rigor" as well as for politicizing the academy.[7] The languages of the cultures of origin are invoked at best as delexicalized and fun mother tongues. The real "other" of Cultural Studies is not Area Studies but the civilization courses offered by the European national language departments, generally scorned by Comparative Literature. It is therefore a real sign of change that the Ford initiative, as reflected in the Volkman pamphlet, seems to bring together Ethnic/Cultural Studies and Area Studies. It remains to be seen if the extraordinary metropolitan enthusiasm in the former will undermine the linguistic rigor of the latter. I will discuss that question in the last chapter. Let us return to Comparative Literature.

Area Studies related to foreign "areas." Comparative Literature was made up of Western European "nations." This distinction, between "areas" and "nations," infected Comparative Literature from the start.[8]

If the "origin" of Area Studies was the aftermath of the Cold War, the "origin" of U. S. Comparative Literature had something of a relationship with the events that secured it: the flights of European intellectuals, including such distinguished men as Erich Auerbach, Leo Spitzer, René Wellek, Renato Poggioli, and Claudio Guillén, from "totalitarian" regimes in Europe. One might say that U. S. Comparative Literature was founded on inter-European hospitality, even as Area Studies had been spawned by interregional vigilance.

One way that the nation-region divide is already being negotiated in comparative literature is by destabilizing the "nation" (s)—introducing Francophony, Teutophony, Lusophony, Anglophony, Hispanophony within the old "national" boundaries; the biggest winner in the United States is "Global English." The effort, recalling the initial Birmingham model of Cultural Studies, is to put some black on the Union Jack or, to put a spin on Jesse Jackson's slogan, to paint the red, white, and blue in the colors of the rainbow.[9] This destabilization follows the lines of the old imperialisms and competes with the diversified metropolitan nationalism of Ethnic/Cultural Studies.

The new step that I am proposing would go beyond this acknowledgment and this competition. It would work to make the traditional linguistic sophistication of Comparative Literature supplement Area Studies (and history, anthropology, political theory, and sociology) by approaching the language of the other not only as a "field" language. In the field of literature, we need to move from Anglophony, Lusophony, Teutophony, Francophony, et cetera. We must take the languages of the Southern Hemisphere as active cultural media rather than as objects of cultural study by the sanctioned ignorance of the metropolitan migrant. We cannot dictate a model for this from the offices of the American Comparative Literature Association. We can, however, qualify ourselves and our students to attend upon this as it happens elsewhere. Here and now, I can only caution against some stereotypes: that such an interest is antihybridist, culturally conservative, "ontopologist," "parochial."[10] Indeed, I am inviting the kind of language training that would disclose the irreducible hybridity of all languages. As I have said elsewhere: "The verbal text is jealous of its linguistic signature but impatient of national identity. Translation flourishes by virtue of that paradox."[11] Other stereotypes are correct but irrelevant: namely, that attention to the languages of the Southern Hemisphere is inconvenient and impractical.[12]

Inconvenient. There are a few hegemonic European languages and innumerable Southern Hemisphere languages. The only principled answer to that is: "Too bad." The old Comparative Literature did not ask the student to learn every hegemonic language; nor will the new ask her or him to learn all the subaltern ones! Can the "native informant" ever become the subject of a "cultural study" that does not resemble metropolitan language-based work? If one asks this question, one sees that the destabilization offered by a merely metropolitan Cultural Studies must exclude much for its own convenience, for the cultural claims of the metropolitan migrant.

Jacques Derrida is the rare philosopher who thinks that philosophical "concepts [cannot] transcend idiomatic differences."[13] Such insights do not apply only to French and German or Greek and Latin. Engagement with the idiom of the global other(s) in the Southern Hemisphere, uninstitutionalized in the Euro-U. S. university structure except via the objectifying, discontinuous, transcoding tourist gaze of anthropology and oral history, is our lesson on displacing the discipline. This is not brought about by the reterritorialized desire of the metropolitan migrant to collaborate with the South, generally through the United Nations by way of nongovernmental organizations (NGOs). As I have argued elsewhere, such collaboration is generally possible only with the class, physically "based" in the global South, increasingly produced by globalization, that is sufficiently out of touch with the idiomaticity of nonhegemonic languages.[14]

What I am suggesting may sound discouraging. I hate to use this word, but perhaps it gives us a certain kind of honesty. It should not paralyze us. We cannot not try to open up, from the inside, the colonialism of European national language-based Comparative Literature and the Cold War format of Area Studies, and infect history and anthropology with the "other" as producer of knowledge. From the inside, acknowledging complicity. No accusations. No excuses. Rather, learning the protocol of those disciplines, turning them around, laboriously, not only by building institutional bridges but also by persistent curricular interventions. The most difficult thing here is to resist mere appropriation by the dominant.[15]

Indeed, the question of the old imperialisms and the new empire is itself different if uncoupled from high-culture radicalism. While I was working on this manuscript, I was also looking at the Report of the Mayor's Task Force on the City University of New York, undertaken in 1998.[16] The question before us was "What is English? Literary Studies in a Public Urban University". The City University of New York was faulted because 87 percent of its incoming undergraduate class was in remedial English. The report separated the old minorities—giving them the code name of New York City public school graduates—from the new—

emergent since Lyndon Johnson lifted the quota system in 1965: "During the 1990's, the white population of New York City declined by 19.3%, while the black, Hispanic, and Asian population have risen by 5.2%, 19.3%, and 53.5%, respectively."

If you sit in on these so-called remedial classes, you perceive the institutional incapacity to cope with the crossroads of race, gender and class—even when the teacher has the best will in the world—to come to grips with the actual play of the choice of English as tongue in the imagination of these working-class new immigrant survival artists. *Le Thé Au Harem d'Archi Ahmed.*[17] As a comparativist I would like to suggest that, just as no "literary studies" in New York City and no doubt in Los Angeles should forget that the answer to the question "What is English?" is that it is more than half the ingredient for producing human capital (the other half being mathematics), so also, literary studies will have to acknowledge that the European outlines of its premise and one of its tasks—positing the idea of the universality of each of the European national languages (the jealously guarded particular domain of the old Comparative Literature)—have, in globality and in subaltern U. S. multiculturalism, altogether disappeared. There are Haitians and West Africans in those CUNY remedial classes whose imaginations are crossing and being crossed by a double aporia—the cusp of two imperialisms. I have learned something from listening to their talk about and in Creole/French/so-called pidgin and English-as-a-second-language-crossing-into-first—the chosen tongue. I have silently compared their imaginative flexibility, so remarkably and necessarily much stronger, because constantly in use for social survival and mobility, than that of the Columbia undergraduate, held up by the life-support system of a commercializing anglo-phone culture that trivializes the humanities. It is time, in globality, in New York, and no doubt elsewhere in the metropolis, to put the history of Francophony, Teutophony, Lusophony, Anglophony, Hispanophony also—not only (please mark the difference)—in a comparative focus.

To pursue this line of thinking further would be to address the question of the thickening of class analysis itself and would take us away from the question of Comparative Literature. I place this parenthesis here so that the reader will take this postponement into account.

Outside of "Gender and Development", the question of human rights is most often confined within trade-related political paradigms leading to military intervention, ostensibly based on game theory and rational choice as unacknowledged theoretical models. If a responsible comparativism can be of the remotest possible use in the training of the imagination, it must approach culturally diversified ethical systems diachronically, through the history of multicultural empires, without foregone conclusions. This is the material that is used to fashion violence in the multiform global imaginary. Pedagogically speaking, such studies are much more successful through language-based literary investigation than through evidence from interested cultural informants, like East Asian capitalist men or South or West Asian fundamentalists.

Again, I am not advocating the politicization of the discipline. I am advocating a depoliticization of the politics of hostility toward a politics of friendship to come, and thinking of the role of Comparative Literature in such a responsible effort.

If we seek to supplement gender training and human rights intervention by expanding the scope of Comparative Literature, the proper study of literature may give us entry to the performativity of cultures as instantiated in narrative. Here we stand outside, but not as anthropologist; we stand rather as reader with imagination ready for the effort of othering, however imperfectly, as an end in itself. It is a peculiar end, for "It cannot be motivated... except in the requirement for an increase or a supplement of justice [here to the text], and so in the experience of an inadequation or an incalculable disproportion."[18] This is preparation for a patient and provisional and forever deferred arrival into the performative of the other, in order not to transcode but to draw a response. Believe me, there is a world of difference between the two positions.

Notes

1. "Preface," in Charles Bernheimer, ed., *Comparative Literature in the Age of Multiculturalism* (Baltimore: Johns Hopkins University. Press, 1995), ix-x.
2. Toby Alice Volkman, *Crossing Borders: Revitalizing Area Studies* (New York: Ford Foundation, 1999), ix. This attempt—to rethink Area Studies after the Cold War—is now somewhat outdated. The watchword now is "Area Studies after 9/11," and the configuration resembles the earlier Area Studies initiative, which I discuss in my text. Here is an excerpt from a spring 2002 [Congressional] Conference Report for the Appropriations

   Act:

   The conferees find that our national security, stability and economic vitality depend, in part, on American experts who have sophisticated language skills and cultural knowledge about the various areas of the world. An urgent need exists to enhance the nation's in-depth knowledge of world areas and transnational issues, and fluency of U. S. citizens in languages relevant to understanding societies where Islamic and/or Muslim culture, politics, religion, and economy are a significant factor.

   Therefore, the conferees have included an increase of $20,478,000 for the Title VI/Fulbright-Hays programs to increase the number of international experts (including those entering government service and various professional disciplines) with in-depth expertise and high-level language proficiency in the targeted world areas of Central and South Asia, the Middle East, Russia, and the Independent States of the former Soviet Union. A portion of these funds is intended to enhance the capacity of U. S. higher education institutions to sustain these initiatives over time. The conferees encourage the creation of distance learning initiatives to provide more universal access to language training, summer language institutes abroad, one-on-one language tutoring to accelerate student progress to the highest levels of proficiency, engaging the language resources of local heritage communities where appropriate, and increased collaboration with the Title VI language resource centers, the centers for international business education and research, and the American overseas research centers with a focus on the least commonly taught languages and areas and underrepresented professional disciplines. (communication to Area Studies institutes holding Title VI grants)

At this point, to withdraw in-depth language learning and close reading from Comparative Literature when it moves to the global South is to decide that the only relationship the United States can have with those areas is based on considerations of security, that the critical intimacy of literary learning must remain isolationist in the Euro-U. S.

3. The statistics may have changed slightly in the intervening years, but the general picture remains the same.
4. George E. Rowe, "50th Anniversary of *Comparative Literature*" and Timothy Bahti, "Impossibility, Free", *Comparative Literature* 51 (1) (Winter 99): 1, 62. Bahti is right, *Premises* is a fine book, and the times are near Fascist, more so than in 1999. The solution is not to go back to an exclusivist Eurocentric comparative literature spawned in the late forties.
5. "Versions of the Margin: J. M. Coetzee's *Foe* Reading Defoe's *Crusoe/Roxana*", in Jonathan Arac and Barbara Johnson, eds., *Consequences of Theory: Selected Papers of the English Institute*, 1987-88 (Baltimore: Johns Hopkins University Press, 1990), 154; the lecture was delivered two years earlier.
6. Charles Wagley, *Area Research and Training: A Conference Report on the Study of World Areas* (New York: Columbia University, n. d.), 1; emphasis mine.
7. These sentiments are expressed in Margaret Talbot, "The Way We Live Now: 11-18-01; Other Woes" *New York Times Magazine*, November 18, 2001, 23, in the wake of September 11.
8. The groundbreaking energy of *Orientalism* by Edward W. Said (New York: Pantheon, 1978) tends to conflate Oriental Studies, Area Studies, and Comparative Literature. Enabled by its initiating impulse, we now make these distinctions.
9. The Birmingham metaphor is taken from the title of a book by one of the most brilliant students at the first Cultural Studies group: Paul Gilroy, *There Ain't No Black in the Union Jack: The Cultural Politics of Race and Nation* (New York: Routledge, 1992 [1987]). There are more differences than similarities here. These differences have been charted by Lawrence Grossberg in *Dancing in Spite of Myself: Essays on Popular Culture* (Durham: Duke University Press, 1997), 191-218.
10. For "ontopologist," see Jacques Derrida, *Specters of Marx: the State of the Debt, the Work of Mourning, and the New International*, tr. Peggy Kamuf (New York: Routledge, 1994), 82. In a back issue of *The New Yorker* (June 23 & 30, 1997), Salman Rushdie refers to all the literatures of India not in English as "parochial."

11. Gayatri Chakravorty Spivak, "Translation as Culture," *parallax* 6 (1) (Jan. Mar. 2000): 21.
12. When I make this point, I often hear "But everyone can't learn all the languages!" Just as the old Comparative Literature did not require learning "all the European languages", so also does this new version of Comparative Literature not ask you to learn all the world's languages. The only requirement is that, when you work with literatures of the global South, you learn the pertinent languages with the same degree of care. As you go toward the already available resources of Area Studies, learn the language with literary depth rather than only social scientific fluency.
13. Jacques Derrida, *Given Time: I. Counterfeit Money*, tr. Peggy Kamuf (Chicago: University of Chicago Press, 1992), 54; the next reference is to 67.
14. "Righting Wrongs." In Nicholas Owen, ed., *Human Rights and Human Wrongs* (Oxford: Oxford University Press, 2003).
15. As usual, Raymond Williams's system of residual-dominantemergent-archaic-preemergent gives me the best handle on mapping culture as process (Raymond Williams, *Marxism and Literature* [Oxford: Oxford University Press, 1977], 121-127). This is why I began with an account of academic memos, a mundane record of the dominant appropriating a social emergent.
16. 1999 Report of the Mayor's Task Force on CUNY, chaired by Benno C. Schmidt Jr., entitled, "The City University of New York: An Institution Adrift." The passage quoted is from 13.
17. Mehdi Charef, *Le Thé Au Harem d'Archi Ahmed* (Paris: Mercure de France, 1983). The phrase is an Arabic transformation of the theorem of Archimedes worked out by a young North African immigrant boy in the low-income housing projects in the outskirts of Paris. This is a typical example of how the underclass imagination swims in the deep waters of metropolitan survival.
18. Derrida, "Force of Law," in *Acts of Religion*, tr. Gil Anidjar (New York: Routledge, 2002), 249: translation modified.

(选自 Gayatri Chakravorty Spivak, Chapter 1 of *Death of a Discipline*, NY: Columbia University Press, 2003, pp. 1-23.)

What Is World Literature?

(节选)

[美]David Damrosch

【导读】

大卫·丹穆若什(David Damrosch，也译做大卫·达姆罗什)，1980年获耶鲁大学比较文学博士学位，历任哥伦比亚大学比较文学系主任(1996—1999)、美国比较文学学会会长(2001—2003)、哈佛大学比较文学系主任(2009—2012)等职。著有《什么是世界文学》(*What Is World Literature*? (2003))、《如何阅读世界文学》(*How to Read World Literature*?)(2009)等著作，并曾出任《朗文世界文学选集》(*The Longman Anthology of World Literature*)(2004)主编。本文节选自《什么是世界文学》一书的结语部分。文中，丹穆若什提出了以世界、文本和读者为中心的世界文学三重定义，并大体对应于著作的"流通"、"翻译"与"生产"三个部分：一是，世界文学是民族文学间的椭圆形折射(elliptical refraction)。"椭圆形折射"是丹穆若什借用物理学术语"椭圆形反射"(elliptical reflection)而自创的、虽没有科学根据却能深刻揭示世界文学特质的一个词语。在一个椭圆形的空间中，一个焦点上的光源会通过反射重新聚焦到第二个焦点上，从而形成双焦点，喻指源语文学与目的语文学(翻译文学作品)双重中心；在文学作品的世界流通过程中，并不存在简单的反射，而是类似于穿越了介质(语言、文化、文明等)的"折射"。正如丹穆若什在"流通"一部分中借以《吉尔伽美什》为个案的考察所揭示的，一部作品要成为世界文学，不仅要被视为文学作品阅读，更要流通到跨语言和跨文化的更大的语境中，世界文学由此成为民族文学间的椭圆形折射。二是，世界文学是从翻译中获益的文学。在世界文学交往中，翻译不仅是桥梁，帮助我们跨越语言和文化的藩篱，在更加宏阔的范围内了解文学；翻译也可能是墙，翻译不可避免地产生某些失落和变形，一部文学作品如果在翻译中失落某些东西，被墙阻隔，那就只能存留在本民族的文化语境当中，相反，如果作品能跨越墙壁，从翻译中获益，则能成为世界文学。在著作第六章中，丹穆若什以卡夫卡作品译本的不断修订，并导致德语原作也在出版修订本为例，说明在翻译过程中，卡夫卡这位原本作为文化超越者的形象(现代主义经典作家)正逐渐为布拉格犹太作家的形象所替代，正因为他契合了当代所关注的问题而在翻译中增值，也使得他的作品在世界范围被广泛接受。三是，世界文学不是指一套经典文本，而是指一种阅读模式——一种以超然的态度进入与我们自身时空不同的世界的形式。在民族文学走向世界文学的过程中，具有不同文化传统、文化背景的读者起着非常重要的作用，某一社会内的不同团体和任一团体内的不同个人将因为自己的阅读而制造独特的文本聚焦体，使之成为自己有效的世界文学"微经典"，我们不是在源语文化情境中与作品相遇，而是在来自迥然不同的文化和时代的作品所形成的张力中阅读，与母语文化保持一定的距离，我们可以清楚地看到一部文学作品怎样从其源点向外伸展、传播。的确，一个作家、一部作品在其他民族中被阅读，会引起新的关注，并赋予其新意，如爱伦·坡不是在美国，而是在法国最早受到重视的。

丹穆若什在全球化语境下重新界定了"世界文学"，其将世界文学视为一种流通模式、一种阅读模式的新观点相当富于启发意义，必将成为我们重新思考世界文学的新的基点。

（李卫华）

Conclusion: World Enough and Time

And so, what *is* world literature? I have conceived this book as a demonstration as much as an essay in definition, seeking to show the kinds of work now in our view and some of the ways they can be approached. I have dwelt on some of the texts that have obsessed me over the years and that seemed particularly suggestive on issues of circulation, translation, and production. In the process, much as Eckermann gives us *his* Goethe, I have given you my world literature, or at least a representative cross-section of it, while recognizing that the world now presents us with material so varied as to call into question any logic of representation, any single framework that everyone should adopt and in which these particular works would all have a central role. A leading characteristic of world literature today is its variability: different readers will be obsessed by very different constellations of texts. While figures like Dante and Kafka retain a powerful canonical status, these authors function today less as a common patrimony than as rich nodes of overlap among many different and highly individual groupings.

Amid all this variety, family resemblances can be found among the different forms of world literature circulating today, emergent patterns that lead me to propose a threefold definition focused on the world, the text, and the reader:

1. *World literature is an elliptical refraction of national literatures.*

2. *World literature is writing that gains in translation.*

3. *World literature is not a set canon of texts but a mode of reading: a form of detached engagement with worlds beyond our own place and time.*

Each of these points merits discussion.

Elliptical refraction of national literatures. For the past half-century, world literature in its North American guises has usually been opposed to national literature. A genial disregard, if not outright hostility, often obtained between the devotees of the two. With most literature faculty based in departments organized along national lines, in many schools "world literature" was treated as an introductory course, suitable for beginning students but fundamentally vague in conception and unrigorous in application, a preliminary stage prior to serious work in a literature major based on close study of a culture and its language. Even the most elaborate comparative scholarship often raised serious reservations among committed specialists. No less a book than Erich Auerbach's *Mimesis* (1946), probably the most ambitious and impressive synoptic study of its generation, was roundly criticized by reviewers based in one or another of the specific areas his book traversed. The classicist Ludwig Edelstein, for example, noted that Auerbach had dramatically foreshortened Greco-Roman literary history, ignoring the findings of classical scholarship to produce his stark contrast of Hebrew and Greek cultures, whereas "in the historical view, even the fifth century is not a unity" (431). Similarly, the medievalist Helmut Hatzfeld criticized Auerbach for reading the *Chanson de Roland* "with the eyes of an enlightened pacifist" rather than with an understanding of what the medieval author would have believed (335). Even René Wellek, in a review filled with faint praise, felt that Auerbach's results were "peculiarly shifting and disconcertingly vague" (305). *Mimesis* won this battle, but it lost the war. Widely admired and discussed to this day, it has had few, if any, successors: Auerbach's own students became specialists in a much more limited range of languages and eras.

Comparatists in the postwar era often returned the specialists' disregard, holding out messianic hopes for world literature as the cure for the ills of nationalistic separatism, jingoism, and internecine violence—and, by implication, advancing the comparatist as the transcendent heir to the narrowness of monolingual specialization. Comparative literature was to be the grand corrective for "the nationalistic heresy," as Albter Guérard put it in a lead article in the *Yearbook of Comparative and General Literature* in 1958. Looking ahead to European unification, Guérard anticipated that "Comparative Literature will disappear in its very victory; just as 'foreign trade' between France and Germany will disappear in the Common Market; just as the 'foreign relations' between these two countries will be absorbed by a common parliament" ("Comparative Literature?" 4). For Guérard, the overriding question in 1958 was "How and When Shall We Commit Suicide?" His answer: "Not just yet: we are needed so long as the nationalistic heresy has not been extirpated." (5)

We can no longer proceed as though this heresy is about to disappear. The European Parliament in Brussels is unlikely to supplant Europe's national governments during our lifetimes, and in an academic context the very great majority of teachers and scholars of literature continue to be located in nationally based departments. What does the ongoing vitality of national literary traditions mean for the study of world literature? An understanding of world literature as an elliptical refraction of national literatures can help to clarify the vital, yet also indirect, relation between the two. With the possible exception of a few irreducibly multinational works like *The Thousand and One Nights*, virtually all literary works are born within what we would now call a national literature. The modern nation is, of course, a relatively recent development, but even older works were produced in local or ethnic configurations that have been subsumed into the national traditions within which they are now preserved and transmitted. A "nation" itself, in early modern English, could designate an ethnic group or culture: in the King James Bible, "the nations" translates the Hebrew *ha-goyim*, the Septuagint's *hoi ethnoi*. Understanding the term "national" broadly, we can say that works continue to bear the marks of their national origin even after they circulate into world literature, and yet these traces are increasingly diffused and become ever more sharply refracted as a work travels farther from home.

This refraction, moreover, is double in nature: works become world literature by being received *into* the space of a foreign culture, a space defined in many ways by the host culture's national tradition and the present needs of its own writers. Even a single work of world literature is the locus of a negotiation between two different cultures. The receiving culture can use the foreign material in all sorts of ways: as a positive model for the future development of its own tradition; as a negative case of a primitive, or decadent, strand that must be avoided or rooted out at home; or, more neutrally, as an image of radical otherness against which the home tradition can more clearly be defined. World literature is thus always as much about the host culture's values and needs as it is about a work's source culture; hence it is a double refraction, one that can be described through the figure of the ellipse, with the source and host cultures providing the two foci that generate the elliptical space within which a work lives as world literature, connected to both cultures, circumscribed by neither alone.

I advance the image of an elliptical refraction as a convenient metaphor, but I don't mean to imply a scientific precision that the extremely varied phenomena of world literature would not support. For those who would prefer a more literary image, I might suggest the two-headed "pushmi-pullyu" from the Doctor Dolittle books. The pushmi-pullyu is an appropriately multicultural animal, related "to the Abyssinian gazelles and the Asiatic chamois, on my mother's side," as he tells the doctor, adding that "my father's great-grandfather was the last of the unicorns" (*The Story of Doctor Dolittle*, 76).

…

This brings us to my second point: *World literature is writing that gains in translation.* There is a significant difference between literary language and the various forms of ordinary, denotative language, whose meaning we take to be largely expressed as information. A text is read as literature if we dwell on the beauties of its language, its form, and its themes, and don't take it as primarily factual in intent; but the same text can cease to work as literature if a reader turns to it primarily to extract information from it, as when George Smith read *The Epic of Gilgamesh* to confirm the biblical history of the Flood, regretting that the account had been "disfigured by poetical adornments". Informational texts neither gain nor lose in a good translation: their meaning is simply carried over with little or no effective change. Treaties and contracts can be complex documents, but if well drafted and well translated, they are understandable to all parties concerned. They may be breached from the pressure of changing circumstances or through misinterpretations that apply to all the document's versions, but treaties rarely fail because of problems arising from translation per se.

At the other extreme, some works are so inextricably connected to their original language and moment that they really cannot be effectively translated at all. Purist views of literary language often take all poetry as "what is lost in translation," in Robert Frost's famous phrase, since whatever meaning a new language can convey is irretrievably sundered from the verbal music of the original. "A poem should not mean/But be," as Archibald Macleish wrote in 1926 in his "Ars Poetica," in lines that convey their own declarative meaning with surprising success. Much poetry, including Frost's and Macleish's, has been translated with great effect into many languages. It is more accurate to say that *some* works are not translatable without substantial loss, and so they remain largely within their local or national context, never achieving an effective life as world literature.

It is important to recognize that the question of translatability is distinct from questions of value. A work can hold a prominent place within its own culture but read poorly elsewhere, either because its language doesn't translate well or because its cultural assumptions don't travel. Snorri Sturluson's dynastic saga *Heimskringla* is a major document in medieval Nordic culture, but it only makes compelling reading if you are fairly knowledgeable about the political history of Norway and Iceland, and it remains unknown abroad outside specialist circles. By contrast, Norse mythological texts like the Elder Edda and Snorri's own *Prose Edda* have been widely translated and much appreciated. They are actually harder to understand than the *Heimskringla*, but they treat themes of broad interest in striking, if often mysterious, language. Equally, a work's viability as world literature has little to do with its author's perspective on the world. There can be no more global work, conceptually speaking, than *Finnegans Wake*, yet its prose is so intricate and irreproducible that it becomes a sort of curiosity in translation. *Dubliners*, a far more localized work, has been much more widely translated and has had a far greater impact in other languages.

Literary language is thus language that either gains *or* loses in translation, in contrast to nonliterary language, which typically does neither. The balance of credit and loss remains a distinguishing mark of national versus world literature: literature stays within its national or regional tradition when it usually loses in translation, whereas works become world literature when they gain on balance in translation, stylistic losses offset by an expansion in depth as they increase their range, as is the case with such widely disparate works as *The Epic of Gilgamesh* and *Dictionary of the Khazars*. It follows from this that the study of world literature should embrace translation far more actively than it has usually done to date. This is not to argue, though, for a return to the kind of ungrounded cosmopolitanism seen a century ago in world literature collections. Too many world literature courses have tended to assume that undergraduate courses should be the last refuge for a high-minded amateurism, a busman's holiday from any real engagement with the works' cultures of origin. Committed teachers of world literature are increasingly finding ways to give students access to cultural context, via corollary readings and through collaborative student explorations of websites and print resources. At the opposite end of the university spectrum, scholars have often feared to touch a work in translation at all as they develop critical analyses for publication. In her article on *Dictionary of the Khazars*, N. Katherine Hayles notes with regret that few people outside Slavic studies have ever written about Pavić, and she urges more to do so, even if they don't know Serbo-Croatian. Admirable as this plea is, it is regrettable that Hayles took her own ignorance of the original language as a license to ignore the book's cultural context outright, even though much information about that context is available in English.

…

And so to the final part of my definition of world literature: *not a set canon of texts but a mode of reading, a detached engagement with a world beyond our own.* At any given time, a fluctuating number of foreign works will circulate actively within a culture, and a subset of these will be widely shared and enjoy a canonical status, but different groups within a society, and different individuals within any group, will create distinctive congeries of works, blending canonical and noncanonical works into effective microcanons. As Bruce Robbins says of a locally inflected cosmopolitanism, it involves not an ideal detachment but "a reality of (re) attachment, multiple attachment, or attachment at a distance" (*Cosmopolitics*, 3). World literature's attachments are multiplied by the fact that it is at once a collective and an individual phenomenon. A large and multilayered group of foreign works that circulate in a given culture, it is also experienced as a private pleasure by individual readers, in ways that may diverge dramatically from the social goals that usually underlie the defining and formal transmission of a literary heritage. The texts themselves exist both together and alone: when we read Dante, we are aware that we are encountering a major work of world literature, one that draws on a wealth of previous writing and that casts its shadow ahead onto much that will follow it. Yet even as we register such connections, we are also immersed within Dante's singular world, an imagined universe very unlike any envisioned by Virgil or by Saint Paul, and one that Milton, Gogol, and Walcott will radically revise in turn for very different purposes of their own.

The individual text's appeal is beautifully expressed by James Joyce in the lines that form the second epigraph to this book: "(Stoop) if you are abcedminded, to this claybook, what curios of signs (please stoop), in this allaphbed! Can you rede (since We and Thou had it out already) its world?" (*Finnegans Wake*, 184). We forget ourselves in reading (the double sense of "abcedminded"); like Hormuzd Rassam and George Smith striving to decipher the signs on a clay tablet they've gotten out of the ground, we enter into a multiple relation with the work, as Joyce suggests by having us "rede" its world. We read but also enter actively into dialogue with the work (German, *reden*: "to converse"), almost as though we ourselves were writing it with a reed pen.

The great conversation of world literature takes place on two very different levels: among authors who know and react to one another's work, and in the mind of the reader, where works meet and interact in ways that may have little to do with cultural and historical proximity. Someone who read *Swann's Way* and *The Tale of the Genji* together is likely to find them resonating in multiple and profound ways, engaging one another at least as closely as a reader who is attentive to national traditions will find Proust engaging with Balzac, or the *Genji* with *The Tale of the Heike*. World literature is fully in play once several foreign works begin to resonate together in our mind. This provides a further solution to the comparatist's lurking panic: world literature is not an immense body of material that must somehow, impossibly, be mastered; it is a mode of reading that can be experienced *intensively* with a few works just as effectively as it can be explored *extensively* with a large number.

Auerbach's great book would not have been much improved if he had added further chapters of the sort he wished he'd had world enough and time to write: a chapter on Apollonius Rhodius, to show Hellenistic fiction in greater depth; a full chapter on Proust, now rather awkwardly shoehorned in as an aside to his chapter on Woolf, to give a more rounded account of modernism. Such additions would of course have added something to his argument, but the book is already long enough at 557 pages. He might have gained more if he had *cut* some chapters: if he had discussed a dozen works, rather than twenty, and made active use of the scholarship of those who were spending their lives on the individual periods and cultures he was passing through.

…

(节选自 Damrosch, David. *What Is World Literature?*. Princeton, NJ: Princeton University Press, 2003, pp. 281-303.)

Conjectures on World Literature

（节选）

[美]Franco Morreti

【导读】

弗朗哥·莫莱蒂(Franco Moretti，1950年生)，先后在意大利和哥伦比亚大学任教，现为斯坦福大学英语文学及比较文学教授，斯坦福大学小说研究中心主任。早在1983年，就以文集《被视为奇迹的符号》(*Sign Taken for Wonders*)一举成名，后相继出版《现代史诗：从歌德到马尔克斯之间的世界体系》(*The Modern Epic*: *The World-system from Goethe to García Márquez*，1998)和《图表、地图、树木：文学史的抽象模式》(*Graphs*, *Maps*, *Trees*: *Abstract Models for a Literary History*，2005)等著作。

《世界文学猜想》(Conjectures on World Literature)一文发表于《新左派评论》(*New Left Review*)2000年1—2月刊，引发了克里斯多夫·普伦德加斯特(Christopher Prendergast)、弗朗西斯卡·奥西尼(Francesca Orsini)、埃弗拉因·克里斯塔尔(Efraín Kristal)、乔纳森·阿拉克(Jonathan Arac)、艾米莉·阿普特(Emily Apter)和杰尔·帕拉(Jale Parla)等人的多方讨论，莫莱蒂随后发表了《世界文学猜想续篇》(More Conjectures)(刊于《新左派评论》2003年3—4月刊)进行回应。

在本文中，莫莱蒂借用了伊曼纽尔·沃勒斯坦(Immanuel Wallerstein)在《现代世界体系》(*The Modern World-system*，1977)、《反系统运动》(*Antisystemic Movements*，1989)和《地缘政治与地缘文化》(*Geopolitics and Geoculture*，1991)等著作中的"核心"、"半边缘"和"边缘"等概念，认为世界文学和国际资本主义体系一样，同时既是一，又是不平等的。它是一个整体，但在这个整体中，不同于歌德和马克思所希望的，它相当不平等，有核心，也有边缘。他还提出了一种与该理论相适应的研究方法——距离阅读(distant reading)，区别于新批评关注文本内部的细读(close reading)方法，莫莱蒂认为，"距离是一种知识状态：它让我们着眼于比文本更小或更大的单位：策略、主题、修辞——或文类和体系"，这种宏观比较法能够更好地把握全球时代文化与文本的复杂流通。随后，莫莱蒂通过世界范围内现代小说兴起的远距观察，阐释了世界文学内部的"核心"和"边缘"运动态势：第三世界现代小说的兴起最初并不是自主发展的，而是外来形式、本土材料和本土形式(外国情节、本土人物和本土的叙事声音)折衷的结果。在文章的最后，莫莱蒂分别以"树"和"波浪"为喻："树"源自达尔文物种起源说的树状结构，描述了从统一性到多样性的发展；"波浪"却相反，它遵循吞噬了最初多样性的统一性，如好莱坞电影征服了一个又一个市场，英语吞噬了一种又一种语言。民族文学是对那些看到树的人而言的；世界文学是对那些看到波浪的人而言的，这就是民族文学和世界文学分化的基础。在2005年的《进化、世界体系、世界文学》(Evolution, World-systems, Weltliterature)一文中，莫莱蒂对自己的"树"和"波浪"的比喻进行了修正，他认为存在着两种世界文学，一种是以进化论为理论基础的("树"的比喻)，这种世界文学是多种独立的地方文化的马赛克式拼贴，具有很强的内部多样性，主要通过分化而产生新形式；另一种是以世界体系分析为理论基础的("波浪"的比喻)，这种世界文学由国际文学市场整合为统一整体，表现不断发展的、时而令人惊叹的相似性，聚合是其主要变化机制。两者并不是对立的，而是具有某种相容性。

(李卫华)

My mission: to say it more simply than I understand it.
Schönberg, *Moses and Aaron*

"Nowadays, national literature doesn't mean much: the age of world literature is beginning, and everybody should contribute to hasten its advent." This was Goethe, of course, talking to Eckermann in 1827; and these are Marx and Engels, twenty years later, in 1848: "National one-sidedness and narrrow-mind-edness become more and more impossible, and from the many national and local literatures, a world literature arises." *Weltliteratur*: this is what Goethe and Marx have in mind. Not "comparative", but world literature: the Chinese novel that Goethe was reading at the time of that exchange, or the bourgeoisie of the *Manifesto*, which has "given a cosmopolitan character to production and consumption in every country". Well, let me put it very simply: comparative literature has not lived up to these beginnings. It's been a much more modest intellectual enterprise, fundamentally limited to Western Europe, and mostly revolving around the river Rhine (German philologists working on French literature). Not much more.

Many people have read more and better than I have, of course, but still, we are talking of hundreds of languages and literatures here. Reading "more" seems hardly to be the solution. Especially because we've just started rediscovering what Margaret Cohen calls the "great unread". "I work on West European narrative, etc... ." Not really, I work on its canonical fraction, which is not even one per cent of published literature. And again, some people have read more, but the point is that there are thirty thousand nineteenth-century British novel out there, forty, fifty, sixty thousand—no one really knows, no one has read them, no one ever will. And then there are French novels, Chinese, Argentinian, American...Reading "more" is always a good thing, but not the solution.

Perhaps it's too much, tackling the world and the unread at the same time. But I actually think that it's our greatest chance, because the sheer enormity of the task makes it clear that world literature cannot be literature, bigger; what we are already doing, just more of it. It has to be different. The *categories* have to be different. "It is not the 'actual' interconnection of 'things'", Max Weber wrote, "but *the conceptual* interconnection of *problems* which define the scope of the various sciences. A new 'science' emerges where a new problem is pursued by a new method." That's the point: world literature is not an object, it's a *problem*, and a problem that asks for a new critical method: and no one has ever found a method by just reading more texts. That's not how theories come into being; they need a leap, a wager—a hypothesis, to get started.

World literature: one and unequal

I will borrow this initial hypothesis from the world-system school of economic history, for which international capitalism is a system that is simultaneously *one*, and *unequal*: with a core, and a periphery (and a semiperiphery) that are bound together in a relationship of growing inequality. One, and unequal: *one* literature (*Weltliteratur*, singular, as in Goethe and Marx), or perhaps, better, one world literary system (of inter-related literatures); but a system which is different from what Goethe and Marx had hoped for, because it's profoundly unequal. "Foreign debt is as inevitable in Brazilian letters as in any other field", writes Roberto Schwarz in a splendid essay on "The Importing of the Novel to Brazil": it's not simply an easily dispensable part of the work in which it appears, but a complex feature of it"; and Itamar Even-Zohar, reflecting on Hebrew literature: "Interference [is] a relationship between literatures, whereby a...source literature may become a source of direct or indirect loans [*Importing* of the novel, direct and indirect loans, foreign debt: see how economic metaphors have been subterraneously at work in literary history]—a source of loans for...a target literature...*There is no symmetry in literary interference. A target literature is, more often than not, interfered with by a source literature which completely ignores it.*"

This is what one and unequal means: the destiny of a culture (usually a culture of the periphery, as Montserrat Iglesias Santos has specified) is intersected and altered by another culture (from the core) that "completely ignores it". A familiar scenario, this asymmetry in international power—and later I will say more about Schwarz's "foreign debt" as a complex literary feature. Right now, let me spell out the consequences of taking an explanatory matrix from social history and applying it to literary history.

Distant reading

Writing about comparative social history, Marc Bloch once coined a lovely "slogan", as he himself called it: "years of analysis for a day of synthesis"; and if you read Braudel or

Wallerstein you immediately see what Bloch had in mind. The text which is strictly Wallerstein's, his "day of synthesis", occupies one third of a page, one fourth, maybe half; the rest are quotations (fourteen hundred, in the first volume of *The Modern World-System*). Years of analysis; other people's analysis, which Wallerstein's page synthesizes into a system.

Now, if we take this model seriously, the study of world literature will somehow have to reproduce this "page"—which is to say: this relationship between analysis and synthesis—for the literary field. But in that case, literary history will quickly become very different from what it is now: it will become "second hand": a patchwork of other people's research, *without a single direct textual reading*. Still ambitious, and actually even more so than before (world literature!); but the ambition is now directly proportional *to the distance from the text*: the more ambitious the project, the greater must the distance be.

The United States is the country of close reading, so I don't expect this idea to be particularly popular. But the trouble with close reading (in all of its incarnations, from the new criticism to deconstruction) is that it necessarily depends on an extremely small canon. This may have become an unconscious and invisible premises by now, but it is an iron one nonetheless: you invest so much in individual texts *only* if you think that very few of them really matter. Otherwise, it doesn't make sense. And if you want to look beyond the canon (and of course, world literature will do so: it would be absurd if it didn't!) close reading will *not* do it. It's not designed to do it, it's designed to do the opposite. At bottom, it's a theological exercise—very solemn treatment of very few texts taken very seriously—whereas what we really need *is a little pact with the devil*: we know how to read texts, now let's learn how not to read them. Distant reading: where distance, let me repeat it, is a condition of knowledge: it allows you to focus on units that are much smaller or much larger than the text: devices, themes, tropes—or genres and systems. And if, between the very small and the very large, the text itself disappears, well, it is one of those cases when one can justifiably say, Less is more. If we want to understand the system in its entirety, we must accept losing something. We always pay a price for theoretical knowledge: reality is infinitely rich; concepts are abstract, are poor. But it's precisely this 'poverty' that makes it possible to handle them, and therefore to know. This is why less is actually more.

The Western European novel: rule or exception?

Let me give you an example of the conjunction of distant reading and world literature. An example, not a model; and of course my example, based on the field I know (elsewhere, things may be very different). A few years ago, introducing Kojin Karatani's *Origins of Modern Japanese Literature*, Fredric Jameson noticed that in the take-off of the modern Japanese novel, "the raw material of Japanese social experience and the abstract formal patterns of Western novel construction cannot always be welded together seamlessly"; and he referred in this respect to Masao Miyoshi's *Accomplices of Silence*, and *Meenakeshi Mukherjee's Realism and Reality* (a study of the early Indian novel). And it s true, these books return quite often to the complicated "problems"(Mukherjee's term) arising from the encounter of western form and Japanese or Indian reality.

Now, that the same configuration should occur in such different cultures as India and Japan—this was curious; and it became even more curious when I realized that Roberto Schwarz had independently discovered very much the same pattern in Brazil. So, eventually, I started using these pieces of evidence to reflect on the relationship between markets and forms; and then, without really knowing what I was doing, began to treat Jameson's insight as if it were—one should always be cautious with these claims, but there is really no other way to say it—as if it were *a law of literary evolution*: in cultures that belong to the periphery of the literary system (which means: almost all cultures, inside and outside Europe), the modern novel first arises not as an autonomous development but as a compromise between a western formal influence (usually French or English) and local materials.

This first idea expanded into a little cluster of laws, and it was all very interesting, but...it was still just an idea; a conjecture that had to be tested, possibly on a large scale, and so I decided to follow the wave of diffusion of the modern novel (roughly: from 1750 to 1950) in the pages of literary history. Gasperetti and Goscilo on late eighteenth-century Eastern Europe; Toschi and Martí-López on early nineteenth-century Southern Europe; Franco and Sommer on mid-century Latin America; Frieden on the Yiddish novels of the 1860s; Moosa, Said and Allen on the Arabic novels of the 1870s; Evin and Parla on the Turkish novels of the same years; Anderson on the Filipino *Noli Me Tangere*, of 1887; Zhao and Wang on turn-of-the-century Qing fiction; Obiechina, Irele and Quayson on West African novels between the 1920s and the 1950s (plus of course Karatani, Miyoshi, Mukherjee, Even-Zohar and Schwarz). Four continents, two hundred years, over twenty independent critical studies, and they all agreed: when a culture starts moving towards the modern novel, it's *always* as a compromise between foreign form and local materials. Jameson's "law" had passed the test—the first test, anyway. And actually more than that: it had completely reversed the received historical explanation of these matters: because if the compromise between the foreign and the local is so ubiquitous, then those independent paths that are usually taken to be the rule of the rise of the novel (the Spanish, the French, and especially the British case)—*well*, *they're not the rule at all*, *they're the exception*. They come first, yes, but they're not at all typical. The "typical" rises of the novel is Krasicki, Kemal, Rizal, Maran—not Defoe.

Experiments with history

See the beauty of distant reading plus world literature: they go against the grain of national historiography. And they do so in the form of *an experiment*. You define a unit of analysis (like here, the formal compromise), and then follow its metamorphoses in a variety of environments—until, ideally, *all* of literary history becomes a long chain of related experiments: a "dialogue between fact and fancy", as Peter Medawar calls it: "between what could be true, and what is in fact the case." Apt words for this research, in the course of which, as I was reading my fellow historians, it became clear that the encounter of western forms and local reality did indeed produce everywhere a structural compromise—as the law predicted—but also, that the compromise itself was taking rather different forms. At times, especially in the second half of the *nineteenth century and in Asia*, *it tended to be very unstable*: an "impossible programme", as Miyoshi says of Japan. At other times it was not so: at the beginning and at the end of the wave, for instance (Poland, Italy and Spain at one extreme; and West Africa on the other), historians describe novels that had, certainly, their own problems—but not problems arising from the clash of irreconcilable elements.

I hadn't expected such a spectrum of outcomes, so at first I was taken aback, and only later realized that this was probably the most valuable finding of them all, because it showed that world literature was indeed a system—but a system of variations. The system was one, not uniform. The pressure from the Anglo-French core *tried* to make it uniform, but it could never fully erase the reality of difference. (See here, by the way, how the study of world literature is—inevitably—a study of the struggle for symbolic hegemony across the world.) The system was one, not uniform. And, retrospectively, of course it had to be like this: if after 1750 the novel arises just about everywhere as a compromise between West European patterns and local reality—well, local reality was different in the various places, just as western influence was also very uneven: much stronger in Southern Europe around 1800, to return to my example, than in West Africa around 1940. The forces in play kept changing, and so did the compromise that resulted from their interaction. And this, incidentally, opens a fantastic field of inquiry for comparative morphology (the systematic study of how forms vary in space and time, which is also the only reason to keep the adjective "comparative" in comparative literature): but comparative morphology is a complex issue, that deserves its own paper.

Forms as abstracts of social relationships

Let me now add a few words on that term "compromise"—by which I mean something a little different from what Jameson had in mind in his introduction to Karatani. For him, the relationship is fundamentally a binary one: "the abstract formal patterns of Western novel construction" and "the raw material of Japanese social experience"; form and content, basically. For me, it's more of a triangle: foreign form, local material—*and local form*. Simplifying somewhat: foreign *plot*, local *characters*; and then, local narrative voice: and it's precisely in this third dimension that these novels seem to be most unstable—most uneasy, as Zhao says of the late Qing narrator. Which makes sense: the narrator is the pole of comment, of explanation, of evaluation, and when foreign "formal patterns" (or actual foreign presence, for that matter) make characters behave in strange ways (like Bunzo, or Ibarra, or Brùs Cubas), then of course comment becomes uneasy—garrulous, erratic, rudderless.

"Interferences", Even-Zohar calls them: powerful literatures making life hard for the others—making *structure* hard. And Schwarz: "a part of the original historical conditions reappears as a sociological form ... In this sense, forms are the abstract of specific social relationships." Yes, and in our case the historical condition reappear as a sort of "crack" in the form; as a faultline running between story and discourse, world and worldview: the world goes in the strange direction dictated by an outside power; the worldwide tries to make sense of it, and is thrown off balance all the time. Like Rizal's voice (oscillating between Catholic melodrama and Enlightenment sarcasm), or Futabatei's (caught between Bunzo's "Russian" behaviour, and the Japanese audience inscribed in the text), or Zhao's hypertrophic narrator, who has completely lost control of the plot, but still tries to dominate it at all costs. This is what Schwarz meant with that "foreign debt" that becomes a "complex feature" of the text: the foreign presence "interferes" with the very *utterance* of the novel. The one-and-unequal literary system is not just an external network here, it doesn't remain *outside* the text: it's embedded well into its form.

Trees, waves and cultural history

Forms are the abstract of social relationships: so, formal analysis is in its own modest way an analysis of power. (That's why comparative morphology is such a fascinating field: studying how forms vary, you discover how symbolic *power* varies from place to place.) And indeed, sociological formalism has always been my interpretive method, and I think that it's particularly appropriate for world literature ... But, unfortunately, at this point I must stop, because my competence stops. Once it became clear that the key variable of the experiment was the narrator's voice, well, a genuine formal analysis was off limits for me, because it required a linguistic competence that I couldn't even dream of (French, English, Spanish, Russian, Japanese, Chinese and Portuguese, just for the core of the argument). And probably, no matter what the object of analysis is, there will always be a point where the study of world literature must yield to the specialist of the national literature, in a sort of cosmic and inevitable division of labour. Inevitable not just for practical reasons, but for theoretical ones. This is a large issue, but let me at least sketch its outline.

When historians have analysed culture on a world scale (or on a large scale anyway), they have tended to use two basic cognitive metaphors: the tree and the wave. The tree, the phylogenetic tree derived from Darwin, was the tool of comparative philology: language families branching off from each other—Slavo-Germanic from Aryan-Greco-Italo-Celtic, then Balto-Slavic from Germanic, then Lithuanian from Slavic. And this kind of tree allowed comparative philology to solve that great puzzle which was also perhaps the first world system of culture: Indo-European: a family of languages spreading from India to Ireland (and perhaps not just languages, a common cultural repertoire, too: but here the evidence is notoriously shakier). The other metaphor, the wave, was also used in historical linguistics (as in Schmidt's "wave hypothesis", that explained certain overlaps among languages), but it played a role in many other fields as well: the study of technological diffusion, for instance, or the fantastic interdisciplinary theory of the "wave of advance" by Cavalli-Sforza and Ammerman (a geneticist and an archaeologist), which explains how agriculture spread from the fertile crescent in the Middle East towards the North-West and then throughout Europe.

Now, trees and waves are both metaphors—but except for this, they have absolutely nothing in common. The tree describes the passage from unity to diversity: one tree, with many branches: from Indo-Euporean, to dozens of different languages. The wave is the opposite: it observes uniformity engulfing an initial diversity: Hollywood films conquering one market after another (or English swallowing language after language). Trees need geographical *discontinuity* (in order to branch off from each other, languages must first be separated in space, just like animal species); waves dislike barriers, and thrive on geographical *continuity* (from the viewpoint of a wave, the ideal world is a pond). Trees and branches are what nation-states cling to; waves are what markets do. And so on. Nothing in common, between the two metaphors. But—*they both work*. Cultural history is made of trees and waves—the wave of agricultural advance supporting the tree of Indo-European languages, which is then swept by new waves of linguistic and cultural contact...And as world culture oscillates between the two mechanisms, its products are inevitably composite ones. Compromises, as in Jameson's law. That's why the law works: because it intuitively captures the intersection of the two mechanisms. Think of the modern novel: certainly a wave (and I've actually called it a wave a few times)—but a wave that runs into the branches of local traditions, and is always significantly transformed by them.

This, then, is the basis for the division of labour between national and world literature: national literature, for people who see trees; world literature, for people who see waves. Division of labour...and challenge; because both metaphors work, yes, but that doesn't mean that they work equally well. The products of cultural history are always composite ones: but which is the dominant mechanism in their compositions? The internal, or the external one? The nation or the world? The tree or the wave? There is no way to settle this controversy once and for all—fortunately: because comparatists need controversy. They have always been too shy in the presence of national literatures, too diplomatic: as if one had English, American, German literature—and then, next door, a sort of little parallel universe where comparatists studied a second set of literatures, trying not to disturb the first set. No; the universe is the same, the literatures are the same, we just look at them from a different view-point; and you become a comparatist for a very simple reason: *because you are convinced that that viewpoint is better*. It has greater explanatory power; it's conceptually more elegant; it avoids that ugly "one-sidedness and narrow-mindedness"; whatever. The point is that there is no other justification for the study of world literature (and for the existence of departments of comparative literature) but this: to be a thorn in the side, a permanent intellectual challenge to national literatures—especially the local literature. If comparative literature is not this, it's nothing. Nothing. "Don't delude yourself", writes Stendhal of his favourite character: "for you, there is no middle road." The same is true for us.

（节选自胡继华编著：《比较文学经典导读》，北京师范大学出版社 2015 年版，第 94-110 页。）

后　记

比较文学是一门面向他者开放的学科，其最初的理念就是要打破文学研究的国别限制，研究世界各国文学的相互交流与影响。美国学派的跨学科研究主张文学向其他学科的开放，中国学派强调比较文学需要向其他文明区域开放。新时期以来，比较文学在中国逐渐成为一门显学，其不仅迎合了后现代文化“持续开发各种差异并为维护差异性的声誉而努力”(利奥塔语)的趋向，而且更主要的在于和中国改革开放的目标相一致；作为一门学科的比较文学，不仅在理论建设上有着重要成就，提出了“跨文明研究”和“变异学研究”等理论主张，并且在学科设置、研究阵地、教材编写等成果丰硕，“比较文学”已经成为中文系和外文系学生的必修课程。然而在教学过程中，学生对比较文学经典文献缺乏必要的了解，教师往往需要将相关文献复印给学生，以便他们能更好地理解教材的内容。

我们在本书中选择了涉及比较文学学科理论发展，以及影响研究、平行研究和变异学研究诸种方法的六十一篇经典文献，力图向学生展现尽可能丰富的比较文学研究成果。在具体编写中，本书体现了三个特点：

一是实践侧重。当代中国的比较文学研究，一定程度上存在着理论的“空洞化”倾向，忽视了具体比较方法的“实践形态”，因而，在具体篇目的选择上，本书除了选有从梵第根、基亚到韦勒克、雷马克再到日尔蒙斯基、康拉德等，从法国学派到美国学派再到俄苏学派关于比较文学学科理论的经典文献以外，我们更注重比较文学研究方法的具体运用，如流传学、渊源学、形象学、类型学、变异学等我们都选有相关的实践性篇目，期望引领、协助学生通过有意识的借鉴和模仿，进行初步的比较文学研究。

二是中外并重。中外并重不仅体现为对具体篇目的选择，如在跨学科研究中，我们不仅选择了玛丽·盖塞的《文学与艺术》、牛顿·P. 斯托尔克奈特的《文学与思想史》等，同样选择了中国学者钱锺书的《中国诗与中国画》、张汉良的《文学与艺术的关系研究》等。中外并重也体现在文献语言的运用上，考虑到学生主要是以英语作为第一外语，我们保留了英文原文的形式，并在文后标明了中文译文的出处。

三是文献释读。在每一篇文献前面，我们都附有由来自于国内各大高校比较文学教学一线学者撰写的文献导读，主要包括作者简介、文献背景、内容梳理等，有助于学生对于经典文献的理解和学习。

由于编写者学力、视野的局限，本书还有许多不足之处，恳请学界同仁批评指正。

曾小月　李卫华

2017 年 5 月